I0645239

Roots of Faith

Roots of Faith

Anthony Jay Cleveland

Roots of Faith

© Anthony Jay Cleveland 2018

This book is a work of fiction. Named locations are used fictitiously, and characters and incidents are the product of the author's imagination. Any resemblance to actual events or places or persons, living or dead, is entirely coincidental.

All rights reserved. Without limiting the rights under copyright reserved above, no part of this publication may be reproduced, stored in a retrieval system, or transmitted, in any form or by any means (electronic, mechanical, photocopying, recording or otherwise), without the prior written permission of the copyright owner of this book.

Published by
Lighthouse Christian Publishing
SAN 257-4330
5531 Dufferin Drive
Savage, Minnesota, 55378
United States of America

www.lighthousechristianpublishing.com

Author's Note ...

This is a work of historical fiction. It follows four southern American families; Cleveland, Cochran, Irvin, and Reed, from their ancient Celtic and Anglo-Norse roots through their migration to the British colonies of America. The story concludes in the year 1863 during the American civil war. It is also a story of the Christian religion and faith in God and how those two things; Christianity and faith have impacted the history of these four families over the course of centuries. As with all works of this genre, I have attempted to be as accurate as possible when the historical facts are known. I have intentionally selected historical events that somehow directly impacted these four families. I have attempted when possible to identify real events in the real lives of the members of these families when that information was available. However, I have also exercised the liberty awarded to fictional authors to create events and narratives that may not have happened exactly as portrayed in the story. Indeed, that's the nature of historical fiction. We write and record what is known and fill in the gaps of our knowledge with creations that hopefully help the reader see the world through the perceptions of the characters, both real and fictitious. I do hope you enjoy it. I also hope it helps to strengthen your understanding and appreciation of the importance of history and the role it plays on shaping the present and the future. I pray this book also aids in enhancing your faith and brings you closer to your God.

Dedication ...

First and foremost, I dedicate this work to the glory of my Lord and Savior Jesus Christ. I also want to dedicate this work to my ancestors who ran the race well and fought the good fight and who now are singing with the angels in glory. Thank you Granny Reed. I occasionally hear you singing *Beyond the Sunset* and while that might bring tears to my eyes; it also brings great peace to my heart. I look forward to our singing together once again. I would like to honor my parents, Jay and Joyce, who brought me into this world and taught me the simple and pure teachings of Jesus of Nazareth as a young lad. They instilled in me at an early age an unquenchable thirst for intimate relationship with God. I would also like to dedicate this work to my daughters, Kathryn and Kristin along with their husbands, Arthur and Aaron. They have brought such joy into my life and have taught me the true meaning of unconditional love. And to my grandchildren, Abigail and Aiden ... this was actually written for you. I hope you find the words written on these pages meaningful. You two were always on my mind as I attempted to weave history and myth, fact and fiction together. I hope someday you will be inspired to remember your ancestors. Remember the sacrifices they have made that you might worship the Lord God in peace and freedom. And keep Jesus in your heart all the days of your lives. And finally, I wish to dedicate this work to my beloved wife, Cheryl. Sweetheart, words can't express what you mean to me so I won't try. Just know that I love you with all my being and will always be thankful to God that He allowed me to spend my life with you.

Chapter One: Strathclyde – circa 600 a.d.

She came here often. It was her private sanctuary. Down by the edge of the river, where mother earth gently touched the flowing waters of the River Nith while being tenderly caressed by the air from the western sea. This interface of air, water and land was a special place for her, she came here as often as she could to quietly sit for a time and allow her thoughts to collect and clarify. She would not have much time this morning. She hardly ever did. Life was constant work for her. She always ran the risk of being caught. After all, she was a slave. She was not meant to take time out of her busy day. And how would she respond if she were to be caught in this act of deep reflection? What would her master say? She was a woman after all as well as a slave. Granted, she was barely a young woman. It was only two seasons ago that she crossed over the threshold from girl to womanhood. But she was a woman. What deep thoughts could she possibly have? Her life was quite simple. She cooked. She mended torn and worn clothing. She tended to the crops in the field. She even learned to handle the spear and the sword. Women were expected to know the weapons of war and fight alongside their men if needed. She did whatever her master ordered done. And she did not need to think about it.

And yet, she did think. She thought all the time. She thought about what her life would have been like had that day never happened. She remembers that day like it was yesterday, but it was many seasons ago. She was a little girl then, just a few seasons old. It was a warm morning. All the people of her clan had been celebrating the night before. The growing season had been good and the hunters had just returned with much game. There would be plenty of food to eat for everyone during the time of the long nights and short days when snow would cover the ground and the world was quiet. She never saw the others until they were upon them. They came quickly into the camp with savage shouts and weapons of destruction. There had been peace in this valley for so long that many forgot how quickly life could be threatened. In the blink of an eye life could change. And that is what happened to her that fateful morning so long ago. Her life changed forever.

When the attack was over, her mother and father lay dead. Much of her tribe had been killed or enslaved. The few lucky ones had managed to escape into the neighboring woods but she never saw any of them again. It was the practice of the Niduari to capture slaves and then quickly trade them for other things more necessary to life. And that is what happened to her.

She was carried by one of them to the western sea. She had never been to this place before. What she remembers is the sound of the wind and the salty smell of the waves. She remembers being so sad and frightened. She could not understand the words of these men. They were speaking to each other and would occasionally point to her or one of the other captives and make gestures or laugh. And then she saw Duncan. He was tall with dark hair and eyes the color of the water that lapped at the sandy beach where they stood. He looked powerful. He carried a huge battle sword with a short knife strapped to his waist. He was young for the hair upon his face was still short. Yet he carried himself with great dignity. It would only be much later that she learned that he was first son of the chief of the clan Erinviene. She found out later her captors planned to take her across the sea to another land and sell her. But Duncan had spied her and had made a deal with these slavers. He bought her and two others, both young boys. She knew she was related to them somehow but had forgotten the nature of the familial connection. The two little boys eventually died of fever. She does not remember what her mother and father looked like or how they sounded. She was so young when she was taken from her tribe. As hard as she might try, nothing of her early past comes to mind.

To the best of her knowledge, she was the last of her people. She had been taken by Duncan and other members of his small hunting group to a place by the river they called Nith. And there she had lived for many seasons being raised by the chief's second wife. Duncan's mother had died giving birth to his younger brother who had also joined his mother shortly after birth.

A few seasons ago, the old clan chief had died and Duncan had become the ruler. This was a horrible time for the Erinviene. The Niduari Picts from whom Duncan had purchased her had gone to war with King Morken of Alt Clut, the land to the north. They were, of course, aided by the kingdoms of Rheged to the south and the Picts of Manaw. It was then she learned she was from Rheged and that no matter how well she was treated by Duncan and his family, she would always be considered an outsider. She would always be a slave.

The Erinviene had to choose a side. Fight alongside their neighbors the Niduari against Morken and his tribesmen or cast their lot with the Britons of Alt Clut. Duncan chose Morken. And the choice had much to do with religion.

The Niduari followed the old customs and worshipped the ancient gods and goddesses of the earth, wind and sea. The people of Alt Clut had mixed beliefs and worshipped numerous gods but the religious power was always held by the druids, a small and elite group of hand selected men and occasionally women who served as spiritual leaders for everyone in the country from slave to King. The druid served the people as priest, poet and counselor. Perhaps the greatest of these Druidic priests was a man called Merlin who lived and died many seasons ago during the days when the people called the Romans occupied the land. This was the time of Arturious, the great king of all Britons. But those days are long past and the bones of Arturious lie silently in his grave.

At the time of the battle between the Niduari and the kingdom of Morken, the druids ruled in Alt Clut. But it was a difficult time, for although the Romans had ultimately fled the land to return home to fight in defense of their imperial city, Rome, they left behind their religion, Christianity.

She did not remember it but has been told the people of Rheged, her people, considered themselves Christian and that she was probably baptized as a Christian. She does not know if this is true or not but does know that once she became a slave in the household of Duncan, there was no more talk of Christianity or of their man-god, Jesus. Duncan had no faith. The few times they had spoken about this subject and, it was rarely mentioned, Duncan explained to her his doubts about the ancient ones. He said they were good stories to listen to at night when sitting around a warm fire after a hard day of hunting but he did not believe there were gods, or fairies, or any of it. When she asked him what he did believe in, he just looked at her and smiled and said, "I believe in life, and my wits and my clan".

When war broke out, Duncan chose to align his little band of warriors with Morken. Morken was not a Christian. For that matter, Morken was not a follower of the Druids either. Morken was only concerned about Morken and he sought only after greater power and the glory conquest would bring him and his family. There were Christians in Alt Clut at this time, of course, but their numbers were small and insignificant. It seems that when the Romans left, the old ways returned and with that, the druids regained their position of power within the kingdom.

The war, as all wars eventually do, came to an end. It was a draw. No one won. No one lost. Yet many good men, women and children on all sides lost their lives. And life went on.

Duncan was a good chief. He was intelligent, fair and wise for his age. Life, once again, revolved around the seasons and the keeping of the cattle, hunting and fishing, planting and harvesting the crops, making music, dancing and telling the old stories over and over again by the light of the evening's fire.

This morning she decided to return to her special place down by the Nith. As she sat on the bank of the river she could hear the birds. She felt the gentle breeze upon her skin. She could smell the flowers of the season as they stretched out their blossoms to capture the life-giving rays of the morning sun. There was much on her mind this day. She had not slept well.

She had never known a man. She knew the other boys in the tribe would not take her against her will because of Duncan's protection. And they also knew she was good with a knife and would use it to protect herself. She did not know if Duncan felt anything for her. But she did for him. Yes, he was older than her and she knew that he had known women in that way. He was the powerful and handsome chief of the clan. He could have his pick of the available girls. In fact, he had been married at a very young age. She had conceived a child but both were lost to death during childbirth. From that day on, Duncan had never publicly expressed any desire to marry again or for that matter to become a father.

On that first day, when she was a terrified little girl, and he spoke to her in such a gentle, soothing and calming manner, she had fallen in love and had loved him and only him ever since. Yet he never showed anything remotely related to attraction let alone passion for her. She was just Bronwyn, a slave girl from Rheged, who cooked and cleaned and did whatever Duncan's stepmother, commanded She knew that soon she would either be given to one of the young men of the clan or perhaps used as a bargaining chip in the constant negotiations Duncan had to establish and maintain with neighboring sometimes friendly but often hostile tribes. It was a complaint he often spoke loud enough for her to hear. "What is wrong with us? Are we not all Britons? Must we continue to war with ourselves?" And yet, no one seemed to know the answer in how to establish peace in the land. So, they fought, bled and died. It seemed so senseless to her. Was there something in the nature of man and woman that caused their hearts to always turn to violence as the means to resolve their differences? She had spoken a few times about this subject with Duncan when they were alone and she could be certain others would not hear their conversation and mock her. He would always politely listen to her. Usually he would just smile, nod his head, and say to her, "Bronwyn, you think too much". Perhaps Duncan was right. Maybe life is really simple. You come into this world kicking and screaming and you go out the same way. And the time in the middle is just one bloodstained event after another. It certainly seemed that was the way of her life. Her parents and the rest of her family killed. Sold into slavery, she had never really known peace. Her life had always been chaotic and unpredictable. She had so many questions and no one around her seemed to have any answers or for that matter seemed to even care. "What was it all about? Why are we here? What is going to happen to me? What does my future hold? Will I ever have a family of my own? Will any man ever love me?" On and on her mind spun out of control with countless questions that appeared unanswerable.

And that is what drove her that morning to the river's edge. It was the one place where she seemed to be able to calm down and relax. She realized danger lurked everywhere. But somehow this place was special even magical to her. She did not really believe in magic contrary to most of the clan. They loved to hear the old stories of Merlin and she would sit by the fire and quietly listen but then would catch Duncan looking at her with that ever-present smile on his lips. She knew he was enjoying the stories but thought they were just that, stories designed to make a cold night seem shorter. He did love his people. But she knew he was often disappointed in them. She knew he was different. He did not always speak what was on his mind but she knew his mind was always at work, calculating, assessing and planning. He knew everyone depended upon him for leadership, for safety and protection. And he willingly accepted that responsibility. But he was alone. He had not yet picked a woman for his bed. That thought troubled her and she tried to command it to leave her mind. She loved Duncan and could not think of him being with another. But she was a slave and the idea that the chief of the clan Erinviene would someday take her for his bride was too much for her to even contemplate.

Then she saw him. Actually, she heard him before he entered her line of vision. He was singing. She did not understand the words of the song but the melody itself was captivating. And the look on his face … that is what she immediately noticed. He appeared to have been in another world. His body was there in the river bathing. But his soul was somewhere else. And his countenance could only be described as being in a state of perfect peace and contentment. She was not embarrassed by his nakedness. She was a slave. She had seen naked men and women before. She was surprised to see him standing in the waist deep water. All the men she had known in her life would rarely come to the river to bathe. Cleanliness was important to her clan. All carried combs with them to manage their hair. And many would wash their face and hands before entering the round wood and thatch shelters in which they slept. But usually only the women would fully bathe themselves in the cool and swirling waters and that only done once every moon after their flow had ceased. But here standing in the River Nith was a full grown elderly man without clothing singing a song so beautiful. It was mysterious the hold this song had upon her.

She glanced around for a weapon to see if he was armed. That was the next surprise. Where was his sword?

Where was his knife? Not even a spear could be seen. The only think he had close by that resembled a weapon was a large wooden staff that he probably used to aid in walking. She was confused yet fascinated by him. He had the longest beard she had ever seen on a man. It was completely white. His aged skin was deeply wrinkled and tanned a deep brown. He had obviously spent most of his time in the sun. His dark brown clothes were of simple structure and lying on the flat of the river bank. He was obviously trying to dry them out prior to putting them back on again after his bath. She stood behind some ferns wondering if she should approach him. And then he spoke to her.

"Hello my child," he said. "I will soon be finished". "Would you be so kind as to look away so that I can leave this chilly water and don my clothing?" She was amazed because he had spoken to her in a language she understood.

"Who are you?" "What are you doing here?" "And what was that beautiful song you were singing?" She asked rapidly. She still did not know if he could be dangerous. He did not appear to be so but she had learned in her life to be cautious at all times especially when approaching strangers, people outside the clan.
"My Christian name is Kentigern. But you may call me Mungo." He said as he stepped slowly and carefully from the water to the dry bank to retrieve his clothes. As he was putting them on, he asked her, "So my child, you enjoyed the song?".

"Yes, very much, it was serene. It brought me peace." She replied.

"Ah … then perhaps I have found a friend?" he answered smiling at her. His smile was like Duncan's but somehow different. When Duncan smiled, she never quite knew his thoughts. It wasn't sinister but distant. This man's smile, this Mungo, as he called himself, his smile was different. Things were not hidden, not mysterious. This was a smile by a man who was at peace. This was a smile of wisdom, of knowledge, and of love. This smile moved her heart like Duncan's had never done. She knew in a moment she was in the presence of a man quite different from any she had ever encountered.

"But who are you … I mean where did you come from and why are you here?" she asked as she realized the tension that she had originally felt in her body was suddenly gone. She was relaxed. She was comfortable in this old man's presence. It was a strange experience for her. All of her life, she had been on alert, waiting for the next moment of danger to materialize. She had never felt this way before. She did not know how to explain it but she knew she did not want this moment to end anytime soon.

"What is your name child?" he calmly asked of her.

"I am called Bronwyn", she responded.

He laughed. And this surprised her. His laugh was not like his smile. His smile was gentle and soft but this laugh was hearty and full of life. It shocked her and she moved away from him a few steps.

"I am sorry Bronwyn to have frightened you. I have been told more than once that my laugh can be a bit overwhelming. You see, when I laugh I like to let all my being enjoy the moment. So I laugh with my whole body … my whole soul. I laugh so that God and His angels know I am happy in this moment. But let me tell you the reason I laughed. The name Bronwyn is from Rheged but we are not in Rheged are we?" he asked.

She shook her head gently from side to side.

"So my dear, you are an answer to my prayers," he stated as he looked at her with his kind and loving eyes.

"Allow me to explain. But first, let me ask you, have you had anything to eat? Are you hungry? I have a bit of oats and a little fish I would gladly share".

"Thank you, kind sir, but I am not hungry at the moment," she answered as she noticed and once again enjoyed the feelings of peace and contentment that seemed to surround her as she came closer to this strange but comforting man.

"Well, if you are not hungry. Let's sit here by the side of the river and I will tell you a story."
She nodded in agreement.

"As I said, my name is Kentigern and I have been sent here by King Rhydderch Hael of Alt Clut to bring the good news of Jesus to all the peoples who inhabit his kingdom. I laughed at you a moment ago because my father was Owain mac Urien, prince and son of King Urien of Rheged. I had been feeling sorry for myself since I am a long way from my home in Clas gu on the River Clyde. I prayed to God, the Father, this morning that He would send me someone or something to lighten my heavy heart and to cheer me up. And then I met you, a daughter of Rheged." He laughed again and this time she did not flinch but smiled at his enjoyment. She stared at him. This was the first time in as long as she could remember meeting someone from her native land.

"But I understand you, you speak our language. How can this be?" she asked perplexed.

"I can see I should start from the beginning. Do you have time? Surely, someone from your family will be looking for you soon." he stated in a concerned manner.

"Kentigern, I am a slave of the clan Erinviene and live in the household of Duncan, the clan chief. No one really cares what happens to me but they will be expecting work from me today," she said quietly and sadly, suddenly remembering the troubling thoughts that had driven her to the river that morning.

"God works in mysterious ways," Mungo said under his breath. "Let me tell you my story and then I will return with you to your tribe's village and explain your absence to your chief." He smiled once again. "I'm sure, once he hears the name Rhydderch Hael, he will understand and forgive you your transgression this morning."

"Duncan is not the problem. It is his step mother, the woman who gives me my daily tasks. She hates me and would like for nothing better than to have Duncan sell me to whomever would pay the price," she stated with more than a little anger in her voice.

"Let's see what God has planned for us," Mungo again said in hushed tones as if he were telling her some important secret of the world that only the two of them would share.

"My father, Owain met and fell in love with my mother, Tenau, at a great banquet held in honor of Tenau's father, King Lleuddin. You see, she was the daughter and princess of King Lleuddin of Gododdin. Owain had been sent there as emissary from the king of Rheged, his father, my grandfather, King Urien. The banquet was supposed to honor the birthday of the king but Urien had another reason to send Owain. The Angles of Bernicia had been sending raiding parties into Rheged and Urien sought an alliance with the Britons of Gododdin to stave off these incursions. He was being pressured on the east and on the south by these troublesome Angles and he desperately needed Lleuddin's assistance of warriors and weapons. Things would have perhaps gone his way until my father met Tenau. My mother, God rest her soul, was a beautiful, intelligent and powerful woman. And unfortunately, power hungry as well. She and my grandfather LLeuddin were constantly bickering with each other over every little thing. In reality, Lleuddin had lost the support of the people of Gododdin and they were looking toward Tenau to rule over them."

"A woman queen?" Bronwyn exclaimed.

"Well, of course, my child. All the Celtic tribes of this island have a long history of great and powerful women rising to the position of leadership when the need arose. Has no one told you the story of Boudicca of the Iceni and her fight against the Roman legions?" he asked incredulously.

"Yes, I have heard of her. I thought it was a myth." She stated this meekly realizing that not only was she in the presence of a good and kind man but that he was of royal blood sired by a prince and born of a princess.

"Yes, they wanted my mother to rule. And when my grandfather found out, he began plotting against her. About this time, my father, Owain enters the story. As I said, when Owain met Tenau, it was love at first sight. And my mother told me before she died that the feeling was mutual. One thing led to another and before long my mother was pregnant. This drove my grandfather mad with jealousy and fear. He realized that the merging of our two kingdoms would drive him out of the picture. Urien would support the alliance in the south and Tenau would rule in the north with Owain as her warlord. So, my grandfather did something that has taken a long time for me to find forgiveness for him though I know this is God's will. He ordered his loyal servants and warriors to break into my mother's room while Owain was in Rheged and had my mother bound and gagged. They then took her to one of the highest cliffs in the land of Gododdin and threw her pregnant body over the side hoping to kill both mother and child in one evil act."

Bronwyn gasped.

"But God had other plans. My mother survived … barely. Some call it a miracle. And perhaps it was. She had friends and one of them was the Christian monk Serf. Through means known only to himself, Serf persuaded Lleuddin to allow her to live. I think Lleuddin was afraid of Serf or at least afraid of Serf's God. Maybe he threatened him with excommunication. Lleuddin was a Christian but in name only. Like your Morken, he was more interested in his own power and fame. I don't really know how Serf convinced my grandfather but he did."

"What happened next?" Bronwyn quietly asked.

"My mother's broken body was taken across the great waters by Serf and his small band of brothers to Culross where Serf and the other brothers and sisters lived. It was there I grew up learning about the Christian faith and seeing it put into practice on a daily basis by the community." He stopped speaking and took a long and deep breath. He looked at Bronwyn for the longest time and then began his story once again.

"With God's grace and the tender and loving help of the Christians at Culross, my mother lived out the rest of her life in peace until the day she died while at prayer. It was a quiet ending. I was around 15 or 16 seasons old and had decided that I would follow in the footsteps of our good friend Serf and become a Christian monk. I was sad at her death of course but my mother had been changed by these events in her life. She no longer seemed interested in the power or glory found in leadership. In fact, she would often gently admonish those who met her and addressed her as my princess or my queen. I can remember her saying to that person, do not bow to me but become a servant of our Lord and Savior Jesus."

"Yes," he said as he slowly nodded his head and looked towards the ground, "I was told many times by Serf my mother had changed. What used to be important to her had lost its significance. She was known as a demanding woman who expected complete obedience from all those she encountered. She was of noble blood. She knew it and acted accordingly."

He chuckled. "Serf once told me … no one would have ever said Tenau was a humble person."
Bronwyn interjected, "But she became humble … you remember your mother as a humble woman?"

"Yes" Mungo replied. "She was the most humble person, male or female, I have known in my many seasons of life. And … I miss her even though it has been many moons since her departure to the bosom of her maker." He spoke slowly and quietly as he rubbed the tears from his eyes. "I have seen such pain and sorrow in my life. Sometimes I wonder why God allows it. Why He allows those he loves to suffer and die."

There was a long moment of silence before Bronwyn spoke, "I too have known sorrow. My mother and father were killed by a raiding party of slavers from the west. They were going to take me across the western sea to another land but I was bought by my master Duncan."
Mungo looked at her with an understanding that only comes from the sharing of the mutual experience of heart wrenching pain. He asked her, "Have you ever seen your family?"

"No", she replied, "the clan of Erinviene is the closest thing to a family I have ever known and while they have been fair with me Duncan's step mother has never let me forget that I am their slave." Now the tears came to Bronwyn's eyes. "I am just a slave. I will always be just a slave. I will die a slave."

At that moment in time, a butterfly danced around Mungo. He stretched out his hand and the butterfly gently landed. He smiled and turned to look directly into Bronwyn's eyes. "My child. You are a slave. There is nothing I can do about that. But I can tell you that Jesus has come to set the captives free."

She stared at him. "What do you mean? Can Jesus free me from the clan Erinviene? Can he make it so that I can go where I please and do what I want?"

Mungo listened intently but did not respond.
She asked him, "What happened to Owain? Did you ever see him? Did he ever come to Culross to see the woman he loved and the child he sired?"

"No, I never saw my earthly father. My mother would occasionally speak of him but that was a rare occurrence. And when she did it was always with a touch of sadness in her voice. Serf told me once when I was about 11 or 12 seasons of age, that Owain was told by the king that Teanu was dead. That she had died by accident. She was going for a walk on a rainy evening unescorted, slipped and fell to her death. Prince Owain returned to Rheged a broken man. It was only after he left the kingdom of Gododdin that king Lleuddin's druid advisors began to spread the rumor that Teanu had been raped by Owain and in great despair had thrown herself off the cliffs of Traipain. King Lleuddin then issued a decree of death for Owain and a handsome reward was offered for his capture. When Urien, the king of Rheged heard about this pronouncement, he declared war on Gododdin. Thus, for the past 30 seasons, there has been a constant state of tension between these two tribes."

She had regained her composure and realized the sun had risen to midday. Duncan's step mother would be looking for her. She needed to return to the village but she could not bring herself to leave this mysterious old man. Mungo continued, "When I was around 24 or 25 seasons, Serf died. It was one of the saddest days of my life. I did not know what to do. He had been my protector, my father, and my friend. I felt lost without him. And then God moved once again in my life. The brothers received a message from King Rydderich Hael of Alt Clut, high king of all the Britons of Strathclyde. The one that is known as Rhydderch the Generous."

"Yes," Bronwyn replied," I have heard of him. Duncan will often speak highly of this king." She proceeded to explain that Duncan had pledged his and the allegiance of his clan to King Morken in the great war with the Picts and the land of Rheged. When Morken died, Rhydderch, a Christian warrior, was elevated to the position of king and all who had formerly established their alliance with Morken continued the bond of loyalty with Rhydderch, his successor. "I always wondered why the druids allowed a Christian to become king?" Bronwyn asked.

"That is a long story. There had always been tension in Alt Clut between the ancient ways and the Christianity of Rome. When Morken died, a power struggle erupted between the people who maintained the old religion versus the Christians, particularly some of the Christian warriors who fondly remembered the days of Arturious and his attempt to defeat the pagan Angles and Saxons of the east. This warrior band was led by Rhydderch. His side won. As Rhydderch took his seat upon the rock of power he stated clearly that God had given him a vision. God wanted Rhydderch to bring the faith of Christianity and the story of Jesus to all the tribes within the land from the Clyde to the Solway and from the western to the eastern sea. Shortly after this pronouncement, the brothers at Culross received an invitation to send someone from their trusted band of followers to evangelize the land. I had already been sent to the Clyde valley. One night, when Morken still held the throne, I too received a message from the Almighty. I was to get up and leave Culross and head west to Alt Clut. There I was to establish a home for the few remaining Christians of Alt Clut. I did that at a place called Clas-gu. And there I lived and taught anyone who would listen about Jesus. Then one day, the druids came with a pronouncement of banishment from Morken. Things were not going well for him in his war with the Picts and the druids blamed me and the presence of the Christians in their midst for the battlefield failures. My life was spared and I fled south to Rheged and met Christian brothers and sisters at a place called Llandu. They were in the process of building a stone church building in the Roman fashion and a community of brothers to support it. Naturally, I joined in and had every intention of living out my days there in peace and tranquility among my fellow believers. And then God, once again, intervened in my life. The brothers at Culross sent me a message. They had selected me to return to the Clas-gu and be the evangelist Rhydderch Hael had requested. And that, my child, is why you found me in the river this morning."

"But why are you here and not up north in Clas-gu?" she asked.

"Rhydderch wants me to focus my evangelization and teaching efforts in the southern part of his kingdom, which he now calls the Strathclyde. Clas-gu is too far for me to travel on a regular basis so I am establishing a community close by here in a place the locals call Hoddam. You know this place?" the old man asked as he bent over to start a small cooking fire for the fish he had earlier caught.

"Yes, I know Haddom. Duncan took me with him one day last season during the time of hunting and we camped in that area. Is was quite a pretty spot." Bronwyn remarked as she assisted him in the preparation of their meal.

They were both quiet for a time. Each lost in his or her own thoughts. Mungo thinking of Hoddam and what he wanted to build there and of the local tribes, wondering if they would be receptive to the gospel and of the people to the west, the ones who lived by the great western sea. Would they also accept the story of the Christ? He knew that the evangelist Ninian had once walked these lands while preaching and teaching about Jesus. The seed had been planted but it had been quite a while since anyone came to check on the harvest. He had found fellow believers here and there during his travels through this southern part of the growing kingdom of Strathclyde. But there was still much work to do. He had been to Rome. He had seen the great structures built there to the glory of God. It was almost overwhelming to his soul to stand in the middle of those vast houses of worship. One could not help contemplating the majesty and power of the Almighty while praying and meditating in these huge buildings. But, in truth, he felt closer to the Lord out here in the land among the simple folk. He saw God in everything. In the birds, the fish, the small animals that darted away from him as he approached. He saw God in the smile of a child. He heard the whisper of angels in the wind. He saw the beauty of the creation and it always brought him closer to his heavenly father. He thought to himself," Jesus was a simple man, a man who knew the land. A man who fished and sat with all manners of people regardless how they were dressed or how much wealth and power they had accumulated during their lives." And one thing Mungo knew with all his heart, he wanted to be like Jesus. That had always been his desire. Not only did he look at Jesus as his savior but as a model upon which he would fashion and shape his life. That was his common simple prayer … "Lord Jesus, make me like you."

Bronwyn's thoughts were elsewhere. She was experiencing a dynamic and chaotic mixture of thoughts and emotions. She had never been with anyone like this old man. She knew she should be concerned about him. She knew she was being childish to trust him he might be dangerous to her or to her clan but, there was something about him she could not articulate but felt deeply somewhere in her spirit. This was a good man, a man who had seen so much more than she in her life. A man, who had experienced that fullness of evil which can be found in the hearts of men and yet, had learned to forgive, had learned to love. She knew she must return to the village. They would be terribly angry with her and may have even sent out a party to find her. She looked at Mungo. She wanted to stay with him. In truth, she wanted to go with him. She wanted to hear more of his life. She wanted to hear more of his stories about his faith. She wanted to understand this hold this Jesus had upon him. She wanted to know why he had given his life to this mysterious invisible God he worshipped.

Just then she heard Duncan shouting her name. He and a few of his men were walking through the woods fanned out searching for her. She didn't know what to do. Duncan had never beaten her in the past although she had seen slaves treated in this fashion. He had never even raised his voice to her. But she was scared. She turned to Mungo and noticed that he had bowed his head and closed his eyes. *Could he be in prayer?* she thought to herself. She did not want their conversation to end and she was concerned about what might happen to Mungo. Duncan had expressed his mistrust bordering on contempt for these men who gave up everything to follow their man-God Jesus. She did not think Duncan would actually harm the old man but she could not be sure about the others in the clan. Most, if not all, were followers of the ancient ways and might react with hostility towards Mungo.

"Be at peace my child." Mungo calmly stated. "This is God at work in our lives."

She looked like a rabbit caught in the snare with eyes quickly scanning the woods searching for Duncan or one of the other searchers. Her breath was coming in quick short bursts.

Duncan appeared in the clearing and immediately smiled. "Where have you been girl? When you didn't return this morning after your walk, I became concerned for your well-being. I asked a few of my men to search with me. Again, where have you been," he stated in a demanding manner.

Mungo spoke up. "Good sir, she has been fishing with me this morning." And he smiled a booming ear to ear grin while pointing to the fish that lay on the ground by the fire. He then looked at Bronwyn and winked. Bronwyn was confused. She was certain there had only been one fish caught but the pile contained at least a dozen fish flopping around in the dirt. "Where did those fish come from?" she thought to herself.

"Who are you and how do you know my slave?" Duncan asked with power and a slight threat in his voice.

"Bronwyn and I met this morning. She caught me in the act of my weekly bath. I asked her to fish with me and we talked away the morning. I'm so sorry. I did not realize so much time had passed. Please, won't you and your men join us and partake of this bounty the Lord has provided." Mungo responded with a calm and gentle voice.

"I asked who you are." Duncan said curtly.

"Of course lad, I was named Kentigern but everyone calls me Mungo."

"So … why are you on my land?" Duncan replied.

And then Mungo proceeded to tell Duncan and his men the story once again of how the king of Strathclyde had sent him to bring the message of Jesus to all the people within the king's dominion in the hopes that fellow believers would begin to worship the one true God and rejoice in the resurrection of Jesus of Nazareth and the salvation of mankind.

Duncan's demeanor changed as Mungo spoke. He appeared to relax. He no longer acted as if the old man posed some kind of threat but Bronwyn could tell he was not completely comfortable in the presence of this strange old man. Bronwyn realized that Duncan was skeptical of what Mungo had to say about his God and the Lord Jesus. As Mungo continued to speak, Duncan would occasionally ask him questions and even challenged him with statements indicating he had doubts about the truthfulness of the stories the old man had to offer. Finally, Duncan brought the exchange to an end.

"Come with me Bronwyn. I have heard enough. It is time to go home." Duncan stated in a commanding manner as he looked first at Bronwyn and then at Mungo. She hesitated and then asked him, "Can we invite Mungo to go with us back to the village? After all, he has been sent by the king… Our king," she spoke in hushed tones not wishing to sound impertinent.

Duncan looked at her for what seemed like a long time to Bronwyn. Finally, he just nodded his head and started to lead the group back into the woods toward the path that led to their home. Mungo gathered up the fish in a small basket and quietly followed them.

The village where the clan Erinviene had settled generations ago had not changed much since the days when the first of the clan arrived after their voyage across the great western sea. The elders of the tribe had told them all of the land to the west that was always green with grass, where the wind was gentle but constant, and there was plenty of food for everyone. Some believed this was just a myth like so many other stories designed to entertain. There was even a story told by some of the elders that the original home of clan Erinviene was a land far to the south and that this gathering of people (for no one knew what they called themselves) were known for their ship building and seamanship. They were said to have traded with the ancient Romans even within their imperial city but were eventually forced by savage war loving men coming from the east to leave their sunny land and flee to the green islands of the north. And it was here they began to call themselves the clan Erinviene, people of the western lands.

When the group of Duncan and the rest reached the village, the children ran out to see this strange man who accompanied them. He laughed and held their hands and lovingly rubbed their heads of hair with his old wrinkled hands. Somehow the children knew this was a kind and good man. Their mothers quickly broke up the gathering and the excitement slowly faded. The people gathered around them and Duncan spoke, "we discovered Bronwyn with this old man down by the river Nith. His name is Kentigern but he calls himself Mungo. He says he has been sent by the king with a message for us. As is our custom, we will grant him lodging and food for the night and, in exchange, he will tell us his tales, as any good druid would do." Duncan smiled as he said this last part while looking at both Bronwyn and Mungo.

Mungo smiled and simply said, "thank you for your kind and generous hospitality. The king will be pleased. I look forward to this evening's time of celebration. But I am an old man and if possible I would like to rest these weary bones for a bit of time. Is there a place I can go?"

Duncan nodded towards Bronwyn and she led him to one of the thatched round cottages that served as home for both the people and their cattle. After Mungo thanked her she found her way back to Duncan who sitting by himself in the middle of the village.

Duncan saw her arrive and motioned for her to sit down by him. He spoke, "I was worried. I thought something evil might have happened to you." His voice expressed concern but also something else, something that Bronwyn had not heard in his voice in the past. Could it be that he did indeed care for her as a man cares for his woman? She dared not allow herself to have that thought that perhaps she was more than just a slave to him.

"Duncan," Bronwyn began, "why were you worried? You know I always walk down by the river early in the morning before my day's work begins. I have always returned after a short time and have always finished all the tasks your mother …"

"Step mother, "Duncan corrected.

"Yes, step mother. I have always done exactly what I have been commanded to do. Have I not?" she replied.

"Yes, you have been a faithful and loyal servant" Duncan responded and then turned to her and looked directly into her eyes. "Bronwyn, I must speak my heart to you. My step mother says it is time for you to find a man and start your family. She wants to sell you to a neighboring tribe. She says we can get plenty of wool and linen for you as a bride and that your marriage to our neighbors to the south across the great forth will bring peace to the land."

Bronwyn was speechless. She knew this day would come but she had always thought, no, always dreamt that somehow Duncan would become her man. Now he himself was telling her that she might be sold to another and would have to move and start life again with strangers. Tears came to her eyes.

"You are crying," Duncan said gently. "I thought you would be happy. You are a grown woman now and it is time for you to begin your family. Why are you sad?"

"Because Duncan, this would mean that I would have to leave clan Erinviene. This place is all I have ever known. It is my home. And," she hesitated to dry her eyes and collect herself, "it would mean I would have to leave you." She looked into his eyes.

"Bronwyn, I told my step mother no. I would not allow the trade to be made. She was surprised and asked me why." He stated.

Bronwyn sat next to him and quietly asked why he was not going to sell her. The sky had cleared from the morning fog. The sun was in the western sky. It was warm. The breeze had died down and everything seemed to be still and motionless.

Duncan looked at Bronwyn. He took her hands in his. He leaned into her and gently kissed her cheek. "Because my love … I want you for my own. I want you to be my wife and rule jointly with me over the clan Erinviene. I want us to have many children and spend the rest of our lives together, grow old together, and someday, die together."

And for the second time that day, Bronwyn was speechless. She looked lovingly at Duncan. She gently kissed his lips. "My Duncan, I love you. How I have longed to hear you say those words to me." And then they kissed again this time with passion. Then she broke suddenly away from his embrace. She blurted out, "but will the clan accept me as your bride? I am a slave! What will the elders say? Will your step mother agree?" She said with deep concern in her voice.

"In the end, it doesn't matter. I am chief and they are my people. We would fight and die for one another. As you know, that is the way of the Erinviene. But, Bronwyn, the clan loves you as much as I do. They have seen you grow from a scared little girl into a beautiful, intelligent and brave young woman. My stepmother will be difficult but it will all work out. You'll see. Tonight, at the celebration, I will announce my intentions and tomorrow, you will share my bed" he said as he held her close to him. And then he winked at her as he said, "And together we will make many little ones."

Later that day, as the sun was sinking in the western sky, the great fire was being built in the circle of the clan gathering. This was to be a night of celebration. The grain had been harvested. It had been a good season. The cattle were fat. New clothing had been made for those who needed their old garments replaced. And there had been peace in the land, something which had not been seen for some time. King Rhydderch now called the Generous was consolidating his power from his throne at Dumbarton Rock. He had found a way to make peace with his enemies through a strategic combination of gifts, trades and threats of retaliation if the peace were broken. He was bringing Christianity to this kingdom and establishing rules and laws based upon the ancient Roman customs. Rhydderch was a student of history and he realized the value of order and stability the ancient Romans had brought to the islands. He wanted to mimic this approach within his own lands. Rhydderch demanded loyalty from the various clan chiefs and warriors throughout his kingdom. And, for the most part, they gladly gave it. They too were tired of war and valued the rule of law Rhydderch was establishing as it spread from the Clyde valley.

As the sun set in the west, the people of clan Erinviene gathered in the great circle located in the middle of the village. It was here Duncan sat as the clan Chief and made his judgments and pronouncements known to his people. This evening, the people were surprised to see a stranger sitting beside their beloved chief.

"My people," Duncan began, "this man is called Mungo. He has been sent to us by King Rhydderch Hael of Alt Clut. The king has ordered his people to listen to Mungo and to hear his words. He has stories to tell us." Duncan made this announcement though Bronwyn knew he was reluctant to do so and was only obeying the king's command because he too was tired of war.

Mungo smiled at the gathered crowd and then rose to speak. Bronwyn sat with the women of the clan towards the front of the group close to the fire. The chill of the night had begun as the sun had now completed its journey across the sky. Bronwyn watched intently the faces of Mungo, Duncan and the clan elders. Although Duncan was chief, she realized that the elders also had tremendous influence over the life of the clan. Duncan had earned their respect and admiration over time through his wise judgments and ferocious leadership in battle. But she also knew the message Mungo was about to share with these people … her people and, she was anxious on how they might respond. Many of the tribe still practiced the old ways and encouraged Duncan at every opportunity to lead the people in the old way of thinking.

Mungo began by telling them the story of his childhood growing up with Serf and the other Christian brothers and sisters at Culross. Then he proceeded to share with them how he had been banished from the kingdom of Alt Clut only to be invited to return by King Rhydderch to tell the people of Rhydderch's land about the one true God and the good news of His son, Jesus the Christ. Bronwyn could almost feel the tension rise within the small gathering as Mungo continued on seemingly oblivious to the unrest his words were causing amongst the elders and some of the men and women of the clan. Finally, one of the elders stood to attention and commanded Mungo to stop. This elder's name was Arwel and he was the strongest proponent of the old ways within the clan. There was a rumor that Arwel's great grandmother had been a lover of Merlin, the famed Druid of the days of Arturious. She had conceived a child who was to become Arwel's grandfather. Bronwyn understood the passion Arwel held for the old ways. To him, the change desired by Rhydderch meant forgetting not only the ancient customs and traditions but his own flesh and blood. This he could not and would not do.

Arwel spoke. "Mungo, you are a welcomed guest in our village. You are a messenger from the king and we will treat you with the respect and dignity such a messenger deserves. However, this thing you ask of us, to believe that there is only one God and that he had a human son who was killed by the Romans only to rise again from death to life. This is too much! I swear by the gods by whom my ancestors swore, I will not support any action by this clan to accept your story. If I break this oath, may the land swallow me, the sea rises to drown me, and the sky fall upon me." And then he sat down for he had said all that he intended to say.

The gathering was quiet. All Bronwyn could hear was the crackling of the wood that had been recently thrown into the fire to keep it burning.

Mungo replied, "I know it is hard to believe. After his death and resurrection, Jesus appeared to his followers and spoke directly to one who had previously expressed great doubt about the resurrection. This man's name was Thomas and when Jesus at last appeared to him in the flesh Thomas fell to his knees and worshipped him as Lord. Jesus placed his hands gently upon the head of Thomas and said, *you are blessed because you have seen me and now believe. Even more, will those be blessed who have not seen me and yet, believe.*"

Arwel stood again and spoke. "Yes, if I saw this man you speak of, this Jesus, I could touch him. I could see him with my own eyes. I could hear the sound of his voice. But I cannot because he is not here. How can you ask me to believe in something I cannot see, nor hear, nor touch?"

Mungo was quiet for what seemed a long time. And then he replied, "With man this is impossible, but with God, all things are possible. I will pray for you dear brother. I will pray that somehow in a way that you will understand and accept God will reveal himself to you and show you the truth of this story and," Mungo paused," the love he has for you and the people of the Erinviene."

Arwel looked at Mungo for a long time. Bronwyn watched quietly wondering if Arwel's thoughts were similar to hers when she first encountered this strange old man. Finally, Arwel spoke, "I can tell there is no malice within you. You are not here to deceive us or to lead us astray but I must tell you I cannot turn my back on the ancient ones and their ways. I just cannot." And then he walked away. A few others stood and followed him out of the circle of light created by the glowing embers.

Mungo spoke. "And that is what the Lord Jesus said would happen. Some would believe and would take up his cross and follow him. But others would reject him and as he has walked back into the darkness they will also walk in darkness. I say this to you who remain. Stay in the light. Walk in the light. Live in the light. Jesus is the truth, the life and the light. His words will bring you light in a world of darkness. Today, we are at peace but all of you know how fragile the nature of peace is. We men and women are sinful creatures. War will return to our land. Brother will turn against brother, sister against sister, parent against children and children against parent. But in the midst of all that is evil, the light of Jesus will bring you guidance and comfort. His truth will set you free from the bondage of your slavery."

At these words, Bronwyn rose from the ground and looked at Duncan to gain his permission to speak. He nodded and she spoke. "I am a slave. I have been a slave since childhood. These people have been a family to me. They have treated me well with kindness and compassion." She looked at Duncan with love in her eyes and he returned her gaze with a gentle and peaceful understanding. She continued, "But, I am still a slave. How can this Jesus free me? Will he come with sword and spear and take me by force?"

"In Christ, there is no master or slave. There is no rich or poor. There is no weak or strong. There is no man or woman. There is only love. Bronwyn, if you accept the story, if you accept the Lord Jesus, though you might be a slave in body, your spirit will be set free. And when you leave this world, you will go to live with him in heaven forever and always be free." Mungo replied with strength and courage.

As Bronwyn heard these words, she felt mysterious and penetrating warmth deep inside her. She had never felt this way before. She could not find the words within her thoughts to express what was happening to her at that moment in time but she would later say to Duncan, it then she finally felt free. She had been released from her chains. Yes, others of the clan might always look upon her as a simple slave girl but she knew otherwise. She did not know how she knew. She just did. And from that moment on, Bronwyn's life, in the blink of an eye, had changed.

At last Duncan rose from his seat of authority. "Mungo, you have come in peace and I shall leave you in peace. You are free to stay or go as you wish. I will think upon your words." And then he left and the clan dispersed each making their way in the deepening darkness back to their small wooden abodes.

Bronwyn was confused. Had not Duncan said he would announce his intention to take her as his woman? What was he doing? Had he forgotten their words of love? Had he forgotten the kiss they shared? She wanted to follow him to his dwelling but she knew she could not. It would not be proper for her to enter his house without him first requesting her. So, she stood there is the darkness as the fire slowly ebbed. Eventually, she turned and returned to her small hut on the outskirts of the clan's village.

Bronwyn arose early the next morning. She had not slept well. She had decided she would confront

Duncan. She had to know if his intentions had changed. As she walked towards his dwelling she saw Mungo quietly leaving the camp. She thought about following after him but was torn with indecision. She had to speak to him about what had happened to her last night but she desperately needed to talk with Duncan and sort things out between the two of them. She stopped for a moment and then suddenly decided to go after Mungo. She thought of calling out to him but decided to just quietly follow him to see where he was going and what he was up to so early in the morning. Little did Bronwyn know but Duncan had also risen much earlier than usual and had already spoken to Mungo. They had both agreed to meet with each other back at the river's edge. Duncan had also had a restless night of sleep and could not get his mind to settle. He was confused. He loved Bronwyn. That he knew. But he was surprised by her statement last night at the clan gathering. How could she still think of herself as just a slave? Had he not told her of his intentions? Did she not realize she was so much more to him than just a mere slave girl? And Mungo's words had offered him no respite. All his life Duncan had been a skeptic. Yes, of course, he had listened to the stories told by the elders of the old ways and of his people's gods and goddesses. As a child, he had enjoyed listening to the tales told by the traveling bards of the fairies and other spirits who inhabited the otherworld. But when he became a man he decided that most of what he had been taught were just entertaining sagas that had been told from one generation to another for as long as his people had been a clan. He had decided long ago that the only thing real was what he could touch, see, smell or taste. Everything else was myth. Stories designed to frighten little ones into obedience and bring a touch of good cheer to old men and women as they huddled around their fires during the long cold nights of the quiet season. Yes, Duncan was a skeptic. But that skepticism had helped him lead his people through troubled times. Duncan's inherent inclination to constantly question everything had given him a personality characteristic that many of his clan would call wisdom. Some even referred to him in that way, Duncan the wise. But Duncan sometimes viewed the skepticism as a curse. Wouldn't life have been so much easier if he were more like a child, trusting what the elders had to say about the ancient ways and accepting their answers as truth? Why did he have to doubt everyone and everything? Why had he been afflicted in this manner? And why had Mungo's words stirred his heart.

Though he did not want to, a persistent thought stayed with Duncan throughout the night," What if Mungo was indeed telling the truth about life and about this one universal God? What if this man-god Jesus had actually risen from the dead? What would it mean for humanity? What would it mean for his people? What would it mean for him … and for Bronwyn? Bronwyn!" Her image jumped into his mind. He knew she was disappointed in him. They had pledged their love to each other. He had promised her he would take her to be his wife. He had told her he would make the announcement last night but then it had all fallen apart. And try as hard as he might, he could not use his great powers of reason to determine why he had not said anything to the clan and elders about his intentions. But he knew this morning he had to speak to Mungo first and then he would find Bronwyn and sort this all out. So, after rising from his bed he quickly sought out the old man and told him they needed to speak in private. Mungo suggested they meet back at the river where they had first encountered one another.

Duncan arrived first. He saw Mungo walking slowly through the woods with his head slightly bowed and he appeared to be talking to someone. But Mungo was not talking to just anyone. Mungo was talking to God. He was asking the Almighty to lead him that day in every way. He was seeking God's guidance. He was asking for His protection from the evil of the world. It was not a formalized prayer. These were not ritualistic words he was speaking. He was talking to God as if He were right there next to him and the manner of his speech was from friend to friend.

When Mungo came upon Duncan he immediately smiled and said, "Well, my friend, here we are once again by the side of this beautiful flowing river. Now, what is on your mind?" His voice was soft yet firm and full of compassion. For God had spoken to Mungo regarding this young clan chief and his slave.

"My sleep was not restful. I am troubled by what transpired last night. I am also confused and I don't like to be in such a state of mind. That is not normal for me," replied Duncan.

At that moment, Bronwyn walked from the woods into the clearing by the side of the river. Both men were surprised to see her and Duncan spoke to her, "Why are you here? Did you follow me?"

"No, I was following him," as she pointed to Mungo. "My thoughts have been filled with his words of last night and I was not able to sleep."

Mungo spoke, "perhaps the Spirit of God is at work within you two?"

"That is what we need to discuss." Duncan said as he looked first at Mungo, then Bronwyn then back to Mungo as if searching for an answer that made sense to his logical mind.

Mungo then asked the two of them to take a seat by the edge of the water. "Let's begin at the beginning. Before the land was, there was God. In fact, before there was anything, there was God. God is eternal. He has no beginning and no end. God is not limited in power nor constrained by place or time. God is in all things yet separate from all things. These are great mysteries which we humans cannot fully grasp or understand. At a time appointed by God, he created the heavens and the earth. He created all the plants and animals of the land and of the sea. He placed the sun and moon in the sky. He made the first man and woman and placed them in a beautiful valley filled with life giving plants. They were happy and God was happy. But they disobeyed God for He had told them they could eat of the fruit of any tree in the valley but one tree was forbidden to them. They did not listen and because of their disobedience God had to banish them from this valley which the children of men called Eden. For only beauty, wisdom and love can exist in Eden. That which is not perfect cannot stay in the presence of God. So, man and woman left and she became with child until generations of mankind had come and gone. One day, God called in His mysterious way, to a man called Abram. God made a promise to Abram, that if he would remain faithful to God and worship only Him and obey His commands, God would bless him and all his descendants. In fact, God told Abram, whose name had been changed by God to Abraham, that the entire world and all of the inhabitants of the world would one day be blessed through his seed. And in the fullness of time, God delivered upon this promise. For, you see, Jesus of Nazareth was a child of Abraham. For generations upon generations, the descendants of Abraham had waited for the promise to be fulfilled. God's Spirit came upon a young woman who had not known man and she gave birth to the child. He grew up in wisdom and love and taught all who would listen how to live their lives in truth, the truth of God. The way God had intended for us to live out our lives in the valley of Eden. But the religious leaders of his time became quite angry with Jesus and plotted with the Roman authorities to take his life. He was killed and all who had followed him became dejected and filled with despair, for they thought it had all been for nothing. And yet, on the third day, the stone the Romans had placed before his tomb had been rolled away and his body was not there. He later appeared to his followers and told them to take his message of wisdom and love and spread it throughout all the kingdoms of the earth. And then God took him up into heaven where he lives with his father waiting for the Day of Judgment when all men and women will stand before him and give an account of how they lived their lives while on the earth. Those found worthy will be granted access into God's heaven and the others will be cast into a fire of destruction." When Mungo finished speaking, he closed his eyes and bowed his head and then sat down upon the ground.

After a long period of silence, Duncan spoke, "Mungo, do you believe this story to be true?"

Mungo looked at Duncan with his eyes full of compassion and the wisdom he had accumulated with the passing of time. "Yes, my son, I believe." And then he looked at Bronwyn. "And what of you daughter, do you believe?"

Bronwyn was lost in a tumultuous sea of confusing and chaotic thoughts. And then the sea calmed, the wind died down, the clouds floated away and her mind became clear, more clearer then she had ever experienced in her life. At that moment in time, she knew absolute truth. And she bowed her head for a moment, raised it and looked directly at Mungo and said with conviction, "you speak the truth." Duncan looked at her. His mouth opened but no words would come to him. He glanced towards Mungo who was looking at Bronwyn with a smile on his face. "Yes, my child, I speak the truth. Flesh and blood has not revealed this to you but the Spirit of God has given you a greater knowledge. You are his now. He has set you free from the burden of sin."

And Bronwyn did feel free. She knew she was still a slave to the clan Erinviene but deep inside her, deep within her soul, she knew that no matter what happened to her now from this moment on she would believe in this truth and that truth had set her free.

Duncan recovered from his shock and spoke to Mungo. "Tell me about this Jesus. What kind of man was he?"

Mungo sat down once again, cleared his throat and began to tell Duncan of Jesus of Nazareth. He told him of the ancient prophecies. He spoke about Mary, his mother and how they fled to Egypt after his birth. Mungo told Duncan that not much was known of the early years of Jesus but that his teachings were recorded in writings the Greeks called the gospels which meant the good news.

At this point, Duncan interrupted, "Tell me what he told his followers. I will judge him by what he taught." Mungo smiled slightly and began.

"One day, as the crowds were gathering, Jesus went up the mountainside with his followers and sat down to teach them. *God blesses those who realize their need for him, for the Kingdom of Heaven is given to them. God blesses those who mourn, for they will be comforted. God blesses those who are gentle and lowly, for the whole earth will belong to them. God blesses those who are hungry and thirsty for justice, for they will receive it in full. God blesses those who are merciful, for they will be shown mercy. God blesses those who hearts are pure, for they shall see God. God blesses those who work for peace, for they shall be called the children of God. God blesses those who are persecuted because they live for God, for the Kingdom of Heaven is theirs."* Mungo continued that overcast morning for a gentle rain had begun to fall. He taught Duncan and Bronwyn the words of Jesus. He taught them about anger, adultery and divorce. He taught them about honoring your commitments by letting your words mean either yes or no. He taught them about revenge and loving your enemies. He taught them about caring for the needy and about not doing good things for show but because you really want to do the right thing. He taught them about wealth and earthly possessions. He told them Jesus wants us to stop condemning each other and to be careful in our judgments. He shared with them that morning what has become known as the "Golden Rule"; to do for others what you would like them to do for you. As Jesus said, *this is a summary of all that is taught in the law and the prophets.* And finally, Mungo taught them about what it really means to be true disciples of Jesus and building your house upon the solid rock of Christ.

And then Mungo stopped talking and looked up into the heavens. The sun's rays were peeking out behind a bank of heavy clouds and in the western sky, he saw a rainbow and said quietly under his breath, "God's promise. He loves us and always will." And then he turned to Duncan. "I have shared with you the water of life, the teachings of the Master. Do you now believe?"

Duncan looked at Mungo and then at Bronwyn. He looked at the rainbow and considered it to be a sign. "What I think Mungo is that you are a good man with an honest heart and this man Jesus of whom you speak was also a good man. And his words are indeed worthy to know. All my life, I have done all that I can to wisely lead and safely protect my people. Can this Jesus help me in that goal?"

Mungo looked at Duncan with a kind and fatherly expression. "He can and he will. Before he returned to heaven, he made a promise to his close followers, to those who had not abandoned him. He told them he would send a Comforter, the Spirit of God who would empower them and guide them in the way they should go. Duncan, why do you think you and I are having this conversation at this moment in time at this place?"

Duncan replied, "It is our fate."

"And who is the author of fate?" Mungo asked.

Duncan was silent and then suddenly smiled in the way only he could. It was his warm and loving smile that had first comforted the troubled heart of Bronwyn. It was his smile that would calm members of the clan when arguments and heated discussion had arisen from time to time. It was his smile that had been a signal to Mungo that no harm would come to him from the clan Erinviene. And as soon as Bronwyn saw that smile once again, on the face of Duncan, she knew something had changed within him.

She moved closer to him and said, "Duncan, you have been a good chief. You are a wise and just leader. Mungo has brought us a gift, the gift of knowledge which is true, something in which we can place our trust. Duncan, my love," she spoke quietly in hushed tones, "Are you persuaded?"

Duncan placed his hands gently on the sides of Bronwyn's cheeks. He looked deeply into her eyes. "Bronwyn, my life is yours to have and to hold. I could not announce last night my intentions after you said you were a slave and would always be a slave. The elders would not permit me taking you as my wife and co-ruler of clan Erinviene. It would have torn our clan in to pieces. And then the night ended abruptly and you left. I returned to my shelter but could not sleep. All night long, my thoughts were constantly of you and of what Mungo had said to us. This morning, I had to speak with Mungo once again. I had to hear what he had to say about his God and this man Jesus. And I had to find you and try to explain my behavior. "Duncan became silent. The wind had picked up and the rain had returned. Mungo was now kneeling on the ground by the river's edge. His lips were moving but no sound could be heard.

Duncan moved closer to Bronwyn and held her in his strong and powerful arms. Mungo stopped his meditation and looked at the two of them. Duncan turned his head and looked at Mungo. "Mungo, this is my woman. I declare that to you and to any who would listen. I also declare that I will do good king Rhydderch's bidding. I would ask that you stay with the clan Erinviene. Stay with us and teach us about this God of yours and his son, Jesus." Bronwyn began to smile and Duncan continued, "I am going to free our slaves. I am going to tell the clan's elders and all the people of the clan, the Erinviene will no longer buy or sell slaves and that all who had been enslaved", he looked lovingly at Bronwyn," are now to be set free. They may join our clan as adopted members of our families or they may depart and go their own way, but the choice is freely theirs. I, Duncan, chief of clan Erinviene have spoken." Bronwyn and he kissed and Mungo threw back his head and laughed along with all the angels in heaven.

Many seasons have come and gone. Duncan instituted his changes and took Bronwyn as his wife. Mungo preached the good news of Jesus the Christ throughout the kingdom of Strathclyde and many became followers and started to refer to themselves as Christians. At a place called Haddom, by the river Annan, Mungo built a stone structure dedicated to the glory and worship of God. A number of brothers came down from the north of the kingdom to help him in its construction and stayed to build a community of believers. And that place stands to this day as a testament of his courage and faith.

Bronwyn and Duncan were happy and had many children. Duncan and she ruled jointly. This was not accepted by all the clan at first but over time the combination of Duncan's wisdom with Bronwyn's compassion became a powerful influence upon the clan and within even the surrounding clans of Strathclyde and Rheged. This was a time of peace. The harvests were plentiful, babies were conceived and born, and the elders laughed often. Christianity was steadily making a positive impact upon the kingdom of Strathclyde and the old Druidic ways were slowly dying out.

Bronwyn had accepted the story of Jesus and her soul felt free. However, she questioned at times the conversion of her husband. Duncan had told her that he also now believed in the one true God and his son Jesus. But Duncan, at times, also confided in her that what he hoped the Christian faith would bring to the kingdom was peace and stability. In Duncan's mind, this is what the old Roman Empire and their domination of his lands had truly meant. The Pax Romana, the peace of Rome, was more than just a mere phrase for at the height of the Roman Empire, it was the reality of this land and his people. And in Duncan's mind, he equated Rome with Christianity. Rome had died but the Christian faith had remained and had strengthened its hold over the inhabitants of what was left of the old empire. And as Mungo and others like him spread the good news of Jesus throughout the kingdom, peace did come to his home. It was not as if Duncan was not being true to Bronwyn or the people of the clan. He had been moved in a strange and mysterious way by the words spoken so long ago by the evangelist Mungo. Perhaps he had been converted? But Duncan was a practical man and was the clan chief. His position of leadership demanded that he always place the security and future of the clan first and foremost in his life. So, his conversion to the faith was a slow and methodical process and it was based to a great extent upon the practical outcomes that this new faith was bringing to his people. It seemed to Duncan that if Christianity could change the hearts and minds of men so that they sought peace and not war, so that they would discontinue the ancient customs of slavery and human sacrifice then, this Christianity was a good thing and he would support it. So, Duncan became a believer in word as well as deed. He sent the brightest of his clan to the brothers gathered at Haddom for instruction in the faith. He ordered that all newborns were to be baptized in the river Nith for it was here by the water's edge that he and Bronwyn first met and heard the words of life taught to them by the gentle old soul.

Unfortunately, peace did not remain in the land. When Duncan was an old man approaching 55 seasons of life, the Britons of Strathclyde led by a new king, Owain, waged war against the Dal Riata of the north. Duncan, as warlord, and two of his sons fought in a great battle at a place far to the north and east of their home. It was to be Duncan's last battle for, it was here, Duncan the wise, chief of the clan Erinviene gave up his life. He died while holding a small wooden cross in his hands, a cross that had been given to him by his precious Bronwyn. The one son who had survived the horror returned to tell his mother that Duncan had died saying her name with a smile on his lips.

Long before this war between Briton and Scot, Mungo had returned to Clas-gu where it was said he died one morning while taking a bath in the river Clyde but not before he had met the great Columba, Christian leader of the Dal Riata whose house of worship was at Iona. This little island had become the center of Celtic Christianity and the home of many evangelists who were sent from the holy place to pagan Angle and Saxon kingdoms throughout the land. Although their visit was brief, they enjoyed immensely one another's company. It was said that Columba loved to hear Mungo laugh.

Bronwyn became a very old woman. She did not know why God the father of all had decided to give her such a long life. She did value each day for what that day brought to her. She watched many of her children grow up and take husbands and wives. Some of them had preceded her in death and this was perhaps the most difficult thing she ever endured. She was so old that her grandchildren were now of marrying age. She was highly respected by the clan although leadership had been transferred by now to one of her sons. At his birth, he was given the name Cumbria to honor the original home of his mother. But she always sweetly and tenderly called him Mungo for it was Mungo and his words of truth that had finally set her free. She longed now for release from this world. She looked forward to her homecoming. She knew, she did not know how she knew, but she knew with all her being, that when she departed from this world, she would be met by a strong and proud young man with eyes the color of the western sea. He would smile at her and welcome her home.

Chapter Two – The North Riding – ca 1030 ad

Thorkil loved this place. He was lying flat on his back looking up into the blue sky. Small wispy clouds were gently floating by and he was using his imagination to assign a name to each passing cloud. There was a horse. And then a dragon with flames of fire erupting from its mouth. Now he saw a long ship sailing the Germanic sea. He could have stayed there all day but he had chores to do. The farm work never ended and his mother, Tasha, would soon be calling after him. As he continued to gaze in to what seemed an eternal blue sky he looked at the cloud once again that he thought resembled a long ship and he thought of his father, Magnus. Magnus was a Norse trader what the local Angles called a Viking. His father said the Angles did not understand what the word meant. To him, to go "aviking" was to set sail upon the water and to travel from one trading point, a vik, to another seeking to gain wealth and fortune in the process. His father loved the sea and loved to travel upon its waves. It was in his blood. Magnus was fond of telling Thorkil that "our people had always been of the water." In fact, Magnus had been born some 40 years ago on a long ship as it travelled across the Baltic.

Magnus's father and grandfather had been seafarers and so had all of his ancestors as far back as any of them could remember. But times were changing and Thorkil did not feel the call of the endless waves. Thorkil loved the land. He loved the feel and the smell of it. He did not want to follow in his father's footsteps and this had recently become a point of tension between them. For Thorkil had just turned 15 years of age and his father, after recently returning from one of his many travels to Jorvik, had informed him that it was time he joined him in his father's work. He told Thorkil that the very next trip he took to sea, Thorkil would accompany him. Thorkil was not pleased. He hated boats. The few times he had been on one of his father's two sleek long ships he had become terribly ill. His father and the other men had laughed at him and that made the situation even more embarrassing. He wanted nothing to do with the sea, nor sailing, nor, for the matter, the life of the trader. Thorkil was a dreamer and a thinker and he desired a simple life. He just wanted to work the farm and perhaps, someday, find a wife and have a family. Although he had been trained by his uncle, Orms, in the weapons of battle, Thorkil was a man of peace. He had never fought in the shield wall as had his father, uncles and most of his cousins. He was not afraid to fight. After all, given the current state of affairs between the Danes and the Northumbrians, war could erupt at any time. And Thorkil knew that should the need arise he would fight to protect his mother and younger sisters and brothers. But fighting did not seem to be of his nature at least not as much as he had witnessed within his extended family during his lifetime. Perhaps his father had been right. Magnus had always told his first-born son that it was in their blood. This desire to fight with whoever opposed them.

One evening after his father and the others had returned to the great hall in Skel from one of their many travels across the German sea, he had sat Thorkil down next to him between Magnus's brothers Orms and Girs. He had been drinking, of course. That was also apparently a part of his people's culture. But he had not consumed enough to where he was not understandable. The singing and the sword play had not yet begun. That would come later in the evening, when fights would break out amongst the men and his father and his uncles would have to break up the brawl and disband the men to their respective farms.

This night, Magnus was sober and he proceeded to tell Thorkil something he obviously considered very important. He told his son he did not really know where their home of origin was located but he did know that the family had originally lived by a fiord named the Kleif in the land of the Norse. For generations, they had annually gone aviking. Sometimes these raids of plunder and pillage and taken them great distances and it was on one of the raiding parties they had stumbled upon the Christian monastery at Lindisfarne. Such wealth his people had never seen so they took it. They killed as many of the monks as they could, they enslaved a few and took all the gold and silver and other precious items as they could carry in their ships back to their homeland. A few years after this first raid, his ancestors returned to the coast of what is now called Northumbria. Magnus did not know why but this time they came not only to raid but to stay. Magnus told his son that night, their ancestors travelled up and down the coast until they found the mouth of the river the locals call the Tees. They landed their long ships on the southern bank and set up camp. Their intrusion was not appreciated by the local Angles and tension was always present. However, the Angles had just endured a long and bloody civil war between the southern kingdom of Deira and the kingdom of Bernicia which lay north of the river Tees. At first, according to this father, the Angles tolerated these newcomers. After all, he told Thorkil, in the beginning, there was plenty of available land and the local population of intermarried Celts and Angles had been decimated by war, famine and disease. But the ships from the land of the Norse kept arriving. They were ships of war equipped with warriors but also contained in their holds cargo of farming implements, sacks of seed and women. They had come to stay. Eventually, the tensions between Norse and Anglo-Celt flared into all-out war and for the next one hundred years small but deadly battles had been waged throughout the land from as far south as the ancient Roman city of Londinium which the southern Saxons now called Lundene to the northern Angle stronghold of Bamburgh in Northumbria.

It was during this time of unrest, Guthrum, a Danish warlord and self-acclaimed king of the Danes defeated a combined force of Angles from the kingdoms of Mercia and Bernicia. It was he who made Jorvik his capital. It was Guthrum's son, Guthfrith, who had established the present boundaries of the north, west and east ridings. The three ridings met at Jorvik and over time quickly filled with both Danes and Norse. Magnus told Thorkil the north riding was settled by his ancestors and concentrated in a hilly area called Cliffland by the Anglish. Uncle Orms said it must have reminded them of their home. In fact, Thorkil's father and two uncles called this land which had become their home Kleifland.

As the night wore on, the conversation turned towards trade, a common topic of discussion. Thorkil had never been to Jorvik. It was more than a day's journey and that was if the weather cooperated. He asked his uncle Orm, his favorite uncle, if he knew the history of Jorvik and why was it so important to his father. Orm said that Jorvik had once been a crucial Roman fortress and after the Romans left this land the Angles came and made it an important center of commerce, culture and religion. As Orm spoke of the Anglish religion of Christianity he spat on the ground as if he had just taken a bite of something sour. Christianity was a not a safe topic in his household. His family was followers of the ways of the Norse. They worshipped Odin and the other gods of his people. Of course, Thorkil knew a little of these Christians and their strange beliefs. His father, uncles and cousins would often encounter them on their many travels and would tell him of strange rituals performed by their priests while inside beautiful structures made of stone lit with candles. But his father did not trust them. Just a few years before Thorkil's birth, a combined force of Anglish and Saxon Christians had massacred a number of innocent Danes who had been led to believe they were attending athing being held in a small hamlet half way between Lundene and Jorvik. To the Danes and Norse, athing was a special meeting called by warring tribes or feuding families to settle their differences in peaceful ways or more often in hand to hand combat conducted by one representative from each side of the argument. In any case, it was tradition to always leave your weapons on the ground while attending athing. Magnus believed the Anglish knew this custom of his people and used it against them to commit this treachery. He might have to trade with them. He might love taking their precious metals and other valuable goods but he would never trust them.

According to Orm, true prosperity came to Jorvik with the rule of Dane and Norse. Jorvik was turned by these seafaring traders into a vik, a place of trade where people of different languages and customs could gather to exchange and barter goods from diverse places throughout Europe. These viks were scattered throughout northern Europe from as far east as Novgorod to Dublin and even went south to Constantinople and on to the shores of northern Africa. Orm had told Thorkil that they were now living in the time of a great Danish empire that stretched in every direction for thousands of miles. All brought together by men like his father Magnus sailing their sleek long warships.

But prosperity did not bring peace to Jorvik. During the time of Thorkil's grandfather's youth, a group of Norse from Dublin to the west attacked and defeated the Danes of Jorvik. This was simply an extension of the great battles being fought at that time between Dane and Norse all over the north of Europe. Unfortunately, this force was too weak to hold back the Anglish and an army of Anglo-Saxon warriors led by the warlord Edred attacked this weakened force and took control of Jorvik. And it seemed for a time that control of this great city would finally revert back to the Anglish. But Jorvik and its trade was too valuable to both Norse and Dane to allow this to happen. King Harald of Norway sent two brothers, Thorgils and Kormak to attack the East Riding and establish an outpost at a place they named Skarthi which the Anglish now call Scarborough. This happened when Thorkil's grandfather was a young man. Then during the childhood of Magnus, Swein Forkbeard, high king of all the Danes assembled a massive army and ravaged the Bernician stronghold of Bamburgh in Northumbria. He then moved his great army south. He died and was replaced by his son, Canute who people now call the Great. It took twenty years but eventually Canute captured the Anglish throne and the Danes were firmly in control of the entire kingdom including the great cities of Lundene and Jorvik.

At this point in the evening, Thorkil intensely looked at his father as if he was trying to understand the inner workings of this complex man. Throughout this tumultuous time, Magnus continued to prosper. He also married well. On one of his many sea travels, Magnus found himself in Novgorod, the land of the Rus. Thorkil did not know the whole story but somehow his father had convinced one of the great princes of Novgorod to give his daughter Tasha in marriage to him. Tasha was of royal and ancient blood being both a descendant of Rurik the first great Rus king of Novgorod and distant cousin to Yarislav the Wise, present ruler of the Kievan Rus. Her marriage brought significant wealth and influence to Magnus. As Thorkil gazed at his father he realized he was looking at a very wealthy man. Magnus of Kleifland had numerous holdings of arable farmland throughout the North Riding, two majestic long ships with which he plied his trade, the ability to call and command at least one hundred warriors in battle should the need arise and perhaps most importantly, the ear of Eric Hiathar, the Norse jarl of Jorvik who had been appointed by the great king Canute himself. To have access to Eric was to have access to the king. Thorkil knew his father was a wealthy and powerful leader of their people and knew how to leverage that power to achieve his goals. And lately, that had become a serious point of tension between them.

"Thorkil. Thorkil, where are you?" Tasha was yelling out to the fields from the door of the great hall of Skel. "Here mother," he responded. "I am here."

"Come to eat child. Your food is getting cold and the sun is more than half way along its journey to the western sea." His mother scolded him with a smile on her face. For Tasha loved Thorkil dearly. She realized her marriage to Magnus was an attempt by both her father and her husband, to increase their respective circles of influence with the growing Danish empire as well as expand the size of their families. Magnus was never mean to her. He did not beat her as some of the men did to their wives regardless of status or wealth. But she did not love him and she deeply missed her homeland. The journey from Novgorod had been long and difficult. It had taken months and she really did not care that much for sea travel. When she arrived in the North Riding, she was warmly greeted by the extended family of Magnus. They were a kind folk. And eventually, she learned to love the great hall of Skel in Kleifland and the surrounding farms and their Norse inhabitants. She was gradually coming to terms with her lot in life and then she became pregnant and gave birth to Thorkil, her first born child and son. Her life was never the same. She loved being a mother. She loved caring for and tending to the needs of her growing family for many others were born to Magnus and Tasha. Unfortunately, not all the children survived and that had been the most difficult experience of her life. She mourned for months after placing the bodies of her little ones upon the small sailing vessels which carried them out to sea after being set afire. Magnus would mourn with her but he would quickly lose himself in his trade and soon be off again on one of his travels. She loved all of her children. She had delivered eight and five had survived thus far. Thorkil was the oldest and tended to be the head of the farm when his father was away. She looked at her son as he approached the barn where the tools and weapons were stored. He was tall for his age and sleek in build. His hair was long and his beard had recently begun to fill out. It was odd. The color of his hair was not golden like his father and grandfather but dark and wavy. Perhaps, she wondered, if he got that from my Slavic ancestors. For somewhere along the passage of time, the golden haired green eyed Rus from the north had intermarried with the local dark haired dark eyed slavs of her native homeland and Tasha represented the mixture of these people. He is turning into a handsome man she thought to herself.

"Hello, mama." Thorkil said to Tasha as he entered the hall.

"Take your seat with the others and let us eat together. I have something important to ask of you." Tasha said to her oldest son as she busied herself ensuring that all her children and the other workers of the fields had plenty to eat. Skel hall was a magnificent single story wooden structure. It was long as was the way of the Norse with a huge fire at one end and sleeping quarters at the other. The walls were hung with tapestries Magnus had secured from his travels and the floors were wooden, a modern invention. In the middle of the great hall were tables made from solid Anglish oak and it was here that family, servants and warriors would all meet and eat their meals. As was the custom of the Norse, there was no rank during this time whether it was a simple noon day meal or a major banquet feast such as Yule held in the deepest days of winter.

"What is it mother? What do you wish to discuss with me?" Thorkil asked.

Tasha hesitated because she knew what she was about to say was a sore subject for her son. "Your father is in Jorvik. He has sent a messenger that he wants you to come and join him there. "She stopped and looked at Thorkil.

Thorkil's eyebrows were raised a notch. "Why? The harvest is not in the barns yet and the butchering has not even begun. I'm too busy. Father knows I have much to do. Why would he call for me now? And why Jorvik?"

Tasha replied, "I thought you would be excited Thorkil? You have said you always wanted to travel to Jorvik. To see the great walls of the city. Your father is a wise man. I know he realizes how much needs to be done here but there are your brothers and the servants. We can survive without you for a little while. Go and see the world. Enjoy this trip." Tasha said this because she knew she had to. But she also knew in her heart that Magnus had every intention of bringing her son into his world and this was the start. A trip to Jorvik to meet all the influential people and to begin the process of making all the necessary trading connections. She was not happy but she put on a good front. That is what was expected of a wife of her stature. The wife of Magnus of Kleifland who could speak directly to the jarl of Jorvik and thus, to the King.

Thorkil was torn. His mother was right. He was excited about the possibility of seeing first-hand the great city of Jorvik. But he was also wise to what his father's intentions were and was not fooled by this invitation. His father had told him recently that it was time for him to follow in his footsteps. It had begun. He could not refuse the call. This was his father and in the ways of the Norse, a father's command must be obeyed. There was no way around it. He was going to Jorvik. He looked at his mother and then smiled slightly. "I guess I am going to Jorvik."

"Good boy. Your father will be pleased." She stated simply and then quietly, "and I will miss you my son." And then quickly turned away so that no one could see the tears forming in her eyes. "You will leave in the morning. I will prepare food and clothing for your journey." She said as she wiped the tears away.

Thorkil kissed his mother and left to return to the work at hand. "I will be back before sunset."

The next morning as soon as the sun had begun its journey, Thorkil took the package of food and clothing his mother's servants had prepared for him.

"Do you want the brown horse, master? The one your father calls Thor's hammer." asked one of the field servants.

"You are reading my mind, Edgar" Thorkil laughed as he followed the servant to the fenced pasture where the few horses were kept. In general, the Norsemen were not the best horsemen. Therefore, they took little interest in horses or ponies. They preferred travelling by waterways. Or simply walking. But the trip to Jorvik was long with no navigable rivers along the way and on such occasions even the seafaring Norse were known to copy the Celts and ride. Although in Thorkil's mind it would not be pleasant.

"Good travels master Thorkil. Odin, guide you and Thor's hammer protect you." Edgar said with warmth for he did indeed care for this young Norse though he himself would never quite understand them. He was a Bernician peasant and secretly hoped that one day, the Angles would once again rise and place one of their own in power.

Thorkil headed south and west. He would follow the hills west until he came to the great pass where he would then turn to the south. He was excited now. He had both dreaded and longed for this day and now it had arrived.

After several hours of travel he saw it before him on the horizon. Odin's mountain, that great elevated area where both Norse and Dane had in the past met to offer thanksgiving and worship to Odin, god of all gods. It was said that in the early days, generations ago, the Norse of this area as well as the Danes to the south would meet here and perform bloody rituals in order to appease the gods. Thorkil thought to himself, the Anglish accused us of sacrificing our captives here on this mountaintop. I wonder if we actually did that or did they just misinterpret what they observed. After all, there was no love lost between Anglish and Norse even to this day. We had conquered them and had become the word of law and holders of power in their land. Of course, they would make up stories about us. They hated us. And I suppose, if the truth be known, my people hated them in the past and hate them to this day. Just then he made a decision. One that he would later recall as the moment when his life began to change. He decided he would walk to the top of Odin's mountain. He dare not take the horse because he was not that good a rider and the way to the top was narrow and filled with small stones which could easily cause the beast to trip and fall taking him with it over the side. What a foolish way to die, he chuckled to himself. So, he tied the horse to a tree and walked.

When he arrived at the top he saw the sun was soon to set and that he would spend the night here. He looked around for a sheltered and safe place. He saw a rock outcropping and thought to himself that he could spend the night underneath it. It would keep him dry should the rains come and he could start a small fire to keep him warm and perhaps heat up some of the food his mother had given to him for the trip.

He walked to the area and looked around. He was surprised to find that it had been occupied and recently. There were remnants of a small fire where someone had been cooking. In fact, the embers were still warm. He moved toward it and noticed that some cooked meat had been placed on a stick and had been obviously quickly dropped by the fire's edge. His intuition was telling him to be careful and he slowly placed his hand upon his sword as it rested in the scabbard... Just then he heard a young male voice.

"Who are you? And why are you here?" asked a young man standing behind Thorkil. His voice was trembling slightly. Thorkil slowly turned around. There before him holding a sword in his hand was a young man about his age. He was of medium height and build, had sandy colored hair and spoke Norse with an Anglish accent.

"Peace friend. I mean you no harm. I am on my way to Jorvik and thought I would stop and spend the night here at Odin's mountain." Thorkil replied.

"You are Norse. What is your name?" the young stranger asked.

"Thorkil and yes, I am Norse. I come from the Kleifland region of the North Riding. And to whom am I speaking?" Thorkil asked with as strong a voice he could muster. He kept his hand on the sword handle. Ready to draw at a moment's notice.

"I am called Cuthbert. I am a Bernician. I am also on my way to Jorvik." He replied.

"You speak Norse. I'm impressed. But what would a Bernician have to do in Jorvik? Isn't that dangerous for you given the current situation?" Thorkil asked. He eased his grip on his sword. This young man did not appear to pose much of a threat to him. In fact, as he gazed at him closely, he looked rather scrawny and a little unkempt. Must be a peasant or perhaps an escaped slave, he thought to himself.

"I am going to Jorvik to visit my distant family who lives there among the heathens. My uncle has invited me to come and stay with his family while I continue my studies." Cuthbert replied while attempting to muster as much courage as humanly possible given his squeaky voice.

"Well Cuthbert, it looks like the three witches who spin our fates have designed for you and I to spend this evening together on top of Odin's sacred mountain." Thorkil replied with a smile as he let go completely of his sword.

"I know nothing of any witches nor do I acknowledge Odin as keeper of this mountain but I wouldn't mind the company!" he said as an ear to ear grin broke out upon his face. He then extended his right hand in friendship and Thorkil took it and gave it a manly shake. Thorkil immediately noticed the small wooden cross hanging from Cuthbert's neck.

"So … you are a Christian, I see? I have heard of them but I have never been this close to one." Thorkil smiled.

"I could say the same for you Norseman." Cuthbert replied while still grinning. Thorkil had to admit his grin was contagious. He felt relaxed in this boy's presence.

"I suggest we restart your fire and fix ourselves something to eat. The sun will soon be setting." Thorkil stated with a calm assurance that came from years of being in the presence of his father the leader of his people.

"Good idea. I have a little meat that I would gladly share." Cuthbert said.

"And I a flask of mead and some loaves." pronounced Thorkil.

"Good" said Cuthbert.

"Good" replied Thorkil.

The two set about the task of preparing their small meal, gathering sufficient wood to keep the fire burning throughout the night and began the conversation that would eventually change the course of both their lives.

As the evening progressed, Thorkil discovered that Cuthbert was named after the Christian evangelist who had followed Aidan from Iona to spread the Christian faith to the Angles of Deira, Bernicia and Gododdin. That was hundreds of years ago, and his ancestors had been followers of this Jesus of Nazareth for all that time. Thorkil learned that despite his appearance Cuthbert was of a powerful Northumbrian family who also traded at Jorvik. He was surprised to learn that Jorvik, while ruled by the Danes and Norse, had a vibrant and growing population of Celts, Saxons and, of course, Angles living within its walls. Apparently, in peace and harmony with one another. Obviously, they lived in different parts of the city and rarely spent time together outside of their mutual business interests but nevertheless had somehow learned to put aside their differences for the common cause of law and order. Thorkil was absolutely shocked to learn the reason why.

"What did you just say?" Thorkil asked in amazement.

"I said it has been much easier to be a Christian in Jorvik since the start of King Canute's reign" Cuthbert replied.

"Canute is a Christian!" Thorkil exclaimed.

"Yes, I'm surprised you don't know that given the connections you say your father has with the Jarl?" replied Cuthbert.

After Thorkil recovered from his shock the conversation resumed. He found out that Cuthbert was going to Jorvik to study with other Christian men there who were beginning to form something Cuthbert called a community. Apparently, this community was made up of all men, who lived in isolation from society with the sole purpose of studying something he referred to as "God's word" and praying and fasting and doing other strange sounding things. And here is where the conversation took a twist.

"Thorkil, I don't really know you but I feel I can speak with honesty?" Cuthbert asked with a subdued voice.

"Go ahead" Thorkil replied.

"I'm not sure I really want to do this." Cuthbert stated as his voice began to crack." I don't think … no, I know I don't want to join this group of monks."

"Why not? You told me that is the reason you are going to live with your Uncle. So, that you might study in preparation for the testing you will be given by the brothers with the community. I assume that if you pass this test of theirs you are in. Correct?"

"Yes, the test is important. But I'm not worried about that." Cuthbert said while composing himself. "You

are going to laugh but, well, the problem is with girls …
women actually" Cuthbert said with a nervous giggle.

Thorkil laughed. "What in the name of Odin do
women have to do with any of this?"

"I have to give them up." Cuthbert stated as a
matter of fact. "And …. I don't want to". Cuthbert looked
at the ground as if he were ashamed of admitting his
imperfections to this Norseman.

"What a strange religion" Thorkil said and then
hoped he had not been offensive to his new friend. "So …
you like women do you?" Thorkil smiled.

"Yes … I love them. I love the look of them. Their
smell. Their soft skin. Oh how I wish I didn't. I wish I had
the ability of the great Saint Paul who told us to be like
him. To be single so that we could dedicate our entire
lives to the cause of Jesus. But Thorkil, I just can't give
them up."

Thorkil burst out in laughter. "I can't believe what
my ears are hearing. You are a man! Of course, you like
women. That is what men do. We lust after women. You
mean to be a Christian man you have to give up women?"
Thorkil exclaimed his sarcasm tempered by his curiosity.

"No, of course not. My father is a good Christian
man and he sired me!" Cuthbert retorted. "But to be a
member of the community of brothers or to be a priest
today you have to be celibate. These are the new rules
straight from Rome. You may desire after them but under
no circumstances can you know them in that way."

"Has your religion always taught this about men in
positions of leadership? It just doesn't sound natural? If
this God you speak about made us both man and woman
then aren't we supposed to enjoy each other's company?"
Thorkil asked half kidding and half serious.

At this point, Cuthbert became rather quiet. After a long moment of silence, he looked at Thorkil and said, "Come with me to my Uncle's house in Jorvik. I want you to meet my family. Will you do that?"

Thorkil was quiet for the longest time. And then he made his decision. "I must first meet my father. I need to tell him something important. Then I will meet with you and your family. I think that once my father hears what I have to say he will not much care what I do or where I stay in Jorvik."

And with that, the conversation came to an end for the evening. The two strangers had become friends. One, a young Christian man torn between his physical yearnings and his desire to please his God, and the other, a young pagan Norseman not wanting to disappoint his powerful and influential father but knowing in the end he simply could not do what was being asked of him. Thorkil sat by the fire deep in thought. And the moon rose full in the night casting deep shadows upon Odin's mountain.

The morning sun rose and the two young men headed southwest towards the great city of Jorvik. Thorkil gave his horse to Cuthbert to ride and was impressed by how the Northumbrian handled the beast. He preferred walking to bouncing around on the top of the powerful animal.

The first thing Thorkil noticed when they approached the city was the great wall that completely surrounded it. He knew, from conversations with his father, the Romans had erected the wall as a means of fortifying their fort against the raiding Celtic tribes that originally inhabited the kingdom. And successive rulers had made the works bigger and stronger with armed guards stationed every quarter mile. Then he noticed the smell.

"By Odin, what's that stench?" Thorkil exclaimed.

"You'll get used to it. That's the way all cities smell, too many people and animals in an enclosed camp with no efficient way to eliminate their waste." Cuthbert explained as if he were a teacher informing his student of some great mystery of the world.

"The city is not for me if that is what you have to endure every day." Thorkil stated with emphasis while curling up his nose at the odor. The wind had picked up and was coming directly at them.

They were stopped at the huge gate and the guard demanded the nature of their business. Thorkil explained who he and Cuthbert were and as soon as the guard heard the name Magnus of Kleifland he opened the massive doors and allowed them inside.

Thorkil stood for a moment and took it all in. There were buildings everywhere and the streets were filled with people. All kinds of people dressed in a variety of manner speaking and shouting and cursing one another in at least three different languages maybe more. It was hard to decipher given the cacophony of sound. The guard had given direction to Thorkil on how to find the great hall of Jarl Eric Hiathar for that is where Thorkil's father had instructed Thorkil to find him. He and Cuthbert parted company but not before agreeing that Cuthbert would first speak to his Uncle and then find Thorkil at the Jarl's great hall in the center of the city. Cuthbert told Thorkil it would be easier and safer for him to have Cuthbert go to him there and then the two could travel together to the Anglish part of the town. What Thorkil did not realize is that Cuthbert knew that Thorkil would be safe in his company while walking through the Anglish side. There was deep and hidden animosity between Dane and Anglish and Cuthbert did not want an incident with Thorkil as they traveled to his Uncle's hall.

Thorkil stood on the outside of the great hall. He was hesitant. He knew what he had to say to his father and did not expect the conversation to go well. He could hear them on the inside. The sun had just begun to set and the great hall was bustling with activity. He gathered up his courage and went inside.

His father saw him immediately and shouted out his name, "Thorkil, my son! Welcome to the Hall of Eric, Jarl of Jorvik." And motioned him to come and sit beside him. Next to Magnus was the biggest man Thorkil had ever seen in his entire life. The man had arms the size of his father's legs and they were covered with bands of gold. At his side was a battle axe that no regular man could ever dream of carrying let alone wield in battle. His hair and beard were long and the color of autumn wheat. His eyes deep blue. And there was a scar that ran down the right side of his face from his forehead to his chin. One look told Thorkil this was a great warrior and not someone he wanted to upset.

Before his father had a chance to say another word, with a booming voice, this giant of a man announced to anyone who would hear, "Welcome Thorkil, son of Magnus of Kleifland. You are welcome to stay and dine with us this evening. I have heard great things about you from your father. I am Eric Hiathar and this is my hall, the Eagle and the Wolf." Then Eric grabbed Thorkil with a massive hand and crushed Thorkil's fingers in a grip of steel.

Thorkil managed to stammer out his thanks and proceeded to sit down beside his beaming father. Thorkil did not know what he wanted to say that evening but he did not know the when or how. He said under his breath a short oath to Odin asking for strength and wisdom. And then he waited.

The evening progressed as Thorkil expected. The men laughed and told stories each trying to outdo the other. And they drank massive quantities of whatever was available and became noisier as the evening wore on. Eventually some of them departed and the hall began to quiet down. Magnus had been busy while deep in conversation with those around him. Thorkil knew those gathered around Magnus and Eric were obviously the important and influential people of Jorvik. They were dressed in different fashions and some of them spoke a different language but the one thing they had in common was wealth. All were wearing elaborate displays of gold and silver and their women were dressed in the finest cloth available. Finally, Magnus turned to his son and said, "let us leave this place and find somewhere quiet. There are things, important things, you and I must discuss." Thorkil nodded and followed his father from the great hall outside to where the horses and been placed for the night.

"Thorkil, I am so glad you have come to Jorvik. There is so much I want to show you and teach you about this great city. It is here where your future lies. It is here where a man can establish his good name and great fortune. Tomorrow you and I will meet as many of the holders of power we can and I will introduce you as my son and my partner." Magnus was grinning from ear to ear. He was filled with pride.

Thorkil swallowed and then said, "Father, I deeply respect you and what you have done with your life. You have provided well for my mother, brothers and sisters. You treat our servants decently and are fearless in battle. All the people of Kleifland respect and admire you. But my father, I am here today to tell you I cannot do what you ask of me. I am not a trader. I am not a warrior. I do not want to lead men in battle. I love the land. I want to farm for the rest of my life and be happy." Thorkil stopped and watched his father carefully to see the reaction to his words. The grin on his father's face slowly faded away. He looked surprised and confused. And then he spoke.

"Thorkil, you have caught me by surprise. I don't know what to say. I don't think you are thinking right about this. Perhaps you are just tired and need a good night's sleep? I'll have one of the servants prepare a place for you to rest. "Magnus said this slowly as he watched his son's face. Magnus was certainly experiencing a variety of powerful emotions but he was also a wise and shrewd trader who knew better than to let his emotions take control. At least until he was in the throes of battle. That was another matter entirely. Then he became enraged with fury. Even at that point he was able to channel all of that emotional energy as he became a powerful destructive force. But trading had taught Magnus that he must control his impulses and be wary on what he divulged during conversation. And this surprise from his son evoked that same cautious and way response within him. As he looked at Thorkil he suddenly realized that standing before him was not a child but a young man. Thorkil had always demonstrated a strong will. It might take him a while to make up his mind but once made he was unstoppable. Magnus then realized it would be a waste of time to try to convince Thorkil of the foolishness of his decision and was simply trying to buy time in the hopes Thorkil would change his mind. Perhaps if he took him around the city and introduced him to the influential people with whom Magnus had established trading partnerships?

"Father, I know what you are thinking. If I go with you over the next few days and see what your life has to offer me, I will change my mind. Correct?" Thorkil questioned his father. "Perhaps you are right? I am tired and I will spend the night here and tomorrow go with you. But, I want you to know that I feel my mind is made up." Thorkil then took his father's hand and placed his other hand on his father's shoulder. Looking straight into his eyes, Thorkil said with conviction and compassion, "I do not want your life. And I must make my own way in this world. I am a man and I must make my own way."

Magnus turned away and motioned for one of the servants. Their talk was over for the evening.

The next day, Thorkil and his father set out to see the great city of Jorvik. As promised, Magnus introduced his son to many of the wealthy and powerful elite of the city. It was clear to Thorkil that his father was well liked and respected by those they encountered. It also became clear to him as the day progressed that he had made the right decision. He simply did not fit with these people. They were concerned about things which mattered little to him. He would never say it to his father but they seemed shallow and superficial and apparently only concerned about wealth and the power that comes with it.

Magnus and Thorkil met Cuthbert by accident that afternoon. They were walking through the western part of the city. Magnus was on guard. Thorkil could tell his father was uneasy being in this part of town. He had even mentioned to Thorkil to keep alert for many Anglish lived in this area and they were not "our friends".

Magnus was startled when Cuthbert suddenly appeared and Thorkil greeted him with a warm embrace. Thorkil spoke to his father, "Father, I would like you to meet Cuthbert. He is a Northumbrian I met on the way here. We happened to spend an evening together on Odin's Mountain."

"Why were you on Odin's Mountain? And why were you there with this Christian?" Magnus remarked with noticeable distaste as he said the word Christian. For he had noticed the cross hanging from the chain around his neck.

"Father, we are friends. Cuthbert is a good man who has come to Jorvik to study his religion while living at the house of his Uncle," replied Thorkil.

"And who is your Uncle?" Magnus said to Cuthbert.

"His name is Uchtred." Cuthbert responded.

"Uchtred," Magnus said with surprise. "I know this man. He is the brother of Ealdred of Bamburgh. Is this not so?" he asked Cuthbert. Cuthbert nodded slowly for he had learned to be cautious when revealing his connections to the Anglish stronghold of Bamburgh.

Magnus turned towards Thorkil and said, "Well my son, you are in the company of Anglish nobility. Ealdred is the Anglish Earl of Bamburgh or at least … what's left of it." Thorkil looked confused by what Magnus had just said. Thorkil replied, "What do you mean, what's left of it?"

Cuthbert interrupted, "What your father is trying to tell you is that my family held the Northumbrian castle of Bamburgh for hundreds of years. This was a stronghold that has withstood numerous attacks by the Danes and the Norse. But that came to an end when my Uncle and father were young boys. King Canute's father, Swein Forkbeard destroyed the place. It was the first place he attacked when he came to this island. Since that time, my family has lived in hidden places scattered throughout the north and here in Jorvik. Obviously," he looked at Magnus, "I am careful who I tell this to".

Thorkil was shocked. He had spent the night with an enemy of his people. More than that, he had become friends with this Christian.

Cuthbert looked at Thorkil and said with hesitation, "I still want you to meet my family. Would you be willing to go with me now and spend the night at my Uncle's home?"

Thorkil looked at his father who was frowning and then quickly decided. "Yes, I will go and father, I will return to you at Jarl Hiathar' s hall tomorrow evening, if that is acceptable to you" Thorkil lowered his eyes when seeking his father's permission.

Magnus hesitated and then agreed. He knew that Thorkil needed to see all of Jorvik including the parts of the city he himself would often avoid. Just be careful he warned his son as they parted company and he gave a menacing glare to Cuthbert that said there would be a heavy price to pay if anything evil happened to his child.

The two of them walked through the inner gate that divided Jorvik into sections. It was clear to Thorkil that as soon as he walked into the area of the town where the Anglish lived, the conditions were much different.

The buildings were of shabbier construction. There were less people. It was ominously quieter and much less show of wealth by those who dared walk in the streets.

They hurried quickly through the narrow passageways until they came upon a simple two story wooden structure which looked desperately in need of repair.

"This is your family's home?" Thorkil asked incredulously. "I thought you were of the Anglish nobility?"

"I know it is not much. But since the defeat of my kinsmen in the north, times have been difficult for us. We survive but, it is a struggle." Cuthbert said as he shrugged his shoulders nonchalantly

Cuthbert knocked on the door and a pleasant female voice bid them enter. Cuthbert turned to Thorkil and said, "I would like you to meet my cousin, Adali. Adali, this is Thorkil, son of Magnus of Kleifland. He will be spending the night with us."

Thorkil wanted to say something but he was transfixed. Standing before him was the most beautiful thing he had ever seen in his entire life. She was tall, almost as tall as her cousin, with long thick and wavy hair the color of the chestnut tree. Her dark eyes sparkled in the afternoon sun and her smile was radiant. She had the healthy body of a young maiden before the tasks of childbearing and the ravages of age had taken its toll. However, what appealed to him most was the sound of her voice. Thorkil had spent his entire life working in the fields and walking through the hills of Kleifland. He thought he had heard the best nature had to offer in the music of the morning birds and the whispering of the summer breezes. But upon hearing Adali speak, Thorkil knew then the sound of beauty. In the blinking of an eye, Thorkil had fallen in love.

"Well say something man. Don't just stand there with your mouth open." Cuthbert chuckled as he teased his new Norse friend.

"Hello Adali. That is a pretty name. Do you know what it means?" Thorkil asked rather sheepishly.

Adali girlishly giggled and replied, "In Bernician Anglish, it means noble. And what of Thorkil?"

Thorkil smiled at her and then finally found his speech once again. He stammered, "It is a Norse name given to boys. I think it means follower of Thor or something like that." He blushed and quickly looked at the floor as he realized he had been staring at her body.

Cuthbert exclaimed, "Adali, I think you have an admirer?" Now it was Adali's turn to blush and look away, for she too had been roving her eyes over the tall and handsome body of this muscular Norse companion of her cousin.

"Come Thorkil, if you can turn yourself away from my dear cousin, I would like to introduce you to my Uncle," Cuthbert said teasingly.

Thorkil followed Cuthbert into the center room of the hall of Uchtred. His uncle had his back to him and was reading something. This surprised Thorkil because he had not encountered many people, Dane, Norse or Anglish who could read. His mother had taught him a few words but that was the extent of his education. He was better with numbers. He guessed he had inherited that from his trading father and grandfather before him.

When Uchtred turned, he stopped suddenly and placed his hand upon the handle of his sword which was hanging in its scabbard on his hip. "Why is this Norseman in my home?" Uchtred said in a calm and steely voice.

Cuthbert immediately responded, "His name is Thorkil. He is a friend of mine. We met on our journey to Jorvik. He is here to see his father, Magnus of ".

"Kleifland," Uchtred interrupted. "Yes, I know who he is. It was his father that led one of the raids on my family's home in Bamburgh. I know all about Magnus of Kleifland."

"Uncle Uchtred. Thorkil is not his father. He is a man of peace. In fact, that why he is in Jorvik. To tell his father that he will not be following him in the way of the Viking. He desires a simple life of the farm surrounded by a wife and children." Cuthbert said in a respectful yet confident tone of voice.

Uchtred looked for a long period of time at Thorkil. He was quietly assessing this young Norse who stood in his home. At last he spoke, "Is this true young man? Are you willing to do what our priest admonish us to do, to turn our swords into plows?"

Thorkil replied, "I am not a Christian sir, but I do desire peace. I love the land. I want to spend my life working it to bring forth its bounty. I have no desire to go aviking with my father and his warriors. I want peace."

At that moment, something moved inside the mind of Uchtred. Later he would tell his family that it was the Spirit of God calming his soul. Somehow he knew right then this young Norseman was telling the truth. He also knew that in some fashion this young man was going to play an instrumental part in the life of his family. Uchtred sat in his seat of honor and looked at Thorkil. "You are welcome here. You are welcome here as long as you leave your sword with one of our servants. You may stay and be my guest in peace for as long as you desire … as long as you obey this rule."

"I am willing to do so and am honored that you would trust me in this fashion." Thorkil replied while unbuckling the belt that held his sword. He handed it to a servant standing by Uchtred. "Let there always be peace between our two houses," Thorkil stated in a solemn manner.

That night, as was their custom, the family of Uchtred of Bamburgh gathered together for the evening meal. Thorkil sat between Adali and Cuthbert. He had a wonderful time. The food was different but delicious. Adali's mother had died a few years after Adali was born. Uchtred had never remarried. Perhaps due to the circumstances, he and his daughter had a close bond and he was watching carefully the interaction between Thorkil and Adali as the evening wore on. At one point, Uchtred leaned close to Cuthbert and said, "Looks like these two are growing rather fond of one another. Not sure if I like that or not. How well do you know this young Norseman?" Uchtred asked of his nephew.

"We just met Uncle but something tells me that he is a good man with a solid future. I know he is not a Christian but in all honesty, he speaks and acts more like Jesus of Nazareth than some of the priests and bishops I've met in my travels." Cuthbert replied with confidence. For what Uchtred did not know was that Cuthbert had travelled far and wide in his young life. He had met many wise leaders within the Christian faith and had developed a keen sense of knowing who was a legitimate believer and who was simply going through the motions for personal gain. Cuthbert had the habit of saying, "you will know them by their fruits", making a reference to one of the teachings of Jesus of Nazareth regarding hypocrisy within the leaders of the faith. Although Cuthbert was young, he was strong in his faith, wise beyond his years and a good judge of character. Uchtred valued his opinion highly.

The evening was coming to a close and Thorkil wanted to speak to Adali alone but did not quite know how to arrange the circumstances to his favor. It was Cuthbert who came to his rescue. He stood up from the table and announced to all that were gathered, "The moon is in full season this evening. Why don't we take a walk outside the city gates and enjoy God's beautiful and majestic creation?" Everyone assembled agreed with the idea and before long Thorkil and Adali were walking side by side a few yards behind the group in the bright moonlight.

"Adali, I am a simple man. I am not good with fancy speech. I speak what is on my mind and I mean what I say. I have had a wonderful time this evening. I have enjoyed our conversation. I would like to see you again. Would you like that as well?" Thorkil asked with guarded anticipation. He hoped to Odin that she would say yes but he was anxious on how a man was supposed to do this type of thing.

Adali looked at him. "I too had a lovely time. And yes, I would very much like to see you again." And then she stood on her tiptoes and gently kissed his cheek. Thorkil grinned and watched as Adali joined her family as they headed back to the hall.

Thorkil did not get much sleep that evening. He tossed and turned the night through. But it was not from a troubled mind. For the first time in his young life, Thorkil, son of the great Norse warlord Magnus of

Kleifland, was in love. Of course, falling for a young and beautiful Anglish Christian girl would no doubt cause significant tension with his father and mother. But somehow in some mysterious way, he knew she was the one for him and he was at peace. He had come to Jorvik to tell his father what he wanted to do and not do with his life and the three witches who spin and sew the fates of every man; woman and child had woven together the lives of these two young lovers. What would their future hold?

Thorkil did not return to his farm the next day, or the next, or the next after that. For one solid week, he arose early in the morning, told his father he was off to see Cuthbert and then spent the day with Adali with Cuthbert as chaperone. Finally, his father told him that they must return to Kleifland the very next day. His mother had sent a messenger. Things were not good at home. A small raiding party of Northumbrians had crossed the river Tees and had ransacked a number of small holdings of Magnus and his brothers. Girs had called his men together and had pursued them back across the river but the damage to crops and cattle had been significant. Tensions were mounting and Tasha wanted Magnus and his men to return home. She also demanded he bring their son home safe and sound.

The next morning Thorkil left the great hall of Jarl Eric and went to the small and humble home of Adali. He knocked on the gate and a servant allowed him in to the interior. Adali was standing before him dressed in her nightgown.

"Thorkil, why are you here so early," she exclaimed.

Thorkil then told her what had transpired in the north and how his father and his men were returning immediately to the North Riding. He had to go with them. It was his duty but he had to see her once again.

Thorkil dropped to one knee, "Adali, I know we don't know each other that well but I am a man who can make quick decision when I know in my heart it is the right thing to do. And I know that I want you to spend the rest of your life with me. Will you be my wife?"

Adali gasped and also dropped to her knees so that she was looking squarely into Thorkil's eyes.

"Thorkil, I have fallen in love with you. I did not mean for this to happen but from the second I saw you I knew. I would be your wife but there are some things we need to discuss and agree upon before I say yes." She spoke with tenderness and love in her voice.

Thorkil looked at her expectantly.

"You must promise me that should the Lord bless our union with children, you will allow me to raise them in the Christian faith. Can you do that?" Adali's eyes were intense and the tone of her voice was serious.

Thorkil looked at her. "I love you Adali. And if this is that important to you then yes, I will agree to your request, but what about your father? Surely, he will not permit his daughter to marry a follower of Odin and a Norseman at that."

Just then they both heard the voice of Uchtred. "Do you think I do not know love when I see it? Daughter, since the death of your mother, I have known this day would come. You would meet some young man and leave me. I never thought it would be a Norseman. Nor did I ever think it would be a pagan." Uchtred looked at Thorkil and then back to his daughter. "But God has spoken to me. I don't really know how I know but I know that God is in the midst of your love and somehow in some mysterious way He has blessed this union. If this is the will of God then who am I to stand in the way?" And with that statement he gently placed his arms around his precious daughter and gave her a quick kiss on the cheek. He then turned to Thorkil and extended his hand in friendship. "Welcome to the house of Bamburgh."

Thorkil took his hand and shook it while grinning from ear to ear. Then suddenly a loud knock was heard at the gate and Thorkil heard his own father's booming voice. "Thorkil are you in there? Son, we must leave at once."

Uchtred looked in a questioning manner at Thorkil and Adali. And as the three of them hastily walked to the gate to allow Magnus to enter, Thorkil explained the situation in the North Riding.

Magnus was surprised to see the three of them together. "Come son, we must get to the north quickly."

"Father, I will ride with you but first there is something we need to discuss," Thorkil said as he glanced at Adali.

"What boy be quick about it!" Magnus exclaimed.

Uchtred interrupted, "Magnus, your son and my daughter are to be wed. But right now is not the time to discuss this matter. I would like to offer my services to you and your men. I realize you may not completely trust me and I understand the reasons why. Perhaps I would be the same if the shoe was on the other foot. But I think I can help. Those men from Northumbria who attacked your farms, they will listen to me. I am the Earl of Bamburgh. They will heed my commands. Let me go with you and speak to them. I will order them to restore to your people all they have taken or destroyed."

Magnus looked at this Anglish Earl. He looked at Thorkil and Adali who were now holding hands. It was obvious to him these two were in love. And no, he would not stand in their way. After all, these unions between Norse and Anglish or Dane and Anglish were becoming rather commonplace. But did he trust this Christian? And then he made his decision.

"You may ride with us. But you will not bring any of your men nor will you be armed yourself. If I am to trust you then you are to trust me. Plus, "he glanced at the young couple, "your daughter will accompany us. I want her to meet Tasha, my wife." And then he smiled. "Agreed?"

"Agreed" said Uchtred.

They immediately set out from Jorvik. The party was led by Magnus and the Earl Uchtred. Jarl Eric of Jorvik had ordered twenty of his best warriors to accompany Magnus and his small group of six men. All were battle hardened but it was a small group and they had no idea what they would encounter in the North Riding or the size of the Northumbrian force gathered across the river Tees. It took them a day and a half to return to Skel hall in Kleifland. When they arrived they found the family had gathered there for protection. Orms informed his brother of the damage that had been done and where the Northumbrians were presently camped. Tasha was silent as Magnus explained the unexpected company.

"And you are convinced this Christian is worthy of your trust? You have brought him and his daughter into our home? And what do you mean they are in love? What does love have to do with marriage? Tasha was frightened and confused.

Orms spoke to one of his men who were acting as scout. He turned to Uchtred and spoke, "You had better be right about them listening to you. My man says there are over one hundred armed warriors across the river and they look like they are beginning to prepare for another raid."

"Take me to them," Uchtred spoke in a calm and dignified fashion.

Led by Orms, Magnus, Uchtred and Thorkil; the group dressed for battle headed to the river Tees. Adali stayed behind with a cautious Tasha and the rest of the women and younger children of the Norse families of Kleifland.

They arrived at the river in short measure. As the crow flies, the Tees is not more than an hour's quick walk from Skel hall. They could hear the Northumbrians on the other side but the thick foliage of the river bank prevented a clear view.

Uchtred turned to the group and said, "Stay here. I will go to the edge of the river and speak to them."

He immediately turned and headed straight for the water's edge. As soon as the scouts on the other side spotted him they alerted their leader. He was a large overweight man with unkempt hair and beard. He came to the edge of the river and spoke in Anglish to Uchtred. "Who are you and what are doing with that Norse scum?" He pointed at Thorkil and his companions.

"I am Uchtred, Earl of Bamburgh. I will be asking the questions this day. And you will be seeking my mercy." Uchtred walked into the river until the water was at knee height.

Immediately upon hearing the words Earl of Bamburgh, the grossly obese man dropped to one knee and lowered his battle axe. The others in the group seeing what their leader had done did likewise. Quiet settled over the river valley. The Earl then spoke to the entire group, "I am Uchtred, Earl of Bamburgh. Many of you know me. Many of your fathers have fought along-side my father and I. And your grandfathers fought with my grandfather at Bamburgh Castle." He waited until he had everyone's attention. "Those days have passed. It is a new age. We have a new king. Yes, he is Danish. But he is also a Christian and he desires for peace in this land, his kingdom." A murmur spread through the Northumbrians. Uchtred continued, "I know injustice has been committed by both Dane and Anglish, by Saxon and Norse, by Celt and Scot. But the days of injustice are over. The king commands it and we shall uphold his rule of law and order. I therefore command you in the name of your king and in the name of the eternal king Jesus to return to your homes in peace. I also command you to return to the people of the North Riding what you have taken from them. Those who do not abide by this command will be hunted down by me personally and brought to the swiftest justice. I Uchtred have spoken."

Slowly at first and then with ever increasing speed the group of Northumbrians came to their side of the river and placed down on the ground all they had taken from the Norse. They then turned north and headed home. Calm filled the air.

Magnus looked at Uchtred as he returned from the river's edge to where the small group of Norsemen stood. "Do you think Canute would have said the same thing? Would he have told these men that it was a new day in this land, that peace has finally arrived?" Magnus said to

Uchtred as he helped him up the steep bank of the river's edge.

Uchtred looked at Magnus, then at his armed men, then straight at Thorkil. "I hope so. I pray so. Enough blood has been shed. Enough of our people on both sides of this river have lost their lives. I'm tired of hearing the wails of mothers who have lost their sons in battle. Yes, we are different, you and yours and me and mine. We are a different people. We speak a different language, dress differently and, live out our lives according to the tradition and customs of our own. But Magnus, deep inside, I know that you and yours and me and mine are all the children of the one true God and it is His desire that we somehow find a way to live with one another in peace, despite those differences." As he said these words, Thorkil looked at his father and the men who would have gladly fought beside him this day. They would give their lives for him. And all of them, to a man, were nodding in agreement with what Uchtred had just said. Perhaps, Thorkil thought, it is a new day. They then turned and headed back to the great hall at Skel.

Thorkil saw his mother and Adali before they saw him. They were sitting outside under the shade of a large oak. Both were smiling and obviously deeply involved in their conversation. Thorkil was almost upon them when at last Adali noticed him.

Oh, thank God, you are all right!" she exclaimed as she ran to him and threw her arms around him. Thorkil's mother anxiously asked about Magnus, "He is safe?"

"Well of course I am woman," Magnus roared as he came into sight of the oak." And we can thank our new-found friend from Jorvik, Uchtred, Earl of

Bamburgh, for our safe return. On his command, the Northumbrians laid down their weapons and returned all they had stolen from us. I still can't believe what my eyes saw and ears heard."

That evening, Tasha and Adali helped the servants prepare a banquet in celebration of what had recently transpired. They celebrated the safe return of Magnus, Uchtred, Thorkil and the other men. Magnus also announced to his family the betrothal of Thorkil and Adali. This was greeted with shouts of acclamation and well wishes to Thorkil and his blushing fiancé. There was music, plenty of food and drink and dancing well into the early hours of the next day. Eventually things quieted down and Thorkil and his father got a chance to sit together and speak in hushed tones.

"So, my son, this is what you want, to marry an Anglish Christian girl and to live out your life as a simple farmer? If that is the case, and it appears to be such, you have my blessing. This man Uchtred is a good man. Since the apple does not fall far from the tree I would imagine Adali is also of similar stock and will make you a good wife and mother of your children." Magnus said as he looked at his on with new eyes realizing how much he had matured.

"Thank you father," Thorkil said as he nodded his head in appreciation of his father's understanding and wisdom. "Tomorrow we shall discuss the marriage as a family, you, Uchtred, mother and Adali but, now, I must rest. Good night father."

Magnus watched as his son walked out of the main hall and into one of the adjacent rooms.

The next day Adali and her father prepared to return to Jorvik. Thorkil had decided he would accompany them for he and Adali had much to discuss about their future and Thorkil wanted to speak with Cuthbert once again.

After a slow but joyous journey of two days the little group found themselves once again in the small home of Uchtred. Cuthbert was there and was extremely happy to see them all alive and well. After Thorkil told him of how his uncle had handled the situation Cuthbert beamed with pride.

That evening, Adali, Cuthbert and Thorkil sat outside the house underneath a large old tree. The evening was pleasant with an air temperature still warm from the day's sun and a slight breeze blowing from the west. The three had sat in silence for a number of minutes as they watched the glow of the setting sun.

"Tell me about this Jesus of Nazareth." Thorkil broke the silence with his question. Cuthbert looked at his cousin who glanced down at the ground while smiling.

Cuthbert cleared his throat and then began in a soft and soothing way to tell Thorkil of Kleifland all that he could about the Christ. Cuthbert began with the story of his miraculous conception and birth. He then shared a number of stories from the Gospels regarding the life and teachings of Jesus. He finished later that evening with the crucifixion and resurrection.

Thorkil listened politely and attentively. "And he said he would return?" Thorkil asked.

"Yes, but no man knows when, not even he himself. Only God the Father knows the timing of the last days." Cuthbert responded and Thorkil lowered his head as if in deep contemplation.

"This Jesus sounds like a good man, a man of peace and compassion. A man who sought justice for the down trodden, a man who lived an honest life and was not afraid to tell the truth. And for that he was killed." Thorkil stated in summation.

"Thorkil, why do you think Canute considers the Christian faith so important?" Cuthbert asked his friend.

"I don't know but I have an idea you are going to tell me, "Thorkil and Adali both chuckled.

Cuthbert grinned and then began, "Canute's grandfather first accepted the Christian faith because he needed the support of the Franks in his rise to power. Later Canute's father sought the help of the Emperor Otto of the Holy Roman Empire to defeat warring Danish jarls and unite the kingdom. In fact, Otto is Canute's godfather. The conversion of Canute's father, Swein Forkbeard, was purely for political purposes to assure critical alliances and prevent powerful Christian neighbors, like the Franks, from attacking his kingdom. It is not for me to judge our king but I have been told by those who should know that Canute is a Christian in name only. Why, he even has two wives, one who lives in the south and the other in the north of this empire. And, of course, you have already heard the terrible stories of what he does to his captives," stated Cuthbert as he shook his head in disgust.

"I am convinced the same is true in the world of the Norse. Men who yearn after glory and power will use whatever means available to avail themselves of such influence, "Thorkil stated as he looked slowly from Adali to Cuthbert. "But surely, the pope, the leader of the Christians is not of such character?" Thorkil asked of Cuthbert.

Cuthbert crossed himself and said, "Sadly Thorkil, the holy father is a wicked man. He has taken the name Benedictus the Ninth and those who have been to Rome and have witnessed his behavior return shocked and disgusted with his immorality. And not only his behavior, but the actions of the cardinals and other important members of the church leadership."

Thorkil took this all in and looked at Adali who was looking at him with an anxious expression.

"So tell me my friend, why are you a Christian? Your Christian leaders seem no different than others who rule this world of ours?" Thorkil asked quite perplexed at the revelations he was learning.

Cuthbert was silent for the longest time and finally stated, "It is Jesus. That is the reason for my faith. It is his recorded teachings and the example of how he lived his life. That is why I am a Christian, Thorkil I am a follower of Jesus of Nazareth and of the God who sent him to us. May his name be praised forever. Jesus taught his followers about this very thing. He said not all people who sound religious are really godly. They may refer to him as Lord but they still will not enter the Kingdom of Heaven. The decisive issue is whether they obey his father God in heaven. On Judgment Day, they will say to Jesus, did we not preach in your name and cast out demons and perform many miracles in your name. And Jesus will say to them he never knew them. He will tell them to go away. Jesus also taught his followers that you could tell a good tree from a bad tree by the fruit it produced. A healthy tree produces good fruit and an unhealthy tree produces bad fruit. Thorkil, I want to be a good tree."

Thorkil looked at Adali, "And you my love, what is your reason for your faith in this Jesus?"

"It is the same. I am not interested in what kings or queens say or do. I care not for wealth or power. I want a simple life. I want a man to cherish. I want children to love and be loved by. And when this life is over, I want to go to heaven to be with my God. And that was the promise the Lord Jesus made to his followers and to any who would believe in him. He will take us to God," Adali responded with a calm and loving voice.

"And I want you Adali for my wife and to be the mother of our children. And we will raise our children in your faith. Adali, I will think about this Jesus. He sounds like a man I would like to know better. Perhaps we Norse can learn something from this son of God?" Thorkil grinned at Adali and Cuthbert.

Adali said with a smile on her face, "Who knows? Perhaps we Christians can learn something of value from you Norse?" And then she burst out laughing and the evening sky was filled with the stars of heaven.

Time pressed on. After much soul searching and intense discussion with his family, Cuthbert decided to become a Benedictine priest. He served under a number of Bishops at York Minster and accompanied Archbishop Ealdred to Westminster in the year 1066 to crown the Norman Duke William, King of England.

Magnus of Kleifland returned to his life of trading and raiding. He drowned at sea during a tremendous storm that had suddenly appeared and engulfed his magnificent long ship. It was a fitting end for a Viking.

Tasha lived out a very long and mainly happy life. She died in the year 1065 and never saw the destruction that came upon her beloved Kleifland and its Norse inhabitants.

Uncle Uchtred lived a few more years after his daughter Adali was married. He lived long enough to see the birth of his grandson named Uchtred in honor of him.

He died while attending mass at York Minster. Those who were present with him said it was a peaceful end to his life. He simply closed his eyes and gave his spirit to God.

Thorkil and Adali became husband and wife. They were married by a priest who was a friend of Cuthbert's and then remarried in the Norse fashion when they returned to Kleifland. God blessed their union with many little ones but only one son survived to adulthood and that was their firstborn, Uchtred. Thorkil kept his promise to Adali and all their children were baptized in the faith and taught daily the teachings of Jesus of Nazareth.

It was a turbulent time for the inhabitants of the North Riding. Five years after their marriage, in the year 1035, King Canute died and war once again erupted in the north. Siward, who had been appointed Earl of York by Canute worked to settle multiple disputes that arose between the Danes of what was now being called Yorkshire and the Anglish of Northumbria. Ealdred the Earl of Bamburgh, not to be confused with Archbishop Ealdred of York Minster, and who was appointed at the death of Uncle Uchtred, was indeed troublesome to Earl Siward. He finally had enough and after hearing of Canute's death had Earl Ealdred assassinated. Siward then declared himself Earl of all Northumbria including Yorkshire. In the year 1055, Siward died leaving a vacuum in the political power structure of the north. King Edward the Confessor, king of the Saxon south, appointed Tostig Godwinson, brother of Harald, Earl of Wessex, to be Earl of Northumbria. Rebellion by the disgruntled inhabitants of the three Ridings broke out against Tostig's rule in the year 1064. In the year 1066, Edward the Confessor who by this time was being called the King of England, dies and Harold Godwinson was crowned King in Westminster. But the hearts of the Danes and the Norse were not with Godwinson. The old citizens of Jorvik and, in particular, the Norse of the North Riding invited Harold Hardrada, King of Norway to invade the north of England. In August of 1066, Hardrada lands in Kleifland which by this time was now known as Cleveland, and prepares to invade the great city of York. At a place called Stamford Bridge on the River Derwent, on the 25th of September in the year 1066, the armies of Hardrada of Norway combined with the Norse and Danes of the three Ridings were defeated in battle by the army of King Harold of England. During this battle, Thorkil, son of Magnus of Kleifland and his son, Uchtred, were killed. It was reported to Adali by those who survived the battle that father and son were side by side when they were slain by an overwhelming group of English swordsmen. Apparently, the story goes, Thorkil died first while trying to protect his son. When death was certain, Uchtred dropped his sword fell to his knees and bowed his head in prayer. His mother was told that he died while clutching the small crucifix that hung around his neck. They did not tell his mother that Uchtred also had the hammer of Thor on that same gold chain.

On October 14th, in the year 1066, William, Duke of Normandy, defeated King Harold and his army. On Christmas day, of the same year, King William the Conqueror was crowned at Westminster.

Uchtred' s son, William was only six years old when all this happened. His mother had died the year before due to fever and Adali had vowed to take him as her own and raise him in the Christian faith. But the three Ridings had no idea at that time how merciless the new King William would pursue those who he considered a threat to his reign. The great "harrowing of the north" would commence in the year 1069 and the devastation would not end until a year later in the year 1070.

In the autumn of 1069 King Swein II of Denmark had invaded England in support of Edgar the Atheling of Wessex. Edgar was the last remaining member of the House of Wessex with a claim to the throne of England. The Danes, as might be expected, landed in Yorkshire and were able to break the hold of William in the north of England. William's response was to completely destroy every threat real or imagined. He systematically devastated the three Ridings with the intention of isolating and eventually destroying any resistance the city of York might put forth. As the city was surrounded, William and Swein came to terms and with bags of English gold in the holds of their long ships the Danes left England for good never to return. With the Danish army out of the way, William continued his harsh lesson to the inhabitants of the area with a specific focus on the Norse settlements in the North Riding along the River Tees. William's army carried out a campaign of general destruction of homes, livestock and crops as well as the means of food production. Men, women and children were slaughtered and many hundreds are said to have died due to the famine that followed. Adali was one of them, but little William managed to survive. Somehow, an old priest by the name of Cuthbert, found the little boy and took him into hiding. The story goes that they lived as hermits for years on the side of what long ago was called Odin's mountain. It was here that William grew to be a man, learned of his ancestors, and followed in the teachings of Jesus.

Chapter Three – Paisley Abbey – ca 1330

William was an old man. He was a very old man. He had outlived all of his adolescent companions. He had outlived all of his friends. He had outlived all of his cousins. He had outlived his wife of 40 years, four of his six children and three of his ten grandchildren. As a young man, he had been taller than most of his companions but now at this age he stooped significantly. While he had kept his hair and beard it was now solid white and oddly excessively long. William had quit cutting his hair after a tragic event that had happened over two decades ago. He did not like to dwell on this time of his life. The memories were painful. He could still see but not well and had lost all of his hearing in his left ear and much of that in his right. For most of his life, William had retained the strength of his youth. As a young man, William could run for miles at a time without tiring. And he could lift extremely heavy stones and easily hurl them across the river White Cart. It was said that only three men in all of Renfrew could wield the broadsword as easily and effectively as William of Cochrane. When his sons were young men, William would wrestle with and easily overpower them. But the ravages of time had begun to show their effect on his body. Some mornings he could barely pick himself up from his straw bed and his body would ache when the cold winds of winter blew in from the western sea. He didn't remember the exact date of his birth but he knew it was in the spring of the year of our Lord 1250. He also knew where he was born. It was here at Paisley. This land had been in his family for as long as anyone could remember. William's father, Osbert, named after one of the early Priors of the Priory at Paisley had told him when he was a young lad that their clan, called Cochrane, had descended from the original Britons of Strathclyde who had lived in the Clyde river valley for centuries. Others in the family said they were descended from a Norse warrior and his family who settled in the land where the Clyde and White Cart rivers flowed together, just a half mile north of where William was born and raised. And still others claimed they originated up in the highlands, across the river Clyde in the land called Argyll. William determined at a fairly early age that no one really knew the truth and for him it did not matter. He knew he was alive and content with his life. He was not afraid to die. In fact, part of him longed for the release death would bring. The church had played a critical role in his life and he firmly believed what the monks at Paisley Abbey had taught him so very long ago. That death was not the end but only the beginning. He looked forward with great anticipation to be reunited with his deceased friends, family and especially his wife, Margaret whom he had loved completely and fully all of his life from the first day he met her to the day she breathed her last. But William's mind was sharp and he enjoyed every day the Lord God had decided to give him. William loved all of this family. He had fought and bled for them his whole life. Each was precious to him. But William had a special bond with the youngest of his grandchildren, whose name was Robert. It was Robert who would come to his home each morning before he set out upon his daily tasks of providing for his young family. Robert would sometimes help William get dressed and gently guide him out to what William called his "sitting spot". It was here by the River White Cart underneath a huge oak tree where William would sit and watch the people of Paisley go about their daily chores. From this vantage point, William could see almost all of Paisley Abbey. He could see all the various structures of the Abbey and watch the monks as they moved from building to building going about what William termed "God's work". William loved the Abbey, and rightly so, for William had spent much of his life in the design and construction of this house of worship. It was here he had been taught to read and write. It was here in this holy place where he had made his life-long commitment to follow the teachings of Jesus of Nazareth, the Son of God. It was here in front of Abbot Stephen he had made his vows to Margaret. And it was here that a life changing miracle had occurred.

William had seen the birth, death and resurrection of this fine old building. The Abbey was a powerful symbol of the majesty of God and His eternal presence. To William, the Abbey represented his own life. In it, he saw himself; the birth, growth and transformation from boy to man. In its stones he saw the continuity of his people. When he touched its walls, he communed with his ancestors who had come to this sacred spot for hundreds of years to pray to the eternal and mysterious God of all. And perhaps most importantly, as William sat here on the side of the river White Cart and looked at this strong symbolic image of the Church of Jesus Christ he felt peace. This was the peace of an old wise man who knew who he was, who knew what God had given him to do and, who had done that task to the best of his ability.

This morning, Robert had arrived early at the simple and humble abode of William. "Grandfather, this day I want to spend with you. I want you to teach me all the things you have seen in your life. I know at times it was not easy for you. I know at times you must have felt that God had deserted you. But still you survived. And now you are the oldest person in all of Renfrew and I want to hear your stories." Robert stated with a degree of seriousness that William did not often find within the lad.

Robert was only 20 years of age. He was the youngest son of William's last son, Walter, who had survived the battle at Stirling Bridge only to die of illness shortly after the birth of his youngest son Robert. Robert had taken an Anglo-Norman wife named Marjorie and she had born two children so far in their young marriage. He was tall like his grandfather and also like his grandfather blessed with a full head of hair that had already begun to turn white. His eyes were the midnight blue of the evening sky. And his teeth were straight and white. He could have had his pick from among the girls of the area but Robert chose to travel to Stirling to work on the castle fortifications that seemed in constant need of repair. It was here in Stirling that he met the young maiden Marjorie daughter of one of the many Anglo Normans who had entered Scotland from the north of England decades ago. Her father was a smithy and was glad to see his daughter married off to a man who knew how to make a living with his hands. Robert had followed in the footsteps of his ancestors who had learned from the Normans how to build with stone. Robert was also good with geometry, could speak at least three different languages and could write in Latin as well as the Norman French of the English courts. Education was important to the Cochranes of Paisley and William saw to it that all of his children and his grandchildren including the girls were exposed to the learning of the day. But, of course, what was most important to William was that all of his family had been baptized and confirmed in the church. To William Cochrane, nothing was more important.

"Come grandfather. Let's sit here in your favorite spot" Robert said with love and admiration in his voice. Robert truly loved this old man and deeply enjoyed the time he spent with him. His daily work on the Abbey did not allow much free time these days. The reconstruction was progressing but at a pace much slower than the Abbot desired.

After the two were settled, Robert asked, "Tell me about the Normans. Why did they come here? And how did they come to be so powerful in our land?"

William looked at Robert with his kind but aged eyes. "Ah yes, the Normans. Where should I begin? Well", there was a long pause for it was common for William to take his time when telling one of his cherished stories of the past. Robert knew this about his dear granddad but Robert was blessed with patience and did not allow the slow storytelling to diminish his enjoyment of that which his grandfather shared with him. William continued, "This country is now called Scotland but, that has not always been the case. Long before the Romans came to the island, we were many different tribes constantly bickering and warring with one another. The Romans brought law and order, at least to the southern part of Scotland. They were never able to subdue the tribes of the north. And then they left. Their imperial city of Rome was under attack by invading tribes from the east and they needed all of their warriors to be brought back home. The Romans also brought the Christian faith. Prior to their arrival, we worshipped many things, seen and unseen. But over time the teachings of Jesus of Nazareth took hold in our land and the vast majority of us considered ourselves Christian. I guess we can thank the old saints for that. Men like Patrick, Columba, Aidan, and good old Mungo whose real name was Kentigern. But old habits die hard and with the departure of the Roman soldiers and courts, we returned to our primitive ways. During this time, we were made up of at least five different groups of people. Those who the Romans called the Picts lived in the large area north of the rivers Forth and Clyde. The Scots, who originally came from Ireland, made their home across the river in what is now called Argyll. The Angles held Lothian while we Britons, the most ancient of tribes, held on to our homes here in Strathclyde, the valley of the river Clyde. And before the Normans came up from the Saxon south, the Norse had settled in Orkney, Shetland, Caithness, Sutherland and the Western Isles. What a mix we were! Constantly at each other's throats. It did not seem to matter if we were Christian or not, the sword and battle axe were how we settled our disputes. Even to this day." William stopped and looked at the ground while slowly shaking his head. "Even to this day," he repeated himself, "when will we ever learn … as Jesus taught his followers, those who live by the sword die by the sword." William was quiet for a brief period and Robert was concerned that he had nodded off. But William was simply lost in the memories of an old man who had witnessed much pain and sorrow brought about by man's inhumanity to his fellow man. After clearing his throat and rubbing his eyes he continued, "But, you asked about the Normans. That story begins with William, Duke of Normandy. You see, the old Danish king Canute had died and those who took his crown upon their heads were weak leaders. There was civil war throughout the Saxon south for years. We were in no better shape up here in the north. Our so-called kings were simply in one grab for power after another and the people constantly suffered because of it. William brought his powerful fighting men with him and on December 25th, 1066, he was crowned King of England. The Anglo-Normans now refer to him as William the Conqueror. Eventually, through their actions on the battle field and, of course, the marriage bed," William smiled, "the Normans had taken over in the Saxon south and even here in Scotland. Dear old king David took the throne of Scotland in 1124 after his brother Alexander had died. David's mother was Sibylla, the daughter of the great Norman King Henry I. So, David was Norman in blood and in spirit. He was a good king. He loved God and he spent much of his energy and the people's money, "William chuckled, "on strengthening the church here in Scotland. He ordered the construction of the great Abbeys at Melrose and Jedburgh. He gave huge tracts of land to members of the Norman aristocracy, families such as de Brus, de Balliol, de Comines and, of course, Walter Fitz-Alan. It was Fitz-Alan who came to Renfrew and was given much of the land to govern here at Paisley. What could we do? David was the king and he was Norman. More than that, he was in love with the Norman idea of fealty. Do you know this word fealty Robert?" William asked his grandson.

"Yes grandfather, the monks have taught me well," Robert replied. "It is from the Latin fidelilas, which means faithfulness or loyalty. But the Normans had a different use for this word. To them, it meant the obligation of fidelity owed to a feudal lord by his vassal or tenant and the sworn oath taken in the name of God to recognize and honor this obligation."

William looked at his grandson with pride. "You have learned your lessons well. Your father would be proud. So, David would give ownership and the monies being generated by these large areas of land to his Norman knights who in turn would pledge their support in arms, if necessary, in the defense of his kingship. Quite a nice little arrangement except it completely ignores the historical claims to ownership of the original tribes … like us". William stopped again and this time gazed out towards the river.

Robert interrupted his time of reflection, "Are you angry with the Normans grandfather? You know, I have married a girl with Norman blood and our children will always have that as part of their heritage."

"No, Robert, I'm not angry with the Normans, "replied William, "For what Satan had intended for evil, God turned into good." William continued while casting his eyes toward the Abbey and gesturing with a sweep of his hand. "The Normans brought us this."

"No, Robert, I'm not angry. Fitz-Alan came to us from Shropshire in England. As High Steward of Scotland, what King David called his dapifer, Walter Fitz-Alan had tremendous power and influence. It was his decision to build a stone church here at Paisley. He brought 13 Cluniac monks from the monastery in Shropshire to assist in this endeavor. Do you know this word Cluniac?" William stopped at looked at Robert waiting on his response.

"Of course, grandfather. The Cluniacs were started at Cluny in Normandy. They were Benedictines intent on reforming the Benedictine brothers. They wanted to restore the traditional monastic life designed by Benedict himself. They taught that those who had been called by the Lord Jesus into the brotherhood were to be educated, celibate, and caring always for the poor and unfortunate of God's children. I even know their prayer. It was drilled into me by the brothers here at the Abbey. Would you like to hear it?" Robert asked his grandfather.

William nodded.

Robert began, "O God, by whose grace we servants, the holy brothers of Cluny, enkindled with the fire of your love, become burning and shining lights in your Church; Grant that we may also be aflame with the spirit of love and discipline and may ever walk before you as children of light through Jesus Christ our Lord who with you in the unity of the Holy Spirit lives and reigns one God now and forever. Amen". William and Robert both crossed themselves as Robert finished the prayer.

"Robert, did you ever consider the brotherhood yourself?" William asked.

"At one time, as a boy, I did consider it. But God works in mysterious ways and He has led me to believe that is not my destiny." Robert responded in a solemn fashion.

William looked at him with deep respect and love. He knew that his days were numbered and soon he would leave this world and enter the next. It gave him great comfort to hear Robert speak these words of faith. Like this great stone building they gazed upon, his grandson's words filled him with peace.

"It was the monks who taught us how to build with stone," William continued with his story. "There had been a church here since the days of Saint Mirin during the rule of the kings of Strathclyde. But it was a simple structure made of wood and mud, nothing as grand or as majestic as this," once again pointing in the direction of the Abbey. "They taught my ancestors how to cut the stones, how to place them in the correct position, how to lay down the mortar and all the other details of designing and building in the Norman fashion. And, once we knew, we passed that knowledge down from generation to generation. My father taught me and I taught Walter your father and he taught you."

"So God has used the Normans to make Scotland stronger and smarter?" Robert asked.

"Without the Normans, there might not be a Scotland," William replied. "But I'm afraid that story will have to wait for another day. It is time for me to rest. But before I do, I want to enter the Abbey and pray. Would you lead me lad?" And with that, Robert took the elbow of his elderly grandfather and led him into this structure that meant so much to them both...

The next morning Robert arrived early at the simple wood and thatch house of his grandfather. It was but a short walk from Robert and Marjorie's dwelling. Much to his surprise his grandfather had already awaken and was busy cooking a bit of fish to eat for his morning meal.

"Ah Robert, good morning lad, I trust you slept well?"

"Like a stone." Robert responded. "I was thinking that today maybe you would accompany me to the Abbey. We are working on the Narthex wall. I thought perhaps you could find a place close by to rest and we could continue our discussion from yesterday?"

"You know me lad, if I have an audience, I could talk for days." And they both chuckled at his comment.

After they had eaten they slowly walked over to the western edge of the building. Many areas were under construction and the workers were already busily at their tasks. The two found a comfortable place for William to sit and Robert proceeded to measure and place stones.

"Tell me about Larg's grandfather. Do you remember?" Robert asked as he was working the mortar.

"My goodness Robert, that was so long ago. Let me think. Yes, I can remember the great battle. I was a mere lad of 12 or maybe 13 years of age. King Alexander II had been in negotiations with King Hakon of Norway for control of the highlands and the islands off the western coast of Scotland. This area had been fought over for hundreds of years going back to the days of the earliest Norse invasions. After the death of Alexander II, the talks had broken off and Hakon, in frustration, had sent a raiding party up the Clyde. His men got as far east as here in Paisley although they mainly stayed on the north side of the Clyde creating chaos all throughout Argyll. Alexander called for his knights and my father and uncles were involved as well. After all, to my family, this was now personal. They had invaded our homeland. Hakon had assembled a large fleet of long ships off the eastern coast of the Great Cumbrae Island but left a smaller group of Norse warriors on the mainland at the village of Largs. Alexander of Dundonald, under orders from his king Alexander III, had assembled a large gathering of Anglo-Norman knights and a number of Scottish infantry, what the King called his *pedisequi patrie*, the foot sloggers of the locality." William laughed slightly at this memory. "We might have been simple foot sloggers but we wielded some fairly large axes and swords. I was too young to join the battle so my father had me stand at the top of a slight rise close to Alexander of Dundonald and his entourage from Ayr. I had a perfect view of the entire battlefield. I have to admit, when I first saw those Norse, I was scared. They were big men carrying huge weapons of war. What I remember most was their hair and beards. It was the brightest shade of red you can imagine, almost orange in color. And they had these huge shields they would hide behind in a tight circle as they slowly moved forward in battle. But they were no match for the Anglo-Norman knights riding upon their massive steeds covered with mail. Lad, those Norman knights knew how to fight! Eventually the weather turned awful and Hakon had to withdraw his men back to his ships and move them to safer waters or the whole fleet would have been destroyed. And after a few days, it was all over. Hakon sailed back to Norway and negotiations resumed between the two courts. In the year, 1266, the Treaty of Perth was signed by both Magnus Hakonarson, the king of Norway at that time and our King Alexander III. This treaty ceded all Scotland's western seaboard to Alexander. A centuries old territorial dispute had at last been settled." At this thought, William smiled and looked up to where workers were standing on scaffolding placing the stones.

As William watched the workers he became lost in his memories of Largs. He vividly remembered the events of that day. There was so much blood. The men were yelling, swearing and crying out in pain. The horses were snorting and stomping at the ground. The storm clouds had rolled up from the west and flashes of lightening were quickly followed by booming sounds of thunder. The rain was torrential. William thought the world was coming to an end. And for many of the men he saw that day, it was the end of their days upon the planet. William prayed to God that day. He prayed for his safety and the safekeeping of his father and other members of his family.

He remembered watching a priest on his knees deep in prayer while the battle raged around him. William was transfixed by this site. How could this man remain so calm in the midst of this chaos? He remembered watching a Norse warrior swing his battle axe down upon the priest killing him in the twinkling of an eye and then the Norseman was surrounded and cut down by the Scots who had joined the battle.

As William stood there gazing up to the workers his eyes moved to the open sky. He saw thin wispy clouds gently floating by and saw birds circling above the trees. He spoke out loud but in a soft distant voice. "Will we ever learn? Why can't we be satisfied with what God has bestowed upon us? Why must the men whom God has placed in authority over us be constantly seeking to increase their sphere of control? What is wrong with us?"

At this moment, Robert had quietly walked close enough to William to hear him speaking. "Grandfather, who are you talking to?"

William looked surprised. "Ah lad, I guess no one. Maybe God. Who knows? Just the ramblings of an old man who has seen more suffering than he cares to."

"The sun is getting high in the sky. Would you like to return to your home?" Robert asked.

"No, Robert, I would like to enter into the church and sit there, if you don't mind helping me? And then you may return to your work," William said with a sigh.

The two of them slowly made their way into the interior of the abbey. As they encountered the workers and monks scattered around the structure, the men would nod their heads with respect and offer a pleasant good morning to William for he was highly respected within the community of Paisley. His age generated some of the respect but, in reality, William was respected for the life he had led, the things he had done and the wisdom he had accumulated. Everyone knew he was filled with great stories and that he loved to tell them.

William sat down near the center of the nave. At that precise moment, the Abbot of Paisley Abbey walked into the nave and saw William and his grandson.

"Good morning William of Cochrane. How are you this fine Lord's day?" asked the Abbot.

"I am well brother John. And how is the Abbot this morning?" responded William while Robert nodded his head and shook the hand of the good brother.

"Well. Thank you. Do you like the progress we are making so far on the reconstruction of this fine old building? What Satan intended for evil, God is using for good. Right Robert? "chuckled the middle-aged Abbot. Father John had come to Paisley as a young priest. He had been brought there by the Abbot Walter thirty-five years ago to teach Latin to the young nobles who had been sent to the Abbey for an education. He stayed and over time proved himself to the congregation of brothers and sisters that were located here and to the gathering of believers who worshipped at Paisley. The now Abbot John was of average height and weight and had lost most his hair early on in adulthood. He was a fair leader who was well liked by almost everyone associated with the Abbey. Perhaps, most importantly, it was to Abbot John and his predecessor the Abbot Roger the responsibility for rebuilding the Abbey and surrounding buildings had fallen after its total destruction by the forces of King Edward I of England during the year 1307.

"Good progress. We are making good progress. God is good." Robert responded while William looked on.

"Father John, when did this holy place become an Abbey?" William asked. "I know it has been decades but I can't remember the actual date."

"Fitz-Alan brought the Shropshire monks here in the year 1169. Work began on the Priory almost immediately and the status was raised to an Abbey in 1219. When that happened, the monks reported directly to Rome. The Abbot was answerable only to the Holy Father, his eminence, the Pope. The first Abbot's name has been lost to history but we do know that William was made Abbot in the year 1225. I would guess that much of the buildings were probably finished or well under construction by that time." Abbot John responded to the old man's question.

"Did they have the same situation we are dealing with now?" Robert asked.

The abbot looked at Robert and replied, "And what situation would that be lad?"

"Two popes," Robert responded with a bit of sarcasm in his voice. At this, William looked at his son as if to urge caution and restraint. Although Abbot John was a kind and gentle man, he was still a very important part of the church's hierarchy and as abbot reported directly to the pope himself. But John saw William's concern and raised his hand as a gesture of peace and attempts to answer Robert's question. "No, Robert, the situation was different during those days. The Avignon papacy did not get its start until the year 1309, 21 years ago. You see, Louis IV, the one people call the Bavarian, became Holy Roman Emperor. And Phillip IV sat on the throne of France. There was constant tension and outright warfare between Louis, Phillip and the Popes of Rome. There had always been this struggle for power between the Church and the State. This goes back to the earliest days of the papacy. The popes really had minimal temporal power so they relied upon the support of various kings and emperors who had sought the church's blessing. There has been a long-standing tradition of holding the coronation ceremony for the kings at Rome. The pope would place the crown upon the earthly ruler's head and then he would prostrate himself before the newly crowned head of state to show his dependence upon the knightly swords of this ruler. Through this symbolic act, Church and State had become one. It was designed to bring unity to the kingdoms of man but instead brought hostility and dissension. There was this constant struggle for power and control. The pope claimed only he had the authority to anoint the king for leadership and, of course, the kings claimed the authority to decide who would be pope. And they had the military strength to support their desires. In the year 1305, Pope Clement V who had been selected by King Phillip of France declined to move to Rome and had his papal court established at Avignon in France. Eventually, the Emperor Louis IV had enough and he installed Nicholas V as pope with his papacy in Rome, this, of course, after he deposed Pope John XXII who had replaced Clement at Avignon. What a mess! Pope Nicholas tries Pope John in abstentia for heresy and in retaliation Pope John excommunicates Pope Nicholas."

Robert interrupts, "So … good brother, who is pope? Who is the head of the church today?"

The Abbot lowered his eyes to the ground and thought before answering, "Jesus the Christ is now and always shall be the head of our church, at least in heaven." Abbot John smiled, "But as far as here on Earth, the answer to that question probably depends upon who is asking it and who is answering it and where the conversation is taking place." And at this comment, all three men roared in laughter. "What I do know for certain is this … last year our beloved King Robert the Bruce died at the manor of Cardross in Dunbarton leaving his 5-year-old son, David upon the throne. The English are once again rattling their swords as they look north towards our land and rumor has it the barons want young David to flee for France. Edward Balliol, King John's grown son, will probably lay claim to the throne and who knows what will happen then. Rome and Avignon are a long way away from Paisley lad but I'm afraid the English will once again be on our doorstep soon." The conversation had turned rather serious and all three men solemnly looked at one another, then at the Abbey and then towards the heavens.

Attempting to change the dialogue to something more pleasant, William gently stroked his long beard and smiled. "John, surely God must be working behind the scenes here. We have rebuilt in 25 years what took the original builders 50. And we did this without help from Rome, Avignon, or anywhere else in Europe for that matter. Look around you. We did this with these good men and women you see in front of you. They put their faith in God and look what we have been able to do."

"Yes, my dear old friend, God has blessed our work here at Paisley." Abbot John smiled as he placed his arm around William's shoulders. Both turned and looked towards the Altar located at the east end of the Nave.

After some time had passed, William broke the peaceful silence the two men were enjoying, "I wish the Wallace had survived to see this day. He loved this place. It would have broken his heart to see what Edward's forces did to this holy building." William said with a touch of sadness.

Robert had been standing behind the two and spoke up when the name of William Wallace was mentioned.

"Grandfather, tell me about him. Tell me about the Wallace." Robert asked respectfully.

"Ah … the first time I saw him, he was a lad of 10. There had been trouble in Elderslie between the local clans and the English sheriff. His family sent him here to the Abbey to keep him safe and also to give him a decent education. The Wallace's were not wealthy nor were they members of the Norman aristocracy but they believed in education, were strong in the Christian faith and desired a good future for their son. Of course, as soon as the monks began to instruct the lad, they saw his keen intelligence and energetic desire to learn all he could about every subject. And, of course, you couldn't help but notice the lad. He was huge. Even at 10, he was already the size of an average man and could wield both the battle-axe and the double-edged claymore. My goodness, the boy was as strong as an ox." William smiled as he reminisced. William sat in silence for quite some time. Robert thought perhaps he had drifted off but soon William opened his eyes and turned to them both and said, "Scotland exists because of him, you know. Without William Wallace, the clans would have never set aside their senseless feuds, the Scottish barons would have never turned against their Norman king and Robert the Bruce would have never become king of a united Scotland. We owe him so much." William's voiced trailed off.

John looked at Robert and then spoke to William. "Perhaps you should rest? Why not sit over there by the central tower. We've not yet finished the roof and there is a warm place there where you could sit in the sunshine." William nodded and the three of them walked to the middle of the nave. William stopped suddenly and stared at the supporting stonewall. "Robert, you need to have one of your masons check out this part," William said as he pointed to a specific spot in the support. "I don't like the looks of the stone placement here." Robert quickly glanced at the abbot. He knew they had been pressed to complete this section quickly and even if his grandfather were correct, there was nothing that could be done. In any event, the central tower wall looked strong to Robert and thought his grandfather was simply taxed from his memories of William Wallace.

"Yes, grandfather, I will check it out." Robert said to his grandfather in a reassuring manner.

Once William found a comfortable location to sit he suddenly smiled and looked at both his grandson and the abbot. "You know, Margaret and I attended his wedding. What a grand occasion that was. People came from all over; Let's see … it was the year 1292. Yes, that's it, 1292."

"I did not know that William," remarked the abbot and he was truly surprised for he had known William for years and thought he had heard all his stories from the past.

"He married a pretty young lass by the name of Marian Braidfute. The wedding party lasted for days. The feast itself was something else …so much food and ale. They were married in Lanark at the church of St. Kentigern. Of course, we all know Kentigern by his Cumbric nickname, Mungo. Anyway, Wallace married her in the same church where he first saw her while attending the mass. Even then, there was tension surrounding the affair. Rumor has it that Heselrig the English sheriff of Lanark wanted his son to marry the lass. Apparently, she had taken over her father's substantial manor after his death and with her marriage the groom would receive the land and buildings. She wasn't extremely wealthy but fairly well off in comparison to most folk. My goodness … those were happy days. William and Marian settled down and that would have been the end of the story had it not been for the ragman roll." William stated while shaking his head. "That's what caused all the fuss."

Robert had heard this story before and knew that his grandfather's memories were accurate. There had been peace in the land during those days. England's Edward was occupied with his desires for French territory and had recently subdued the defiant Welsh. Unfortunately, this all changed with the untimely death of King Alexander III of Scotland who fatally fell from his horse while hunting. He left no living sons and this initiated a struggle for control among the Anglo-Norman Scottish nobles. Bishop Fraser of Glasgow appealed to Edward to intercede and Edward proposed a marriage between his son and Alexander's granddaughter, Margaret, known as the Maid of Norway. This seemed to appease most of the Scottish nobility and perhaps would have been a peaceful resolution but Margaret suddenly died in Orkney. Into this vacuum John Balliol pledged his fealty to Edward in exchange for his support of Balliol as King Alexander's replacement on the Scottish throne. For this action, Balliol earned the nickname Toom Tabard which meant empty coat implying he was a king with no power to rule. Scotland erupted into civil war. In reality, it was simply the ancient feuds coming to life once again. Except this time the strife was on a much grander scale and involved the powerful King Edward of England himself. In order to save face with his aristocratic Scottish supporters and perhaps show them he was not Edward's lap dog, Balliol entered Scotland into a treaty with France, Edward's sworn enemy. This enraged the English king and he gathered his armies for an invasion of Scotland. His troops devastated Berwick and the surrounding lowlands of Scotland. He eventually left but placed John de Warrenne and Hugh de Cressingham, two faithful Anglo-Norman knights, in charge of the king's peace. Edward's intention was to bring Scotland, at least the lowlands, under his dominion. Of course, this led to all-out war. Due to the superiority of the English forces and the fact they had established strong fortifications at strategic locations throughout the countryside the Scots originally fought a hit and run type of warfare. And the Wallace's excelled at this type of fighting. In fact, all the clans of the ancient kingdom of Strathclyde eventually rose in rebellion. It happened slowly however involving small skirmishes between English soldiers and various lowland families. Things came to a head in 1296 when Edward demanded those who would pledge their loyalty to him sign what's become known as the ragman roll. Robert knew that his grandfather William had signed the detested document because he mistakenly thought it would bring peace back to his homeland. But it did not. It only increased the tension between English and Scott. The Wallace clan refused to sign and for that they were singled out for an example of Edward's wrath, as members of William Wallace's family, including his father, were murdered by the local English forces.

Wallace was incensed by this action and vowed vengeance upon any and all English unfortunate enough to be in Scotland. He became a wanted man. There was a price on his head.

William suddenly spoke to Robert and John, "you know the Wallace's had a daughter. Her name was Elizabeth. When the troubles began, she was sent here to the Abbey for safekeeping. My wife and I would often feed her and keep her company. You don't remember her Robert. You weren't born yet. So sad, what happened to her mother and father. Do you two know the story?" William looked at John and his grandson.

John spoke first, "All of Scotland knows the story. The English sheriff Heselrig of Lanark attempted to use the wife of William Wallace to trap him in the town of Lanark. When that failed and Wallace and his clansmen managed to escape with the help of his wife, Marian, Heselrig had her executed on the spot. Wallace was crazed with grief and anger. He sent out word to all the neighboring clans and a strong force was assembled, which then attacked the town where Heselrig was located. I have been told that Wallace personally cut off the head of the sheriff himself. Yes, all of Scotland knows the story."

William looked slowly at John and then towards his grandson, "And your father was there. He did not want me to go. He told me I needed to stay here in Paisley and look after the family. But he was determined to help Wallace seek justice for what had been done. He stayed with Wallace throughout the war. By this time, all of Scotland was in arms. Even the highland clans had come down out of the mountains to join the fight. It was William Wallace who ignited the spark and it was

William Wallace who united the people of Scotland. In September of that year, 1297, we defeated Edward I and his English forces at the Battle of Stirling Bridge. Yes, I was there. And I will never forget that day. On that day, we became Scots, all of us, united against a common enemy. And on that day, I lost my son. Your Uncle died during that battle. I did not see it happen but was told later that a Welsh arrow had pierced his heart and he died instantly. I was overcome with grief and filled with anger. To this day, I will never understand how the Welsh, a people very much like us, could offer aid to Edward's forces."

The three were quiet for a time. Workers would come and go. The monks tended to their daily tasks and everything would occasionally come to a stop as the hours of prayer were followed. Everything in the village was directed by the scheduled hours of prayer and meditation. In fact, all manner of life was planned according to the rituals associated with the Abbey and its parish church. So many of the local inhabitants had invested so much of their energies into reconstructing the main buildings, attending the services at the appointed times and in general uniting with the community through mysterious bond of the Abbey. It was as if the building was alive. One could almost feel the presence of the spiritual kingdom while still maintaining residence in the physical world.

After some time had passed, the Abbot asked William "was William Wallace a religious man?"

William thought a moment before answering, "I suppose good brother, the answer to the question depends upon how you define religious? Was he a saint? Heavens no, William Wallace was no saint. He could be vindictive and blinded by his rage. Although he yearned for peace and a simple life, he was a product of his times. Our world is a violent place where death is just around the corner and can happen at any moment. William was a survivor. I don't think he put much stock in the teaching to turn the other cheek." William said this with a slight smile on his lips. "But he was not an evil man. Was he a sinner? Yes, of course, as we all are. But I think his heart was in the right place … most of the time. There is a troubling story about him that he once had an English soldier skinned alive and wore that skin around his waist like a belt. I hope that is not true but I do know from first-hand experience that if the Wallace lost his temper with you, there would be no safe place to hide." William was quiet once again as if he was deep in thought. "What was it that you taught us one mass … ah yes, I remember now, it was something Saint James wrote about in the New Testament …Pure and lasting religion in the sight of God our Father means that we must care for orphans and widows in their troubles, and refuse to let the world corrupt us. Did I get it correct brother John?" John nodded while smiling. "Yes, wise one, you must have been listening that morning?" John said with a gentle laugh as a loving parent might tease their child.

"Oh, I listen to you brother, even when my eyes might be closed." They all laughed at this comment. "Of course, "William continued, "I don't always agree with what you say but I do listen." William smiled and tugged at John's beard. "No, Wallace was not religious as some might define the word. But if I understand the good James correctly, true religion is measured more by what a man does as opposed to what he says. It is easy to say I am a follower of the Christ. It is another thing to demonstrate that through your actions. So … if I consider what William Wallace did with his life and how he did it then I must admit, he was a religious man, indeed. He worked so hard to ensure that justice was had by all not just the wealthy or powerful. Stories have been told of his feats in battle but you do not hear the stories of the young man I once knew. How he gave away a prized family cow one day to a family in the community who had lost theirs due to a fire. No payment expected and none could be offered. How one day, he dove into the Clyde trying to save a boy who was trying to swim across from Argyll. He managed to save the child and carried him home on the back of his horse. You see, this is why men followed him into battle and gave their lives for him. I suppose historians will write that it was because of their desire for Scottish independence. And that may be true to a degree but no, it was Wallace himself. It was the man who inspired all of us. It was his character, his spirit." And at this, William once again became silent until finally Robert said, "And perhaps that is a good definition for what it truly means to be religious? It is not what we say but how we live out our lives. I wish the powers of this world understood that lesson. Grandfather, are you angry with the English and their king? After all, it was upon Edward's orders that Wallace was killed in that horrible and humiliating fashion. It was upon Edward's orders that Scotland was put to the torch and the famine that resulted from the burning of our crops took the lives of many innocent people. It was upon Edward's orders that this beautiful house of God was burned to the ground. Does that not make you angry even after all these years?"

William looked at his grandson for quite a while before answering, "of course, when the troubles began, I was furious with Edward, his nobles and all the English people. I lost so much to him. And when they destroyed this Abbey, I thought my soul would shatter into pieces. I have given my life to this holy place of worship. And yet, time has a way of healing even one's shattered soul. No, I will never have my son again by my side. King Edward, William Wallace and the war took him from me. But we did rebuild this place. And we built it well. We built it to last. We built it to be a testimony for those who come after us of how important God was to us. We, all the people you can see working around this glorious building, and all those who have toiled in the past and have since died, we all have left this thing at this site to be a memorial of our lives. This is how they will remember us. They will think those were the people who gave all they had to construct this Abbey to serve as a beacon of light in a world of darkness. Good things have happened here my son, and good things will continue to happen here. Babies have been baptized here, young lovers have been married here, last rites have been said over the dying here and the bones of my good wife and some of my children and grandchildren lie over there," as he points in the direction of the graveyard, "in that sacred ground. This is truly a house of God. This is where heaven meets earth and the two intermingle so that we mere mortals can have but a glimpse of the heavenly majesty that awaits us."

"Well said William of Cochrane … well said" responded the Abbot. "And now, I must leave you two." And he ambled away to tend to one of the many duties an Abbot has when managing an affair of this magnitude and importance.

"Grandfather, are you hungry?" asked Robert.

"You know me, I can always eat," responded William with a smile.

The two walked out of the nave and into the tent which had been set up to prepare the meals for the gathered workers. There was an empty bench and the two sat down. Robert went to the woman working the large kettle hanging over the fire.

"Well Muriel, what sumptuous delight have you prepared for my hard-working men this fine day of God's creation?" asked Robert of the elderly woman who was stirring the concoction with a large heavy wooden spoon. Muriel had been working at the Abbey way before Robert had been born. She was not nearly as old as William but had been around there when Edward's troops had put the torch to the place. Muriel was a constant fixture on the Abbey grounds. She was loved by all and always seemed to have a smile on her face and a good word for those who would bother to take the time to stop and chat. The rumor was that she had once been in love with William but he had chosen another. Muriel never married and, of course, was childless. When asked she often just responded that she should have been a nun but didn't like to work indoors. No one pushed for the real reason but most guessed it had something to do with William and her undying love for the man.

"Robert, my lad, it's good to see you looking fit and apparently, hungry. Today, I'm cooking up my special stew. It smells delicious. Can I get you and your grandfather a bowl?" she asked as she glanced over to where William was sitting. He was motionless with his eyes closed. Must be praying she thought to herself. The man does know how to pray.

"What Muriel? Were you speaking to me?" asked Robert.

"No lad, I'm just speaking to the heavens … of course, I'm speaking to you. Do you want a bit of stew for you and your granddad?" chuckled the cook. "How's the old man today? Did he sleep well last night? You know, he is aging well. He doesn't look a day over 100." Both she and Robert laughed with gusto.

"Ach … the old man is doing fine. He's been rather talkative this morning. Telling the Abbot and I about the old days … Wallace and Edward an a that." Robert replied with a look of concern on his face.

"I see," said Muriel. "Those were difficult days for him … for all of us. Difficult days."

Robert took two bowls of stew from Muriel. "Muriel, this looks and smells good … what's your secret?"

"Would not be a secret if I told you now would it" Muriel replied with a wink. "It's just a mixture of leeks, onions and cabbage with a little meat thrown in for good measure. Oh, and some garlic and rosemary for spice. Now, take it over to William and enjoy."

Robert did as he was told and soon both he and his grandfather were licking the bowls to gather up the last bits of tasty meat. "I feel like another," Robert said to William. And he walked back over to Muriel and her pot of boiling stew. "Can I have some more?" he pleaded.

"Of course, I've made plenty this day," Muriel said as she beamed with satisfaction. As Robert stood by the pot and watched Muriel fill his bowl once again, he asked her a question, "Were you there Muriel? Were you there when it happened?"

"When what happened, lad?" Muriel responded.

"When Edward's troops burned the place to the ground and grandfather … lost his mind" Robert said this last bit quietly and under his breath as if he were embarrassed to speak of such matters.

"The man never lost his mind. He was just so-filled with shock, grief, and, I suppose, anger that he did things that some might think peculiar," Muriel responded with what was obvious tremendous respect and tenderness for William.

"Tell me what happened? Whenever I try to bring it up with my mother she just changes the subject and, of course, the one time I tried to talk to William about it, he just grunted, nodded his head and closed his eyes as if he were in prayer," Robert explained.

"Well … it was a long time ago. You had not yet been born. The Wallace had been captured and brutally executed on orders from Edward himself. Let's see … that would have been in 1305. With Wallace out of the way, Edward decided he could turn his attention to other pressing matters of state. However, Robert the Bruce saw an opportunity and he took it. He killed his competition for the throne, John Comyn, and was crowned King of the Scots at Scone in the spring of 1306. This infuriated Edward and he sent Percy and Valence from the north of England over the border to ravage the land once again. This time it was even more brutal than before. Edward wanted every Bruce supporter driven from his lands. He viewed them as traitors. He ordered death and destruction. It was devastation on a grand scale. And one of the targets was, of course, the Abbey. Not too many know this part of the story. You see, the Wallace had a daughter, Elizabeth. Well, your grandfather, God bless him, agreed to hide her here in Paisley at the Abbey after the murder of William Wallace's wife. She was only three years of age at the time. Edward sent spies to find her but they never did. The clans took it upon themselves to keep moving her around from one holy house to another in secret. Not even the locals knew what was going on right under their very noses. Anyway … that never did sit well with the old King so when he finally had a chance to seek his revenge on us he took full advantage of the situation. By this time, he was, of course, too old and sickly to lead the forces but he was the one who gave the ultimate order to burn it to the ground. I guess it was some type of payback in his twisted mind. When they arrived, most of the monks and the locals fled across the Clyde up into the hills of Argyll. They knew the English wouldn't follow them. The English were more than a little afraid of the highlanders. But your grandfather stayed. We pleaded with him to come with us but he would not be moved. Even by this time, he was one of the oldest people around these parts. His wife had been dead for years and, as you know, he had buried a few of his children, as well. I guess he thought if he was meant to die, he was going to die right here protecting his beloved Abbey." At this point, Muriel tries to fight back the tears but she can't as they trickle down each cheek.

"The English came and they did what Edward had sent them to do. They destroyed it. Did not leave one stone unturned. William resisted as well as an old man can. At one point, he even managed to escape their grasp on him and he ran into the burning nave screaming in some incomprehensible language. Rumor has it that he had been possessed by the Spirit of God and was crying out to the angels to come and protect this holy place from the followers of Satan. I don't know about that … I do know your granddad and I think he was probably just cursing those English dogs in the old Cumbric tongue of his youth. Robert, your grandfather did not lose his mind but, he did lose his temper and my God lad when that man got angry well … you had better run for the hills" At this point the tears had stopped and Muriel and Robert both were laughing. She continued, "He could not stop it from happening of course, And eventually. He walked back out of the burning building. But something had happened to him while he was there in the midst of the flames. None of us really know for sure and William rarely spoke of it. All any of us could get from him was he saw something or someone and heard a voice." Muriel stopped and looked at Robert whose mouth had dropped open in amazement for he had never been told this part of the story. Perhaps his mother was not even aware, for surely, if she had known this would she not have told him so?

"I can tell lad from your reaction that this part is new? Ah well, 'tis time you knew the whole of it. The voice told him to stop resisting his enemy. The voice told him to stay alive and find a way to make peace in order to rebuild. Yes, Robert, the voice told him it was his job to rebuild the Abbey. And that is exactly what he dedicated the rest of his life in doing. And … the voice told him something rather strange. The voice said to let his hair and beard grow uncut. He was not to take a razor or knife to it for the remainder of his days. And he did as he was told." They both turned and looked once again at the long white beard and hair of the old man who had seen so much in his life. As they were looking at him, he raised his head from his prayers and looked at both of them and smiled ever so sweetly and gently. It was like he knew at that moment the nature of their conversation. And then he nodded slowly and closed his eyes.

"So, there you have it Robert. That's all I know. That's all he has ever shared with me and it took years before I was able to extract even that from him." Muriel looked once again at William as he rested after his simple meal of her secret stew.

Robert looked at Muriel and said, "You have always loved him haven't you?"

Muriel seemed somewhat taken aback by Robert's directness. "Yes, if the truth be told, I suppose I have, ever since I was a child. He was old enough to be my father but I didn't care. I knew it would never amount to anything. He dearly loved his Margaret. That was a terrible loss for him when she passed. "

"But Muriel, that's been years ago. Surely, he must have known your feelings for him. Did you two ever talk about what could be?" Robert asked as he looked into the old woman's eyes.

"Oh, once or twice, we talked a wee bit but he always made it clear that although he was quite fond of me he truly only had room in his heart for one woman and now she was waiting for him in heaven. So … we became close friends and, of course, we are bonded together by our faith and this land." Muriel looked off into the distance and rubbed away the one solitary tear that was trickling down the side of her face. She then crossed herself in prayer and walked away from Robert saying as she walked, "Robert, I've got things to tend to and I imagine so do you lad."

Robert watched her walk into the building where much of the rations were stored. He wondered about her and his grandfather. Why hadn't love sprung forth from this obviously fertile territory? He did not remember his grandmother. She had died shortly after his birth. Thus, he had no way of understanding the depth of love his grandfather felt for her even to this day. Just then the bells rang. It was time for the monks to stop their work and head into the great nave for a time of communal prayer and meditation. During this time, all work ceased on the structure so that an atmosphere of reverential quiet could be achieved. Robert walked over to where William was resting.

"Have a nice chat with Muriel?" William asked pleasantly.

"Yes, I did. She told me something I never knew about you." Robert responded. He then waited in silence to see how his grandfather would react.

"Oh … that. Well lad that was a long time ago." William spoke with a quiet tone of voice and a heavy heart.

"So … that is why you do not cut your hair or beard. You were told not to as an outward sign of what transpired that day?" Robert asked in a quizzical fashion.

"Yes," was William's simple response, "When God speaks, one must listen."

"You think it was God who spoke to you?" Robert asked in a soft and respectful manner.

"Actually Robert, I think it was the Lord Jesus. I could tell immediately it was the voice of a person, a person like you and I. And I knew it was a male voice. I also immediately knew that I had no choice but to listen and obey what he told me. It saved my life. I was able to work on the Abbey and now God has given me the years to see my efforts coming to fruition. And," William paused for a moment, "the Lord has blessed me a life long enough to see you come into this world and watch you grow into a good man, a man of God." At this Robert's eyes began to water and he had to look away to maintain his composure. "Come with me boy, I want to show you something." And he grabbed Robert by the arm to steady himself as they walked along the gravel path.

"Where are we heading?" asked Robert.

"You'll see. Let's walk down to the edge of the river," replied William.

The two walked slowly away from the Abbey west to the edge of the river White Cart. It was summer and the water level had dropped somewhat from its earlier springtime high. Robert guided William right up to the edge where the bank dropped off quickly into the swiftly flowing water.

"Now turn around and tell me what you see?" directed William.

"It's the Abbey grandfather. You can't miss it. It fills the whole scene from here," replied Robert.

"But lad … what do you see?" asked William once again with strength in his voice.

"The Abbey," Robert responded slightly frustrated but then suddenly he stopped and smiled realizing this was a lesson he was being taught by this wise old man so he asked, "Grandfather, what do you see?"

William smiled from ear to ear. "I see life. I see the beauty and majesty of the Almighty. I see that which can't be seen with human eyes. I see all of our ancestors. I see my mother and father. I see my Margaret. I see my sons and daughters and grandchildren and great grandchildren. I see the Wallace and his daughter Elizabeth. I see the past. I see the present. I see the future. I see our family gaining in numbers and spreading throughout the land. I see great oceans filled with terrifying beasts. I see long ships filled with many people leaving this place and following the setting sun in those ships. They are frightened but are praying to God and God delivers them from all harm. I see you Robert as an old and happy man. I see the angels of heaven as they sing praises to the one who is holy and eternal. I see the Lord Jesus standing at the right hand of God his father. I see the Spirit of God moving over mother earth and through her air and deep into her waters. I see my death but with no fear. And most of all, I see love. That my precious grandson is what these old eyes see."

The two of them stood there side by side gazing at the great Paisley Abbey. Robert was moved beyond words with what his dear grandfather had just shared with him. He wanted this moment in time to last forever. For it was peace he was experiencing. Not the peace brought about by the workings of flawed and mortal men but the perfect peace of the eternal God created only by the presence of His son Jesus the Christ and sanctified by the Holy Spirit. Robert knew in a moment that he was in the presence of the holy and this place was indeed sacred ground. William slowly dropped to his knees as Robert assisted him. Then Robert also knelt. William placed his hand in Robert's and together they recited the prayer Jesus had taught his disciples to pray … "Our Father in heaven, may your name be honored. May your kingdom come soon. May your will be done here on earth, just as it is in heaven. Give us food for today, and forgive us our sins, just as we have forgiven those who have sinned against us, and do not let us yield to temptation but deliver us from the evil one." Both men crossed themselves at the amen. Then William added, "Lord Jesus come soon, I am ready." Robert could hear the birds singing to one another. He could feel the air as it gently caressed his face and hands. He felt alive. He felt connected to this old man. He felt the energy of the earth move up from the ground and into his body, into his soul. He was at one with all things. He was complete. He was whole. After what seemed like an eternity but was probably only a few minutes Robert turned to help his grandfather rise from his kneeling position.

"Grandfather, it's time to head home," spoke Robert gently to the old man. There was no response. Then slowly William opened his eyes and spoke to Robert, "help me lie down lad." So, Robert helped his grandfather lie down on his back. William looked up into Robert's eyes, "My time has come Robert. Tell your Mother that I love her." William's breathing was weak and labored. "Tell all of my family that I love them." Robert's eyes began to fill with tears. "Do not cry for me son. We all must come to this moment in our lives. I go now to be with my Lord. I have lived a long life. I have tried to run the race well. Bury my body next to my Margaret." The color of William's face was slowly fading as he continued to struggle for air. "Robert ... keep the faith." These were the last words spoken on this earth by William Cochrane. But as the life was slowly ebbing from the body of this very old and tired man once again William heard the voice. Welcome home my son, it said. And a smile came to William's lips as he breathed his last.

William's body was buried as he wished next to his loving companion. For weeks, the brothers and sisters of the Abbey, William's family and all the inhabitants of Paisley mourned the loss of this good soul. But as time passed people moved on with their lives. The bells continued to call the monks to prayer. The priest conducted the mass. Robert and his workers returned to the reconstruction of the great building. Even old Muriel, who perhaps was impacted the most by the death of her trusted friend and not so secret love found she was able to once again smile and laugh while serving the Abbey workers their daily meal. Muriel had insisted on preparing William's body for his burial and she had shocked those gathered for the internment when they saw that William's long beard and hair had been neatly trimmed. When asked about it, she responded that this was something William had requested of her some time ago. She told everyone the voice had said to him to take this action at his death. She told everyone that William had completed his mission given to him by the Lord and that the cutting of his beard and hair was symbolic of the completion of this divine task. Everyone agreed and they all smiled when Muriel had said that William told her he wanted to be presentable when he met the King of all Kings.

Life went on. Robert and Marjorie had many children and quite a few survived to adulthood. Edward Balliol did manage to get himself crowned king of Scotland and gave away to England much of Scotland's southern territories in an attempt to bring peace to his troubled land. After his abdication, governing Scotland became increasingly difficult as the powerful nobility became increasingly intractable. This was very much the situation during the reigns of Robert II and Robert III both elderly men when they first sat upon the throne.

Abbot John was replaced at his death in the year 1347 by Abbot James. That was the year plague came to Europe eventually making its way into Scottish territory by 1350. Roughly one third of the Scottish population died from what became known as the Black Death. However, work continued on the Abbey. It was the Abbey that stood strong. Be it a ravaging English king, near starvation due to weather induced famine or a devastating plague, it was to the Abbey that the people turned when the troubles came. Her walls remained standing. The bells continued to ring. The monks prayed without ceasing. And the spirit of William Cochrane lived on blessing all those who would enter her sanctuary of peace.

Chapter Four – Guisborough Priory – ca 1400

Ann Whitby had a secret and this was a secret no one outside the immediate family could ever know. In fact, only her brother, the Lollard priest John Whitby, knew the incredible nature of Ann's tightly kept secret. Ann could read. Her brother had taught her and she would be always grateful. For although women of the highest ranks, especially those of the royal court, could read some Latin and, of course, speak, read and write in French, the Whitbys of North Yorkshire were certainly not of that social standing. The family had managed somehow to scrape together enough wealth to have one of their brightest children, John, attend Balliol College at Oxford. They were like many of the of the middling class of this area, rich in land but poor in actual accumulated wealth. However, their father, named William, had dreamed of his exceptionally intelligent son entering the priesthood after a challenging education at one of the finest universities in all Europe. And that is exactly what happened to young John Whitby. He had so impressed the local priests at the priory of Guisborough; they had sponsored him and helped his family convince the local Anglo-Norman nobility to lend financial support to the benefit of John's education. This was highly unusual. Only the truly wealthy could afford to send one of their own to Oxford or perhaps Cambridge. But father James and a monk by the name of Peter had spoken to the de Latimer, de Percy and de Neville heads of household and somehow through a combination of pleading and much prayer convince them the money would be a wise investment. After all, they said, how often do we here in the far north of Yorkshire, get a parish priest who actually understands the Latin language of the mass? And, appealing to the political ambitions of these Anglo-Norman families had not hurt the cause. For when John was sent to Oxford at the tender age of 15, King Richard II had just come to the English throne at the age of 10. Obviously, he was under the guidance and protection of his Uncle John of Gaunt, the third son of King Edward III. Richard would be the 9th king of the Anglo-Norman House of Plantagenet. As always, the royal courts were simmering with intrigue and the closer one was to the center of the kingdom the better. So, the reasoning went, let us send this bright young lad to Oxford where, who knows, he might encounter members of the royal family and impress them. Surely that can't hurt the aristocratic Norman families of this far-flung part of the kingdom. Families whose loyalty unfortunately was always suspect. Little did they know at the time that John would meet someone who would drastically alter the course of his life but, it would not be a member of the royal household? The man John Whitby would meet had come to Oxford himself at a relatively young age. In fact, he had hailed from the North Riding of Yorkshire. His name was John Wycliffe.

By the time John Whitby enrolled at Oxford, Wycliffe was an Oxford Don who had earned his Doctor of Divinity degree two years before in the year 1372. His research placed an emphasis on the inward aspects of religion and the mystical source of grace which the Bible revealed to all of God's people. He was a brilliant scholar of the early Greek and Latin texts as well as biblical Hebrew. In addition, he had the sharp mind of a student of canon law. In the year 1374, John of Gaunt hired Wycliffe to present his scholarly works upon the subject of civil authority as it pertains to the role of the Church. Wycliffe defended the authority of the Crown over the Church in civil matters and this, of course, was highly regarded by the king's Regent. Over time, Wycliffe became a regular legal consultant for the Crown.

As Wycliffe gained in prestige and influence, his more radical teachings came to the forefront. He questioned the concept of religious pilgrimages which had been generating significant revenue for certain towns throughout the kingdom. He questioned the idea of private religious shrines. But his most controversial work was in the area of transubstantiation. This was the idea that during the Eucharist, as the priest blessed the bread and wine it became the body and blood of the Lord Jesus Christ. Wycliffe also firmly believed the Scriptures needed to be translated into the more common English language and spent much of his last years doing just this very thing.

He became quite a popular figure among the theologians at Oxford and his fame began to spread throughout the kingdom. And while he initially had the support of King Richard II trouble was indeed brewing. And the trouble was called Lollardy by the citizens of the realm and eventually heresy by his Holiness, Pope Gregory XI. The word Lollard was the derogatory term given to those who followed the teachings of John Wycliffe and others of like mind. Ann did not know the origins of the word but suspected it had come from the continent. Her brother John had once told her that it was a word the Dutch used to label people perceived as heretics. John said the Dutch borrowed it from the Germans who had burned a Franciscan monk named Lolhard at the stake in Cologne for his preaching against the Church of Rome. Who really knows she thought to herself but it did stick and now anyone in England who was perceived as someone who taught, or even thought, the English church was somehow wrong in doctrine received this label. And once you were labelled a Lollard life became rather difficult.

Ann did not know her bother as a young man. He was 19 years older than her and the oldest of the ten children of William and Marian, her mother. Marian had died shortly after Ann's birth and she was essentially raised by her older siblings. Her father had never remarried and seemed quite content with his lot in life. But her brother John was a different story. Her earliest memories of him were after he had returned to Yorkshire to begin his duties as a priest here at the parish church of Guisborough. Controversy seemed to surround John wherever he went. John was filled with enthusiasm for Wycliffe and his teachings. Shortly after his assignment by the Bishop at York, John began to include ideas of Wycliffe in his short homilies during the mass. This was highly unusual. No one could remember as time when the priest would dare to address the locals in their native tongue. The mass was always held in Latin and there was little if any interaction between the priest and the people during the entire process. Eventually word of this made its way to York and before long John had lost his position. Now, he simply roamed the countryside teaching all those who would listen what he had learned from Wycliffe. Ann's father was terribly disappointed with his son. And, of course, the noble families of this area who had funded his whole education were quite distraught with how things had developed.

But Ann loved her brother. He was like a second father to her. He had always treated her with kindness and affection. And he seemed to respect her for the bright mind she had been given. Ann loved learning and had always been an inquisitive child. Perhaps that is why John was so fond of her? After his dismissal, John and she would often walk the lonely paths of the windswept Yorkshire moors talking about God, the church, or life, in general. Ann respected John's intellect and more than that, he was a good and decent man full of wisdom. It was on one of these long walks that John proposed teaching Ann to read. She was amazed and thrilled. To be able to decipher the squiggly lines of Latin or French and to make meaning out of them had been a dream come true for her. And once she began the process, she could not stop. She constantly begged John to give her more of the Wycliffe tracts that he had smuggled out of Oxford. One day, on her birthday, John surprised her with a copy of the Bible Wycliffe had translated to English. She cried with delight. From that moment on, Ann never lost sight of this precious book and read it daily. Latin was hard to read but to be able to speak and understand the scriptures in her native tongue was in her mind a miracle. She and John both knew they were treading on thin ice. Ann's ability to read was a secret and her possession of her own Bible was something that no one, not even her father or other siblings could ever suspect. Public knowledge of this fact, given the current situation in the North Riding would mean disaster not only for her but for John and all her family.

How had it come to this? She often puzzled over that question. John had told her that in the early heady days of Oxford when he first encountered Wycliffe he thought the man was a lunatic. But after time passed and John got over his initial shock of Wycliffe's teachings he realized that what Wycliffe and some of the other professors at the school were teaching was simply a new way of looking at the faith, a faith they believed had been corrupted and tainted by the politics of power and unchecked avarice. Greed had permeated the church at all levels from the lowliest priest to the pope himself. And the people of all the Christian kingdoms had suffered. And those that suffered the most, the poor and destitute, were those whom Jesus had most identified with during his time on earth. John had said that Wycliffe was just teaching what the scriptures taught him to teach and nothing else. And for this, his teachings had been condemned by Pope Gregory XI who had returned the papacy from Avignon France to Rome in the year 1377 and eventually ordered the burning of all Lollard heretics. Perhaps Wycliffe himself would have died at the stake but the Lord God took him home in 1384 after suffering a stroke.

"There you are my little sister", John's powerful booming voice called out to her as he walked towards the Priory.

"John, you know you are not supposed to be here," Ann exclaimed with caution in her voice, "and I'm not so little anymore" adding with a smile.

"They know my every move. Don't think they don't. The bishop has his spies scattered throughout Yorkshire. I see them everywhere. It's like a game of cat and mouse. And I," John smiled ruefully, "am the mouse." He then brushed the hair from Ann's forehead and gave her a swift kiss on the cheek. "Good to see you again Ann."

"Oh John, you know my heart always sings a little song of joy when I hear your voice," Ann replied. "How goes the work?" she asked. She said this quietly under her breath. John and she both knew that these were difficult times for the followers of Wycliffe. John of Gaunt had died and Richard II and been deposed last year by his cousin the new King Henry IV. And the new king desperately needed the support of his nobles. And these nobles had been dreadfully alarmed when the Lollard movement took an interesting turn and became a social as well as religious statement. In the year 1381, inflamed by the rhetoric of the radical cleric John Ball and led by the now infamous Wat Tyler, the peasants of England revolted against their aristocratic masters. From that moment on, the Lollards lost any support they might have had among the powerful and wealthy elite of the kingdom. Ann had been an infant when the events transpired but she grew up hearing the stories of Wat Tyler's rebels and how they had sought an end to excessive taxation by the agents of the Crown, the removal of the King's biased courts and most controversial of all, the end of serfdom. This last item came directly from the teaching of Father John Ball who spoke publicly that "from the beginning, all men by nature were created alike and serfdom had come into God's world by the oppression of naughty men". For this John Ball was hanged, drawn and quartered on July 15th, 1381. Ann had learned at an early age that words were powerful and if not chosen correctly could lead to a cruel death. Ann realized the peasant's revolt had changed England. People no longer trusted one another. Things were unsettled and unclear. Life had lost its stability. You could not predict what tomorrow would bring. And Ann knew that somehow her brother and other people like him were responsible for the changes that were happening. A fire had been lit in the hearts of the oppressed and it would not be put out easily.

She spoke to John, "Do you think he knew?"

"You are speaking of Wycliffe?" John asked in reply.

"Yes," she said as she nodded her head in affirmation.

"Knew what dear sister?" John asked again.

"That his teachings would cause such a stir among the people of the kingdom," She responded.

"I don't know. But I suspect that Wycliffe, being as smart as he was, certainly had an idea that what he was teaching his students and writing in his notes was going to force people to think about how things are and maybe … with God's help … change them." John replied with a distant look in his eyes. Ann had seen that look in her brother's face before. It happened when he became serious about a topic. John usually had a smile on his face and kind words for all he encountered in his life. But occasionally her brother the kind and gentle priest transformed into the idealistic and passionate preacher who courageously told the world of their sins and the need to repent from their ways. Now that Ann could read the Bible she had discovered the stories surrounding the ministry of Jesus and her brother John reminded her of John the Baptist, the one who came before the Lord telling all who would listen to repent for the time was at hand. She thought it was quite ironic that both were named John. That is how she viewed her brother. He was now a prophet of God. And it brought fear to her heart and tears to her eyes when she realized that her dear sweet brother's life might be taken in similar fashion to that of John the Baptist.

"So, what brings you back to Guisborough?" she asked. The family knew he was in the area and had suspected that he would try to see them but did not know if and when that might occur.

"I've been to the North, all the way to Scotland. There are Christians there, especially in the western part, who would hear the truth about God's word and what it means for them. As usual, the authorities put an end to our meetings and ran me out. I'm heading south to York. There is a small group of Lollards there who are growing in numbers even in the midst of this persecution. I hope to meet with them and discuss what we should do next now that Henry is on the throne." John replied while glancing about to see if anyone had seen him speaking with his sister. He loved her dearly and knew that by just talking to her he might be placing her in jeopardy.

"Can you come to the farm John? Can you stay a few days with us? Father and the rest of your family would love to see you once again." Ann asked as she tried unsuccessfully to keep the tears from gently falling down her cheeks.

"Not this time, lass. These are dangerous times for me and for anyone associated with me. As the Lord commanded, I must be gentle as a dove but wise as the serpent. I can't risk putting you and the family in anymore danger." John replied while reaching out to hug his beloved sister. "Do not cry. I am doing the Lord's work. His Spirit will guide and protect me … until my task is done." He said these last few words with a heavy heart. As if he could see the future and what it would bring for him and the other Lollard brothers.

"Let me at least run to the house and get you some food to take on your journey?" Ann asked her brother as she attempted to regain her composure. She wanted to be strong for him. She knew he would worry and fret about her and the others. She did not want to place any more burdens, then what had already been placed, upon this man's strong shoulders. Her brother was not a large man but he was well muscled and strong as an ox. His health was good. He had been born in the year of the last plague, what the people called the Black Death. It had brought death and devastation throughout the kingdom. Not a family in Yorkshire had escaped its wrath. Some had estimated that over 30% of the population had been killed by the disease and most families had suffered tremendous financial hardships. Ann's father had told her that if the Black Death couldn't kill his little boy than neither could the Bishop of York. He also told Ann it had planted the seeds of the peasant revolt. For the Church seemed helpless in the face of the plague. And as Ann's father had said to her, if the Pope himself can't put an end to this pestilence, then is he really God's vicar on earth? That thought, as troubling as it might have been to the faithful, permeated the minds and hearts of the English peasant as well as the rest of European Christendom both rich and poor. In fact, few truly had any respect anymore for the Church leadership. The year 1378 marked the beginning of what was now called the Western Schism.

Gregory XI died that year. The Cardinals elected Urban VI who decided to return the papacy to Rome. Urban was also a reform minded leader who quickly irritated the very Cardinals who had elected him to office. They united against him and announced to the Christian world that Clement VII was now pope and he immediately proceeded to return the papal court back to Avignon France. There had been popes and antipopes before but this was the first time in Christian history that two popes were elected simultaneously by the same body of Cardinals. What resulted was chaos. All the kings and queens of Western Christendom had to now pick a side to support. France and Scotland preferred the papal court at Avignon and thus considered Clement VII the one true head of the church. While dear old Henry IV, King of England, chose to support the Roman pope, Urban VI. His support of the Roman pope was probably based upon his mistrust of the King of France and his desire for French lands much more so than any theological dispute. Trouble was brewing over all of Europe. Actual battles had taken place in the north of France as well as Portugal and only God knew what the future might hold for England.

Ann thought of the state of the kingdom as she raced back to the house to secure some food for her brother. She thought to herself that all of this confusion within the church was brought on by its total moral collapse. She felt quite strongly her brother was correct. The church was in dire need of reform. Change needed to happen and it needed to happen now. It was confusing and highly frustrating to her how others could not see what appeared to be so simple and clear to her. The crown was temporal and the church was spiritual. But both had somehow lost their way and became entangled in one another's affairs. Yes, she firmly believed the Pope was the head of the church, but which Pope? And what really did she mean when she said the church? She was deep in thought and did not see the young man walking slowly by the side of the road with his head bent towards the ground and his eyes downcast as if he were searching the ground for a lost item. The two were within 50 feet of one another when suddenly Ann stopped startled at his presence.

"My goodness, I almost ran right into you. I did not expect to see anyone on this trail this day. It leads from the priory at Guisborough to our farm in the valley below town." Ann explained with shortness of breath and then immediately wondered why she felt the need to explain herself to this stranger.

"You don't remember me, heh? I remember you. You are Ann Whitby and your family lives just over that ridge," the young man smiled as he pointed in the general direction of the small Whitby farm.

"Who are you?" Ann demanded and then stopped and took a closer look at the man. He was young but older than her. She guessed maybe he was around 25 or 30 years of age. He was a good-looking fellow. Tall with long dark hair and deep brown eyes. He was obviously a working man for his hands were callused and bruised and his skin had the deep tan of someone who spent much of their time in the hot sun. But it was the sound of his voice that got her attention and made her heart skip a beat. His deep baritone voice carried through the air and instantly put her at ease. It was both soft and firm at the same time. She had been to the sea a few times in her life and she had always enjoyed the gentle yet constant sound of the waves hitting the beach and crashing upon the cliffs. That sound had brought her peace and now she felt peace once again in listening to this young man. "Wait a minute … I have seen you before but I just can't remember where …. Oh … now I remember, you were at mass last Lord's Day. You were standing at the back next to Lord de Neville and his family. Correct?" Ann asked and wondered why her voice right then sounded so terribly girlish and immature.

"Aye, lass, that was me. Robert Cleveland is my name and it is a pleasure to finally get to speak to you in person." He bowed in a courtly fashion as his eyes twinkled with delight.

She curtsied in response as was the fashion of young maidens of the day. They both began to speak at once.

"Where are you off to in such a hurry this fine day?" Robert asked.

"What brings you to Guisborough?" Ann asked.

They both chuckled with embarrassment. "You first my lady," Robert spoke and bowed slightly once again.

Ann hesitated. She did not know this young man and was not about to tell him about her brother and the task she was on. She finally said, "I'm late. I usually go for a walk in the early morning before I start my daily tasks and lost track of the time. I need to return home. My father will want his midday meal soon." Once again, the girlish voice came out of her mouth and Ann was becoming quite frustrated with herself. *You idiot*, she thought to herself. "Why can't you speak normally to this man?" She turned to Robert and said, "Your turn. Why are you here in the North Riding?"

"That's a long story girl. But the short version goes like this … This land, as far as you can see in any direction once, a long long time ago, belonged to my family." Robert began.

Ann stifled a laugh. "Sure it did. And I'm the Queen of England," she said half mockingly.

Robert's back stiffened and his chin jutted out. "No, seriously, Ann, this was all ours."

Ann looked at him and then it dawned on her, yes, of course, "You said your name was Robert Cleveland and …the people around here call this place the Cleveland hills. You are that Cleveland?"

"Yes, I am. So … as I was saying before you decided to scoff at me"

"Please accept my apology," Ann replied somewhat sheepishly.

"None required. Anyway, this land was once my ancestors. But they chose to fight on the wrong side when William came to England from Normandy to claim his crown. As you probably know, he brought his Norman knights and they stayed. He was particularly nasty with the Angles, Danes and Norse inhabitants of this area, including my family. Do you know the castle at Skelton? That was once the great hall of the man from whom I am descended." Robert pointed to the northeast where Skelton castle was located.

"Of course, I know it well. It has belonged to the de Brus family for generations and now is cared for by the Latimers, if my memory serves me well." Ann replied.

"Yes, all these Norman sounding names. They all came over with William."

"What happened?" Ann asked, for the young man's story had caught her attention. Not only was he handsome but intelligent as well, with a good knowledge of history.

"Life happened. History is written by the victors. We lost. They won. We left. It is pretty much as simple as that. Oh, some tried to stay and adjust to the new situation but no matter how hard they worked at it my people were never really accepted here as equals. We had money. We had land. But we weren't Norman. So, eventually, my ancestors left. Not all of them. Some stayed and today you can find them here and there squeaking out a living from this hard soil or down in Hull living off the sea but most of them headed to York and even further south. I have been told that I have relatives as far south as Leicester. I don't know if that is really true as I have never laid eyes upon them. But there was quite a few of us and surely some of them must have survived by hook or by crook." Robert laughed at this last statement. He liked this girl. He knew that from the moment he first saw her during the mass at Guisborough. He had asked Lord de Neville, who was that stunning lass and, he had told him all about her, her family and her Lollard priest brother John who was currently in trouble with the bishop of York. Not that he cared that much for religion. He didn't quite understand what all the fuss was about. Yes, he believed in God. Yes, he had been baptized as an infant in a Christian church in York. And yes, he occasionally attended the mass basically to establish and maintain his business connections. For Robert was a practical man. He lived in the moment. His feet were firmly planted on mother earth and he did not concern himself with the highly theological debates of the day. His primary task was to provide for himself, his widowed sister and her two small children and, of course, his little Elizabeth, a daughter that had been born to him by his first wife, also named Elizabeth who had died during the birthing of their child. His daughter Elizabeth was now ten years old and would soon be crossing the step from girl to woman herself. And that is what brought Robert Cleveland to the North Riding of Yorkshire. He was looking to find a suitable husband for his daughter. And in the back of his mind he had a dream that someday a Cleveland would once again reign in the Great Hall of Skelton. He had only openly shared this dream with his sister one time. She had laughed at him and it had hurt but he kept his feelings to himself. That is another thing the experiences of his life had taught Robert. Never show how you truly feel. Keep it all inside. Robert's father had been a carpenter in York taking what jobs he could find in order to put food on his family's table. Robert had decided at an early age that he wanted something different in life. So, he learned to fight. The king, his nobles and the Lord Mayor of York, a position appointed by the king, were always looking for men at arms and Robert was good at it. He knew how to wield the sword, battle axe and even the Welsh long bow for which he had a fondness as a weapon of war. He had joined the king's army and had been involved in battles in France, Scotland and even far away Portugal. He had learned to kill. It did not come easy to him but he did what had to be done. He was rewarded as all victorious soldiers were with the spoils of war. Due to his military prowess, he had been named a vassal of the Yorkist nobility and had been granted a small holding of land in the East Riding. The land he worked was not all that fertile but it was much better than what the many English peasants had to survive upon. Families of seven to ten people often with three generations under one roof trying to exist upon the produce of small farms of ten to thirty acres. Robert's holdings were not much larger at fifty acres but it was enough to get him accepted into the next highest social class of knights, vassals and even some of the smaller land holding nobility, such as the Latimers and Faucenberges of the North Riding. Robert was not proud of how he came into his small holdings but he was not paralyzed with guilt. Life was hard. You had to fight to survive and if that meant others had to die then so be it. Robert had a family to support and that is how he found himself in the parish church of Guisborough celebrating the mass with Lord de Neville, one of the most powerful men of the North Riding and, possibly of all of Yorkshire. Robert had escaped the town of York and for that he was thankful. But Robert was an ambitious man who wanted more. Land meant wealth. The more land you owned in the service of your lord who was in the service of the king himself, the wealthier you were. Robert knew that the only way to acquire more land was to have his daughter marry into the aristocratic social class of the kingdom. Only then would he be satisfied. This had been Robert's dream for most of his life, to be the lord of some great manor and perhaps someday have an audience with the king himself. And he had set his sights on the aristocratic Norman families of the North Riding. To Robert, these families had stolen his ancestral land and he was going to gain a piece of it back through the wise wedding of his precious daughter to one of their noble sons. The de Neville's, in particular, had twin sons around the age of thirteen or fourteen, Robert was not quite sure, but certainly close to the marrying age and their father, the Lord de Neville himself would be casting about seeking good breeding stock for the next generation of his family.

"Well, I must be on my way," Ann said to Robert quickly bringing him out of his inner thoughts.

"Must you leave in such a hurry? I had heard from Latimer that you had a controversial brother as priest … what was his name… oh yes, I remember, John … John Whitby. Is that so?" Robert asked nonchalantly.

Ann's immediately became suspicious. "Yes, I have a brother. And yes, he is a priest, trained at Oxford. But I don't know if he is all that controversial?" she spoke with caution in her voice.

"Relax Ann. I don't work for the Bishop. I'm just asking about him. I'm trying to get to know the people in this part of Yorkshire better and it happened to come up in a conversation I had with Latimer. That's all." Robert could sense her anxiety and the last thing he wanted to do was generate any king of tension between her and him.

"So, why are you here? Really, why," Ann asked in a frank and straightforward manner. Her brother had once remarked that she could be like a bulldog at times when either threatened or if she suspected someone was being less than completely truthful with her.

Robert looked directly into her eyes. He was transfixed and for a moment speechless. He had not felt this way in a long time. His wife, Elizabeth had died almost ten years ago and Robert had never considered the possibility of remarrying. For one thing, marriage and the life of a man at war did not mix. He had only been married to Elizabeth for three months when she conceived and the king called upon his troops once again for battle in France. Elizabeth had moved in with her sister and had delivered their first and only child there while Robert was fighting across the sea. By the time he had returned to York, she had died and the baby girl was sickly and not expected to survive. That was a hard time for Robert and he vowed then and there to his little girl that her life would somehow be easier and more comfortable than his had ever been. How he loved his little Elizabeth. He would still have to at times leave her and do the king's bidding but he always returned and she was always thrilled to see him once again. They had a deep and special bond which might be considered by some as highly unusual. Roughly half of all children born during this time survived to adulthood and parents often just simply viewed them as extra labor. There was not a lot of love to be shared in English families in the year 1400. Survival was the first priority and that often took every ounce of physical and emotional energy anyone had to spare.

"Ann, may I walk with you awhile? I would like to tell you about my farm down in the West Riding and my daughter Elizabeth," Robert asked with hopeful expectation.

"Oh … you're married then?" responded Ann unable to disguise the disappointment in her voice.

"Widowed, my wife passed away shortly after giving birth to our daughter," Robert replied with a touch of sadness in his voice.

"Oh, I'm sorry." Ann responded with kindness.

"It's all right. It has been ten years now. Most of the pain has gone away but every once in a while, when I'm looking at my little girl, I see her mother and it brings me back to the short time we had together." Robert cleared his throat and rubbed the slight tear from his eyes that had quickly formed. He was a soldier hardened by war but he had a soft and gentle heart.

Ann made a quick decision. "Yes, you may walk with me; our place is just over the hill, maybe a couple miles from here." She regretted what she said as soon as she said it. She didn't know this man. What if his story was a lie? What if he really was a spy of the Bishop sent to uncover the whereabouts of her brother, John? She would never be able to forgive herself if something bad should happen to John on account of what she said or did. But there was something about this young man that led her to believe he could be trusted.

They walked slowly down the lane and up over the next hill. As they looked over the top, she could see the little thatched farm house she called home and her father was walking to it from the fields. "Ach … he'll be hungry and I've not even began to prepare the meal," she exclaimed to her companion. "Come Robert, we must hurry." And so they ran together down the hill. Suddenly Robert slipped, stumbled and fell. Ann almost fell on top of him but somehow managed to catch herself. Ann giggled at him for he was quite a sight lying in a puddle from last night's rain. As he was lying on the ground looking up at her, he began to laugh uncontrollably. At the sound of a man's voice, Ann's father grabbed his pitchfork and ran up the hill towards them. "Be at peace father. This is Robert Cleveland of York and he means us no harm," Ann spoke quickly to her father as he came to a halt just a few feet in front of them. By this time, Robert had picked himself up from the ground and was bowing to Mr. Whitby while attempting to brush the dirt from his clothes. "Good day to you sir, as your daughter has said, I am Robert Cleveland," Robert bowed deeply while removing his hat in a sweeping gesture. Whitby extended his right hand and grasped Robert's with his powerful grip. "I've no use for courtly ways, here in the north we men just shake hands," Whitby said while smiling at Robert.

The three walked into the small cottage the Whitbys called home. "It isn't much but you are welcome to stay and take a meal with us," Ann's father said to Robert as he motioned for him to sit at the large oak table in the center of the main room. As the two men sat, Ann scurried off to the fireplace where a large black kettle hung from the wall. She immediately began to prepare the food while listening to their conversation.

"So, young Mr. Cleveland, what brings you to these parts of Yorkshire?" asked Mr. Whitby. Robert proceeded to inform him of the reasons he had travelled to the North Riding. "And your daughter, Elizabeth is only ten years of age? That's a little on the young side to be planning her marriage, wouldn't you say so Annie, "he glanced towards his daughter who had been keeping herself busy but her father knew she was taking in every word that had been said between the two of them.

"Yes, father, it seems young but you know how short life is and in just a few years she will be ready to start a family so I suppose now is just as good a time as any to begin the search," Ann said not quite sure she actually believed what she had just said. She couldn't explain why but she liked this man. But she also thought he was not being realistic. In the short walk from where they had met to the moment he tumbled down the hill, Robert had told her everything. He wanted his daughter to marry into one of the ruling families in order for his descendants to reclaim the land he perceived belonged to them, but, what about the people who held the land prior to the arrival of Robert's Norse ancestors? Didn't they have just as much of a right to it as he and his descendants did? This seemed rather silly to her. All this concern over land, titles and everything else associated with the accumulation of wealth.

Just then there was a slight tapping at the door. Three quick knocks, a pause followed by two quick knocks, another pause followed by one quick knock. It was John. That was his signal to let them know it was him standing outside their closed door.

Ann and her father simultaneously jumped to their feet and tried to answer the door together. Father and son grabbed each other in a bear hug while Ann waited patiently for their emotional reunion to subside. John was smiling from ear to ear and then he saw Robert sitting at the table. His countenance quickly changed. "Father, who is this man?" John asked quickly while considering how he might escape if trouble were brewing. He wondered if he had been followed but then quickly decided he had been careful and was confident he was alone before approaching the house.

"Rest easy my son. This is Robert Cleveland and he is a guest of your sister's and now, mine," John's father stated slowly while nodding and smiling at the three of them. At this point, Robert extended his right hand to grasp the hand of John Whitby. As the two locked eyes, a friendship began to immediately develop. Through some mysterious process, both men knew at that moment in time they were in the company of a friend and someone who could be trusted. John would say years later that the Spirit of God had moved within him when he met Robert for the first time and that the Spirit had immediately calmed any anxiety he was experiencing upon meeting this stranger in his life.

The four of them spent the rest of the day together chatting about all the things people usually talk about, weather, health and local happenings but then the conversation turned towards religion.

"John, I know you are a Lollard. I know the Bishop of York wants you to recant of Wycliffe's teachings and shy of doing that, at least temper your public pronouncements, "stated Robert. "I also know that given the opportunity he will turn you over to the authorities to be tried for treason against the crown."

"Yes, that's true. I have no argument with King Henry or any of his officials for that matter. I leave that to my colleagues at Oxford and Cambridge. They have taken up the debate about the power of Church and Crown. No, what troubles me most are the current teachings of the Church and how they appear to have strayed from the simple and straight path of the teachings of our Lord Jesus as it is written in holy scripture." John replied while looking off into the far horizon.

"And that is what I don't understand," replied Robert. "How can the Church have strayed from the original teachings of Jesus if they are the ones who have written the scriptures to begin with? Doesn't the Bible belong to the Church?"

"A common argument, one that I hear often in my travels, it goes something like this … the Church came first and then the Bible was written by men operating within the framework of the Church. So, the argument, goes, it is the Church that decides what goes into the Bible and what does not." John replied thoughtfully. "And I thought that too until I went to Oxford and sat at the feet of Wycliffe and heard him expound about the word of God in my native language. In words that not only I but any English person, man or woman," John glanced furtively at Ann while saying this last part, "can understand. And when you read the words yourself you begin to see that many of the practices and teachings of the Church are in error when compared to scripture."

"Give him an example John," chimed Ann.

"Robert, did you know that the papacy is not found anywhere within the Bible. Pilgrimages are not mentioned and. confession to a priest is unnecessary for salvation of one's soul." His voice grew in intensity for he was passionate about his faith and had grown accustomed to speaking loudly outdoors to gathered people due to his banishment from the churches.

"I had heard that you Lollards taught that the bread and wine are not really the body and blood of the Lord Jesus? If this is the case, no wonder the bishop is angry with you, "Robert stated while seeking agreement from his new friend.

"On the surface, that may appear to be the true issue … but it is not the issue that has the leadership of the clergy as well as the crown upset with the Wycliffe followers." John replied.

"What, pray tell, could the issue be if not the holy sacraments themselves?" asked Robert.

"The issue is warfare and Wycliffe's ideas that it is not permitted for a Christian to be a warrior nor is it condoned by God for members of the clergy, including the Pope himself, to have a standing army, to participate in any military action or, for that matter, to even endorse the use of violence by one state over another, or … one person over another." John said this last statement with a calm but precise manner as if he had conducted this discussion before on numerous occasions which indeed he had. And he knew from prior debates that this was the real sticking point. It was not Wycliffe's questioning of Church doctrine that had stirred up the hornet's nest. To Wycliffe and to those like John Whitby who followed in his footsteps the issue was the Christian's involvement in the temporal affairs of this world. "To Wycliffe the problem actually began when the Emperor Constantine of the Roman Empire had first accepted Christianity and had made it the official state religion of Rome. Yes, of course, the persecutions of the early Christians ended, but, Wycliffe would argue, look what transpired. The Church itself became mired in the affairs of the world and the leadership of the Church ultimately was corrupted by those same things that princes and kings all over Europe go to war over; power and wealth. Just look at us now. Henry fights the French, the Scots, the Welsh and whoever else stands in the way of an English empire. We have two popes … why? … because both are puppets of different and opposing rulers. And why do these so-called men of God allow themselves and the holy mother church to be sullied in this manner … because they too are enamored of the things of this world, power and wealth. They might wear the vestments of the clergy but underneath all that finery they are no different from any member of the aristocracy."

The room became deathly silent as John finished. I have said too much to this stranger thought John to himself. But it is what it is and I can't help but speak the truth to any who might listen.

Robert broke the silence. "I understand now the Peasant's Revolt and why the clergy and the crown both turned against Wycliffe and his Lollard followers. This is more than religious doctrine. This is an attack on the way things are throughout Europe. This cuts to the very core of the foundation of our society." Robert said slowly and quietly as he attempted to process this new idea.

Ann did not know what to think. She loved her brother but she had never heard him speak this way before. This was treason. To speak of changing ones understanding of church procedure and doctrine was dangerous but understandable but this… what John was now teaching… this went against everything she had been taught throughout her young life. There was structure to society. Everyone had a place and knew that place from lowest peasant up through the social layers to the king and on top of this pile of humanity was the Pope himself. And he reported directly to God. If she understood her brother correctly, he was saying the Church had been in the wrong for well over a thousand years.

Finally, Robert spoke. "Is this what Wycliffe taught when he was at Oxford?"

"No, not this controversial, he might have thought these ideas but Wycliffe was careful. He was favored by King Richard at the time and had used that monarchial influence to try to slowly make changes within the structure of the Church and the clergy. At first his teachings were widely accepted by merchants, the gentry, lower clergy and even some knights of the royal household of England. People had seen the corruption of the Church leadership at the highest levels and were ready for change. But then something happened. The movement took on a life of its own. And Wycliffe was changing as well. He began to preach the Bible should be given to the common people in their own language. And others used Wycliffe and his teachings about Church doctrine to attack what they perceived as a corrupt social system filled with injustice for the poor and downtrodden. They took to heart the teachings of Jesus and wanted to do away with the current structure of both king and pope. So … in the end … the revolt happened. Thousands of poor peasants invaded London with sickle and axe hoping to change their world. Of course, all of you know how the story ended. Power and wealth won and the king's soldiers put an end to the lives of hundreds of the leaders of the commoners."

Once again quiet overtook the room. At last Robert spoke, "John, I am one of those soldiers. I have travelled far and wide in the service of the king. I have had to do things I do not like to think about. I consider myself a Christian. Are you saying my faith is in vain because of what I have done in the name of the king?"

John was quiet. He took his time. And before he answered, Ann spoke up," the Bible teaches us that all men and women have sinned and fallen short of the glory of God. That means all men Robert, be they peasant or King, priest or soldier … all of us… Me… You… John…all of us…"

"And sweet lady, how would you know what it says in the Bible, unless your brother has taught you?" Robert looked quizzically at John who was shaking his head and mouthing the word no to Ann.

"Because dear sir," she said in a half mocking tone, "I can read it for myself."

"What," Robert exclaimed while Ann's father and brother both exclaimed, "Ann that is a secret only for members of the family to know."

John interjected," Obviously, my sister trusts you Robert. For you realize what problems this might cause her should it become known that a common farm girl knows how to read and to top it off is reading holy scripture."

Robert chuckled, "Rest easy brother John. I have no desire to bring any trouble upon this house and certainly have would not want to cause your fair sister any discomfort. Ann, your secret is safe with me.," Robert said as he smiled gently in Ann's direction. Both John and Ann's father knew that look. It was the look of man who had been smitten. Right before their eyes this Robert Cleveland was falling in love with their precious Annie and neither was sure they enjoyed the experience.

"So, John what happens now? Do you stay on the run? Preaching and teaching to those who would listen to your words of revolution?" Robert asked John in a sensitive manner. He had not yet made up his mind about the beliefs of John Whitby but, he had certainly made up his mind about Ann. She was fascinating. She was pretty. She was intelligent. She could read. She was courageous. He was impressed with her like he had once been impressed so many years ago when he first met Elizabeth's mother. What was happening here? He had come to the North Riding to find a future husband for his daughter. One that would escalate she and him into the upper echelon of English aristocracy and in doing so, return the land of Cleveland to its rightful owners. But then fate or was it God had intervened. He had met Ann Whitby, sister of the hunted Lollard preacher John Whitby. For these Whitbys were not his original objective, they were simple farming people. They had no great wealth. They had no powerful influence within the community. What good would come of this he wondered? And yet, he could not keep his eyes off her.

Ann's father spoke, "It is getting late Robert. Are you staying at the inn in Guisborough tonight?"

"I had not made arrangements as of yet but that was my intention," Robert replied.

"You shall stay with us and I won't hear any objections from you. You are our guest and we simple folk of the North Riding know how to treat the travelling strangers amongst us, "he said with a smile. "I assume Ann that will be alright with you?" Ann's father winked at John as he said this to his now blushing daughter.

"If it pleases Mr. Cleveland … that would be fine" Ann said as she looked sweetly towards Robert. Ah yes, thought Ann's father, Cupid's arrow has found its mark.

Early in the morning the next day Robert had accompanied Ann on her walk to Guisborough for it was market day. The little town would be filled with all the local farmers plus the local merchants trying to sell their goods to each other. It was also a good time to meet with neighbors and catch up on the local gossip. As they walked along the lane to town both were light hearted and in a merry mood. Neither of them had expected what had transpired in their lives. Robert had been in the king's service the past decade of his life and the thought of marrying again had not entered his mind. Ann, at twenty years of age, had felt she was past the prime marrying age and doubted she would find a suitor interested in a farmers' old maiden daughter. Both were wrong. God works in mysterious ways and apparently it was their destiny to find one another at this moment in time and space. So on towards the town they walked completely engrossed in the conversation and consumed with curiosity about the other. Finally, as they approached the town, Robert said, "Ann, I would like to ask a favor of you."

Ann looked hesitantly at him. They had only met yesterday but she could tell she was falling deeply in love with him and did not want to be hurt by some strange request he might make of her. She looked at him and gave a slight nod of her head to indicate he should just go ahead and ask the favor he had in mind.

"I would like to know how to read. Would you teach me?" Robert asked as a child might ask her mother for a cup of milk.

Ann hesitated briefly and then said, "Why yes, of course, I would be honored to teach you how to read. I guess I just assumed that someone like yourself who has seen so much of the world would already know how." She regretted saying it that way as soon as the words had come out of her mouth. She did not want to embarrass Robert.

Robert smiled slightly and replied, "Yes, I have seen some of the world. But, no, I never learned to read, at least, not very well. I can make out my name and a few limited words but that's about it. I would understand if you choose not to. I'm a fairly old student." He winked at her in a playful manner and she knew immediately that this was a kind man who did not take himself too seriously.

"Yes, I'll do it but it will take time. I assumed you would be returning soon to your home and daughter?" Ann asked while holding her breath. She was in quite a state. She wanted him to stay but knew that he would be yearning to return to his home.

"I've been giving that some thought. I have to travel to Guisborough on occasion. I thought perhaps I could plan on coming back every month or so until I mastered it … the reading that is." He looked at her with great affection in his eyes. Robert knew that he was quickly falling for this young woman. He did not actually know how he was going to make this work but he knew he was going to try … and Elizabeth would just have to understand, so the two of them made an agreement that morning. Robert would return to the North Riding once a month for a few days and during that time would stay at the Whitbys farm while he made his connections in the town and then she would tutor him during the evening hours. This went on for around six months. Winter had come and gone. Robert was beginning to be known in and around the community as a trusted vassal of the king as well as an experienced wool trader who was simply trying to expand his sphere of influence. He and Ann maintained one another's confidence. No one in town suspected she was teaching him how to read and few really understood the ultimate motivation of Robert Cleveland to secure his family's ancient land holdings through the strategic marriage of his daughter.

One spring morning in the year 1401, Robert managed to arrive earlier than expected at the Whitby farm. He had something he wanted to ask Ann and, of course, her father. He wanted to bring Ann back with him to York to visit his family and meet his daughter. But before he did that he wanted to seek her father's permission to ask Ann to marry him. He loved her and he knew she felt the same for him. But he also loved his Elizabeth and would want her to meet Ann and tell him that their marriage would be acceptable to her. This was highly unusual for a grown man and father to allow his daughter that much say in his affairs but that was the nature of Robert Cleveland. Although a warrior in training, in his heart, he was a man of peace and wanted to avoid conflict within his family at all costs.

"Ann, you look surprised to see me. I know I'm a few days early." Robert said to Ann upon meeting her in the grassy meadow outside the cottage. Ann ran into Robert's arms with tears streaming down her cheeks. "Oh Robert, I have missed you so but my distress is over my brother. King Henry has issued an edict … de heretic comburendo … which means he will order the burning at the stake of any Lollard heretic who dares to continue to preach anywhere in the English countryside. I know my brother. He is a man of passion. He will not stop. He thinks he is doing God's will and I'm afraid of where this will all end." Ann began to sob as she informed Robert of her concerns.

"Ah lass, Henry has his hands full with Owen Glendower in Wales right now. I doubt if your Lollard brother is that much of a concern to him. He is just trying to keep peace with the Pope in Rome who he supports against the French pope located in Avignon. And the only reason Henry supports Rome and not Avignon is he hates the French king and wants to topple him from his throne. This is about political power Ann, not religion." Robert tried to soothe her as he held her gently in his muscular arms.

"That may be my love but the bishops have tried the Lollard preacher William Sawtray and found him guilty of heresy. He is scheduled to be burned at the stake. He will be the first Lollard to die under this new edict." Ann began to sob once again. Robert placed his hand under her chin and raised her mouth to his. He kissed her gently on the lips and said, "Ann, marry me. I love you and I think you love me. I was planning on trying to make things go smoothly with your father and my daughter but I realize now that I love you Ann and I want you to be by my side every day of my life for the rest of my life." Then he kissed her again this time with passion.

Ann broke away first. Gasping for her breath she exclaimed, "No, Robert, we must not take this any further. I love you and I ache for you as surely you must ache for me but we can't do this until rightfully wed in the eyes of man and God"

Robert regained his composure and quickly replied, "Yes, my love. I am truly sorry to take advantage of a lady in distress. I can wait for you for I think it will be worth the wait." And then Robert let out a whoop of joy and both of them began to laugh.

They heard the horse at the same time and turned together to look up the lane to see a rider coming at them at a gallop. "Good Lord! It's my cousin William from York. What in the world could he be doing up here?"

William reined in his horse and jumped off the great beast right in front of Ann and Robert. "Good day cousin. I have news. Edmund, Duke of York has ordered his knights, vassals and all available Yorkshire men to join him as he joins our good king Henry in his battle against the Scots."

"What? When did this happen?" Robert exclaimed.

"Henry rides north now as we speak. He is leading a huge army gathered from all over the kingdom. He has grown tired of the continual harassment of his lands in the north by the Scots and aims to put an end to it." William explained.

Robert turned to look at Ann whose face registered the shock and anguish that Robert was feeling. "Ann … I must go. I have to return to York and get my affairs in order. I have to make sure my sister will continue to watch Elizabeth for me while I am away."

Tears were forming in Ann's eyes. Will we never know peace in this land, she thought to herself. This king wants that and that Bishop wants this and the one constant is the misery of the people stuck in a land where bloodshed and death is the only answer.

"Why, Robert? Why go and fight for a man you do not know? Who does not know you nor cares for you. He only desires more land, more power. Why Robert why?" she burst into tears as she pleaded with him.

"Ann, try to understand. It is the way of things. I was given my land holdings in exchange for my service to the king. And when he beckons … I must answer the call. My king needs me." Robert said half-heartedly. For Robert did not quite believe what he was saying to her. Robert was changing and it was Ann and her Bible that was doing the work. Ann had insisted that Robert and she use the copy of the English Bible her brother had given to her in secret as a way for Robert to learn to read. And as the lessons continued, not only did Robert learn to read his native language but he learned to truly think about what the holy words were saying to him. At first, he dutifully sat through the lessons struggling mightily to understand the markings on the pages. But after time he began to read for knowledge and with that knowledge came understanding. He was a changed man from when he and Ann had first begun their lessons together. Where did Jesus order his followers to rise up and slay their enemies? Did not the master say just the opposite? Robert's favorite part of the New Testament was what Ann called the 'I am' statements. *I am the bread of life. No one who comes to me will ever be hungry again. I am the light of the world. If you follow me you won't be stumbling through the darkness, because you will have the light that leads to life. I am the good shepherd; I know my own sheep and they know me.* And perhaps Robert's favorite passage … *I am the resurrection and the life;*

those who believe in me, even though they die like everyone else, will live again. They are given eternal life and will never perish. Robert had come to believe in the power of these words. So now he felt as if he stood at the crossroads of his life. If he followed his cousin back to York it would lead back to his previous way of life, a way that indeed had brought him some standing in this world, a way that had opened the closed doors of society so that he and his daughter might have a better life and, a way that could possibly help him seek justice against those who had taken his ancestral lands. But was that what he really wanted out of life? The other pathway was dark and narrow. He could not see where it might lead. It was a pathway that required much faith and trust in God. If he did not walk down that one, he would be walking away from everything he had learned from this good woman who had such a gentle heart. A woman who loved all she encountered even the most difficult, a woman who was trying as best she could to bring the teachings of Jesus alive in her life. To Robert, Ann was a true follower of Jesus and worthy of the title Christian.

"Make haste cousin, The Duke awaits your arrival." Robert's cousin William said as he flung himself back upon his horse and turned the beast back towards the west … back towards the great city of York. Back to where he was respected as a member of the king's own. Back to where his precious daughter awaited him with open and loving arms. Robert felt as if his soul was being torn into pieces. What should I do? he thought to himself. Just then William turned to Robert and asked, "Cousin, may I have a word in private with you?"

Robert walked close to the horse and William bent down so that Ann could not hear his words.

"Be careful Robert with these Lollards. Henry plans to use them as an example. You and I know he is under tremendous strain to keep his throne. There have been assassination attempts. There is rumor upon rumor of revolt. He is particularly suspect of us here in the North. He does not trust the great northern magnates, especially the House of Percy of Northumberland. He will charge these Lollards with treason and turn them over to the Church who will burn them as heretics. Be wary my cousin." Then William sat upright and spurred the great beast upon which he sat. "Do not tarry, Robert", he shouted over his shoulder as he rode away leaving a cloud of dust in his wake.

Robert turned and looked at Ann. The bond between them had grown over the months. She had stopped her tears. She did not say anything but just looked into his eyes as if trying to touch his very soul with her love for him. And then, he knew what he must do. It came to him as if struck by a bolt of lightning. He would state later that the Spirit of God moved within him at that very moment and helped him to see the light. The light … did not Jesus say he was the light of the world? That dark narrow path was now brightly lit.

"Ann … we must marry. We must marry now and you must go with me. "Robert said with determination in his voice and love in his eyes.

"Yes, my darling. I will eventually marry you but as we discussed, there is the matter of my father and your daughter", Ann spoke with tenderness.

"No, Ann, we don't have time. It has become so clear to me. You are not safe here anymore and I won't leave you to fight once again for Henry. I'm tired of the bloodshed Ann. I'm tired of saying goodbye to the people

I love and care most about. I'm tired Ann. I just want to live out my days with you by my side. Maybe God will bless us with children? Who knows? But whatever happens to us I want it to be us together and not apart. My cousin William reports to the High Sheriff of York. He gave me a warning that your brother is in danger. Henry wants to make an example of the Lollards. He's using them as a scapegoat of course but that doesn't matter. Ann, he is the king and with that crown comes the power of life and death. We need to get away from here. It is not safe here for you." Robert was excited and his words were coming fast. His mind was moving at an incredible speed for his only objective now was to get this woman he loved to safety.

Ann was very quiet. She looked at the ground and then up to the heavens. "What about my family … my father, my younger sisters and my brother John?" She began to cry softly as she thought about all of them.

"We will take them with us." Robert declared. "Ann, I don't know where we will end up but I do know who will be leading us. For the first time in my life, I am placing my faith in the Lord. I know it is scary. But look at it this way … God, in His infinite wisdom has allowed our paths to cross. Surely, He will not abandon us now when we so desperately need His guidance and protection." Robert could not believe the words that were coming out of his mouth. It was as if someone else had taken over his mind. But the strange thing was he firmly believed in what he was saying. He was committed to following this path that had been lit for him and he was at peace.

"I love you Ann. What do you say … yea or nay?" Robert looked at her waiting for her reply.

"I love you Robert and I say yes." She flung her arms around him and kissed him passionately. It was Robert who broke the embrace this time. "We have much to do and perhaps little time to do it." He said with the steely voice of a man who had been in combat. "Where is your father?" he asked. "Right about now he should be coming in from inspecting the fields." Ann replied. "Let's go" he said as he grabbed her hand and turned toward the little cottage located over the hill.

At times in life things become rather simple. This was one of those times in the lives of Ann Whitby and Robert Cleveland. A primitive survival mechanism had become engaged within. They raced back to the cottage. They told Ann's father what they had planned. As if planned by God, John, Ann's Lollard brother was also with their father for he had been traveling by secret throughout the countryside continuing to teach the ideas of his mentor, John Wycliffe. When Ann informed him of the danger they were all in he broke into tears explaining that he never wanted to place his precious family in jeopardy. Robert stopped him and informed him with military precision that there would be time for tears later but now required action. He asked John to marry them right then and there, for although John had been deposed from his parish church he was still considered an ordained priest and had every legal right to pronounce them man and wife. And so, on that day standing in the meadow just outside the little cottage of her childhood, Ann married Robert with John saying the fateful words, 'let no man put asunder what God has bound together." Afterwards they immediately packed a few of their belongings and tried to convince Ann's father to go with them or at least allow them to take Ann's two younger sisters. Her father agreed to have the younger children go with Robert and Ann but he refused. "Annie, my wife lies in the ground over the hill. I'll not leave her. God will protect me until it is my time. And when death comes, by whatever means, they will bury my bones next to her but our souls will be reunited finally in heaven." John was adamant about staying. "I have a job to do given to me by the Lord God Almighty and I pray He gives me the strength to endure whatever is to happen to me while doing His will," he spoke these final words with conviction and Ann knew this might be the last time she saw her beloved idealistic brother. John did ask Robert, "What are your plans? Where will you go that your family might be safe?"

"I don't know. For now, Ann and I are heading to York. There I will collect Elisabeth and a little money I have placed in my sister's hands for safe keeping. There is no reason to return to my farm. As soon as the Duke realizes I am not joining the march north he will have the sheriff possess it and all our belongings in the name of the king and probably have me branded a traitor to the crown." Robert replied with all seriousness in his voice.

"I have a suggestion, "John replied in response while looking at both Ann and his new brother-in-law.

"We are all ears dear brother, speak what is on your mind," Ann responded her voice tinged with anxiety and concern.

"Go south to Leicester. I know it is a Lancastrian stronghold. The support runs high for King Henry in those parts but I also know the Lollards are numerous in that county and there are farms that I can direct you to that will keep you two and the children safe … for a while. Perhaps this will all blow over after a time and we can return to our peaceful manner of life?" John doubted what he was saying but at the moment he was doing his best to give encouragement and hope to these two people, one of whom he dearly loved and the other who he was learning to love. John continued, "I know some men there. I could write a letter of introduction for you Robert explaining the situation. I'm confident they would find a way to keep all of you safe from harm. What say you?"

Robert and Ann looked at one another and both slowly nodded their heads in affirmation. "What are we doing," Ann thought to herself. "This is madness. I love Robert and I know I will come to love his daughter but how will we live. What will happen to Robert and his Elizabeth when the king hears of his disloyalty? What will happen to me and my sisters? Can we trust these men John mentions?"

As Ann and Robert packed food and what clothing they could gather together for the trip south, John and his father worked on the wording of the letter he would give to Robert. Working with haste, the two were, at last, prepared to travel. John handed the letter to Robert and spoke to both of them. "When you arrive in Leicester, ask to see a blacksmith by the name of William Smith. If he is not available, seek out either, the cobbler, John Anneys or the lawyer, Thomas Tickhill and his wife Agnes. I know these people. They are good Christians and are working to spread the teachings of Master Wycliffe. The letter explains the situation here in the north and why you two are on the run. Robert, I did not say much about your personal convictions. I'll leave that for you to explain when you arrive. You can trust these people. I do every time I travel south." At this last statement, Ann raised her eyes in surprise as she was not aware that her brother had these types of connections all over the kingdom. John looked at her and said, "Annie, if you only knew. There are so-called Lollards everywhere. People are hungry for the word of God and no man no matter how powerful will be able to stop them from having it. Go now and God be with you." Finally, Ann kissed her father and brother a tearful goodbye knowing full well it may be the last time she sees them alive. Ann's father replied, "I'll not say goodbye to you my darling but just until we meet again."

Robert and Ann and her two younger sisters travelled lightly. John had given Robert his horse and Ann's father had tied it to a small cart that he often used around the farm. Ann and Robert rode in the front and the girls held on for dear life in the back as the road was rutted and the ride quite bouncy. As they approached the great walled city of York, Robert could immediately tell that Henry was within the walls with his usual entourage of advisors and men at arms. Robert decided it would be too dangerous for Ann and the girls to enter through the gate so he decided to secure them in a great meadow just south of the city. Robert paid a wool merchant to allow him to travel in the back of his covered wagon as he hid underneath a pile of goods ready for market.

Robert knocked softly on the door of his sister's small house. His daughter Elizabeth answered the door and squealed with delight when she saw her father. Robert gathered her up into his arms and smothered her with fatherly kisses. At last his sister appeared and with a look of concern upon her face asked him, "Why are you here my brother? The king has called for all of his vassals to join him in an attack upon Scotland. You should be preparing for battle. Should you not?"

"I do not have a lot of time. So, I need you both to listen to me very carefully and do as I command," Robert replied with military precision. Both of the young women looked at one another and then at Robert with anticipation.

"Elizabeth, as you know, I have been calling on a young woman in the North Riding by the name of Ann Whitby. I will get to the point. We were married by her priest brother John." At this announcement, Robert's sister gasped but Elizabeth appeared to take this news in stride. She smiled and said, "If that makes you happy, daddy, then I am happy. When do I get to meet her?" the young girl asked in innocence.

Robert replied, "That brings me to the second point. For reasons that I can't take the time to explain fully, my wife Ann and her two sisters are waiting for us in the great meadow south of the city."

"For us?" Elizabeth asked. Robert's sister interjected, "What do you mean Robert? This is all very confusing!" she exclaimed.

"Sister, I love you and I'm so deeply appreciative of you for looking after Elizabeth while I was away but, things have changed and we, Ann, her sisters, I and you, Elizabeth, are heading south today," Robert replied with certainly tinged with apprehension as look at his daughter.

"Why!" Robert's sister stated with an alarmed voice.

"I am not going to shed any more blood for King Henry. I'm done. And my wife Ann has opened my eyes by teaching me how to read and more importantly, to read the Bible. I have learned by reading with my own eyes and thinking with my own mind how far the church has strayed from the simple yet profound teachings of Jesus of Nazareth, the risen Christ," replied Robert

"Robert ... you can read?" asked his sister incredulously. "This is all a bit overwhelming. I need to sit down."

"We don't have time to waste. They will begin searching for me soon. And they are already hunting for Ann's brother John. He is a Lollard priest who travels the countryside teaching and preaching the word of God as he understands it. He was a student of Wycliffe at Oxford and that experience transformed him. Elizabeth, sweetheart, pack a few things for the travel but be quick my dear." Robert spoke to his daughter who was staring at him with wide eyed amazement.

"Brother, where are you going?" his sister asked as she helped Elizabeth gather her belongings.

"I can't tell you. It is better that you do not know. That way, should they ask you, you will not have to lie," replied Robert.

Soon father and daughter were heading out the southern gate of the walled city of York. Robert had cautioned her to not say a word should they be stopped. They travelled through the gate past the guard unnoticed as there was much traffic at that point in the day and they were just two people in a large group of people conducting their affairs in this busy northern city of England. They quickly found Ann and her two younger sisters. Introductions were made and if either Ann or Elizabeth were uncomfortable with the circumstance nothing of their countenance revealed that discomfort. They headed south.

It took them almost three days to complete their journey. They entered the town of Leicester late in the day just as the sun was beginning to set. Their little group was stopped at the town's gate by a guard who enquired of them Robert asked politely for directions to the blacksmith. When the group first saw William Smith, they were amazed at his size. Smith's arms were the size of small trees and the muscles bulged every time he moved. At first Smith was hesitant engaging in conversation with them but as soon as the name John Whitby was mentioned his face transformed and he became extremely helpful. Smith led them to the home of the Tickhills who immediately invited them in for supper and to rest that evening with them. It was Agnes Tickhill who took control of the situation. She informed Robert and Ann that they, the Tickhills had a small rundown farm that had been given to them by Agnes' late brother and that they could rent it from her at no charge of course until Robert found some type of employment. When Agnes determined that Ann could read she informed her of a Lollard school that was meeting every Tuesday and Thursday and would she be able to help read and teach the Scriptures to those who attended. An offering would be taken and Ann could have the proceeds as payment. Thomas Tickhill, an Oxford trained lawyer informed the group that many folks in Leicester considered themselves Lollards and even though King Henry had forbid translation of the Latin Bible into English, there were probably as many copies of the English Bible in Leicester as there were sheep in Yorkshire. Being from Yorkshire, Robert laughed at the joke. In fact, he and Thomas Tickhill became friends rather quickly. For the time being, he felt safe.

The days turned into months. The months inevitably turned into years. Robert took up carpentry work and because he was skilled with the bow would often lead small hunting parties into the surrounding forest for wild game. They combined this income with Ann's weekly contributions. They managed to survive. Only a few people actually knew the whole story of the Clevelands and those that did kept it to themselves. Those that had considered telling the authorities   only had to take one look at the massive William Smith and realize he and Robert Cleveland had become close friends. That was enough to keep their silence. After all, people reasoned, they were a good God fearing family who just wanted to live out their days in peace.

In 1403, the Percy family of Northumberland revolted against King Henry IV. The plan was to join forces with Owen Glendower of north Wales and raise Edmund Mortimer to the throne. However, these plans came to naught with the death of Henry "Hotspur" Percy at the battle of Shrewsbury.

In 1405, the now Archbishop of York and Robert's old nemesis, Richard le Scrope, joined forces with the elder Percy, the Earl of Northumberland and attempted, once again to overthrow Henry. This uprising was crushed by the Nevilles of York. The Earl fled to Scotland and the archbishop was executed by command of the king. This would have probably led to the excommunication of Henry by the church but it was in the midst of the great schism that had developed with the two competing popes keen on King Henry's support; it protested but took no action.

As King Henry had his hands full with the troubles in the north, he appeared to relax somewhat his persecution of the Lollard movement. Life went on in Leicester and the rest of the nation as it had for ages. Couples fell in love, married, had children, watched those children grow and then left this world to stand before their maker. Little Elizabeth Cleveland grew up and married Walter Gilbert a Leicester Lollard of some means who had made his wealth in the building of carriages and other finery for the aristocracy of the surrounding area with some of his customers coming from as far away as London. Unfortunately, both of Ann's younger sisters died from unexplainable illness which was quite common at the time. Ann and Robert had five children of whom two boys, John and William survived to adulthood.

In 1413, King Henry died and was succeeded to the throne by his son, King Henry V who was to become obsessed with reasserting his claim to the French throne he had inherited from Edward III. Perhaps because of this redirection of the King's attention, the Lollards, although identified as trouble makers for the established church, had managed to continue to grow in size as their message of a pure and simple gospel spread through the country, particularly in the midland and southwestern counties.

All this changed with Sir John Oldcastle. Oldcastle was a Lollard knight who had befriended a young Prince Henry, later King Henry V. In 1404, he became a member of the Parliament and in 1408 after marrying into an aristocratic and wealthy family; he became Lord Cobham and a member of the House of Lords. While Oldcastle was rather outspoken about the corruption he saw within the English church his friendship with the Prince who would be king offered him a degree of protection from the church officials. In 1414, Oldcastle's home was searched by agents of the Archbishop of Canterbury, Thomas Arundel, where they found an English bible and some written documents supporting Lollard beliefs. After some legal arguments, Oldcastle agreed to a trial in hopes that his friend the new

King would gladly intervene on his behalf. That did not happen. King and Church were still intertwined in each other's affairs and Henry needed the Church hierarchies support in his quest for the crown of France. So, Oldcastle was quickly found guilty of heresy and sentenced to be burned at the stake as a heretic. While awaiting his execution at the Tower of London he escaped with some inside aid from Lollard sympathizers. While on the run Oldcastle decided to organize active Lollard resistance against the Crown and led an uprising of Lollard men willing to fight against the Lancastrian king and corrupt church officials. The goal was to topple the current system and replace it with a kinder more democratic form of government with social reforms including the English church. Forty-four-year-old Robert Cleveland heard the call and responded with his sword. He did know Oldcastle but he had heard of him and liked what he heard. Here was a man of principle who was willing to place his life on the line for what his belief. While Robert's faith had grown tremendously after his marriage to Ann and their resettlement within the Lollard community in Leicester he still had lingering doubts about the path he had chosen. Should he have stayed in the north and fought against Henry then? Should he have surrendered to the king's officials and taken whatever punishment they wanted to deliver upon him and his household? He was not one to often second guess his decision but these thoughts nagged at him. He was not a coward. He had fought bravely in a number of battles and he knew that what he had done he had done for Ann and Elizabeth as much as he did it for himself. But still he lived in doubt and now, finally, to him at least, a righteous reason to fight back. Here was a nobleman who shared in his belief of a purified church with justice for the common man. Here was a man of God he could follow once again into battle. His son William was only four years of age and John; the baby had just been born last year. He knew what he must do but first he would have to share his decision with the most important person in his life, his dear sweet wife, Ann.

Robert walked the three miles from the town to the humble cottage he and Ann had called home for the last fourteen years. He was surprised to see a strange horse in the yard. He usually did not carry his sword to work but always kept a short-bladed dagger stuffed in his shirt. He touched it and then walked into the house. There before him was Ann's brother, John Whitby whom neither had seen since they left the North Riding so many years ago. John let out a yell of amazement as Robert walked into the main room. They hugged one another and then started to speak at the same time.

"My God John, I never thought we would lay eyes upon you in this world again." Robert exclaimed.

"It is good news that brings me back to the south. Oldcastle is calling for rebellion. And I am planning on joining his forces as chaplain. We are in communication and he will be here in Leicester soon," John explained with great excitement in his voice. Ann was smiling and crying at the same time.

"Ann, dry your tears. This is good news. God has sent us an avenging angel to lead the people in revolt against a corrupt king and even more corrupt church, "Robert spoke lovingly to his wife.

"Perhaps it is the Day of Judgement, Ann," John spoke to them both as Ann cradled little John to her breast for he had started to cry.

"If I read my Bible right good brother, will not Jesus himself return to defeat the powers of Satan on Judgement Day?" Ann responded. "And you dear husband. I suppose you have a mind to take up the sword once again?" Ann looked into her husband's eyes as if willing him to say no, he would remain a man of peace and stay at home. But even as she thought that she knew this time he would go and fight. She could see it in his eyes. She knew of his doubts he had harbored all these years but had never dared to bring them up to him. She was just silently glad that he had chosen her and had tried to make a stable life for all of them.

"Ann, you know I must join your brother. Don't you?" Robert asked while trying to hold back his tears. "I have to. I have no other choice. Before I met you, I was a simple warrior. I did what I was told and never thought much about it. And then you came into my life and all that changed. You taught me how to read. You taught me how to think for myself. You taught me how to love again after my Lizzie had died. And for that I will be ever grateful. But Ann, deep down inside, I am still a warrior. And now through Oldcastle, the Lord is calling me to once again pick up my sword and this time to fight for justice and righteousness. This time I fight not for sinful king and corrupted country but for God." Robert looked into the eyes of this woman whom he dearly loved. He knew that if she said no, he would not go. He waited.

Ann did not speak for the longest time. She had her head bowed as if in prayer. Suddenly, she turned to her husband. "Go Robert. Do what you must do. The boys and I will be alright. Perhaps Elizabeth and William will take us in until this is over? But if not, the Lord will provide. Go my husband. Do your duty." Ann tried to put on a brave face as she said these last words but the tears were now freely falling down her cheeks. The baby began to cry. Little William continued to play with his toys not understanding what had just transpired in their little cottage.

The next morning the two of them headed out. And that was the last time Ann ever saw her husband Robert or her brother John. Robert died a few weeks later in a small skirmish between Oldcastle's followers and the king's knights. How he died was not known but someone later found a small English bible in his coat with the name Ann written on the inside front cover. Ann was overwhelmed with both joy and sadness when at last it was returned to her by a good friend of Walter Gilbert, her son in law. John was caught trying to hide in Oxford where he had first heard the teachings of Professor Wycliffe. He was hanged in the large yard in front of where he used to listen to Wycliffe's lectures. Oldcastle and his dwindling rebels fought on but eventually he was captured and quickly taken to the royal court in London where he was tried and found guilty of treason and heresy. Oldcastle was hanged and his body burned at Saint Gile's Field in the winter of 1417.

After the Oldcastle rebellion was brought to a bloody end, the English Lollard movement went underground. It lay there simmering for decades like embers in a fire that someone thought they had extinguished only to catch flame again when the conditions were right. And the day would come when those embers would explode with intensity and sweep over the nation.

Ann lived to be an old woman. She never remarried. She saw both of her sons marry and raise a family. To family and friends, to everyone in the county who knew of her, she was just the old woman known as "Granny Annie". But Ann had a secret. She had lived her entire life with secrets. She was comfortable with keeping them. A few years after Robert's death, Ann had travelled to Guisborough, a long and dangerous journey for a woman of her age. But she was on a secret mission which she completed and then returned to live out her days at the small cottage she and Robert had called home. Years later, as her earthly life was coming to a close, she decided to tell her grandson, Alexander about her secret. As she lay dying she called out for him and told everyone else in the small cottage to leave them alone for a few minutes. She motioned for Alexander to come close to the bedside and bend over so she could whisper something to him. He did as she requested for he did dearly love his granny and was terribly sorry to see her leave this life.

"I buried it Alex. I buried it in the North Riding on his ancient land. There with the bones of his ancestors. I buried it there. A part of him will be there to the end of time." Ann whispered to her grandson as she struggled for breath.

"Buried what, granny?" Alexander asked somewhat confused by his grandmother's dying words.

"His English bible … and my name … written in it." Ann Cleveland weakly smiled at her grandson and then breathed her last.

Chapter Five – Annandale, Dumfries ca 1513

"In nomine Patris, et Filii et Spiritus Sancti," the priest slowly chanted these words as he made the sign of the cross and threw a clump of dirt on the freshly covered graves. Then one by one men of the western border clans of Bell, Carlisle, Carruthers, Johnstone, Armstrong, and, Yrwyn, stopped in front of the graves of their fallen kin and paid their final respects. At first, they had talked of burying their dead across the border in Northumberland near the actual battlefield of Flodden outside the town of Branxton. But the remaining chiefs of each of these western clans, and there were few who had survived, decided their fathers and brothers must be buried in Scottish soil. So, they gathered up the bodies and headed west to the little town of Yetholm, one mile due west of the northern border with England. It was here, at the Kirk of Yetholm, built in the 13th century, where they buried their dead.

Flodden had been a disaster for the assembled troops of King James IV of Scotland. The King claimed that he was merely seeking revenge for the murder of Robert Kerr, a Border warden murdered by a member of a reiving English clan called Heron in the year 1508. But no one actually believed that story. Reiving had been a part of life for the English Scottish border region since the days of Edward I and William Wallace. This land and its people had not known peace for over two hundred years. The pattern was fairly simple to explain. During the summer months, the border clans concentrated on attempting to raise their crops in less than fertile soil while sending their herds of cattle and sheep onto upland pasture land to graze. During the winter months, when darkness provided sufficient cover and hungry bellies ample motivation, they raided the stored crops and cattle or sheep from across the border and occasionally from one another. Murder was not commonplace but this was a troubled land where a man's honor was often put to the test with the resulting bloodshed sometimes leading to death. This was the land of the feuds where sons and daughters were taught from a very young age who was kin and could thus be trusted and who was an outsider and therefore could not. The only time this pattern was not followed year after year was when war had broken out once again between Scotland and England. And this happened with a certain degree of frequency.

So no one, at least not any of the border families, believed the reason for this current war with England had been the murder of one unfortunate warden. No, the real reason lay in France and his name was Henry VIII, King of England. Scotland and France were allies. This was the auld alliance often mentioned by the Anglo-Norman aristocracy who had taken power in Scotland shortly after the invasion of William the Conqueror. It really meant nothing to the vast majority of poor Scots who were simply trying to survive. But it could serve the Scottish kings and his barons when it seemed advantageous. And, to James, the time seemed right.

Henry, who claimed also to be the overlord of Scotland, was in France with the Emperor Maximilian as they attempted to defend Italy and the Pope from the French. The Pope had excommunicated James but he was not troubled by this action. Henry had earlier attempted an invasion of Aquitaine. In his mind, it would be the first of many actions which led to his crowning as King of France. He had leveraged the English relationship with

Spain in order to secure the necessary troops and treaties but the whole thing fell apart since Ferdinand, King of Spain was naturally not entirely supportive of Henry's desires for European Empire. However, Henry had pulled off a diplomatic coup by convincing the Emperor Maximillian to join the Holy League in defense of the Italian state of Venice and the Pope. For this he was promised the title of Most Christian King of France by Pope Leo X, who had just been elected the Supreme Bishop of Rome in March of this year but, of course, King Louis stood in the way. Since Henry was tied up in France, James saw his opportunity and invaded Northumberland with a huge force of over 40,000 Scottish nobles and infantrymen equipped with horse as well as cannon taken from the walls of Edinburgh Castle.

Catherine of Aragon was acting as Henry's Regent in England while he was abroad in France. She issued warrants for the property of Scotsmen in England to be seized. She also ordered Thomas Lovell to raise an army from the Midland counties of the English kingdom. The Earl of Surrey was appointed to lead the English into battle. The Scots, in typical Scottish fashion went on the offensive as their nobles and clan chiefs led each group into battle with little organization or control. The English simply waited for them at the bottom of the hill and ultimately surrounded the Scots. The English generals stayed behind the lines of battle and directed the attack. The Scots did not and numerous Scottish leaders fell in the first wave of the attack which meant there was no one left to coordinate a retreat when the battle turned against them. It was an overwhelming English victory and the Scottish losses were huge. On the field of battle lay James IV plus twelve Earls, fifteen Lairds, an Archbishop and numerous lowland and highland clan chiefs plus thousands of Scotsmen including many of the Yrwyn fighting men from Dumfries. In fact, the Clan Chief of Yrwyn, William, whose seat was at Bonshaw Tower overlooking the river Kirtle and most of his sons were killed. It had been estimated by the survivors that the Scots lost nearly half of their original 40,000 troops. The English suffered loss, of course, but only to the tune of around 5,000 men.

"Well, that's done. Let's go home," said William Johnstone to his childhood friend Christopher Yrwyn of Bonshaw.

"Tis a sad day Willie, a sad day indeed for Clan Yrwyn, I never thought I would live to see such a thing, my father, Edward and all my brothers lying lifeless on the ground. God preserve their souls." And Christopher crossed himself as he said these words quietly to his dear friend. "What will become of the clan?" he pondered aloud as the two of them joined the rest of the small band of Scotsmen heading west to their homeland.

"Ach laddie, someone will rise to the occasion. Perhaps it will be Edward from those of your clan who live up the river Annan across the hills from Maxwell land. They are your kin?" William asked his friend.

"Aye, kin they are. But they've got their hands full with the Maxwells. You know that Willie. Your people have used them as a buffer against the Maxwell clan for generations. Edward is a powerful man and I've heard rather ambitious but will your Chief let him move a day's journey to the east to take over Bonshaw? It's not looking good right now for what's left of my family. I fear a power struggle looming and bloodshed will surely come of it." Christopher looked down at his feet as he made this prophetic pronouncement.

"Christopher, you might be the youngest lad of the bunch, but as a son of Edward of Bonshaw, are you not entitled to the position of clan Chief?" William asked his childhood friend. He knew Christopher did not want to lead his small band of Yrwyns. Even though both were only 12 years old Christopher was wise for his age and understood completely the great responsibility carried upon the shoulders of clan Chief.

"Willie, there are at least six different families of Yrwyns in Dumfries. You have my people at Bonshaw then there are Yrwyns at Hoddam, Luce, Pennersax, Stakehugh and Skail. Each of these branches claims to have descended from the same Annandale man but no one is certain of his name or of his woman's. We don't even use the same spelling of the clan. Those who can write, and they are few, sometimes will write Yrwyn, sometimes Irwyn or Irvine and even Irving. If we can't agree on something as simple as that how in heaven's name will we agree on who should lead the clan at Bonshaw Tower? Mark my words my friend, good King James may have thought he was doing the right thing by invading Northumberland but the results of our defeat will be disastrous for my kin. There will be blood shed" Christopher looked into the eyes of his closest friend. He saw understanding. Willie also had lost most of the fighting age men of his family including two of his three brothers. But the Johnstones were a united, large and strong clan led by Willie's father, Adam, and they seemed to get along with each other better than most of the Scottish clans of eastern Dumfries. Rarely did feuds break out between them and other clans on this side of the border. With the notable exception being the Maxwells, who held much land west of the river Annan and, of course, were keepers of the huge fortress known as Caerlaverock Castle.

"Bloodshed … of course, there will be bloodshed," Willie responded sarcastically. "It is all we seem to know how to do … kill one another. I do grow weary of it my friend. I do grow weary …" William's voice trailed off as he looked towards the western horizon. On the crest of the adjoining hill, in the direction they were walking, the boys saw a banner swirling in the bright noon day sun. At first, the image was rather fuzzy and shimmering as if a mirage. Christopher exclaimed," do you see what I see Willie? Is it not the royal banner of our good King James?"

William replied, "It is … it's the Red Lion rampant on a golden background. But, how can that be! I saw James' cold dead body. With my own eyes, I swear it Christopher." And then as suddenly as it had appeared it disappeared. Years later, Christopher would hear the tales of the survival of his king and think back to that day when he and his wearied companion saw the banner on the top of the hill unfurled in the strong westerly wind. He did not believe the legends of course, it was simply the yearnings of a downtrodden people for some semblance of pride and comfort in the face of utter defeat. Both young men knew what was coming next to their land. The English troops would ravage the countryside. No, they would leave the great port cities alone. They were well fortified and could withstand a lengthy siege. And they dare not touch the great fortifications of the Scottish nobility. But they would play havoc with the small land holding clans of the border region. Christopher imagined that Bonshaw would be razed to the ground along with the smaller less fortified seats of other Scottish border clans. Then Christopher chuckled, "of course if they don't do it to us, we will do it to ourselves." William asked what he had said but Christopher just shook his head and smiled. "No sense lamenting the condition of my world. It is what it is," he thought to himself.

After days of steady travel, Christopher and William saw home. The English had not yet arrived and things from a distance looked peaceful. He saw his mother and younger sisters first. They were working in the fields. Williams' twin sister, Margaret was there with them. She was tall for her age of twelve. She had a gracefulness about her that other girls of that age did not share. William constantly teased his friend about how he looked at Maggie, which is what everyone called her. "Stop staring Chris, your eyes will fall out of your head." This was William's usual response when he caught Christopher looking at his sister. But it was always said in jest accompanied with a lot of laughter and good natured jostling between the two close companions. The two had never really had a fight break out between them. Of course, being of Scotts border blood, the anger could quickly surface upon a disagreement but their friendship was deep and lasting and neither would ever think of actually hurting the other.

"Mother," Christopher called out to his mother. Upon seeing this rag tag band of survivors, the girls ran to greet them. Maggie was the swiftest and reached them first. She gave her brother a huge hug and kissed him on the cheek. In her excitement, she did the same to Christopher and then realized what she had done. Both were red with embarrassment but the mood quickly became somber as Christopher's mother suddenly realized that the boys were not accompanied by Christopher's father or brothers.

"Where are the lads? Where is your father?" Christopher's mother spoke with great anxiety for she knew already before her son shared the sad tale that they would not be coming home. She began to cry. And then her daughters suddenly realized what Christopher's unchaperoned appearance meant and they joined their mother in her grief-stricken wails. As the women stood before them in tears, Christopher realized the serious implication of what had befallen them. There would be a vacuum of leadership within his branch of the clan. Other Yrwyn men would step forward to claim authority. His mother and sisters would somehow survive. They would probably be used to cement stronger alliances with neighboring clans through marriage but what would come of him? Would they be fair to him? Would they ship him off somewhere? Or worse yet, would he end up in the Annan with a dirk in his back? The reivers of the borders were not known for their mercy or kindness. This was a hard land and times were harsher still. Only the strong and wily survived and death was a constant companion. He had lost his father and brothers and many of his friends but he knew he could not dwell on that loss. Life goes on and he was bound and determined to survive against all odds. There was one man still living in all of east Dumfries that Christopher Yrwyn trusted and could depend upon for guidance and direction in this troubled time. And he was a Franciscan Greyfriar from Dumfries town whose name was Gilbert Broun. Everyone in these parts simply called him Friar Broun and he was the only Christian evangelical for miles around. It was hard to find men of the cloth who would work in the border region. It took a certain and special type of person. There were small parish churches scattered here and there and, of course, the abbeys at Dundrennan and Sweetheart plus the Hoddam monastery. But the monks kept to themselves in their well-structured buildings making their ale and tending to their crops of barley and rye. The few ordained priests of the Annandale region did not stray far from the safety of their small priories. It was the mendicant friars who taught, preached and in many other ways brought the gospel of Christ to the reivers.

Christopher had known Friar Broun all his life. He was once told the story of how the good Friar came to Dumfries. It was long before Christopher was born sometime in the 1490s. Broun had been a student at the newly formed University of St. Andrews on the eastern shore of the sea. He had been told that Broun was a bright and energetic student. However, Gilbert Broun was an independent thinker and although he was studying for eventual placement in the Scottish priesthood he had voiced some rather public and negative opinions about the Church hierarchy and, in particular, the behavior of some of the priests he had encountered growing up in the vicinity of Edinburgh. Gilbert was a bright lad from a middling class burgher who had high hopes for his one son. And Gilbert loved to learn and did want to have his father be proud of his accomplishments. But Gilbert spoke the truth as he saw it. And the truth to him was the current church needed change. Gilbert learned to read at an early age and as he progressed in his understanding of Latin he was able to read the scriptures for himself as opposed to many Scots who depended upon their local priest for interpretation. The more he read of the teachings of Jesus, the more convinced he became that somehow the church had lost sight of its original purpose and mission. He would grapple constantly with what appeared to him the large discrepancy between the current church's accumulated wealth and the obvious poverty of Jesus and his original followers. Eventually, his inner thoughts became public while he was at the university and this is where the trouble began for him. He alienated most of his professors, many of his fellow students and the local church leadership. Finally, the powers to be had enough and they asked him to leave. He offered to become a mendicant friar. Christopher learned the word mendicant is derived from the Latin mendicare which means to beg. The mendicant friars were bound by a vow of poverty and dedication to an ascetic way of life, renouncing property and traveling the land to preach a simple gospel of the love of Christ and mercy of God. The mendicant movement had started in France and Italy and had become popular in the poorer towns and cities of Europe at the beginning of the thirteenth century. However, their refusal to own property and thus pay taxes threatened the stability of the established church which at that time was in the middle of the crusades which needed to be financed by tithes.

Friar Broun was a Franciscan. The founder of this order was Francis of Assisi who's only commitment in life was to imitate the Lord Jesus. Francis attracted followers who sought a renewal of the original message of Jesus and the purity of his lifestyle. Many Franciscans were like Friar Broun, men of learning and religious zeal. No one really knows how or why Friar Broun ended up in this part of Scotland but that is what happened and for some reason the Yrwyn clan of Bonshaw considered him to be their connection to God and highly valued his wisdom and knowledge. According to what Christopher had been told, it was not an easy relationship at the beginning when the good Friar stumbled upon the lands of Dumfries. He had joined the order and had requested to be sent to the most difficult place in the kingdom thinking he would be sent to the far north. But it was in southwestern Scotland where he ended up and attached himself loosely to the abbey at Dumfries. He did not report to the Abbot, that was not the structure of the mendicant friars but they did allow him to stay and he began to go out into the neighboring countryside to preach the gospel and live the life he thought Jesus demanded of him. He went from farm to farm and from clan to clan simply trying to be a good example of the Christian faith to all he encountered. He had first met William, Christopher's father after the Yrwyn men had returned from one of their many raids into England. It had been a costly excursion as one of Williams' brothers had been killed and two of his own sons had been seriously injured. Friar Broun had met the party on the road outside the Bonshaw Tower. At first, William threatened to have him drowned in the local pond but Friar Broun convinced him that he could help mend his injured sons. And in that he was successful. As the two young Yrwyns regained their strength William and Friar Broun began to develop what could be considered a strong and lasting bond of friendship. The Yrwyns, including William, were no stranger to the message of Jesus. They had all been baptized by a traveling priest but until the arrival of Friar Broun religion and faith were not common topics of conversation. After the Friars arrival, things slowly changed for William and his clan. At first, they simply tolerated the eccentric old friar but with the passage of time, trust between the Yrwyns and this man of God grew and united them in friendship. Friar Broun would never accompany William and his men on any raids or participate in defending the Tower from attack by marauding members of Clan Maxwell. He had sworn to follow the example of Christ and that meant being a pacifist. But he was always there for the clan when they needed his help. And during those times when he offered tangible help for the sick and wounded, he would minister to their souls. Christopher had grown up hearing the many Biblical stories Friar Broun would convey to the family when gathered around the warming fire on a cold winter's night. Christopher learned of Adam and Eve and the Garden of Eden and their banishment by a holy God and of the murder of Abel by his brother Cain. Friar Broun had an uncanny way of somehow weaving the Biblical stories with the daily lives and events of the lowland border clans. Christopher liked Friar Broun and over time grew to consider him a trusted friend to whom he would often pour out his frustration and confusion with the way things were in the border region, for Christopher was a thoughtful, kind and considerate young man who really did not understand the incessant need for violence and bloodshed of his people. Of course, Christopher Yrwyn was a son of the clan chief and therefore was expected to learn how to fight at a relatively young age. And learn he did. It took quite a lot of irritation for him to lose his temper but when he did no one was safe. It was as if he had lost his mind and went berserk with anger. Consequently, other boys in the family would often give Christopher a wide berth hoping to not upset him or provoke him in any way. Although his father William was actually rather proud of this wild streak in his son, Christopher was often ashamed of his inability to control his temper and felt guilty afterwards for the mayhem he had committed. It was then he would seek out his dear friend Friar Broun and confess his sins. The good Friar always had a sympathetic ear and wise words of advice for the young boy soon to be a man. Broun knew this was a dangerous land and these were dangerous times.

As Christopher stood there with his bereaved kin Friar Broun appeared. He had a knack for being in the right place at the right time. As soon as Christopher saw him the tears came to his eyes. He had lost his father and older brothers and the Friar was the only grown man he now had for comfort and guidance.

Friar Broun placed his arms around Christopher and spoke to him gently, "there laddie, you are home now, you are safe." Christopher's body went limp in the man's embrace and the tears turned into a fountain. Friar Broun simply stood there holding onto this grieving young man and continued to speak softly and gently to him. After a while, Christopher regained his composure and cleared his throat to speak.

"It was awful. They went like lambs to the slaughter. Wave after wave cut down by the English using their bills. Our men used the pike. It was no match. The English stayed in formation and obeyed the commands of their superiors who were positioned behind the front lines. And the English cannon devastated and scattered our men. When it was over, thousands lay dead and dying on the field including my father and brothers." At this point, Christopher began to cry once again. And once again, the good friar comforted him.

Christopher's mother spoke up, "Friar Broun, what is to become of us? All our men save young Christopher have been slain. Who will step forward and become the head of the family? Who will lead our clan?" And she began once again to wail to the heavens with a heart torn into pieces by her grief and anguish.

"God will provide, my children. God will provide," Friar Broun responded with a look of confidence and love. He did love these strange folk of the borders. He did not know why. They were challenging and frustrating to say the least. Kind and tenderhearted to a fault and then in an instant filled with blinding and murderous rage. But somehow, down through the years, they had become his sheep and he was their shepherd, black sheep perhaps, but his to keep nevertheless. And so, it stood to reason that now when this calamity had befallen them they would turn to him for solace and guidance. And with God's help, he would lead these poor souls as best he could.

"Come. Let's head to the Tower. We need to prepare it for whatever Satan has planned next." The good friar stated as he led his small entourage out of the fields and back onto the one stone road leading to Bonshaw Tower.

That evening as the cooking fires began to slowly wane into embers, the Yrwyns of Bonshaw Tower gathered around Friar Broun. He took stock of what he beheld. One elderly grandmother who could no longer see nor hear, Christopher's mother and her three remaining daughters, Christopher and a few other families now all led by women who called Bonshaw home, nineteen people in all, sixteen women, two baby boys and Christopher, who was now, technically the oldest man and chief of this branch of the clan Yrwyn, and, of course, himself.

"Although it may not look like it, we are not alone," Broun began, "We are surrounded by a cloud of witnesses, those of our number who have gone on before us to their heavenly reward. And the Lord Jesus is here with his army of angels. And of course, on his throne sits the almighty God, giver and keeper of life itself. We have nothing to fear." The Friar slowly moved his head around the room and softly spoke these words as he gazed in to the eyes his little flock. "I know that nothing can separate us from the love of God, death can't, and life can't. The angels can't and the demons can't. Our fears for today, our worries about tomorrow and even the powers of hell can't keep away God's love. Whether we are high above the sky or in the deepest ocean, nothing in all creation will ever be able to separate us from the love of God that is revealed in Christ Jesus our Lord. This I believe."

He continued on, "Tonight we will try to sleep and rest our bodies. I will pray for God's guidance and direction. Tomorrow we will see what the day brings and with God's help and protection, we will be ready," and with that final statement he motioned for everyone to find their sleeping place and to lie down and close their eyes and rest their weary bodies.

The next morning a light rain was falling. Christopher was up early as was Friar Broun. As they scaled the Tower steps to the lookout perch located at the very top of the fortress they looked to the west where night was slowly turning into day and were shocked by what they saw. Coming slowly towards them were three men all riding great steeds of battle and all were dressed for war. Friar Broun immediately recognized the man in the center as John Johnstone, a leader of the northern branch of his clan. He was accompanied by Michael Irving of Pennersax and to their amazement the third man was none other than William Maxwell, the Laird of Caerlaverock Castle. Maxwell was holding the small white flag of truce. They had come to speak and not to raze the Tower to the ground as Friar Broun had suspected but did not tell any of the family the night before.

The threesome stopped just outside reach of an arrow. Johnstone spoke first, "Hello Yrwyns of Bonshaw. We come in peace. We have come to negotiate. Send out the one called Christopher along with the Friar. On my word, nothing evil will befall them."

Christopher looked at the good Friar with concern. "What should we do?" he asked. "Trust the Lord," replied Friar Broun and with that quick and terse statement opened the gated door and began to walk outside the Tower towards the three armed and dangerous men. Christopher followed behind wondering if this was indeed the right thing to do.

Johnstone spoke first. "So, you are the brave young lad who fought the mighty English forces at Flodden? You don't look big enough to wield a pike or a sword."

"I was assigned to the cannon detail. My job was to keep the barrel cool with water and fetch cannon balls when the supply ran low." Christopher responded with caution.

"Relax son. We mean you no harm. I heard about your father and brothers. I've been told they died bravely fighting for their king and for Scotland," Johnstone spoke. He was obviously the assigned spokesman of the group but everyone there knew that the aged Maxwell had the highest ranking and the most power behind him. His son, John Maxwell, was a Lord of the Scottish Parliament and had died fighting with his king at Flodden. Michael Irving, who had miraculously survived the carnage at Flodden, spoke next, "Christopher, we are kin. We belong to the same clan though we live in different places. We share a common ancestor. I am not here to do you or your family harm. We are here to help."

Maxwell finally cleared his throat and raised his deep bass voice. "Listen to me both of you. The English are heading this way. They aim to finish us off. We are not going to let that happen. I have sent messengers to all the neighboring clans on the Scottish side of the border. I have asked for a state of truce between the clans. We need now to band together to fight our common enemy. Many of the chiefs or whoever has been left in charge after the disaster at Flodden has responded favorably. We are all setting aside our feuds. It is time now for peace between Maxwell and Johnstone, between Douglas and Graham, between Kirkpatrick and Elliot. We must now come together as Scotsmen and fight to protect our freedom and way of life. Given what has happened to your men," Maxwell looked at Christopher with a curious mixture of sadness and disdain, "the three of us have decided that we will all send men to help protect your Tower when the English raiding parties arrive. Plus, we have agreed that you Christopher Yrwyn though only a wee lad of twelve will be named chief of Clan Irwyn at Bonshaw Tower. Johnstone has agreed to act as Regent on your behalf until you come of legal age. Then he will retire from those duties to leave you manage the affairs of Bonshaw as you see fit." Maxwell stopped speaking and looked at both

Friar Broun and Christopher. "Do you understand me son?" he continued.

"Aye, sir" Christopher dutifully responded. Maxwell began again, "And you Friar. Since you are the closest thing around these parts to a man of God we ask that you act as witness to this understanding. We also ask that you cease from your travels and stay here at Bonshaw until Christopher reaches the age of 18 at which time you may leave if that is your desire. Do you agree with these terms?" Maxwell looked solemnly at the friar.

Gilbert Broun was reluctant to agree because it was not the way of the Franciscans but he knew in his heart he could not abandon this boy and his family to the whims of these border chieftains. He looked first at young Christopher and then at the three war lords. "Aye, I agree. I witness before God and man this agreement and I agree to stay with Christopher and his clan at Bonshaw until he assumes full leadership of his people, "Friar Broun stated with clarity and conviction in his voice.

"Good," said Maxwell. "Now that is settled, would you mind Master Christopher if we entered your home and expressed our condolences to your mother and remaining kin? I would like to personally thank them for the sacrifice their men have given for the nation of Scotland and the people of the borders."

Time passed. The English did come but their hearts were simply not in it. It was if their passion for war and bloodshed had run its course. They burned a Tower here and there, stole a few cattle, and held drunken feasts in a few villages celebrating their victory. Then they went home and peace came to a land that had not known much peace for as long as anyone could remember. It was a strange time. It was a time of expectation and ceaseless worry. These Scots knew how to make war. It was in their very blood. But making and keeping the peace was an entirely different matter. That was an unusual state of affairs for the men and women of the borders however, things were happening in a faraway land called Germany that would ultimately bring an end to this tenuous peace.

Martin Luther was born on November 10th, 1483 in Eisleben Saxony a part of the Holy Roman Empire. He was baptized the next morning on the feast day of St. Martin of Tours. His father, Hans, was determined to have his oldest son, Martin, become a lawyer. Being of middling stock, he was able to have Martin educated in the trivium; grammar, rhetoric and logic. In 1501, at the age of 19, he entered the University of Erfurt and received a master's degree in 1505. In keeping with his father's wishes, he enrolled in the school of law but dropped out shortly thereafter for Martin was drawn to theology and philosophy. He soon became dissatisfied with philosophy's emphasis on reason and reason alone. Luther felt that reason alone could not lead men to God which to him was the first objective of life. That could be done only through divine revelation and he considered Scripture to be that revelation. On July 2, 1505, a lightning bolt struck close to Luther as he was riding back to the University during a thunderstorm. He made a vow to Saint Anna that if he survived the storm he would become a monk and that is what he did much to his father's displeasure. Luther entered a closed Augustinian friary in Erfurt on July 17, 1505. In 1507, he was ordained to the priesthood and in 1508 went to the University of Wittenberg to teach theology. He earned a Bachelor's degree in Biblical studies in 1508 and in October of 1512, he was awarded the Doctor of Theology degree. In that same month, he was called to the position of Doctor of Bible at the University of Wittenberg.

The controversy began with the sale of indulgences. Church theology taught that faith alone cannot justify man in the presence of a holy God. Justification depended upon an active faith, one that demonstrates its veracity through charity and good works; fides caritate formata. And, of course, the benefits of good works could be obtained through the donation of money to the church which is what it desperately needed to rebuild the Basilica of St. Peter in Rome. These donations were called indulgencies and the concept annoyed and irritated Luther. So much so, that on October 31, 1517, Luther wrote to his bishop, Albert of Mainz, protesting the sale of indulgences. Within this letter he attached a copy of his "Disputation of Martin Luther on the Power and Efficacy of Indulgences". Luther's 95 Theses was eventually translated from Latin to German and then into the other European languages including English. Eventually copies were being secretly shipped into Scotland including the border region.

"Christopher, have you seen this statement of Luther's?" Friar Broun asked of his young scholar. Christopher was now seventeen years old and although not legally the head of Bonshaw Tower everyone considered him as the chief of this small band of Yrwyns. The family had grown. Christopher's sisters and cousins had married and had added little ones each year to the size of the clan. The time of peace had brought some semblance of prosperity to the region. For the most part, the Scottish clans had maintained the truce and the raiding upon each other had diminished noticeably. However, the English farms across the border were still considered fair game and many winter's nights were filled with the shouts of men leading stolen cattle or sheep back into Scotland. Christopher and Friar Broun had become quite close more like father and son than teacher and student but the good friar had much to teach his able and willing student. He noticed that Christopher had a mind of his own. While he would never react in a disrespectful manner to his beloved teacher he did not always agree with what the man said. Even though their discussions about politics and religion often exasperated and frustrated both, in the end, their love for each other overcame any lasting hostility. As Friar Broun would often state, "Well, I guess we must simply agree to disagree and leave it at that." He would then usually smile at Christopher and both would begin to chuckle.

"No, friar, what have you stumbled upon now, another rant against the pope or maybe our young king James?" Christopher replied with a sarcastic smile upon his lips.

"Listen to this … Why does the Pope, whose wealth today is greater than the wealth of the richest Crassus, build the basilica of St. Peter with the money of poor believers rather than with his own money? What do you make of that lad? I'll bet that raised a few eyebrows in Rome." Friar Broun chuckled as he read the pamphlet.

"Where did you get that?" Christopher asked suddenly a little concerned. He knew Gilbert Broun was a man not afraid to speak the truth as he understood it and sometimes at the most inappropriate times.

"I have my sources. You don't need to fret over how I got it. Just listen to what this man Luther writes. Forgiveness is God's alone to grant and those who claim indulgences absolve the buyer from all punishment and grant them salvation are in error. Amazing, isn't it. Kind of reminds me of my days at St. Andrews when we were allowed for a short while to study the teachings of Wycliffe."

"Not him again, that man has been dead for over a century and people still read his blasphemy!" Christopher responded somewhat in jest but also somewhat serious. Christopher Yrwyn considered himself a true follower of the holy church and while he was no theologian had decided long ago that every successful organization needs one true leader and for the church in Christopher's mind that was the pope in Rome. "You need to be careful my friend," Christopher cautioned. "They burned heretics in England and it could happen here … be careful."

"Alright, so you don't want to talk religion tonight what about politics? Have you heard the latest regarding the English king Harry? Apparently, the child Mary lives. I guess she would be about two now? I have heard that Henry keeps a number of mistresses and Catherine just looks the other way. If she doesn't give him a son soon there will be trouble brewing in the southland and, what about right here in Scotland? Our good King is now five years of age and who rules the kingdom? First it is his mother and then Stewart and now Robert Maxwell. The poor child is in Stirling Castle as we speak but I've heard plans are to move him to Holyrood in Edinburg. All the Scots nobles and aristocrats are jockeying for position. They all want to be able to say they had a hand in caring for this lad in hopes it will pay off for them when he takes the crown. What men will do for money and power? It sickens my Franciscan soul." Friar Broun ended his mini speech and drank deeply from his cup.

"I'm tired my friend. I'm bound for the kingdom of sleep." And with that, Christopher went to his room and fell fast asleep. Friar Broun sat in the shadows for the longest time. Yes, he had probably had too much to drink but he was deep in thought. He had read and reread this pamphlet of this German Luther. His words had troubled him. Luther had been able to put together in a written language the thoughts that Gilbert had harbored hidden in his heart for years. Thoughts he dare not reveal to anyone including his trusted friend. What if Luther was right? What if it was all a sham, just a way to make money? How could a holy God condone such a deceitful scheme? As he slowly fell asleep in front of the fire with these troubling thoughts in his head he did not hear the English assassin sneak into the room with his dagger drawn.

The murder of Friar Gilbert Broun was a mistake. The assassin's target was young Christopher Yrwyn. But the attacker, a member of the Bell clan on the English side of the border became confused in the darkness of the poorly lit room and plunged his dagger into the heart of the old friar. Once he realized his mistake, he panicked and left quickly the way he had originally entered the Tower structure. His identity was never revealed although he left a small piece of cloth colored with the regalia of Clan Bell and the English flag of battle. He obviously intended to send a message to the Scottish border clans and it was a message well received. The peace that had lasted for a few years was broken and all the clans on both sides of the border reverted back to their tried and true ways of violence and bloodshed. Christopher had become enraged by this cowardly act and vowed to seek vengeance on the perpetrators. In fact, he became filled with a simmering rage that no amount of violence was able to satisfy. Of course, no one understood how he had felt about Friar Broun. The old man had become a father and closest friend to the young clan Chief. Christopher had placed his ultimate trust in Friar Broun and had continuously sought his wise counsel as he transitioned from boy to man. And now he was gone. And Christopher Yrwyn teetered on the brink of madness.

Eventually, the border clans become mired once again in their plots of intrigue and violent reiving and, of course, the old feuds erupted into a flaming firestorm of hostility. No one was truly safe in the region and death was a constant companion. The land once again became a place where the only law was the law of might enforced by the sword. Evil reigned.

But in the midst of this darkness, God's light of truth was attempting to shine into the hearts of the Yrwyn men and women who called Bonshaw Tower home. And the source was rather surprising. Maggie Johnstone had blossomed into a beautiful young woman. And her beauty was matched by her wit and wisdom. She and Christopher had fallen in and out of love a number of times during their childhood and adolescent years but as adulthood approached both had decided they were a good match for one another and had been married by a priest from Annandale in the year 1520.

Two years later, Christopher was a father and had been granted sasine or Scots deed to the lands of Bonshaw and Dunbratane in the region of Annandale and was now recognized as chief of the clan. In an attempt to bring unity and peace to his clan, Christopher began to sign his name as Irvine. This suited many members of the clan but others refused to conform and thus many spellings of the clan were still in fashion with the two main being Irvine and Irving.

Maggie and Christopher had a number of children over the next ten years but unfortunately only five survived infancy. Edward, named after Christopher's father was the oldest male, followed by Ann, Mary, William and finally the youngest also named Christopher. By the year 1532, the Irvines of Annandale had become a powerful force with which to be reckoned and their alliance with the Johnstones had given Christopher significant influence in the region. However, Bonshaw Tower was not a happy place. There was considerable tension between Maggie and Christopher over the topic of religion and the battle ground was often the table at which the family ate its one daily meal together.

"Why won't you at least listen to me you stubborn man," Maggie said with a deep sense of exasperation. She truly loved this man who she had known since both were wee bairns.

"Because this type of conversation has already caused enough bloodshed. Look what they did to poor Patrick Hamilton. Burned at the stake for his public preaching of Lutheran principles. The church has all the power and the Pope is the head of the Church and God is the head of the Pope and that's the way it is and ever shall be." Christopher stated this firmly but knew in his heart it was a lost cause. Maggie was a Lutheran. Granted she had never espoused this new doctrine outside the Tower walls but Christopher knew his wife and he knew that it was only a matter of time before she said the wrong thing to the wrong influential person in Annandale and then there would be the Devil to pay. He was the chief of his clan. If called upon by his king, he could raise 103 Scottish warriors who would follow him into battle. He had to be careful. These days no one really knew who was friend or foe. The borders had once again erupted into chaos. It was Scot versus English and at times, Scot versus Scot He looked at his children and shook his head. They have never known peace in our land. All they know is drum and fire and sword.

It had started with Hamilton. Patrick Hamilton was the second son of Sir Patrick Hamilton of Kincavil and Catherine Stewart, daughter of Alexander, Duke of Albany and second son of King James II of Scotland. He was born at his father's estate in Lanark outside of Glasgow. In 1517, he was appointed titular Abbot of Fearn Abbey in Ross. The income from this appointment paid for his education at the University of Paris where in 1520 he was awarded the Master of Arts. It was at this University where Hamilton first came in contact with the writings of Luther and it dramatically changed his viewpoint on many things including the established church doctrine. He returned to Scotland and joined the faculty of St. Andrews. He began to preach the Lutheran concepts to students and whomever else would listen. James Beaton, the Archbishop of St. Andrews ordered him to stop and when he did not, ordered that Hamilton be formally tried for heresy. Hamilton fled to Germany. He returned to Scotland later that year and stayed with his brother near Linlithgow. But he would not remain silent. While in Germany he had written and published Patrick's Places stating his support of Luther's ideas of salvation by faith and the authority of scripture. With his return to Scotland, this work which was translated from Latin into everyday Scots spread from person to person in pamphlet form thus introducing into the hands of the everyday

Scotsman the teachings of Martin Luther. He was convicted of heresy by the assembled council of St. Andrews under the direction of the Archbishop and handed over to the state for his execution. The sentence was carried out the same day of the trial to ensure that his noble friends would not attempt to rescue him. According to those who witnessed his death, his last words were, "Lord Jesus receive my spirit."

Maggie had one of those pamphlets in her possession and she was now waving it at Christopher. "Just read what the man had to say, Christopher. That's all I ask of you. Take it and read it and tell me you don't think Hamilton had it right," Maggie slumped to her seat. She had said what she needed to say and was now finished talking. She had not been feeling well lately and was becoming very tired with the least amount of physical exertion. Christopher was becoming worried about her. He smiled at her, "Truce, my love. I will read young Lord Hamilton's work … but not tonight."

"You promise?" she looked at him with love in her eyes.

"Aye, I promise." Christopher nodded in affirmation and just like that the argument between these two ended as it always had with a short kiss and hug. Since the death of his beloved friend and confidante Gilbert Broun, Christopher never let the sun go down with anger in his heart towards those he loved.

"Come girl, let's go up to the top of the hill and watch the sunset." Christopher smiled at his wife. At first, Maggie was hesitant. She did not know if she had the strength for the climb. But it was a lovely view from the top and she felt good inside about how the conversation had concluded.

There was much on the young chief's mind this evening. Trouble was brewing once again with the neighbors to the south. He had heard through the rumor mill that King Henry had sought a divorce from his first wife Catherine. The Pope had denied him this action. Henry then arranged to have Thomas Cranmer, the Archbishop of Canterbury rule that his marriage to Catherine was null and void and Henry had then secretly wed his mistress, Anne Boleyn. "This is not going to end well for the Tudor king" Christopher said out loud to no one in particular as he, his wife and their children trooped up the hill to watch the western sun sink into darkness.

As they reached the crest of the hill, Christopher noticed that Maggie was having trouble breathing and the color had washed from her face. Not wanting to alarm the children he took her by the arm and safely guided her to a flat rock where she could comfortably sit and watch the sunset. He put his arms around her shoulders. "You are cold my love. We should have brought a blanket. I forget how chilly it gets up on top." And he pulled her closer to his body. She looked deep into his eyes and smiled," I love you Christopher Irvine".

"I love you too Margaret Johnstone Irvine." The sun was sitting low in the horizon and it was indeed a beautiful sunset. The colors were rich and vibrant and slowly changing as the light rays bounced among the clouds rolling in from the western sea.

Maggie coughed and said, "I wish this moment would never end. Perhaps this is the way heaven will be? Just one eternal beautiful moment of peace and love. "

"Aye, lass, that would be heaven," Christopher gently kissed her cheek. It was still cold.

The family took their time returning to the Tower. It was obvious to everyone now that Maggie was ill. And her body was no longer cool to the touch but rather warm. About half way down the hill side she had collapsed into Christopher's arms and he had carried her back with the children gathered around them. When they returned to the Tower, other family members quickly took over the situation. They got Maggie into her bed and diverted the attention of the children. Young Edward, the oldest refused to leave his mother's side and Christopher allowed him to stay but ordered Ann to take the younger children with her and go into their room to play quietly. Minutes turned into hours and hours turned into days. Maggie's fever worsened and she drifted in and out of consciousness. Eventually her temperature subsided and she called for her children and husband.

"What day is it? How long have I been in this bed?" she asked weakly.

"It's been three days lass. Are you hungry?" Christopher looked relieved and exhausted. I'll have your sister bring a bowl of something warm. We have all been worried about you. The children would not leave your side."

"Christopher, I must tell you what happened to me," Maggie suddenly stated as she looked wide eyed at her husband.

"I know what happened to you lass, you became ill with fever and we nearly lost you," he responded.

"No, not that. I mean I must tell you what happened to me while I was in the fever. I think I died Christopher. I know I left my body and somehow traveled to a place far from here. I met your father and many of our deceased kin." She spoke with another-worldly voice as if she was in some type of trance state of being. "Friar Broun came to me and told me things I shall never forget."

Christopher looked at his wife and thought to himself surely this must be some strange working of the fever upon her mind. What could she be talking about? But as he gazed intently at her he realized she was deadly serious.

Maggie continued, "Friar Broun gave me a message for you and a warning for the border clans." Maggie stopped and looked into the eyes of her husband. "You must believe me Chris! It's important that you believe me and that you listen to what I have to say."

It was the intensity of her passion that convinced Christopher that Maggie was attempting to explain to him something which happened to her but could not be explained with the mere words of man. And so he nodded his agreement and encourage her with his eyes to go ahead with her story.

"It was a green place … like a garden. There was a gently flowing river there in the middle and I was walking or floating alongside the river as if the water and I were one, then, all of a sudden, Gilbert Broun appears but his appearance was dramatically different. He was bathed in white light. It was so powerful all I could make out was his face and his eyes. His eyes shone like two sparkling diamonds. I could not speak in his presence. He spoke to me. He said I would not be able to speak to him but I was simply to listen to him and take his message back to you first and then to the people of the borders. He said he had been purified and that was the reason I could not speak in his presence. So together, we just floated along the side of the river and he gently spoke to me in a soothing way the things I must now tell you."

"I am listening my love … go on." Christopher responded with awe in his voice.

Maggie continued, "First, for you. Gilbert said it is time you set aside your doubt and placed your trust in God. He is your creator. He has given you life and he has expectations for you. He has a plan for you Christopher and Gilbert told me you will not be happy until you pursue God's plan for your life. He said you are to pray every day for one year. You are to ask God to lead you on the pathway of truth and justice for your people. He said this pathway will not be easy to follow but the reward at the end of the journey will be great. And then Gilbert's countenance changed and his face became like fire and I felt the heat coming from him. His voice changed and he told me of the future. He said I was to tell the people that God was not happy with their behavior. That God loved us but was dissatisfied with the choices we were making in our lives. He wants it to stop. Times of trouble are ahead of us. Gilbert said the Lion of the South will rise up and strike at us and we will suffer much sorrow. But we are to not lose our faith. We are to pray daily and to seek God's will for our lives. It will be difficult but the faithful will endure to the end. Gilbert said that angels will be sent to our shores from other lands and they will be carrying the words of truth and love. We are to accept them as messengers from God. They will be bringing change. Change in how we act. Change in how we think. God wants change. The last thing Gilbert said to me before he suddenly disappeared was this, return to the simple teachings of Jesus. Love God with heart, mind and soul and love your neighbor as yourself. Upon these words rest all the law and prophets of old. And then … I returned to my body and woke up to find you standing here beside my bed."

Silence filled the room. Finally, Maggie spoke. "Do you believe me my love?" Christopher was slow in his response. He walked to the door and looked outside at the land of his people. He thought of all the things he had seen with his eyes over the course of his life. His mind was flooded with memories of the past and his heart was filled with sorrow. He saw his father's body lying in the rain soaked ground of Flodden. He heard the cries of mothers and daughters who had lost husbands and sons during the many raids he himself had led. He saw the dead body of Friar Gilbert Broun and the priest standing over the grave chanting the final Latin words of internment. And then Christopher looked up into the sky and was amazed at what he saw. There in the clouds were three angelic beings. In the middle was the figure of a man immersed in the brightest light and as he gazed upon this person a deep sense of peace filled his soul. And then he heard in his mind a gentle voice saying to him, believe and be set free. He turned quickly back to Maggie lying in her sick bed.

"Yes, my love. I believe you," running to her side and engulfing her in his arms. He placed his head upon her shoulder and sobbed. The tears were tears of relief for his soul. It was as if a heavy overwhelming burden had been lifted from his body. The tears were tears of joy, for Christopher had been set free by the power of Jesus of Nazareth, the Christ … God incarnate.

Life continued on as before but something obviously had changed within the Irvines of Bonshaw. Christopher's personality was slowly but steadily changing. His immediate family noticed it at first then those of the clan who interacted with him on a repetitive basis and then eventually all who had contact with the man. And Maggie was also quite different. Both seemed to outside observers calmer and more content with life. Christopher was slowly learning to manage his volatile temper and the dangerous angry outbursts happened less frequently and when they did with less ferocity. Maggie had started to teach her small collection of followers about the Lord Jesus. They were not hearing what the priests had been saying to their respective flocks for hundreds of years. This was a much simpler and easier to understand message. Maggie was teaching that Jesus was simply about learning how to love God and others even in the midst of sorrow. Loving others even when they did not deserve your love. That was her simple straightforward message and amazingly it was having an effect. Slight at first but as the years wore on the impact of her teaching and the example of Christopher's changed behavior was having an impact upon the border clans of southwestern Scotland.

But Satan would not release his mighty hold upon this land or its people. There were still feuds, raiding and bloodshed but things were slowly almost imperceptibly changing. The clans were beginning to use the rule of law to settle their differences and the practice of religion, while historically a highly formal and essentially private affair among the border Scots, was slowly evolving into public displays of passionate love for the Creator. The seeds of the simple teachings of the Lord Jesus had found fertile ground. Many of the border Scots were tired of the old ways and were ready for change. People were beginning to openly discuss the Scriptures and some even had copies that either they could read or someone in a gathering could read on behalf of those who could not.

Of course, this did not go unnoticed by those in authority either within the Church or the Nobility. And, in general, they were not pleased. Perhaps it was fear of change that prompted their response? Some, like the friends of Christopher Irvine said it was the not so hidden intent of the Scottish and English kings to keep the border region in a state of war as a means of destabilizing that critical interface of both countries. Or perhaps it was simply that men are indeed sinful creatures and following God's commands to love each other was not in their innate ability. Whatever the reason, peace when it would come to the border region was often short lived and hard as they might try Christopher and Maggie and their small group of followers were simply too few and too powerless to change the ultimate destiny of this troubled land. As the vision of Gilbert Broun had once told Maggie Irvine, "the Lion of the South would rise and strike" and that he did.

The Lutheran teachings had caught on in Europe and were spreading to the British Isles by inspired messengers who risked all for their cause. At first, both King Henry VIII of England and James V of Scotland along with the established church hierarchy resisted the movement. The spread of the Protestant doctrines spread from south to north and, of course, encountered strong pockets of resistance. But this changed quickly due to Henry's thirst for power and his desire for a male heir to his Tudor line. In the year 1534, Henry was named Supreme head of what was now being called the Church of England. Two years later, the staunchly Catholic north revolted when Henry dissolved the legal and economic rights of the English monasteries. Along the same time, Henry's second wife, Anne Boleyn was found guilty of adultery and high treason and was beheaded at the Tower of London. On the same day of Anne's execution, Henry married Jane Seymour who soon gave birth to a baby boy named Edward VI. Jane soon died after the birth of Henry's male heir and the child itself was considered rather sickly and many questioned whether he would live long enough to actually sit on the throne of England. Thomas Cromwell, Henry's principle legal advisor and the true mastermind behind Henry's battle with Rome, arranged for Henry to marry Anne of Cleves based solely upon political and religious perspectives. Unfortunately, Anne was not nearly as attractive as the picture that had been sent to Cromwell and as soon as the King laid his eyes upon the real woman her fate was sealed. She was quickly set aside for wife number five, Catherine Howard. Catherine was of the powerful and noble Howard family who held sway in the north of England. The Howard's, of course, were faithful to the Roman church and this combined with Lutheran inspired uprisings in Germany and elsewhere convinced Henry that perhaps he had made a mistake placing so much trust in Cromwell's guidance and constant anti-papal advice. And for this, Cromwell was executed in the year 1540. But Henry had his eyes on lands in France that had once belonged to England and still considered himself the rightful ruler of France as well as defender of the faith. Henry desperately needed money and the surviving English monasteries was a rich plum ready to be picked. By the King's edict the last of the English monasteries lost their independence from the crown and the north erupted once again into revolt. This time, as predicted in Maggie's vision, the trouble spilled over into the border region of Scotland.

The battle of Solway Moss on the English Scottish border was a disaster for the Scots. Christopher Irvine had been given command of the Light Horse of Scotland. There had been relative peace at Bonshaw Tower for a few years and he was reluctant to return to the violent behavior of his past. But he felt forced by the circumstances and accepted the command given to him by none other than the King of Scotland himself. The issue, as usual, was a lack of coherent leadership. The Lords Maxwell and Sinclair bickered over who was actually in charge of organizing the defense of the lowlands and consequently, no clear plan of attack or defense was implemented. Hundreds of Scots died in the short battle but what was most troubling were the thousands who drowned in the River Esk due to poor battlefield tactics upon the part of the Scots. Hundreds were also taken prisoner including Christopher Irvine. Eventually, he was released but only after signing a pledge that he would never again fight against the English. The old Christopher would have laughed at this agreement but the transformed Christopher believed he had taken this oath under God and planned on maintaining it for the rest of his life. However, the very next year, in 1543, Bonshaw Tower was burned to the ground by the English troops of Lords Dacre and Wharton. This action convinced the Irvines the English could never be trusted to keep their end of a bargain and Christopher no longer felt bound by his oath.

James V was so completely devastated by the Scots loss at Solway Moss that he died a few days later. His daughter, Mary, heir to the Scottish throne, was only six days old when he died. Henry VIII had tried to convince James to join him in his Protestant cause. There had even been a meeting arranged to be held at York for the two sovereigns to work out an arrangement in making Scotland a Protestant nation. But James had refused to attend. His wife, Mary of Guise, was French and a faithful Catholic. She convinced her husband that Henry simply wanted to weaken the alliance Scotland had with France and that if he tried to bring the Protestant cause to Scotland, the people would rise in revolt. Of course, neither realized that this was only partially true. Yes, many of the highland chiefs of the north and members of their respective clans would remain faithful to the church however; many of the powerful barons and lords of Scotland who held much of the good farming land combined with the rising merchant class of the cities would have supported James in a move towards the Protestant faith. With James' death and Mary of Guise ruling as regent in Scotland until the young Mary reached adulthood, Henry felt it was the right opportunity to once again place his plan into action. He decided Mary should be wed to his young feeble son, Edward VI and thus unite Scotland and England into one powerful nation which could then possible defeat France once and for all making the Tudor line invincible.

For the next four years, there was violent bloodshed in the border lands. Armies from both England and Scotland would invade each other, ravage the countryside and then return safely across the border until the next engagement. The locals had begun to call this time the "Rough Wooing of Mary, Queen of Scots".

Maggie looked across the field at her husband as he stood beside their eldest son, Edward. Edward had been named the legal heir to Christopher and Maggie

Irvine ten years earlier and the time had come for him to take his position as chief of the clan. Maggie thought to herself, "those two look alike but they are as different as day and night in personality." Whereas Christopher was often torn between his belief in the Lord Jesus and his teachings and the horribly violent way of the world in which he lived, his son Edward, was a realistic young man with no illusions about making the world a better and more peaceful place. He had professed a belief in God and in his son Jesus but his actions did not always support his stated belief. Edward was utilitarian when it came to achieving what he desired. He would do anything to be successful whatever the costs. Maggie was afraid that his faith was superficial. He would talk about his faith when it served him well but she wasn't sure that her son really meant what he said. She knew in her heart her husband's transformation and conversion was real. She saw his pain when the troubles would erupt and he once again had to don his sword and shield for King and country. Christopher was tired of it all and just wanted to be left alone to live out his days in quiet reflection and prayer. But Edward was different. It was as if he yearned for a fight. Maggie had sometimes remarked to her husband that their son was like water being heated in the kettle … over time it would explode with steam and scalding heat. But as she looked across the field of barley she thought to herself, "I love them both so very much. Somehow, I wish they could find peace."

But peace was elusive in this father son relationship and it was the same within the nation of Scotland. For the teachings of John Calvin had come to Scotland from the continent and they were taking hold in many places throughout the land. There was tremendous discontent within the ruling classes and the sides were being drawn up. A few nobles had led an action to agree to a marriage between Mary and Edward but another faction, led by Mary's Catholic mother influenced the Scots Parliament to establish legal protection of the mass.

And this had become a source of tension within the Irvine family. Maggie was firmly convinced that Rome had become corrupted beyond repair. It could not be reformed. But she could not support what the English king Henry had done. In her mind this was simply a replacement of one power hungry flawed and dangerous man for another. She didn't feel there was any real change in the way the faith was being practiced by either the followers of the Pope or of Henry. For Maggie, to be a follower of Jesus meant exactly that, one gave up self for others. A true follower attempted to put into practice as difficult as it might be at times, the practice and to her simple teachings of Jesus. Christopher, on the other hand, saw the need for stability and firm leadership within the church and was not quite ready to give up on the idea of a reformed Catholic church. After all, if he could change, so could the Pope and so could the king or queen of Scotland. Their son Edward was ultimately motivated by wealth and the power that comes with it. What he saw in the Calvinist movement was freedom. Freedom from the unfair taxation of the nobility. Freedom from the burden of financial support to an organized church laden with corrupt officials from top to bottom. Freedom to make your own way in the world and not having to bow in obedience to any man or woman just because they were born in a castle and you weren't. Freedom is what mattered to Edward.

Obviously, with these three very different types of philosophies, there was bound to be heated discussions at times and significant opinions on how one was to live out their life. However, there was one thing they all agreed upon, family came first. It was a tradition within these lowland Scots that was as old as the hills upon which they roamed. And it had kept them alive for hundreds of years.

Edward may not agree with the religious or political thoughts of his parents but he did love them and he knew if he had too he would fight and possibly die to protect them.

"Here they come," Maggie said to no one in particular as she continued to gaze across the sun-drenched field. "I wonder if they're in a fair or foul mood?" she thought to herself as she finished folding the sheets she had been washing. One of the young Irvines that lived-in Bonshaw had been delivered of her new born the night before and although Maggie had assisted in the delivery and was exhausted from being on her feet for hours she still felt the need to clean up as much as she could before the men returned from the fields. "They'll be hungry for sure," she thought to herself and turned to call out to one of her daughters and also a niece who had just moved in with them. "Girls, the men are returning, set the table for supper." Maggie felt a sharp pain in her head. She became quite dizzy and fell to the floor of the Tower. By the time the girls had reached her still body, Maggie Irvine had given her soul back to God.

The unexpected death of his wife caused tremendous grief and anguish for Christopher. He was at a lost as to what he should do next. Maggie had always taken charge of the small important details of their lives together. A quiet somber stillness settled over Bonshaw

Tower. Not many smiled anymore and no one, not even the little children laughed for weeks after Maggie's death. After a slightly heated discussion, Christopher agreed to have one of Edward's Protestant friends officiate at Maggie's internment. Christopher knew his wife would not have wanted a priest but he was still reluctant to agree to Edward's suggestion. The young man's name was Hamilton and he and Edward had become close through a mutual business partnership they collaborated on in Glasgow. It had something to do with building ships but that was pretty much all Christopher knew about it. Hamilton claimed to have been trained at Edinburgh and convinced the family that he had the church's authority to conduct Maggie's services. Her body was to be buried at the top of the hill where she and her young lover had often sat and watched the setting sun.

As the small group of Irvines and Johnstones trudged their way up the hillside it began to softly rain. "God is crying," one of Christopher's granddaughters happened to say. Christopher turned to her and smiled "Nay child, those are not tears from God. God is happy because one of his own has returned to him. The rain is a gift from your grandmother. When she got to heaven she convinced the Almighty the hillside needed a good washing before they laid her old bones in it. That's all." The grandchild looked up into the soft and gentle eyes of her grandfather and then ran off to play with her Johnstone cousins.

"Do you believe that father? Is mother in heaven?" Edward asked wiping the tears from his eyes.

"Aye lad, I do. If there is a God and I think there is. And if he lives in a place called heaven and I think that be the truth as well. Then your dear old mother is certainly there. If your mother doesn't deserve a place there, then who does?" Christopher looked at his son. Yes, although they looked so much a like they were quite different. But Edward had always placed his family … his kin … his clan first before anything else. And as he looked at his son he knew that he would be a good leader of his people. He just wished that his faith was stronger … like his mother's.

"Father, I know you worry about me. I know you and I don't always see eye to eye on certain matters of religion and politics. But you must surely know that I am trying as hard as I can to do what I think is the right thing for me and for my family?" Edward looked at his father. As he continued to look at him it dawned upon him that he was looking at the end of an era in Scottish history. There was change in the wind. You could almost smell it. You could certainly feel it in your body. Christopher Irvine was a man of the past, a good man, for sure, but he represented what needed to change in Scotland. Edward thought to himself, "I am the future of this land. I understand my ideas are new and radical. I understand people will be resistant but we must change. We must change or we will never know how good life can be for us here. We don't have to wait to die to go to heaven we can make it right here in this very land. It will happen when all people are considered free and equal. When your birthplace will not determine your destiny. When freedom will allow a man to go where he pleases and do what he desires without restraint, that's when heaven will come to earth. And I think the future will not be in the hands of kings or popes but of the simple hard working people of the land." "Freedom father," Edward said to his father as they walked down the hill back to the Tower. "That is what and where heaven will be. Not up there in the sky someplace but right down here …. In Scotland." Edward looked at his father and smiled.

"Perhaps you are right my son. But for today, this land holds my Maggie's lifeless body but her soul," and he stopped and pointed up to the sky," is up there and that's where my heaven is … with her."

In the year 1547, Christopher Irvine led one more charge of his Scots Lighthorse raiders into England. Rumor had come to the region that old King Henry was approaching death and the Scottish barons in charge of the realm along with the Regent Mary of Guise had decided to take advantage of the political instability within their southern neighbor. So once again, the call came to lead his clan into battle. He knew it would be the last call to arms for him. It was also personal. Once again, an English force had come across the border and had burned Bonshaw Tower to the ground. Thankfully, all had escaped to the north but still the financial loss was crippling. Edward was off in Glasgow trying to scrape together enough funds to rebuild. "He thinks the salvation of man is through commerce and trade. Ach, he is so confused but he is still mine. I will show him how I deal with this type of English nonsense." Christopher said to himself as he buckled on his sword. Little did he know what was to befall him and his fellow Scotsmen when they crossed the English border.

Christopher woke up in a fog. His head hurt and he felt weak. It was dark wherever he was located. He tried to speak but his throat was parched from thirst and he could not speak any intelligible words. Finally, his eyes adjusted to the darkness and he realized he was in a dungeon cell. Then a man came towards him carrying a small lantern. The light hurt his eyes.

"Ah, I see Scotsman you are back among the living. We had bets you would not make it. I lost. Oh well … easy come, easy go." The English guard chuckled to no one in particular.

"Where am I being held? What happened to my men? Who has my horse?" Christopher asked in rapid fire succession as soon as he regained the ability to speak.

"You are in the dungeon of the Lord Dacre's castle outside the town of Penrith in Cumbria. Your men either deserted and fled or are lying dead in the fields outside Carlisle. I have no idea who has your horse nor do I care. Does it really matter anymore? You are a Scottish reiver and will probably hang for your crimes." The old guard chuckled again as he filled Christopher's bowl with bread and soup.

"What crime have I committed? England and Scotland are at war and I'm simply a loyal Scots soldier doing his duty for king and country." Christopher looked at the man in earnest and thought to himself, "I can probably overpower this one but how many were outside those doors?"

"Don't even think of it. Many have tried and all have been shot down by the guards posted on the Castle walls. There is no escape from this place. Either you will be executed or exchanged for an unfortunate English member of the aristocracy who stupidly got himself caught by your Scots cousins. You fellows are all related to one another, aren't you? Marrying your cousins and what not." Another chuckle.

Days passed and turned into weeks which turned into months. Christopher was kept alive but in isolation.

Eventually he developed a somewhat friendly relationship with his guard who let slip out that old King Henry had died and had been replace by his nine-year-old son, Edward VI. He was the son of Henry and his third wife, Jane Seymour who had died shortly after the child's birth from complications resulting from the delivery. The guard had informed him that the real power was now held by his uncle, Edward Seymour, Duke of Somerset who was head of a Regency Council designed to run the government until Edward was old enough to rule. He also learned from the guard that Thomas Cranmer, Archbishop of Canterbury, was leading major reforms in the organization and practice of the Church of England. England was now a truly Protestant nation. The Cranmer reforms had included the abolition of clerical celibacy, the Mass and the imposition of compulsory services. In Scotland, young Mary had been sent to France and in her place her mother, Mary of Guise in cooperation with the official Regent of the Kingdom, James Hamilton, 2nd Earl of Arran, and next in line to the throne after Mary. At first, the guard informed Christopher; Hamilton had urged the marriage of the little Mary to Henry's son Edward but soon changed his position and strongly endorsed the wedding of Mary to the Dauphin of France. On this, Mary of Guise and Hamilton agreed. So, Scotland reneged on the deal they had originally struck with Henry and was now firmly Catholic while England was in the Protestant camp. So, even after the death of Henry, the war continued between the two nations and, of course, Christopher was, once again, caught up in the violence. Only this time, his capture by the English Lord Dacre had made matters much worse. There was an obvious power vacuum within the English realm and no one actually knew who would ultimately be victorious. The English of the north were resistant to the conversion of the nation to the Protestant cause and silently plotted against Edward to replace him with his half-sister, Mary, a devout Catholic. Similar intrigue was underway across the border in Scotland but with the roles reversed. The Scots barons and other members of the aristocracy were slowly being converted to the teaching of John Calvin and they were rather openly plotting the removal of Mary of Guise and her daughter. Being true to form, they could not agree however, upon a successor. Being a prisoner of the English meant that Christopher like other Scots land holders were pawns in this social upheaval.

His family, in particular, his son, Edward never gave up trying to buy his father's freedom. But every time an agreement had been settled upon some new outbreak of violence would disrupt the proceedings. The world was in chaos just as had been predicted by Maggie years ago.

One evening Christopher felt very tired and fell asleep quite early which was highly unusual for him. As long as he had been an English captive, and it was now approaching four years, he had trouble falling and staying asleep. His captors were not barbaric but the conditions were definitely taking its toll on his aging body and mind. He had last seen his son over three months ago and the suspense was slowly making him lose his mind.

He lay down on the bed. After the first year of captivity he had at last been transferred into the main tower of Castle Dacre and had been given a small room of his own. But a guard was always present day and night and although he had plotted a thousand times, an opportunity for escape had never materialized. He looked about his small quarters and slowly closed his eyes. A deep sleep overcame him and soon he was dreaming. It was his usual custom to offer up a simple prayer that God watched over his kin and allowed him to see the morning sun a free man. But as the months turned into years, Christopher had come to the conclusion that his God had abandoned him. Perhaps it was just he had decided. After all, he had done many awful things in his life to those who had threatened his family and land. Perhaps this was the way God worked? He rewarded the good and punished the evil. This night before he fell asleep his prayer had changed, "Lord, have mercy upon me and let me die a free man but if that is not your will then just let me die and be done with me. I can take no more. Amen."

At some point in the night, Christopher began to dream. He was walking through a meadow. The heather was in bloom and as far as he could see in any direction, the hills were covered with a fine purple haze. This is heaven he thought to himself. I must have died and gone to heaven. It was such a peaceful place. He felt no distress during the dream, only a sense of complete and total peace and relaxation. At last he woke, or thought he was awake and looked across the room and saw a young girl looking intently at him. She must have been around eleven or twelve years of age. Her silken hair was long and golden in color. Her angelic face was serene. They looked at each other for the longest time and then he wondered if he were still dreaming.

"No, Christopher, you are awake. Be not afraid. I am a messenger and have been sent to you by the king of kings." She spoke softly with a melodious voice. It was not childlike but did not sound like the voice of an adult woman either. It had its own strange and unique nature. It was not a human voice. There was purity to her and her countenance that he had not encountered during his life.

"Who are you? What is your name?" Christopher was finally able to speak.

"I am called Faith. And as I said, I have a message for you. Now, you must be quiet and not interrupt me while I share my message with you." She spoke once again and lifted he index finger to her mouth in a symbolic gesture for quiet. Christopher nodded and she began once again.

"I have been watching mankind for a very long time. I was sent here to tell you what I saw happen many thousands of years ago. The Creator had set into motion the powers of nature that brought your ancestors into existence. He was happy at the beginning. Your ancestors were given a choice on how they were to live out their lives and they chose badly. This planet, your home, became filled with violence. The Creator and we messengers observed the total extent of the wickedness of humanity and it brought great sorrow and anguish to each of us. The Creator's heart was broken and He spoke in heaven that He wished He had never set the creative process in motion upon your planet. He let it be known that He would destroy every living thing upon the Earth. He could no longer bear to watch what was transpiring. But one of my fellow messengers, who was given the name Hope, brought the man Noah to the attention of the Creator. The Creator was pleased with Noah's blameless living. Noah was not perfect, you see, but he would strive for perfection and he always balanced his judgments with mercy and compassion. He was a man who could be trusted to keep his word and to always tell the truth. Yes, Noah was a good man. I am glad the Creator decided to save him and his family from the destruction." The angel Faith stopped for a moment and looked at Christopher. His eyes were wide. He, of course, had heard the story of the great flood before but had never given it much thought. To him, it was simply something that happened a long time ago and had little significance to him in his daily affairs.

"You see, Christopher, our Creator is a just and merciful God who wishes nothing but the best for His creation but during this time of terrible violence, He could no longer watch his beautiful creatures turn upon each other in their aggressive and wicked ways. And so, He started over again with a man and woman who He thought would bring peace and joy to the world. But alas, this was not to be the case. Over time, sinful violent men and women once again brought evil into the world and all humanity suffered because of it. Think, Christopher, of all the tragedy your own eyes have witnessed in your lifetime and that is such a short piece of the total history of your people upon this Earth. Eventually, when the time was right, God came to the Earth himself in the form of the man, Jesus of Nazareth. Yes, I know you call him the Son of God and in a way you are correct. Jesus represents the Son, the Daughter, the Father and the Mother. He represents the words of God. He is the wisdom of God. He is the compassion of God. He is the love of God. He humbly came to the earth to give all mankind an ideal human model. His life was to set an example on how all of you were to live out your lives. And he came to tell you the message that all that you see is not all that exists. That there is more to the creation than what meets the eye and that there is existence beyond the grave. He simply asked men and women to believe in him and to live their lives by his example. Doing that would enable each human to approach the death of their earthly bodies without fear. Christopher, God has heard your prayers. Tomorrow you will be set free from this prison. But you will not be free from the prison you have created for yourself. This prison was created by you and can only be destroyed by you. This is the prison of vengeful violence. Yes, it was one into which you were born and perhaps you know no other way of living. But the Creator grows weary of the pain and sorrow that you and your countrymen have heaped upon each other. The cries of the innocent shout out to the heavens and God hears them. Christopher, the Creator is patient and long suffering but His patience does have a limit and I and the other messengers can see that limit is near. Turn from your violent ways. Seek peace in all you do. Follow the earthly teachings of Jesus of Nazareth, the king of all kings. Do not fall into the temptation of constantly seeking after worldly wealth. Let that not be your priority. Be pure in spirit and humble in your opinion of self. Seek always after justice but temper every judgment with mercy and compassion. God has given you a choice Christopher … choose wisely." And with that she disappeared.

Christopher rubbed his eyes. He was very sleepy and soon it was morning. He had fallen into a deep sleep and for the first time in his captivity had a restful night. The next morning as soon as the sun had begun to rise in the eastern sky, there was a knock at the door of his room. Lord Dacre entered in followed by a number of his personal guards.

"Irvine, you are a free man. Gather your things and follow my men. We have a fresh horse for you outside the gate of this place. You will get on it and ride back to Scotland and never return. You hear me old man, never return. For if you do it will mean your life. ", and with that pronouncement, Dacre wheeled around and marched swiftly out of the room which had served as Christopher's home and prison for the last four years of his life.

Christopher Irvine gathered his meager possessions and did as he was told. He said not a word to any of the guards as he walked slowly down the tower steps and out into the courtyard where he saw a horse waiting for him. He rode it slowly away from Dacre Castle and never looked back.

Christopher returned to Bonshaw Tower or what was left of it. For the endless war with England had once again taken its toll on the border lands. Buildings had been razed to the ground. Fields had been destroyed. Cattle had been stolen. Though peace had finally been struck between the two warring nations the price both countries had paid was immense. And there was still trouble in the political and religious air. Young Mary, Queen of Scotland, was still in France being raised a staunch supporter of the Catholic cause and firm in her belief that the Protestant Lairds of Scotland were a threat to her ultimate reign. The English king Edward's policies and laws designed to make England a permanently Protestant nation were all overturned after Mary, his half-sister, came to power in July of 1553. Mary, who after a while had earned the nickname "Bloody Mary" for her treatment of Protestant preachers, including Church of England Bishops and members of the nobility, had restored as much as she possibly could the Catholic faith to England. Although peace had finally come to the borders, it was indeed a fragile one and one that would quickly be tested by events that were soon to transpire with Mary's death and the crowning of Elizabeth as Queen of England.

But Christopher Irvine was a changed man. Yes, he was older and the years in prison had left their mark upon his body. But his mind was clear and his soul had been set free. Although his son and other members of the clan could not or would not understand this change Christopher would never again pick up the sword. He had fought his last battle. He wanted no more blood on his hands when he met his Creator face to face. Leadership of the family had passed to the next generation and many in the family thought the old man's mind had succumbed to the pressures he had endured throughout his life. But Christopher was not demented. He was not filled with remorse or vengeance against the English over his treatment. When asked by his companions, he simply replied, "The Lord causes his rain to fall on the just and unjust. Blessed is the name of the Lord." And then would gently smile and give out a little chuckle. For Christopher's heart had been changed.

One autumn day in the year 1555, old Christopher Irvine struggled as he walked to the top of the hill where years ago he had buried his beloved Maggie. He walked over to her grave and sat down on the ground beside her. "Well, my love, I think my time has come to leave this land. I will miss it but I have an idea that where I am heading is a much better place and I think," he winked" I'm going to very much enjoy the company." And with those words, Christopher Irvine closed his eyes and breathed his last.

Chapter Six – Under the Wall, Edinburgh ca 1586

"Janet, you know how to write in a way that others can actually read what the words say. My handwriting is awful. That's one thing the friars in Dundee were never able to improve upon. But oh, how they tried. Would you sit here by my bedside for a wee bit and take down my words?" The sick and dying man raised himself up by his elbows and weakly smiled at his young wife.

"Aye, my dear husband. I will take down your words." Janet said as she attempted to hold back the tears forming in her eyes. She found a small piece of parchment and gathered up her writing quill and ink and then pulled a chair and table close to his bedside. His voice was weak and she knew he was fading fast. She leaned in and encouraged him with her smile to proceed.

"My name is John Reid. I know very little about my early years. I don't even know the names of my parents. But I do know I was born somewhere near Dundee in or around the year 1538. I know that because the friars told me I was about six years of age when they took me in to raise me. Plague had once again visited the land where I lived and this time it took most of my family including both my ma and pa and, to the best of my knowledge any brothers or sisters I might have had. Down through the years I have always looked for any of my relatives but the name Reid is rather common in this part of Scotland and whenever I asked one of that name that I might chance to meet they usually just shook their head and say they knew of none of their clan who lived in Dundee. So, I can't pass on to my boys any knowledge about their family's history. But there is one story I can tell them and … it is quite a story." John began to cough and had to stop his dialogue with his wife. After the coughing spell came to an end, he smiled at her in his loving way and started in again.

"As I was saying, after the plague hit in '44 and destroyed much of the population of the town, I was left entirely on my own. I imagine being a child of but six years of age I probably did not do much but sit in the dirt and cry. But God took pity upon me and sent a Dominican friar to my rescue. I will never forget his name, Robert Abercrombie. It was his wealthy grandfather who had originally given the land to the Dominicans to build a small friary in Dundee. His intention was to establish a way for the good brothers to help the poor of the area. And that is exactly what they did. Robert's father was not happy with the choice his son made to become a Dominican but I think his granddaddy was smiling in heaven. Anyway, Robert was a young man when the plague devastated our region and he gathered me and a few other youngsters who were now orphans together and brought us to the friary on the west end of the town. And that became my home for the next nine years of my life. All in all, they were good years. The brothers treated me and the other children well and taught each of us how to read and write as well as skills that would enable us to survive on our own when it came time to leave that holy place. Education was very important to the Dominicans. They were considered defenders of the faith and believed that knowledge was the key to keeping heresy at bay." John grew silent as he remembered back to his days with the Blackfriars. Janet knew that he was lost in his inner world of thoughts and memories and perhaps the writing would be done for a time. But after a short rest, John seemed to regain his strength and began to speak once again.

"All us bairns simply called him Brother Robert. He was a small man in stature but big in heart. It seemed like he was always looking for ways to help others. There was a constant smile on his face and often he was humming or whistling some tune he knew would calm our weary souls. Most everyone in the village liked him but because he was a Dominican and given the times we were in things did not always go well for him or the other brothers. Do you remember Janet? Do you remember what those days were like?" John looked expectantly at his wife. Without saying a word, she gently nodded her head and lowered her eyes to the floor. "Yes," she thought to herself, "I remember those days well. We were so full of ourselves. We thought we had all the answers. We thought we needed to tear everything down and start fresh. We thought only we had the truth and it was our God given task even right to bring the truth to Scotland. Did we do the right thing? I guess only time will tell. One thing is for certain. We made history. We changed this country … I hope for the better." Janet was struggling internally with the doubt about what and how things had transpired. She and her young husband had played a small but important role in the sweeping changes that had overcome her nation. But now the dust was beginning to settle in Scotland and she was wondering if it had been the right thing to do?

"Where are you my love?" John lovingly teased his wife. "I don't think I have your undivided attention now do I?"

Janet meekly smiled and quickly brought her pen to the parchment. "Speak, my love, and I will write down and cherish each and every word."

"In general, life was good at the friary. Yes, it was hard work. Everyone had to pull their fair share and the brothers were insistent that we learned everything they taught us and learn it well. I can't tell you how many times my hands were smacked or my ears pulled when I fell asleep during the time dedicated to teaching. Then, of course, there was the time for religious instruction and prayer. Then when we weren't doing any of those things, we were working either in the fields or in the barns. That's where I learned my trade, how to make good whiskey from barley, yeast and water. That was Brother Thomas's specialty and he took me under his wing so to speak shortly after I arrived and convinced Brother Robert that I would make a good maltman. And, I guess," John coughed once again, "I did become pretty good at it." Janet laughed at this understatement. "Ach, you are too humble, John Reid. Your whiskey was the best in Edinburgh. Everyone said so … even the Queen Regent would send for a case or two of your finest on special feast days to be shipped to Stirling Castle."

"Ah, the Queen Regent, Mary of Guise … French to the core … French till the day she died. I wonder how things might have turned out if she had not been in the picture. Or, if she had simply listened to her people?"

"Or had been honest about the fates of Methven, Christison, Harlow and Willock?" Janet interrupted.

"They knew the danger. They understood the risks associated with what they were doing." John responded. "They felt called by God to preach the gospel as they understood it and that is what they did."

"And for that, they were declared outlaws and fugitives by her majesty," Janet retorted.

"Aye, they were indeed. And perhaps that is what started the fire that eventually consumed us all?" John responded in his quiet humble manner. Janet looked at the body of her husband. She knew the life was slowly but persistently leaving it. She dearly loved him and hated to see him go but knew she needed to be strong not only for him but for their three children.

"Anyway, back to my story. When I turned 14 or maybe it was 15 the brothers decided I had to leave the friary and start out on my own. That's how I ended up in Edinburgh. The brothers knew a man in the city who was looking for an apprentice. He owned a fairly large still, in fact, operated a number of them … some legal and others … oh well; let's just say that my original master was a cunning businessman who did not care to pay his hard-earned money to the Queen Regent and her nobles. His name was Hamilton. Mr. James Hamilton and he claimed to be kin to Patrick Hamilton, that poor soul who was burned at the stake at St. Andrews on orders from Cardinal Beaton. Today, he is considered the first martyr of the Scottish reformation."

"Do you think James Hamilton was really related to Patrick?" Janet asked.

"I don't know. But, if they were, it must have been a distant connection. Those two men were as different as day is from night. James Hamilton did not have a religious bone in his entire body. His God was money pure and simple. What a rascal he was." John started to laugh and that brought on another coughing spell.

Janet gave John a glass of whiskey to help him clear his throat. He sipped at it as he always did. The great irony was that although John Reid was a master maltman he really did not like to drink his product. He had seen too much pain and suffering brought on by its over consumption. He gave the empty glass back to his wife, wiped his lips and smiled. He chuckled and said to Janet, "Aye, tis a good product I made."

"Edinburgh was quite a change for this lad from Dundee. There were so many people and so much activity day or night. It seemed as if the place never really got quiet. Except, of course, when he was preaching, then the streets were empty. Everyone wanted to hear this man who had worked in Geneva with the great John Calvin, who had convinced Elizabeth, the Queen of England to invade Scotland and who had called the young Mary, Queen of Scotland a blasphemer and idol worshipper … and had lived to tell the tale." John's voice lowered in intensity as he remembered those early days of the movement.

"When did you first meet him?" Janet asked.

John was quiet. She could tell he was deep in thought.

She asked him again a little louder this time, "John, when did you first meet John Knox?"

John looked at his wife and his countenance changed ever so slightly. "It was the night of May 3rd, 1559. He had arrived a day earlier in Leith. He had travelled by boat from France. We all knew he was coming home, we just did not know when or where. He had been in Geneva since leaving England in 1554. He had to leave you know. Queen Mary I of England wanted him dead and she had sent out orders to find him, arrest him and have the Church trial him for heresy and, of course, treason. Then she would have had him burned at the stake. I did not know he had snuck into Scotland in 1555 to marry Marjorie Bowes. I found that out later. I did know he was a wanted man and I assumed a dangerous man. It was said that he had been a personal bodyguard for George Wishart. As a young man, he followed Wishart around with a huge claymore strung to his back ready to defend the outcast Protestant minister with his life if necessary."

"He was a big man, wasn't he love." Janet stated matter of factly.

"Aye, he was. With a full beard and eyes dark as coal. I can remember his fiery sermons. Those eyes seemed to blaze with intensity. He would always start out slow and calm but as he got himself worked up into a frenzy, his voice sounded like thunder rolling across the Forth of Firth and those eyes, my God, how they would shine with power and passion. Tis no wonder he inspired the people the way he did."

"Aye inspired them he did." Janet agreed with her husband. She knew that John had mixed emotions regarding the famous John Knox and she knew why but she waited patiently to see if he brought up that part of their history together. She thought to herself, "no since tormenting his poor soul anymore about what happened. I thought it would kill him outright, but somehow he survived. He is a tough old bird." She looked respectively at her dying husband. "Yes, indeed, he is a tough old bird."

"I had been with Hamilton around a year or a year and a half when he first asked me to smuggle some of the product up north in an attempt to get around the Royal fees. He knew I was originally from the Dundee area so I guess it made sense to him somehow that I would be somewhat familiar with the terrain and people. I tried to tell him I didn't think it was a wise idea but there was no dissuading him once his mind was set. So, I did what I was told. He was master and I was servant. It was as simple as that. I knew if I got caught, they would extract a pretty good fine from Hamilton but I would probably hang. So, I made it my business to not get caught. I got pretty good at it. I could make my way by either land or sea but I preferred the water route. Once I evaded the guards at Edinburgh and slipped my small fishing boat into the waters of the Forth, I set sail for the northern coast. I would sail straight across the Forth and then hug the shore while moving east and north. Then I would do the same across the Firth of Tay. I would aim to land somewhere just east of Dundee and there meet my contacts who would pay me and they would be responsible from that point on for delivering the goods into the pubs and shops of Dundee. They never told me their names and I never shared mine. We would use special bird calls and animal noises to communicate with each other as I was preparing to land. And our business was always conducted in the dark. Going by land was much slower and had a greater chance of being discovered by the Royal authorities. I can't tell you how many time I thought I had met my end. The wind would pick up and the waves would splash over the sides of my little boat and I was sure I was going to drown at sea. The thing I thought about most was if that happened no one but old Hamilton would know about it. I had no family. I would not have had a soul to mourn my passing. At times, I felt so alone." John stopped and looked at his wife. She returned his gaze with a smile.

"And then the Lord, in his mercy, brought you into my life," John returned Janet's smile and lifted her hand to his lips and gently kissed her fingers.

"I remember Johnnie, I remember that day as if it were just yesterday," Janet replied. "My you were a good-looking thing. And full of yourself." They both chuckled.

"Aye, tis true. I was young and strong and had a few coins in my pocket. On top of the world, I was. It was … let me think … on a Sabbath day in March in Dundee in the year …." John's voice trailed off.

"The year of our Lord 1557," Janet finished his thought for him. She knew he was tiring quickly and thought perhaps he should rest but she knew that once he closed his eyes this time it might be for the last time. So, she just sat quietly and patiently waited for him to continue.

"Aye, '57, I was nineteen and you a pretty young lass of sixteen. Janet, I fell in love with you the moment I first saw you."

"More like lust I'm afraid," Janet interrupted with a soft laugh.

"No my dear … oh well, aye, it was some of that for sure … but nay, there was something about you … the way you carried yourself as you walked out of the kirk that afternoon. You were confident. You were poised. You were quite mature for your age. And then when you looked at me and our eyes met, I knew immediately, you were the one God had planned for me. Of course, I probably didn't think it was God's doing at the time. I had kind of fallen away from the teachings of Friar Robert and the rest of the good brothers. Religion wasn't something that Hamilton encouraged. He taught me to keep all that stuff to myself. I can remember him saying often to me …

a man's religion is a private matter and one he should work to keep to himself. But you Janet, you taught me that we are to live out our faith. To put into practice the teachings of the Lord Jesus everyday of our lives in whatever endeavor we undertook. You taught me that my love." And this time John gently stroked the cheek of his wife and sighed. Janet took his hand to her lips and gently kissed his tired and worn fingers.

"Did I do the right thing, Janet? Did I? What will the Lord God say to me when I stand before him on Judgment Day?" John looked and spoke to his wife with a deepening anxiety in his countenance and voice.

"Rest easy, my husband. Our God is a merciful God. He will see in you what I have always seen in you. A wise man driven by loyalty combined with a constant yearning to do what was just and noble. There will be a seat for you at the table of paradise." Janet spoke with loving conviction.

John smiled at her. She had always had a way of calming his fears and today was no different. "Well, if true, I'll certainly save you a chair right next to mine."

They were both quiet for a while. They heard the bells of St. Giles ring out the noon day time.

"At least, they didn't destroy the bells." John said with a quiet and sad voice.

"You didn't know John. Quit blaming yourself for what happened. Go back to that night when you met Knox. You were given another smuggling job to do … correct? You were just doing what your master had instructed." Janet stated.

"Aye … I just did what I was ordered to do. It was raining cats and dogs that night. There was a loud knock at the front door of the shop. I ran to the door expecting it to be Hamilton. I was surprised to not only see him standing in the doorway but also three other men whom I did not know from Adam."

"And one of them was John Knox?" Janet asked.

"Aye, there he was in front of me in the flesh. You were home with your mother in Dundee expecting our first child at any moment. Hamilton knew I was itching to get back to you and he knew I knew how to sneak objects out of the city. So, when he was approached by one of the elders of the local private Protestant conventicle with the task of getting Knox safely to Dundee where the Lords of the Congregation were gathering he put two and two together and gave the task to me. Of course, he didn't share any of the money that elder gave him for Knox's transport. Took that to the grave with him I guess. The Queen Regent had put a price on Knox's head. As soon as word spread to Stirling, and it didn't take long, that John Knox was back in Scotland, Mary declared him an outlaw and ordered his arrest. You see, Knox had come back to show his support for the four protesting priests that the Queen Regent had decided to place on trial for heresy and treason."

"That would be Methven, Christison, Harlow and Willock?" Janet asked although she already knew the answer.

"Aye, the same." John replied. "I didn't know it at the time, but thousands of Protestants from the Mearns, Angus, Fife and Lothian were gathering in Dundee. I'm sure, the Lords of the Congregation were behind it all pulling the strings of the local pastors of each of the private conventicles to set the whole thing in motion. I had heard later that even the Abbot of Paisley had travelled across the entire country to show his support for what folks now call the reformation movement. It was a keg of powder ready to explode and John Knox was to be the spark that ignited the whole thing." John began to cough violently.

Janet became alarmed, "Rest husband, rest now."

"Nay, dear wife, I've not much time left and I want you to write this down so people will remember what really happened at the beginning." John spoke weakly as the coughing slowly subsided. He took another sip of the whisky.

"It took almost a whole day to make that trip. The weather was not cooperating and I had to stay close to the shore to keep us from capsizing. You could tell the two who were accompanying Knox on this journey were afraid for their lives but Knox just sat calmly in the middle of the boat. The man was not afraid. Some said he feared nothing but God and the temptations of Satan. I have to tell you Janet, he did not have a pleasant countenance. He seemed stern to me. Others have since told me that was not his true nature. That deep inside he was a kind and gentle hearted soul who simply wanted to restore the church to her earliest pristine and pure days. I did get a chance to speak with him a bit during the journey and what he said made a lot of sense to me at the time. The Kirk was in need of purification he said. It had lost its way. The reformed kirk would put all faith in the Word of God as the ultimate authority. That nothing was to be done in worship that could not be found in the Bible. That the kirk's task was to educate those who had been called by God in the ways of God to be faithful disciples and that required daily discipline not just of the monks and nuns but of all the elect of God. He talked about a priesthood of all believers and that the word nor the position of Pope could be found in the Scripture. Those who called themselves Christian were to encourage one another and to be entirely dependent upon the leading of the Holy Spirit of God. These were all the things he told me that night as our boat bounced along in the storm."

"Why do you think he came back to Scotland when he did?" Janet asked.

"Don't know for sure, but I reckon it had something to do with Archibald Campbell, the Earl of Argyll, for he had sent his brother Colin with many of his highlanders to Dundee prior to Knox's arrival. So, he must have known what was going on with Knox and the rest of the Lords of the Congregation well before Know returned to Scotland. I counted at least 200 of them. What a sight it was a Janet! Their pipes were playing, banners were swirling in the wind and all of the men dressed in the kilt of Clan Campbell. What a sight." John sighed.

"And, I imagine, quite a sound as well if the pipers were at it," Janet blurted out and both of them chuckled since they both knew of Janet's lack of fondness for the sound of the bagpipe. "Sounds like something dying" is what she often said whenever she had the chance to hear one playing.

John smiled as he said, "Aye, they can make quite a racket but you know it gets our blood flowing. I don't know if tis true but I've been told that the ancients would send them ahead of the warriors to scare off the evil spirits before a battle would commence."

"Ach, highlanders… what a superstitious bunch they are but I reckon no more than the rest of us Scots," Janet replied.

"Well, I thought this was supposed to be a secret mission so you can imagine my surprise when our little boat docked in Dundee and crowds were already there shouting out Knox's name to the heavens. If the Queen Regent wanted him she sure knew where to find him. But then again, he was now protected by the Lords of the Congregation and their loyal troops. So, what could she do?" John spoke quietly as his mind drifted back to that fateful night and the days that followed.

"Were they all there, Johnnie, all the Lords gathered together?" Janet asked.

"As best as I could tell, aye, they were all there or they had sent a representative. Janet, what happened in Dundee after Knox's sermon might have been spontaneous but his arrival in Scotland had been planned and carefully orchestrated by the Lords. I saw the Earl of Glencairn, Alexander Cunningham. And James Douglas was there, the Earl of Morton along with John Erskine of Dun and, of course, Colin Campbell, Archibald's brother. And armed men as far as the eye could see. There were dozens of Protestant preachers scattered amongst the troops preaching and teaching as they walked along handing out food and drink. And, of course … there were scores of the poor and downtrodden of Dundee and Angus, all of them waiting expectantly to hear the great John Knox speak the words of God. It reminded me of the stories the friars would teach us about Moses when he brought the tablets down from the mountain to the people of Israel. Here was the new Moses bringing the word of God and the people were ecstatic with religious zeal ready to listen and do whatever he commanded of them." John began to cough once again and it was quite some time before he was able to continue. Janet had watched him with concern but soon the spell passed and John found his voice once again but he spoke in a quiet and subdued manner.

"Why did it all happen, Johnnie? Why would so many of the Scottish barons and lairds fight against their Queen?" Janet asked.

"Ah lass, tis always about two things with that lot … wealth and power. Oh, I'm sure some were truly sincere in their desire to reform what they perceived to be a corrupted church. Maybe all, I'm not God and I have no right to sit in judgment upon them. But I know the wealthy. They can speak all day long of their desire for a pure and undefiled return of the Christian faith to Scotland but be not deceived, their principle concern was and always shall be keeping the wealth and powerful influence their ancestors had accumulated within their grasps. And they were frightened of France and the French king's desires to rule in Scotland through his marriage to Mary. At that time, she was still in France and betrothed to the Dauphin, son of King Henry. And that is why her mother was in Scotland running the kingdom as her Regent. But the Lords knew who was really pulling the strings, Archibald Campbell and to a lesser degree, James Stewart, the illegitimate sons of the deceased King James V. God rest his soul. But it was Campbell who was grabbing at and gaining power in the chaos. Just look at how he vacillated between positions. At first, he was loyal to the Stewarts and to the queen Regent and then later on, who but the Earl of Argyll negotiates with the English. You tell me Janet … what does the man truly believe?" John shook his head. Janet knew that discussing the politics of Scotland always troubled her husband. He just could not understand the shifting sands of loyalty within the Scots nobility. For John Reid was loyal to a fault and once he swore his loyalty to a person it was theirs for life. This was why what happened at Dundee troubled him so deeply.

"John, what happened next?" Janet refocused her husband's train of thought.

"On that very day, Knox marched into the Royal court at Dundee to show his support for the four priests on trial. And he was joined by scores of Protestants from the Mearns and Angus. A messenger from the Queen Regent then told the court that the trial would be halted while her advisors consulted about the merits of the case. Knox considered that a small victory and went to the home of a local preacher to rest from his trip. The man was not young and the whole affair was taking its toll upon him. Of course, you remember what happened next. I went to see you at your Mother's and things were starting to calm down until a few days later when the Queen Regent's representative arrived from Stirling with news that the four priests had been declared outlaws and fugitives by the Regent with total support from all her French advisors. This infuriated Knox and he strode into St. John's Church and preached a fiery sermon denouncing the Pope, his church, and the French nobility who supported him including, of course, the Queen Regent, the young Queen Mary of Scotland and her French court. Knox called for a purification of the kirk of Scotland and those words lit the powder which set off the explosion." John looked at Janet with misty eyes. She knew this was the part that deeply saddened her husband. She was torn. She wanted him to tell the story as he remembered it but she feared the effect it might have upon his failing health. Finally, John spoke.

"I was there. I heard his message. I saw the fire in his eyes. I saw the impact he had upon the people of Dundee. His message truly went straight to the hearts of the poorest and they responded. I don't think even Knox knew at that time how the people would react. But that's the way a fire does what it does. Once it gets started, it is hard to contain and almost impossible to put out. The crowds started to tear down from the Church walls all the things it thought represented the corrupted Church of Rome … the paintings, the tapestries, the crucifixes, all of it and they started a huge bonfire outside the building and just kept throwing the items on the flames. Then someone yelled out, to the friary, and the mob headed to the west end of town where the Dominican friary was located. I was shocked. This had been my home. These men had taken me in when I had no place to go. They fed me. They clothed me. They took care of me when I became ill. They taught me my trade. They taught me to read and write. It was there at the friary where I first learned the gospel of Jesus Christ. And this crazed mob was heading in its direction with the sole intent of destruction." John stopped suddenly. Janet noticed the tears in his eyes. She held his face between her two hands and gently kissed his forehead as a mother might try to comfort her hurt child.

Time passed and silence was their only companion. Once again, the bells of St. Giles rang. Both of them turned their heads towards the window and listened. Janet spoke first, "pretty sound isn't it?"

John looked at her and smiled. "Aye, tis a lovely sound," he said while nodding his head slowly.

"Perhaps we should stop for the day love?" Janet asked.

"Nay," John replied immediately, "these things must be told. I'm alright. It happened and there's nothing I or any of us can do about it now. We just have to get on with the living of life. Do you remember that afternoon Janet?" John looked expectantly at his wife.

"Aye, I do. I was at home with my ma. I was just beginning labor and dared not go after you but I could tell from the noise in the street outside that things had taken a turn for the worse. I was so worried about you Johnnie. I didn't know what to do?" And now Janet began to cry gently as she continued to pat her husband's hand.

"The mob, and that's what it became, marched toward the friary. I tried to stop them. I pleaded with Knox and the other leaders to use their influence … to somehow calm them down from their fury. But they would not listen. It seemed to me they had all become obsessed with zeal for the task at hand. People kept shouting purify, purify and Knox just kept nodding and looking sternly at the crowd. It was as if the Spirit of God had taken over his mind and he had become an avenging angel, an angel of death. People now say that Knox wasn't to blame for what transpired that day …. Maybe they're right but I have my doubts. It was John Knox who stirred them all up that day and it was John Knox who marched with them to the friary."

"Could he have stopped it John?" Janet asked although she herself felt the answer was no. Janet had committed to the Reformation cause long before she had met her husband and while she did not approve of what happened in Dundee that day, she felt it was inevitable. In her mind, it was the will of the Almighty.

"Probably not. Too much fuel had been thrown on the fire and now it had become all-consuming destroying whatever lay in its path. The mob quickly reached the friary and some of the ringleaders pounded on the door. I was shocked when I saw Brother Robert open it and stand calmly before them. He did not look frightened or concerned. In fact, he looked completely at peace. He was the same brother I had known all those years before, with a constant smile of his lips and a song in his heart. And then one of the rabble grabbed him and threw him to the ground. Men gathered around him and began to kick him and beat him with whatever they had in their hands at the time. Finally, Erskine of Dun sent his troops into the mess and liberated the poor friar. He was beaten and bloody but still displayed the same countenance of peace. The crowd had moved into the building and had chased all the inhabitants out into the street. I remember it had started to rain and the thought crossed my mind that the heavens were now weeping. It was chaos. They ransacked the place, destroying any religious art or other icons. They even gathered up all the books the friars had kept in their library and threw them into a large pile in the middle of the street and set them on fire. By this time, I had fought my way through the crowd to be at the side of Brother Robert. He had been able to maintain his composure throughout the entire attack but when he saw them burn the books he began to weep. And I joined him. The poor man knelt in prayer in the dirt of the street and wept asking God to somehow save their books from destruction. But God was silent and the books burned." John suddenly stopped speaking and once again tears filled his eyes. Janet silently and patiently waited for the tears to subside.

"What happened to the brothers?" Janet asked, although she already knew the answer.

"They fled. I heard some headed into the highlands where Catholic lairds provided a safe haven for them. Some even escaped across the sea to France and then on to Rome. But, a few, just drifted from place to place and we lost track of those. I heard that one of them had thrown himself into the Forth and drowned. I don't know if tis true but God knows." John replied after drying his eyes.

"And Robert?" Janet asked as she looked at her quill not wanting to look her husband in the face.

"He died right there in the street, in my arms. Folks say it was from apoplexy. Perhaps they're right? Me … I think it was from a broken heart. Robert loved reading. He loved his books. He loved sharing the knowledge contained within them to anyone who would bother to sit at his feet and listen. He was a wise and gentle teacher." John became silent and then began again, "the mob had moved on. After Robert had given up his spirit to God, I looked up and saw Knox standing beside us. I will never forget that moment or what he said to me. There were tears in his eyes and sadness in his voice. 'This is not what I wanted lad,' he said to me. 'I have come to purify the kirk of Scotland, not destroy it'. He helped me carry Robert's body to St. John's. We placed it inside one of the side rooms and told one of the young lads there to fetch a priest and the undertaker. They buried Robert's body in a small grave next to the ransacked friary. The old priest officiated. Knox refused to say anything over the body. He said it was better for one of his own to send him to God's seat of judgment. What a complex man he was… cold as stone one moment and then committing an act of tender kindness the next."

"Have you forgiven him Johnnie?" Janet asked her husband with a hushed voice.

"Aye, love, I have. I think he like the rest of us are all victims of forces beyond our control. We come into this world totally dependent upon others for our very survival. We look to others for guidance. That makes us easy to be led. And we are all led by something or someone. The poverty-stricken folks of Dundee wanted to believe in something or someone and John Knox was their answer. What happened after his sermon was just the product of man's fallen sinful nature. Knox did not make them sinners. They already were…. Who knows, perhaps Knox was right, maybe it was God all long setting the stage and putting into motion everything that had to transpire for the Reformation to happen here in Scotland?" John looked upwards as if he was trying to see God in heaven.

"Would that make God the author of sin?" Janet asked.

"Nay, lass. God is God and I want to believe with all my heart that our God is a good God and one that has our best interest as his goal …. But I don't understand him. I don't understand why a good man like Friar Robert had to die for the so-called purification of the kirk of Scotland." John looked at Janet with a questioning expression as a child might look toward a wise parent.

Janet returned John's gaze. "I can't answer your question my love. I suspect no one can. What person of flesh and blood can truly understand God? God is eternal, has no limit to power and knows all there is to know. How can any of us mere mortals really understand that?" Another long period of silence followed as the two lovers enjoyed the physical and spiritual presence of one another.

"Are ye hungry husband? I've got a stew in the pot. I can get you a bowl if you like?" Janet asked.

"Aye, I could eat," John replied. Janet smiled for she knew this was a good sign. John's appetite had been failing and this was the first time in a number of days that he indicated he was hungry. She hurried over to the fireplace and ladled out a bowl of steaming stew form the large black kettle that hung by the side of the fire.

"Be careful John, tis hot." Janet warned her husband as he took the bowl from her with his shaking hands. John and Janet sat quietly as John slowly ate his food.

After time had passed, John sat down his spoon and bowl and began his story once again, "I have told you all this so that you may have peace in me. Here on earth you will have many trials and sorrows. But take heart, I have overcome this world."

"From the gospels, John?" Janet asked him.

"Aye, from the Gospel of St. John, and one of my favorite teachings of the Lord Jesus. It seems rather fitting to this story doesn't it girl?" John looked at Janet as she slowly nodded her head.

"But what I don't understand is when the trial and sorrow comes at the hands of believers, those who profess to follow the Lord Jesus. I can't find it in my heart to believe that Knox knew ahead of time what his sermons would unleash upon Scotland. There is no way he could have known the anger and frustration that had been building amongst the people, particularly those without wealth or influence. For as long as I can remember, the rich have been getting richer in this land and the poor poorer. Knox came and blew air on embers that were ready to explode into flames. And explode they did. But … the lairds … now that's another matter entirely …they knew what was up. They had been part of the problem all along. The battle between the French Queen Regent with her Catholic supporters and the Protestant Scots nobility had more to do with power and money than faith. Both simply wanted control and both used religion as a shield to operate behind in their quest for domination. But Knox's heart, I think, was pure. He truly wanted to reform the kirk based upon what he had experienced in Calvin's Geneva."

"Dear Johnnie, don't you think at least a few of the Lords of the Congregation had purification of the Church as their prime motivation. Surely, they all couldn't have been as you say …" Janet looked with a questioning yet loving look about her.

"Perhaps … perhaps … God knows and in the end God will sit upon his seat of judgment and deliver his verdict." John replied.

"How bad did it get, love?" Janet asked.

"The mob went from town to town looting and burning religious icons and razing some structures completely to the ground. They destroyed a Dominican convent including the Nun's chapel in Fife. And the destruction spread quickly across the country. Soon, word had arrived to us that the purification movement was being carried out in a variety of places across Scotland including Glasgow and even here in Edinburgh. The only places that weren't rising in smoke were out in the islands of the Irish Sea and, of course, in and around Stirling, where the Regent and her French forces were gathering. When word arrived that the Regent was gathering her troops to invade Perth it seemed the whole country was on the verge of civil war. The Lords of the Congregation warned the Queen Regent that if she attacked they would rise in defense of Perth and the Protestants located there. But by this time Protestant congregations in the West Country, Fife, Perth, Angus and Dundee, plus the Mearns and Montrose were arming themselves and preparing to defend their faith with their own blood if necessary. Then on June 1st, we were amazed at the news that the great highland Earl of Argyll himself plus Lord James, Queen Mary's half -brother and other prominent Scots noble holdouts had informed the Regent they too were joining the Protestant cause in Scotland. The Queen Regent was losing her hold on her daughter's nation and she knew it. About this time, the Protestant leaders at St. Andrews called for Knox to come and preach at the great Cathedral. This had been the heart of the faith for hundreds of years in Scotland and it was truly an amazing symbolic gesture for Knox to occupy the pulpit against the wishes of Patrick Hepburn, the Arch bishop. I was there Janet. I heard his sermon. He seemed like a man possessed. By now, Knox realized what was transpiring in his homeland and I think though he might have had mixed feelings about what was happening all around him, publicly he stayed the course and continued to preach purification of the Scots Kirk as the will of God. And the people ate it up. The next day, the mob in St. Andrews gutted the Cathedral and burned the attached monasteries to the ground. There was now no going back."

"What did the Regent do?" Janet asked in a hushed voice.

"Well … she ordered her French troops to march on St. Andrews, one of the holiest places in all the land.

And then she died. No one really knows what caused her death. Of course, the French say she was poisoned and the Lords of the Congregation say her death was the will of the Almighty. The doctors attending to her at Edinburgh Castle said it was dropsy. We heard that her body just swelled up to enormous proportions and her heart stopped beating. Only God knows what really happened but her sudden death swiftly changed things. The French commanders in the field lost their nerve for the fight and disbanded to return home to France. Of course, it probably helped to cement their decision to retreat to a safer place when they heard of 10,000 English troops gathered together on the border ready to come to the aid of the Scots Protestant nobility. Apparently, the story goes, and I have no way of knowing if true of not, that Knox himself had pleaded with Queen Elizabeth of England to send troops into Scotland to help make this a Protestant nation. Would he have really done that knowing how the Scots people would react? More likely it was John Erskine of Dun or Lord Maxwell or maybe even Campbell himself. Those three certainly gained from the so-called purification movement."

"So, did things quiet down after her death?" Janet asked while placing another blanket over John for he had started to shiver once again though it was not particularly cold outside. The rain had stopped and the sun was shining brightly.

"Aye, for a time, things did quiet down. The General Assembly, which at that time was meeting twice a year, invited Knox and three other influential preachers to join them in the writing of what is now known as the Scots Confession. And this is where the trouble began between Knox and the Scots nobility. You see, John Knox had been to Geneva and what he saw there convinced him this was the direction Scotland needed to take in order to become the most truly reformed nation of Europe. It was never his intention to just change the kirk. He wanted the entire country to be modeled upon what Calvin had done in Geneva. Of course, changing a country is not the same as changing one town and Knox quickly found out he had supporters, of course, but he also had enemies who had no intention of giving up their wealth and powerful national influence. Men like William Maitland and the Earl of Morton did not approve of the Assembly's desire to turn over the lands and accompanying wealth of the old church to be used solely in support of the new kirk and Knox's desire to relieve the impoverished as well as support education for all the people. Knox wanted a truly Christian nation run by men elected by the congregations and confirmed by God's Holy Spirit. Knox wanted to bring about heaven upon earth but he ran into the greed of the Scots nobles. Knox had on one or two occasions likened Scotland to ancient Israel. In his mind, we were to be a covenanted nation led by men ultimately under the direction of holy ones inspired by God, the brethren of the General Assembly. In the eyes of many of the Scots lords and lairds, this was taking the purification movement in the wrong direction and so they resisted and in the end, they won. The very next year, they invited young Mary, daughter of James V and Mary of Guise, to return to Scotland from France and claim her crown as Mary, Queen of Scots." At this point John began to laugh.

Janet asked him, "What's got you so tickled, love?"

"I was just remembering the first time I saw Queen Mary. She was a bonny lass indeed. But I had been ordered by her steward to provide some of my whiskey for her court and so I did. But Mary had never tasted Scottish whiskey. I guess she had grown up with French and Spanish wines. So, the look on her face when she drank down in one swift gulp the whiskey I had provided was hilarious. I dare not laugh but could not help but start to giggle as did others surrounding the young queen. Eventually even she did and by then the whole court was laughing uproariously. She was a good sport that girl. Tis a shame what happened to her."

"But John, she wanted to take the country back to the Catholic faith" Janet stated as a matter of fact but she knew that her husband had a soft place in his heart for his Queen. Janet knew that John Reid was a loyal follower of the House of Stewart and though, Protestant like her, he did not share in her radical views of how the people should be governed. For Janet remembered how excited she was when the General Assembly attempted to take the reins of power and was terribly disappointed when the Scots nobles won out and invited Mary to return to Scotland. Janet was a dreamer and had envisioned a new Scotland where the people had a real say in how they were governed and that true men of God would be in charge. And maybe, even some day, women of God … but she kept that radical thought to herself for she knew her husband would be shocked and dismayed if he ever knew how she truly felt about the political situation in their homeland. This was her largest complaint with Knox … he did not value the contributions of women nor think they should hold positions of power over men. He truly felt they were inferior and had no greater calling than to be wife and mother. But alas, neither Knox's idea of a Geneva like Scotland nor her dreams of equality for all came to fruition. As much as things change, they remain the same.

"What's that, my love? What did you say? I only heard remain the same" John asked.

"I was just thinking to myself dear. I didn't realize my thoughts had slipped out." Janet responded with a smile as she placed a cool wet cloth on John's forehead.

"She was a mere lass when she came back home. Her young French husband, King of France dies of an ear infection and she loses her powerful position. At the same time, many of the most powerful of the Scots nobility wanted her back so ... back she comes and arrives in the midst of a storm. And although intelligent in her own way, she was no match for the intense passion and wise debate of John Knox, a man many years her senior. The poor girl was just a pawn in a game of chess being used by first one side and then the other. You know Janet she had a rightful claim to the English crown ... perhaps more so than Elizabeth herself. Mary's great great grandfathers were King Edward IV of England and King James II of Scotland."

"Can you imagine that ... a Stewart sitting on the throne of England!" Janet exclaimed. And Janet and John both knew this was one of the major issues between the Queens of England and Scotland. Elizabeth had never married and had never given birth to an heir to the throne. She was quite concerned with Mary's legitimate claim to the throne which was strengthened by Mary's marriage in 1565 to her first cousin, Henry Stewart, Lord Darnley. Stewart was also of the royal bloodlines of both Scotland and England. Their marriage infuriated Elizabeth since Henry was an English subject with land holdings in Scotland and she felt he should have requested her permission to marry the Scots queen which she probably would have denied given the fact that any children born to the two would have an even greater claim to the English crown. Although both Mary and Henry were practicing Catholics, they were first cousins and needed a special dispensation from the Pope to be wed. They did not bother to secure that papal pronouncement. Janet knew this was a marriage of passion. For the first time in her young life, Mary was in love and no power on earth or heaven would keep the two apart.

"What did Knox think of this Mary and her marriage to Lord Darnley?" asked Janet of her husband.

"I don't really know. I do know that he met with Queen Mary on five separate occasions and I have been told by those who should know that with the conclusion of each session the two grew further apart, Knox became adamant that she should abandon her papist convictions and convert to the true reformed faith. Mary refused and eventually, perhaps out of youthful spite, threw all of her Protestant advisors out of the court and surrounded herself with Catholic supporters including, of course, Henry Stewart. This was the beginning of the end of her rule here in Scotland." John began to cough again. This time his body was wracked with a severe and painful reaction to the coughing spell. It troubled Janet to see her man in such pain and she thought to herself, the end must be near. How much more of this can his body take? But she stayed strong and held him close to her until the coughing subsided once again.

"I don't know how much time I've left lass," John said with a weak voice. He managed somehow to smile at her though and the smile told Janet that he had not yet given up. He wanted to finish his story.

"What happened to Knox?" Janet asked in a hushed and slow manner. She knew the answer but she wanted John to tell it as he saw it.

"John Knox was ill. The fight had taken its toll. Despite his weakening condition, he married again. He had been a widower for a number of years. We were all surprised when he announced his betrothal and marriage to Margaret Stewart, who in an ironic twist of fate was a distant relative to the Queen. And ... she was only 17 years of age! They made him the principle pastor at St. Giles as well as St. Andrews and he continued to do the work he thought the Lord God had called him to do. He wrote, taught and preached the same message wherever and whenever he occupied a pulpit. The Kirk of Scotland was to become the most reformed church in all of Christendom and the nation of Scotland was to be a leading example of the Protestant movement in all of Europe. John Knox made that happen within the Kirk but not within the hearts of the Scots themselves. It seemed to me it was a theological battle between the power brokers of our country but the poor really had little say in the matter. So ... the wealthy Lords and Lairds of Scotland divided themselves into two groups, those who held to the ancient ways of the old faith and those who now followed the reformed movement of Calvin and Knox. And that led to civil war. James Stewart, Mary's illegitimate half-brother, who by now was called the Earl of Moray joined forces with the Protestant Earls of Argyll and Glencairn and forced Mary to raise the troops loyal to her and her Catholic cause. They chased each other around the country but never had a major battle. By this time, there was trouble in the marriage between Darnley and his wife. He was no longer satisfied to be King Consort but demanded to be a co-equal ruler with Mary. She refused and their marriage grew strained. He had also become quite jealous of Mary's private Catholic secretary, the Italian David Rizzio. Darnley murdered Rizzio in front of his pregnant wife at Holyrood Palace. Mary never forgave him. She eventually had an affair with James Hepburn, the Earl of Bothwell. They had known each other from their time together at the French court and Mary had clearly been fond of him for years. Bothwell was accused of Darnley's murder but found not guilty due to a lack of evidence presented at his trial. In April of 1567, Mary visited her infant son at Stirling Castle for the last time. On her way back to Edinburgh, she was abducted by Bothwell and his men and taken to Dunbar Castle. He had divorced his wife Jean Gordon just 12 days before this event. Some say it was consensual others claim rape but whatever happened the two returned to Edinburgh and were married according to Protestant rites. This was the final straw. Her Catholic supporters considered the marriage unlawful since they did not recognize Bothwell's divorce or the validity of the Protestant service. Her few Protestant followers were shocked that she should marry the man accused of murdering her own husband and the father of her son. Twenty-Six Scottish peers, now known as the Confederate Lords raised an army against Mary and Hepburn. Mary tried to raise her troops to meet in battle at a place called Carberry Hill but so few men showed up to fight on her behalf that she eventually surrendered and was taken captive by the Confederate Lords. In July of that year she was forced to abdicate the throne. Her son, James, was now King James VI of Scotland and James Stewart, Earl of Moray was made Crown Regent. Hepburn fled to Denmark where he died in prison. I was told that Mary had a miscarriage while at Loch Leven Castle. Some say it was twin boys. I don't know for sure as I was not there." John stopped speaking and closed his eyes. He was quiet for a long time and Janet thought maybe he had lost consciousness. But after a while, John opened his eyes and turned to Janet and spoke once again.

"The poor girl was only 25 years old. Can you imagine how abandoned she must have felt? How alone in this world? But she still had allies. George Douglas, brother of Sir William Douglas freed Mary from Loch Leven and helped her raise an army of 6,000 troops. She met the Earl of Moray's troops at Langside but this time her army was totally defeated and she had to flee the country. Loyal followers who lived in the border region of Dumfries helped her safely across the Solway Firth into England where she sought the aid of Elizabeth. I guess she thought good Queen Bess would help restore her to her Scottish crown but that is not what happened. She has been a virtual prisoner all these years and now I hear that she has been implicated in another attempt by the Catholic north of England to force Elizabeth from the throne and replace her with Mary." John stopped. His breathing was labored and the color was vanishing from his face.

"What do you think will happen to her, John?" Janet asked as soothingly as she could muster in the face of John's discomfort.

"I don't know. I hope they release her and maybe send her in exile to France or Italy. But only God truly knows our fate? There are certainly men on both sides of the border who want her dead but I can't believe in my heart of hearts that Elizabeth will order the execution of a fellow Queen." John grew silent once again. Janet knew his time was quickly approaching.

"I wonder what I will say to him." John muttered suddenly.

"Say to whom, my love?" Janet said as she leaned in closer to John's body for his voice was now barely audible.

"To old Knox … when I see him in heaven. Assuming he's there and, of course, assuming God has mercy on my soul and Peter lets me past his gates." John smiled weakly as he looked with love at his bride of all these years.

"Ach Johnnie … if anyone is getting in, it'll be you." Janet said as she tried unsuccessfully to hold back her tears.

"Ah lass, don't be crying none for me. I've lived a good long life. I've had you in it for most of it. You've given me all your love and three beautiful bairns. Plus, I've stood in the presence of those who have made Scotland's history. Aye, I've run a good race. I do wish I had a bit more time … but would I ever be ready to leave you, even if it is only temporary … doubt it." John attempted to laugh but he was growing weaker by the minute. He continued, "Knox passed from this world to the next in November of 1572. I remember the day cause that is when you gave birth to our baby, Mary. Poor lassie didn't last the week. Well, she'll be the first one I'll look for…" By now, Janet had stopped trying to hold back her tears. She hated death. But she knew it was the end of all life in this world. She also knew it was the beginning of true life in a far better place with the Lord Jesus as dearest friend and deepest companion.

John interrupted her train of thought, "I would ask him if he thought it was all worth the effort …all the tears and sorrow … all the blood, shed in the name of Christ … was it worth it John Knox .. Is your conscience clean … what did the Lord say to you when you first met him … ah … Janet, so many things I want to discuss with the man. But then … we'll be in glory … will I even care anymore what happened here in Scotland … in Dundee? It's getting dark girl, you had better light a candle." And those were the last words spoken by John Reid.

Janet sat outside the little shop in Under the Wall Edinburgh for what seemed a long time waiting for the undertaker to arrive. She was lost in her thoughts. She had hoped their eldest son, William, a maltman in Dundee, of all places, would have arrived in time to say goodbye but she knew the mail was not always on time and he probably did not receive her letter informing him of his father's failing health. Her other son, Christopher had joined the Protestant movement and was in training to be a Presbyterian pastor at the University in Glasgow. It had taken almost all of the family's accumulated savings but John gladly gave all that he had to educate this bright young lad and he would have given more were it available. And the third one, James, was somewhere sailing on a merchant ship between here and the continent. He was just a mere lad of 15 but he had firmly told his father this was what he wanted to do with his life and though it broke his pa's heart he gave him his blessing and wished him Godspeed in his journeys.

As Janet sat there it began to rain. The water from the sky mixed with the tears on her cheeks. And she remembered what John had said … "the Lord Jesus taught any who would listen, in this world, you will have trials and sorrow … but take heart, I have overcome this world." She thought to herself, "You now know the truth Johnnie. You now know what tis like on the other side. Our land, our Scotland will never be the same and you lived right in the middle of all the change that happened. You saw it all. The joy and the sorrow. The pleasure and the pain. Rest in peace my love … until we are once again in one another's arms." The undertaker arrived. Janet got up from her seat and entered the shop shutting the door behind her. The gentle rain continued to fall.

Chapter Seven - Castlederg, Count Tyrone, Ulster Plantation ca. 1625

They both heard the warning bell and simultaneously turned in the direction of the Castle. Francis was the first to react. "Christie, run, get on your horse and head for safety … quickly lad." Francis shouted to his 11-year-old son, Christopher Irvine. But the stern command was not necessary for Christie had already dropped his rake and was running with all his might to where he had tied up his horse early that morning when the Irvines had ridden to the fields to tend to their crops. Their home was a modest structure in Learmore in the Barony of Omagh West where Christie and most of his siblings had been born. However, all the residents of the parish of Urney including the Irvines headed for the safety of the Castle when the warning bell was sounded. The Castle was a bell tower built over a hundred years ago by the powerful Irishman, Earl O'Neill, one of the many clan chiefs of the O'Neills, the original inhabitants of this section of Ulster. But much had changed in the past quarter century with the coming of the English and Scots to Ulster in King James' "Irish plantation" scheme. And the castle had been given to the English appointed Attorney General, Sir John Davies in 1608 and had served ever since as a shelter for the immigrant Scots and English Protestants who had been transplanted to this part of Northern Ireland. While those in King James' administration located in London and Dublin believed the Irish clans of Ulster had finally been subdued the folks living in Ulster knew the reality of the situation. These native Irish were a stubborn and proud people and had never really given up even though their leaders had fled the country to seek exile in various parts of Catholic Europe, an episode now known as the "flight of the earls". The raiding and trouble making was constant. Especially here in the west of Ulster close to the larger concentrations of Irish natives in County Donegal. But that is exactly why the Irvines were here. This border warfare was in their blood. Back home in Dumfries, Scotland, they had been constantly skirmishing with the English across the border and with one another on the Scottish side.

"Pa, get on your horse and let's go." Christie shouted out to his father. He was nervous. He had been prepared for this day, of course. From as far back as he could remember, he had been taught how to act should the warning bell sound when he was outside the protection of the thick walls. He thought to himself, "Run if you can, hide if you must but always be ready to fight". That had been something his father had drilled into his mind over and over. And they had practiced every week on what to do should they be attacked by a marauding band of natives. And the day had come to put the practice into action.

Christie was too young to carry a sword or pike but he was given a dirk to wear and taught how to use it if necessary. His father, being the Cousin of the influential Christopher Irvine of County Fermanagh, the owner of Castle Irvine, was given a position of leadership within the small militia of the parish of Urney and was allowed to carry multiple weapons with him at all times including a snaphance, a hand-held gun that fired a ball with killing velocity but limited accuracy.

"Can you see them, yet?" Francis asked his son. "Which direction are they coming from?" he asked as his gaze spanned the horizon. Suddenly his head jerked to a stop. "There they are, by the side of the river Derg and heading this way fast. Come on lad, let's ride" And with that he swiftly kicked his horse into a gallop and headed for the castle gate. Christie followed on his heels along with a dozen or so men and women who had been tending their fields. As Christie looked ahead, he saw that men had already begun manning the Castle walls and were swinging their small cannon in the direction of the raiding party. It was only one piece of artillery but could play havoc with the enemy if the aim was accurate which it often wasn't. The border Scots were used to hand to hand combat often on horseback and had little use for established European military tactics. But it wasn't just border Scots living in this area. It had become a melting pot of English, border Scots, Scots from Edinburgh and Glasgow, as well as the Anglo-Irish faithful to the Protestant King. So, they had to learn to live together and that meant learning and employing the battle tactics of the English.

The gates of the castle were quickly closed after Christie and his father entered the structure. At that moment, the cannon exploded with a blast of powder and shot. The Scots manning the gun let out a yell of celebration and Christie assumed that they hit their target. By the time Francis and his son had retrieved their weapons and manned their station on the castle wall, the battle was over. The cannon had found its mark and had hit the middle of the Irish raiding party shortly after they came into range. Apparently, this was enough bloodshed to cause the raiders to quickly turn their small shaggy ponies around and head back to the west.

Francis and Christie arrived at their post just in time to see the attackers ride away into the setting sun. "They'll be back," one of the Scots posted with them managed to blurt out in frustration. "Aye, they always come back don't they," responded Francis.

As things calmed down, routine returned to the castle but the folks inside knew they would not be returning to their farms and cottages that evening. This was unfortunate because under cover of darkness the raiders would be tempted to raid their farms, destroy their crops and steal their cattle. Some of the men talked about heading out in a group to track down the raiders but were persuaded by their wives and mothers that it would be foolish to pursue them in the quickly approaching darkness of nightfall.

Finally, Francis spoke up. People listened to Francis Irvin. Not just because of his blood relationship to his more famous cousin. There were many Irvines who had travelled from Dumfries to this part of Ulster at the behest of their King James. His kinship with the clan Irvine was not the reason. Folks trusted Francis' intelligence and battle hardened experience. He was a natural leader. So when he spoke, people generally listened and heeded his advice.

Francis spoke to the small gathered crowd of men, women and children. "We have hurt them with the cannon. I imagine they weren't expecting to suffer any or at best few losses. They will be using the darkness to gather their dead and wounded and recover from the surprise of our preemptive strike. But they will seek revenge. Of that, we can be sure. We don't know how many of them are out there. I suggest we wait until first light and then send out a few of our best riders on the fastest horses and scout out the area. I also suggest we send one of the youngsters who can ride south to Castle Irvine and alert my cousin. I will write him to request he assemble the militia and come to our defense. Christie, you can ride out in the morning." Francis looked around the crowd and saw the nodding heads indicating they were in agreement with this plan. Christie was bursting with pride. His father had never given him such an important task to do. He would not let him down. He would ride like the wind south to County Fermanagh and would not stop until he reached the gates of Castle Irvine.

Francis spoke again to the little crowd of anxious but determined Scots and English settlers. "I suggest we post a guard on each wall tonight. We will take turns. Two hours on duty then two hours to rest. Any trouble, sound the alarm. Everyone sleep tonight with your weapons by your side." And with that, the group disbanded and the first guards on duty went to their designated places while everyone else headed for the interior of the old tower to find a place to spend the night. The women had already started up the cooking fires and the smells of food were slowly wafting through the air.

After inspecting the preparations, Francis entered the main tower and sought out his family. They were all present and safe. His wife, Mary and his children, Christie plus their newly born baby girl, Elizabeth, were settled in by one of the cooking pots. Christie was sharpening his dirk and daydreaming of his big upcoming ride. Mary was nursing the little one. Francis thought to himself, "The poor girl has lost her last three infants. I pray to God this one survives." He glanced upwards to the heavens and quickly made the sign of the cross. Francis was not a strongly religious man but he did believe in God and turned to him in prayer during difficult times. Like all his neighbors, he considered himself a Protestant and a loyal servant of King James VI of Scotland who was now King James I of Ireland, Wales, Scotland and England. But he tended to not get involved in the numerous theological squabbles that would often break out amongst this mixed group of Anglican and Presbyterian planters. Quite frankly, he didn't know whose theology was more correct and in reality, he didn't care. Francis Irvine was grandson of "Black Christie" Irvine, one of the most feared warriors of the Scots English border region, Laird of the Irvines of Bonshaw and surrounding area. Upon his command, 150 men would assemble to fight as he directed. And, perhaps most important, "Black Christie" Irvine was a friend of James Stewart, King of Scotland and now all of Great Britain. So, when James decided to finally stabilize the border region of his newly united country, he naturally turned to those who he trusted. He soon realized he could "kill two birds with one stone" by relocating the most loyal and battle-hardened clans to Ulster to help subdue once and for all the rebellious Irish of his new kingdom and in doing so, he just might bring peace to this part of his war weary kingdom, the Scottish English border. Francis was a young boy himself when the good King James himself actually travelled to Bonshaw to dine with his grandfather and lay out his plan for the Ulster Plantation. "I remember that day like it was yesterday." Francis thought to himself as he stood watching his family. "There he was in his entire splendor, the king of all Britain standing in the home of my birth speaking to my grandfather as if they were old friends. And perhaps they were? After all, the Irvines had been loyal to the Stewarts from the beginning." But the king knew what he was doing. This was more than a friendly chat. James in his polite and nonaggressive manner was making it fairly clear for the Irvines that there really was no choice in the matter. Peace must come to the border region and James needed these men and women who had been born and raised in a life of constant warfare to relocate to another part of his kingdom to help pacify and bring stability to it. Old wise "Black Christie" saw the handwriting on the wall and agreed with James that he would send two of his three sons, their families and servants to Ulster to help "the cause". And that was that. The king and his entourage left the very next day, probably to speak with other troublesome border clans on both sides of the border to not so subtly recruit troops for the Protestant conquest of Northern Ireland. And they all obeyed their king. They travelled at first by the dozens and then by the hundreds and eventually by the thousands, flooding into the counties of Derry, Tyrone, Fermanagh, and Armagh. These would soon be joined by thousands of Scots from the areas surrounding Edinburgh, Glasgow and Dundee as these folk settled in the neighboring counties of Antrim and Down. Once there, this combined Protestant force of English, border and lowland Scot and noble Anglo-Irish families would expand into the historical counties of Monaghan, Cavan and Donegal. Even some of the highlanders from Argyll and the islands elsewhere got in on the land grab as long as they pledged their allegiance to King James I and took an oath of loyalty to the Protestant cause.

Francis remembered the trip. He was recently married and was eagerly looking forward to starting his farm in this new land and raising his family. At the time, he knew it would be difficult but he rationalized to himself that it could be no worse off than staying in Dumfries where sudden and violent death was a constant companion. Perhaps it would be better? Perhaps this would be a land of peace? But Francis and the hundreds of others who eventually called Ulster home underestimated the tenacity of the native Irish. This had been their home for a thousand years and even though their leaders had taken flight for the sanctuary of Catholic Europe, they were not going to give in without a fight. Stripped of all legal rights and powerless to join in the growing prosperity of the linen markets, they resorted to hit and run tactics that the border Scots and English had used so effectively for hundreds of years. And that is what life evolved into in Ulster, long stretches of anxious peace disrupted by horrific and unpredictable acts of vengeance. This forced the Scots and their English allies to build fortifications throughout the countryside which served as havens of safety when the natives attacked. Francis and his family had settled close to one in Tyrone named Castle Derg. It was small but afforded the locals all the protection they needed at least so far. The Irish had not yet been able to mount a major offensive in this part of Ireland and the number of Scots in the Counties of Antrim and Down were growing by leaps and bounds. The military objective became in Tyrone and Fermanagh to simply hold out and try to survive these quick hit raids while waiting for loyal English troops from Dublin or their fellow Scots from the east to come to their rescue. Of course, being border Scots, Francis and his kin often would go on raiding parties of their own seeking out local Irish farms who they suspected of harboring Catholic Irish supporters. They would evict the poor families, confiscate the land and all their earthly possessions while burning the buildings to the ground thus leaving the poor natives to their own devices many of whom would eventually starve or be forced to flee to the Southern sections of the island where they might find temporary refuge. To Francis this was considered justice as it had been practiced in the border region for as long as anyone could remember.

And so he sat down as he watched his little family. "Tis a hard life we live here but it has its good moments" he thought to himself and smiled at Mary his wife as she stirred the black kettle containing the meal they would all eat that evening. That night he slept well. For Francis was a man who lived in the moment and was not one given to worry about what might happen tomorrow?

The sun rose early the next day. It was close to midsummer and the days were long. Christie was up at dawn for he had hardly slept a wink the night before. He had been given a mission and he was excited about it. As he walked to get upon his horse, his mother handed him a leather pouch containing some food along with a flask of whisky. His father helped him on the horse and then much to Christie's surprise handed him his weapon. "I pray son you'll not need to use this but if you do aim where I taught you and take a deep breath before you gently squeeze the trigger" Francis said with solemnity as he shook the hand of his eleven year old boy. "Go with God lad" and then Francis gently slapped the rump of the big horse and off they galloped to the south down the road towards County Fermanagh and Castle Irvine. It would be a quick trip. A man at full gallop could probably get there before sundown but Christie knew his horse would tire before long and he would have to find a safe place to hide in the event the Irish raiders were somewhere nearby.

The trip was uneventful. As Christie approach Castle Irvine he was stopped by a guard standing in the watchtower. "Identify yourself and state your purpose young man," the guard yelled down to the boy on horseback.

"I am Christopher Irvine from County Tyrone sent here by my father Francis, Cousin to the Laird of this castle," Christie managed to speak up with as manly voice he could utter although he was tired and weary from the anxiety he had experienced the entire trip. His imagination had played games with him and he saw Irish raiders behind every tree and just knew he would encounter them over the next rise on the road. But nothing happened. And so now he arrived at his destination, tired but thankful to be safe amongst his kin.

Soon the gates opened and Christie's oldest relative, Christopher Irvine, Laird of Castle Irvine walked up to greet him. "Christie lad, by all that's holy, it is good to see you but what brings you here. Where are your father and the rest of your family?" Irvine asked in a booming voice that was used to barking out commands which were immediately obeyed. This Christopher was much older than his father Francis.

"We were attacked by Irish raiders and my father sent me to inform you of such and to request you send men to our aid." Christie blurted out, his voice cracking as he tried to hold back the tears.

The older Christopher became serious very quickly. "How many were there and when did they attack? Did you suffer any losses?" he asked concerned.

"Nay, not a one but I think we got some of them with the little cannon the English gave us. One shot and they scattered. But my father thinks they will return with a larger force," Christie responded.

"Aye, probably will. I'll give the orders to some of my men to join you. I can't spare them all. We'll need some here to protect our folk and lands if the Irish be rising. But I can spare a dozen or so. That'll have to do for now." And with that the elder Irvine wheeled around and marched back into the Castle barking out orders as he walked inside the gates. "Come on lad," he shouted over his shoulder at Christie. "You'll need to rest and eat. Tomorrow lad you'll lead a dozen of my best warriors back to Castle Derg."

Christie sat on his horse. "That's it," he thought to himself. "…A dozen men. I rode all the way here through enemy infested territory to bring a mere dozen soldiers back to my father, and not a word of congratulations for safely making it here, risking life and limb." Christie tried to hold back the tears but the frustration was overtaking him at this point.

Suddenly, the elder Christopher stopped and whirled around. "Well, lad, what are ye waiting for, a medal and piper to pipe you in here. Aye, ye have done well on this day. Ye have done your family proud. Now get off that old nag before she dies of exhaustion. You must have ridden her hard the whole way. And I suspect you didn't see any Irish, correct? Probably a small band of starving farmers looking to steal some meat from your family farm, I imagine. But I will send my men just to be on the safe side. We wouldn't want dear old Francis to think his cousin had abandoned him in his time of need now would we?" and with that final comment, Laird Christopher bellowed in laughter and it was joined by many of the men and women who had gathered around him to see what all the commotion was about.

What Christie did not realize, could not have realized at his young age, was the historical tension that had existed between his father and the Laird. The issue started in Scotland shortly after the King had left Bonshaw. Francis was the eldest son of his father, Edward Irvine, who was the eldest son of the "Black Christie". Since he was the eldest of the eldest, Francis always felt he should have had the first pick of the available Ulster lands but the issue was Mary, Francis' wife. The Irvines had always been faithful to the Stewarts but they had not always been Protestant. In fact, Francis himself was named after Francis, the young Catholic King of France and husband of Mary, Catholic Queen of Scots. It had been the Irvines along with other loyal border families who had helped Mary escape across the border into England when being pursued by the Presbyterian nobles of Scotland. This might have been one of the reasons the current King James had decided to personally visit the seat of the clan Irvine at Bonshaw.

Mary, Francis' wife, however, was a staunch supporter of the Presbyterian cause and an advocate for the teachings of John Knox who had desired a reformed government in Scotland as well as a reformed kirk. This was too much for old "Black Christie". So, in retaliation, he gave the choice of Ulster lands to his second son, John who's first born son Christopher, named after his grandfather, inherited the title of clan Chief and was now Laird of Irvinestown and keeper of the Castle Irvine. Francis was given a smaller piece of holding in the northwestern area of Ulster where the farmland was not as rich and productive. It had led to bitterness between the different segments of the clan but this was not uncommon among the border families. And so, with time, tempers cooled and the families learned to live in a civil fashion with one another. The relationship became more complex with the wedding of Christopher and Blanche, his cousin. For Blanche was the daughter of Edward Irvine, son of "Black Christie" and father of Francis. Blanche and Francis were brother and sister. Not only was the Laird Christopher, Francis' cousin but also his brother –in-law. Kin relationships were always complicated amongst the border Scots of Ulster.

It was Blanche who greeted the lad Christie with a huge smile, hug and peck on the cheek. "My, how you are growing, like a thistle in the fields."

Christie loved Blanche. She was his favorite aunt and a little younger than his father. That made her considerably younger than her husband, the Laird but this was also not unusual in Ulster. Life was hard, brutal at times and one had to find love and companionship when and where they could.

"Come, wash the dust of the road off yourself and set down to the table. I've made a rich lamb stew. It's delicious if I don't say so myself." And with that comment, Blanche giggled and covered her teeth with her hands. This was a habit of hers that had started when she was a child. Blanche had very large front teeth and was self-conscious about their appearance.

"Thank you Aunt Blanche. I'm starving." Christie said in reply as he made his way to the table in the middle of the main hall. However, Christie came to a sudden stop when he saw sitting at the table a man wearing the black robe of a Catholic priest. He was suddenly alarmed and confused at the same time. But before he could speak,

Blanch cleared her throat and said, "Christie, I would like you to meet Father …er … I mean Brother Paul." She glanced at the man and smiled weakly. "Paul, this is my nephew, Christie Irvine from Castle Derg up in County Tyrone." The man extended his arm and shook Christie's hand. The first thing Christie noticed about this man, other than he was wearing the clerical garb of a Catholic priest was his size. He was very tall, much taller than most men around these parts and extremely skinny. He looked like a bag of bones and the smell of his body and breath was atrocious. Christie took a couple of steps back instinctively as the stench of the man reached his nostrils. "Brother Paul is our guest Christie and he has traveled far, all the way from the western edges of County Donegal. He has brought important information to the Laird about the Catholic Irish settlements in that part of Ulster." Blanche spoke in a matter of fact fashion as if this should be no surprise to anyone. Christie quickly put two and two together. This man was a spy. He pretended to be a Catholic priest as he travelled through Catholic held areas picking up tidbits of information about potential troublemakers and future plans of armed assaults on the English and Scottish communities of Ulster. Christie immediately did not trust the man and from that moment on was very cautious about what he said in his presence.

The sun was quickly setting and it was time for sleep. The last thing Christie saw as he tried to keep his eyes opened while fighting back the exhaustion was the Laird Christopher shaking the hands of Brother Paul and slipping him a pouch of what sounded like coins. Then sleep overcame him and the next thing he knew his Aunt Blanche was gently shaking his straw mat attempting to waken him from a   deep sleep. He had been dreaming of leading a brigade of Scots and English troops against an assembled army of wild Irish natives. The pipes had been screeching out their sounds of battle and the drummers were beating the sounds of the battle formation. Christie was out in front of the massed forces ready to lead the massive charge. And then his Aunt Blanche woke him up.

Just then, Christopher Irvine's booming voice bellowed from outside. "Get the lad up and feed him quickly. My men are ready to travel. We are wasting daylight."

And before you could say the Our Father, Christie was back astride the old nag that had brought him to Castle Irvine and was leading the dozen fighting men back to the north along the road to County Tyrone and Castle Derg.

There was not much conversation between Christie and the men. They were servants and small farm holders who had come to this part of Ulster from various places in Scotland and England. But the one thing they had in common was the experience of battle in fighting the natives. They kept to themselves and while the unsuspecting person might not have noticed, each of them had one eye on the horizon constantly scanning for potential trouble. This was the way of Ulster. Peace was fleeting and danger lurked behind every tree or over every ridge. Only those who were constantly on guard had a chance for survival and these men were survivors. Suddenly Christie saw the spy amongst them. He did not know what to think. Questions flew through his mind. Why was he with us? What was his purpose? Did his father, Francis know about this man? What would his father do when they arrived at Castle Derg?

Time moved on and eventually they saw the Castle in the horizon. Everything looked as he had left it the day before. People were out working in their fields. There were a couple of men who obviously had been stationed as lookouts posted on the castle walls but if you had not known the recent history you would have never suspected there had been an attack just two days ago. And that was also the way of Ulster. As quickly as violence flared up, it receded and people got about the business of living their lives.

The lookouts spotted the group of armed men and quickly sounded the alarm bell but Christie spurred his horse into a gallop and shouted out to them that he was returning and that these men were allies sent from the Laird Irvine. Francis walked quickly out of the gates and greeted his son before he had a chance to dismount. "Welcome back lad. Glad to see you are safe and sound. And you've brought help. I was wondering if our cousin Chris would oblige my request for assistance." Francis stated with a slight amount of sarcasm in his voice. But in his mind, he knew his kin … his clan. No matter what the circumstances, family came first. And when one of your own needed help, you moved heaven and earth to do so with no exception. That was also the way of the border Scots.

Just about then, the black garbed Paul got off his beast of burden and strode up to Francis. Before he opened his mouth, Francis grabbed him in a huge bear hug and shouted out his name, "Robert Hamilton, sweet Jesus, it is good to see you once again. But, my God, man you reek. When is the last time you bathed?" And the two of them laughed as if old friends. For indeed, that is what they were. Francis called his son over to them. "Christie, do you know who this is?" Francis asked with a huge smile on his face.

"Aye, father, he is a Catholic spy working for our cousin Christopher," Christie responded.

The two men exploded with laughter. "Well lad, you are partly correct. Yes, he is a spy. But he is no Catholic. Hamilton here is a graduate of the University of Glasgow with a Master's degree in Divinity. And he speaks Gaelic better than the Irish do. The man is a Presbyterian through and through and is on a mission to convert as many of the native Catholics as he can before the Elders call him home to Glasgow."

"Or some wild-eyed Irishman runs me through with a pitchfork," Hamilton interrupted. And once again, both men laughed with joy.

"But I thought your name was Brother Paul?" Christie asked in deep confusion. This was a bit much for an eleven-year-old boy to take in even if he was quite mature for his age.

Hamilton turned toward Christie and smiled, "That's an alias lad. When I am in "enemy territory" so to speak, I go by either Father or Brother Paul, depending upon the circumstances. Once it becomes clear to me that I'm in generally safe company, I let them know my real identity and we talk about God and his word."

"But I saw the Laird pay you coins. I thought it was for information you had gained while spying." Christie asked Hamilton and noticed that both he and his father were once again smiling.

"Aye, lad, the Laird did give me money but it was not for payment of services rendered. It was a donation. We are trying to build a church here in Tyrone and your cousin Christopher gave a generous donation for the initial construction. But, aye, you are right, when I come upon information that I think he needs to know to ensure the safety of his lands and people, I do pass that on to him if I have the opportunity. But I take no payment for that information." Hamilton stopped and looked sincerely at Christie.

Christie thought to himself, this man still stinks but I think I may have misjudged his character and suddenly laughed quietly to himself.

"What's got ye tickled lad," his father asked.

"Nothing pa, nothing important" Christie responded. And with that, the conversation ended and the three headed inside to sit at the table of his mother Mary.

As the family gathered around the table, Mary asked Robert if he would say grace before they partook of the meal she had prepared.

"Aye, let us pray," Hamilton began as the assembled group bowed their heads in prayer.

"Merciful and powerful God. We give you thanks for this food. May it bring strength to our bodies, wisdom to our minds and love to our hearts. We pray for those this night that are going without. We pray you will have mercy upon them and fill their hungry bellies with sustenance and fill their minds with your words. We pray for this land you have given to us. We pray we will be an example of the truth of Christ to all we encounter here. We pray for our good King James. We pray that you will always guide him that he might continuously seek the truth and do right in your sight. We pray for those whose eyes you have not yet opened and whose hearts you have not yet set straight. We pray for those who might wish us harm. May their plans for evil not bear fruit of any kind? We pray you have mercy upon our souls. Amen." And with the word amen everyone began speaking at once and enjoying the bounty of food that Mary had lovingly prepared for her small but close knit family.

The dinner conversation transitioned over a wide range of topics but everyone sitting around the table knew eventually Mary would bring up the topic of the King and his apparent attempt to move the Church of England and the Kirk of Scotland closer together in structure and, most importantly to Mary, in theology.

"So, Robert, what's the latest word from London? Is our good king James still bound and determined to make us all Anglicans?"

This was obviously a touchy subject with Mary so Robert proceeded with caution. Since coming to Ulster, Robert Hamilton had learned to weave his way carefully through the bog and swamp of religion and politics. If the truth be known, what had evolved in Ulster was a type of Protestant religion Robert liked to call Prescopalian, a sort of mixture of Church of England and Kirk of Scotland.

"Well Mary, as long as Bishop Usher is in charge of the Church of England here in Ireland, I think we Presbyterians will be allowed to worship as we choose with minimal interference from the Bishops." Robert continued, "It is certainly true that James is surrounded by men who would like to unite the two distinct Protestant movements together and I guess I can see their point." At which point Mary gave a derisive snort. "Robert Hamilton, you who have been called by the almighty to spread the true gospel, how could you dare say such a thing?" Mary was stinging in her retort. "The only thing the Anglican bishops want is exactly what their Catholic predecessors wanted … more wealth for the church and political power for themselves within the realm." Francis looked at Mary and smiled. He knew she was a kind and loving woman who had been a good companion to him and a wonderful mother for their children. But when Mary talked about religion and politics sparks would fly from her as if she were on fire. "Knox knew this. That is why he taught what he did. He wanted to recreate Geneva, first in Scotland and then eventually within the rest of the kingdom." Mary waited on a response from her guest but Hamilton had been here before with Mary Irvine and knew he was treading on thin ice.

"Mary, what if Knox had succeeded in changing Scotland? What would that have meant for us? For you and Francis and the rest of the Irvine clan." Robert asked politely and cautiously.

"It would have meant the end of the reign of King James … or any king or queen for that matter. It would have meant that God's spirit would select our rulers just as the Elders are picked today in the true reformed church." And with that statement, the room became quickly and totally silent.

Francis spoke first, "Be careful woman. Some might interpret your words as treason against the king. You are among family and friends here but please; please do not make such statements in the marketplace. I love you Mary Irvine and want nothing evil to befall you."

"Husband, I am of God's elect. What happens to me is His will. You know that!" Mary responded to her husband's admonition. Now she was truly stirred. She continued her speech to her captive audience. "Francis, you and Robert know that the only reason we border Scots are here is to fight against the natives and bring some semblance of stability to the region. James is no Presbyterian and he can barely tolerate us and our ideas."

Francis interrupted, "Mary, I don't think James wants to destroy the kirk of Scotland. I do think the man wants peace in his kingdom for all his subjects, be they Catholic, Anglican or Presbyterian."

Mary jumped back into the fray, "Nay, husband. The king is surrounded with men lusting after wealth and power and they see a united kingdom with one united church as the answer. What, pray tell, do ye think will happen when the good king dies? He's no spring chicken now, is he?"

Robert Hamilton attempted to answer the question in his soft-spoken manner, "When James passes from this world to the next, he will most likely be replaced by his son, Charles. I have not met the man, of course, but have been told that he is above average intelligence but not a scholar like his father.
While he does enjoy the arts and liveliness of the court...."

"You mean the ladies of the court," Mary derisively intervened.

"Well ... yes, I suppose so ... at least he likes women as opposed to his father's inclination towards young men" and with that Mary blushed as Christie looked quizzically at his father who just looked down at the wooden floor and shook his head slightly. Robert continued, "I have been told that Charles is somewhat pious and fairly tolerant in his views on the matter of how one practices' one's faith. So, I suspect we'll not be troubled by him or his father for that matter, should God decide for James to remain with us for a few more years."

"I think you are both dreaming, "Mary spoke up to the men. "There is a time of tribulation coming our way. God, in his righteousness, has decided to reform the church and I'm afraid it will be with bloodshed and not just words spoken from the pulpit…. Or the throne. Mark my words, when old James dies, this fragile peace that now exists in the kingdom will quickly come to an end. The wolves will bear their fangs and the fighting will be fierce." Mary stated with a firmness that impressed both men and Christie who always sat in on these dinner conversations with open ears. Christie was bright for his age and was able to follow the give and take of these nightly discussions and very rarely asked questions or offered any comment. But tonight, would be different.

"Ma," Christie began haltingly, "have you had one of your visions?" Silence surrounded the table. Everyone in the close-knit family knew that Mary had been given the gift of what the Scots called second sight or what a Presbyterian Elder might call the gift of prophecy. Mary bowed her head and was still for a moment. Then she looked directly at her son and said, "Aye, lad, I have." Now, the tension in the room began to mount. Francis loved his wife dearly and had the deepest respect for her as a mother and wife but in his heart, unbeknownst to Mary, he had his doubts about her so-called visions. Robert Hamilton, on the other hand, had been a witness to Mary's gift in the past and had come to accept and fully believe that Mary Irvine had indeed been given a special gift. But he was extremely careful about with whom he might share this knowledge. These Ulster Scots were a superstitious bunch and unfortunately, some might claim that Mary's abilities were not of heaven but from Satan himself. They might accuse her of witchcraft. The consequences of that were too horrible to contemplate.

Robert leaned in closer to Mary and asked her in a hushed tone, "What has God told you sister?"

Mary looked at her husband. Their eyes locked and he nodded. Mary looked at Robert and then at her son. "The king will die soon. His son, Charles will take the crown. At first, things will have the appearance of tolerance for various religious opinions. But then Charles will appoint a man to be Archbishop of the Church of England. And Charles will have instructed this man to weed out any who oppose his right to rule both his kingdom and his church as he sees fit. Civil war will erupt. There will be bloodshed. The streets will run red with blood." Mary finished her prophecy. The silence deepened. She spoke again, "That is all the Lord has shown me. I do not know the timing. I do not know how it will start. I do not know how it will end. But I do know it will involve the deaths of many of the faithful." And with that, Mary looked down at the baby in her arms and began to weep.

After what seemed like hours but was only minutes, Francis broke the silence and said, "Mary, it is getting late. Perhaps we should all try to get some sleep. The raiders might decide to attack at daybreak and we all need to be rested and ready should that happen."

"Aye," Robert stated and nodded to Christie to head to his bed while he helped Mary with the little one. Francis headed outside to check on the men who had taken the first watch of the night.

Christie lay in his bed but sleep would not come upon him. He had too many unanswered questions.

As soon as the morning light broke through the overcast sky, Christie was up and helping his mother gather sod for the fire. He wanted to speak with her. He had many questions he wanted to ask her. They walked outside the castle and headed for the sod field. Here they would take a sharp knife like tool and cut the sod into squares. Then stack it to let the sun dry off the moisture. Once fully dry, it could be used to keep the fires burning throughout the fortress. This was tough work but Mary was a strong woman and would often sing hymns while working in the field. Christie loved this time with his mother. She had laid the baby in the crib so he had her all to himself this morning.

"Ma, I have been thinking a lot about what you said last night," Christie began.

His mother smiled and replied, "I thought you might. And what are these thoughts you have been having?"

"Ma, why are we here in Ulster? I mean … I know what pa says about "Black Christie" and all that but why are we really here?"

"Lad, we are here on this earth to serve God. To do His will to the best of our ability," Mary replied.

"And we can't do His will in Scotland? It must be here in Ulster? Ma, no one wants us here. The Protestant Anglo-Irish look down their noses at us. The English laugh at us behind our backs. And, the good Lord knows, the native Catholics want us all dead or to leave. So why stay? Why don't we just go home?" Christie looked at his mother with love and concern in his eyes.

"Christie, this is our home," Mary's reply was short and direct.

"But Ma, didn't this land belong to them way before we ever arrived? What right do we have to come here and take their land from them? Isn't Ulster their home?" Christie asked his mother once again with the perplexed look of a young boy transitioning to manhood who could not yet grasp the complexities of the world into which he had been born.

Mary put down her sod cutter and wiped the sweat from her brow. "Christie, do ye remember the stories I told you about the ancient Israelites and the Promised Land? Do ye remember the story of Moses and of Joshua?"

"Aye" the boy said.

"God decided the Israelites were to fulfill His purpose and plans by moving onto the Promised Land. But this land was occupied by other tribes. These tribes did not worship the Lord our God. So, God took the land from them and gave it to His faithful … the sons and daughters of Israel, thus keeping a promise He had made a long time before to Abraham. Do ye remember all that my son?" Mary was looking directly at Christie now with deep love in her heart for this young man her only son.

"Aye, ma. Joshua led many men into battle as he cleared out the Promised Land for settlement by the Israelites." Christie replied as a student would respond to his teacher.

"Lad, many of us feel that God again has intervened in the history of mankind. Many of us, including myself, feel that God has chosen us to be the messengers of reform and that we are to take this new kirk wherever He leads us. And some of us feel that God has given Ulster to us. Just like He gave Israel to the Hebrews. Can ye follow that logic? Does it make sense to you?" Mary waited for a reply from her precious boy.

"I understand that is how we Scots feel. But how do the natives feel about it. They pray to God too ma. Isn't He the same God we pray to?" Christie said with some apprehension. He knew this would be a difficult question for his mother to answer but he had to know what she really thought even if it meant upsetting her.

Mary looked at her son. It suddenly dawned on her that he was growing up. That he was no longer a mere child but had become a man with an intelligence that would not be denied. These were good questions and she wasn't quite confident that she had sufficient answers for him. In truth, she sometimes wondered the same thing and had similar concerns in her heart but she dared not share them with her husband.

"Have you spoken to your pa about this subject?" Mary quietly asked her son.

"Nay, do ye think I should," Christie replied.

"Aye, if the opportunity presents itself. In fact, I would like to hear his answers myself." Mary smiled at her son. Christie loved his mother's smile. He didn't often see it. Life had been quite a struggle for her … for all of them.

They both saw the man on horseback at the same time. He was riding quickly towards the castle. He was alone and did not seem to be brandishing a weapon but he was definitely moving as fast as his steed would take him. Without communicating a word both mother and son began running back to the safety of the castle walls.

When they arrived a few minutes later everyone was buzzing with the news. Robert Hamilton saw them first and exclaimed, "Have you heard the news sister?"

"News … about what" they both said.

"James has died. Charles is King of Britain. The king is dead. Long live the king." Robert said in reply.

Mary and Christie were shocked. It was just as Mary had predicted last night. Christie looked at his mother in astonishment and wonder. He thought to himself, "Tis true … God spoke to my ma."

Francis came running up to the three of them. "Well, you've heard the news I see. What do you make of that!" he exclaimed.

But Mary had fallen to her knees and was deep in prayer. It was as if she were in a trance and was paralyzed. Francis dropped to one knee and placed a gentle hand on her cheek. "Are you alright love?" he asked with great concern.

Mary looked up at her husband. Tears filled her eyes. "The Lord moves in mysterious ways. Blessed be His name."

Francis helped her to her feet as she dried the tears from her eyes.

"I must tend to the bairn. She is surely awake and hungry by now." And with that statement, Mary walked away from Francis, Robert Hamilton and Christie.

Robert was the first to speak. "We must tell no one and I mean no one of Mary's prophecy. Agreed?" as he looked sternly at the other two men.

"Aye" they both said in unison.

Meanwhile, a small group had gathered around Francis. They needed to hear him speak. They needed to hear his reassurance that all would be well. King James had been king of Scotland for a long time. For everyone gathered in this small colony, he had been the only king they knew. Of course, they had grown used to change. Things happened quickly in Ulster and these Scots planters had become accustomed to rapid changes in their day to day existence. But this was different. James was dead. Their king was dead. As most of them knew, James was the reason why they had been sent here in the first place. Now, what would happen? Their king was dead. And Charles, his son, had taken the throne. What would it mean for them? What would it mean for all the Protestants in Ulster? Would Charles continue with his father's plans? Would he even keep the kingdom Protestant?

Francis could almost read their minds. Perhaps because he had similar thoughts. He cleared his throat and then spoke to them all with a firm but kind voice.

"Yes, the king is dead. And yes, Charles is now our king. And I know that causes many of you concern. But be not troubled. God is still our God and reigns over us all from His throne in Heaven. Jesus is still our Savior and the Spirit of God dwells within us. Be not troubled. Nothing can separate us from the love of our God." Francis heard a few muffled "amen" from various people in the crowd gathered around him. "Eventually, we will all learn what this will ultimately mean for the plantation of Ulster. But for now, we have fields to attend to, children to nurse and teach and lives to live. So, I suggest we get about our business and let tomorrow take care of itself." The group responded with a loud aye and began to disperse. Everyone went back to what they had been doing before the messenger arrived. And soon it seemed as if nothing out of the ordinary had occurred on that day. But deep in Francis's heart, he knew the world, his world, had changed. And it did concern him. He always worried about the safety and welfare of his little family and his fellow Scots here in the parish of Urney. For some strange reason, he felt responsible for them all. He knew that wasn't really the case. But that is how he felt. And he knew, in his wisdom, what his people needed now was stability. He was thankful his cousin had sent the dozen men to aid in the defense of the castle against the raiders. It was possible that as the news of the death of James spread throughout the realm, the Irish might see it as an opportunity for a mass revolt against English rule. If that happened, Francis knew he would need every man his cousin could spare. He prayed that would not happen but decided it would be for the best if they prepared for another attack, this one perhaps much larger than the last. He also had a fleeting thought that they may have to flee back to Scotland if things got out of hand. He had not been back to the land of his birth since before the birth of his son Christie. He knew they would take them in but it was not a meeting he looked forward to. In some strange way, it would appear that he failed in his mission. He would have let down his king. But more importantly, he would have failed his family … his clan. And that thought was almost too much to bear. He needed time to think. To consider what their next move should be. But his mind was foggy and filled with anxiety. Then Francis heard a still quiet voice come from somewhere inside his soul …. "Francis …. Francis …. Be not afraid. I am with you. I will never abandon you. Place your trust in me. I am with you." And then just as quickly as it had come to his mind, the voice left and then silence. Francis did not know what to think. He had prayed to God before but God had never answered him. Francis had even recently begun to wonder if there was anything out there he was actually praying to? He had never shared that doubt with anyone but the truth was that he did doubt. But now suddenly he was calm inside and the doubt was gone. The events of his life had not changed but his perspective indeed had. He was not alone. He was not alone.

During the early years of the reign of Charles I of England, Ireland, Scotland and Wales a tentative peace was maintained throughout the realm while the continent of Europe became engulfed in a war of tremendous magnitude. This war would last for decades. This conflict, originally confined to Bohemia, spiraled into a wider struggle which the people of Britain viewed as a polarized continental fight to the death for supremacy between various Catholic and Protestant rulers. Charles married the fifteen-year-old French princess Henrietta Maria in front of the doors of the Notre Dame Cathedral in Paris. Many members of the House of Commons opposed the king's marriage to a Roman Catholic, fearing that Charles would eventually lift the restrictions which had been placed on those who were practicing Catholics. Although he told Parliament that he would not do so that is exactly what he promised to do in a secret marriage treaty he made with Louis XIII, King of France. Charles was crowned on February 2, 1626 at Westminster Abbey but without his wife at his side because she refused to participate in a Protestant religious ceremony. And this set the tone for his reign.

English Anglicans along with Scottish and Ulster Irish Presbyterians did not trust Charles. He had publicly supported the anti-Calvinist theology of Jacob Arminius and many felt he would eventually attempt to reinstate Catholicism throughout his realm.

Another constant source of tension between Charles and his Parliament was his belief in the divine right of kingship. Charles felt strongly, as had his father before him, that the Almighty specifically appoints the rulers of the world. Therefore, he, Charles had been appointed by God himself to rule over all Britain and no one had the right to question his ultimate authority.

The trouble in London eventually infiltrated the entire realm. Life continued on for the Irvines of County Tyrone and Fermanagh but the fragile peaceful existence of their lives was often explosively interrupted by the violent extremes of religious fanaticism. Farms would be burnt to the ground, crops destroyed and peoples' lives forever disrupted by sword wielding men on both sides of the theological debate.

By the year 1633, Christie Irvin was now a young man of nineteen. He was much taller than either, father, mother or any of his relatives. The hard and steady work on the farm had given him powerful muscles and it was said of him that he could toss a twenty-pound stone farther than anyone in the county. As an Ulsterman, he, of course, now knew how to use all the weapons of war granted to a man of his station and had on occasion throughout his adolescent years been forced to defend his family and friends from marauding Irish native's intent on destroying their little community. At least that was the propaganda the English government officials would spread throughout the province after one of the many local "Irish uprisings" had been dealt with in a vicious and unmerciful manner. However, Christie knew the truth. The Irish natives were slowly starving. In his mind, they were only doing what any decent man would have done who loved his family and did not want to watch them die a slow and painful death of starvation. These so-called uprisings were simply attempts to steal food or livestock from the much more prosperous English and Scots planters in Ulster. They were trying to stay alive. Christie understood that and did not blame them for it.

But his perspective on the matter was not shared by the majority of his fellow Ulster Scots. Many of them believed, as his mother had told him years before, this land had been promised to them by God and with God's help they would keep it and turn it into a New Jerusalem. The old Knoxian idea of a reformed state as well as kirk would not die. In fact, the concept seemed to gain in strength as more Presbyterian Scots moved to Ulster bringing with them a more militant version of their Presbyterian faith and pastors who were not reluctant to preach fiery sermons against Catholicism and by association, the poor Irish natives who happened to also be Catholic.

"What a mess," Christie said out loud as he and his father were riding out to their expanding fields one early morning.

"What's that lad … I dinna hear ye … Ye ken, I'm losing my hearing. You'll have to speak up son." His father responded in a huff.

"Tis nothing pa. I was just thinking about Ulster. I was wondering what the future will bring for us?" Christie said in a reflective manner. One thing Francis Irvine knew about his son was that he was a thinker. His mother Mary had called him the philosopher of the family. For although Christie had grown into a mountain of a man his was a gentle soul with a kind heart who would much rather talk than fight. Although, like most of his border ancestors, if forced to fight, Christie Irvin was a powerful force with which to bargain and many of the other young men in the county would think twice before taking him head on.

They rode their horses slowly that morning as the sun was just beginning to rise as neither really want to arrive at the fields before enough light had lit the rough worn path they had to follow through the bogs and swamps that separated sections of arable land.

"Pa, what do you truly think of the Irish … not the Anglo-Irish who have pledged their allegiance to King Charles but the other Irish … the poor natives whose land we have taken?"

"You mean the Catholics?" Francis responded with a question.

"Aye, Catholic they are, but more than that, Pa, aren't they just people like us, trying to scratch out a living from this poor sod?" Christie looked directly at his father as he spoke. He knew this was dangerous territory for a conversation with any fellow Ulster Scot but Christie had always been able to speak his mind in the presence of his father though they might not always agree.

Francis lowered his voice and looked at his son. "What's on your mind, lad? Something is troubling ye … that I reckon."

Christie was quiet for a while and when he spoke it was with a strange mixture of confusion and confidence. "Pa, they are just people like us. Did they ask to be born here in Ulster? Nay, they did not. Did they ask to be born as Catholic? Nay, they did not. Did they ask to be born at this time of history in the midst of all these troubles? Nay, they did not. They are just like us. Did you decide when and where you were to be born or into which kingdom or …. Religion? Nay, you did not." Christie waited for a reply.

"I understand what you are saying lad but what's your point? As far as I can tell, not a soul on God's green earth is given a choice as to when or where they are born. That's the way it is. That's the way God has ordained life for each of us. You know what the pastor preaches. God has predestined man's life and nothing will change what God has set into motion. One thing I know lad...I'm not God. Yes, sometimes I wonder why He makes the decision He makes. Why this one prospers and that one lives a life of poverty. Why this one is healthy and that one sickens and dies? Yes, I have questions. But at the end of all my questions is simply silence. God is silent on these matters. So, I reckon we just have to accept things as they are and do the best we can with what we have been given … and be thankful for it." Francis smiled at his son but Christie was not smiling in return. He had heard his pa's philosophy about life many times and although it seemed to give his pa some peace of mind it just created more confusion and dissonance for him.

"I've been reading the Bible a wee bit, pa." Christie said.

"Now, that could be dangerous lad, "Francis said, trying to make a joke to release some of the tension that had crept into the conversation.

"I've noticed that our pastors tend to focus on the Old Testament … the scriptures of the old Hebrews but rarely do they preach about the teachings of the Lord Jesus. Have you noticed that pa?" Christie looked expectantly at his father.

"Nay, can't say that I've given that much thought to the matter. Preaching is preaching and quite frankly, I just try to stay awake until it's time to go home. Now, don't you dare tell your ma that …" And with that both father and son laughed out loud.

"She would boil you alive if she caught you sleeping during the message." Christie responded while trying to reign in his laughter.

"Aye … that she would," Francis nodded while chuckling. Both of these men loved and respected Mary Irvine yet both realized that Mary's Presbyterian outlook was unflappable. She was a devoted student of John Knox and believed their God given task was to turn Ulster, Scotland and the rest of the British Isles into a Calvinistic nation whereby God himself would come down from heaven to dwell.

"It just seems to me Pa that the Jesus of the New Testament has a different story to tell then the old God of the Hebrews," Christie said to his father while closely watching for his reaction.

"Aye, lad. I've had those thoughts myself from time to time." Francis responded with quiet respect for his son's intellect and insight.

"Pa, the Jesus I've read about told his followers to love their enemies, to pray for those who brought them trouble, and to forgive seven times seventy any offense," Christie spoke in an earnest and honest manner now with his father. He continued," but our pastors … they seem to always want to focus on the God of the Hebrews … a God who demanded complete and total obedience and one who appears to me to condone the violence of his chosen people against their enemies. It just doesn't make any sense to me Pa. Who are we praying to when we pray? The ancient God of the Hebrews or this kind and loving Jesus?"

Francis thought for a moment before responding, "I think the pastor would tell you they are one and the same. God the father, God the son and God the Holy Spirit. Jesus was both God and man. And remember he got angry himself from time to time. Didn't he even run all the moneychangers out of the temple? Seems like that is a story I remember hearing from the pulpit once."

Christie looked at his father and then turned his gaze to the horizon. He was deep in thought and Francis decided to let him be. He knew his son was more a philosopher than a farmer and certainly not designed for the quasi-militaristic life here in Ulster. But he loved him dearly and truly valued the wisdom he displayed on occasion. He was as some might say an old soul.

"Pa, perhaps God sent Jesus to us because the ancient Hebrews did not truly understand the God they worshipped?"

"I don't quite follow you lad. What are you driving at?" Francis asked politely.

"I'm not sure I even know. I've got so many thoughts jostling around up here, "as he tapped the side of his hat covered head," sometimes things don't make sense to me until I talk them out or write them down. But I've been thinking that God's timing is not like the timing of men. He sees things way out into the future. Things we can't see or if we saw would not understand. So, I was thinking, maybe. God is just feeding us bits and pieces of the truth down through history as we can handle it. Just like a mother feeds her little one breast milk until they grow teeth and then she switches the bairn over from milk to solid … but even then she might chew up the meat or cut it up into small bite size pieces so her little one won't choke. Maybe that is how God has worked in the history of men and women. He doesn't want us to choke on the truth so he gives it to us in bits and pieces."

"Well, lad, that is a mighty interesting thought you have there, "Francis said as he scratched his head and wiped the sweat from his brow. The sun had started to rise and the day was going to be one of the warmest of this growing season.

"Pa, what if Jesus came to teach us what the real truth is about God?" Christie asked his father.

"And what might that be?" Francis replied.

"That it is all about love. That God created us out of love. That He gave us rules to follow out of his desire to keep us safe. And that He simply wants us to learn how to get along with all of His creation … to love those we encounter during the short stay we have on this earth. What if that was the real message of Jesus?" Christie said slowly and with emphasis on the word love.

"Well … do you think we are supposed to love even those who commit evil against us lad?" Francis asked.

"Aye father … I do. Even the Irish deserve our love. That is what I think Jesus would say if he were here right now and had joined in our conversation. Even the Catholic Irish deserve our love." Christie said as he looked deep into his father's eyes. These thoughts had been formulating within Christie's mind for some time but today was the first time he could clearly articulate them. For at this moment, Christie Irvine came to the conclusion that everyone, the Irish Catholics, the English Anglicans and his fellow Ulster Scot Presbyterians had gotten it wrong when it came to understanding the words and teachings of Jesus of Nazareth. "We all got it wrong", Christie said to himself.

Francis was looking at him with a mixture of emotions. This was his son. His own flesh and blood. In his veins was the blood of the Border Scot … the Reivers, as the English called them. For hundreds of years his people had known nothing but violence and bloodshed.

To fight any who went up against them and to fight to win no matter the method was all that he had known his entire life. It was what he had been taught to him by his father who had been taught by his father, the great "Black Christie" and so on back into the mists of time. And now here was his precious son sitting on his old grey mare telling him it had all been wrong in the eyes of Jesus, the son of God. Francis did not know whether to shout at his son in anger or to hold him in love. Before he realized what was happening tears were flowing down his face into his long scraggly beard. Christie did not notice the tears or if he did refuse to acknowledge them out of his deep respect for his father. The two plodded along on horseback for a time riding silently together.

Finally, Francis responded, "Christie, we … I mean I … know of no other way to live my life. This is all I know. I have had to fight for every inch of land I have been given. I have had to be on guard against anyone who might come and steal away from us what meager possessions we have. Our very survival has depended upon our ability to strike back against our enemies, whomever they may be, with such devastating ferocity that they might be terrified and thus think twice before striking at us again. This is the way I have lived my life and lad … this is the way of our people. Your people son. Fighting is in your blood. It courses through every muscle and bone of your body. And, "Francis paused for a moment as he gathered his thoughts," this apparently is what God has destined for us. It is His will and as the preacher says, let His will be done on earth as it is in heaven." Francis looked at his son. He loved this young man. He was proud of him. But he could not find it in his heart to agree with this radical outlook on life. They continued to ride in silence.

"Pa, I mean no disrespect but I can't help but say what is truly in my mind and on my heart. I don't understand why I have these thoughts. But there they are and they won't go away. I know I am different from the other lads. I have always known that. They like to prove their manhood through their ability to fight with each other. I will fight when I have to but I would much rather sit down with my adversary and try to reason with him. And pa, I think we Ulster Scots need to try to do that with the Anglican English and …. with the Catholic Irish. I think pa that is what Jesus would have me do … would have any of us do who call ourselves a follower of him … to love others as we love ourselves … to do unto others as we would have them do to us. Pa, what would we have done if the shoe were on the other foot? What if the Irish had come to our land in Dumfries and had forced us off the ancient land of our ancestors. What if they would have come in overwhelming numbers and changed the laws so that we might not own land, might not vote for members of Parliament, and not even be able to worship God as we saw fit. What would we have done pa?" Christie became quiet as he waited for his father's inevitable answer.

"We would have picked up our swords and fought" Francis replied with certainty in his voice. "But lad that is not what happened. And because that is not what happened then surely God must have ordained what did happen to have happened. You must believe that don't ye?" Francis looked expectantly at his son. Christie just looked at his father. It suddenly dawned upon him that a gap had developed between the two of them. They had come to a place in their relationship where no amount of reasoning would change the position of the other. Christie had been here before with friends and family members. He simply did not see the world as others appeared to see it. And no amount of talk was going to change the way others felt about the situation in Ulster. He could see it all so clearly now. James had become king of Ireland, Scotland, Wales and England and he wanted peace throughout his entire kingdom. And King James viewed the north of Ireland as much his kingdom as his very own castle in London. He needed to bring peace between Scotland and England and had to resolve the constant warfare in the border region. In a brilliant strategic move, he moved the Scot and English from their border home to Ulster and used them to subdue the native Irish. And what truly became clear to Christie was that religion was the excuse James used to motivate everyone to do his bidding. James was a wily and intelligent king and he understood the deeply motivating power of religion. He knew that if he could convince the parties involved that the plantation of Ulster was ordained by God himself then he could simply step aside and allow the religious leaders of his people, the Presbyterian Elders and the Anglican Bishops to do his work for him. And that is exactly what transpired. At that moment, Christie realized that the Christian faith had little if anything to do with the plantation of Ulster. This was about power. In truth, this was about money. And had he not just the evening before read in the gospels about the teaching of Jesus regarding the love of money being the root of all evil. "The root of all evil" Christie muttered under his breath.

"What's that lad? I could not hear you." Francis asked.

"Nothing pa … nothing at all," Christie replied and the two of them rode slowly and silently toward their fields. The sun was quickly rising in the east. It was going to be a very warm day.

And on that very day, at that very moment, hundreds of miles away in the court of Charles I, King of all Britain, Mary Irvine's prophecy became fulfilled. Developments at the court were heading towards an inevitable course of violent bloodshed for the Presbyterians of Ulster and their native Scotland. For on that day, Charles appointed William Laud as Archbishop of Canterbury.

Chapter Eight – Parish of Hinckley, Leicestershire, England circa 1633

"And so, in conclusion my brothers and sisters, I read you the words of St. Paul … *The law is good, then. The trouble is not with the law but with me, because I am sold into slavery, with sin as my master. I don't understand myself at all, for I really want to do what is right, but I don't do it. Instead, I do the very thing I hate. I know perfectly well that what I am doing is wrong, and my bad conscience shows that I agree that the law is good. But I can't help myself, because it is sin inside me that makes me do these evil things. I know that I am rotten through and through so far as my old sinful nature is concerned. No matter which way I turn, I can't make myself do right. I want to, but I can't. When I want to do good, I don't. And when I try not to do wrong, I do it anyway. But if I am doing what I don't want to do, I am not really the one doing it; the sin within me is doing it. It seems to be a fact of life that when I want to do what is right, I inevitably do what is wrong. I love God's law with all my heart. But there is another law at work within me that is at war with my mind. This law wins the fight and makes me a slave to the sin that is still within me. Oh, what a miserable person I am! Who will free me from this life that is dominated by sin? Thank God! The answer is in Jesus Christ our Lord* ... go now in peace my brother and sisters. In the name of the Father, the Son and the Holy Ghost, Amen" And with those concluding remarks, Thomas Cleveland, the Vicar of Hinckley made the sign of the cross and dismissed his congregation.

Thomas saw his brother John standing at the back of the church. He had entered late after the service had already begun. Thomas knew he was coming from his home in King's Stanley, Gloucester. John had sent a letter and had paid a rather expensive postage to have it mailed upon King Charles's royal mail coach as it travelled from the western parts of the kingdom to London. And Thomas knew what was in the letter for he had read it immediately. He had not seen John since the incident with their father William and that had happened years ago. They had briefly kept in touch with one another at first even though their father William had forbid it. But over the years, the correspondence had dwindled away. It had been at least seven or eight years since any contact between the two. He knew John had married and had at least two children one of whom died shortly after birth … a girl, I think it was he thought to himself. And then last week, on Tuesday, the day after the royal mail coach had stopped in Leicester, a young lad had brought him his brother's letter addressed to the Reverend Thomas Cleveland, Vicar of Hinckley parish. He had paid the boy a little money for his troubles and then stepped into his poorly lit office where he began to read. The words he read had troubled him and brought tears to his eyes. John's wife, Elizabeth, had suddenly died. No one was sure of the cause. The local physician in the small town of King's Stanley had simply said her heart stopped working and that was the end of the matter. That had happened over six months ago and John had been trying to cope but apparently not doing so well. After John had left their childhood home in Leicester, he had looked to apprentice himself in the Gloucester wool trade. He had found someone who took him on, a trader by the name of Williams, who had connections in Bristol and London. And he eventually learned the business of trading wool on the London, Paris and Amsterdam markets. But all was not peaceful in John Cleveland's life. He had met a girl in Leicester a pretty young lass by the name of Elizabeth Martin. They had fallen in love and had engaged to be married. But there was a problem. Elizabeth was from a non-conformist family. In other words, they were not Anglican. They were not Catholic that was a relief to be sure to their father, William Cleveland, who had left his boyhood home of Ipswich due to a falling out he had with his parish priest over the direction the English Reformation had taken. William was indeed, a supporter of the movement. He had been baptized a Catholic during the reign of Queen Elizabeth but had converted to the Church of England when James Stewart came to the throne. William was a strong supporter of James. In his eyes, he could do no wrong. Thus, he was in these times considered a strong royalist. And he expected his sons and daughters to follow suit. And all did with one exception, John. John never was really a very religious man nor did he care much for politics. Thomas remembered his younger brother as a simple boy who loved to laugh and play games. He remembered his father often shaking his head and saying under his breath, "that boy will never amount to anything … he's lazy". Thomas did not know if John ever heard what his father said about him but he surely must have known that he was not the favorite son. That distinction fell to him, Thomas Cleveland, the eldest son of William and Mary Cleveland. And William took every step possible to give his son an opportunity to advance in his station. He even somehow found the money necessary to send his son to Cambridge. "And I did go to Cambridge, and did rather well. Earning a Master of Arts and eventually became ordained." Thomas thought to himself as he walked up to his long-lost brother.

"John, my God, man, how long has it been? I was shocked to receive your correspondence. I'm terribly sorry to hear about Lizzie. I pray she did not suffer?" Thomas shook the extended hand of his brother and then both quickly dropped their hands to their sides.

"No, Thomas," John replied, "she did not suffer. She died quickly … in her sleep. The night before I kissed her cheek and told her I loved her and… the next morning …. She was gone. Just like that …gone." John looked down at the dusty floor of the small parish church in Hinckley. Although Leicestershire had prospered in the past couple of decades, this part of the county seemed to lag behind. This was a poor parish and John knew his brother was dissatisfied. "How could he not be," John thought to himself. "The poor boy was put under such pressure by our father to succeed. Scraped together every penny the old man had to send him off to Cambridge and where does he end up … in poor little Hinckley parish serving maybe 100 people at the most and that on Easter if they all came to service. How is this man surviving? And how, in God's name did he come up with the funds to educate his oldest son, John at Cambridge?" John looked up at his elder brother. Except for the years that separated them, the two could have passed as twins. Both had dark thick hair, blue eyes and thin lips. Thomas was ten years his senior but John looked as old if not older. The past years had been hard on him. The wool business had suffered with the uniting of the countries of Wales, Ireland, Scotland and England with the kingship of James the VI of Scotland who became James I of the developing empire of Britain. It meant a larger supply of high quality wool and the demand had not risen as expected. Thus prices had fallen and everyone in the wool trading business had suffered including John Cleveland. And then his wife had died unexpectedly. But that was the way it was in England at this time. Death was always just around the corner and it came swiftly and often silently to the least suspecting. In fact, at this very moment, an outbreak of plague was devastating Wales and the southwestern shires of England. Everyone was praying it would not come east and north. But they all understood that should it arrive it would decimate the population.

"I read your letter John. I must admit, I was moved to tears but I'm not sure if I can honor your request." Thomas gazed away as if he were embarrassed by what he had just said for, in truth, he was. John had asked him to help him secure an apprenticeship in Leicester for his only surviving child, a young man of thirteen called Alexander. No one knew why he was called that. By custom, he should have been called either William or Robert, the names of his two grandfathers. But when he was born his mother decided to name him Alexander. When John questioned his wife as she held the newborn son in her arms, she had only responded with a smile and said, "tis a noble name for a fine young baby boy". So that became his name. His parents would often refer to him as Alex when at home but everyone outside the family including Alex himself addressed him as Alexander.

He was now thirteen years old and the time had come for him to get about the business of doing something with his life. He knew he did not want to follow his father into the wool trading business. Alexander loved the sheep but not the business associated with the bartering of their wool. In fact, he loved the farm. He enjoyed working in the fields, tending to the farm animals and watching the sun rise and fall over the hills of Gloucester. He was a smart young lad but no intellectual. Life to him was rather simple. You slept. You woke up. You worked and ate. And then the next day you repeated the process. And occasionally, you read the Bible and went to the service. Reading the Bible was a major requirement in the household of John and Lizzie Cleveland. Not so much because of John's religious nature but due to Lizzie's firm hand on the spiritual development of her little family, for Lizzie Cleveland was a secret follower of John Smyth, an English Baptist, who had fled the country in 1616 to seek religious and political refuge in Amsterdam. And that was the issue that had arisen between her and her father-in-law. William Cleveland believed in the King's right to rule and his right to determine the faith of the people. And in William's eyes there could be only one true church and that was the Church of England. He had little tolerance for the Scots Presbyterians and despised all others, including the Puritans, Catholics and, in particular, the Baptists or Anabaptists as they were called on the Continent. So, when John had announced his attention to marry Lizzie, William had nearly had a stroke. The words became heated and eventually William demanded his son leave his household and take his non-conforming bound for damnation and hellfire woman with him. And those were the last words William ever spoke to his son. A few years ago, William did indeed have a stroke. He survived but never regained the ability of speech. Currently his only form of communication is a series of grunts and gesticulations. He had even lost the ability to write although he for some reason had retained the ability to read and that is how he spent his days in the small house of his son, the Vicar, reading everything he could get his hands upon. One day, in an attempt to heal the rift between father and son, Thomas had silently left a tract of Smyth's explaining the Baptist position. Thomas watched aghast as William came upon and quickly through it in the fire before him reading the first word. That was the last time Thomas attempted in peace making.

"Thomas, I would not be here with my hat in my hands if the situation was not dire. The boy needs a future. I've no money to educate him nor does he have the inclination. But he has a strong body and works hard at those things he enjoys doing." John looked over his should at his young son who right at that moment had fallen asleep sitting upright in the back pew of the church. "God, how he looks like his mother, such a handsome boy," John thought to himself.

"But John, what do you expect me to do with him? This parish is small and we have no need of a young lad to work the grounds." Thomas explained as gently as he could but with a firm tone in his voice.

"It's not here I was thinking about," John replied.

"Well, pray tell, what then, what do you want me to do with him?" Thomas asked.

"I want you to get him connected with those who have influence in this county. And you know who these people are. You and father, before his stroke, would hobnob at the holidays with all the rich and powerful upper crust. I know you, Thomas Cleveland. You might come across as a simple country parson but you've got big plans for this family. That's why you sent your son, John to Cambridge. By the way, I hear he is making quite a name for himself … as a poet, of all things." John smiled at his brother. Although he often wondered why he did not come to Lizzie's aid when their father drove them out of the community, he still loved his older brother and truly hoped he could help his son.

"How is the old man?" John asked.

"'Bout the same … just sits all day reading every paper and book he comes across and occasionally grunts at us to fetch him something … Not much of a life, heh?" Thomas responded.

"Do you think he would see me? Do you think he would see his grandson? John asked as tears formed in the corner of his eyes

"I don't know, John. I really don't know. You know how set in his ways he is. A few years ago, I tried to get him to at least read something Smyth had written about you Baptists but he just angrily threw it in the fire and that was the last time I tried," Thomas looked at the floor ashamed of himself. He was a vicar, a man of God, and he could not patch up this fissure between his own father and brother. What would God say to him when he stood before him on Judgment Day?

"I've rented a room in town for Alex and me. As you can see, he's worn out by the trip here. We had to walk most of the way," John stated as a matter of fact.

"Walked! My God, John, that's over ninety miles," Thomas exclaimed.

"I've no money for a coach Thomas. Times are hard right now. That's why I'm here. You think I want to see my boy go off and work for some rich stranger doing God knowns what! I'm desperate brother. I need your help. I don't know where else to turn." John looked away trying to keep the tears from flowing down his face into his bushy beard.

Thomas looked at John and then looked at his still dozing son. He thought to himself, "looks so much like his mother. It is uncanny." And then Thomas made a decision, one that he might later regret but one that ultimately changed the course of the lives of all three.

"John … you and Alex are coming home with me. It might kill the old man but I'm not leaving you two begging on the streets. You are family. And you are my family. Welcome home brother." And with that the two brothers hugged and the tears began to freely flow.

John and Alexander waited outside the small parish church as Thomas gathered his things and locked the front door. It was a habit he had recently begun out of necessity. Times were difficult everywhere and even churches had been broken into where desperate men would take whatever might be sold on the black-market? Thomas hated locking the doors of the church and he wondered why he was doing it … there was not much to steal. But it was his sense of justice that motivated the behavior. This was a sacred place in his mind and one that should always be open to the public. However, with the rapid decline in the local economy and with it the apparent morality of the locals, he was bound and determined to protect as best he could this humble house of God. So he began to lock the doors whenever he was away.

It was a short walk to the parsonage. It wasn't much to look at from the outside but Thomas's wife and daughters had turned the inside into a clean and well maintained abode for him, his disabled father and the rest of the small family. This family had known heartache.

Thomas and his wife had lost two young children and his wife had miscarried two other times but God had blessed them with a number of children who had survived and his oldest, John, was doing quite well in his academic pursuits. John had earned a BA at Cambridge in 1631 and was now enrolled at St. John's College where he was studying theology, law and physics aspiring to attain the Master in Arts degree.

Thomas saw his father sitting beside the fireplace trying to stay warm though the weather outside was actually rather pleasant. He called to the old man who at first did not appear to hear him and then slowly turned to look. William Cleveland's eyes opened wide as he gazed at his son John and the other younger man who he did not recognize. William could not speak, of course, but his physical response was easily assessed. At first, his face registered shock. Then he appeared to calm himself down and the tears began to flow down his cheeks. He motioned with his left arm and hand for John to come close to him. William extended his left hand and John gently took it into both his hands and humbly bowed his head in the presence of his father. Tears were now flowing down the cheeks of all that were gathered in that little parsonage. For without a word being uttered, the rift between father and son had disappeared and the two hugged each other in silence. After he was able to regain his composure, John spoke, "Father, I would like to introduce you to my son, Alexander … your grandson." At this moment, Alex stepped forward and extended his right hand grasping the feeble left hand of his grandfather and squeezed it gently. Alex was a strong boy but he knew when to be gentle and he exhibited this gentle side of himself as he met his grandfather for the first time of his life. Through his tear-filled eyes, William appraised the tall young adolescent standing in front of him. Although he could not articulate it, he thought to himself, "My God, he looks just like his mother." He attempted to speak but was only able to offer a slight grunt combined with a mangled smile. There was silence in the room for quite some time and then finally, Thomas spoke.

"Father, John has returned home in hopes of finding work for his son. I told him things were rather difficult right now but that he and Alex could stay with us until something developed."

At this, the old man nodded his head with enthusiasm. He motioned with his left hand for his quill and parchment. He wanted to write something down. Thomas's wife quickly procured the writing instrument and gently placed it in the old man's hand. Although he was right handed, after the stroke, William had forced himself to learn how to write with his left hand and while the quality of his penmanship was poor it was legible at least most of the time. William focused his attention and scribbled two names on the parchment ... Herrick and Skipwith and then handed the paper to his son, Thomas. Thomas picked up the parchment and read the names out loud. William nodded in affirmation.

John was puzzled and of course, Alex, being thirteen years old, was bored. Alex loved the outdoors and did not enjoy remaining for too long inside any building in particular this small and somewhat stuffy parsonage. John asked, "What does Herrick and Skipwith have to do with my son finding a trade?" John knew of these two men or more importantly of their families and standing within the community of Leicester. Both families were wealthy, influential and politically connected to the king and his advisors. Herrick was a rare story. His ancestors were traders in iron and from those humble beginnings his grandfather and father has amassed a small fortune in trading of a number of goods which included a stake in the newly developing fishing off the coast of Newfoundland. In fact, Herrick owned a share in at least three sailing vessels which were used to fish the bountiful waters of the North Atlantic. The fish were salted and shipped back to the southwestern counties of England where the demand for the product was high. The Skipwiths had a long and distinguished family history that dated back to the days of Richard III. In fact, the surviving heir of the Skipwith fortune had just been made a Baron by King Charles. While his father, who was now dead, had Puritans tendencies, Baron Skipwith was a loyal Anglican and devoted to this king. "But," John thought to himself, "What could these two significant members of English society have to do with his young son?"

Thomas knew the answer to the question as soon as he was able to decipher his father's writings. Recently, Herrick and Skipwith had combined forces to use their fishing vessels to transport people to the new world. It was the elder now deceased Skipwith's idea. His allegiance to the throne was not nearly as strong as his allegiance to the Puritan cause and this has caused a degree of tension to develop between himself and the royal house of King James, Charles' father. The Puritans were an interesting group of English Anglicans who had decided the English Reformation had not gone far enough and were concerned about King James' desire to strengthen his control over both secular and religious elements within his kingdom. Over time, the Puritans split into two factions; the one group and by far the largest, wanted to simply continue the reforming process within the English church and were perfectly willing to work alongside and in collaboration with James and his advisors. The other, however, now known as the Separatists, had lost all hope for changing the nature of English rule and religion and had initially sought the refuge of liberal Amsterdam to practice their faith but then quickly saw the new world as an opportunity to advance their cause by establishing an English colony in what was being called New England. Here they would be allowed to worship in accordance with their beliefs and not be disturbed by the King or his supporters. A few years ago, they had established an English colony at a place called Plymouth in New England. And Skipwith had played a role in transporting those early Puritans to their new home. Financially, it made sense. The ships that he and Herrick had invested in were already sailing in those waters and had developed navigable routes from the coast of what was now being called Massachusetts to Bristol in Gloucester. The vessels would leave England laden with the Puritan Separatists, drop them off in New England, fish the waters off the coast of Newfoundland and then return with their bounty of the sea back to Bristol to repeat the process. It was making both men rather wealthy. And then the elder Skipwith died and his oldest son became Lord of the manor. Whereas, the old man was inclined philosophically with the Puritans, the son was quite different. He wanted nothing to do with them but saw their removal to New England as a way of ridding the English church of their presence. So, he accelerated the rate of transportation by reducing the cost of crossing Atlantic passage by increasing the number of runs his ships made during the fishing season thus generating even more revenue for both he and Herrick. Although Herrick personally liked the elder Skipwith, he was not a seriously religious man. His motivation was money pure and simple. In 1633, King Charles, son of the deceased James I, appointed William Laud as the Archbishop of Canterbury and this radically changed the religious and political environment within the mother country. Under the rule of James there had been a certain degree of religious toleration for the Puritans but, with the appointment of Laud all that changed. Laud, with the support of the king, instituted significant changes in the church structure and practice. He made it a personal goal to rid all of the king's dominion of any religious and/or political dissent. And Charles loved him for it. Due to Laud's autocratic strategy to purify the kingdom, tensions were rapidly rising throughout the land. Thomas could almost physically feel the anger and hostility against the crown. He heard it from the members of his parish and through the connections his father had established over the years. And to complicate matters, Charles desperately needed more funds. His empire was growing but it was in competition with the stronger empires of Europe, in particular, Spain, France and the Dutch. In addition, the relationship between crown and parliament was rapidly deteriorating. As his father before him, Charles felt strongly in the divine right of kings to rule according to his own conscience. In fact, a few years ago, Charles had disbanded parliament and sent the members home. He now ruled England without the aid and consent of the men who initially had been his strong supporters. He had implemented a new tax structure that many felt was unjust and excessive. He had married a Catholic and had failed to support the Protestant cause in the Thirty Years war that had, in particular, created chaos and devastation within the small feudal states of the German people. This failure to act had caused many radical Puritans and staunch Presbyterians to become quite alarmed. Thomas did not know how this was going to end but the future looked grim at the moment.

Just then, the old man William reached out for the parchment and quill once again. John handed it to him and he once again scribbled down a single word … Virginia. John picked up the parchment and read the word Virginia out loud. He looked at his brother with great puzzlement. "What could this mean?" he asked Thomas who quickly came to the conclusion that his father wanted him to convince his brother to send his only son, a thirteen-year-old boy, to the new English colony of Virginia.

Thomas spoke out loud, "Father wants Alexander to go to Virginia." He turned and looked at John and then at his young son. He could tell it simply wasn't registering what the old man was suggesting.

The Virginia colony had recently discovered how to successfully raise tobacco. When it was first brought to England in the early 1600s, no one knew what to do with it. But that quickly changed and now tobacco was in high demand not only in England but on the continent as well. But life in Virginia was brutal. The climate was exceedingly challenging to the English who were used to a much milder weather. And the natives while initially friendly had decided the English were not to be trusted and had begun to violently and repetitively attack their small English landholdings. Life spans were short for the few English who managed to survive the trip across the ocean thus there was a constant need for more people to live and work the growing plantations. So, Herrick had recently begun to ship the English to Virginia and then return to Bristol with tobacco instead of salted fish from Newfoundland. The money continued to flow into his hands and by now he was one of the wealthiest men in the county.

Thomas looked at his brother, John, and spoke slowly and clearly, "I think what our father is saying is to send your son to the English colony of Virginia." Thomas waited for that idea to sink into the mind of his brother so that he might fully comprehend the implications.

"What!" John exclaimed. "He's too young. He won't survive the voyage and even if he did how would he stay alive once he arrived. Where would he sleep? Who would feed and care for him? No! Absolutely not! Surely, there must be another option?" John said emphatically while shaking his head.

Alexander had stepped back from the three older men and was looking out the window. He was listening to the conversation but his thoughts were directed to the sight outside. He was looking at a beautiful and large garden full of flowers and vegetables with tall majestic trees lining the area. He loved the land. As long as he could remember, he and his mother had always been outdoors, rain or shine, working in their small plot of land trying to grow enough food upon which to survive. Alex could remember his mother singing hymns and telling him the great Bible stories while the two of them spent hours at work. Of course, his younger sister was there until one day she suddenly died of the fever. That had deeply saddened him. He had loved her just as he had loved his mother. And now both were gone. Some of what was transpiring between his father, grandfather and Uncle he heard and understood. They were going to send him to a place called Virginia and it would involve getting on a ship. That part seemed exciting to him. But then he thought to himself, *where is this place, Virginia? How long will I have to stay there before I can come back home to King Stanley? Will papa be going with me?*

Because William could not carry on the conversation, Thomas intervened and began to explain the situation to his brother.

"John, listen to me. The economy is in sad shape. There is no work here in Leicester. People everywhere are on the move looking for work. John, people are starving to death. And to make matters worse, the king's indifference and inaction has alienated many of those with means who might be able to help him navigate these rough waters. Now, he has appointed this Laud fellow as Archbishop. You remember he started out in Gloucester where you are from and the people there despised him. Now, for the love of God, he's the Archbishop of the Church of England! John … I'm afraid we are headed towards civil war. There is no future here for Alexander. You will have to indenture him to some wealthy family with holdings in Virginia. They will pay for his passage and feed and care for him when he arrives in exchange for seven years of labor."

John began to shake his head but Thomas continued, "He'll learn a trade John. He'll grow up in a place where he will have so much more opportunity for advancement then he ever would if he stayed here. Even if he travelled to London, there would be no guarantee of success. He would end up a beggar or be forced to lead a life of crime for survival. Is that what you want for him John? Is it?" Thomas looked into the eyes of his brother and saw all the sadness and heartache he had been carrying for so long. It broke his heart but he knew this was the only reasonable solution. If he had the money, he would have somehow found a way to keep father and son together but as he had said, the times were harsh and he barely had enough to keep a roof over his own family much less take on two more mouths to feed.

John grew quiet. He had wiped a few tears away from his eyes. Finally, he spoke while looking at both his father and brother, "you two must understand. Alexander is all I have left. If I put him on that ship to Virginia. It will mean I will never see him again. I don't think I could survive that …" And then the tears returned and ran down his face into his shaggy and unkempt beard. "My only son … that's what you are asking of me God … my only son" John said in a hushed tone to no one in particular. In an instant he realized that his father was right. The only future for Alexander and many other poor Englishmen lay across the ocean in a strange and mysterious place called Virginia.

He turned to his son who was now looking back at him. Alexander did not like to see his papa cry. But tears and pain had become a part of his life and somehow through some power he had but knew not the source he spoke to his beloved father with tenderness and wisdom beyond his years, "Papa, Grandfather Cleveland is right. My destiny lies in Virginia. I will give the next seven years of my life to whomever will take me on … and then I will return home to you and take care of you as you have taken care of me." With that pronouncement, everyone gathered together in that small humble parsonage knew the decision had been made. Alexander Cleveland was bound for the Chesapeake colony of Virginia. None knew how this was to happen but all knew it would happen. It had to. There were no other options.

Thomas finally broke the silence. "I will speak with Lord Herrick this week and make the necessary arrangements. He's not a bad man. His heart is good. And more importantly, I trust him. He will guide us in these matters. Until then, John, you and Alexander will stay here with us."

He spoke to his wife who quickly fled to her kitchen trying unsuccessfully to hold back the tears. She thought to herself, "God, go with this young lad. Guide him and keep him safe from all evil."

The arrangements were swiftly made. With the growing trade in tobacco, Herrick's fleet had grown and his business was strong. King Charles was taxing heavily all the shipping in and out of the colonies but there was still plenty of money to be made. Families with means were buying land in Virginia on speculation and sending hundreds of indentured servants to work their prosperous fields. New settlements had developed up and down the western coast of the Chesapeake. It had started in Jamestown but now there were at least eight separate and distinct shires in the colony. They were huddled close together but were quickly spreading out into the surrounding farmland as the demand for the tobacco crop grew steadily. It had been decided and contracted that Alexander would be indentured to a family from Devonshire by the name of Armistead. Specifically, Sir William Armistead, Lord of Axminster would be Alexander's master. The Armisteads were a fairly well to do family with ancient origins in the West Riding of Yorkshire. But of late, through the hard work of his grandfather, Roger and then of his father Anthony, their estate in Devon had grown to a point of substantial wealth and influence. As was often the case, Sir William was a third-born son and thus, due to English law could not inherit his family's estate. Approximately 25% of the Virginia colonies English inhabitants would have origins similar to Sir William. Latter born sons who had to find different means to accumulate wealth. On his behalf, the family had purchased from the greedy King's ministers a parcel of land in the shire known as Elizabeth City and he was soon leaving to start the construction of an appropriate dwelling and farm buildings to support the growing of tobacco. Soon these places came to be called plantations. The other 75% of the Virginia colony population were men and a few women whose situation was very similar to Alexander's. A minority was, indeed, convicted criminals but the vast majority were simply strong and healthy young people who had little chance for advancement in English society due to a variety of reasons, primarily, to whom they were born. For Alexander, it was simple. His father was not Thomas Cleveland who could afford to send his son John to Cambridge. His father was John Cleveland who unfortunately fell in love with a beautiful woman that simply held a different religious perspective than the powerful patriarch of the family who had banished them both from his sight. And now, close to death and the judgement seat of the Almighty, he was trying to make things right by leveraging his family's ancient Yorkshire connections to find a place in this world for his grandson.

Alexander had never been on a ship before. In fact, he had never been on any type of water craft in his young life. He stood by the side and gazed down at his father, Aunt and Uncle and his cousins who had come to

Bristol to see him off. Grandfather Cleveland had taken a turn for the worse and was not able to make the trip but he had given Alexander something just before he left. It was a piece of parchment upon which William had scrawled the Latin phrase... por Deo et Patrio ... for God and Country. William had hoped his grandson would keep this writing with him at all times and to read it when he wavered in his confidence or faith. William hoped his grandson understood that this was the real reason why he was going to Virginia ... for God and Country ... and to never forget it. William was highly frustrated that he could not speak his thoughts directly to Alexander and hoped that he would someday understand how proud he was of him. William felt deeply that Alexander and the many young English men and women who were setting sail for the colonies were doing their part to help expand the Empire of the Commonwealth of England, Scotland, Ireland and Wales. In the old and feeble body of William Cleveland was a strong and vibrant mind and in this mind was the firm thought that Alexander Cleveland was serving his God, king and country.

Alexander waved at his family as the ship left the dock. He had promised himself that he would not cry. He would be strong like his father who stood on the wooden docks and gave a slight wave of his hand and nod of his head and then quickly turned and walked away. John Cleveland did not want his son to see the tears that had formed and were freely falling onto his cheeks. This was too much for him to bear. In his life he had suffered. He had lost wife, daughter and now son. He knew that even though he had told Alexander they would meet again, it was a lie, and he knew it even as he was saying it to his son. For John was slowly dying. The cough and started on the trip from King Stanley. And shortly after their arrival at Hinckley, the intermittent fever had begun. He had been fairly successful in hiding it from his family but he knew his days were numbered. The same thing had happened to his daughter and then to his wife. John waited until he was sure his son could no longer make him out in the crowd of well- wishers who had assembled at the dockside. He then turned and watched the ship as it slowly made its way out of the harbor and headed out to sea. John looked up into the heavens. For a moment, he thought he saw the smiling face of his beloved Lizzie. She was smiling and crying at the same time. He spoke to her, "I tried my love. I tried to keep him safe and sound. God knows how I tried but … there he goes. Now it is up to you and the angels. Watch over him. Keep him from evil." John then quickly looked out to sea. By now the ship was a small dot on the far horizon. Most of the people milling about had left the dock but John walked up to the edge of the side. He wanted to get as close to the water as he could. And then John shouted out with all his might … "I love you Alexander Cleveland … never forget that … I love you." Then John turned and slowly made his way back to the inn where his brother and sister in law waited patiently for him.

Alex stood on the side of the ship for a long time. He was deep in thought. Finally, a firm male voice spoke behind him, "Well, Alexander, are you ready for this great adventure?" Alex looked and saw Sir William Armistead standing behind him. Armistead had been born in 1610 and was ten years older than Alex. He was a young man himself but carried himself with the dignity and sophistication of the aristocratic class to which he had been born. He was dressed in fine and expensive clothing, not like the other men who at the moment were quite busy with the tasks of sailing this vessel safely across the Atlantic. There were approximately 100 souls on board. A small crew of fifteen including the Captain plus a few wealthy Virginia land speculators like Sir William. The vast majority of the passengers were indentured servants. It was highly unusual to be traveling with your master. Usually they simply purchased vast tracts of Virginia land and sent their servants under the direction of the taskmaster to establish and run it. Alex understood this as he looked around at his fellow passengers. Most were young men with a social status similar to his. Here and there were a few young women who most likely would be put to work in the kitchens and laundries of the landed gentry. The boys would work the farms and learn various trades associated with making a tobacco plantation a successful financial investment. What they did not know at the time was that a few of them would become ill and die quickly upon arrival and the rest would live short and brutal lives in a wilderness setting while their masters became exceedingly rich from the labor of their hands. There was one Anglican priest on board. His name was Samuel Johnson. He appeared to be about the same age as Sir William but he did not carry himself with the same noble bearing and air of importance. In fact, to Alexander, he seemed weary and worn out for a man so young. At the moment, he was standing next to Sir William and the contrast between the two was quite noticeable.

"Yes, Sir William, I am ready for whatever he future may bring," Alexander answered his master. "You look sad Alex," said Armistead in reply. "Be of good cheer. Your Uncle has done well for you by bringing you to the attention of my father and elder brother. They are financing this expedition, of course. But we will essentially be on our own once we arrive on the shores of Virginia. And I have full confidence in you and the rest of our lot that we will make a great success in the new world. Who knows, maybe someday, you'll make enough money to send for your family?"

"Yes, Sir William, that's what I pray for … to be able to see my papa once again … of course, that is after I have worked off my indenture to your house." Alexander said as manly as he could for being so young. Sir William laughed and then turned and headed for the other aristocrats who were gathering together at the far end of the ship.

"So, lad," Parson Johnson spoke to Alexander, "what crime have you committed that would cause your being placed on this ship to hell?" Johnson seemed depressed to Alexander and indeed, he was. What Alexander did not know about Samuel Johnson was the fact that he had been a priest without a church for some time now. It seemed innocent enough to Samuel at first as he had begun to initially question in private and then speak in public about his doubts regarding the Church's teachings and, in particular, the influence the King had over it. Johnson was not a Presbyterian nor was he an Anglican Puritan. But as his homilies became more controversial he became noticed, and not in a good way, by his church superiors. Eventually he was called to task for his statements and in failing to recant and renounce his developing beliefs; he was "assigned" to be a parish priest for the brand-new parish of Elizabeth City, Virginia. He was devastated by this action and his family mourned him as if he had died. And, to Samuel Johnson, being sent to Virginia was like dying. But he had decided this was ultimately God's will and he would make the best of it. As he looked around the ship he suddenly realized "all of us are literally and figuratively in the same boat". In all honesty, there wasn't a single person on this craft, with the possible exception of the ship's captain and some of his crew, that really wanted to be here sailing for this strange new land. Everyone was either running from something, like the British form of criminal justice for some, or sheer abject poverty, for young men and women like Alexander or, they were running toward something, like Sir William, born into an upper crust English family but with the misfortune of not being the first born male child. "Yep," Samuel spoke out loud to know one in particular, "we are all in the same boat". And then he burst out laughing.

Alexander asked him, "What is so funny?"

"Oh, dry your tears lad. Crying will do nothing for you and the older boys will poke fun at you all the way to dry land." Samuel responded.

Alexander wiped his eyes once again for what seemed like the hundredth time. He missed his papa so much so it physically hurt and the tears just came upon him often unexpectedly. But he knew that Samuel was right. If he were to survive, he would have to be strong, on the inside as well as the outside. So, he made up his mind right then and there that Alexander Cleveland would survive. He would survive this trip across the sea. He would survive whatever the colony of Virginia had in store for him. He would survive the next seven years of indentured servitude to the Armisteads. He would survive.

The hours turned into days. The days turned into weeks. Alexander and Sir William developed a polite but distant relationship. Even in these tight quarters, everyone remembered their station in life and it would not have been socially acceptable for the Master and servant to fraternize. However, as the ship sailed slowly towards the new land of Virginia, Alexander did develop a friendly and fairly close relationship with the Reverend Samuel. One bright sunny morning as the ship rolled from side to side due to the immense waves generated by the strong winds, Alexander spotted his new friend kneeling at prayer. After he was finished, he stood up and pulled out a Bible where he began to read. Alexander walked up to him and asked nonchalantly, "what are you reading Samuel?"

Samuel looked at his young friend and started to read out loud, "Do not be afraid, for I have ransomed you. I have called you by name; you are mine. When you go through deep waters and great trouble, I will be with you. When you go through rivers of difficulty, you will not drown! When you walk through the fire of oppression, you will not be burned up: the flames will not consume you. For I am the Lord your God, the Holy One of Israel, your Savior." Samuel closed his Bible and turned toward Alexander with a smile on his face. "What do you think about that, my young friend? Words of comfort, heh? At least, they bring me comfort in this vast wasteland of water. My God, how I long to stand upon the good Earth once again. I'm so tired of this constant bouncing about."

Alexander smiled at Samuel. "Yes, they are good words. From where in the Scriptures did you read?"

"The forty-third chapter of Isaiah," Samuel answered.

"Samuel, I have a question for you," Alexander asked in a deeply serious fashion which was rather unusual for him. He was not one given to deep theological discussions but Samuel could tell something was pressing on his mind.

"Go ahead, Alex, what's your question?" Samuel replied.

"My mother called herself a Baptist. My father stayed true to his Anglican baptism but really never practiced his faith. He didn't attend services and he often grumbled about the taxes and other monies the local parish church demanded of him and his fellow traders. Papa complained constantly. But mama never said an evil word about anyone for as long as I can remember back into my early days as a child. But she would get all worked up when he and papa would discuss the King and dealings with the Church of England. She called him a papist and said he would be the ruin of our country. I never could quite understand what all the fuss was about. It seemed to me that God is God and however you pray to Him, He will listen. And I never understood mama's insistence on baptizing only those who could confess with their own mouths their belief in Jesus as the Christ, the Son of God and Savior of the world. Samuel ... what is this all about and why do people get so riled up about religion anyway?"

"Goodness, Alexander, it is a wonder your head did not explode from all that thinking." And then Samuel laughed deeply and fully. He kept laughing so much that eventually he had Alexander laughing with him. Right about then, Sir William appeared and pointedly asked the two, "What's so funny? Tell me, I'm in need of some humor to lift my spirits. I must tell you, I'm sick and tired of being stuck on this ship. I swear I will never again leave land once I return to it."

Samuel replied, "Sir, young Mr. Cleveland here had a question about religion"

"Is that so," replied Armistead. "And I hope you set him straight. There is but one true faith and that is the Church of England with both King and the King's appointed Archbishop at its head."

Samuel turned to Alexander and said, "you see Alex, for some people, it's rather simple … but for others, like your mama, it's a bit more complicated." And then he winked at Alexander who smiled in return.

Armistead moved on and the Reverend Johnson spoke once again to Alexander. "The issue at its fundamental core is all about authority. Yes, that's it in a nutshell. Before Luther came along, no one dared questioned the authority of the Pope. People might have grumbled about what was happening at their local parish church with their incompetent priest but no one questioned the Pope as the head of the universal church. That's actually what the word catholic really means … universal. But after Luther … well my boy, things changed. Luther, whether he realized it or not at the time, put the whole question of authority front and center. His often-used Latin phrase, sole scriptura, became the rallying cry for religious dissidents throughout all the empires of Europe. Now, according to Luther and all those who followed in his reforming footsteps, anyone could read the Bible for themselves and make up their own minds as to what it says and, perhaps more importantly, what does it mean. Who needs a pope? In a way, we are all now "popes" according to the more radical elements. I wonder if Luther ever fully thought out the far-reaching implications of what his actions would start within Christendom."

"Mama said he didn't go far enough … and I guess that's why she became a Baptist … but we were never supposed to tell anyone that … it was our family secret. Mama and papa and me and my little sister would attend the service at our local Anglican parish church... to be counted like sheep papa always grumbled … but then afterwards, mama and sometimes papa would sneak off into the countryside and listen to a Baptist preacher drone on for hours about what must you do to be saved from the fires of hell." Alexander stopped suddenly. He was remembering those times and it brought a deep sadness to his soul. He missed his mother and father and even his little sister so much. He usually tried to think about something else whenever a memory would escape from somewhere deep inside and bubble up to the surface of his awareness. A single tear formed in his eye and dropped onto his smooth beardless cheek.

"I can see this conversation is troubling you son. Let's move on to a better subject shall we?" And with that statement, Samuel brought Alexander out of the past and into the present.

Just then, they all heard the shout of a man's voice … Land Ho … Land Ho. Everyone rushed to the starboard side of the ship and peered out into the horizon. The spotter was in the crow's nest high above the main deck and had seen land. And then suddenly as if by magic, there it was before them. Land! A cannon roared out its welcome from somewhere on the shore. And the ship's captain ordered a saluting blast in response. The flag of England flew over the encampment. Word quickly traveled through the ship …they were looking at Virginia. They had made it. This was their new home.

Life in Virginia proved to be very difficult for Alexander and the rest of the ship's passengers. The hot and humid summers and cold wet winters was a drastic change from the mild English climate of their origins. Disease was rampant. While there was plenty of wild game and fish to eat. Going hunting meant you would be traveling in territory filled with the natives who were unpredictable at best. It seemed to Alexander that the least offence set them "on the warpath" and violence would often break out between colonists and native. But just as suddenly as the enmity had erupted it would cool and things would return to a quasi-peaceful state between these two quite different groups of humanity, although many of the English settlers refused to consider the natives as truly human, often referring to them in various derogatory ways such as "Injun savages" or worse. By the time Alexander had reached his eighteenth birthday, over half of the original passengers on his ship had died from various causes. Even his friend, the Reverend Johnson had been killed by a tomahawk thrown in anger by one of the natives. This had once again set off a small-scale war that only ended after numerous men on both sides had lost their lives or been severely injured. And the work never ended. And it was indeed hot sweaty back breaking work attempting to turn the less then fertile soil of the Virginia coastline into a profitable tobacco plantation. Alexander worked in the fields from sun up to sun down. He was well kept. The food was ample and steady and Sundays were a day of rest. But even then he was expected to tend to the animals and mend tools as he waited for the next week to commence.

The Armistead plantation grew in size and profitability. It seemed as if Mother England could not get enough of the tobacco plant. And so each year, Sir Armistead increased his land holdings and planted more tobacco plants thus increasing the workload on Alexander and his fellow indentured servants.

But Alexander had a real talent. He was skilled in handling the farm animals. He seemed to be able to know exactly what to do with each of them to gain the most effective output from them. He also appeared to have a knack at healing them should they become lame or otherwise infirmed. Eventually, other plantation owners heard of his expertise and would often send for him to help them with their own creatures. Alexander also knew how to farm. He loved working in the soil and getting his hands full of dirt and dust. Sir Armistead often bragged to his friends of Alexander's ability to make tobacco grow "out of a rock, if need be". He and his master got along most days. Occasionally they would butt heads, usually about how to do a task related to the care of the plantation but, the tension between the two would quickly pass, and peace would return to the little household.

The one thing that had changed in the past five years was the marriage of Sir William. Women were a rare and precious commodity in the English colony of Virginia. In the early days of the colonization process, it had been primarily men sent to the new world. But soon everyone saw the need for women to arrive to help populate the land with brand new English bred Virginians. And so they came from the ports at Bristol and London. Many were poor and had their passage paid by the men who expected to claim a bride when they stepped off their arriving ships. Many were indentured to work as house servants in the big houses of the planters. And a few, like Anne, the new wife of Sir William

Armistead had come from a West Riding Yorkshire family of means. It had been an arranged marriage put together in England by the two original families and after some correspondence the union had been agreed upon by both parties and Anne had set sail for Elizabeth City and the Armistead plantation. But she did not travel alone. Alexander was quite surprised when Anne arrived at the plantation one early spring morning accompanied by Sir William's youngest sister, Lucy Armistead, whom everyone called Fanny although not Alexander, of course. He simply called her Lady Armistead and felt she was the most beautiful thing he had ever seen in his entire lifetime. In reality, Lucy was not a beautiful woman. She was short and on the plump side with a pear-shaped body plus her teeth looked as if someone had just thrown them into her mouth with little regard for placement. It was for this reason she often subconsciously covered her mouth when she smiled or laughed out loud. She was quite self-conscious regarding her appearance. But as Alexander was to discover, Lucy had a heart of gold and was perhaps the kindest person England had so far sent to the shores of the new world. Lucy was only sixteen years old but she and her soon to become sister-in-law had become inseparable and the decision was made by the patriarchal heads of both families that Anne should not travel the high seas alone and, if the truth be told, Lucy did not have much of a future in England. What few outside the Armistead family knew was Lucy had been betrothed a year earlier at the young age of 15 but the engagement had been broken off by her father when it was determined that her suitor was essentially a man without means of support He was seeking to increase his station in life by "marrying up" as they say... And to make matters worse, he had strong Puritan tendencies in his religious views. This did not go over well with the Armisteads, staunch supporters of King Charles and the Anglican Church.

Sir William and Anne were quickly married by the Reverend William Wilkerson, the Rector of St. John's Anglican Church in Elizabeth City Parish. Wilkerson had been sent by the bishops in England to take the place of the deceased Johnson. Wilkerson did not like Alexander and the feeling was mutual. Alexander found him to be arrogant as well as a little ignorant of theological matters. The few times he had tried to engage him in conversation regarding some religious topic, Wilkerson had seemed rather bored and quickly changed the subject to one of his two favorite topics, loyalty to King Charles or horse racing. The man knew a lot about the racing of horses.

The days passed into weeks and life continued on the plantation as it always had. For Alexander that meant lots of work with very little free time. Occasionally, and always on a Sunday afternoon, he would slip off by himself and make his way down to the water's edge. He would turn and face the east. He knew that somewhere in that direction lay England. At times, he missed it so much. He yearned to see his father once again. And if he allowed himself to think much about it, he missed his mama. During these times of solitude at the water's edge, his mind would drift back in time and he would remember the times of laughter they had all shared. And then he would remember the illness and death that soon followed, first of his precious little sister and then his loving mother. At times, he would speak to them all. He told his mama how much he loved her and that he missed her and that he was trying to be good so that he could be reunited with her when it came his time to leave this world. One

Sunday afternoon in the autumn season, Alexander was sitting on a log by the water's edge gazing towards the eastern horizon when he suddenly heard a cough behind him. He grabbed his matchlock gun for he was never far from it and swirled around quickly to do battle with what he suspected was some renegade native out to take his scalp. Much to his surprise, there before him stood Lucy Armistead. The sun was behind her and it made her features difficult to see but he knew immediately it was Lady Armistead. He quickly bowed and politely said, "My lady, you startled me. I could have shot you by mistake! What on earth are you doing out here this far from the plantation?"

Lucy looked down at the ground for a moment and glanced around to make sure they were alone. She then stepped close to the young man, closer than she ever had before, and smiled at him. "Alexander, I've been watching you these past few weeks and I've seen you take off and then return later in the day. It seemed mysterious to me so I just had to find out where you went and what you were doing?" She stated in a matter of fact manner although she could feel her cheeks starting to blush. The truth was she liked the boy. She had from the moment she was introduced to him by her older brother. So, she gathered up her courage and decided to follow him after the service was concluded at St. John's.

Alexander looked stern. "My lady, you should not have followed me here unaccompanied. There are still native savages about and the woods are filled with wild creatures. It's not safe."

"You are angry with me Alexander?" Lucy asked flirtatiously.

Alexander did not know how to respond. No, he was not angry. He could never be truly angry with her. "I … was worried about your well-being, my lady." He managed to stammer this out with some degree of difficulty.

Lucy threw her hands up into the air, "Would you please quit calling me my lady. Lucy will be fine or better yet, just call me Fanny like everyone else in the family does" And then she smiled at him and her eyes seemed to sparkle in the setting sunlight. Alexander felt as if he had been struck with lightening. It wasn't just the change in address from the formal to informal; it was the way she looked at him now and the sound of her sweet girlish voice and the sparkle in her eyes. He wanted to grab her into his arms and tell her how much she was on his mind, but he dare not be so forward. Her brother would have him shot or at least branded and sent off to fend for himself in the wilderness. He began to stammer once again.

"Oh Alex … may I call you Alex" Lucy asked and then with a quiet voice after he nodded his affirmation of her new name for him, "we are not in England anymore. This is a new world and we are building it the way we want it to be. You and I are the future of this new world. We can take from the old the customs and traditions that we want to maintain and discard the rest. For me, I want freedom that I never had as a woman in England. What do you want Alex from this new world?"

Alexander was quiet. He had never been spoken to this way by someone from the upper classes. Yes, Sir William was kind and all, but he never really asked his opinion about deeper subjects. And now here was this young lady really just barely a woman asking him what he wanted out of life. Incredible. It took some time for him to think about his response.

"I too want freedom my lady … I mean Lucy … I mean Fanny" He smiled and continued, "I want to have my own place. It doesn't have to be as big as the Armistead plantation. But I want it to be mine. I want to be able to walk around in freedom upon my own land and decide each day of my life what needs to be done and what can wait until the morrow. Yes, that's what I want. I want to be free to decide my own fate." Alexander finished his little speech. Lucy was somewhat taken aback since she had never heard him put together more than two sentences since she had first met him months ago. She responded with a soft womanly voice, "and what about companionship Alex … do you want a wife and children on this land of yours? Or do you just want to be free of all human entanglements?"

"Oh no, "he replied quickly, "I want a family … a big family with lots of little children around. Back in England, I had a family, a small one, but now …" his voice dropped off.

"So … you'll be needing a wife then … to the best of my knowledge that's how a man gets children … first comes a wife." She was openly flirting with him now and he knew it and loved it.

"Yes … I reckon I'll be needing a wife." And then he blurted out … "Got anyone in mind?"

"Why Alexander Cleveland, some girls might take that as a proposal." She replied as she feigned being shocked but inside was delighted with how the conversation had turned.

"It's getting dark. We had better head back to the house or your brother will skin me alive." Alexander quickly changed the subject.

Lucy was obviously disappointed but agreed to return to the big house. After they walked a bit in silence, Alexander slowly touched Lucy's hand. "Lucy, it would never work. Your father would never agree to our wedding. You are from one class and me another. Besides, I have absolutely nothing to offer you. I still have two years of my indenture to your brother and then what?" He raised his arms and shrugged his shoulders in frustration.

"Alex, are you asking me to be your wife?" Lucy said in her matter of fact manner. "Because if you are, that's all that matters to me …that's all that ever really matters. Do the two people want each other as husband and wife until death breaks their bond? "

Alexander stopped and turned and took both of her hands into his. Her tiny hands disappeared into his large work hardened and earth stained farmer's hands. "Yes, Lucy Armistead, I want you to be my wife. I want you to be the mother of my children. I want to grow old with you. I love you. I have from the first time I saw you. Will you marry me?"

"Yes, Alexander Cleveland, I will marry you." Lucy responded as she threw her arms around his neck and their lips met for the first time.

Later that evening, Lucy and Alexander stood before her brother, Sir William Armistead. Although Alexander nervously initiated the conversation by asking for Lucy's hand in marriage, Lucy did most of the talking for the two of them. Sir William was quiet for what seemed like an eternity of time and then he finally spoke,

"Alexander, you have been a good and faithful servant. And I believe that I have treated you fairly in all our dealings?" To which Alexander nodded in affirmation. "But what you ask of me today is more …. I just simply can't agree to it lad." Alexander's head dropped down and Lucy gasped in surprise. "It's not me, you see. If it were entirely my decision I would wish you well on your journey as husband and wife but it's our father, Lord Axminster who must have the final say. You two must wait while I send a letter to him in which I will plead your case. Yes, that would be the proper thing to do." Sir William spoke to them as if he was trying to convince himself that he was correct in this action he proposed.

Lucy spoke up, "brother, how many times have you yourself told me "this was a new land and we will make of this land what we will"? How many times William have you said that to me? Well, I'm telling you as one of those who are making this new land my home that I want to marry this man and quite frankly I don't care if father agrees or not." Lucy said with pugnacious tenacity. William had seen this side of his sister before and he knew to tread softly. Lucy Armistead was a determined young woman when she decided she wanted something. Alexander's color had drained from his face. He did not quite know what to think of his young love. My … she had spunk. And inside he was so proud of her at this very moment. She was fighting for them. But he also realized that Sir William was by law his master and he had to obey him. He cleared his throat as if preparing to speak, "My lady …er, I mean Lucy, perhaps your brother is right? Maybe we should wait to hear from Sir Anthony regarding our plans? That would be the proper thing to do for English gentlemen and women, would it not?" he looked at her lovingly as he spoke these words in his deep and kind voice.

Lucy spun around and looked directly up into his eyes. "Hogwash! Alexander Cleveland, do you love me?"

"Of course I do" Alexander replied looking down at the floor like a scolded puppy.

"And do you want to be my husband?" asked Lucy impatiently.

"Yes, my dear, I want that more than anything else in this dear world." Alexander looked deep into her eyes and said this in such a sincere and moving manner that Lucy caught her breath while William smiled. Lucy spun around and looked at her brother.

"Tell my father that I am with child. And tell him that for the sake of our family's honor you thought it best that we become husband and wife as soon as possible to prevent any scandal that might befall the house of Armistead."

"What" exclaimed William while poor Alexander was speechless. He looked at his master and said with his eyes "nothing like that degree of intimacy had ever transpired between them" but, the words would not come out of his mouth.

"Oh you silly goose," Lucy poked the ribs of her beloved and began to laugh. "I'm not really pregnant. But father doesn't know that. And if you William will compose the letter as I direct you to do so, it will convince him that our immediate marriage is the best thing under the circumstances." Then she laughed once more this time even louder. She was enjoying herself.

Alexander finally found his voice and said rather quietly, "but surely, word will eventually get back to Sir Anthony that you are indeed not … carrying my child"

Alexander said these last few words in a hushed tone as if he were too embarrassed to speak of such things in public.

Lucy looked at him. She looked directly into his humble face. She smiled sweetly and said, "Well, my dear soon to be husband, I guess we'll have to do something about that now won't we …."

And with that statement, William burst into laughter. His entire body shook from head to toe. Alexander did not know quite what to make of it all but after a few moments he too began to smile and finally laughed heartily along with both of them. He now had a family and it filled him with utter joy. As he laughed he looked at Lucy. He was impressed with her and he knew at that moment how deeply in love with her he was. Yes, this indeed was a new world and it called for a new way of living. And the Lady Armistead soon to be Lucy Cleveland, known by all her friends and family as Fanny, would perhaps show them all, the way it was to be done?

Marriage in Colonial Virginia was often a simple and quick event. In the first couple of decades, women were in short supply. In fact, back in the early days, a ship from London had arrived at Jamestown with nothing but young women aboard whose passage had been provided for by the men who intended to marry them. The two, man and woman, simply stood in front of witnesses and exchanged their vows with one another and that was that. Eventually, over time, as the planter class developed and carried over the ocean their English customs, marriage became more of a formal affair with an Anglican rector officiating at a church service followed by a feast sponsored by the bride's family which often lasted for days. The Armisteads were no different and Lucy's "condition" was not that unusual. Even in the mother country, it was often said that over half the young women who walked down the center aisle of the church were already carrying the next generation of aristocrats. So, although Sir Anthony Armistead, Lord of Axminster, was indeed shocked upon reading the news of his daughter's plight, the Colonial Virginians took it in stride and treated the new family like anyone else who had decided it was time to fill this new land with good English men and women. Of course, only Lucy, Alexander and William knew the truth nor did they care what others might say behind their backs. It was a ploy to gain their father's approval for a marriage between an English noblewoman and her indentured lover and it worked. To Lucy, that was all that mattered. She was now free of her past. She was now free of the stifling old customs of the English aristocratic class. She had decided who she was to marry and it made her feel strong and independent. She was a new woman living in a new world.

As part of the wedding arrangement, Sir William reduced Alexander's length of indenture to the time he had served. He was now a free man. In addition, as dowry, Sir William, acting on behalf of their father, gave the new young couple 500 acres of undeveloped land in an area that eventually would be called York County. It was rather primitive and sparsely settled. The natives had recently moved out of the area thus leaving those few Englishmen who called it home in relative peace. The land was facing the York River to the north and Williamsburg was a day's ride to the south and west. Of course, Alexander would need help in starting his farm and Sir William loaned him two indentured servants and three dark skinned Africans. Alexander remembers the shock he felt upon seeing the Africans for the first time.

Initially they had been brought to the Virginia colony from the islands of Barbados and were considered indentured servants just like him. But over time, the laws were changed so that these Africans would never escape their indentured status … thus … over time slavery came to Colonial Virginia. The English planters actually preferred the African slave over the English indentured servant for obvious economic reasons. And they would not run away as the natives would after capture. How could they? They did not know the lay of the wild frontier any better than the English settler. But, of course, the natives did know the land well and as soon as they could would drop their farm tools and head for the woods to freedom. Occasionally, Alexander would hear of a runaway African servant but they were often found a few days later hungry, cold and frightened by their unfamiliar surroundings. This was, after all, he reasoned, a new land to them as much as it was to his fellow Englishmen.

Life in York County was difficult but not much different from what he had known since arriving in the colony. He didn't mind the hard work. He kept his musket close by and always ready to fire. He had also learned how to handle a tomahawk, the apparent favorite weapon and tool of the natives. He and Lucy quickly set about the business of building their first home, a simple structure of three rooms with a massive fireplace at one end for cooking and heating the house during the cold Virginia winters. Then they built a barn for their livestock and a tobacco barn for the crops they would eventually plant and harvest. Life was good and Alexander, perhaps for the first time in his life, was truly happy.

And then everything changed one cloudy afternoon when Sir William arrived at the farm on horseback. Lucy saw him first. "Brother William, what on earth brings you here today? You look as if you had seen a ghost. We weren't expecting you until next month."

William stopped his horse suddenly and jumped down to hug his sister. He suddenly stopped dead in his tracks and looked at her belly which was just beginning to show the signs.

"Oh, close your mouth man. Haven't you ever seen a pregnant woman before?" Lucy laughed as she ran up to her brother and hugged and kissed the side of his whiskered face. "I told you to tell papa I was with child. Now … we couldn't lie to him now … could we?" And she giggled like a little school girl who had been caught doing something naughty.

"When do you expect the arrival?" William finally managed to get out the words.

"Not for a while. Probably sometime in the fall or early winter." Lucy replied.

"So … what brings you to our humble home?" Lucy asked once again.

"Dear sister, I have received two letters from England and I am afraid they do not bear good tidings for you or for Alexander." William stated as the laughter between them quickly faded.

"What has happened brother? Tell me? Is it father?" Lucy demanded to know.

"We need to fetch Alexander. Where is the lad?" William asked.

"In the barn, we've got a cow that's having a hard time giving birth and he is teaching John, one of the servants you loaned us, how to tend to it." She replied with concern on her face and in her voice.

Just then Alexander appeared. He had heard the commotion of the horse and wanted to check things out. He was standing behind Lucy with his musket draped over his shoulder. He never went anywhere without it.

"I'm right her Lucy. William, so good to see you. What brings you to this piece of paradise?" he said with a huge grin on his face.

"I'm afraid I'm the bearer of bad news, Alex." William said stoically. "I have just received two letters from England, one from my father and the other from your Uncle Thomas." He handed Alexander the letter from his Uncle and waited for him to read it. Alexander read it out loud so that Lucy might know the news as well … "Dear Nephew, I regret to inform you of the passing from this world to the next your father John. He followed your grandfather into death within two weeks' time. Both left this world peacefully in their sleep. It was your grandfather's wish and your father agreed to it that they be buried side by side in the old parish churchyard. And that is what we did. Your father had been ill for quite some time and we thought the end would come at any day. But he would repeatedly recover his health and return to work and then the sickness would come upon him once again. His strength of will was incredible. This happened over and over the past five years. My father, your grandfather, had suffered numerous strokes during this time and eventually ended up completely paralyzed and bed ridden. As I have written, they both died within two weeks of one another. Alexander, they both wanted you to know they had patched things up between them and had died as friends. They also both wanted you to know how proud they were of you. I do pray this letter finds its way to you. In deepest sympathy and heartfelt kindness... your loving Uncle Thomas". Alexander stopped reading and slowly let the letter fall to the dusty ground. He looked at Lucy who had tears streaming down her cheeks.

"Oh don't cry my love. He didn't die alone. And now he and mama are together for all eternity." Alexander said in hushed tones as he gently smiled at his loving wife. He touched her swollen belly. "Just wish the little one had been able to get to know their grandfather. They would have loved him … like I did." And with these words, Alexander collapsed into the arms of his wife and sobbed.

Lucy was the first to regain her composure. "William, you said you also received a letter from our father?"

"I did girl … and it's not good. Trouble is brewing in England. Father is quite concerned. It began with the Scots. As the both of you already know, the King tried to enforce Anglican observance in Scotland. And the Presbyterians would have none of it. Two years ago, the Scots adopted the National Covenant and many of their nobles and merchants signed it. It essentially said that although they did desire to remain faithful to their king the Scottish Kirk would always remain reformed and they would not comply with the King's commands. They kicked out the bishops and repealed the laws of episcopal authority that old King James, God rest his soul, had implemented decades ago. The Scots would have nothing to do with Laud's Book of Common Prayer or his attempt at reinstating the altars in places of worship and all the rest of the liturgy. Well, again, as you already know, Charles needed money to go to do battle with them and enforce his will so he called for Parliament to assemble …

the first time in years. And they refused to grant him the tax revenues he desired so he dissolved them and sent them home. You both knew that … well … looks like he tried to invade Scotland all by himself with a meager supply of troops and ammunition and, how do I say it tactfully with Lucy present … got his butt kicked. On top of that the Scots have now seized Northumberland and Durham and our threatening York of all places. Can you imagine that! The Scots in York! So, Charles has summoned Parliament once again but father says it does not bade well for our King. Parliament now, at least the House of Commons, is comprised of many Puritans and even some Baptists, "William glanced at Alexander, "and they are demanding the King address their grievances before they will raise one farthing for the defense of the country. He's got the House of Lords, of course, on his side, or at least most of them. But father says the Commons is united behind men like Pym and a younger fellow by the name of Cromwell. Father concluded his letter by saying it might mean civil war. In fact, the Parliamentarians are busy organizing themselves into units readying for battle. Father says the West Country and the north are behind Charles but London and the east are staunch supporters of the Parliament. The midlands are divided and that is probably where the conflict will break out."

"Which means my Uncle will be caught in the middle of it all." Alexander stated clearly as if he could see the future developments in his homeland.

"And your cousin John, the poet, will probably be placed under arrest, if they can find him." William commented slowly.

Alexander thought about his cousin John. He really didn't know the man. He was an older son of his Uncle and knew he had gone on to Cambridge, or maybe it was Oxford, he did not really remember which one. But he did know that this John had made quite a name for himself as a Royalist poet famous for his biting sarcasm of the Puritans and even more so of the Scots Presbyterians and their fanatical hyper-Calvinism. If the truth be known, Alexander had never read one word from the pen of his famous cousin. In this wilderness, he didn't have a lot of free time to read and when he did find the time he would usually pick up an English Bible and read some of his favorite passages, verses that he could remember his mother reading to him when he was young lad.

Just then, Lucy let out a groan. She then doubled over in pain and grabbed her pregnant belly. Alexander reached for her but she had collapsed and fallen to the ground writhing in pain. "It's too soon, it's too soon," is all she managed to barely get out before completely losing consciousness.

She regained consciousness the next morning. She found herself in bed surrounded by her young husband, her brother and an old African woman whom William had called to the Cleveland homestead as soon as he was able to send a message to his plantation.

Lucy began to cry for she realized immediately something terrible had happened to her baby. Alex patted her hand and kissed her forehead trying to hold back his own tears. They had lost the child. It was a girl. They had decided ahead of time that should they have a girl she would be named Henrietta Elizabeth; Henrietta, after the wife of King Charles and Elizabeth, the name of both their mothers.

William spoke, "Lucy this is Sadie. She's going to be staying with you for a few days, just until you can get back on your feet." The African slave who had been given the name Sadie could speak a little English but she just looked at Lucy nodding her head and smiling in a comforting fashion. Lucy looked into the eyes of her husband and began to cry once more. "I have failed you my love. I have failed you miserably," Lucy lamented.

Alexander fiercely shook his head no. He could not speak but he wanted his young wife to know she was not to blame for what had transpired.

It took a few days before Lucy was back on her feet again but something had changed in her personality. She was somber and quiet with eyes downcast. She stayed this way for weeks. Not speaking to anyone unless spoken to first and then with only the absolute essential words of conversation. This was not the bubbly outgoing energetic Lucy Alexander had come to know and love. This Lucy was alive but seemed dead inside. Alexander did not know what to do. He was also taking the loss of their first child quite hard but he could tell he had not been impacted to the degree his young wife had suffered.

Finally, after weeks had passed, Lucy woke up one morning and asked Alexander if he would walk with her down to the edge of the river. It had been a while since the two of them had strolled along the bank of the York. Although he many things to do that day he quickly agreed and that seemed to brighten somewhat her countenance. She packed them a little food for the journey and off they set with Lucy riding the old mare and

Alexander walking beside her with his ever-present musket slung over his shoulder.

They walked this way in utter silence until the river came into view. Then Lucy spoke, "Do you think God has punished us for lying?" Alexander was startled somewhat by her question but he quickly recovered and responded, "No, my love, the little one's death was not due to the punishment of God".

"How can you be sure, my husband, we lied. We lied to our families about being pregnant in order for us to be married. If father had known the truth, he would have never agreed to it. I broke at least two commandments. I dishonored my father and I lied to him." Lucy was on the verge of tears once again.

Alexander stopped the horse and helped his wife to the ground. He wrapped his strong arms around her and kissed her cheek. "Lucy, bad things happen all the time. Bad things happen to bad people and bad things happen to good people. And I don't think it means at all that God is behind it."

"But God knew our child was going to die didn't he? And if he is all-powerful, why didn't he put a stop to it. Why didn't he save our little one?" Lucy began to sob and Alexander just hugged her more tightly.

"I'm not God my love. I do not know why God allowed this to happen. But I do remember something my mama told me before she passed from this world to the next … what Stan intends for evil, God will turn into something good … Lucy, we must simply have faith that our little girl was not meant to live here with us. I believe with all my heart she is right this very moment in the arms of her loving grandmother. And Lucy, I believe someday she will meet us at the gates of heaven."

"But she wasn't even baptized before she died. Doesn't the church teach she died in a sinful state and will spend eternity in hell?" Lucy had managed to regain her composure and pose this question of her husband.

"I know what the church teaches. But I also know what is in my heart. Our God is not a God of hate and vengeance. My mama taught me that not only with her words but by her actions. I saw God at work in my mama. And because of that, I know this God we worship is a God of love and compassion. Just look at his son. Look at how Jesus treated the children. He even said, "let them come unto me, for of such is the kingdom of heaven."

Alexander looked deeply into the eyes of his beloved. "No, my dear, if God loves our little girl as half as much as I do, then there is no way he could banish her to the fires of hell for all eternity. And if I, a mere mortal, can love a little baby to that degree, can you imagine the love our God, the Creator and Giver of life has for her … for you … and for me. Dear sweet Lucy, this is a bad thing that has happened. And no, I do not understand the why of it. Perhaps, someday, when I meet God face to face, I will understand but this I know … the Lord Jesus said we would have trouble in this world but to take heart for he had overcome this world." And with those words Alexander softly cried out his pain. His tears mixed with Lucy's and dropped to the bank of the river where they formed small circles in the dust … circles of pain and heartache.

The seasons came and went. The days turned into weeks, then months, then years. Lucy and Alexander tried to conceive once again but to no avail.

It seemed to Alexander that God had abandoned him. First came Lucy's miscarriage. This was followed by a poor growing season. Although the demand for tobacco continued to grow, the harvest did not meet the demand. Prices went up but few planters benefited because of their reduced ability to supply. Then the colony received news from England. Things were not going back home. King Charles, in an attempt to generate more funds for his war with the Scots had called once again for the parliament to assemble. This would prove to be a fatal error on his part. For this parliament was comprised of zealous Puritans who wanted to abolish many of the policies the King and his Archbishop had implemented regarding taxation and religious practice within the church of England. To complicate matters, a rebellion broke out in Ireland. This country's Catholic population, which was the majority, were appalled by the prospect of a Puritan parliament achieving political control in England. They had watched the Scots defeat Charles and his royalist forces and thought the time ripe to rise against their own English and Scottish landholders. Several thousand English and Scottish men, women and children had been killed or forced to flee to the safer shores of southwestern Scotland or northwestern England. Some had even decided to immigrate to the New World. Two years ago, Charles had raised his royal standard at Nottingham and the country had erupted into civil war. The men of Cornwall had risen with Charles but most of the south of England was in the control of the parliamentarians, who were now simply known derisively as the roundheads. Charles made peace with the Irish Catholics and this caused the Parliamentarians to enter into an alliance with the Presbyterian Scots. The combined Scots-Parliamentarian force crushed the Royalist army in the ferocious battle of

Marston Moor. The king had lost his loyal subjects in the north of England.

Of course, all this trouble in the mother country had spilled over into the colonies. Trade had been severely and negatively impacted. Pirates now roamed the seas off the coast of the colonies and the King's weak navy was barely able to maintain links with the colonies. He was quickly running out of money and to Alexander, the obvious end of the story seemed inevitable. What Alexander found interesting in all of this was the rise of the man known as Oliver Cromwell. Apparently, he had come from a rather middling sort of East Anglian folk and had been elected to parliament before the troubles broke out. Also, he seemed to be a military genius or, as Alexander thought, was pretty good at self- promotion. For whatever the reasons, his star was rising and he seemed to have the greatest influence in the Parliament.

He was deep in thought one morning as he walked toward the tobacco barn. "What will the future hold for us?" he thought to himself. "What is going to happen to Lucy and me? What if the King's troops are unable to put down the rebellion? Will the colonies be sold to another country to generate funds?" The poor young man's mind seemed ready to burst with all the questions and anxiety those questions generated. And to top it all off, Alexander had begun to question his faith. He would never actually voice his doubt to anyone, not even his loving wife, but he truly wondered about God. This morning he found himself looking up into the heavens and talking to God as if he were a friend who had for unknown reasons severed all contact with him.

"Where are you? Are you there? If you are there, do you hear me? Can you hear me? Or do you not even care anymore?" Alexander gazed upwards into the clouds that were beginning to develop. A storm was brewing and it was coming from the east. Not a good sign. In the past, when these storms had blown in off the ocean they had brought with them massive winds and torrential rains. Alexander looked to the east. The clouds were thick and menacingly dark. He could see lightening and began to hear the booms of thunder. He decided he needed to head back to the house and check on Lucy and Sadie. The African had become a fixture in his home and he was truly glad. It seemed that Lucy and Sadie had developed a close relationship. "In a way," he thought to himself, "Sadie has become Lucy's mama and Lucy her daughter." Even with the language barrier the two had somehow managed to communicate and, of course, with time, Sadie began to slowly learn some of the English language and in return taught Lucy some of the mysteries of the culture she had carried with her from the plantation in Barbados where she had been born. Sadie's parents had been born in Africa but that's all she really knew about them since she had been sold to a sugar planter when she was but a girl of three. There was something about this whole idea of bringing the Africans to the colonies that didn't sit well with Alexander. He couldn't articulate what it was that was troubling him but deep down inside he questioned the whole concept.

Just then, he heard Lucy shout out his name. He tightened his grip on his musket and began a trot to the house which he could now see.

"A storm is coming love," Lucy said to him as he approached her standing in the open doorway. "You had better secure everything down. You remember the last time this happened. Anything that wasn't securely fastened was lost. "

"Yes dear," Alexander responded. And then he stopped and looked at his wife.

"Why are you smiling woman. The sky is about to let loose and you're standing there grinning like the cat who ate the mouse?"

"Alexander … I'm with child." Lucy spoke it quickly as if she didn't really think it could be possible true.

Alexander rushed to her and grabbed her up into his arms. And then he gently set her back down. "Are you sure … positive?"

"Oh yes, my love, God has heard my prayers and He has given us life once again. Praise His name," she looked at her husband through tear soaked eyes.

Alexander went outside where the wind was beginning to howl. He dropped to his knees. He began to cry. "Forgive me Holy One … for my doubt. Forgive me … Creator of all things and Giver of life. And thank you … thank you…. thank you" The moisture laden clouds had unleashed their precipitation and the rains were pelting Alexander has he knelt in the ground of his humble homestead. Lucy stood in the doorway and just watched. Sadie came up behind her and in her broken English said, "What was lost has now been found. Praise be to the God of us all."

The pregnancy went smoothly. Alexander worried every day of it but Lucy seemed unnaturally calm. And Sadie worked busily around the little house preparing for the entrance of the little one into this world. In the spring of 1645, Alexander and Lucy Cleveland looked into the little face, for the very first time, of their brand-new baby boy. "What are we to call him?" Alexander asked his wife. "I think we should name him Roger, after my grandfather Roger Armistead." Lucy replied. Alexander thought a moment and then smiled and said, "Well, hello Roger Cleveland … welcome to Virginia. I need you to grow up and be big and strong son. You and I have a lot of work to do." Lucy smiled at them both while Sadie pretended to busy herself by the cooking kettle hanging in the fireplace. But Sadie was really offering a tearful prayer of thanksgiving to this mysterious invisible God of the light skinned people she served. There were many things in this new world Sadie did not understand including this God of the English. But during her long sorrowful life, and Sadie's life had been full of unbearable heartache, she had learned that a newborn child, regardless the color of its skin, was precious. And on this morning, Sadie saw the joy in the faces of her master and his young wife. Joy brought to them by this little one. As Sadie witnessed Alexander humbling himself while kneeling in the downpour of rain to worship this God in thanksgiving, something stirred inside her. Sadie did not understand the ways of this God. The stories Lucy had told her about how his son Jesus came to the earth as a man and died upon a tree for the sins of mankind left her in a state of confusion. Why would an all-powerful God allow such a thing to happen to his only son? Yes, this was a mystery to her. But that morning Sadie was strangely moved by what she saw and she decided right them and there that she would learn more about this God and his son, Jesus. "Who knows," she thought to herself, "maybe someday, I will feel as strongly for this God as do Alexander and Lucy?" Maybe someday she would come to truly know this Jesus and learn to love him? Time would tell. For the time being, there were potatoes that needed peeling and a floor that needed sweeping. And that would have to do … for now. Sadie looked once again at the three of them; mother, father and newborn child. She saw the love that filled that cabin that morning and she smiled. She began to quietly hum a tune from her childhood. She had long ago forgotten the African words that accompanied it. But the tune somehow always brought peace to her heart and comfort to her troubled soul. At that moment, she remembered from her distant past the face of another young mother, this one with very dark skin and a beautiful smile on her face. Sadie kept smiling but the tears had begun to flow down her cheeks. And Sadie thought to herself, "ain't that the way of life … tis both bitter and sweet … often at the same time." Then she picked up her broom.

Chapter Nine – Parish of Kilbarchan, Renfrewshire Scotland, c. 1647

Thomas sat on the edge of Lochwinnoch. He had walked miles that day and needed to rest. He could have taken the horse but she was needed to plow the spring fields and the family could not spare her for the trip he had to make. The clan Chief, William Cochrane of Dundonald had sent word to all the leading male members of the clan to meet at his castle in Dundonald in Ayrshire.

Thomas was 31 years old, a husband, father of three little bairns and one on the way and had lived most of his life in and around the ancient barony of Cochrane. Land that been in his family for as long as anyone could remember. Thomas was tall with curly reddish brown hair and bushy beard with green eyes. His mother, Jonet Broun, had told him he got his coloring from the ancient Norsemen who had settled in the highlands of Argyll centuries ago. Perhaps she was right but everyone else in the family had the same darkish gray hair and blue eyes. The prematurely gray hair seemed to be a trait of those whose ancestry was connected to the area surrounding Glasgow. Thomas wasn't sure his mother had been correct. He had grown up with many different stories surrounding the origin of the Cochrane family. One of his Uncles swore they came from across the Irish Sea and another said they had been there in the Kingdom of Strathclyde before the Romans came to Britain. Whatever the origins, the family had been here for quite a while and had flourished and done well for themselves. There were Cochranes scattered from the River Clyde to as far south as the town of Ayr and as far east as Stirling Castle. In fact, it had been told to Thomas that one of his ancestors had helped to design and build the Castle for James II ... or maybe it was the James III ... he could not remember. He knew it was one of those Stewarts. His clan had always been faithful to the Stewarts or Stuarts, as sometimes they liked to be called, given the late Queen Mary's French connection. He knew they had been instrumental in building the Abbey at Paisley. In fact, stone masonry seemed to run in the family, that, and making music. The Cochranes loved to play their fiddles, sing and dance. And, of course, fighting was in their blood. And that is why he had been called to Dundonald.

As Thomas sat by the edge of the water, he thought about his homeland and what had transpired over the past few years. The way he saw it, the trouble began when King Charles, son of James VI of Scotland who was also James I of what James himself liked to call Great Britain ... the combined kingdoms of England, Wales, Ireland and Scotland ... and parts of France ... Although, the French would never admit to that fact ... which caused Thomas to chuckle ... selected Laud to be Archbishop of Canterbury. Thomas wasn't truly convinced that Laud was the actual problem. After all, it had been James who had reintroduced the bishops back into the leadership of the Kirk. All Charles was trying to do was foster uniformity between the Anglican Church of England and the Presbyterians of Scotland. But it was Laud's imposition of the Book of Common Prayer in 1637 combined with other changes in the liturgical practices that sparked rioting throughout the country. The trouble began in Edinburg at St. Giles and then spread like fire to the west and south. The highlanders were tenaciously holding on to their Catholic faith and traditions and had never truly converted to the Reformed

Kirk. But they were often fighting amongst themselves and thus were not a significant factor on the national front. But the major trading towns of Glasgow, Edinburgh and Dundee had definitely risen in defiance against the king's interference in the religious matters of Scotland. And that prompted the National Covenant, a document which was signed by a vast majority of the Scottish nobles, major landholders and wealthy merchants. To sign the Covenant meant you were opposed to any changes the King might wish to impose upon the true Reformed Kirk of Scotland. And, of course, this ran directly counter to the ancient Stewart belief of the Divine Right of Kings to rule both the religious as well as secular functions of their governments. Charles truly believed that he answered only to God. He had even disbanded the Parliament years ago. They had become overrun with Puritans, some Presbyterians and even a few Baptists. Charles disliked what he called the nonconformists and despised the Baptists, so Parliament was no more.

Charles was angry at Scotland and decided to teach her a lesson. He managed to put together a force of some 20,000 English men who came across the border. That's when the Earl of Argyll and other like-minded Scots nobles and lairds like William Cochrane decided to oppose their sovereign and gathered an army of some 12,000 Covenanters. "I was called into action," Thomas thought, "but we saw little action". The King backed down with the Pacification of Berwick treaty in which he agreed that all disputed questions should be referred to another General Assembly of the Kirk or to the Parliament of Scotland. "Another mistake on his part," thought Thomas. For the Scottish Parliament completely abolished all forms of Episcopacy within the Kirk and declared itself free from the control of the Stewarts. Now Charles was forced to take major action against this part of his kingdom in rebellion. He recalled Parliament because he needed their support and tax dollars to finance a major war. In 1640, the so-called Short Parliament convened but demanded redress of grievances, the abandonment of the royal claim to levy a tax on merchant ships and a complete change in the ecclesiastical system. This new Parliament was now dominated by Puritans who demanded a reform of the English church. Charles refused these conditions and sent the grumbling men home. He, once again, dissolved the English parliament. The Scots saw their opportunity and took it. They crossed the River Tweed and overran the whole of Northumberland and County Durham. They were knocking at the gates of York.

"I remember those days," Thomas said aloud although no one was nearby. He was lost in his thoughts. So much had happened to him in such a short period of time. "It was the summer of 1640. I was 24 years old, newly married with our first bairn on the way. I was working in the fields when a rider came up to the farm and told us all that the Duke of Argyll had once again raised his standard and was gathering his clansmen to attack royalist clans in the Highlands. I had to go. I had no choice. I was a Cochrane and we had always fought when the Campbell pipers began the call to arms. "

"My poor wife will be wondering where I am. I must be getting on towards home," thought Thomas. And with that, he gathered up his things and began the final three-mile leg of his journey. It was a simple trip really. He just had to keep the Black Cart River to his right and follow it all the way home.

His wife, Jennie, saw him first and called out his name, "Thomas, dear husband, you've come home safe and sound" as she ran to him. He saw her and the thought came to his mind, "she is as pretty today as she was the first time I laid my eyes upon her." Back then, she was Jennie Guild of Clackmannon Parish. (It was quite a distance from Kilbarchan to Clackmannon almost 50 miles as the crow flies.) The constant warfare and religious troubles had brought the two together. Thomas was young and on the march with his fellow Cochranes. They were headed to the castle at Stirling. A rumor had been started that Charles was planning a naval assault on Edinburg and, if successful, would then land a huge force which would attack the Scottish midlands including the important site of Stirling Castle. Needless to say, none of that was true. So, the gathering of the forces was in vain but it did allow Thomas and Jennie to meet. It was love at first site and although Jennie's father, a teaching Elder in the Kirk, was quite reluctant to have her move clear to Renfrew in the end he relented because as he said to his new son in law, "what man alive can resist that smiling face and those pretty blue eyes." Thomas chuckled as he remembered the conversation he had with his father in law. That had been years ago. He and Jennie had taken up a small bit of good fertile land in Kilbarchan given to him by his grandfather and had settled down to raise a family.

But they had not known peace. Somehow, between the constant bickering between the King and Kirk and the seemingly ever present call to arms by the clan chief, they had managed to start a family. In fact, Jennie was pregnant right now with their fourth bairn. According to Jennie, she should deliver within the month. That was one of the major reasons she was so frustrated with the current situation in Scotland. She needed Thomas around the house to keep track of things as she went into labor and then to help out after the delivery. She was exceedingly happy to see her husband this day but was concerned about what the future might hold for them and their little ones.

"How are you my love?" Thomas asked sweetly of his wife as he held her in his arms.

"Fat and miserable," Jennie exclaimed but with a deep sigh of relief at having Thomas home again.

"Aye, ye may have put on a few pounds while I was gone but you're looking grand as ever lass," Thomas said with a wide grin on his face and a twinkle in his eyes. "And how are my little ones?"

"Good. They miss their daddy. But your sister is helping out. But you know Thomas she has her hands full with her own lot and that man of hers …" Jennie's voice trailed off. No one much cared for the young lad that had married Thomas's sister. He was often drunk and did as little as possible around their farm.

Suddenly Thomas remembered why Dundonald had called the clan together. "Jennie, listen to me sweetheart. I've got some news which you're not going to like." Thomas swallowed hard as he prepared himself for what was about to happen.

"What!" Jennie demanded.

"The clan is going to join Leslie and Argyll and cross the English border. I have to go." Thomas stated as quickly as he could knowing full well how his wife would respond. But Jennie surprised him. She did not explode in anger as he had anticipated. She began to sob. This was a surprise. His wife was an emotional woman but rarely did she cry.

"You have to leave again! With me like this …" as she pointed to her swollen belly. And then the tears abruptly came to a stop and Jennie announced, "I'm going home to Clackmannon and I'm taking the children with me. I can't stay here anymore trying to keep the farm running and the kids fed while you are off once again fighting for …. whatever it is you men insist upon fighting about. This is ridiculous Thomas. The Covenanters handed Charles over to the English Parliament in January... did they not? Then what more is left to fight over? This battle between Kirk and King is over and it looks like to me the English Puritans have won the day." Jennie dried her tears and stared defiantly at her husband.

Thomas had seen that look before. He knew that once Jennie made up her mind, it was set in stone and there would be no further discussion. He also knew he was at one of the moments in life where the next decision he made would have a long-lasting impact upon his life. He was quiet for the longest time and then he spoke, "Jennie, my love. Your happiness and comfort are more important to me than anything in the Lord's creation. I agree. Let's return to Clackmannon."

A huge smile broke out upon her face. "I love you Thomas Cochrane."

"And I love you Jennie Guild Cochrane," Thomas replied.

Then Jennie blurted out with a sudden realization of what they had just decided together, "but what of the farm? Will you sell it? What should we do?"

Thomas was again quiet for the longest time. Finally, he spoke, "I can't give it up lass. That land has been in my family for decades, maybe centuries of time.

No, we'll leave it lie. It will rest fallow … until we return." He looked at his wife and she stared back at him. He went on, "Jennie our home is here in Kilbarchan. I agree you are in no condition to run the place and raise bairns while I'm fighting for the cause. So, I think we should make this a temporary arrangement. We'll move back to your parent's farm in Clackmannon but only for a time." He said this with a question in his voice. He wasn't sure how she would react.

Now it was Jennie's turn to be quiet. Finally, she spoke, "Aye, tis the right thing to do. Our home is here in Kilbarchan. But as long as these troubles continue, there will at least be some stability in the lives of our children if we go back to Clackmannon. My mother and sisters will be able to help me out with the delivery and keeping the bairns clean and fed and you can help out my father and brothers around the farm. Until, of course, Dundonald calls you once again." She could not help saying this last sentence with a touch of anger and spite in her voice. Jennie thought the situation in Scotland was simply absurd. Killing one another because of how some men in far-away places interpreted the Bible. She knew her husband was loyal to his clan and King. And being the daughter of a teaching Elder in the Kirk, she realized how important these theological matters were perceived by her father and those like him. But, in her heart, she had always questioned killing in the name of Christ. And so much killing had taken place over the past few years, not only here in Scotland, but elsewhere in the kingdom, in England and, of course, in Ireland. That had been bad … very bad. In 1641, the Catholic Irish had revolted against the rule of the English in Ulster. Thousands of English Anglicans and Scots Presbyterians had been massacred.

Argyll and the other Scots Earls along with the Lairds like William Cochrane of Dundonald had sent thousands of men like her husband to Ulster to subdue the rebels. She was convinced then she would never see her Thomas alive. She remembered the utter joy she had experienced when she saw him that day walking over the hill safe and sound. And that had been just one of many times her precious man had been forced to drop everything and leave for battle. She just simply did not understand this hold his allegiance to his clan had upon him. But Jennie was a Scot and she knew that at the end of the day, only God mattered more than one's family and clan. That's the way things are and she guessed the way they had always been.

Jennie had hoped and prayed that after the Irish rebellion had been put down, peace would return to her land. But that was not to be the case. In August of 1642, King Charles I went to war with his own Parliament. England was at war with herself. The Scots were torn by this development. Many of the Covenanters believed God was intervening in history once again to ensure the true Reformed faith survived in Scotland and perhaps even spread throughout the rest of the Stewart kingdom. At least that was the position of Jennie's father. And it was something that he was apparently preaching from his pulpit. That is what her mother had written in a letter to her. "Your father is ecstatic about the developments in England. He believes God has judged Charles and found him wanting. I told him to be careful in what he says. There are still many Stewart supporters even though they have signed the Covenant." But Jennie's father had apparently been correct in his prediction. In August of 1643, the Scots General Assembly offered their support to the English Parliamentarians in exchange for their acceptance of a Solemn League and Covenant in effect ensuring that England would become Presbyterian should the King lose the civil war. However, this did not go over well with a number of the more moderate Covenanters, like the Cochranes of Dundonald. In February of 1644, Charles appointed the Marquis of Montrose as head of the forces in Scotland who decided to remain loyal to the Stewart crown. And Thomas had been sucked into the whirlpool of religious war once again. Thomas fought with Montrose when he captured Dumfries for the Royalists but then was quickly defeated by Cromwell and his English Puritan army at the battle of Marston Moor. And then the highland McDonalds accompanied by 2000 Catholic Irish rose against the Campbells of Argyll. So, the Cochranes quickly switched their allegiance back to the Earl of Argyll and followed him into battle against the Royalist army of Montrose made significantly larger and stronger with the addition of these highlanders. Thomas was so confused and torn by this turn of events. He had written Jennie in a letter, "I really no longer understand who we are fighting or for that matter why we are fighting anymore? I'm so tired of it all. I just want to come home and be with you and the wee little ones. Why can't we Christians find a way to make peace with one another? Do ye think God really cares about all of this?" Jennie pondered upon the current situation as she moved about their small simple dwelling gathering items for the trip to Clackmannon. Her parents would be expecting her. She had written them in a letter that she would soon be returning home to finish out her pregnancy and childbirth. At the time she wrote the letter, she did not know if her Thomas would be accompanying her or not. It troubled her that her parents would not be expecting him but she realized they would warmly embrace him into their home and would soon put Thomas to work in the fields.

The next morning, they set out for Clackmannon. It had not taken long to pack what items they could carry with them on their cart which was pulled now by the big gray mare. And, of course, behind the cart they had tied their cow and her recent calf. Jennie had told her sister-in-law to keep their chickens. They were too much trouble for the trip and the children would pester them all the way to her parents' home. She didn't need that type of aggravation … not right now. She realized they had made a hasty decision but it still seemed right after a good night's sleep so off they went, heading east and north. The trip would take a couple of days assuming all went well and they did not encounter any difficulties along the way. These were troubled times in Scotland and people were always on the move, seeking a better life for themselves. And, unfortunately, there were always those who would prey on the weary travelers. But Jennie knew that Thomas was a skilled warrior and most trouble makers would have heard of his reputation or just take a good look at his size and the sword he kept at his belt and would quickly seek out an easier target for their evil work. She spat onto the ground. "God have mercy on their souls … because I don't," she thought to herself. Her father would probably be disappointed in her lack of mercy but the times had turned his little innocent daughter into quite a fighter and one with little patience or forgiveness for those who might consider troubling her or her family. Life had not always been this way for Jennie Guild. She had grown up in a loving home with two doting parents. She had learned at an early age to play the clasarch … the Scots harp, as some called it. And she played it admirably. Plus, the Almighty had gifted her with a pleasant voice and when she sang and played her harp, people said the birds would stop their chirping just to listen and enjoy. Jennie would often play at the small parish Kirk where her father preached and taught. He had been a man of God for as long as she could remember. He had trained at the University of Glasgow and had quickly been hired by the Elders at Clackmannon soon after his graduation. It was there where he married Jennie's mother and raised their small family of five, Jennie being the youngest of the three bairns. My how her life had changed after Thomas Cochrane had entered into it. She had never traveled far from Clackmannon and her parents were deeply saddened when Thomas announced he would return to his family's ancient clan lands along the Black Cart River in Renfrew. But she was his wife and every Scots woman knew that the husband made these types of decisions. She never regretted her decision to marry Thomas. She loved him dearly but she did indeed miss her family. So now, that they were heading back to Clackmannon her heart was full of joy, so much so she burst into song. It was one of her favorites … The Water is Wide. She sang in her lowland Scots brogue … "O waly, waly up the bank, and waly, waly doun the brae, and waly, waly yon burn-side, where I and my true love wont to gae." It was a song full of melancholy with a haunting tune that stirred the hearts of all young lovers. Her father would have died on the spot had he heard her sing such a provocative tune but Jennie was not in the Kirk right now and this is what came to her soul and thus she sang. Thomas smiled at her and soon joined in. The children loved to hear their parents sing together and make music. Thomas could play the pandole and was learning how to play a new instrument from the Continent something everyone was beginning to call the fiddle although its original name was viola. He had found one lying beside a dead Englishman once and figuring the lad had no need of it where he was going, picked it up and put it in his sack. "To the victors, go the spoils" Thomas thought as he walked alongside the cart carrying his wife and family.

"What did you say love?" asked Jennie as she sat in the slow-moving cart heading back to Clackmannon.

"Oh, nothing important … just thinking about my life and how the strange twists and turns have brought me to this point … leaving my ancestral lands and going with you and the bairns to Clackmannon," replied Thomas.

Jennie was silent but after some time had passed she asked her husband a question, "Thomas, are you glad you wed me and had these little ones?" She looked at him with a slight smile on her face as if to convey she was only joking but he knew this woman. Thomas knew that she was concerned about him.

"Aye, love … wisest decision I've ever made. I would have been a fool to let you slip away." Thomas chuckled and gave his wife a gentle tap on her arm. "Sing some more for me, Jennie. The world needs to hear more music about love and less the sounds of battle." And so Jennie sang.

The trip was uneventful, perhaps the best kind given the current situation in Scotland. Jennie's parents and siblings with their families all gathered together in the old homestead and celebrated the safe return of the young Cochranes. The evening included prayers of thanksgiving and singing with Jennie playing the harp. After things quieted down and the wee ones were put to their beds, the adults gathered around the big table in the center of the room and discussed the events that had brought them all together.

Thomas liked his father-in-law and valued his wisdom on matters of theology. However, Thomas was struggling with the current situation in his life and he had asked Jennie's father on his opinion of the current religious strife that ran throughout the nations of Europe.

Jennie's father smoked his pipe slowly and took a sip of his wee dram before answering, "Lad, you stated earlier that you thought God cannot be happy with how his children continue to slaughter one another "He took another large puff on his pipe and a little more whiskey. "But what if we are not all God's children? What if God has chosen sides in order for His will to be made known and done? Do ye ken that possible?" Jennie's father asked Thomas.

Thomas looked at Jennie's father and then at his wife who was placing a finger to her lips and shaking her head no as if to tell Thomas to not go down this path. But Thomas was a Cochrane and was not known for surrendering without a fight and more importantly, Thomas was confused and deeply struggling with his faith. The last few years had hardened him. And he had begun to doubt. He didn't doubt the existence of God as some of his companions had shared with him on the battlefield. But he did doubt man's interpretation of the will of God. And that is where he began his response to Jennie's father, "Elder Guild, you know I respect you and value your opinion and I mean no disrespect for what I'm about to say." Suddenly a deep quiet came over the little gathered group of family and close friends and Jennie held her breath ever so slightly. She knew her father could be set in his ways and could easily bring down "fire and brimstone" on those he thought were teaching blasphemy … which could be anyone who disagreed with the basic theology of John Knox and the Presbyterian Kirk.

"What if we got it wrong? What if our understanding of the will of God does not actually represent the true will of God? After all, don't our theological positions come from the workings of the minds of men? How can we be so sure that when we take the lives of other people, we are doing the will of God? And if we are wrong, then what will God say to us on the Day of Judgment?" Thomas finished his mini-speech and cast his eyes to the floor for he did not know how this group would react. In some places in Scotland, a man could be burned at the stake or thrown into the river to be drowned for making such statements. He was questioning the foundational understandings of those who led the Kirk. He waited for the response.

Jennie's father sat in silence for what seemed like an eternity. Then he smiled and looked directly at Thomas. "Lad, you remind me of me when I was a much younger man." And with that simple statement, the tension in the room was broken and everyone, including Jennie, relaxed with relief. Jennie's father continued," Of course, we are humans and are flawed in our basic nature. That is the premise of Augustine in his concept of original sin which … by the way, I think is well grounded in scripture. Therefore, the answer to your question regarding getting the will of God wrong is yes … absolutely and emphatically yes. However, if the decision-making process were entirely left up to us as mere mortals then everything we do would be in question, would it not?" Thomas slowly nodded his head. He knew the old man was about to make a point but he didn't know what that point might be. "But lad, we are not alone in this deciphering the will of the Almighty. Jesus promised us he would send his Spirit to act as our guide. And that is what the Session of Elders believe when they gather together to determine the direction of the Kirk. We pray for the Spirit to guide us, and … most of the time, I think it does so." Elder Guild stopped speaking and looked first at Thomas and then turned toward his daughter. "Do you agree Jennie? Do you think the Spirit of the Holy One guides the leadership of the Kirk?"

Jennie looked at Thomas and then stated boldly, "Yes, I do think the Spirit of God is alive and well but I am not convinced that every pronouncement of the General Assembly comes directly to us from the mouth of God. I think there is always the possibility of hidden motives and secret agendas when it comes to the ways of men, in particular, men who have much to lose in the way of earthly gain if certain decisions of the Kirk do not go their way … so to speak." Jennie hesitated with that last statement thinking to herself, "Ach girl, ye have gone too far this time." She waited for the expected explosion of righteous anger from her father. But it did not materialize. Instead the old man began to smile. This turned into a chuckle and before long he was rolling in laughter. Finally, after he had composed himself, he said, "I do love you Jennie. I love the way you are not afraid to speak your mind come heaven or hell." And then he laughed some more and this time, everyone in the family including Jennie and Thomas joined in although Thomas was thinking deeply about what his young wife had just said. He was impressed, for he had similar thoughts but had kept them to himself for fear of retaliation by the leadership of the Kirk. He looked sweetly at his wife and thought, "Aye, your father is right, you are indeed a courageous woman …a true Scot… and I'm proud of you and so deeply in love with you."

The next morning came early to Jennie Cochrane. She had started the labor of childbirth. Jennie had done this before she had given birth four times with three of the children still alive. But she felt differently. Something was wrong. The pain began to worsen and did not periodically leave her body as it had in the past. This time, the pain came and stayed and became more intense with each passing minute. After tossing and turning in her bed for some time she got up and woke her mother. Jennie's mother took one look at her directed her back to her bed and said to her husband, "Go fetch Isobel and make it quick. Something is terribly wrong with Jennie and her wee one." Jennie's father hesitated and her mother replied preemptively, "Look. I know what the elders say about the old woman but Isobel is not a witch. She is a healer and knows the ways of the ancient ones. Our daughter is in trouble and you need to get off that high and mighty judgement seat of yours, saddle up the cart and bring Isobel here as fast as the good Lord will allow…. Now" And with that final command she turned and walked into her daughter's room where the moaning sounds of pain were starting to become louder. By this time, Thomas was awake and up and had gathered his three bairns together. Jennie's mother said to him, "Take the wee ones to Jennie's sister, Martha. She'll watch over them until this is all over." Thomas knew all along that was the plan but he did not like the appearance of his wife and wanted to stay with her. Martha's farm was only a couple of miles away so he reasoned that he could get the children over to her place and get back in time for the birth of this next new child. None of them fully realized the dire predicament of Jennie and her unborn child.

The old woman Isobel lived in an old rundown stone cottage that had been there longer than anyone could remember. The cottage was located alongside the River Forth around three miles from the Guild farm. Jennie's father knew it would take at least an hour to get there, convince the old woman to come with him and return to Jennie's bedside. He was anxious. Not only was he nervous about his daughter but he was more than a little concerned about enlisting the help of Isobel. He had certainly heard the rumors about her and he was troubled by what his fellow Elders might think of him should it become public that he sought the help of someone many in the parish considered a witch. And he knew there would be no way to keep this quiet. Things like this traveled like water going downhill through his little parish. And how would his parishioners react to all of this he wondered. He needed this posting. It didn't pay much but it certainly supplemented what little earnings came from their small farm. And on top of that, he liked being in the pulpit. He enjoyed bringing the Word of God to his wee congregation. But he knew these people. Although he had his doubts about witchcraft, he realized that many of his parishioners were a superstitious lot including some of the more vocal and influential ones … the ones that probably could influence the decision to keep or get rid of him. "So, what do I do?" Jennie's father asked himself as his cart pulled in front of the old woman's cottage.

"Hello?" he called out. The place appeared to be empty. He started to shout out again and then suddenly stopped. As if by magic, the old woman startled him by speaking from behind him, "Save your breath Elder Guild."

Jennie's father whirled around and was face to face with Isobel. He stammered as he tried to introduce himself. She cut him off with a curt … "I know who you are and I know why you are here. Let me go into my house and fetch my bag. Then we can ride back to your daughter. She is running out of time." And with that she disappeared into the cottage and quickly returned with a small satchel filled with an assortment of ointments, herbs and various other medicinal items.

Jennie's father was in shock. "How did you know? How do you know me? Have we met?" Questions came pouring out of his mouth.

Isobel turned to him and grinned. She was missing a few teeth and her breath was rather strong and offensive. "Don't you know brother … I'm a witch." And then she let loose with a hearty laugh that spooked the old mare into a trot.

The two of them just sat silently side by side as the little cart rolled over the rocky lane. Finally, Jennie's father asked, "Are you really a witch?"

Isobel responded, "Do you believe in such things Elder Guild?"

Jennie's father responded, "I don't know. Part of me has my doubts but another part …. Well, let's just say there are strange things in this world of ours."

Isobel cackled, "You old fool. I'm no more a witch than this old mare pulling your cart. Sure, I have a gift. I can heal when others have tried and failed. And yes, I know things about people before they know them. I study people. I watch them very closely and they give off little tell-tale signs that expose the secrets their trying to hide."

Jennie's father looked at her and asked, "How did you know it was me that had come to your place? And how did you know it was about my daughter?"

Isobel chuckled, "I told you. I watch and listen to others. Everyone in this valley knows your daughter is expecting any day now and, of course, I know who the teaching elder is at the Clackmannon Kirk. So … I just quickly put two and two together and there you go."

Jennie's father asked, "How did you learn the arts of healing?"

Isobel responded, "Well, it wasn't from old Satan, if that's what you're thinking." She chuckled once again. "It was from an old woman who took me in when my parents died in the last outbreak of the plague. She was a healer and a strange old hoot but she gave me a warm bed to sleep at night, kept my belly full with food and taught me how to use the things of the earth to bring about healing in worn out bodies. She taught me how to ease pain, the pain of the heart as well as the pain of the body."

Jennie's father became silent once again but his mind was racing. The idea of witchcraft was a serious charge in Scotland. He knew from his studies at the University that while the idea of witches and Satanic worship was as old as the Christian faith itself it was only during the recent reign of King James that the identification and punishment of witchcraft had become an obsession with the Scottish people and its Kirk. It indeed had become an obsession and one that had easily developed into something rather ugly. Jennie's father knew of women and men who had annoyed their neighbors and subsequently been accused of witchcraft for which a number were executed by drowning or, more frequently, were burned to death. Some said thousands had lost their lives all over Scotland and England as well. Jennie's father did not know if that was true but he had certainly seen his fair share of witch trials and unfortunately the outcome of those trials. He didn't doubt the idea of witches or Satan followers but he had serious doubts about a number of the cases that had been brought before the gathering of Kirk Elders at Clackmannon. He had gone along with the other leaders because quite frankly he was afraid of the personal consequences if he chose to speak up and against the ruling of the Session. He had seen careers of his colleagues ruined when they decided to turn against their ruling Elders. These men felt they were being led by the Holy Spirit of God. They would tolerate debate but only to a point. In the end, it was expected that any decision made and presented to the congregation represented the unanimous opinion of these Spirit led men. And those with differing ideas were told to keep their opinions to themselves. "All for the good of the Kirk, of course," Jennie's father smiled slightly as this last thought escaped from his mind and into the surrounding air.

"What's that you say, Elder Guild?" asked Isobel.

"Oh nothing … just thinking about what my fellow Elders would say if they saw me sitting here in this cart next to you." Jennie's father became immediately embarrassed by what he had just said. He certainly didn't want to irritate this woman. She might be his daughter's only chance for survival.

Isobel just laughed. "Well, I have a good idea as to what they would think and probably say … but maybe not to your face, heh?" And then she laughed some more and this time with gusto.

Jennie's father couldn't help but like this old woman.

"So, Isobel, have you ever been married or had children of your own?" he asked innocently.

Isobel became very quiet and sat in silence for some time. "His name was Robert. He was my little boy. But he didn't live long. Just a few months and then I had to bury his body. Just started coughing and I couldn't get it to stop. Finally stopped breathing and that was the end of it."

"I'm so sorry for your loss. Did you and your husband try again?" Jennie's father asked.

"Never was married. I was raped by one of these Scots who were going to war with the English or whomever else they were fighting at the time … always fighting … always dying." Isobel looked off into the horizon. This part of her history still hurt deeply though it had been decades since those tragic events of her life.

They both rode in silence for the remainder of the trip.

Finally, they crested the hill and both could see the Guild farm and little cottage sitting quietly next to the small burn that ran off the River Forth. And the closer they got they could see and hear that Jennie's condition had worsened.

Isobel barely waited for the cart to come to a complete stop when she flung herself off the seat with her satchel of potions. She ran into the bedroom where Jennie lay groaning with pain while clutching her belly. Isobel went to work immediately barking out orders to the other women who had gathered. She knelt down by her satchel and opened it up. She reached inside for a small container holding a white viscous liquid.

"Here child … drink this," She said to Jennie. Jennie's mother looked nervously at the other women.

Jennie took the potion and within minutes the pain had left her body and she closed her eyes and began to sleep. At the same time, Isobel had removed the covers in order to check the progress of the labor. She then began to frown and moved back to her satchel where she produced two metal bars that were long and curved on the end.

"What in God's name are those and what are you planning to do with them?" Jennie's mother asked with fear and immense concern.

"The bairn is coming out the wrong way. I've got to turn him if I can or they both die." Isobel's voice was stone cold with no emotion. And without delay she went to work on Jennie's body.

Thomas was waiting outside with the other men who had assembled. A number of them were in prayer led by one of the Elders at Clackmannon. Thomas looked at them and thought to himself, "I hope God hears you men. I don't know what I would do if I lost my Jennie." And with that looked up into the heavens as if to plead with the Almighty for the life of his young wife.

And suddenly everyone heard the cry of a new born baby. Thomas rushed into the house going straight to Jennie's bedside.

Mother and newborn son were lying quietly together. Jennie was smiling. She was exhausted but she was alive and happy to be holding her newborn son. Thomas looked at Isobel who was gathering up her equipment and establishing order in her satchel. Jennie's father was standing behind Thomas and smiling from ear to ear.

Thomas said to Isobel, "How can I ever repay you for what you have done for us today?"

Isobel just shook her head and smiled. "No need for payment but I wouldn't mind some of that broth you've got in the pot. I'm hungry."

Jennie's mother looked at her daughter and son-in-law. "Well, the bairn is a man-child. What shall you call him?" And without hesitation Jennie's father interrupted and stated in a clear and loud voice stated, "His name shall be Robert," and then glanced at Isobel. She smiled and gave a slight nod of thanks. Thomas looked at Jennie and they both said, "Robert it is."

The days turned into weeks. The weeks turned into months. For the first time in his adult life, Thomas felt at peace. Things were still unsettled in Scotland. Charles was essentially in English custody and many Scots were troubled by this development. But Thomas had not been called to battle by Dundonald and so he was content to live in Clackmannon and watch his little ones grow while he tended to the farm of his father in law. Then one evening, this peace was shattered.

It had started when one of the cows owned by an elder of the Clackmannon Kirk had died. And then another one died. And then two more from a neighboring farm. One thing led to another and before long the whole community was convinced witchcraft was the cause of these untimely deaths. A rumor was started that someone had seen the old woman Isobel by the barn of one of the dead animals. It wasn't true, of course, but the idea spread quickly. The people were scared and they needed a reason for the deaths of these animals to help alleviate their anxiety.

Thomas had just come in from the fields and was setting down to his supper when a loud knock was sounded at the door. A voice shouted, "Elder Guild … Elder Guild … are you in sir?"

Jennie's father went quickly to the door and opened it wide. Much to his surprise he saw a number of the members of his church gathered outside and in the middle of the group bound by rope was the old woman Isobel. The husky voice shouted out from the crowd, "This woman is a witch. She is responsible for the deaths of our cattle. She must die. We need you to sanction this action and tell us the mode of death."

Jennie's father lost all color in his face and felt his knees weaken as if he were about to fall to the ground. He started to stammer … "No … no … you are mistaken. This woman is no witch. Her gifts of healing are from God above … not from Satan."

But the crowd, which had now grown to well over twenty people, would not be satisfied. They grabbed Jennie's father by the arms and drug him outside. The husky voice said loud enough for all to hear, "Elder Guild, you are our chosen teacher. You have preached from the pulpit the evils of sin and the fires of hell that await those who commit wrong doing in the eyes of the Almighty. This woman has been found guilty of witchcraft. She must be put to death. And we need you to sanction this action."

Jennie's father had regained control of his senses and now could see that in the crowd were some of his fellow elders of the Kirk of Clackmannon. And they were looking at him suspiciously. He knew they had the power to remove him from his position and throw him and his family out of their parish home. He would be a minister with no pulpit. "How would we survive?" he thought to himself. He began to shake and perspire with dread. He was troubled deep in his soul. He knew Isobel was no witch. He knew Isobel had probably saved the lives of his daughter and new grandson. But how could he refuse the Session of his Kirk. And the crowd was gathering in size. Now there were around 50 angry yelling people gathered around him and poor Isobel. She stood ramrod stiff with no expression on her face. She had been bound by thick ropes and one of the largest and angriest men was holding the end of the rope that tied to her and thus prevented her escape.

Jennie's father made a decision that he would regret the rest of his life. He raised his hands in the air to quiet the crowd. Stillness came over the angry mob. Jennie's father spoke with a tremble in his voice, "I see many of the Elders are here and I assume you men have consulted with one another regarding this spiritual matter?" He looked at each of them and they all nodded. "And you are all in agreement this woman is a witch and is responsible for the deaths of the cattle?" They nodded in agreement. "Then I have no option but to rule in favor of the leaders of the kirk. The witch must die." And with that pronouncement a mighty yell of excitement laden with blood lust came from the assembly. The group quickly drug Isobel to a nearby tree and tied her to it. Then as if on cue some men began to throw small pieces of kindling and dried grass all around the tree and Isobel.

"My God," thought Jennie's father, "these fools mean to burn her right here on my land in front of my family." It was one thing for him to give his blessing to the destruction of what the Session had deemed was a witch. It was another to have to watch them perform the execution.

Someone produced a lit torch and was about to set the grass on fire when a masculine cry came from behind the tree where Isobel was bound. For those who knew warfare, they had heard this cry before. It was the battle cry of the Scots warrior and it was meant to strike fear in the hearts and minds of those who heard it.

It was Thomas Cochrane who screamed this ancient Celtic battle cry and raised his mighty claymore high above his head. With one fell swoop he cut through the thick ropes that bound Isobel to the tree. "This woman is no witch. She saved the life of my wife and son. And I'll run this blade through the body of anyone who dares harm her." Thomas shouted defiantly at the mob. He pointed his sword slowly at the large man who still held on to the end of the rope that had been tied around Isobel. "And you will be the first to die." Thomas said in a deadly voice as he moved slowly towards the large farmer. The man was big but he had never been in battle with a Scots warrior. And everyone in the Kirk knew about Thomas Cochrane. He had been to war many times since becoming a man. He knew how to kill and would do so in the blink of an eye if necessary. The man quickly dropped the rope and began to rather quickly slip into the crowd. The crowd began to disperse. One of the Elders as he was leaving the scene shouted over his back towards Jennie's father. "This is not finished Elder Guild. You will be hearing from us." Thomas began to walk more quickly towards the Elder who had spoken to his father in law and that man turned around and ran as fast as he could away from the Guild farm. There would be no witch burning that day.

After the crowd dispersed, all that remained were Jennie's father and mother, Jennie, their oldest son, Hugh, Isobel and, of course, Thomas still holding the claymore with fire in his eyes. Jennie had seen that look before in the eyes of her husband. She knew what he was capable of when in this state of being. Jennie's father's eyes were downcast and he began to mumble." I'm so ashamed of myself. I'm so sorry Isobel. I did not do the right thing and come to your defense. I was afraid of how the other elders would view me. I was afraid of losing my position in the Kirk … I'm so ashamed." And then he began to cry. Jennie's mother attempted to comfort him but he stepped away from her. Jennie looked at Isobel and then at her husband. He had begun to calm down. His anger was slowly being replaced with pity. He actually felt sorry for the old man. Then he spoke, "Isobel, it is no longer safe for you to stay here at Clackmannon. I want you to go with Jennie and me." Jennie looked shocked as what Thomas had just said registered with her. She thought, "He is leaving. We are leaving. He is asking me to return back to Kilbarchan." Then she looked at her husband and knew immediately what he was thinking. Thomas spoke up to the group, "It won't be safe here for any of you. That group will go away but they will return with reinforcements. It wouldn't surprise me if the Elders meet with the Magistrate in Stirling and demand the trial of Isobel as a witch and, of course," as he turned to Jennie's father, "you might survive all of this since you were willing to go along with their madness." He stopped to spit onto the ground as if removing something distasteful from his mouth. He began again, "You and Mrs. Guild are welcome to come with us if you don't want to stay. The choice is yours. But," as he turned and looked at Jennie," as for me and my family … we are going home to Kilbarchan." He looked at Jennie, their eyes met, and for a brief moment she hesitated and then dropped her gaze to the ground nodding her head in affirmation. She thought to herself, "He is right of course. They will be coming back for both Isobel and her husband. They had to leave. They had to leave now. He was her man. He was the father of their children. And he had been right in her heart and her father … had been cowardly." It hurt deeply for her to admit that last thing but she knew in her soul her father had taken the easy way out of the situation. It didn't make him a bad man in her eyes … just human. Perhaps she would have done the same? But for now, time was of the essence. She spoke, "I'll start packing and we'll leave first thing in the morning. Isobel, do you need help packing?"

Isobel shook her head. "I'll not be going with you, though I appreciate the offer. I really do." Jennie and her mother began to protest but Isobel raised her hand to silence them both. "Clackmannon is my home. My son is buried here. And soon, I shall be also." Then she turned to Jennie's father, "Elder Guild, I have one thing to ask of you. When the time comes, make sure you have them bury my bones next to my son's grave. I'll show you tomorrow morning where it is hidden up in the hills. Will you promise me that?"

Jennie's father looked at Isobel and saw such courage in her. He was once again overwhelmed with his guilt and shame. Through the tears that had begun, once again, to fall, he said," Of course, Isobel. I'll grant your wish …and it will be a Christian burial."

Isobel smiled. "I suppose that will be alright. If I do meet the good Lord after I die, it won't hurt to have someone say a few good things about me, heh?" And then she cackled so loudly it frightened the birds that had gathered in the tree to which she had been shackled.

The night went by fast and the morning came quickly. Jennie and her mother had spent most of the night tending to the children and packing the cart. Thomas was sharpening his sword, dirk and drying the last bit of powder he had for his musket. He had no idea what lay in store for them as they fled this area but he was going to be prepared to defend his little family to the death if need be.

The parting was sorrowful. The children were too young to understand the situation but even they could feel the tension in the air surrounding their parents and grandparents. Sometime during the night Isobel had returned to her cottage. She had left a note for both Thomas and Jennie's father but on the outside were instructions that neither were to open and read the notes until her death. Both men placed the notes safely in their cloaks and both obeyed her instructions.

Ben Cleuch loomed ahead for Isobel. She had left early before daybreak and had already traveled a good distance by foot. She wanted to make the top of the mountain before sunset. She had spent the night preparing for this her final journey. She had left notes for both Thomas and Jennie's father. She had packed her satchel with the necessary ingredients took one final look at her home for the past forty years and gently shut the door.

It did take her most of the day but eventually she reached the summit some 2300 feet above the valley below. She had been to this place once before in her life. It was here she had buried the remains of her infant son.

And it was here she planned to die. She knew what would happen to her once the Elders of Clackmannon sat together with the most influential members of the Kirk. They would decide she indeed was a witch and the community would be safer with her gone. And she knew how the Scots had handled witches. And she had decided she did not want to die that way. So she had prepared a powerful potion that would at first put her to sleep and then eventually stop her heart. She knew all along this day would probably come. She had mixed feelings. She would not miss this lonely world of sorrow and pain but she didn't really know what death would bring. Were the fire and brimstone ministers correct? Would she be brought before God and cast into the pit? Or, would she just simply go to sleep never to wake again? And after a few years she would be forgotten.

She sat down on an outcrop of rock that looked out over the valley below. It was a clear night and the sun was just setting in the west. Ben Cleuch was the highest point in all of this part of Scotland. From this vantage point she could see Edinburg to the east and Stirling Castle to the south west. She could almost make out the steeples of Glasgow far away to the west. It was an amazing site. It brought both joy and sadness to her heart. "I guess I might miss this old world after all", she thought to herself. Then she raised the vial containing the toxic potion to her lips.

At that moment, she heard a voice. "Isobel … Isobel … do not drink the potion you have prepared. Throw it on the ground." The voice was masculine but gentle. It was a command but it seemed so natural to her to do as she had been told. The vial dropped from her hand and broke upon the rock she stood upon. As she gazed in the direction of the voice, she was suddenly blinded by a bright intense white light. She had to shield her eyes. The light was so intense it hurt to look in its direction but she felt compelled to stare at this apparition. The light was beginning to take the shape of a man. Isobel asked with a trembling voice, "Who are you? Where did you come from? I made sure no one followed me up here."

The voice responded, "I am who I am. I am the way, the truth and the life. Those who believe in me though they taste death, they shall survive."

Isobel was stunned to silence. She didn't know why but she dropped to her knees and bowed her head.

The voice continued, "Isobel … do you believe in me?"

Isobel replied, "Are you the one the people talk about? Are you God?"

The voice responded, "I am the Christ, the risen Savior of mankind. The father and I are one."

Isobel looked into the white light and felt tremendous peace and contentment such as she had never experienced before in her life. "Do you not know Lord the Elder and the people of the Kirk of Clackmannon think I am a witch?"

The voice answered, "I too was accused of being a follower of Satan. My accusers were wrong. Your accusers are wrong."

Isobel began to cry for she knew she was standing in the presence of absolute truth and purity. "What is to become of me? If I don't take my life this evening, they will find me and put me to the flames. I do not want to die that way."

The voice replied in a gentle and comforting manner, "Isobel, you will die tonight but it will not be by the hands of sinful man. I have come for you. I am the alpha and the omega the beginning and the end. Isobel, I ask you again, do you believe in me?"

Isobel looked through tear stained eyes into the gentle and loving face of Jesus of Nazareth. "Aye, Lord, I believe."

The voice responded, "I have brought someone with me, someone who wants to see you and speak with you." And at that very moment, a young lad who looked to be around five or six years of age stepped out of the bright light and walked over to Isobel and said, "Mommy, it's fun where we are going. You will like it there."

Isobel clasped her hands to her mouth and shouted with joy, "Oh Robbie my dear sweet Robbie … it is you … my boy… my son." Little Robbie took his mother's old and wrinkled hand and gently led her toward the bright light surrounding the Lord Jesus. "Welcome home my daughter," is what she heard and then the light quickly vanished. All that was left that evening on the top of Ben Cleuch was the cold dead remains of Isobel. On her face was a smile. Next to her body was the broken vial of poison she had intended to use but never did.

It was Jennie's father who found the body of Isobel. He had read her note earlier that day and had immediately set out for Ben Cleuch. He hoped he could arrive at the destination Isobel had described before she had committed her one final act but such was not to be the case. Her note had informed him that she was to be buried by the body of her long dead infant son. He looked around and saw the cairn off to the side not more than twenty feet from where Isobel had died. He knew what he must do. If he returned her body to the Kirk, it would be burned with the ashes probably scattered into the muck pit behind the town. She certainly would not have a Christian burial in the Kirk's yard. Elder Guild had made a decision that if he was not in time to save her life he would abide by her final wishes and build a cairn of stones for her besides her infant son. It would have to remain unmarked in order to keep her tragic ending a secret. But that is what he had planned to do and that is what he did upon finding her lifeless body. Once he placed the last stone of the cairn, he bowed his head and offered up a prayer to God asking for His mercy upon the soul of Isobel. He was ashamed that he didn't even know her last name or if she had any remaining kin that should be notified. He looked up into the storm clouds that were just beginning to form. "Tis fitting," he thought to himself, "heaven is sad and sheds a tear for this poor lonely creature." And with that he wiped a small tear from his eye that had dropped upon his cheek, turned around and headed back down the mountain to his home. He would never again visit this cairn nor would he ever again speak of the circumstances surrounding the woman whose body was buried there on the top of Ben Cleuch. His heart was filled with anguish and his mind overwhelmed with the guilt he felt for not saying what he knew should have been said in her defense. He hoped that one day he would be able to forgive himself for his cowardice.

Thomas and Jennie had pushed the old mare as hard as they thought they could and not break her. They both wanted to put as much distance between themselves and Clackmannon as possible. By evening their little packed cart had traveled as far as the outskirts of Stirling Castle. Thomas knew they could not make it the rest of the way in the dark. They had to find shelter for the night. It was summer and the storm that had accompanied them as they began their journey had blown to the east and the night sky looked clear and calm. So they simply pulled the cart off the trail into a flat meadow close to a burn and settled down for the evening. Thomas kept watch over his family as the sun set in the west and the stars began to shine bright in the ever-darkening sky. He bowed his head and said a simple prayer asking God to watch over them through the night and guide them tomorrow safely home. "Home," Thomas thought, "will we find peace there or am I doomed to a life of instability and chaos. I thought we would find peace at Clackmannon but I was wrong. Will Jennie ever forgive me for involving the family with Isobel and the Kirk? I know she is a faithful wife but because of my actions she has had to leave once again her childhood home and who knows what the Kirk might do to her father. God be with them all."

The morning sun woke them all and they immediately began about the business of feeding the children and gathering fresh water from the burn. Thomas quickly got everyone on the cart and started to walk besides the laboring horse. They returned to the cart path that would take them southwest to Kilbarchan. They had been traveling about three to four hours when they saw a rider heading in their direction. Thomas pulled the cart to a halt and quickly removed his musket and sword from its hiding place. He wanted to be ready. Thomas' face broke into a smile when he was able to make out who it was. He spoke to Jennie, "Tis John Hutchinson from Glasgow. We have fought together many times. He is friend and not foe." Jennie relaxed her hold on the small dirk that she had hidden in her dress.

Hutchinson pulled on the reins of the great white stead upon which he rode. "Greetings Thomas, I've been sent by the Dundonald to find you and the other Cochrane warriors. I am surprised to see you on this side of Stirling. I was told you were living with your in laws in the Clackmannon area?"

"Tis a long story John. You are looking well and I must say that is a fine specimen of an animal you ride," Thomas replied. "What does the Dundonald want now?" Thomas asked although he already knew the answer. It meant he would be off once again to battle some new or perhaps old foe of the clan. He looked at Jennie and saw the recognition in her face and eyes of what this message meant to her and the little ones.

"King Charles has been arrested by the English Parliament. He has sent secret messages to his loyal supporters in the southwest to gather troops and free him from captivity. The Dundonald and other clan leaders from Dumfries and Ayr have joined forces and are heading south to the English border. The Dundonald has sent out the message to gather all available warriors and meet at the border and then head south to Lancashire. Our spies tell us that is where the King is being held captive. Thomas, now that I've found you here, I'll ride with you to your home in Kilbarchan. It's just another two hours due east from this point. Then together you and I will head to the borders to join the Dundonald and the men who have gathered in the name of the King. I have heard that Duke of Hamilton and the Earl of Callendar are leading this attack. I have a fine strong stallion for you to ride. You'll like him. He's a beast of a horse. Just the sight of him will put the fear of God in those English Puritans." Hutchinson laughed loudly. John Hutchinson was from a fairly well to do family in Glasgow and he loved to fight. His father was a doctor, trained at the University but John did not inherent his father's love of intellectual pursuits. So, he had found his way in life as a mercenary soldier fighting for one side or another. To John, it did not really matter the cause. He just enjoyed the battlefield and all it symbolized.

"What of the Marquis of Argyll?" Thomas asked. "Is he bringing his warriors to join in with us? Those Campbell's are fighting men. We'll need them on our side if we are to teach the English a thing or two."

"Nay. word is he staying out of this one. Apparently, he has become rather radical in his Presbyterianism and has turned his back on King Charles. It's reported that he and the English Parliament have struck a deal. He gets Scotland in exchange for Charles' head," Hutchinson replied.

Jennie gasped at this last exchange between the men. She spoke up, "Surely, they would not harm the King, one of God's anointed?"

John replied, "The Elders of the Kirk in Edinburgh have tasted power and are now not satisfied with just the elimination of Charles' episcopal policies. They want him out of the picture completely. Will they really put him to death? Who knows but your chief and others loyal to the Stewarts are not going to sit by and watch while this happens to the King of Scotland. They aim to free him from the grasp of the Puritans and set him upon the throne in Stirling Castle from where his forefathers ruled." Thomas interjected, "I imagine we'll be joined the English Royalists after we cross the border? If that is the case, our numbers will swell but ..." he hesitated and looked at John knowingly, "then a power struggle will erupt between the Scots and English aristocrats to see who actually is going to manage the battle strategy and tactics. Heh, Johnnie?"

"Aye, tis true. But in the end, we'll outnumber them and we'll defeat them … once and for all," Hutchison replied with arrogant confidence.

And there it is, Thomas thought to himself, "the ever present problem with we Scots. We squabble so much amongst ourselves over who will lead and who will do this and who will gain glory for that feat … how in the world will we ever be able to work with the English to defeat these Parliamentarians?" Thomas had heard about this Oliver Cromwell and his ability to lead men in battle. He had a foreboding thought as he looked at Jennie. "Aye, lass," he thought to himself, "this may be the one that puts me in the ground … and so far from my home. I do not want to die on foreign soil. I want to live to see my bairns grow old and have babies of their own. God save me from this mess." But not a word of this was uttered to either John Hutchinson or his dear wife Jennie. Thomas kept these thoughts and the dissonance it created within his mind. In his soul, he knew there was no escape. He was first and foremost a Cochrane warrior and when called he and his clansmen answered … even if they did not agree with the reasons. "Such stupid people, we are … brave, aye … but so stupid," he thought to himself as a faint smile crossed his lips. "Oh well, what is that the minister always harps on about … we are the clay and He is the potter … perhaps tis so … but why must it be so hard. Could it be that we are doing all this killing in His name while he is crying upon His throne?" Thomas mused. "Aren't the English as much His children as we Scots? Or for that matter, aren't the McDonalds as much His children as the Campbells … and on and on ….." Thomas looked at the ground and a single tear dropped from his cheek. He looked at Jennie and in a second she knew. Her husband did not want to go and it filled her heart with joy. The two of them had been through so much pain and sorrow in their short time together as husband and wife. They had started their family and God had blessed them with strong healthy infants. She looked at little Robert who was fast asleep in her arms. She thought to herself, "What kind of world have we given to you my little one? Will you know peace? Will you know joy? Or will it be more of the same …. Battle cries and the clanging of swords and the sounds of cannon … the cries of dying men and the wails of new young widows and orphaned bairns. God help us."

The three of them headed to Kilbarchan. Thomas and Jennie never spoke another word while Hutchison talked incessantly. It was obvious he was energized and excited about the thought of going across the border to do battle with the English.

They eventually came over the top of the last hill and saw the valley below and there in the midst of the scene was their little stone cottage. Although they had been gone for some time, it looked as if they had never left the place. Thomas brought the cart to a halt and the little ones ran off with their mother to inspect the home. Jennie quickly ran inside and just as quickly popped her head out the door to tell Thomas all was well inside.

That evening, after they had put the little ones to bed, the three adults gathered around the one table that served many purposes. Thomas had a Bible opened to the 6th chapter of Genesis. He started to read "Now the Lord observed the extent of the people's wickedness, and he saw that all their thoughts were consistently and totally evil. So, the Lord was sorry he had ever made them. It broke his heart." Thomas stopped reading aloud and then continued, "The earth had become corrupt in God's sight, and it was filled with violence. God observed all the corruption in the world and he saw violence and depravity everywhere." Thomas stopped reading and then looked at John who had gone suddenly silent. Thomas spoke quietly into the darkness that surrounded the lit candle in the middle of the table, "then he told Noah to build a boat".

"John, I'm thinking I might be done." Thomas looked at his friend and fellow warrior and then he looked into the eyes of his beloved Jennie.

"What do you mean, done, Thomas," John asked.

"Done means done. I'm tired of it all. The constant warfare … the blood shed John … I'm done with it. It no longer makes any sense to me. Why are we going to England once again? Because some high and mighty laird says we must? They speak and we do as we are told … no questions asked? This is madness John … madness … and based upon what I just read … it breaks the heart of God." John looked down at the straw covered floor. He couldn't look his friend in the eyes.

John looked at Thomas, then Jennie and then back at Thomas. "Listen old friend. I understand. You've a wife and a family. It's only natural that you would not want to leave them yet again. But this time Thomas … this will be the last time. I can feel it in my bones. We will free Charles from the grip of those fanatics. We will place him on his rightful throne back here in Scotland where he belongs. He and the Kirk will iron out their differences and finally Thomas … finally peace will come to our land." John was smiling as he said these words to his good friend. He truly believed in what he had just said. He believed this would be the last battle for him and his fellow Scots. Peace would finally follow their victory. John continued, "Think of your clan … think of your reputation Thomas. You are a warrior. You are good with the sword. You have always responded to the call. I know there is no cowardice within you but if you fail to heed the Dundonald's call to arms … they will call you a coward and brand you a traitor to your clan and country. Your life will be ruined. They will run you and your family out of this little cottage and then where will you go and how will you survive? You know I speak the truth." John stopped and looked with great intensity at his friend and Jennie. Thomas was silent.

Jennie's voice broke the silence, "Husband, it is time for bed. Tomorrow will come soon enough … and then you can decide." She said these last words as the tears filled her eyes. She knew her man. She knew that John's word had struck home. She knew he would once again prepare for battle and leave them waiting for his return. In her mind, she hoped and prayed he would not go but in her heart, she knew.

Thomas sat in his chair the entire night. He dare not sleep with his bride. Her touch would only make his decision that much harder. He knew his friend had spoken difficult but truthful words to him. This was the only life he knew, the life of the farmer-warrior. He had not asked to be born into this place and time but here he was and he knew he had no say in the matter. He also knew that his logic was sound. He was no theologian but he could read the Scriptures as well as any man on the planet could and how could anyone read the story of the destruction of the creation by the Creator and not think the same thoughts he was thinking. He thought to himself, "we broke his heart then and we have continued to break it down through the history of mankind. And now," he stood up from his chair and rubbed his lower back," I go to break it once again. God have mercy upon my soul."

As the morning light filtered into the small stone cottage, Jennie was already about the business of preparing what she could for her husband and John to carry with them as they headed south to join the rest of Dundonald' s men. "It isn't much but it will at least get you to the camp." She said as stoically as she could muster although her voice was cracking with the pent-up emotions of sorrow and fear. She was the wife of a fighting Cochrane. She would do her part.

John had placed his gear upon the back of his horse. "I'll leave you two alone now to say your good byes. Thomas, I've left your horse tied to that tree over yonder. I'll meet you at the top of the hill." And with that final statement he bowed to Jennie and jumped on his horse and headed for the hilltop.

Thomas watched him leave for a few minutes and then turned and took his wife in her arms. They kissed and kissed again. Tears were streaming down Jennie's cheeks. She wanted to be strong but she just couldn't stop the tears. Thomas hugged her body close to his.

"Jennie ... my love," he began to speak. "Shh", she replied, "just hold me"

The two young lovers stood that way for as long as they could hoping against all hope that this was some sort of horrible dream from which they would awaken. But then reality set in and Thomas pulled himself away from her body and looked gently into her eyes.

"I love you lass. And I'm coming home to you. You hear me girl. I'm coming home to you and the bairns." And with those final words, Thomas wheeled around and strode to where his horse was tied. He mounted the beast and looked back only once to wave at his wife and children. "Be good to your mother. I love you all." He quickly turned the horse and spurred her into a gallop as he headed off in the direction John had gone.

Jennie watched him ride away until she could no longer make out his image on the horizon. "Go with God my love … go with God." She turned and headed back into the cottage where little Robert had begun to cry for his morning meal. The other little ones followed her back into the cottage and the oldest one gently shut and locked the door.

Thomas caught up with John at the designated meeting spot and the two rode in silence heading south for the Scots-English border. They had been on the path south for two days when they encountered trouble. A group of men from Ayr and Galloway had formed up under the direction of a local laird who was a Covenanter and fanatical in his loyalty to the Scots Kirk. The locals began to call them Whiggamores which in the local dialect meant the "riders of mares". What John or Thomas did not know at the time was the name the locals had established for the Dundonald and his followers. They were called engagers, Covenanters who wanted to engage with the deposed King Charles and hopefully restore him to power in Scotland. So now the war with England had turned into a Scots civil war based upon your loyalty, or lack of, to the Stewarts. It was Whiggamore versus Engager.Of course, all were dyed in the wool Presbyterians and most if not all had signed the Covenant.

Once again, it was Scot versus Scot fighting and killing each other for absurd reasons. At least they seemed absurd and ridiculous to Thomas but he kept his thoughts private and rode on.

There had been heated words between John Hutchinson and the leader of this small band of Whiggamores but Thomas was able to keep his temper in check and was able to keep the peace between the groups by citing their universal loyalty to laird and land. This seemed to appease the leader and, if the truth be known, neither man was looking to fight that day. So Thomas' interjection gave the potential combatants an excuse to back away from one another without being accused of cowardice.

After they had ridden for another hour or so, John finally spoke, "You know I could have taken him. He wasn't that much bigger than me."

Thomas laughed, "Aye, that may be true but did you happen to notice the other six men standing behind the big loaf?"

John laughed and said, "Aye … guess it was a wise thing you did back there. Probably saved our lives, heh?"

And both men chuckled as they continued to ride south.

Finally, the two tired and hungry men stumbled upon the camp of Dundonald. They were greeted with great appreciation and ushered immediately in front of the Laird.

"Greetings Lord," Thomas spoke. "We've ridden here to heed your call to arms. I hear we're marching into England to set the King free?"

"Aye, lad," the Dundonald replied. "The king is God's anointed and we are God's people. So … we go to war."

Thomas thought to himself, "And in your mind old man, tis as simple as that isn't it?" But he just nodded and shook his kinsman's extended hand.

"You'll find food over yonder. Set up a tent for the night. Tomorrow we march south." And with that the old noble leader of Clan Cochrane turned and headed out for another part of the camp shouting orders right and left as he moved through his assembled troops.

As Thomas stood on the side of the hill he took in this assembled group. "What a rag-tag bunch we've got here," he thought to himself. These men did not look like the warriors he had fought with in times past. In fact, what Thomas did not know was that the Kirk had refused to sanction this attempt to intervene in England on behalf of the King. Therefore, David Leslie and thousands of experienced officers and fighting men had declined to respond to the call of the Engagers.

That evening, Thomas spoke quietly to his good friend. "John, have you taken a good look at these men?"

John nodded, "Aye, I have and it's a worry. Nay many have fought before. They are young and inexperienced."

Thomas added, "And undisciplined … they will run when they meet the trained troops of Cromwell and the other Parliamentarians. This is a mistake John. Many of these boys are going to die in England … maybe us with them?"

John nodded solemnly, "Aye … maybe this is the end of the line for us?" And then he began to hum a tune from his boyhood. Others sitting around the campfire knew this familiar song and began to join in. Soon hundreds of men were singing softly of a young lass at home waiting for his Johnnie to return.

The battle of Preston in the year 1648 did not go well for the Scots who fought there on that day. It was not the numbers of troops employed. The Duke of Hamilton had over 9,000 men and Cromwell had similar numbers. Some say around 8500. The main issue was Hamilton's inexperience in battle. He had allowed his troops to become strung out whereby the end of the line was many hours march from the front. He thought it was a necessary strategic maneuver to maintain a connection to his supplies in the rear. Many of his men were starving and without proper battle equipment. And he ignored critical tactical information regarding the whereabouts of Cromwell's crack troops. The first shock of Cromwell's attack happened at Preston Moor and within four hours it was all over. The Scots had been outflanked and eventually surrounded. They were dying by the hundreds. Hamilton had no choice but to surrender the remnant of his troops on August 25th. Preston was the death blow to the Royalist hopes.

Thomas and John fought bravely. Thomas saw his childhood friend fall and knew he was gone. At that moment, something in him snapped and he turned and joined the rest of the clan who were running for their lives. He had never done that before in battle and even as he was running from the English he was filled with anguish and guilt. He knew the alternative was death and as he was fleeing the carnage he had a vision of Jennie and the wee ones. And that is what sustained him over the next couple of weeks as he headed home. It was not easy. A small group of those who had escaped capture were attempting to make their way north to safety. Thomas advised them to split up. It would be easier to sneak back across the border that way. They said their goodbyes and Thomas headed off towards the hills. He was alone. He would travel only during the night and find a place to shelter and stay hidden during the light of daytime. He wasn't quite sure where he was but he knew if he kept heading north he would eventually end up in Scotland and perhaps there find his way home. He ate what he could find and drank from cool mountain streams. His thoughts were continuously of Jennie and their little ones and the stone cottage that served as their home. He prayed constantly. All he wanted was to arrive safe and sound … to place his arms once again around his beloved wife and to kiss her lips and feel her warm body next to his. He wanted to live. He was determined to live. He prayed that if God would deliver him he would never again take up the sword against his fellow man. He just wanted to be home.

One night as he sat in the cold on top of a hill he heard a distance in the sound. "Was that a piper?" he thought to himself. He strained to hear and then thought, "Aye, by God, that is a piper playing a Scots tune!" He had made it. He was in Scotland. "Thank you Lord Jesus," he exclaimed. He walked toward the direction of the music and as he crossed over a slight ridge he saw a young lad of around 13 or 14 years of age with his pipes. Thomas startled the lad and he started to run but Thomas waved at him and said, "I mean you know harm lad. Can you tell me where I am at? Where is the closest town? Forgive me … my name is Thomas Cochrane."

The lad stammered, "You were at Preston. You fought Cromwell for the King's release."

Thomas replied, "Aye lad, tis true. And if you know that much of the story you'll know we were beaten pretty badly. And who, pray tell, are you?"

"My name is Jackson Armstrong. My friends call me Jocko." The lad extended his right hand and shook the hand of Thomas.

"You are close to the town of Langholm. This is Armstrong country. You are in Scotland." The young piper replied.

"Aye, tis Scotland I'm in then …. I'm almost home." Thomas spoke as a tear began to form in his eye but he would not allow himself to cry in front of this young lad. "Lad, can you point me in the direction of the town. I need food and a hot bath might not hurt either." Thomas asked.

"Sir, it would be an honor if you would come with me to my family's cottage. My ma would gladly feed you and provide all the comforts you might need for the remainder of your journey." The lad responded with a huge grin on his face. This man was a warrior. His family would want to meet him. He would be the envy of his friends. "Look at the size of that claymore he carries on his back. I wonder if he'll let me swing it?" young Jackson thought to himself.

Thomas thought to himself, "I want to get home but, I am so tired and hungry. I'll just stay the night and start up in the morning." And that is what he did. The small cottage he stayed in that evening was filled with Armstrongs … wee little ones and old decrepit ones. But all were friendly and wanted to hear over and over again the tale of the Battle of Preston. Thomas did not elaborate and simply told the facts as he knew them. The Scots fought bravely but were poorly led and there was significant miscommunication between the English Royalist forces and the Engagers from the north. Finally, one of the aged members of the family said it was time for sleep and the gathering came to a close. Thomas slept like a log that night. It had been quite a while since he had lain on a real bed. His belly was full and when morning sun came he was packed and outside ready to travel. The Armstrongs had told him to take the river Esk north to its end and then go west to the town of Moffat. From there he could walk the much-travelled Carlisle to Glasgow road back home to Kilbarchan. Someone might even offer him a ride in their cart?

It took Thomas three more days to finally reach the hills surrounding the wee village of Kilbarchan. The closer he came to his home, the harder he pushed himself. He almost ran up the last hill. And then he crested the top and there down the lane he saw it, his little cottage. He couldn't believe his eyes. He had made it. He was home.

Jennie saw him about the same time he saw her. She dropped the basket of linen she was carrying down to the burn to wash and ran as fast as she could toward Thomas. She wanted to yell out his name but could not find the voice to do so. She just ran and he ran towards her. When they were ten yards from each other they suddenly stopped and slowed to a walk. Jennie spoke first, "tis you … tis really you …"

"Aye, my love, it is" Thomas aid as the tears streamed down his face and into his bushy beard.

He grabbed her with both arms and swung her around in the air. "Oh praise God … I never thought I would get to hold you once again, my dear sweet lass, my Jennie," Thomas spoke with his voice choking.

Jennie looked up into his eyes. Tears were running down her soft cheeks. She could not speak. She just looked at her man and gave thanks to God. He was home. He was alive and well. He was home. By then the bairns had heard the commotion and led by the oldest all ran out to see their father. The oldest lad was carrying the baby Robert in his arms. Robert was sound asleep. Thomas thought to himself, "my children … my precious bairns," and once again offered up a silent prayer of thanksgiving to the Almighty.

One of the children asked out of the blue, "Daddy, are you home now for good?"

Thomas looked at the little ones and then looked at his wife and spoke, "Aye, I'm home for good." He then bent down to one knee and gathered all his wee ones up into his massive arms. Jennie placed her hands on his head and cried tears of joy. After a few moments had passed, she looked up into the sky. The sun was beginning to set in the west. The earlier rain clouds had parted and a beam of yellow sunshine could be seen. In the distance, she made out a beautiful multi-colored double rainbow and thought to herself, "And God said, I have placed my rainbow in the clouds. This is the sign of my covenant with all the creatures of the earth." Then she smiled.

Chapter Ten – City of Dundee ca 1651

Scotland was in turmoil but Elspeth would not let it bother her today. Not today. For in just a few days she and the most handsome lad in the entire kingdom were to be wed. His name was Alexander Reid. He was an apprentice to his father, John, a maltman and candlemaker for the city of Dundee. He was just 19 years old, intelligent, witty and although tough when he needed to be was really quite a compassionate and gentle soul. Elspeth loved him dearly and the feeling was mutual. Friends and family had all had agreed this was a marriage made in heaven.

Elspeth's heart was filled with joy this day but the same could not be said for the surrounding countryside. The trouble began with the execution of King Charles I by the English parliamentarians led by Oliver Cromwell. That was in January of 1649. The very next month, the Scots Parliament proclaimed his son, Charles II, the new King of Scotland. Thirty days later, England declared itself to be a Republic with Cromwell established as its "Protector". England and Scotland were, once again, at war. And, as had been the case for all of Elspeth's young life, it was the explosive mixture of religion and politics that had ignited the flames that now threatened to consume her country.

Elspeth was a young bride being only 16 years of age. But she was a mature 16. In her short life she had witnessed much and those experiences had an accelerating effect upon her development. Her mother had often told her, "Lass, you take life too seriously. You need to lighten your load a bit, frown less and smile more." But it was in Elspeth's very nature to take on the cares of the world. She didn't know why she was like this way she just knew this was who she was and it had always been the case with her. Even when she was a wee lassie, she was constantly fretting over and caring for the sick animals she might encounter while out at play or would listen with wide eyes and nodding head when the Minister would occasionally preach on the need to care for the poor and tend to the less fortunate.

Elspeth loved attending the services at the local parish kirk. She had been attending for as long as she could remember. After her father died at an early age and left her and her mother to fend for themselves, the kirk and the local congregation became a stable force in her young life. She loved the building. It seemed like a special place to her. Her mother said it was God's house. Maybe that is why she felt so at peace when there? And she could sit for hours and listen to the minister deliver his sermon. She knew how to read thanks to the parish school but her education had abruptly stopped when her father died and her mother needed her to work in the fields to make a little extra money. But her education would have stopped soon anyway. In Scotland, only the boys got to go on in school. The boys learned all about how to write, they studied the ancient languages of Greek and Latin and even Hebrew for those destined for the clergy. They also got to study other subjects like Physics and Philosophy. But not the girls. The girls were taught to read, of course. After the reformation in Scotland it became expected that all the citizens at least knew how to read the Bible. And they were taught the traditional domestic duties of sewing, weaving and other such things. Most of which bored Elspeth to tears. Elspeth was very intelligent. Everyone who had encountered her throughout her life either told her parents about her brilliance or would make off handed comments to her directly about how smart she was. But then under their breath would often mutter something about it being such a shame that so much intelligence was wasted on a poor girl destined to be a farmer or shopkeeper's wife.

Elspeth was frustrated by the situation but she would not allow it to get her spirits down. She had always had a smile on her face and a tune in her heart. She loved life and enjoyed living it to the fullest. She also had a secret. Her young lover, Alexander Reid had taught her how to write. It wasn't much at first. Just a few simple things like how to spell and write her name correctly. But then once the magic of the English letters had been opened to her mind, her brilliance took over and she had quickly mastered the art. She even kept a hidden diary where she would enter her deepest and private thoughts and ideas about life and love and, of course, God. Elspeth loved writing about God and his son, Jesus the Christ.

Elspeth felt a special kinship with the Lord Jesus. She always started her day out with a quick prayer to him and finished the same. And throughout the day, she felt his constant presence and that brought her great comfort particularly when her father died. She was only a young lass of ten and the illness had taken him rather quickly. But after the initial shock and sorrow had passed, Elspeth once again found her anchor in Jesus. For he indeed was her anchor throughout the storms of life. She sometimes felt that he spoke to her or at least made his thoughts known to her in some mysterious fashion she could not explain. Nor would she try. People would laugh at her at best and perhaps even accuse her of witchcraft. After all, she was only a young girl and everyone knew that Jesus had surrounded himself with men to do the work he left for them after his rise to heaven. Why in the world would he have some kind of special word for little Elspeth? So she kept these matters to herself and did not even speak of them to her friend and soon to be husband. She thought he would understand but in her mind since there was no immediate need to divulge the nature of her relationship with the Lord she would just simply keep quiet on this matter.

But Elspeth did find it difficult to keep quiet when she disagreed with something being said from the pulpit. And, more often than not, she frequently took issue with what was being preached. It wasn't that she thought the minister was an evil man. On the contrary, she loved him and looked forward to hearing what he had to say to the congregation week after week. But she sometimes wondered if he was reading the same Bible she was. Or could their interpretation and understanding of scripture be so far apart from one another? Perhaps she was wrong in her viewpoint. After all, hadn't the minister been educated at the University? Surely, the learned men assembled there had correctly interpreted the words of God with the Spirit of God directing them? She had gently approached this subject one evening while sitting alone with Alexander. Which wasn't often, after all, they were only betrothed and not yet husband and wife. But occasionally, when her mother was busy off doing some important task, she and Alex would walk down to the river's edge and sit and chat for what seemed like hours, and every once in a while, she would let him kiss her … but that was all. She knew the passions of young men and if the truth be known she was fully aware of her own fires burning deep within her especially for this young lad of hers. But she had every intention of remaining chaste until their wedding night. Alexander didn't like it but he accepted it. He knew that once his Elspeth had made up her mind about something, it was cast in stone.

She remembered that conversation they had one of those rare evenings down by the river when they were alone. "Alex", she started," I have a question for you. Do you think the minister is always right in his understanding of God's word? Do you think what he is saying, all of what he is saying, has been ordained by God himself?" Alexander sat quietly by her. He loved this girl with all his heart and would give his very life to protect her from the evil of this world. "And, unfortunately," Alexander thought to himself, "there is much evil in it." But tonight the air was warm, the sun was slowly setting over the hills to the west of Dundee, there was no sickness in the town, and a relative blanket of peace had settled upon it for the evening. He could have sat here for the rest of his life just looking at Elspeth and listening to the melodious sound of her voice. "Perhaps that is what I like about her the most," he thought, "her voice. When I hear it, no matter the mood I'm in or the troubles I'm facing the sound of it carries me away to a tranquil land where all have food to eat and no man hates another because of his faith or politics." And that summed up Alexander's belief system. He was a bright lad but he really did not concern himself all that much with either religion or politics, the two subjects that to him seemed to cause more grief and start more conflict than much of anything else with the exception of cattle thieving. To Alexander Reid, cattle thieves were the lowest of the low and while he was in general a kind and merciful young man he had little tolerance for those who would steal some poor family's only source of food.

"Alex, are you listening to me?" Elspeth asked somewhat impatiently. "You know you do that sometimes. I'm chattering away about something I think is pretty important and you sit there looking at me with that smile on your face but then I wonder where your mind is … where is your mind Alexander Reid?" she demanded jokingly.

"Ach, lass, you don't want to know what I'm thinking about right now," he laughingly responded as he swooped her up into his arms and planted a huge kiss upon her lips. She kissed him back and then quickly broke free of his grasp while gently poking him in the ribs. "Patience, my love, patience" she said to him as she attempted to steady her heart and regain her composure.

"Now, back to my question," she quickly interjected to change the subject and the tenor of their interaction. "Is the minister always correct in his discernment of God's words?"

"Well, Elspeth … that's a deep subject," then he laughed at his own joke but quickly got serious when he realized Elspeth was not amused. "I think he tries the best he can. And surely, he must pray a lot before he enters the pulpit to make sure that what he is saying is pleasing to God. Don't you think so?"

"I would hope so. But wouldn't the Anglican priest do the same and for that matter the Roman priest?" she asked innocently enough.

"Quiet girl! Talk like that will land you and me in a lot of unwanted trouble." Alex lowered his voice and made it as stern as he could not because he was mad at her but because he was concerned for her safety. In

Scotland these days, one had to be very careful what you said and with whom you said it.

"It's just you and I here Alex. And I trust you that what I say to you will be kept in your trust. Aye?" she asked with a raised eyebrow.

"Aye" he said nodding his head in affirmation.

"It seems to me the more I read the words of our Lord Jesus, the less I think the man actually studies them. Oh, don't get me wrong. He knows his Old Testament. And he is certainly one to spend quite a bit of time on the eternal fires of hell."

Alexander interrupted, "you must be paying attention to that part" and then winked at her with a coy smile on his lips and mischief in his eyes.

"Oh stop that … you men are all alike… one thing on the mind… I swear … Alexander … I'm serious. I think our minister doesn't read the New Testament or if he does he certainly skips out on the parts that Jesus spoke … at least the parts that I read and have touched my heart." She stopped suddenly and looked out to the river. The sun had set and the gloaming was leaving its serene cast on the water's quiet surface.

"Tell me my love," Alexander said in his strong masculine voice, "what words of our Lord touch your heart?"

"Oh Alex," she began, suddenly with soaring spirits, "there are so many. Let me see …hmm … *I am the light of the world. If you follow me, you won't be stumbling through the darkness, because you will have the light that leads to life. And .... Don't be troubled. You trust God, now trust in me. There are many rooms in my Father's home, and I am going to prepare a place for you. And … I am the resurrection and the life. Those who believe in me, even though they die like everyone else, will live again. They are given everlasting life for believing in me and will never perish.* And … so many others Alex. His words give me such comfort deep in my soul." Elspeth looked up into the night sky. The stars were starting to appear as day gave way to night.

Alexander looked at his young bride to be and knew that she was now gone. Yes, she was physically present but her soul had flown away somewhere to a mysterious place to which only she could travel. He could try to interrupt her moment of transcendence but he would not. He knew she was safe and in communion with someone or something greater than anything he had ever encountered. His faith was not like hers. He knew that and often wondered if there was something wrong with him. His was a practical faith that matched his practical outlook on life. He had never been caught up in the spirit as Elspeth had described it. He knew that right now though she sat next to him and gazed up into the night sky, her soul had drifted somewhere far from this world of sorrow and pain to a place or state of being that was indescribable. He didn't really know what it was she was actually experiencing but he knew she would soon return to him and that was all that mattered. And when she returned there would be a smile on her face and a song in her heart. She would be happy and that was all that mattered to him. As he looked at her he knew in his heart she was all that mattered to him.

"It's late lass. Time to head for home." Alex spoke to his young wife to be with a gentle and kind voice. He knew she would be disoriented for a while and would require him to lead her back on the path to their respective cottages located the village. "We'll have to get a move on

… they'll be closing the gates soon." And picked up his pace as the two tightly held hands. She did not speak. She rarely did after these moving spiritual experiences. But there was a glow to her face and a look in her eyes that told Alex that once again his gentle sweet Elspeth had encountered the other world. This was a world he had never experienced. It was Elspeth's and hers alone. He sometimes wondered if there was something not quite right about her but he quickly banished those thoughts. Elspeth was intelligent, witty and articulate. And, of course, she could write. That was the secret the two of them guarded closely. He had taught her and if the authorities found out they would hold them both accountable for this terrible misdeed or as one teacher had once told him, "Teaching a lassie to do something she will never need in her entire life was a total waste of precious time." Alexander disagreed, of course, but one had to be careful these days what you said in public in particular if it went against the accepted community standards of behavior or thinking. The Kirk of Scotland had fought long and hard to gain the position of power it currently held and it was ever watchful for any whom it considered "outside the faith" which meant anyone who might even slightly disagree with the ruling or teaching Elders. After all, these men, were led by the Spirit of God … at least that is what they wanted everyone to think.

By the time Alex had escorted Elspeth back to her home and then jogged home it was completely dark. He had only been stopped once by the night watchman. But the old man knew him and let him pass without any trouble. As soon as he entered the door of his humble home however, his mother was waiting for him. She was sitting at the one large table that dominated the main room of the house. A single candle shone on the center of the table giving a faint and glowing light to the room. She was holding a letter in her hand and the look on her face told Alexander immediately it was not good news.

"Where have you been lad?" She asked.

"With Elspeth. We walked down to the river together and time slipped by us. Sorry for being late" Alexander lowered his eyes to the floor while waiting for the admonition from his mother. But she sat there in silence just holding the letter.

"Son, you need to read this. It's a letter from your great Uncle Christopher Reid. Came all the way from Glasgow. Took a fortnight to get here" her voice trailed off and then she gently spoke, "which means we don't have much time left."

"What do you mean mother?" Alexander asked as he took the letter from her hand. He read the first sentence and then stopped and then quickly read the remainder. It was short and to the point. It was addressed to him.

"My dear nephew. I pray this letter reaches you in time. Cromwell has instructed General Monck to lay waste to Dundee. He intends to set an example. He has grown weary of Dundee's Royalist allegiance. Truth is he wants all the gold held in the royal depository. My informant in London tells me that Monck will attack somewhere around the 30th of August or the 1st of September. There will be no mercy shown to the inhabitants. Do not be misguided by those old fools who think they are protected behind the thick walls of the Dundee. Monck will find a way in and heaven help those who are inside the city when he releases his English troops upon them. As you must surely understand, I write this with great risk. If my messenger is caught by those loyal to Cromwell, I will hang. But you are my kin. And you lad are the head of your household. Take everyone who is dear to you and flee the city immediately. Do not generate suspicion. Do not pack much. Take enough food and supplies for your family to travel to Glasgow. Meet me at the University. I will find you and yours safe shelter from the coming storm. Cromwell has grown mad with power and he will not let anyone or anything stand in his way of complete domination of the kingdom. May God be with you!" It was signed, the Reverend Christopher Reid, Glasgow Parish.

Alexander slowly turned and looked at his mother whose eyes were filled with tears. "What are we going to do?" she asked with an anxiety laden voice. Alexander didn't respond immediately. He was thinking. That was his nature. In particular, when he had to make a decision and much depended upon the outcome, he stopped all external interaction and went inside his analytical mind. He was weighing out his options. He could ignore the letter. He had not seen his great Uncle in years. Could he trust what the old man had written? Had he grown senile over the years? He was quite old after all. But what if he was telling him the truth? If so, then he and Elspeth and their families were in immediate danger. He couldn't risk it. They had to leave and leave at once.

He finally broke his silence. "Mother, we must leave Dundee tonight."

"But Alex, this is my home … our home. Your father's body and the rest of your ancestors lie in the Kirk yard, and what about our business? We can't just up and leave. It will mean our financial ruin. And where we would go? I haven't seen nor heard from old Christopher

Reid in ages. Perhaps it's all a mistake? Maybe the old man has lost his mind?"

"Mother, we can't take the risk of staying. Listen, if he is wrong and the city holds, then we'll return and set up shop as usual. But if he is right and Monck manages to break through the walls of the city, then you and I both know what will happen to us and all those who live here. We must go. We must go now."

Alexander's mother dried her tears and looked at her son. She loved him dearly and knew in her heart he was correct. But she wasn't going to leave her home. She said, "Alexander, you take Elspeth and her family and flee to Glasgow. I'm not going with you. I just can't leave. This is my home. I grew up here. I married your father here. I gave birth to you here. And Alex, if it be God's will, I will die here and be buried next to my husband while we together await the return of the Lord Jesus and the resurrection of the dead. No lad, don't look at me that way. My mind is made up. Now … pack a few things and head over to Elspeth's place. You'll need to leave tonight so as to not raise much suspicion." And Alex knew his mother had set her course from which she would not be swayed.

He quickly grabbed a few precious items and some food and placed it in a sack which he slung over his shoulder. He kissed his mother and without glancing back headed down the lane to Elspeth's. He knocked on the outer door as quietly as he could but had to knock more forcefully when no one at first came to the door. Finally, Elspeth's older brother answered.

"Alex … what are you doing here? It's the middle of the night." Elspeth's brother exclaimed. Alex marched into the room and shoved his Uncle's letter at him. "Read this and then help me wake everyone." But by this time, the commotion has caused the entire family to awaken from their sleep to see Elspeth's beloved standing in the middle of their cottage. The family gathered around Alexander and he told them his plans. Elspeth looked at her young lover. She knew immediately he was serious and that this was his intended action. Elspeth's brother was shaking his head. "I'll not run. If the English want a fight then I'll be ready", as he grabbed his sword and buckled it to his belt. Elspeth's mother's hands were shaking and her voice trembling as she looked first at her son and then at Elspeth. Finally, she managed to speak directing her words towards her son "don't be foolish lad. Monck's forces are many and strong. I want you to go with Alex and your sister. They'll need your sword and your strength if they are to make it to Glasgow safely. I'll go to Alexander's house and stay with his mother. Perhaps this will blow over and Cromwell will change his mind. After all, he has conquered the south and Edinburg. Maybe he'll decide to leave us alone?"

Elspeth looked at the three of them, Alexander, her brother and mother. She loved them all. But she knew in her heart, her mother was not going with them and that she was trying to save her son as well as her daughter from whatever calamity the future might bring. She knew in an instant that this was their destiny. Without saying a word, she started to gather up a small quantity of food items and other precious objects from her childhood but only taking what she knew she could carry herself. Her mother watched her for a moment and then quickly went to a large chest nestled by the side of the wall away from the daily traffic. She opened it and motioned for her daughter to come closer. She swiftly pulled out a wrapped article of clothing and then lovingly placed it in her daughter's hands. She whispered, "I wore this dress on the day of my wedding. I want you to have it." The tears were slowing sliding down her cheeks as she kissed her daughter on the forehead. "I love you Elspeth. Never forget that." Elspeth couldn't speak. The words became choked in her throat. She was overcome with emotion.

"Then it's settled. I'll hitch up the wagon we use to cart the big whisky barrels to Edinburg. I'll drive the beast and you Elspeth and your brother will hide under a blanket in the cart between the barrels. We have to move slowly as to not alert the guards. I think they'll let me pass through the gates since they have seen me do this a hundred times before." Alexander stated as he took charge of the little entourage.

"Aye, but not in the middle of the night. How will you explain that to the guard at the gate?" Elspeth's brother asked.

"I will tell him we received a rush order from some of our pub customers in Edinburg and need to leave now in order to make it there by daylight tomorrow." Alex responded.

In fifteen minutes the three of them were heading towards the main gates of Dundee. As expected, they were stopped but by this wee hour of the morning the night watchman had been hitting his cup a little too hard and never even stopped to question them. He just ordered the gate to be raised and within minutes they were on the road heading west to Stirling and eventually to Glasgow. It seemed too easy. The tree of them sat in silence for hours until the sun was beginning to peak through the eastern clouds. Elspeth's brother spoke first, "we're going to look pretty silly if this is all for naught."

"Aye," Alex said, "silly but alive. And if what my great Uncle said was the truth then we'll be safe."

"And our mothers' dead at the hands of those English dogs," retorted Elspeth's brother.

Elspeth hushed them both. "Only God decides who is to live and who is to die and when and where and how. Our mothers were not leaving Dundee. We all know that. My spirit tells me we are doing the right thing. We are following God's will. Don't ask me how I know. I just know." She looked at Alexander who was gently smiling at her. He pulled back on the reins of the big horse that had the tough task of carrying them all to Glasgow.

"Why are we stopping?" Elspeth and her brother asked simultaneously. Alex didn't say a word but went straight to one of the large barrels that were sitting upright towards the back of the wagon. With one swift movement he pulled off the fake top and reached down to help his mother out of the contraption. Her mouth had been gagged and it was obvious she was terribly angry. Before he removed the ropes that bound her, he quickly moved to the next upright barrel and proceeded to produce his future mother-in-law, also bound and gagged. She seemed angrier then the first woman. Elspeth and her brother looked on in amazement as Alexander gently removed the wraps from the hands, feet and mouths of both the women. They seemed shocked to see one another and then suddenly Alexander burst out laughing so hard it hurt his belly … Slowly but surely, the surprise and anger of the two mothers turned to smiles and then before long all five of them were laughing hilariously.

"Ye dinna think I could ever leave me ma and ma to be … now did ye lass" He winked at Elspeth as everyone slowly regained their composure. Elspeth and her brother were simply too shocked to speak and eventually tears of joy flowed down everyone's cheeks.

Alexander jumped back into the driver's seat of the wagon. Elspeth finally regained her ability to speak and just said one word, "How?"

"That is probably a topic better we not discuss right now. Grab a seat ladies and gentleman … we've miles to go before we sleep." He smiled at his soon to be wife who returned the gesture with all the love in her heart she could muster. She didn't know how but he had done it and she was praising God in her heart for this man He had brought into her life.

Alex then turned in his seat, clucked at the horse to pick up the pace. Alexander Reid looked towards the west and his future.

Just as Uncle Christopher's letter had predicted, on the first of September, in the year of our Lord, 1651, the storming of Dundee and the siege by the forces of General Monck began. Cromwell was outraged by the Royalist resistance in the north of Scotland and he intended to make Dundee an example for any in Scotland or Ireland who might continue to resist what was quickly becoming a dictatorial rule. Dundee was completely surrounded by a thick wall and many of its inhabitants falsely believed it was a fortress that could withstand anything the Parliamentarians had to offer. They were deadly wrong. To this day, no one really knows how Monck's troops breached the thick stone walls. Some say there was a secret passage that innocent children had unknowingly revealed to Monck's troops. Others say Dundee's guards had a habit of being drunk by midmorning and that is when Monck's troops attacked. The guards did not see and respond to the attack until it was too late to raise the gates. In any event, Monck's troops went on a rampage.

It was to be the worst massacre ever committed on Scottish soil. The men who attempted to defend the town were rounded up and killed without mercy. Women were raped. Some say almost a third of the inhabitants of Dundee or around 2,000 people were killed. Even the Governor, Robert Lumsden was executed, beheaded and then had his head placed on a spike displayed high atop one of the parapets of the Kirk steeple.

After three days Monck's troops were exhausted from their pillaging and their general called an end to the slaughter. A fleet of 60 ships many of them stolen from the Scots were used to carry the vast amount of Scottish treasure back to England. Rumor had it that the collection contained over 200,000 gold coins. However, a mighty and freakish storm suddenly developed and most of the fleet went to the bottom of the sea never to be recovered. Many faithful Scots believed the storm sent by God as judgment upon the evil actions of Monck and his men.

Alexander and his little group of Dundee refugees finally arrived at Glasgow University a week after they had fled the town in the middle of the night. They had travelled the slower country trails and were highly careful when they encountered others along the way. This was a difficult time in Scotland when a person could not really know for certain if they were dealing with friend or foe. In general, the south including the major cities of Edinburg and Glasgow had fallen to the Roundheads … the name that had been given to them by their enemies, the Royalists. It mattered little that both claimed to be Christian. Both sides believed that God was on their side and that the atrocities they committed in the name of God were ordained by the Almighty and represented His judgment upon a fallen people. In times like these, people reverted back to the old ties of family. At the end of the day, it was the clan, the bloodlines of your family that truly mattered. And so, Alexander rekindled his connection with his great Uncle Christopher Reid.

"I now pronounce you husband and wife, in the name of the Father, Son and Holy Ghost. What God has joined together, let no man put asunder … Amen" boomed the voice of Alexander's elderly but still powerful and vibrant Uncle Christopher. And the small congregation gathered responded with a hearty "amen". The young couple turned from the pastor and towards the people. "May I present to all of you, Mr. and Mrs. Alexander Reid." A piper began to drone and the couple walked swiftly out the front door of the Kirk and into the bright midday sunshine. As English soldiers looked on, the couple kissed their mothers and climbed into the newly rented coach. Their bags had been packed for days and they were headed into Renfrew. They were going to spend a little time in the country with one of Christopher's grandsons, a Robert Reid, of Eaglesham parish. After that … they were a little unsure of the future but for the time being would return to Glasgow and stay with Uncle Christopher who had graciously opened his home to the five who had escaped the slaughter of Dundee. Alexander had thought he might try to set up a candle making shop in the town and perhaps even a small distillery. After all, it is what he knew how to do.

Elspeth was content and happy. She had married the man she loved. They were alive and safe in Glasgow. Though it was loosely held by Cromwell's English troops, the inhabitants of the town were faithful Presbyterians and had managed to put aside their differences of opinion regarding the claim of Charles II to the throne. Although some were more Whiggish than others in their political leanings, both agreed that an Anglican King who had signed the Presbyterian covenant as ruler was better than a Puritanical English tyrant like Oliver Cromwell. So, in time, Glasgow and Argyle to the west remained a fairly safe place for practicing members of the reformed Kirk of Scotland, although the religious and political tensions remained high.

Alexander, Elspeth, her brother and the two mothers eventually settled into a small cottage on the outskirts of Glasgow parish. Alex's Uncle Christopher was able to secure employment for him as a candlemaker in one of the existing shops in town. Elspeth's brother was indentured to a large landowner in Ulster and left for the north of Ireland shortly after the New Year of 1652 began. He would learn the trade of linen manufacture. The older women kept busy in the small house Uncle Christopher had found for them through his Kirk connections but Elspeth was unsettled. She had conceived a child twice but in both cases had miscarried before much time had passed. She desperately wanted to give Alexander a child but was beginning to wonder and doubt if it was the will of God. This difficulty led her into a number of fairly deep theological discussions with Uncle Christopher. She would often take him a midday meal and meet him in the Kirk where he kept a small office located at the back of the building. He would build a warm fire and the two of them would sit for hours and discuss various and diverse topics. The old man was a kind and gentle soul and though they never spoke directly concerning her inability to carry a child to term, he knew that was a major struggle for her and his nephew. He prayed often to God that she might give birth to a healthy child. But, so far, God had remained silent. One secret Elspeth kept from him was her ability to write. She didn't think he would be all that bothered by it but didn't want to take the chance that somehow it might interfere with their growing relationship.

One cloudy afternoon in the depths of the winter Elspeth asked Christopher a question. It was a question that had been on her mind for some time. She had briefly brought the subject up with her husband but then quickly dropped it when he seemed disinterested in the topic.

"Uncle Christopher, do you think God should pick those who rule over us or should we common folks have a say in the matter?" Elspeth asked in her quiet and gentle way.

"What an interesting question, lass. Whatever brought that to your mind?" the elderly man responded. Christopher knew his great nephew's young wife was as smart as she was pretty. He respected her which was saying a lot because the Reverend Christopher Reid like most men of his time and culture did not think highly of the female gender. He believed and taught from his pulpit that women were to refrain from too much mental activity and focus on their daily household duties. He taught his congregation that women were to be good helpmates for their men. To run the household, of course, but to let the more important matters of religion and state be handled by the men. Reverend Reid said this is what had been established by scripture and good Reformed churches were to follow this practice. Yes, of course, they needed to learn how to read. How else would they understand the goodness of the Almighty if they couldn't read the old stories for themselves? And, of course, in many Scots homes, it was the mother who taught her children to read by reading from the Bible. But the husband was the head of the home just as Christ was the head of the church. This was the way it had always been and should always be according to his interpretation of Paul's letters in the New Testament. The old man would have been totally shocked if he knew about Elspeth's writing ability and even more so had he the opportunity to read her private journal. It was there Elspeth allowed herself the freedom to express her deepest ideas and thoughts about her faith and her journey through life with the Spirit of God as her guide. She still had her episodes, as Alexander liked to call them, brief moments of time where she seemed to disconnect from the world of material things and entered into a spiritual realm of utter peace and love. Elspeth rarely spoke of these events but when she did she would often cast her eyes up to the heavens and smile then nod her head in affirmation as if an angel or God himself had just spoken to her. She would try to explain to Alexander what these episodes were like but was unable to sufficiently articulate in detail what she was experiencing. She would just shrug her shoulders, smile and tell him "God works in mysterious ways, His wonders to perform." And that would be the end of the conversation.

"I was just thinking dear Uncle. Did God choose for Oliver Cromwell to rule over us or has he chosen Charles? And, if so, why has Charles fled to Holland? It just seems so difficult at times to truly discern the intent of the Holy One." Elspeth looked at Christopher with an innocence perhaps not fully grasping the significance of the statement she had just made.

The old pastor was quiet for the longest time. He let out a deep sigh and smiled at Elspeth. "I wish I knew the answer to that one child. I truly do. I must agree with you. We Scots have tried to remain faithful to His guidance and direction. And it seems like all we have gotten in return is pain and sorrow. I don't know the answer to that question. Has Cromwell been sent to test us or to convert us? Is he God's instrument or Satan's?"

Elspeth continued with her questioning. "Why, dear Uncle, do we even need a king? Has it been ordained by God that the Stewarts are to rule over us until Jesus returns? Perhaps Cromwell had a good idea in rule by the Parliament but became corrupted by his own lust for power? And, if he has been misguided by Satan then why would our loving and faithful God not intervene and bring peace to this war-torn land? I know my God exists. I know in my heart this to be true. And I have placed my trust in his Son, the Lord Jesus, as my Savior. But I sometimes wonder … why does he tarry? Why not send the Lord Jesus back to the earth to rule over all mankind once and for all?"

The old man rubbed his whiskered face. He was deep in thought. Finally, he opined, "I don't think it is within man to rule himself. God must be our guide. His Spirit must lead us from the darkness of our sins to the light of holiness. But God must use man to bring about his will. At least that is how he has worked in ages past. Think of Abraham and the promise. Think of Moses, the giver of the Law. And, of course, King David, who brought stability and prosperity to the kingdom of Israel."

"And who sinned with Bathsheba" Elspeth quietly interjected.

Christopher suddenly stopped and looked at her and then laughed out loud. "Yes lass, David were a sinner. We are all sinners in need of a savior. Praise God for his love that he sent his son to show us the way."

Elspeth smiled. "Yes Uncle, praise God for His love for us His children." And then she stood up from her chair and said, "It is getting late and I must return to put supper on for Alexander. He'll be home soon and hungry he will be."

"Aye, the lad loves to eat" Christopher said as he rose from his seat to walk Elspeth to the front of the Kirk. "Tomorrow then … we'll continue our discussion?"

"Aye Uncle … until the morrow." Elspeth kissed him softly on his cheek, turned and was out the door and walked quickly to her little cottage. But she was deep in thought and oblivious to her surroundings. She almost stumbled into a group of men who were reading the latest news from London which had been nailed to one of the posts used to tie the horses of the many carriages that traveled throughout the growing town.

"What's it say man?" One of the gathered men asked in a husky masculine voice.

The other responded, "it says that Cromwell has announced a Tender of Union. This gives us Scots 30 seats in a united Parliament in London. He has also appointed General Monck the Military Governor of Scotland and instructed him to build a series of defenses to ensure control over the entire country of Scotland."

A voice in the back responded, "The Lord Cromwell giveth and he taketh away". This comment generated a number of chuckles and outright laughter.

Elspeth had stopped and was listening to the conversation and the chatter the posting had started amongst the gathered crowd.

She heard a woman's voice in the crowd, "Aye, and what will the General Assembly have to say about this action?" "Nothing good, I'm sure" came a quick reply.

Another masculine voice could be heard within the growing crowd "Better a Protestant dictator than a Catholic King …" And then quickly a shoving match erupted between men who were loyal to the Stewarts and those who thought rule by Cromwell and his now mixed Parliament was an improvement. Elspeth quickly extricated herself from the group and ran for her cottage.

As soon as Alexander returned home she met him at the door with the question, "Have you heard the news?"

"Aye lass … be at peace … it doesn't really involve us. Life will go on as before." He said in his soft but husky voice attempting to calm his obviously anxious wife.

Elspeth smiled at him and seemed to relax somewhat. The business of the crowd pushing and shoving troubled her. She thought to herself, "Are we not all Scots here? Why would we turn on one another like that … because of what one man in faraway London has decreed? Who cares if he is allowing Scots to sit in in Parliament? He still rules with an iron fist. And if Charles was a true leader worthy of the title King of Scotland, why has he fled to France? I suppose afraid he'll follow in his father's footsteps and lose his head to the executioner's ax."

Suddenly Elspeth's mother entered the room. "I miss Dundee." And with that statement, she slumped to the floor. Her heart had beat its last.

It took some time for the little family to recover from the shock of the sudden passing of Elspeth's mother. Alexander's great Uncle presided at the funeral service and Elspeth's mother was buried in the adjoining yard of the Kirk. This, perhaps more than anything had deeply saddened Elspeth since she knew her mother had wanted to be buried next to her husband's body back in Dundee. Eventually Elspeth resigned herself to the fact that this was the will of God but she did grow quiet and withdrawn from her husband, mother in law and even the kind old Uncle Christopher. Time passed. The seasons came and went.

In May of 1652 the last Royalist stronghold in the eastern side of Scotland, Dunnottar Castle near Stonehaven fell to General Monck's troops after an eight-month siege. The crown jewels of Scotland had been stored at Dunnottar for safekeeping until the return of the rightful King of Scotland. Monck thought there capture would be a symbolic ending of the Stewart dream of restoration and thus, end the continuous flare up of rebellion that occurred sporadically throughout the land. In particular, the Highland clans were deeply loyal to Charles and continued to fight back against what they perceived as English tyranny.

However, after the Castle fell, the jewels could not be found. Apparently, they had been smuggled out and were safely buried somewhere in the surrounding countryside. Only a few trusted souls knew the location and no power on earth could make them reveal the location of these precious symbols of Scottish independence.

When Alexander pressed his great Uncle for information, the old man just smiled and touched the side of his nose. "They're safe" would be his only comment.

In the summer of 1653, the general Assembly of the Kirk of Scotland in St. Giles' Cathedral in Edinburgh was attacked by Cromwell's troops. The Elders and their families fled for their lives and were scattered throughout the land. They were hidden in a multitude of cottages and small farms as well as the large estates of the ancient nobility. And not a single person was turned over to the English despite the fairly hefty sum of money that had been offered as payment for information leading to their arrest.

Finally, in the spring of 1654, Elspeth conceived once again and this time it looked like she would give birth. After some intense discussion between Elspeth and her mother in law they demanded of Alexander that he take the three of them back to Dundee. Elspeth had said, "I want my child to be born in Dundee, the land of his ancestors." And Alexander's mother had sealed the deal when she stated emphatically, "I am going back to die there. You may come with me or stay but that is what I intend to do and you won't be able to tie me up and stick me in whiskey barrel to stop me this time."

So, one late spring morning, the three of them, led a full wagon of goods out of the parish of Glasgow, their home for the past three years, and headed east to Dundee. Alexander pleaded with his great Uncle Christopher to join them but the elderly man simply smiled and said, "This is where I have lived my entire life lad and this is where I'll breath my last. Go with God. You will all be in my prayers constantly." It was only when he smiled and hugged Elspeth did the tears start to flow down his cheeks and into his shaggy dark gray beard. Christopher was an old man and he knew this was the last time he would see them in this life. Elspeth seemed to read his mind and looked up into the gentle eyes of this good servant of God and said, "tis not goodbye Uncle but until we meet again … beyond the sunset."

Alexander did not know what to expect. They had heard little news from Dundee since they had escaped the rampage of Monck's troops. He thought to himself, "How will our neighbors greet us? Will we be shunned and branded as cowards and traitors for saving our own skins while hundreds of them died in the destruction of the city? Will they let me start up my business once again? Is our little home and shop even standing or has it been destroyed or perhaps occupied by someone else? After all, we left no notice of where we had gone to … for all they knew, the five of them had died at the hands of Monck's troops somewhere outside the city walls."

It was evening when they finally arrived at the hills overlooking Dundee. They were shocked at the sight. The massive walls had been destroyed. An English flag flew over the green in the center of the town. English soldiers were everywhere and boats sailing the English flag were moored in the bay. Some rebuilding had occurred but much of the place lay in ruins. And the people … what a sight. This was not prosperous and thriving Glasgow or royal Edinburgh. Dundee had paid the price for her resistance to Cromwell's iron rule. And it had been decided by Monck and his commanders to leave things as they were to be an example for any who might contemplate rebellion.

Alexander turned to Elspeth and said immediately, "We can't live here. There is no here left." Suddenly Elspeth let out a gasp of pain. She managed to say through clinched teeth, "Ye may be right husband but, it appears our child has decided it will be born in Dundee." Elspeth had gone into labor and her contractions were frequent and strong. Alexander's mother had participated in the births of many wee ones and knew immediately that Elspeth would be giving birth soon. She took command of the situation and had Alexander find a stand of woods off the main road. It was a secluded and hopefully safe place for the child to be born. Alexander quickly took items off the back of the wagon and spread out a blanket on the floorboards. It wasn't a comfortable bed but given the circumstances it would have to do. And within the hour Elspeth gave birth to a son. Alexander's mother wrapped him in a blanket and handed him to his father as she tended to Elspeth.

"What shall we call him?" Elspeth asked her loving husband. Alexander shook his head. He had not given it much thought. Elspeth thought for a moment and then said, I would like to give him two names .... Alexander and Christopher, if you agree my love, his name will be Alexander Christopher Reid."

Alexander looked at his wife through tear stained eyes and then at his mother who was nodding in agreement.

"Then that is what it will be. Welcome to the world Alexander Christopher Reid." The new father proudly stated to anyone who would hear.

The young family decided to not stay in Dundee. It took some, at times, heated discussion but eventually they were able to convince Alexander's mother to return with them to the west. It had been decided that the little family would travel back to Eaglesham in Renfrew just ten miles south of Glasgow. They had spent some time there visiting the grandchildren of great Uncle Christopher when the young couple first became husband and wife. Robert Reid, one of Christopher's many grandchildren, had told them at that time that Eaglesham needed a good maltman. Alexander was hoping the offer was still good for he was quickly running out of funds.

And so the parish of Eaglesham in East Renfrew became the new home of this little branch of the Reid clan. And it was here that little Alexander Christopher grew up along with his brothers James and Robert and sisters, Martha and Mary. Alexander had opened a malt shop in the little burg and made and sold candle as well. His business met their meager financial needs for they lived a humble existence but one would never accuse them of being prosperous.

During this time of relative stability for this growing family, Scotland continued to be convulsed by the winds of religious and political war. In 1658, Oliver Cromwell died and was quickly replaced with his son who soon proved to not be the ruthless leader his father was and was eventually removed as Protectorate of the Kingdom by act of the English Parliament. The kingdom was in chaos. Strife driven by religious divisions was rampant and numerous small uprisings against the government threatened the very foundation of Anglo-Scottish society. Eventually, the radical puritans had been displaced from Parliamentary power and the newly elected members of Parliament, many of whom were some of the wealthiest landholders in all of England called for the restoration of the monarchy. In an ironic twist, General George Monck, who had been named Military Governor of Scotland by Cromwell himself, led his loyal troops south to London to restore Charles Stewart, Charles II to the throne. It was said by many a cynical Scot that Monck saw the handwriting on the wall and decided if the monarchy were to be restored it would be a Scotsman from the ancient line of Stewart, and, thus, his change of heart. This cunning action on his part probably saved his head as well. For soon after Charles II returned to London from Holland to reclaim his father's lost throne, heads, literally began to roll. In England, the radical Puritans who had initially supported Cromwell and the execution of Charles I were rounded up and subjected to a mockery of trial where the result was assured. Hundreds were beheaded and some drawn and quartered before they tasted death. Even the body of Cromwell was exhumed from his grave and symbolically beheaded.

In Scotland, things did not go well for the Presbyterians who had forced Charles II to sign the Act of Covenant years ago in exchange for their support of him as rightful King of Scotland. Charles appointed the Earl of Middleton, a Royalist and Anglican as Head Commissioner of the Scots Parliament. In March of 1661, this Parliament revoked every law passed since the year of Charles I's accession thus rolling back the Covenants and restoring ultimate power to the King in London. In fact, throughout the year of 1661, Charles II continued his purge of the English and Scottish nobility and other wealthy landholders who had in his mind turned against his father. The Marquis of Argyll and a number of extreme Presbyterian leaders were executed for the role they had played. And finally, in September, the new King restored episcopal government to Scotland by royal decree. This single act inflamed the passions of Scottish men and women whose ancestors had worked so hard to bring about the Reformation of the Scots Kirk over a century ago. Throughout the land, alternative religious services, called conventicles, often held in the open air and directed by clergy faithful to the Presbyterian cause, sprang up almost as if overnight. Nowhere was this more evident than in the southwestern part of Scotland, from Glasgow south to the border and west to the Irish Sea. Eventually this type of outdoor service was declared illegal by the King and its leaders were sought after and, if caught, executed.

And, once again the Reid family found itself dragged into this quagmire of religious tension and outright rebellion. Although Elspeth tried desperately to raise her family in peace and harmony, there was constant turmoil in their community. One could not trust anyone. Elspeth, in order to keep her young children safe and somewhat insulated from the external forces at play had learned to keep her passionate opinions confided to within the walls of her own home. They attended services at the local Kirk which was now being run by an Anglican priest sent there from the north of England. And she warned her husband and children to not talk of religion outside the home but inside when the door was closed tight and the family gathered together to read the Bible, Elspeth let her thoughts be known. In fact, she had begun to write some of them down. She realized this was a dangerous act but she desperately wanted her descendants to know her inner most thoughts and ideas about God and her savior Jesus the Christ.

Elspeth was so disappointed. She just simply could not accept the fact that men and women on both sides of the issue were using the Scriptures and the name of the Holy One to justify their wanton acts of violence and mayhem against each other. Elspeth knew that her Lord Jesus was crying in heaven when he cast his eyes upon Scotland. So much turmoil and chaos perpetrated in the name of God had had sometimes caused her to wonder if there was indeed a caring and loving Creator. How could God just sit back and watch all this unfold and not take some type of action. Had he not destroyed all mankind once before due to the evil violence in the hearts of mankind? But then, when she least expected it; Elspeth would have one of her experiences and would suddenly realize the truth of God and, of course, His love. She could see it in her writings. She would write angrily full of doubt and then her words changed as her soul had once again been refreshed and delivered from the insanity that appeared to enslave her world.

Even in the midst of the turmoil, Alexander's business continued to thrive. As he was fond of saying, "all men, be they Presbyterian Whigs or Anglican Royals take a wee dram every once in a while. And, of course, they need candle light so they don't drop their whiskey on the floor". Then he would chuckle and shake his head at the strange and misguided ways of his countrymen. Alexander certainly believed in God and in the Lord Jesus but his theology was much simpler than his wife's analytical perceptions. Although he would never say so in front of his dear wife or precious children, he firmly believed that no one man had the absolute truth regarding the Almighty and that the love of the Creator covered a multitude of sins, those committed with intent and perhaps, more importantly, those more often committed out of sheer ignorance. For Alexander believed men, in general, were pretty stupid when you got right down to it. "Ach, we are driven by our passions and they often lead us where we should not tread." Then, in keeping with this personality, would chuckle, smile and think about his great Uncle Christopher who had since left the world of the living. "Ah, old Christopher," Alexander thought, "you now know the truth … don't ye? All the things we mere mortals think are so mighty important pale in comparison to eternity."

And so, for years, this is how they lived, keeping their heads bowed and their eyes downcast while in public, trying as hard as they could to offend no one and doing their level best to keep their little ones safe. And then gathering each evening by the candle light of the candles Alexander and his sons had made in their shop to read the Scriptures and hear Elspeth attempt to interpret them in truth and purity.

Then on May 3rd of the year of our Lord 1679, their lives and the lives of all Scots changed with one fatal action. On that day, Archbishop James Sharp, the Primate of Scotland, appointed by the King himself was attacked and killed while traveling through Fife on his way to St. Andrews. Rumor had it the men who carried out the deed were actually waiting for the Sheriff of Fife but were ecstatic when given the unexpected opportunity to murder the very man responsible for leading the forces suppressing the Covenant in Scotland. His death seemed to be a rallying cry for all Covenanters everywhere. Scotland had been a powder keg ready to blow and Sharp's death lit the fuse.

Sir Robert Hamilton, a distant relative of Alexander, became a leader in the local movement and defeats a small force of Royalist troops at Drumclog in Ayrshire. Huge numbers of Covenanters gather at Bothwell near the River Clyde but can't agree to a common manifesto. Charles II instructs the Duke of Monmouth to crush the rebellion.

Elspeth is worried about her children who are now emerging into adulthood. In particular, she is concerned about her two youngest sons. Alexander Christopher, who they now simply called Alec, had married and moved back to Glasgow where he and his young bride ran a small pub furnished, of course, with an ample supply of his father's golden stock. His wife had given birth to two wee bairns but sadly both had perished after a short life measured in months not years. Although she thought of Alex and his wife often and missed them much her major concern was centered upon Alec's younger brothers James, 19 and Robert, who had just turned 16. Neither men had wanted to follow in their father's footsteps but there weren't a lot of options. James was bright enough to go to University but did not have the desire and Robert loved to spend his time in the outdoors hiring out for odd jobs in the surrounding farms of the Renfrew countryside. So both ended up working sporadically with their father in his shop but they were restless. And both were drawn to the radical elements within the Presbyterian faith. Elspeth thought perhaps she was to blame for their religious zeal. After all, she had been the one leading the regular Bible studies in their little home and had encouraged all her children, boys and girls, to freely speak their minds on topics of a theological nature. But that was then. And now all of Scotland had erupted into what would prove to be a climactic upheaval which future historians would refer to as the "killing time". Elspeth was torn. She loved the fact that her sons were so strong in the faith but constantly worried about their safety given the current situation. The Presbyterians were becoming an underground movement of resistance to both crown and government and she knew both her young lads had somehow been caught up in the whirlwind.

What Elspeth did not know was the extent of the involvement in this new movement of her two precious sons. For both had pledged to support the overthrow of the monarchy and the establishment of a purely reformed Christianity throughout the entire kingdom of Britain. They were members of a secret messenger team transporting information about the location, strength and movement of Royalists troops to Covenant strongholds in the southwest of Scotland, the highlands of Argyll and even to pockets of resistance within Ulster across the Irish Sea. In fact, James, under the guise of visiting Elspeth's bother in Ulster, had taken secret messages from Covenants in Ayrshire to Antrim in Northern Ireland. What Elspeth did not know and could not know was that two of her sons were spies for the Covenanters and if caught would surely die a horrible death.

"Are you a Cameronian?" Elspeth demanded of her son, James. Elspeth was both angry and frightened for her son. He had been traveling much lately and when gone would be gone for weeks at a time. When he returned, he said little of his travels other than he was conducting business in Ulster on behalf of linen buyers in Glasgow. Elspeth had her doubts from the beginning but her son's latest adventures had convinced her that his travels across the Irish Sea had something more dangerous to do with than the trading of linen from the farmers in Antrim to the weavers in Glasgow. She has seen him slip letters to the Elders during services at the local Kirk. And she had found sealed letters from these same Elders in her son's possession. She had never dared open these confidential documents but the time had come for her to confront James regarding his activities.

"No, mother, I'm not a Cameronian. But, what if I were? Richard Cameron was a brave man whose only sin was a desire to return Scotland to her reformation roots." James responded rather angrily.

"Richard Cameron was a radical Presbyterian who led an uprising against the King and was killed in the process," retorted Elspeth. She knew her son was involved in something which he would not share with her and that alone made Elspeth unsettled. She changed her tune, "James, lad, you are my son and I love you dearly. I just can't stand the thought of losing you. I realize your love for the faith is strong. But these are dangerous times and many of our people are being thrown in prison or worse for a simple slip of the tongue. Please tell me what activities are constantly taking you to Ulster? I know it's not just the linen trade." Elspeth stopped speaking suddenly and looked at her second oldest boy. James Reid was the second male and fourth child born to Elspeth and Alexander. OF all their children, James seemed to be the most independent and had always been that way from the beginning. Even as a wee bairn, Elspeth would tell her husband, "Our Jamie … now that one has a mind of his own … and he's not afraid to tell ye what's in it." And James had always been strong in his desire to learn of God and the gospel of His son Jesus. Even when he was little, James could often be found hanging around the old

Kirk after services had finished not wanting to travel back to the family's small cottage in the country. Both Alexander and Elspeth had thought he would enter the University and pursue a career in the clergy but that desire was not within the lad. He did not want a life as country pastor. James craved excitement and adventure and knew the established daily life of the country pastor would bore him to tears. Now, Robert, the youngest son could certainly live the simple clergy life but he lacked the intellectual skills. Robert loved the farming life and had every intention of living out his days as a farm laborer.

"Mother, I cannot lie to you. But you must promise me that what I am about to tell you must never be repeated outside this household. You must promise me. Too many lives depend upon you maintaining my secret. Are you able to keep that promise?" James' voice became steely cold and sounded much older that his years.

Elspeth looked at her son, swallowed and said simply, "Aye."

"Mother, I am a messenger for the Kirk … but not the Kirk whereby we attend services. That Kirk has been corrupted by the influence of King Charles and his Anglican puppets. I am a messenger for the secret Kirk of Scotland … the one true keeper of the Reformation. And I take critical information back and forth between these parts of Scotland with our brothers and sisters in Antrim and Down in Ulster."

"What kind of information?" Elspeth whispered to her son.

"The kind of information that someday will prove valuable when we are in a better position to do God's will." James replied.

"So … you are a Cameronian?" Elspeth let out a small gasp and tried unsuccessfully to hold back the tears.

"Richard Cameron was a good man. His faith in the one true reformed Kirk was strong. But Richard Cameron was not a very smart man. Look what happened. He and many of his followers ended up dead because he acted without intelligence regarding the strength of his enemy. He did not know how many he faced or where they were located or the degree of their provisions. When we act, we won't be so stupid." James said with his face set in stone and his eyes boring into his mother's soul. Elspeth had seen that look many a time before in this lad's life. And she immediately realized there would be no talking him out of this dangerous scheme.

"James, I know you. I know your mind is set. But pray lad listen to me just for a few minutes. I'll only say this once to you and then you may do as you please." Elspeth lowered her voice but her gaze into her son's eyes was steady and full of love and kindness. "I have been reading of late the words of George Fox."

James' eyebrows arched somewhat in surprise as he blurted out, "Fox, the Quaker?"

Elspeth continued on, "I think they refer to themselves as Friends but, aye, that's the one. Fox came to Scotland once, way back in '57. I never met the man but I have met a few of his followers along the way and they strike me as decent folk. Somehow, one of them gave me a tract of his principle teachings. I never thought much of it until the other day I came across it in one of my journals. I started to read it and could not put it down. Now … don't be looking at me that way, James Reid. I'm a Scots Presbyterian through and through but Fox writes things that I have always known in my heart to be true but was never quite able to articulate the way he has done."

"Such as …" James interrupted.

"I'll get to the point. James, you know that I times I am caught up in the Spirit as your Father likes to say." Elspeth stops and James responds, "Aye. We all know that but even you have told us to keep that within our family and not to share it with strangers." James looked at his mother while shrugging his shoulders in a questioning manner.

"Well … Fox writes of these things. He calls it experiencing the Light. He says it is the Light that is Christ Jesus and is within every man and woman and that if we sit in silence the Light will lead us on the path of righteousness. Fox says we don't need organized religion … in fact he goes on to say that all the religious organization of man are corrupt. That all believers in Jesus as the Christ whether they call themselves Presbyterian, Baptist, Anglican, or for that matter, Roman Catholic, can be led by the Light if they surrender to its holy guidance. Fox doesn't believe in an ordained clergy or cathedrals or any of what he calls the trappings of sinful pride. He calls for a simple life of faith led by the Light." Elspeth stopped to draw in a large breath and collect her thoughts.

James used this interlude to ask, "This is all fine and dandy Ma but what does any of this have to do with me? I'm no Quaker nor do I plan on ever becoming one."

"Oh my precious Jamie … tis what the man says about wielding the sword in the name of Christ. He calls for all of us who claim the name of Jesus to put down the weapons of war and to treat all we encounter with kindness and love." Elspeth suddenly began to cry for

Fox's long lost writings had touched her very soul. She continued, "Nay, I'm no askin ye to convert to the Quakers … but heed what the man says about the love of Christ. For too long lad, we Scots have been letting our violent passions rule our minds as well as our hearts. For too long, we Scots have taken innocent lives in the name of our faith. James, it is all I have known my entire life. It was all my ancestors knew of life in this troubled land. And now, to hear of your actions and how they will do nothing but to continue this cycle of hate and violence … laddie … my precious boy … it breaks my heart." And once again the tears began to flow down her cheeks.

James was quiet for the longest time. Then he looked at his mother and gently took hold of her two hands in his. "I love you Mother. I always have and I always will. I will think upon these things you have shared with me this day. I will pray to our God and seek His direction. But this I must tell you. Many men, women and children are suffering this night because of their faith and our King's stubborn resistance to change. And many of those poor folk depend upon me and others to do our jobs and help prepare for the coming Day of the Lord when true justice and mercy will flow throughout the kingdom like the rivers of this land. When, at last, we will be truly free to worship our God as we see fit in perfect peace. Fox is a dreamer. Let him have his dreams of heaven on earth. But I see no way we can bring about the changes that need to happen in Scotland without blood being shed. I'm sorry Mother to make you cry. That breaks my heart. And, I do promise you, I will think on these words you have shared with me from your heart. But I must tell you … I have set my hands to the plow."

The next morning James set out for Glasgow. There he would board a boat which would take him across the Irish Sea to Antrim. In his possession were secret documents which would someday release the hounds of war. There were tears in his eyes as he looked back towards the land of his birth.

Chapter Eleven – Clady, Urney Parish, Tyrone County, Ulster, ca 1688

The land Jamie Irvine was standing upon was owned by Theophilus Hastings, the 7th Earl of Huntingdon. It made no difference to the ruling Anglo-Irish aristocracy that a member of the Hastings family had never once stepped upon this land. Jamie had no idea what the Lord Hastings even looked like. The Hastings huge country estate was located across the Irish Sea in the northwestern section of Leicestershire, England. A place Jamie had never visited nor had any intention or desire to do so. The simple fact was that most of Northern Ireland, what most of the inhabitants simply called Ulster, was owned by very wealthy absentee English families, powerful men who supported the monarchy and the Anglican Church with their money and, thus, had tremendous influence in both Westminster and Canterbury.

With the restoration of the English monarchy by Charles II in 1660 and continued by his brother James II upon the death of Charles in 1685, the Stewarts were firmly in control of not only England and Wales but also Scotland, Ireland and, of course, the constantly developing British colonies across the Atlantic. The Stewarts ruled what was becoming the Empire of Great Britain. And they ruled with an iron fist.

Things had not gone well for the Irvine clan located in county Tyrone for quite some time. The trouble began way back in the year 1641. That was the year the native Irish Catholic had risen in rebellion against their English and Scottish rulers. Jamie did not blame the Irish for their behavior. "After all," he reasoned, "we Scots would have done the same had the tables been turned." He realized the roots of the 1641 rebellion lay in the failure of the English Anglican state to assimilate the native Irish elite in the wake of the Elizabethan conquest and plantation of the country. Her son, James I, exacerbated the situation by bringing thousands of Scots Presbyterians from the border region of Scotland and England to Ulster, at the time, a region which held tenaciously to its Gaelic ways and Catholic Church. Tensions between the three groups, Anglo-Irish Church of England aristocrats, poor native Irish Catholics, and middling class Scots Presbyterians were constantly simmering and in 1641 boiled over.

The Irish rebellion against English Protestant rule began in October of that year and resulted in several months of violent chaos. Led by Hugh MacMahon and Conor Maguire in the south and Phelim O'Neil and Rory O'Moore in Ulster the Irish planned a complete overthrow of the existing Anglo-Irish government. While the leaders had initially hoped for a peaceful usurpation of what they considered a foreign power, things quickly got out of hand and violence soon filled the entire island with Ulster turning into a blood-filled battleground between native Catholics and planted Protestants. Thousands of innocent men, women and children on both sides of the issue were slain and thousands more expelled from their homes, Christie Irvine, Jamie's grandfather, being one of them. Christie fled with his young wife and children along with other members of the small band of Irvines located in county Tyrone from their home in Castlederg back to Scotland. The Irvine men returned the next year as part of a fighting force of Scottish Covenanters led by Major-General Robert Monro. The Ulster Irish were quickly defeated with swift retribution and no mercy shown to any Catholic civilian. Hundreds of Catholic women were raped. Thousands of innocent Catholics were savagely beaten and tortured to death. In some areas, the fighting in Ulster was simply a continuation of the old clan feuds carried on for centuries within the Scottish Highlands. Sir Duncan Campbell of Auchinbreck ordered his men to throw McDonald men, women and children over the cliffs of Rathlin Island. No one knows for sure how many died that day but most folk believe the number was in the hundreds. The war raged on between the forces of the Ulster Catholics led by Owen Roe O'Neill and the Scots Covenanters led by Robert Monro whose troops were also aided with the addition of English Royalists sent by King Charles I. The Irish rebellion however soon evolved into a squabble between the old Anglo-Irish aristocracy who were known as the Catholic Confederates versus the poor Irish peasants led by men like O'Neill. This led to a stalemate as full scale battles were replaced with hit and run attacks from both sides. The Irvines knew this type of fighting from their 300-year experience in the Border region of Scotland and England. While this was happening, England eventually erupted into a civil war of its own with Charles losing his head and the Puritan Oliver Cromwell becoming Lord Protector. Cromwell landed in Ireland with his New Model Army and quickly put an end to the rebellion. Cromwell's troops were well supplied, well trained and battle hardened. It was no contest.

The end of the formal Irish resistance however did not mean the end of the troubles in Ireland. Small units of Irish troops, now called Tories, continued to torment the local Protestant inhabitants. This created poor economic conditions which were aggravated by outbreak of bubonic plague. The Irvines returned once again to their ancestral homeland of Dumfries.

Then in 1660, King Charles II was restored to the crown in England. He immediately began a policy of religious toleration for the Catholics of Ireland. They still could not own land, hold public office or vote but the century old tension had definitely subsided and the Irvines, blindly loyal to the Stewarts, were allowed to return to Ulster and reclaim their lands in county Tyrone, Fermanagh and elsewhere.

But trouble in Scotland was developing at this time between Anglican supporters of the King and Scots Presbyterian Covenanters. Many of these Covenanters fled from their homeland in the southwestern part of Scotland across the Irish Sea to Ulster. It was a short trip by boat and for hundreds perhaps thousands of years it had been a common practice for trade and travel between these two areas. So when the lowland Covenanters came under tremendous persecution for their faith in their native Scotland, it was only natural for them to move by the thousands into the semi-fertile lands of Ulster. The Scots who had been part of the plantation of King James welcomed them and their Presbyterian convictions with open arms. But the Ulster English, Anglican and fiercely loyal to the throne of Charles and then, in succession, to his brother James, established diverse types of punitive laws and social constraints intending to keep the Scots legal and economic power in check.

Scots could lease land and participate in the local commerce while paying unfairly high taxes but, they could not hold public office, teach or be in the local militia. Unless they belonged to the local Church of

Ireland parish, which was, of course, Anglican, they could not be buried in the local church yard nor were their marriages considered sanctioned and thus, any children born to them were considered illegitimate. Ireland, under the Stewarts, had become a three-class society with the Aristocratic Anglo-Irish on top, the Scots Presbyterian in the middle and the poor Irish Catholic native who survived anyway they could on the bottom. Often, they worked on the leased farms of the Scots or, if lucky, at the huge estates of the wealthy Anglo-Irish.

It was into this culturally divided Ulster that Jamie was born in his father's rented cottage on the side of the River Finn in the parish of Urney. Jamie's grandfather, Christie, had long since passed from this world to the next and he had left quite a large family. His third son, John had married a distant cousin, Mary Hamilton, and had learned the trade of blacksmith. He had managed somehow to set up a small shop in the town of Clady and had leased a small cottage attached to the back of his smithy. On the west side of the river lay County Donegal, a part of Ulster but largely inhabited by the native Irish Catholic. On the east side of the river, the Clady side, lay the county of Tyrone, inhabited by a mixture of Scots Covenanters and English Anglican planters with a few native Irish scattered here and there throughout the countryside. The original Irvine holdings had been in and around Castlederg six miles to the south. And it was to this stronghold the Scots and English Protestants would send their families when the native Irish mounted one of their increasingly less frequent attacks. This was common knowledge among the inhabitants of Clady but in reality Jamie had actually never had to flee from his home while under attack. Since the coronation of King James II, things had become rather settled and somewhat peaceful in the Ulster countryside. Of course, there was always an underlying tension of mistrust among the inhabitants along the River Finn but it seemed for the time being they had exchanged their swords for plows and were just trying to make a living out of the rocky and not so fertile soil of this land. The growing of flax or what some called linseed had become a major crop in this cooler climate of Northern Ireland and trade with the linen manufacturers in Dublin and Glasgow was growing at a healthy pace. It wasn't going to make any of them rich by any means but it might keep food on the table. And farmers needed tools made and repaired so that kept Jamie's father busy.

Jamie was not the world's hardest working blacksmith apprentice. In reality, if Jamie had his way, he would have gone to Dublin or perhaps Glasgow or Edinburg to study law or maybe even theology. But his family did not have the means nor the motivation to send him away to a university. His father had once said to him, "Lad, we Irvines work with our hands." And that had been the end of the discussion regarding furthering his education. He knew how to read, of course. Most Scots Presbyterians could read and were expected to read their Bibles on a daily basis. But the more Jamie read his, the more questions it generated. And no one around Clady seemed to know or care about the answers. So, Jamie felt adrift in the sea of life. And that caused him to often walk along the side of the River Finn casting small pebbles into the water as he walked and thought about the bigger questions of life.

That's where he was and what he was doing the first time he saw her. Actually, he heard her first before he caught a glance of her. She was singing. It was in

Gaelic. That much he knew but he didn't understand the lyrics because he didn't know the language of the native Irish. He just thought it was the most beautiful thing he had ever heard. And so he followed the sound of her voice until he came to the edge of the river close to a stretch where it widened out and slowed down its current somewhat. She was on the other side kneeling down by the water's edge. There was a basket of something which he assumed were clothes by the look of it. Obviously, she had come down to the water's edge to clean what looked like to him were bed linens, a fairly common practice in these parts. He crept softly to the edge of the river remaining hidden behind a stand of small bushes. He didn't want to be rude and be caught staring at her but he could not help himself. He had never seen such a pretty young lass in his entire life He was smitten. She stood up and stretched out her back giving him a view of her entire profile from top to bottom. Her clothing was plain. She was obviously a local farm girl or perhaps hired house help in one of the nearby large estates. There were some of them in this area but not many. *No*, he thought to himself, *it's too far away from the closest English landlord's estate. She must be a poor Irish farm girl.*

"So, lad. Are ye gonna stare at me there all the day long or are ye gonna introduce yerself like a gentleman would?" She shouted across the river in his direction.

Jamie was stunned. He didn't know how to respond.

The lassie continued, "Is there something wrong with your hearin? I asked ye a question?"

Jamie managed to speak but it sounded like a garbled mess, "My name is Jamie … Jamie Irvine of Clady … And who might ye be?" Jamie was slowly regaining his composure but his voice sounded childlike and right now he wanted to come across as a strong and grown man not some week laddie staring at a pretty lassie while hiding in the bushes.

The young girl walked up to the water's edge. As she did so, Jamie came out of his not so effective hiding place and also climbed down the bank to his side of the River Finn.

She spoke in a softer more feminine and melodious tone, "My name is Niamh O'Donnell. Do you speak Gaelic?" Niamh asked.

"Nay … well I ken a few words but in the village and at home we all speak the King's English … or try to anyway. Our English neighbors constantly laugh at me. Tell us we destroy the language with our Scottish tongues."

"The English," she almost spat the word out of her mouth, "wish they would all die and rot in Hell."

Jamie was taken back by her hostility. "Why, what did they do to you? Why would you have such hatred for them?"

"Jamie Irvine … you must not be too bright. Surely, you know the history of this land? The very land you and I are standing on once belonged to one of my ancestors, Sir Niall Garbh O'Donnell of Castlefin. And then the English came, helped by you Scots, and took it away from my people. The castle is all but a total ruin now and the descendants of the once proud and mighty Nial O'Donnell squeak out a livin any way we can. I am a milk maid for one of your Scots Presbyterian ministers who hold a lease on a small plot of land up the river a couple of miles. The Reverend Anderson he calls himself. Of course, he can't conduct services in a real church …

just has his little flock gather where ever they can find a clean and dry space."

Jamie had heard of Anderson. He was holding illegal worship services in barns, homes and even out in the countryside. Although it was against the Irish law … only the ordained Anglican priests of the Church of Ireland could conduct the worship service inside an official church building … nobody seemed to care all that much about Anderson and his small gathering of Scots Presbyterians. As long as he didn't stir up too much dissent with his messages, the powers to be left him alone.

Suddenly Niamh stooped to gather up the basket containing her washings. "Tis getting late. I've got to get on home before the Reverend starts a worry 'bout his cows. They'll need a milkin' soon."

Jamie did not want her to leave. He was overwhelmed by her looks and the sound of her voice. He tried desperately to think of some way to continue the conversation. Suddenly, he blurted out, "What was the name of that tune ye were singin' before?"

Niamh stopped and turned back towards Jamie, "So ye heard that did ye now … It was a song me mother sung to me while I was a wee lass. She's long gone now, died a few years ago from the fever. Da tried to get a doctor from Castlederg to come and tend to her." Her voice suddenly trailed off and Jamie interrupted, "but he couldn't save her?"

"Didn't even try... was one of your kin I think … name was Irvine and said that he didn't have the time nor the inclination to care for us Irish. Slammed the door on me Da's face he did and that's the end of it. Ma died a couple days after that. Listen, I've got to go or I'll be in trouble." Then Niamh picked up her basket which was obviously very heavy due to all the linens she had washed that afternoon.

Jamie had what he thought was a brilliant idea, "That basket looks heavy. Why don't ye let me carry it home for ye? You said it wasn't more than a mile or two south of here, aye?"

Niamh stopped walking and looked at Jamie long and hard. The sun was shining in his eyes so he really couldn't see her well but she could see him. And, she liked what she saw. Jamie was tall with dark thick hair and his eyes the color of the Irish Sea. He was slim but muscular, obviously worked with his hands which now hung loosely by his sides. She smiled at him and said, "That would be mighty nice of you but how will ye cross this river … unless you propose to walk on the water like our Lord?"

Jamie laughed and was in the river in a second. He knew where the stepping stones were located and was able to cross over rather quickly. The water came up to his chest at one time and the current was flowing rather strongly but he managed to get across in one piece and soon stood a few feet away from this breath taking Gaelic princess.

Niamh looked at him in his soaked clothing and laughed. "Ye are a determined young lad?"

Jamie answered, "That I am. When I know what I want, I go after it." He stopped his speech for a second thinking that perhaps he had said too much. She obviously knew he was taken by her but he didn't want to be rude and offensive.

Niamh just smiled and said, "I like that in a man. They know what they want and they go for it. Well, here's the basket ye wanted to carry." And she handed

Jamie her load of wash. Their hands briefly brushed each other and Jamie felt a spark of excitement and wondered if Niamh felt the same. He looked into her eyes and they confirmed what he hoped … she was smiling sweetly at him and twirling her hair with one of her free hands. Their eyes locked for the briefest moment but in that moment, they both knew something wonderful had just happened to them and their lives would not be the same. After they had walked away from the river and up to the edge of the path that ran south to the Anderson's Niamh said to Jamie. "Jamie, it might be easier if we both carried the basket. You take one side and I the other," all the while smiling sweetly at him. "My goodness," she thought to herself, "he does have such handsome eyes and look how big and strong his hands are."

The two of them walked down the dusty path heading to the Anderson cottage. They walked in silence but soon Niamh began to sing softly the tune she had been earlier singing when Jamie had first appeared. And Jamie Irvine smiled for although this lassie was Irish and probably Catholic, he had fallen in love with her and knew in that moment he wanted to spend the rest of his days listening to her sing.

When they arrived at the small cottage leased by the local Presbyterian pastor, Jamie hesitated and Niamh noticed it immediately. "What's wrong, Jamie?"

"Anderson is a Presbyterian and he knows my ma and da," answered Jamie.

"Aye, that's probably true." Niamh responded, "So, what's the problem?" And then it dawned on her. "It's me isn't it, because I'm a Catholic, a native?" She looked into his eyes while waiting for his response.

"Aye," Jamie answered and lowered his head and gazed at the dusty ground beneath them.

Just then the Reverend Anderson's booming voice shouted out to them from the field, "You two over there, I could use some help." Jamie looked in the direction of the minister's voice and found him trying to dig up some potatoes that were ready for harvest. He was covered in dirt and sweat and obviously quite tired from his work. Jamie and Niamh quickly walked over to where he was located and grabbed some of the tools from the small cart to help dig up this amazing vegetable that had helped to revolutionize the Irish agrarian landscape.

"Ach, the Irish call these blasted things the gift of the Spanish, but I wonder if they're not a small token of Satan's appreciation for getting us all kicked out of the garden," Pastor Anderson chuckled as he struggled lifting the heavy load of a pitchfork full of healthy and large potatoes.

Anderson was a kind-hearted middle aged man whose wife had been unable to bare children. In response, he had become the father of all the local children both Scots Presbyterian and Irish Catholic. In his eyes, they were all children of God. He was well liked on both sides of the River Finn. In fact, although this was a little-known fact in the community at large, Kenneth Anderson had a long lasting and deep friendship with Father Patrick O'Neil, the local Catholic priest. O'Neil had learned from experience to work in the shadows as he ministered to the small Catholic community located where the counties of Donegal and Tyrone met. And the same was true for the Reverend Anderson. Being an ordained Presbyterian minister meant he was significantly constrained by the official Anglican Church of Ireland. He could not preach in their buildings nor could he baptize, marry or bury the members of his flock in the Anglican cemeteries. Perhaps this is what brought these two men so close together. Many an evening was spent by the two of them discussing some theological point while agreeing the current situation was untenable and needed to change. "After all," Father Patrick often stated, "are we not all followers of the Lord Jesus Christ? Yes, we have our differences of opinion upon how we worship and on and on but in the end, we all pray to the same God. What's the problem?" And then, of course, after a wee dram, the two would venture away from religion and talk about politics and the real issues facing all of Ireland including Ulster. Kenneth would often comment, "Patrick, it's this us versus them attitude we are up against. It has plagued my Scots ancestors for all recorded time. We just can't seem to be at peace with our neighbor, no matter who it is. Look at my border ancestors. First, we fight each other. Then we fight the English. Then we fight each other again. Then we fight the Irish. Then we fight the Irish and the English. And then, of course, we end up fighting each other once again." And by this time during the conversation both men are laughing at the sheer stupidity of it all. And then the mood would turn solemn as Patrick stated the obvious, "all this bloodshed … for what purpose … for King … for country … for God, why, my dear brother, why?" And that is usually where the conversation would end with the two men hugging one another then parting company, Kenneth back to his cottage and loving wife with Patrick heading back to his safe house in the Donegal countryside.

Kenneth suddenly looked at Jamie and Niamh as if he had just seen them. He smiled and thought to himself,

"Here lays the answer … love". For the wise pastor could see what the two youngsters standing before him perhaps could not or were not quite ready to admit. They were a couple. It hadn't taken long. On the short walk from the river while carrying together a basket of laundry they had fallen in love with one another. And that was the answer to the troubles. Then suddenly a frown came over his countenance as he thought, "But it will never be accepted by her family or his. Too much blood has been shed by both sides of this issue. You poor souls, you have no idea what cupid's arrow has done to you, do you?" He continued to stare at the two of them until Niamh was uncomfortable.

"Mr. Anderson," she interrupted his thoughts. She always called him Mr. Anderson and never Pastor Anderson and certainly never by his Christian name, Kenneth. "What deep and terrible thoughts are plaguing ye now? Yer face is as if a cloud of storm has come upon it." The young lass innocently asked.

Kenneth started to respond and then thought better of it. "Ach, girl, just thinkin' bout how I'm gonna get all these taters to Clady on the morrow?" He looked at Jamie, "Any ideas lad?"

Jamie looked up at the sun which was beginning its slow descent into the western horizon. "I must be on my way Pastor Anderson. Me ma will be worried. But I'll return tomorrow and help you cart them to town. Will that do?" And then he glanced at Niamh and caught a glimpse of the smile that had come across her face as he mentioned he would return the next day.

"Aye lad that will do just fine." The pastor stuck out his hand and shook Jamie's hand with a firm and warm embrace. And then to Niamh he said, "And ye will have to spend the night lassie. Mrs. Anderson has some knitting she'll be needing yer help with. Is that alright?" Niamh nodded her head in the affirmative. Since beginning her employ with the Anderson's it had become quite common for her to spend the night when her tasks had taken most of the day and it was too late in the evening to return the six miles to her home. She glanced at Jamie and this time caught him smiling when he realized he would once again get to see this pretty lass and soon. Her heart skipped a beat. She thought to herself, "he likes me and I think I like him … a lot." Then Jamie headed back down the trail to the River Finn and the town of Clady while Mr. Anderson and Niamh went inside the small cottage warmed by the fireplace Mrs. Anderson had set for the evening's meal.

This was to become the pattern of behavior for these two young lovers over time. They would meet in secret at the edge of the River Finn or sometimes in the fields surrounding the Anderson cottage. They were both careful to ensure they were not being followed and never were seen together at any public gathering such as market or feast days. Their families would not understand their romance and certainly would never condone a marriage between Catholic and Presbyterian. It simply was not done. The tension between these two social groups was ever mounting and the aristocratic Anglo-Irish rulers did not help matters by enacting ever more stringent and punitive laws against those who were not faithful members of the Anglican Church of Ireland be they Irish or Scots.

But Jamie Irvine was a man who knew what he wanted and one of the things he wanted in this world was to take Niamh O'Donnell as his bride. Finally, he gathered up the courage to ask her and she answered with a simple nod of the head and a brief quick kiss. It was done. They would be husband and wife. But how might they accomplish this? Could they announce to the world their love for each other and thus their intentions to marry? Or was that simple lunacy in this day and age?

One bright spring morning in the year 1689, Jamie spoke from his heart to the Reverend Anderson, "Pastor, I want to marry Niamh and, she wants to marry me. I have learned the skill of the blacksmith and I could provide a modest living for the both of us and any bairns with which God might bless us. But …." Jamie stopped mid-sentence as if he did not know how to articulate the situation. But, of course, the good and wise Reverend had seen this coming weeks ago and said gently and in hushed tones to Jamie, "Listen lad … tis no secret ye love the lass. Both Mrs. Anderson and I can see that for ourselves and so does Father Patrick. In fact, Patrick and I have discussed your situation at length and we have a proposal for you two to consider. None of us can marry in the Church of Ireland. But Patrick and I both consider ourselves ordained by God himself and no one on this planet can take away that responsibility. Jamie, you are a Presbyterian Scot. Niamh is an Irish Catholic. Your families will not condone your marriage. You will be scorned by your neighbors and friends. You two will be all alone. But Patrick and I both think the only way to bring lasting peace to this ravaged land is to encourage love to replace hatred and what better way to start then to marry together you and Niamh. What do you say lad? Are you up for that idea?"

Jamie had been listening intently to the good pastor. And as he proceeded to explain the proposition,

Jamie's face broke into a huge smile and his eyes lit up with excitement. "Aye, Pastor Anderson. Aye, please marry us. But how and where and when?"

"You leave that to the Mrs. and me and, of course, Father Patrick. It will be a quiet ceremony officiated by the both of us. We're going to tie that knot so thick and strong that no power on earth or in hell itself will be able to break it apart." Kenneth was laughing so hard tears had started to stream down his face. Jamie was happy but he did not quite understand the significance of Kenneth's response. To Kenneth Anderson, this was an act of disobedience to the Church of Ireland and to King James II of Great Britain. And he reveled in the thought. He was a Presbyterian minister ordained by God himself and if he chose to marry these two young lovers then that is what he was going to do … and heaven help those who might stand in his way.

At that moment, Niamh walked into the barn where Jamie and Kenneth had been discussing their plans. Jamie looked sheepish but the Reverend Anderson continued to smile and chuckle softly. Niamh looked puzzled. Finally, Kenneth broke the silence. "Ach, Niamh, Jamie here tells me the two of you desire to become husband and wife. Is that so?" Niamh was shocked at first and then looked at Jamie. She thought her heart would burst. "Aye, Mr. Anderson. That is what I want with all my very being, to be this man's wife." She smiled and moved closer to Jamie. She placed her hand in his.

"Jamie … do you want to tell her or should I?" Pastor Anderson winked at him as he motioned for Jamie to speak up.

Jamie cleared his throat and then spoke, "Niamh, I love you. I want us to marry. I want us to live out our lives together as husband and wife. I want to have children. I can't offer you a life of ease or riches. You know how our families and neighbors will react to this action. But … I don't care. I love you Niamh … and, in my mind, that's all that matters." He slowly moved closer to her and gently kissed her.

"Whoa there lad," Kenneth said with a chuckle. "We need to make it official first."

Niamh spoke up, "but I don't think I can be married by a Presbyterian minister … can I?"

"In this day and age under these circumstances," Kenneth spoke, "the law would not permit either of you to be married in a church officiated by an ordained priest of the high and mighty Church of Ireland. And yet we Scots and you Irish continue to marry one another and bring little ones into this sad old world. So … I've spoken to Father Patrick and he has agreed to a ceremony in a location of your choosing where both he and I will officiate and together pronounce you husband and wife. Patrick's bishop won't like it but, Patrick has a bit of an independent streak within him … kind of like someone else we all know, heh?", and looked at Jamie as he spoke these last words. The three of them were smiling from ear to ear.

Niamh had a thought and immediately spoke it out loud, "Jamie, let's be married by the side of the River Finn at the place where you and I first met last year."

Jamie thought for a second and responded, "Sounds like a brilliant idea! But when my love, when she would do this?"

Just then a voice from the back of the barn said, "How about right now?" It was Father Patrick. He had been standing in the area where Kenneth's cow was locked away every evening. He had been there since early morning. One of his parishioners had taken quite ill the night before and had eventually left this world for the next. Father Patrick had been summoned for the last rites. Since the old man who had died had lived not too far from the Anderson cottage, Patrick had just decided to spend the rest of the evening there in the barn and had just woken up when the conversation between Jamie and Kenneth had begun.

Kenneth turned to Patrick and said, "How much did you hear old friend?"

Patrick responded, "Enough to know that God is in the midst of this union and I am honored to be able to participate. If ever a man and woman were meant for each other. It's these two. I say we head down to the River Finn and make this happen."

The four of them were silent. Jamie looked at Niamh and after a short period of time, she gently nodded her head. But then she said, "Jamie, I can't be married in this old work dress. Look at me. I'm covered with filth. My hair is a mess."

Kenneth Anderson broke into their conversation, "Never mind that lass. We'll stop at the cottage and tell Mrs. Anderson what the plans are. I'm sure she will help you prepare for your wedding and I know she has a dress that will fit you so that you might be a proper bride. I know this because she wore it on the day we were wed. And how about you lad, I reckon you'll need to wash up a bit and maybe find one of my old suits you can squeeze into?"

They were all smiling as they left the barn and headed to the cottage. Mrs. Anderson was overjoyed with the idea and helped Niamh prepare for her wedding more than the young bride to be could have imagined. Father Patrick assisted Jamie and when all was ready the five of them headed to the river.

They were all smiles and laughter as they stood by the edge of the Finn. And, as promised, at the exact time in the ceremony, both the Reverend Kenneth Anderson and Father Patrick O'Neil said simultaneously, "by the power invested in us by the Almighty God, we now pronounce you husband and wife." And as Father Patrick made the sign of the cross, the Reverend Anderson said in his booming baritone voice, "in the name of the Father, and of the Son, and of the Holy Ghost. Amen."

Little could this small group of kind hearted and loving Christian people know what was happening that very moment at the Chateau de Saint Germaine en Laye, France. And yet, what was happening there would soon have a major and horrible impact upon all of them.

During the month of April in the previous year of 1688, King James II had re-issued his Declaration of Indulgence ordering his Anglican clergy to read it in their churches. James had issued this proclamation once before in the summer of 1687. His intent was to negate the effects of English laws which punished Catholics and Protestant Dissenters. He also set into motion legal action to provide some support to Catholics in Scotland and Ireland. But James was reluctant to grant freedom of religious expression to the Presbyterians in Scotland and Ulster. He was still furious at the Scots Presbyterians for their rebellion against his rule led by Archibald Campbell, the Earl of Argyll in 1685. In an attempt to gather and maintain support for his actions, James instituted a wholesale purge from government and church offices those who opposed his liberal attitude in particular his stance towards the Catholic Church. By now, James had married the Catholic Mary of Modena and it was widely known that he also was considered a faithful member of the Roman Catholic faith. His purge included the major colleges of education, the military and significant positions of authority and power throughout his administration. He replaced many of these men with Catholics or those Anglicans who were more tolerant of religious differences. When seven bishops of the Anglican Church plus the Archbishop of Canterbury were arrested and tried for sedition, the Anglican English aristocracy had had enough. The tipping point was the birth of James and Mary's son and heir to the throne, James Francis Edward on June 10th. The Prince's birth substantially increased the probability that the next monarch would also be Catholic. James had two daughters who were Protestant. But by law, they would not be first in line to inherit the crown. Several wealthy members of Parliament plus other influential men from diverse places in the kingdom entered into secret negotiations with William, Prince of Orange to come to England with an army and to take by force if necessary the crown from James. On November 5th, of 1688, William and his Dutch army invaded England. Many of the Protestant nobility including Churchill defected and joined William as did his own daughter Princess Anne. James lost his courage and declined to resist with his own loyal forces. He attempted to flee to France was captured but released by William on December 23rd. William had no desire to make James a Catholic martyr. His cousin and ally, Louis

XIV offered him a palace and pension. So James fled to France. The Parliament ruled that James had abdicated his crown and therefore it was now vacant and could be offered to anyone they chose. They chose James' Protestant daughter, Mary to be Queen and dictated she would rule jointly with her husband William of Orange as King. This happened in February of 1689. The new monarchs in concert with their loyal Parliament established that henceforth, no Roman Catholic was ever permitted to ascend the English throne nor could any English monarch ever again marry a Roman Catholic.

On that warm spring day Jamie Irvin and Niamh O'Donnell became husband and wife, James Stewart, the former King James II of England and Ireland who was also considered to be King James VII of Scotland, supported by a contingent of French troops landed in Ireland. The Irish Parliament had not followed the example of their counterparts in London. They declared James King of Ireland and passed strict punitive laws against any Irish that opposed him. At James's urging, the Irish Parliament passed an Act for Liberty of Conscience that granted religious freedom to all Catholics and Protestants in Ireland.

When word of these activities arrived in Ulster, the tenuous peace that had existed in the north between Irish Catholic and Scots Presbyterian collapsed and violence erupted throughout the north country.

Jamie and Niamh had already decided to keep their marriage a secret from both of their families prior to the start of the hostilities. But with the outbreak of the fighting, the two young lovers lost all hope of ever living openly as husband and wife. Every evening found them in separate cottages longing to be with the other. Jamie's home was in Clady while Niamh went to sleep every evening in her small cottage across the River Finn in County Donegal. The distance that separated them was only six miles as the crow flies but to them any distance was as good as a thousand miles when they could not be together. Their love was under attack by forces they could not truly understand nor control.

They would meet in secret at the crossing of the river where they had first met and fallen in love. The marriage had been consummated but the event was not memorable at least not the way Niamh had imagined it would be or the way Jamie had intended things to go. But in their minds, they were now truly husband and wife in the eyes of God and nothing could sever that bond.

In the early summer, a force of some magnitude comprised primarily of native Irish Catholics from counties to the south in combination with the French forces accompanying King James attacked Ulster.

Jamie and Niamh were lying side by side next to the cool running water of the River Finn looking up into the blue sky of mid-day. Jamie rolled onto his side and took his young bride's hand into his. "I love you Niamh. I love you with every ounce of my being." They kissed slowly and passionately. Suddenly Jamie jerked back and put a finger to his mouth to tell Niamh to not make a sound. He whispered, "Did you hear that?"

Niamh whispered back, "Aye, I did. What was it?"

Jamie replied, "Cannon fire. Listen … there it is again." He crawled up to the side of the top of the river bank and looked west across the river into Donegal. He was shocked by what he saw. Stretched out before him as far as his eyes could see were troops of foot accompanied by men on horseback waving the flags of France and Ireland. And the cannons were aimed right at them.

"My God, Niamh. We're under attack. They are firing at Clady. We have to get out of here …now!" And with that, he grabbed Niamh by the arm, pulled her to his side and began to run as fast as the two of them could travel together back down the lane to the tiny village of Clady. His mind was racing as the noise from the cannons got louder. It wasn't but a couple of miles from the crossing to the center of town but as soon as they rounded the curve where he had a clear view of the town he could see the cannon had already had an effect. People were screaming and running everywhere. Men were assembling at the town center and the women and children were being placed in horse drawn buggies and carts presumably to take them east to safer territory. He ran holding Niamh close to his side until he reached the blacksmith shop. He ran right into his father.

"Jamie, thank God, lad. You need to grab a weapon of some sort. The Irish are rising and we have to defend Clady. We've sent the women and children south to Castlederg. They'll be safe behind its walls" Then Jamie's father stopped in mid-sentence as it suddenly dawned on him that his son was not alone. "Who is this?" He asked.

Jamie stopped but only for a moment. "Da, this is my wife … her name is Niamh. Aye … she is Irish and I don't care what you have to say about it. We love each other. We have been married by two men of the cloth. And …" before Jamie could finish his thought a cannon ball exploded on the rooftop of the blacksmith shop. Sparks of fire and splinters of wood and metal flew everywhere. Smoke quickly filled the interior.

Jamie's father fell to the floor. A sharp piece of shrapnel had entered his back and had exited out his chest obliterating his heart. He died instantly. Niamh screamed and Jamie grabbed her hand and turned and ran. They ran as fast as they could to the road that took them south and east to Castlederg.

"Why, Jamie? Why is this happening?" Niamh pleaded with her young husband. But Jamie did not respond. He had one thing on his mind and that was their survival. He had never been in battle before but the blood of warriors coursed through his veins. He knew instinctively they needed to get out of Clady as fast as possible, stay out of sight as long as possible and somehow make it safely to the Castle. After they had run for what seemed like hours he finally slowed to a walk. Niamh was exhausted and he was half carrying her until finally he couldn't go on. He spotted a section of jumbled boulders which could provide some cover for the two of them while they rested. He picked up Niamh in his arms and carried her to the rock where he managed to find a safe place to hide. Niamh had fainted and he gently laid her down on the hard surface. He then crawled slowly up to the top of the ridge where he could get a clear view of Clady, the River Finn and the road to the south. What he saw he kept in his memory for the rest of his days. Clady was burning to the ground. The Irish and French troops were crossing the River Finn and were heading south along the road to Castlederg. He knew in a moment his ma and all the rest of his kin would soon be overtaken. "God help them," he thought to himself. He realized that they could not go in that direction. He looked again at the troop movements and realized in a second their only chance for survival was to sit tight, let this band of troop march past them and then circle back around to the road out of Clady that headed north to Strabane. He thought to himself, "If we can get there, we can make it to the fort at Derry. We'll be safe there." Niamh stirred and Jamie rushed back to her side. "Shh … my love … rest now and don't speak a word. Our lives depend upon our silence." He looked into her eyes and she nodded her head to signify she had heard and understood their predicament.

Jamie had decided they would travel at night and hide during the day. Unfortunately, Jamie did not know at that time the gates of Derry had been shut since the beginning of the year due to unrest in the surrounding countryside. Even if he and Niamh managed to elude the roaming Irish and French soldiers they would be unable to enter into the safety of the town which would soon be under siege by the forces of James II. As soon as the sun began to set in the western sky, Jamie and Niamh left their rocky hiding place and headed north to Strabane. The small village of Clady was deserted and that enabled them to stop at Jamie's cottage and gather up a few items of clothing and food. Jamie also grabbed his father's butchering knife and, of course his blacksmith's hammer. He wanted to bury the body of his father but knew that time was precious and so he simply covered it with a blanket and laid a few stones over the top. It was the most difficult thing he had ever had to do in his young life. He didn't feel right doing it but he also took one of the small ponies from a farm on the outskirts of the village. He placed Niamh with a little bundle of their possessions on what had become a beast of burden. The pony resisted at first but Jamie was determined to get to Strabane. The moon was full and bright enough to light the dirt path that led from Clady north to what he hoped would be a safe place.

After they had travelled a short distance from town Jamie spotted a lone individual walking in their direction. Jamie brought the pony to a halt. He handed the knife to Niamh and placed the hammer in his strong and powerful right hand. When they were approximately 30 feet apart from one another, the stranger called out in Gaelic in the darkness of the night. Niamh gasped and exclaimed, "Father Patrick, is that you!"

"Aye 'tis me and is that you Niamh and your man Jamie?" Patrick responded trying to see the two in the growing darkness.

Jamie answered, "Aye, Father, tis us. Why are you on the road this late at night? And where are you heading?"

"I was just about to ask you two the same question?" Patrick replied.

"Clady has been attacked and burnt to the ground. My da is dead. Killed by a French cannonball and me ma is probably gone as well. We are heading to Derry to find shelter behind the walls of the town," Jamie replied still in a state of shock from what had transpired. Niamh slid off the pony and stood by Jamie in stony silence. "Father," she asked, "what in God's name is going on?"

Father Patrick came close enough to them to see the fear, sorrow and anger on the young couple's faces.

"James II has returned from France. He has invaded Ireland with the help of his French troops and local Irish supporters. He intends to reclaim the crown from King William and Queen Mary. You can't go to Derry." The priest explained in hushed and urgent tones.

"Why not?" asked Jamie.

"It is surrounded by Irish and French troops. In fact, most of James' forces have gone north to surround the Presbyterian holdout. The band of them that came through Clady is a small off shoot of the main force. We would be better off heading south. I have been told that hundreds … maybe thousands of Scots Presbyterian and English Anglican soldiers are gathering at Enniskillen. If we can get there we might have a chance at surviving this madness?"

Jamie took a step back from the priest. "You said we, father. Surely, you can't think you would be safe with us in the midst of a group of Presbyterians ready to shed the blood of any Irish Catholic they encounter, especially a priest?"

"And what of your wife Jamie? Is she not an Irish Catholic? How were you going to keep her safe?" Patrick responded. "Listen to me lad. I'm not a supporter of this … using the pure and simple teachings of our Lord Jesus as an excuse to take the lives of innocent men, women and children. You need to get to Enniskillen. Between here and there are dozens if not hundreds of angry Irish men who see this as an opportunity to get even with the English and, I'm sorry to say this, Scots landholders who have kept them in bondage for the past century. They would kill you and Niamh on the spot, you for your Scots blood and Niamh as a traitor to her faith. Let me go with you. Niamh and I speak perfect Gaelic and we can tell strangers you are her mute brother. I will tell them I have been called by my Bishop in Dublin and I'm bringing Niamh to enter the nunnery and you will be indentured as a servant to a wealthy Anglo-Irish landholder … who happens to be Catholic. That should get us safely to Enniskillen. Once we arrive, you two can enter the gates and reverse the roles. Niamh becomes a mute sister. Once inside you'll both be safe until this bloodshed ends."

Niamh spoke, "But if we do make it, what will happen to you Father? Where will you go?"

Patrick managed a small smile, "Why lass, a priest can't lie … I'm off to Dublin. I've been called to start teaching at a small Catholic school for the wealthy aristocrats who think James will somehow be victorious. As if William and Mary are just going to stand by and watch as part of their Empire falls to an abdicated King with French support. Ha … what fools men can sometimes be."

"Father Patrick, what of Kenneth Anderson and his wife, are they safe?" Jamie asked.

Patrick became quiet. He finally shook his head no and looked first at Niamh and then at Jamie before he spoke," I'm sorry to inform you of this but both are dead." Niamh gasped and clung to Jamie for support. Tears streamed from her eyes. Jamie was doing all he could to be strong for her but could feel the tears welling up in his own eyes.

"I had just left their cottage. I heard gunfire and saw smoke rising from their home. I ran back to their farm and hid behind a tree on top of the hill looking down upon the scene. It was horrible to watch and one I will never forget as long as I live. Those French dogs had drugged them both from their cottage. Kenneth with just his nightshirt on and his wife covered with only a blanket from their bed. One of the French officers, I assume he was an officer since he was giving the orders asked Kenneth a question in broken English. I couldn't really make out the question but it had something to do with the one true faith. I didn't hear Kenneth's answer but then to my surprise and horror the officer took his sword from his scabbard and ran it completely through his body while his poor wife screamed to the heavens for mercy." He stopped and looked at Niamh. "Discretion prevents me from speaking of the awful things those dogs from hell did to the poor woman before they took an axe and cut off her head. May God's judgment be swift and certain for those who participated in this heinous and barbarous act." Patrick then began to sob and looked at the ground. "And I was too frightened to come to their aid … I'm so ashamed of myself." He spoke through the tears while gasping for breath as if retelling the story had forced him to relive the vivid scene once again.

At last Jamie spoke, "there is nothing you could have done. They would have killed you and based upon what you have told me about them it probably would not have been a quick and merciful end." Jamie looked at Niamh. "Well, my love, north to Derry or south to Enniskillen? I do have kin between here and there. Perhaps some of them are still alive and we'll find safety amongst them?"

Niamh looked at Jamie. "You are my husband. I go where you lead. But I do think we take Father Patrick with us?"

"Aye," Jamie responded and with that the three of them turned around and headed back to the burned-out village of Clady and then south on the road to Castlederg.

AS the crow flies it was only a half day's journey to Castlederg. They could hear small cannon booming in front of them as they approached the Castle. They had released the pony and made their way on foot to higher ground where hopefully they could get a look at what was happening ahead of them. The Castle was under attack.

But the force, as Father Patrick had said was a small detachment and equipped with one solitary cannon. The inhabitants of the Castle were holding their own. They had two small mortars and were firing them into the scattered French and Irish troops. It appeared to be a standoff for the time being. Jamie now knew that if he could somehow get ahead of these Frenchmen, they had a good chance at making it to safety at Enniskillen. But Jamie also knew that somewhere in that Castle now being bombarded were his ma and the rest of his family. Jamie was helpless and that made him extremely frustrated. His da was dead and maybe his ma too. He didn't really know if she and the others had arrived safely to Castlederg or if the French had caught them before they reached its walls. And, as hard as it was for him to admit, he could not know. It would be impossible for him to enter into the Castle now while it was under bombardment.

"We'll wait here until night falls. Then we'll head due south and then turn to the east. Maybe we'll get around them safely?" Jamie spoke to Niamh and Patrick and both nodded their heads in agreement. "What else could they do?" thought Niamh.

As the sun set upon the three of them the battle had started to quiet down. Perhaps the French were giving up and heading back to the north? Perhaps, God forbid, the inhabitants of Castlederg had run out of ammunition, whatever the reason an eerie silence fell over the battlefield.

They had walked about five miles through the moonlit night when suddenly they heard a masculine voice shout to them in Gaelic to stop and stand still with their arms raised in the air. Jamie didn't understand, of course, but he carefully followed Niamh's behavior.

Quickly, Father Patrick engaged the man in Gaelic. After a rather lengthy and sometimes heated discussion, Niamh lowered her hands and Jamie followed her action. Patrick turned to them and spoke in Gaelic. Niamh took Jamie by the hand and quickly led him past a small group of Irishmen armed only with pitchforks, sickles and hammers. These were not seasoned troops but there were at least six of them that Jamie could count and he kept his head lowered and eyes to the ground as they walked by. When they were out of hearing range Niamh spoke first, "Jamie those men were scouts sent out by the French to watch for reinforcements coming from Enniskillen to Castlederg. They said King William's forces had been spotted at sea and it was a mighty armada consisting of English, Dutch, and Danish warships. It appears that William will attempt to land in Ulster first and then make his way south to the capitol at Dublin. Jamie … do you know what this means?" Patrick was smiling and as soon as the message sunk in Jamie allowed a thin smile to cross his lips. "Aye, lass, we're going to be safe." And then he hugged her and kissed her and then he embraced Patrick. "Thank you Father. Had we gone north and not south, only God knows what would have happened?" Jamie spoke to the priest with complete trust and honesty. This man was a good man. He had risked his life to save his and Niamh's.

Patrick was nodding his head. "Aye, you two are safe … for now. But do not tarry. Travel as fast as you can to Enniskillen. I know these Irish. They are my people. They will not give up without a fight. And now, we must part and go our separate ways. He said something to Niamh in Gaelic. She smiled and they embraced. He then took Jamie's hand in his. "Lad, take care of her. Walk always in the path of righteousness. Live long and happy lives together and bring many little Irvines into this world."

And with that, Father Patrick O'Neil turned and headed due south. He would travel across the open fields and pastures until he reached the road to Dublin. Jamie and Niamh watched him walk away until he was no longer in their sight. Then Jamie took Niamh by the hand and turned to the east and headed towards Enniskillen and what they hoped and prayed would be safety.

The next few months of the lives of this young couple would be filled with danger, chaos and uncertainty. While Enniskillen managed to hold out against the combined forces of French and Anglo-Irish loyal to King James II including a few Anglican Scots landholders like Sir Gerard Irvine a distant relative of young Jamie, it was not without sacrifice and bloodshed. Thousands of Protestants would gather at Enniskillen and venture out into the Irish countryside in assault and counterassault tactics. Eventually, King William's forces did land at Carrickfergus and liberated Ulster including the besieged towns of Derry and Enniskillen plus numerous small towns and villages between the Irish Sea and the Atlantic Ocean. In July of 1690. William's forces met James at the Boyne River just thirty miles north of Dublin. In this war between the kings, thousands of men died in battle and countless numbers of innocent men, women and children died as their homeland convulsed with the agony of war. Finally, a year later, it was all over. James and 14,000 Irish soldiers went into exile to France and joined the French army never to return to their native soil. The reign of the Stewarts in Great Britain had come to an end.

At first, Jamie and Niamh had followed Father Patrick's advice. Jamie's surname of Irvine had been enough to grant them entrance and once the leaders of the town found out that he knew the trade of the blacksmith, his services were in high demand. But Niamh played the role not of his sister as the original plan had called for but as his wife who unfortunately had lost the ability to speak after witnessing the slaughter of her family in Donegal. The story was true enough that Niamh rarely slipped up. She did however occasionally speak a word or two in her native tongue but any who might have heard her seemed to ignore it. After all this was a time of war and strange things often went unexplained. Her pregnancy may have also had something to do with her neighbor's tolerance of her lack of language. With so much death and devastation surrounding them people were in general quite excited to consider the possibility of love and new life in their midst. So life went on for the Irvines. Niamh, silent during the day when out in public became quite the chatterbox in the evening behind the closed doors of their little cottage attached next to the blacksmith shop. But now that she was expecting, she knew they would not be able to keep up the charade much longer. It was Niamh who made the suggestion.

"I will convert." She said one evening as she was filling her husband's plate with food.

"What?" Jamie exclaimed. "What did you say?"

"Jamie, my love, I can't go on living like this. I won't go on living this lie. Not with me about to become a mother and all." There were tears in her eyes as she spoke gently but with firmness to her husband.

"Niamh, I have never asked that of you nor would I. I know how important your faith is to you. Once the war is over, we can just be ourselves again. You'll see." Jamie said as he tried to muster up a degree of optimism which quite frankly he did not have.

"Nay, husband. You and I both know the truth of the matter. There has always been tension between the Protestants and the Catholics here but with this last outbreak of warfare atrocities have been committed by each side that will not soon be forgotten. I fear this land will be drenched in blood for decades …. Centuries to come. You know I speak the truth. And this is not our home. We belong in County Tyrone. I miss it Jamie. I want to go home I want our baby to be born at home. Our home." Niamh became quiet and looked at her young husband with loving but determined eyes.

"Goodness woman. That's the most words I've heard ye put together in some time now." And he thought to himself "and that's a good thing". He had become worried about Niamh. He knew she was happy about being with child but she was unhappy with the current situation of their lives. He looked at her and his heart was filled once again with the love he had felt on that first day by the River Finn.

"Well … I guess you had better start packin' yer things, heh?" Jamie smiled and waited for her response which was quick. She literally leaped for joy and ran into his arms. "Ach, lass, there's a wee bit more o ye to hug now," Jamie said teasingly. Niamh softly punched his arm and said, "Not the right thing to say to a pregnant woman, lad." They smiled at each other and then kissed.

It took them a few weeks to prepare their plan and begin its execution. Jamie had spoken to his distant kinsman, Sir Gerard Irvine, who had changed sides when it became obvious that James was going to lose the war.

Many did not trust him from that point on but he was a knight of the King and more importantly, from Jamie's perspective, Sir Gerard owned large parcels of land in and around Castlederg. It wasn't Clady and the River Finn but the Castle walls had withstood numerous attacks by the combined Irish and French forces and perhaps, most importantly, they needed a new blacksmith for the old man who used to serve the community as the smithy had died and had left no sons to take his place. Jamie and his distant cousin struck a deal. He would be given ten acres of land to farm as he saw fit. Gerard would take ten percent of each year's earnings and Jamie would be given the old blacksmith's shop inside the walled town itself. Any profit he made could be his to keep. The matter of Niamh's conversion would be a slightly more delicate and somewhat difficult matter. Thousands of Irish men and women were being forced to convert to the Anglican Church of Ireland but what Niamh wanted to do was for Jamie to remain a Dissenter and stay faithful to his Presbyterian roots. And that is the church to which Niamh wanted to convert. It was one thing to go from Catholicism to the established Anglican faith. It was an entirely different matter to become a Presbyterian as an adult convert. In particular, for a young highly pregnant girl who looked very much a native and spoke flawlessly the Gaelic language.

But Jamie had made friends during the couple's stay at Enniskillen. And one of those friends was the Reverend Thomas Wilson, a Presbyterian minister, ordained by the Elders of his home parish in Glasgow. Famine had broken out in Scotland and hundreds of Scots were fleeing their homeland by making the short journey across the Irish Sea to Ulster. And most of them were fiercely independent and loyal to what they considered the one true reformed Kirk of Scotland. Thomas Wilson was sent to guide a newly formed flock in none other but Castlederg Tyrone County Ulster.

For weeks Wilson had been coming into Jamie's small blacksmith shop securing supplies for the trip to Castlederg. One day, after securing the papers from his cousin to the land and shop in his new home, he approached Wilson with his wife's issue of conversion.

"So, Jamie, you tell me she is not really a Scot. She didn't see her family slaughtered by the Catholic Irish. She really can talk. She is seven months pregnant. And she wants to convert to the reformed Kirk of Scotland. Did I get that right, lad?" Wilson looked at the young blacksmith with incredulity.

"Aye, pastor. That's about the size of it." Jamie looked at his new friend. He had taken a chance with Wilson. It could mean disaster for he, his wife and their wee soon to be bairn. But Niamh had been set in her ways. And he had already learned in their short-married life that once she made up her mind there would be no going back. He waited for the Pastor's reply.

"I must speak to your wife in private." Pastor Wilson replied. Jamie knew that Wilson was a kind and gentle man but Jamie really had no idea the thoughts that only Thomas shared with himself. Thomas knew that eventually once peace was firmly established in Ulster, good old King William and Queen Mary would soon forget the aid his Scots brethren had provided in the war with King James and the French. He knew that soon the old Anglican ways would reestablish themselves and we Presbyterians would go back to our second-class citizenship, not only here in Ulster but back home in

Scotland as well. In reality Thomas, even though trained at the Reformed Seminary, was not really much of a Reformed theologian. He had always been drawn to the simple and pure teaching of Jesus of Nazareth. To Thomas you could sum up the good news of Christ in one word … love. It was his understanding that Jesus told his followers to go into the entire world teaching them to obey what he had commanded and what he had commanded had been rather simple, you are to love the Lord your God with heart, mind and soul. You are to love others as you love yourself. Upon these two commandments rests the law and the prophets. It was and always would be about love. And somewhere in time, Thomas reasoned with himself, we who call ourselves Christians, followers of Jesus of Nazareth, had lost track of that fundamental concept. So he had privately and secretively dedicated his ministry to remind his flock and all those who would listen what the message of Jesus was truly about.

"You want to speak to her in private?" Jamie interrupted his thoughts.

"Aye, in private." The minister responded. Jamie looked at Thomas. Did he trust this man? What choice did he have at this point? He knows the truth. With that knowledge alone, he could destroy his family.

"Then so be it. When?" Jamie responded.

"Now is as good a time as any. She's at home, I reckon?" Thomas Wilson asked.

"Aye" Jamie acknowledged. I'll walk with you and wait outside out cottage. He trusted the man but he wasn't going to let any man be with his woman alone.

The two of them walked to Jamie and Niamh's house and Jamie rapped on the front door. Niamh opened it and stepped back when she saw her husband was accompanied by his friend, the Presbyterian pastor.

"Thomas knows it all Niamh." Niamh clutched her swollen belly and gave out a little gasp of surprise. "We have to trust someone if what you want to happen is going to happen." Jamie looked at his wife with tenderness and compassion.

Niamh nodded and Thomas Wilson walked inside the small cottage. He closed the door softly. Jamie looked surprised. "I thought you said this discussion was to be in private."

"I did. But I changed my mind. After all, we'll need an earthly witness," he looked up towards the ceiling, "as well as a heavenly one."

Jamie nodded and took a seat behind Niamh.

"Niamh, I have but three questions for you?" Thomas raised an eyebrow as he sought her affirmation.

In her gentle and knowing way, Niamh nodded her head and smiled.

"Niamh, do you love the Lord your God with all your heart, mind and soul and do you believe that He sent His son Jesus to be our Savior?" the pastor asked.

"Aye" Niamh answered.

"Niamh Irvine, do you love others as you love yourself?" the pastor continued with his questions.

"Aye … at least I try to Reverend" She smiled and Jamie chuckled in the background. Pastor Wilson smiled.

"And finally, the last question and perhaps to me the most important … Niamh do you promise me you will allow love to flourish in your home … for yourself, your husband and any wee bairns with which the God above decides to bless this union? And in doing so, fill your heart with the Spirit of God and treat all you encounter with gentleness, compassion, and honesty?" the Reverend Thomas Wilson looked at Niamh expectantly.

"Aye, pastor, with all my heart and with God's help." Niamh replied as a single tear dropped upon her cheek.

"Niamh, daughter of man … welcome to the family of God."

Jamie looked at the two of them. "Amen"

Pastor Wilson picked up his hat which he had removed out of courtesy when entering their home. "I'll see you two at the gathering this coming Sunday I think it is being held in Johnston's barn this week? Have a good day Mrs. Irvine." Niamh looked at Jamie smiled and spoke in Gaelic … "buann gra gach rud… love conquers all".

"Aye love", replied Jamie, "it surely does."

Chapter Twelve – Parish of Paisley Abbey, Renfrewshire, Scotland ca. 1726

They were all gathered at the estate of William's Uncle, the Laird of Ferguslie. His father, Alexander and mother, Agnes and his younger brothers and sisters along with many others of the Cochrane clan of Renfrewshire were there. His uncle the Laird, also named William, had just entered the great hall of Ferguslie carrying an opened letter in his left hand. The look on his face told everyone in the room the news was disturbing. He nodded to one of the house servants who rang a small bell announcing to the guests that it was time to enter the dining room where a holiday feast had been prepared for the gathered family and friends. It was Hogmanay, the Scottish celebration of the New Year.

Young William knew that he had a large extended family but he didn't realize just exactly how large it was until the moment his family had arrived at his Uncle's estate. There were people everywhere. Every which way he turned he saw men, women and children from wee bairns up to young lads and lassies who must have been around his age of sixteen. As his family's carriage came to a gentle stop in front of the estate William couldn't help but notice the towers of the nearby Kirk. As he had done a dozen times before, his father leaned over to him and said, "Lad that is the Abbey of Paisley. Your family was on this land when it was being built. In fact family legend has it that we Cochranes were responsible for selling the land it resides upon to the original monks who built it … with our help, of course. Many of your ancestors are buried right over there in the Kirk yard," as he pointed in the direction of the adjacent cemetery.

"Some have headstones that date back over three hundred years. There are others … but the markings have been weathered away. Only God knows whose bones lie there now." And with that last comment his father smiled and chuckled at his attempt at humor. William could tell his father was nervous. The whole family was. Although his father and Uncle got along with each other well enough they were not close. Alexander was not really close with any of his aristocratic brothers and sisters. They had all married well but according to the family at least, Alexander had not. He had married a woman by the name of Agnes Scott. Agnes had been orphaned at a wee age and graciously taken into the home of one of Alexander's distant cousins, a man named John Cochrane, who lived in the small village of Lochwinnoch, eleven miles south west of Paisley as the crow flies. She was treated well by this humble man and his loving wife and she was perfectly happy living a simple life in Lochwinnoch. And then she met the man of her dreams, Alexander Cochrane of the Cochranes of Ferguslie. It was love at first sight and no power on earth or in heaven could stop the two from marrying. Of course, Alexander's father, William the Elder and then laird of Ferguslie was not pleased to say the least. That was the start of the tension that existed between Alexander and his extended family, that, and the fact that Alexander was not William's first born male son. By law, Alexander's oldest brother, William was to become laird at the death of their father. Fate had intervened and William the Elder had suffered a debilitating stroke which left him unable to maintain his duties as laird. His son, William took the position of leadership. He had done well. He was investing in the linen trade in Glasgow town and was in the process of adding to his father's collection of trading ships that frequently traveled between Scotland and Ulster. The ships had even, on occasion traveled as far as the coast of Holland and northern France. The Irish linen business had been good to the family. But Uncle William's wealth had turned him into a snob who looked down his long aristocratic nose at anyone, friend or otherwise who did not share his high society views. In particular, William of Ferguslie had a critical test for any and all he allowed into his inner circle. Were they loyal supporters of the Stewart family? For William of Ferguslie was a Jacobite. A name that had been given to those Scots and others scattered throughout the British Empire that had great difficulty in accepting the Hanoverians as rightful kings and wanted to restore James Edward Stewart, son of James II, to the throne. With the abdication of James II, the Act of Union of 1707 which essentially erased the legal sovereignty of Scotland and united her to England, and the death of Queen Anne in 1714, the British political scene had changed dramatically. William of Ferguslie had kept a low profile. Although his politics were important to him they were not nearly as crucial as protecting and developing his growing trade business. So, he did not actively participate in the Jacobite rebellions of 1715 and 1719 and that turned out to be a wise move on his part. The ring leaders of those rebellions were rounded up and systematically executed or shipped off to the American colonies. William of Ferguslie was a sharp businessman who many suspected of having no heart due to the ruthless way he conducted his affairs.

His brother, Alexander, was very different. His was a gentle soul. He was not known for his wit or business savvy. Alexander was a man of peace and of the land. He and his wife had been given a small farm within the parish of Paisley Abbey but not close enough that his brother, the laird, would have to interact with him or his family on a daily basis. They lived on the fringes of acceptable society. Alexander loved music. He had a strong baritone voice and enjoyed singing. He also played the pipes and any other musical instrument he could get his hands on. His wife, Agnes, was also talented with musical abilities and each evening the two of them would often sing duets to their little flock of bairns as they gathered around the supper table for Bible reading and prayers. For this little branch of Clan Cochrane took their faith rather seriously. Of course, all the Cochranes of Renfrewshire were tithing members of the Reformed Kirk of Scotland but to the laird, his religion was a way to strengthen his influence in the community and thus enhance his business opportunities. To Alexander, however, his relationship with God was his first priority and he stressed this point daily to the children.

This was the world into which Alexander's first born child, named William after his grandfather, was born. It was a simple life. One in which faith played a critical role. And the relationship between Alexander and his son was strong. But the lad William was quite different in one aspect from his father. He had an unquenchable curiosity about the world. He wanted very much to travel on one of his Uncles' grand sailing vessels. William wanted to see the world and perhaps discover what God had intended for him to do with his life. He was restless. After all, he was sixteen years old. He considered himself a man and was ready to get about the business of being an adult. This had ultimately become a point of tension between him and his father as well as his loving and doting mother. Any time he mentioned the possibility of him leaving the parish they quickly changed the subject or in their not so subtle way made it known to him they were not supportive. In fact, it had been a topic of discussion once again last evening at supper.

"But father," pleaded William, "why can't I just ask Uncle William if he could perhaps find a spot for me on one of his ships? I could learn to sail. Perhaps even one day become Captain?"

"William," his father said while shaking his head no, "we've had this discussion already. I need you here on the farm. Your brothers are too small to help me. And, anyway, it would break your Mother's heart." As both men looked towards Agnes and she nodded slightly with a smile on her lips.

Alexander knew the connection between his son and his wife was strong. He knew he was not fighting fairly in this argument but he didn't care. The thought of having his son leave on one of his brothers' ships was unbearable. "We'll not speak of this again … understand." Alexander looked expectantly at his son for he knew that although this urge to see the world was strong within him William was an obedient child and would ultimately do what he was told. William nodded his head in defeat. Supper that evening was quieter than usual.

The next day they had all boarded the carriage that had been sent for them from the estate and headed to Ferguslie. Now the butler was ringing the bell for supper and the dozens of family and friends that had gathered for this year's Hogmanay celebration were slowly making their way into the great dining hall and looking for their selected places to sit and enjoy this feast the laird's cooks had prepared. And what a feast it was. The table was spread from one end to the other with all manner of delicious edibles. Alexander and his wife Agnes found their spot at the far table away from the center of attention, the laird and his immediate family. William sat next to his mother. The laird rose and silence fell over the group.

"I want to thank everyone this glorious day for blessing us with your presence. I do hope you enjoy this humble spread that has been prepared for you." The laird began his speech but his voice was cracking and his hands were shaking. Alexander had never seen his brother this upset in public before and wondered what in the world was wrong. Apparently, others in the room sensed that something was amiss. Finally, someone sitting at the center table asked the laird if he was alright.

The laird rose once again and spoke in a serious tone, "I hate to dampen our festive spirits this holiday but I'm afraid I've just received some rather disturbing news from my cousin in County Down, Ulster." He was still holding the recently read letter in his trembling left hand. Another cousin sitting at the main table asked the laird if he would be able to read this troubling news to the gathered family. "After all," said the elderly man, "if it was bad news for the laird, it was bad news for the entire clan and should be shared." The laird thought for a moment and then nodded his head. He cleared his throat. "The letter is from my cousin Hugh Cochrane. Most of you know of him. His great grandfather left Dundonald, the seat of our Clan, with many troops, decades ago to put down the Irish rebellion of 1641 To make a long story short, after peace was restored, Colonel Cochrane purchased significant acres of land in County Down and established a working estate upon it. Cochranes have lived on that land for almost eighty years. Apparently," the laird looked at the letter," things have gone from bad to worse for them and our fellow Scots in the area. Please allow me to read what our cousin Hugh has to say about the situation ... *Dear Cousin William, Honorable Laird of Ferguslie. I wish you well on the eve of the New Year. However, it is with great desperation and anxiety that I write these words to you. The situation in Ulster has been difficult for some time as you well know. The trouble began with the Test Act of 1704 created by her majesty Queen Anne and enacted into law by both the English and Irish Parliaments. Again, as you well know, this intolerable act has severely tested the faith of the loyal members of our Presbyterian Kirk. With one signature of the pen, we were made second class citizens of the Kingdom. We were stripped of the right to hold office, to be married, baptized or buried in the Church of Ireland. Our ministers' credentials are ridiculed and they have been constantly harassed and tormented. A Catholic priest is considered comparable to an Anglican vicar but not the Elders of the true reformed Kirk. To make matters worse we have suffered terrible droughts off and on for the past decade significantly reducing the flax crop and thus reducing our ability to effectively operate within the linen trade. But the greatest offense by far has been the relentless raising of the rents that our tenants pay to the Anglican Anglo-Irish landholders. After the original thirty-one-year lease expires, if the land is leased by a Scot, the rates are tripled and more. The average Scots flax farmer can't begin to pay these exorbitant rates. So, the local Irish Catholics go together as families of four or five and take up the leases. These people are living on farms that can only sustain one family at best. Poverty abounds throughout Ulster. As you well know, many of our fellow Scots have headed to the colonies. The first great migration happened around 1715 and 1716. Thousands of Presbyterian Scots left for Penn's colony or New England. I thought that if we could just hang on here in County Down and simply survive things would improve. Surely, our faithful God would not abandon us? But, alas, such was not the case. Once again, land prices continue to rise. In addition, the poor Irish Catholic will work at rates no decent Scot would ever accept. Our people cannot find work. My dear cousin, we are slowly but surely dying here in Ulster. In a few years, I doubt if there will be any Presbyterian Scots left in this part of Ireland. This brings me to my request of you. I know you are in the linen trade. I know you have a fleet of sailing ships with captains that know the way to navigate the seas around our islands and beyond. I beg you to send as many ships as you can spare so that we might embark upon them and sail west to America. We will pay you what we can but the coffers are indeed running low. Have mercy upon us dear cousin and send what help you may. These words are sent to you with deepest kindness and with ultimate trust in the good grace of the Almighty.* It is signed Hugh Cochrane." The laird stopped reading and looked at the assembled crowd. Silence overtook the room.

It was the laird's mother, Bethia, who first broke the silence. "We must send them help son." The laird looked at his mother whose health was rapidly failing. She had spent the last few years taking care of her stricken husband and it had taken a toll upon her well-being. She rarely spoke at these public gatherings and never interfered with the running of the estate by her son. However, this time, she felt compelled to intervene. The laird looked at her and simply said, "the costs to send these people to the colonies would be excessive … and what would I … we get in return … very little from the sounds of this letter." A slight gasp escaped from the assembly. The laird was not going to send help. A few of the elderly men began to shake their heads yet some nodded in agreement. One cousin spoke out, "the laird is right. Yes, these people are Cochranes but they've lived in Ulster for three generations. Are they really part of the clan anymore? Why should the laird take on such a perilous journey at tremendous costs and gain nothing in return?" A number of the crowd agreed with this man and offered him and the laird their vocal support.

Just then, Alexander rose from his seat. His son William was amazed. Alexander's wife looked concerned. She had no idea what her husband was about to say but given the history between he and his brother it would probably not go well.

"Dear brother, "Alexander began, "it is true, you may not profit much if any on this undertaking. And yes, it is true they are distant relatives at best." He cleared his throat and his baritone voice deepened and became stronger. "But we cannot turn our backs on fellow Presbyterians who are calling out for our aid. All of us in this room know the blood that has been shed and have experienced the flowing tears of our clan and many others who have stood up for the true Kirk of Scotland. In fact, some of you in this very room have lost loved ones in the past battles fought here on our land. And some of us," as he looked at his wife, "had family members who were martyred for their faith in the Lord Jesus. Think on this brother … Penn's Colony and perhaps New England offer our people the opportunity for the first time in our history to practice our faith as we so desire without the fear of retaliation from those in authority who cannot accept the one true faith. These poor people are being squeezed by forces beyond their control and are simply asking for us … for you to do the right thing and help them escape from this religious tyranny." Alexander looked straight at his brother and then slowly took his seat.

William had never been prouder of his father. He was old enough to realize that his Uncle William was a man driven first and foremost by profit. And this voyage to America would be expensive with little in return to show for it. But, William reasoned, his father was right. These people … our people were asking for our help and in his eyes this was the will of God.

The laird was silent for some time and then spoke. "I am not a man to make rash decisions, in particular, when it might cost me … us … a fortune. But I will honestly think on it and make my decision in the morning. Now … let's return to the reason we are all gathered here today and continue with our celebration." He turned to the assembled musicians and motioned for them to play something. They began with a waltz and before long the mood had changed once again from somber to festive as the people began to eat, drink and, in the words of the laird "be merry".

Young William could not sleep that night. He tossed and turned and finally gave up and went to the room of his parents. He gently knocked on the door. His mother answered, "Willie, my goodness lad, what are you doing up at this hour? It's the middle of the night."

"I must speak with you and father." William replied. He disliked it when his mother called him Willie instead of what he perceived to be the more masculine William. But he knew that to her he would always be her wee Willie. To her it was a term of endearment and love.

By this time, Alexander had roused himself from his sleep. "What is it lad? And why can't it wait until the morning sun is up at least?"

"If Uncle William decides to send a ship to Ulster, I want to be on it." William said with as much conviction he could muster. His father and mother both looked at one another and spoke in unison, "No, lad, you can't go."

William raised his hand in slight protest, "Hear me out … I believe this is the will of God for me. No, I'm not being called to the ministry but I do think that in a way that is exactly what is happening. I don't know how right now but, God wants me to somehow help this poor folk, travel to the colonies. Either, I go with your permission and blessing or I'll just sneak upon the ship. One way or the other, I'm going to America" The young lad looked with defiance and determination at his parents. Alexander looked at his son. He thought to himself, "My God, he is me. So idealistic and headstrong and a little naïve." Alexander looked at his wife and saw the tears slowly developing in her eyes.

"Listen lad, I think you are getting the cart before the horse aren't you? After all, what if your Uncle decides to not fund the trip, then what?"

William was silent for some time. Then he turned to his father and said, "I know we are not to put God to the test but I will test the faith of my Uncle. Can we all agree that if Uncle William decides to support this request it must be a sign from God and that means you'll allow me to leave with your blessing?"

Alexander quickly interrupted, "And if my brother says no … that is also a sign as you say meaning you stay here with your mother and I and continue to work the farm. Agree?"

William's mother finally spoke, "Willie, I can't bear the thought of you traveling away to the colonies but your father is my husband and I will abide by his wish. I will agree to his proposition. If in the morning, Uncle William decides against the trip … you'll stay at home. Can you agree with this? Shall we leave this up to the Lord?" William's mother had wiped the tears from her eyes. She knew this day would eventually come but she was not quite ready for her oldest child to leave the nest. Not yet. And both of them knew Alexander's brother. They were both silently and secretly betting on his greed. Neither thought he would fund this costly trip to America … not when there was so little profit in it.

William looked at his parents and finally nodded his head in agreement. He shook his father's outstretched hand and said," Agreed."

Alexander spoke, "Well then, I suggest we all return to our beds. It's at least two or three hours before sunrise and we probably won't see Uncle William until mid-day at the next meal."

Alexander was right. Although Uncle William was an early riser he had locked himself away in one of his drawing rooms and was busy discussing matters of his business affairs with a couple of his cronies.

Young William was not able to sleep that night and quickly rose as soon as the first flicker of sunshine had entered his room. He quickly dressed and went looking for his Uncle. He asked one of the maids where he was and she informed him to wait outside the closed doors until his Uncle was ready for a public appearance. And this is where he was when finally, the doors swung open and standing before him was his Uncle William with a couple of men he did not know.

"Then it's settled," Uncle William said to one of the men," we take three of our fastest and largest ships to Ulster. Take these cousins to wherever they want to go in those God forsaken colonies. Then you take the ships to French Quebec and buy as much beaver fur as the ship will hold. You take that fur to the London exchange and sell it for top dollar. You and your crew get thirty percent … I get the rest. Is that understood?" Both men nodded their heads in agreement and then shook Uncle William's hand to seal the deal.

William's heart skipped a beat. Had he heard his Uncle William correctly? If so, that meant he was going to America. And suddenly he was overwhelmed with emotion. He knew this was God's will for him but now that it seemed like it was going to come true, he was anxious and saddened at the thought of leaving his home. Perhaps never to return?

Just then Uncle William saw his nephew and looked at him with a quizzical expression as if to ask him what he wanted of him so early in the morning? And to make matters worse, Alexander strolled around the corner obviously intent on finding his brother before his son did.

"Well, good morning to both of you. Now, if you don't mind, I have business to attend to … what with the holiday feasting and all that …" Uncle William shut the door of his boardroom behind him and began to walk away from father and son. William found his voice and said to the back of his Uncle as he walked away, "Excuse me Uncle William sir … I could not help but overhear your conversation. You will be sending ships to Ulster to transport our kin to America?"

"Aye lad … that I will. I was planning on making an announcement at the next gathering of the family during the mid-day meal." William smiled and started to turn away.

"Brother," Alexander spoke now, "I think my son has a request to make of you?" He looked at his son with fierce pride mingled with sorrow in his eyes. It seemed like overnight he had become a man.

William needed no further encouragement, "Dear Uncle William, I would like to sign on as a deck hand on one the ships taking the folks from Ulster to the colonies. Do I have your permission, sir?"

"Why in the name of all that's holy would you want to do that lad?" exclaimed Uncle William.

"It is the will of God for my life," William stammered and stumbled over the words as he spoke them but he was able to get his point across to his Uncle.

Uncle William looked at his brother, "You and Agnes are acceptable to what your son is proposing?"

Alexander looked first at William and then back to his brother, "Aye … we're not happy to see the lad leave but he feels strongly about it and I think he'll be in good hands on one of your experienced ships. Perhaps he'll find the sea to his liking and make his living by sailing?" Alexander attempted to put a smile on his face but grimaced instead.

Uncle William looked at his nephew as if looking at him for the first time in his life. He looked up and down at the young man as if he was measuring him. Finally, he spoke, "Aye, perhaps he'll find a home at sea. You'll sail on Captain Wilson's ship seven days from today. Pack your bags lightly … there won't be much room on her once we pick up the folks from Ulster. And … be at the dock at least twelve hours before we set sail. Wilson will have to assign you some menial task to keep you busy and help you earn your way amongst the men. They are a rough lot, lad. Are you ready for it?"

William was ecstatic. "Aye," he said with a huge grin upon his face. He shook his Uncle's hand who quickly turned and left father and son alone.

"I am proud of you lad. I am also saddened and anxious. But I know that if this indeed is the will of our Lord then you will have a safe and successful journey. God will protect you and guide you in His ways." Then father and son hugged one another tightly. William did not want his father to see the tears streaming down his face nor did Alexander want his brave young son to see his.

The week passed quickly for the young man. The day finally arrived. He sat on the small sack containing all his earthly possessions. He was deep in thought when he heard the voice of a young girl behind him. "So, it's true then," the young girl said. William looked around and stared into the childlike face of Helen Wilson. Helen was the twelve-year-old daughter of Captain Wilson, the man who would be responsible for steering this ship safely across the Atlantic. William and she had essentially grown up together and had been playmates as young bairns. Mrs. Wilson and William's mother were close friends and would often sit together during services. Often when Captain Wilson was at sea, Mrs. Wilson and her children would dine with the Cochranes. The families had grown close over the years.

"I wish I was going," Helen said. "I miss my father when he's at sea. And he has told us this is to be a long journey … all the way to America and back. He'll be gone months." Helen started to cry softly.

William stood up and hugged the young lassie. He was tall for his age and towered over the girl. "It will be alright Helen. God will watch over us," William tried to sound brave and fearless but inside he too was sad and by this time rather frightened of the unknown that lay across the great Atlantic.

"William, I have something for you," Helen said as she dried the tears from her eyes. She stuck her hand into the pocket of her dress and pulled out a locket. She handed it to him and pressed it into his open hand. "May I open it, "he asked softly.

"Aye … and when you do…think of home … and me," her voice falling to a whisper with the words "and me". William looked at Helen and then at the locket. He opened it slowly and smiled. It contained a small purple thistle and wrapped around the stem of the flower was a lock of Helen's brown hair.

"This is your hair, I assume," William said trying to be manly but sounding very childish.

Helen looked surprised, "Well, ye silly lad, whose hair do you ken it would be if not mine?" Then she giggled and William laughed. He hugged her and then gently kissed her cheek.

"I will keep it with me always. It will remind me of home … and of you." The two locked eyes. William had never looked at Helen in this way before. They were no longer children. Something had replaced that relationship. Something neither understood but both felt deeply within their souls. He was nervous and so was she but he knew that if he did not kiss her now he might not ever get the chance again in his life. So he slowly bent his head down towards her upturned face. She closed her eyes and gently their lips met. And in a second, Helen Wilson was in love.

"Ahem, "the voice sounded deeply masculine and somewhat perturbed. It was Captain Wilson, Helen's father. William jerked away from Helen's body as if struck by lightning. "Well lad, are ye ready for a journey?" asked the Captain.

"Aye sir," William almost shouted although the Captain was standing but a few feet away. Captain Wilson chuckled slightly and then turned to his daughter, "I thought I had said good bye to you at home … but I'm glad you are here. Gives me another chance to do this," and with one sweeping motion he grabbed up his daughter and spun her around in the air while squeezing her tightly. "I love you Helen. Take care of your mother while I'm gone." Then he winked and said, "And don't be kissing anymore lads while I'm gone, ye ken?" Helen began to blush and said, "Love you daddy" turned and ran down the dock back towards their little cottage.

William's family had said their goodbyes at their little farm on the outskirts of Paisley Parish. It was a mutual decision to say goodbye at this location. Alexander had said to his son, "It's too much for your mother to see you off at the dock so … we'll just say our goodbyes here at home. William, I want you to know that there will always be a place for you at my table and a roof over your head should you need it." His father was trying unsuccessfully to hold back the tears. William had looked at his father and simply nodded his head, picked up his bag and headed north to the docks at Glasgow Town. He heard his mother's voice, "Willie, wait … I've something to give ye …" Agnes walked up to her son and handed him a letter and a Bible. "The letter is for you to read when you are at sea. And the Bible is to read every day of your life from this point on. I've marked in the cover some of my favorite passages. I pray they will bring you as much comfort as they have brought me. … I love you Willie. Go with God." She hugged him tightly and then quickly kissed both his cheeks and turned and ran into her cottage. She did not want her son to see the tears.

The voyage from Scotland to Ulster did not take long. When the wind blew, the small trading vessel made good time and headed straight for the new port of Belfast. William was excited. He loved everything about the sea and sailing upon it. He was a good student and was quickly learning the ropes. But when the ship docked at the port in Ulster, William was shocked by what he saw. There were hundreds of people waiting around the area hoping for a vessel to take them to the colonies. They seemed to be arranged in groups of families, neighbors and friends. Usually there was at least one minister with each group but a few of them were without religious leaders. William had not really known what to expect but whatever he had expected it was not what he was witnessing. These people were desperate. You could see it in their faces. You could hear it in their voices. The talk was the same as he moved from one group to another, "Aye, we are going to the Promised Land … to America … where we will be free to tend our farms and raise our children in the faith of our fathers without hindrance or harassment. God will lead the way." He could tell these distant kin of his were not extremely poor. Some did have substantial goods to load upon the ships waiting to take them to sea but many were selling their goods to brokers at the docks trading them for passage and there was a line of men and women who were selling themselves and their families into indentured servitude in order to pay for the passage. But whatever their economic station one thing had brought them all together … their faith and their desire to practice that faith in freedom. Both rich and poor had but one objective … to travel safely to America and to start a new life in a land of "milk and honey". William, along with the rest of the crew helped those who could afford the passage onto their ship along with the possessions the Captain allowed on his vessel. Everyone quickly learned that Captain Wilson's words were the law at sea. No man or woman did anything without first seeking his permission and William understood the need of such authoritarian leadership. Many of the seasoned crew had warned him of the travails that lay before them. And, of course, what many on board did not know was that even though Wilson was an experienced seaman this would be his first transatlantic voyage. Uncle William, however, had been wise enough to hire a few extra hands that had made this journey safely before and Wilson had quickly come to depend upon their wisdom and knowledge. His Uncle was a shrewd and canny businessman and he meant to protect his investment as best he could. If this trip proved successful, there would be others and the Laird was already counting the silver he would be adding to his coffers.

After a couple of days to get everyone aboard and make the ship seaworthy, it became time to set sail. It took almost a whole day of travel to get around the little island of Ireland and head west. William stood aft looking back to the east. He wondered to himself, "Will I ever see you again? Will I ever see my family once again? Will I ever again stand on the soil of Scotland? Will I ever see Helen?" The thoughts almost brought tears to his eyes but he knew the other sailors were watching him and he dare not let them see his weakness. William had quickly learned that any sign of weakness was considered an opportunity by some of the more sketchy types on board to tease him without mercy.

The journey was difficult. Some days the sky was clear and a strong wind at their back made for quick movement across the water. Soon many people were seasick but not William. He loved the constant rocking and rolling of the ever-present waves. He loved the feel of the air in his face and growing beard. He loved the smell of the saltwater. But there were days when the wind disappeared and it seemed like they had been forsaken by God himself to be doomed to die upon this vast wasteland of water. It was during one of those phases of the weather when the wind was absent and the boat moved little that William finally took out the letter his mother had given to him weeks before as he left his childhood home. He had read the Bible daily as his mother had instructed but had been hesitant to read her letter. He didn't ken why he just knew that it contained information that his mother thought important for him to know and apparently, it was something she had not been able to tell him face to face. He went to his small sleeping quarters and opened the sealed letter. It began …*My dearest Willie. The day you were born was the happiest day of my life. I have loved being your mother and I pray to the Almighty that He has found me worthy of the task. I know we might not ever meet again this side of heaven. That very thought brings tears to my eyes even now as I write these words. And if that be the case, there is something about me you need to know. Something I have carried in secret all of my adult life. Very few know of this secret. Your father does and I suspect, so does his brother, the laird William. And, of course, the man and woman who raised me as their own. You know me as Agnes Scott, an orphaned child raised by John and Ursula Cochrane of Lochwinnoch. And that part is true. I was orphaned as a wee bairn and I was indeed raised by the man and woman I call my father and mother. But the secret is how I came to be an orphan. My precious son, my natural father was a cousin of my adopted father John Cochrane. His name was Thomas Cochrane and he was a wild and free thing until he met my mother, a pretty young lassie by the name of Maggie Wilson. Maggie was the daughter of a Covenanter minister who had lost his flock when he refused to sign the Oath of Abjuration of 1685. That oath required all Covenanting ministers to swear loyalty to the new King James II and renounce the Covenant. Those who refused, as my grandfather did, were hunted down and tortured to death. During all the chaos that went on during the killing times my mother became pregnant by Thomas though they had never wed. I was born illegitimate. John Graham, Laird of Claverhouse had sent many troops to this part of Scotland to root out the last remaining covenanters. And they were ruthless. That is why even to this day, he is called "Bluidy Clavers". Apparently, the troops came to my mother and grandfather's wee cottage. I was but a few weeks old. She saw the troops approaching and handed me to a neighbor woman with instructions pinned to my blanket to take me to her lover's cousin John who lived miles away at Lochwinnoch. That action saved my life. Graham's troops killed my mother and grandfather and when my natural father, Thomas heard about it, he went on a killing rampage himself. When I was old enough to understand, my "father" John told me they cornered Thomas in a pub but he took four of Graham's troops with him to the grave. His body was cut into pieces and burned with the ashes taken and thrown into the Solway Firth where many dozens of Covenanters had been previously drowned the year before. My illegitimacy and the circumstances surrounding the deaths of my natural mother and father have been kept a family secret to this day. But now ... you know the truth. I pray you will not think less of me? I had no choice in the matter. We are born into the world in which we are born. Perhaps now you understand why my faith has played such a major role in my life and why I impressed it upon you and your younger siblings. My faith is all that I have left of my natural mother and father. My dear sweet lad, stay strong in your faith and let it be your constant companion. It is all that I can give you. It is the one precious gift that can't be stolen by another but take heed, it can be tarnished by your own actions. Let that never be the case and we shall meet once again in God's beautiful paradise. You will be in my mind always until I breathe my last.* It was signed, *all my love, Agnes, your mother.* William was sobbing by the time he had finished reading the letter. Once he regained his composure, he gently folded it and placed it in the center of his Bible. He walked out onto the deck of the ship and looked up towards the heavens. He heard some of the passengers singing. It was a song about the fire that consumes the hearts of the faithful. He had not heard this song before but the words seemed to somehow bring him comfort. He waited until the voices had quieted and then he headed back to his quarters and tried to sleep. The wind picked up during the night and the mighty ship headed west once again.

Early one morning, after being on the ship for almost three months, William saw a bird in the sky and he immediately realized where there were birds there must be land. Everyone sensed the change in the environment and the excitement began to build. Finally, the cry "land ho" was shouted down from one of the lads in the crow's nest. They had made it. A great shout of relief and thankfulness went up from the passengers. Not all who had started on the trip had survived. Those who had died at sea had been buried at sea. It was so sad for William to watch the families of the deceased as they said goodbye to their loved ones as their linen shrouded bodies were lowered into the Atlantic. The crusty sailors on board muttered under their breaths about "more feed for the sharks" but never loud enough for Captain Wilson to hear. Such impertinence might ensure you walked the plank into the depths of the deep as well. Wilson ran a tight ship.

William saw Boston Harbor and the town of Boston for the first time in his life. It had been decided that the Ulster Scots would try New England at first and if that proved unsuccessful they would go by land (or by sea, if they could stand it again) south to Philadelphia to Penn's Colony where many of the initial Ulster Scots had emigrated a decade earlier.

Hugh Cochrane of Down had heard that the small town of Londonderry had been settled earlier by Ulster Scots and he thought he could arrange for travel from Boston to Londonderry for his group of countrymen. He had approached William to see if he would like to accompany them but William was homesick by now and wanted to return to Scotland. He dearly missed his family. He missed his homeland. And, if the truth be known, he missed Helen, although he would never dare tell anyone that fact. And so, he respectfully declined and told Captain Wilson he would be returning with him. Wilson then had the unfortunate responsibility of reminding William they were not returning directly back to Scotland. William had forgotten of his Uncle's plans to trade Canadian furs on the London exchange. But that would mean at least another four months at sea and then travel from London back to Glasgow. Was he up for that?

William hesitated before giving a response. He dearly wanted to go home to see his loved ones. But he also wanted to see what this brand-new land might have to offer for him. He was torn. So he told Captain Wilson, "Sir, if you don't mind, I would like to think on it for a wee bit. Perhaps seek God's guidance on the matter? Can I give you my answer in the morning?"

Captain Wilson smiled and said, "Aye lad … in the morning then. Sleep tight." And with that Wilson walked back to the Captain's quarters.

William looked at Boston Harbor. He had permission to leave the ship and walk about the town so that is what he did. Unfortunately, no one warned him about the press gangs that were roaming the docks looking for young sailors to impress into His Majesty's Royal Navy. Impressment of sailors from privately held trading vessels had been going on in England since before the days of King Henry VIII but Scots were usually left alone, until the Act of Union of 1707. Then Scottish seafarers became active targets for the press gangs who were basically thugs working on behalf of the British navy. They searched the taverns and pubs along the wharfs on both sides of the Atlantic taking whoever seemed to know their way around a sailing vessel and before the lad could complain to his family or employer he was at sea sailing under the flag of Great Britain. Usually impressment was utilized only during times of warfare and England and Spain were once again fighting over the Gibraltar Straits of Spain and certain ports of call in the Caribbean.

William never saw the blow coming. He lost consciousness immediately and woke up the next morning on a large British warship that had already set sail. He was confused and frightened out of his mind. When he finally regained some semblance of control over his thoughts he roused himself up and walked towards the front of the ship. Whoever had kidnapped him had simply dropped him on the deck of the ship. He was not alone. By his count, there were six or seven other lads about his age that were milling about wondering what had happened. Finally, someone in authority shouted at them to stand in a straight line at attention and "do not move an inch or ye will be swimmin' with the sharks." That got their attention and William did as he was told. The voice continued, "I am Lieutenant Johnson, and that man standing over there is Captain Harris. The ship's Master is Jones. And this vessel is called the Queen Anne. You men are now members of the Royal Navy of his majesty King George. You will be paid but your pay will be held in arrears until the conclusion of this present conflict with Spain. You each will be assigned to a work detail. Learn your job well and stay out of trouble and you will do just fine. Cause trouble and you will find it. Is that understood?" All the new recruits including William responded with a vigorous, "aye, aye sir." And that was that. William was assigned to the powder room. It was dangerous, dirty and sweaty work. He reported to the head Gunner whose name was Lewis and happened to be a Scot from the highlands. Luckily for William, Chief Gunner Lewis was a decent older man seasoned by years of naval service. He was easy to talk to and although firm with his men was just. The same could not be said for Captain Harris. William quickly learned from the others on board to stay as far away from Harris as possible and only speak to him if and when he spoke to you first.

William was stuck and he knew it. He was angry and frustrated but given the circumstances there was little he could do but to try to do his best, stay alive and at the first opportunity jump ship. The desertion rate for impressed sailors was quite high and for this reason they were watched very closely any time the ship needed to dock for resupply.

Over the next twelve months, the Queen Anne sailed up and down the eastern seaboard of the American colonies spending much of her time at sea in the southern waters of the Caribbean. Her mission was to provide protection to British trading vessels in the area and to engage with force any Spanish warships she might encounter. It was a long and dangerous year for William but an educational one as well. He witnessed his first slave ship as it brought Africans to the colonies. The Queen Anne provided protection for it as it headed into Charleston Harbor but kept a distance from the vessel due to the stench. William enquired about the odor and was told the conditions on the slaver were horrible with the Africans kept in cages stacked four or five deep in the hold. Harris told him, "they lose as many as they bring over ... disease, madness, you name it ... those poor souls suffer it." And then would shrug his shoulders and turn back to his task at hand. But William was both fascinated and disgusted by what he saw. He thought to himself, "Aye, things were bad in Ulster for our folk but ... nothing like this. They are being treated like animals. God in heaven have mercy upon them."

And just as suddenly as his life as a Royal Navy sailor began it abruptly came to an end. The war with Spain ended and his services were no longer required and to his amazement he was actually paid his back wages. The Queen Anne headed for the port of Philadelphia for dry dock and repairs and William was deposited with the rest of the impressed Scots sailors at the wharf.

To his surprise and delight he stumbled into Captain Wilson whose ship happened to be in the Philadelphia port at the same time. Wilson saw him first, "My God ... is that William Cochrane I see?"

William whirled around at the sound of the familiar voice. A huge smile broke out upon his face, "aye sir it's me and you are a sight for sore eyes."

"So lad ... what's next for your life. Are ye staying here in Philadelphia?" asked Captain Wilson. "You can catch a ride home with me if you like?"

"Home," thought William, "I could go home ... but to what would I be going ... what have I accomplished?" William became rather silent with his eyes downcast.

Captain Wilson was somewhat taken aback by this lack of positive response so decided to change the topic, "Did you see much action, lad. I heard things got rather hot off the Spanish coast in the Mediterranean."

This brought William out of his trance. "Nay spent almost a year on the Queen Anne and only fired the cannons one time and that against some pesky pirates that had been troubling the trading from Charleston in the Carolina colony. Most days it was pretty boring. But I did get to see much of the coast of the American colonies and, of course, all the major ports of call … Boston, New York, Philadelphia, Jamestown, Elizabeth City and Charlestown." And then it hit him. He truly felt that Scotland was no longer his home. "Here is my home," he said out loud not realizing that the Captain would hear him.

"What lad … what's that you say?" asked the Captain somewhat bewildered?

"Captain Wilson, it has suddenly dawned on me that Scotland is my past. I will always have a soft place in my heart for it. But it is my past. These fresh new colonies … this is my future. This is where I belong. So … I think I will turn down your most generous offer. I'm going to stay here in America." William was as much surprised by his words as Captain Wilson. But he knew in his heart he had made the correct choice. He had to at least give it a try. Everything here was new and exciting. Back in Scotland, everything was as it had been for centuries. And since the Act of Union, English influence and control was growing in his homeland. He needed the newness and the freedom of the colonies. He needed the opportunity this new land offered to him and perhaps to his children one day if God should so bless him.

"Well lad. I'm surprised but I do have a suggestion," replied the Captain. He was fond of William and, of course, he knew his daughter, Helen would be soon old enough to marry and he thought she had her eye on this young lad. He wondered if there might be a way of keeping an eye on William on behalf of his daughter should she decide he is indeed the one for her. "Why don't you travel with me up the coast to Boston? I hear the Ulster Scots in Londonderry are looking for strong young men to help build up the place. In particular, they want to build a new church … one that would rival anything built so far in the New England."

William thought about the suggestion. It seemed to work for him. Perhaps this is what God had intended for him all along? So he agreed to the proposal and the two set about making plans for the trip.

Travel to Boston from Philadelphia by boat was by far the easiest and safest way to travel. The overland route was often rugged and overgrown with plants and trees of the upcountry woodlands. There were mountains to negotiate. And, of course, danger lurked behind every tree with the local natives, who people were now calling Indians. The peace between native and colonist was often tentative and easily broken. And once one of the tribes went on the warpath chaos reigned in the land. Usually it was hit and run affairs between small groups of nearby communities that had somehow offended or threatened the hunting grounds of the local natives. Here in Penn's Colony, the English Quakers would try to settle the matters quickly through diplomacy and payments for the territories that were being gobbled up by incoming shiploads of Ulster Scots, German Anabaptists or Calvinist French Huguenots. But it was the Ulster Scot who was placed on the frontier's edge to serve as a buffer between the Indians and the coastal communities. Fighting was in their blood. The centuries' long border wars between England and Scotland combined with their most recent experiences with the Catholic Irish of Ulster had turned them into a body of people who at a moment's notice could drop their farm implements and grab their weapons. They already knew how to fight and how to be brutal in combat. The Indian taught them the hit and run tactics of woodland fighting. And they were good at it.

Londonderry was approximately 45 miles north and slightly east of Boston. To William it was actually easier traveling from Philadelphia to Boston then from Boston to the frontier settlement of Londonderry. He didn't know what to expect but he was prepared for whatever task God put before him. He had written a rather lengthy letter to his mother and father attempting to explain his rationale for staying in the colonies. He hoped they would understand. He had also taken the liberty of writing a short but tender letter to Helen. It was not a proposal per se … she was still too young to entertain such matters hut he did hint rather strongly that he would be waiting for her here in American should she decide to emigrate when she came of marriageable age. He prayed she would understand and eventually follow him to this new land.

William was greeted with warmth and tremendous hospitality. He stayed with his distant kin and worked on building the new kirk during the day while keeping everyone awake at night with his tales of the sea. He learned to love his new home. The air seemed cleaner and the folks much more open and kind hearted then what he remembered from Paisley. But still there was something missing in his life. He prayed every day for guidance and attended services regularly. He certainly met numerous eligible and available young lassies from the surrounding farming country and was often encouraged by his family to entertain the possibility of choosing one and settling down to start his own family. But whenever he thought much about it his mind and heart returned to Helen. He had never heard from her again. Of course he had never returned to Boston to see if perhaps a letter had arrived for him. He just assumed with the passing of time she had found another. That may be the case but he could not get her out of his mind.

One day, after spending almost a year in Londonderry, William made up his mind that it was time to move on. He had heard through the network of Ulster Scot families scattered along the frontier from New England to the Chesapeake Bay that new lands were being planned for settlement in the south. Virginia was often mentioned and just a few months ago North Carolina was declared a Royal colony. But his cousin Hugh had informed him of the great need for stone masons and other builders to travel to Chester County in Penn's Colony to help build churches, schools and other buildings needed by the new Ulster Scot communities springing up along the western edges of the county. Within a week, William was off with his bags packed. He was excited. Once again, he had felt the Spirit of God tug at his heart and he knew he was heading in the right direction with his life. He travelled south to Boston hoping to catch a passenger ship heading down the coast to Philadelphia. While in Boston, his heart turned again to thoughts of home and of Helen. He wondered if she had become engaged by now. Surely, if he was still in the running for her hand she would have sent some type of message to him. But there was no message for him in Boston and it had been weeks since Captain Wilson's vessel had been in port. He was unable to secure passage upon a vessel heading south and to make matters worse press gangs were working the Boston docks seeking unsuspecting men for service in the royal navy. To be on the safe side William decided to take the King's highway which ran from Boston south along the coast through the major ports of New York, Philadelphia, Charles City and ending in Charles Town in the province of South Carolina. It would be a long and grueling trip. But it was relatively inexpensive travel and he would have different companions along the way as he made his way south.

When the stagecoach finally arrived in New York, William was exhausted and sought out a secure tavern in which to spend the evening as he prepared for the trip to Philadelphia. The next morning, he met a new traveler, a young man by the name of Thomas Wade, whose father had been one of the early English Quaker settlers in Penn's colony. Thomas routinely made a business trip from Philadelphia to New York and return. This was William's first face to face encounter with a Quaker. After a few minutes of trivial social engagement, the conversation turned to theology. William was quite curious.

"So, Mr. Wade, what can you tell me of the Quaker faith?" asked William, "I've been a member of the Reformed Kirk of Scotland all my life. I guess others might refer to me as a Presbyterian. And, quite honestly, although I have certainly heard stories about William Penn and his colony of Quakers, you are the first one I've had the privilege to encounter."

"Where should I start ...? "Wade said as he gently rubbed his long beard. "We consider ourselves Christians but as our founder George Fox wrote ... we do not place much emphasis upon the certainty of theological interpretations as some others do … we rely on the Inner Light to guide and direct our thoughts and behaviors. We view all people including women, Africans, Indians, etc. as equal recipients of God's love and guidance. We are a peaceful people and consider all men our potential friends and brethren. I would like to think we are a faith born out of love and motivated by love." Thomas Wade smiled slightly as he said these last words. He had learned on his travels that religion can be a touchy subject with some and he always proceeded with caution when engaged with someone regarding his own beliefs.

"I mean no disrespect Mr. Wade, "replied William," but I don't think the Indians who tried to wipe out our settlement in Londonderry actually loved us, or if they did … they sure had a funny way of displaying it." William said with a slight sarcastic chuckle at the end. "However, what you say is indeed quite appealing. In my short lifetime, I have seen so much pain and sorrow brought upon decent and kind people by other decent and kind people all in the name of Christ. I have often wondered what Jesus must be thinking about all of us who profess to be his followers? The way we tear at each other. The way we so quickly pick up the sword to defend our beliefs. The downright meanness of spirit and lack of tolerance we have for those who are different. "

"Mr. Cochrane, you are not alone in your questions. Perhaps this is why thousands of your countrymen are now fleeing the north of Ireland and coming in droves to Penn's colony? Perhaps it is a truer religion they seek?" Thomas spoke and then looked at William with his gentle and somewhat downcast eyes.

"Aye, perhaps, but I think it has more to do with starvation than religion although the fact that my kinsmen can practice their faith as they desire without fear of harassment from the Quaker authorities is certainly a factor. The Presbyterian Scots are being run out of Ulster due to economic disaster combined with their fierce loyalty to the reformed Kirk of Scotland."

Thomas Wade chuckled, "for one so young you have certain wisdom about the nature of mankind. Here is my card. When we arrive in Philadelphia, I would very much like to introduce you to my family and … by the way … we are always looking for gifted tradesmen in the city. There is so much to be done … new building and such. Are you good with your hands?"

"Aye, it's in my blood. Cochranes have been workers of stone and timber since before time began." William smiled as he took the card from the outstretched hand of Thomas Wade.

And for the next year, William Cochrane was kept very busy by the Wade family and their Quaker associates. He had decided to settle on a small farm just outside the town of Philadelphia in order for him to be close to his work within the city yet being able to dwell amongst his Ulster Scot friends and family moving into Chester County. However, land prices were beginning to rapidly rise as more and more immigrants from Ulster combined with Rhinelander Germans and French Huguenots. And it appeared to William everyone was seeking the same thing, relatively inexpensive farming land where people could raise their families and practice their Christian faith in a peaceful and stable environment. People were now coming to Penn's Colony by the thousands. Each day, a new boat filled with immigrants would arrive at the docks of Philadelphia. And the native Indians were not happy yet, they continued to barter with the Quaker authorities trading their precious hunting grounds for English goods they coveted, but, could not manufacture themselves lacking the basic technology and know-how. Tension between the groups was rising and something had to give. William knew that at any moment the Indians could "go on the warpath" and once again his peaceful existence would be shattered.

And then one day, God once again, intervened in his life. He was in the city transporting goods from the Wade's candle shop down to the docks to be boarded for a small ship to sail them up the coast to New York and Boston. He noticed a rather large vessel docked at the edge of the wharf. The sun was shining so intently that day he could not make out the name of the vessel then he heard a familiar voice behind him.

"Praise be to the Almighty … is that William Cochrane who stands before me?" the husky voice said with command.

William whirled around to stand face to face with his old friend and mentor, Captain Wilson. He almost fainted from the shock. He was indeed speechless. As he stammered out a reply Wilson grabbed him and gave him a bear hug literally lifting him off his feet. "Lad, it is so good to see you safe and sound and in one piece." Wilson laughed as he released his vice like grip on William.

William finally found his voice, "Aye, Mr. Wilson. It is good to see you once again sir. So much has transpired since we last met in Boston. I have found work in Philadelphia and am leasing a small farm just west of the town. Life has been good here but things are starting to become difficult. With all the new immigrants moving in the landholders are raising the rents and, of course, there is talk of another Indian uprising. It has gotten to the point where many of the Ulster Scots are heading farther west to York in Lancaster County. I'm wondering myself if that is where I should go as well?" William stopped speaking suddenly as he caught sight of someone else walking toward the Captain. Wilson noticed William's change in demeanor and then smiled. "Ach, laddie, I see you've seen my surprise."

And then Captain Wilson stepped aside and there she was standing immediately behind him. It was Helen, the Captain's daughter. The last time William had seen her was at the dock in Glasgow when she was only twelve years old. Four years had passed and Helen had completed the transition from girl to woman. And to William's eyes, never a prettier sight had he ever seen.

Helen spoke first, "Hello William. My father thought our paths might cross again here in Philadelphia. It's been a long time …. "Helen smiled, looked quickly at her father and then ran into William's outstretched arms.

"I tried to write you so many times," William began, "but the words just never came out right. And after the passage of so much time I just assumed you had grown up and found another." William was nervous and stammering over his words but his heart was on fire. Here she was in flesh and blood and she was holding on to him as tight as he was to her. William glanced at Helen's father and saw him smiling. He knew in an instant what he must do. He broke the embrace with Helen and gently pushed her away. He then stood directly in front of Captain Wilson and said, "Mr. Wilson, I would like to ask you sir for your hand's daughter in marriage," and then he looked over his shoulder at Helen and said out of the corner of his mouth, "if she will have me, of course?"

Wilson looked at his daughter and raised one eyebrow as if to ask the question. Without hesitation, Helen nodded and said, "of course, you silly lad, why do you think I've sailed all this way. Rest assured young man, I'm choosing you as much as you are choosing me."

Then Captain Wilson looked at William and said, "William Cochrane, do you promise me on your word as a Christian that you will always love and remain faithful to my daughter until you breathe your last? Do you promise me on your word as a fellow Scot that you will always defend and protect her in all circumstances? Do you promise to bring me lots of grandchildren? If so, answer aye."

"Aye … aye, indeed," exclaimed William.

"Then I grant you the right to marry my lassie Helen," Captain Wilson said with his customary loud laugh. "Of course, lad, you must know that was my intention all along," he said with a wink and more laughter.

William turned to Helen. He looked into this face he had not seen for four long years. "I love you Helen Wilson. This is the happiest day of my life." And then he grabbed her again in a tight hug and swirled around the Philadelphia dock as he done in Scotland years ago when they had parted. He glanced at his soon to be father in law. Wilson laughed and said, "Well, kiss her, lad. That's what I would have done with her mother, God rest her soul." William turned back towards Helen and their lips touched in a tender and gentle kiss. Helen then backed away and said, "Now, that's decided. Where, pray tell, dear husband to be, are we to call home?"

William did not know how to respond or what to say. He had been alone since he had left his home in

Scotland. Since that time, he had been like a leaf blowing in the breeze going wherever the wind took him. Of course, he had always considered the wind to be the Spirit of God. For the last four years of his life he had simply trusted God to lead him in the direction he should go. But now, in the year 1730, at the age of twenty, he was to take a wife and settle down someplace … permanently. Many thoughts quickly ran through his mind. Should we go back home to Scotland? Should we stay here in Philadelphia? Return to Londonderry where other Ulster Scots had put down roots? Or perhaps move west to Lancaster County where some of the Cochranes from Down had settled?

Captain Wilson saw the confusion on the face of his son in law to be and decided to offer a suggestion, "It's just a suggestion mind ye, but I often take my ship into the ports at Jamestown and Charles City in the colony of Virginia. Up the river they call the James there is a place called the Falls. It is as far as sailing vessels can travel. But the country west of this navigable point is quickly developing into good tobacco land. Wealthy English Virginians are buying huge segments of land and raising tobacco upon it. However, they still need a way to transport their crop to England. That's where their major market in located. So, they need tradesmen that can build warehouses and hogsheads for shipping the tobacco and all manner of things at this place called the Falls. Perhaps William, that's where you and my Helen could settle? You are good with your hands. You could get work helping to build up this part of the colony. Or, "Wilson lowered his voice as if he was about to say something he did not want to say but knew he must, "ye both could come home to Scotland?" The good Captain spent more time at sea then on the land but he knew that if his daughter remained in the colonies he would stand a better chance of seeing her from time to time then if she moved back across the Atlantic to Paisley. The laird's business just did not require Wilson' ship to be there as often as it was here running up and down the coast of the American colonies.

William was deep in thought … "Scotland … land of my ancestors … land where my mother and father lived … should I return to that land?" And then he looked at Helen and asked, "Helen, where do you want to live and raise our family?"

Helen surprised them both with her answer. "Not in Scotland. Aye, I will be sad to not return home. But our future, Willie, is here in the colonies and not back there. I want my children to be born here in this new land where a person can be truly free to move about as they please and to worship and pray to God in whatever way they choose. Scotland is the past my love. America is the future. I say we go to Virginia. From what my father says, the opportunity to make a good life is there. That's where we can raise our family," and then she blushed as it dawned upon her what she had just said in public in front of her father.

William looked at his young fiancé. She had called him Willie. No one but his mother had ever used that name with him. And he loved hearing her say it.

"Ye called me Willie," William stated with a grin.

"Aye, love … is that all right," replied Helen.

"Aye love, tis more than all right," and he smiled at her and kissed her quickly on the cheek.

"Aye then … Virginia it is," said William Cochrane to his bride to be with her father standing close by her side. All three were smiling from ear to ear. None of them knew what the future held for them but they knew who knew the future. And they had an unbreakable trust and life-long faith in the One who held them in his hands.

Chapter Thirteen – Blue Run, Orange County, Virginia Colony, ca. 1745

"Benjamin, where is your younger brother? I told you to keep an eye out for him. Lad, I'm gonna tan yer hide if something has happened to that youngin'" Benjamin's mother said in a tone that indicated she meant business.

"Momma, I reckon he has run off again down to the creek. You know how he gets. He's probably chasing a butterfly. The boy has no sense at all." Benjamin responded to his irate mother. He knew he was treading on thin ice. His mother had a temper and everyone in the family knew it and kept their distance when she was "riled up" as his daddy was fond of saying.

John or Johnny as everyone in the family called him was two years younger than Benjamin and although Benjamin was only seven he was still expected to watch over his younger brother. Momma was expecting again and had her hands full with Elizabeth, who was three and little Robert, who had just turned two.

"Well, young man, "stated Benjamin's mother, Martha Cleveland, "you better find him and fast. Your daddy's out in the fields and I'm cooking supper. He'll be home soon and be expecting food on his table. So get …" And with that she swept her hand in the direction of the Blue Run, the small creek that meandered its way north into the Rapidan River which eventually entered the Rappahannock eight miles to the north and east of John Cleveland's small tobacco plantation. From there the Rappahannock headed southeast until it emptied into the waters of the great Chesapeake Bay. The Clevelands had made this trip by water numerous times since Martha's family was located in Essex County. Water travel was safer and more reliable than overland trips although the development of a patchwork of dirt and cobblestone roads was rapidly occurring throughout the eastern counties of the Colony of Virginia. Martha's grandfather, John Coffey, had settled in Essex after making the arduous journey from Ulster across the Atlantic to Philadelphia and then south by boat to the Rappahannock. Her mother's family, the Powells had settled in Elizabeth City parish almost a century before, when Martha's great grandfather Thomas had come across the Atlantic from Suffolk, England. The marriage of Martha's mother, Ann to her father Edward was frowned upon by both sides of the family and, of course, the issue, as always, was religion. The Coffeys were Presbyterian while the Powells were Anglican. It wasn't so much that both families were faithful members of their respective churches … if the truth be told... they weren't … it's just that everyone expected you to marry within your class of people. The Powells, being of English descent, looked somewhat down their noses at Edward Coffey's Scottish background even if he had decided to become an Anglican so that he might wed Martha's mother in a proper church setting. This had led to tension between the families and Martha even as a young child was continuously aware of it. She had decided as a budding adolescent that the man she would someday wed would take her away from this constant bickering between English and Scot. And then one day she met John Cleveland, the young man who would eventually take her for his bride. John had been born in Gloucester County in the year 1714 to a family that had deep ties to England. They were Anglican, of course, but Martha discovered over time that John's family, not unlike many of the middle to upper class Virginians of the day, leveraged their church membership primarily to establish and maintain business contacts. In fact, that is how the two met.

John was working some new lands purchased decades ago by his grandfather, Roger, in what was to become Orange County. The lands around the Chesapeake were quickly losing their fertility for the growing of tobacco thus pushing the English further and further west into the Virginia frontier. Roger had bought as much of the Indian lands as soon as they became available. Eventually, the old man died and his sons and their families took over the small plantations. They weren't rich by any stretch of the imagination. But they had been able down through the years to gradually accumulate more and more land upon which they grew the ever-present tobacco plant plus the other crops necessary to sustain life. John's father, Alexander, had never been able to see his dream come true of building a large stone house by the Blue Run but he had passed this dream onto his son who was working hard to make it a reality. And that is what brought John for the first time to Essex County. It was here where John would float down the Rappahannock on a flat barge loaded to the brim with hogsheads of dried tobacco ready for shipment to England and the northern colonial ports of Philadelphia, New York and Boston.

It had been in the autumn. The days were getting shorter and the leaves on the trees had begun their change of color. The air was cool with a hint of what was to come. John was standing on the dock's edge next to his barge. It had been emptied of its cargo and John was counting the money he had made off the trade. They happened to see each other at the same time. Martha was walking along the river's edge. She had been to a neighbor's farm in order to trade eggs for a new piece of fabric the neighbor had just received from England. John stared at her. He bent in front of her sweeping the ground with his quickly removed hat. He had been taught this is how an English gentleman should act when greeting an aristocratic lady of means.

"I'm afraid you are mistaken kind sir. I'm a simple lass on a mission of trade. You've no need to bow before me like I'm the Queen of England." Those were Martha's first words to the man who would eventually become the love of her life. A few weeks later, John asked her father for her hand in marriage and he agreed to the arrangement. Martha was thrilled. She would be moving to the Cleveland lands in Orange County. It would be close enough to visit on occasion but far enough away to hopefully free herself from the constant family tension that she had endured her entire life. She realized they would be moving to the frontier. It was at the edge of English civilization. But there had been little trouble with the native Indians the past few years. Most had simply picked up and moved farther west or had somehow blended into the encroaching English society. Plus, the backwoods were quickly filling with the Ulster Scot along with newly arrived Germans taking the Great Philadelphia road south to the piedmont region of the colony of Virginia. What used to be the Virginia wilderness was quickly filling up with white European settlers some of whom had the means available to purchase significant acres of available land. Others, the less fortunate, simply travelled to the end of the road and then headed west towards the Blue Ridge Mountains. When they could go no further they stopped and called it home. The established easterners referred to them disparagingly as squatters but it was a title the immigrants bore proudly. In particular, the Ulster Scot had travelled to the American colonies seeking economic opportunities and religious freedom and when they came upon fertile land that had never felt the plow they told themselves it must be in God's plan for them to settle here and turn this wilderness into productive farmland. Never mind, of course, the lands they were possessing were considered the sacred hunting grounds of the native Indians. Thus, the newly arrived Ulster Scot as they worked their fields and planted and harvested their crops learned to keep one eye on the neighboring woods constantly on guard for a hit and run Indian raid. Easterners who travelled to the western edges of the Virginian frontier would often remark it was quite common to see an Ulster Scot farmer with a hoe in one hand and his musket in the other. But the Scots quickly wised up to their situation and began an interesting pattern of development. They would often travel in groups of five to seven fairly large families. Once they arrived at a place that looked inhabitable with fertile soil and clean water close by they would build a fort. Then they would slowly build their simple wooden structures along the various paths leading to the fort. Once it appeared that the settlement was to become permanent they would come together and build a church first and then a school house. However, often, the church would serve as the school during the week. They were simple structures, made entirely of wood usually covering no more than a space of land sixteen by twenty feet. Their houses were even smaller and always made of disposable wood. These were a people that for at least two generations had been on the move. It made no sense to them to invest in long lasting brick or stone structures since they might not be there the very next year. Cheaper and readily available land was always just over the next ridge south and west. These were an adaptable and flexible people who looked upon the eastern English gentry with suspicion and mistrust. After all … they were English and Anglican … and that combination had meant serious trouble for their Scottish ancestors. So the tension in Martha's family was not without cause. The conflict was as much cultural as religious. And then, of course, there was the concept of slavery. The newly arrived Ulster Scot would often see his or her first black African slave when their ship first docked in Philadelphia. Coming to terms with this new reality would often take some time of adjustment. It became even more of a shock to them as they travelled into the southern colonies of Maryland and Virginia where they would often see black African slaves working the tobacco fields of the wealthy English aristocrats who owned vast acres of land and used their slaves to tend to the task of growing and harvesting tobacco. Within a generation after the first slaves arrived, owning a slave or slaves became a status symbol. They were viewed as property by the Virginia planter and, of course, in Colonial Virginia, the more property one held, the higher in the local social circles one climbed. Only the truly wealthy became the powerful members of the House of Burgesses or other official positions within the royal colonial administration of King George. And here in Virginia, being a member of the Anglican Church and giving the tithe no matter how meager your earnings… that was the law. Of course, that exceedingly annoyed the freshly arrived Presbyterian Ulster Scot and Lutheran German who resisted this intrusion in a variety of ways.

Martha thought she had escaped all of that when she married John and moved or rather fled to Orange County. It wasn't the slavery issue that bothered her. Although her father's people were not slaver owners, the Powells certainly were as well as her husband's family. In fact, the old man Cleveland had left his grandson a number of slaves to help work the fields and even one, an older woman named Sallie, helped Martha with her household duties including childrearing. In fact, in some of the larger newly built brick and stone mansions that nestled along the James or Rappahannock, black African house slaves actually lived with their masters in the "big house" and took on active and intimate roles such as nursing the Massa's children. Martha thought that was going too far. She would nurse her own thank you very much but never the less she did find Sallie's help highly beneficial from time to time and all the children did appear to love her dearly.

No, to Martha, the issue wasn't slavery. It was religion. And she thought she had escaped that prison when marrying John and moving west. But the issue followed her. John himself was not a seriously religious man. Yes, he did attend Anglican services. You were fined if you didn't. And yes, he did pay the tithe. That was the law and once again, you were fined if you somehow forgot to do so. And as a dutiful wife, Martha went along with him with their children in tow. Every Sunday, John would hitch up the wagon to one of his huge plow horses and they would clop clop clop the four or five miles to the local church, St. Ann's, spend the entire day there and then turned around the old mare and head home before the sunset. Only in winter when the weather was sometimes awful or news of an Indian uprising would permeate the County would they not follow this habitual pattern. Yes, Martha was obligated as a wife, mother and citizen of the colony of Virginia to fulfill certain observable behaviors when it came to the Christian faith. However, Martha's heart was elsewhere. It wasn't that she did not believe the stories she had grown up with or that she had been told by her mother about God and his son Jesus. She did believe. "Look around at what Nature has wrought," she would often think to herself. "All of this could not have just happened? There must be a Creator. And if there was or is a Creator then wouldn't that being want us the Creation to know of its existence?" This was Martha's reasoning. She was an intellectual believer but quite frankly Martha's system of religious practice did not move her emotionally. She actually felt closer to God when working in her garden or nursing her child. It was in those moments when she felt as if she were collaborating with the Creator in maintaining the life force upon the land that she felt closest to her God. She just didn't understand what all the fuss was about. Of course, she knew her history as a recent descendant of Ulster Scots. And she knew that to her parents, religion was the ultimate priority. Yes, they also attended the Anglican services even though they were of Ulster Scot descent. There was no choice in the matter. But at home, behind closed doors and in private, Martha's parents longed for the plain worship services of what they considered the one true church – the Reformed Kirk of Scotland.

Just then, the door to their little cabin swung open and her son Benjamin stood in the light of the afternoon sun holding the hand of his younger brother, Johnny.

"Well, it's about time gentlemen. I was thinking I would soon have to go out and find you myself. And that would not have made me too happy." Martha scolded and wagged a pointed finger at them although as she stood there looking at them she knew she wouldn't stay upset very long. She dearly loved both of these boys even though they were as different as day and night. Benjamin was a strong-willed child. He always had been right from day one. He was large for his age and was a natural born leader. He would often accompany his father on his trips to the fields or on hunting excursions into the neighboring woods. He knew how to shoot and could already skin a deer. He was very concrete in his speech. Benjamin was a boy of few words and when he did say something it was direct and to the point. And then there was dear sweet and kind Johnny, only five years old but clearly showing signs that his world was a world not of labor and sweat but one of thoughts and ideas. Yes, Martha knew he would eventually learn to fend for himself with the knife and gun. Every young man had to learn these basic necessities of life on the Virginia frontier. But Martha knew that had they been in England or Scotland, this boy would grow up and go to the University to study law or theology or some other lofty subject. Johnny was a thinker and would often communicate his deepest thoughts even at his young age to anyone who would care to listen to him. Johnny would often ask the strangest questions about life in general. "Where does God live? If Jesus is alive, where is he at right now? Why are rainbows colored? Where does the sun go when it leaves the sky?" The boy was constantly asking interesting questions on a variety of subjects. His father pretty much ignored him and "that's a shame" Martha thought to herself. She could tell that Benjamin was his favorite. Benjamin was practical, down to earth and capable of fending for himself if need be. But Johnny was different. "What will become of him?" she thought to herself. "We can't afford to send him back to England for an education" thought Martha and heading up north to Harvard was out of the question given Martha's views on the Puritan church of Massachusetts. She had heard recently of Tennant's Log Cabin College where young men of some means were being sent to prepare for a life of ministry in the Presbyterian Church. "Perhaps that will be an option someday?" she thought as she gathered her two young boys to her side and gave both a hug and kiss on the tops of their heads. "Now go wash up for supper." She demanded. "Your daddy will be home soon."

That Sunday, John hitched the buggy up to one of his large draft horses and the family headed to services at St. Ann's. The church was located around five miles away so it took the family about an hour to make the trip. As usual, it was an uneventful trip. Although John kept his musket close by his side and over the years had added the Indian style tomahawk to his collection of weapons, he had never once had to defend himself or his family from attack. It was just a precautionary and habitual behavior that he and all his neighbors committed. It had been wild and unstable when John first brought his growing family to this part of the Virginia colony but with the opening to the west of Augusta County and the massive peopling of that new county by predominately Ulster Scots from across the sea by way of Pennsylvania, tensions with the natives had eased or had moved further west. The

Virginia frontier was slowly but persistently evolving from rugged woods to cultivated pastureland with the ever-present tobacco plant.

The family settled into the pew they had purchased and prepared to hear another long and tedious sermon delivered in a monotone voice. Much to everyone's surprise a new face occupied the pulpit. The stranger was introduced by the rector as Samuel Morris from Hanover County and what he had to say that morning radically changed the hearts and minds of many of those gathered there including Martha Cleveland. It was not Samuel's oratorical abilities that inspired his audience for he simply read a sermon that had been delivered by an itinerant Anglican minister by the name of George Whitefield. But it was the words of the Reverend Whitefield's message that so moved Martha and many of the others gathered together that morning.

Whitefield along with others such as Theodore Frelinghuysen, a Dutch reformed Pietist and the father and son team of Presbyterian ministers, William and Gilbert Tennent had unleashed a storm of religious revival in the newly formed English colonies during the 1740s. They were continuing on the work of the New England Puritans started by the revivalist preaching of Jonathan Edwards. But a significant difference had developed in the ten years between Edwards and Whitefield. While both men saw the need for a passionate devotion to Christ and his message of salvation, Edwards was still quite concerned with maintaining a pure form of Calvinistic theology. Whitefield was not. Whitefield focused on the unmerited grace of God available to all and not just the predestined. This variation in theological thought was not new. The Anglican Church had always taught that any could be saved from God's awaiting wrath but it could only be done by practicing an ascetic lifestyle while living a life that God found worthy. Here is where Whitefield challenged the prevailing Anglican theology. He taught and preached from pulpits (when allowed) that God's grace was free to all … one only had to accept it. That morning Samuel Morris read the following from one of Whitefield's messages, "Oh what joy – what unspeakable joy- joy full and big with glory was my soul filled when the weight of sin came off and an abiding sense of the pardoning love of God and a full assurance of faith entered my very being." At this point, Morris began to cry and many in the audience joined him including Martha Cleveland. After Morris regained his composure he turned and looked at the audience and Martha felt that he was staring right at her. He then asked the eternal question, "Do you believe that Jesus of Nazareth was and is today the Christ, the Son of God? If you answered yes to that question, then know in your heart that you have been set free from the bondage of sin and decay. Know this day that you will conquer death through the aid of your Lord and Savior Jesus and that your soul will live with Him forever in heaven."

Someone from the back of the sanctuary shouted "amen" and another "hallelujah". John and Martha and the children had never experienced anything like this before in a worships service. In the past things had always been done in a controlled and orderly fashion. Never had they heard such spontaneous and emotional reaction from their fellow parishioners. John was not pleased. Martha was overjoyed. This had been her yearning … to be moved by the words spoken from the pulpit. This is what had been missing in her spiritual quest … to truly know the love and care of a God … not some distant unknown all powerful being ready to strike you down for the commission of some random mistake or error on your part but a loving God who wished only that His children turned to Him for safety and protection from the evils of this world. "A God who loved me … yes, that is what I want with all my heart … a God who loves me for who I am and not because of some perfection I cannot attain," thought Martha to herself.

The wagon ride home was quiet. Each was lost in his or her own thoughts. Finally, Benjamin spoke up, "Daddy, what did you think of what Mr. Morris read this morning?" Martha thought to herself, "of course, it would be her little courageous and honest Benjamin to ask the obvious question of his father," as she waited for her husband's reply.

John thought deeply for a moment or two and then said, "It was interesting, I'll grant you that. Did you see how the people reacted all weepy and going on," he said while shaking his head. "That ain't the church I grew up in. Church is supposed to be a quiet place where you come into the presence of the Almighty God and seek His forgiveness for the sins you have committed. And did you see how the rector reacted? I reckon we won't be seeing or hearing much more of old Mr. Morris … at least not from the pulpit of St. Ann's." John stated this last part as he was smiling at his son and did not notice at first the tears streaming down the cheeks of his wife, but, little Johnny saw them and for the rest of his life he remembered that one Sunday service and how it moved his mother to tears.

Apparently, John Cleveland was not the only Anglican in Virginia who had concerns about this new movement. Later that year, Virginia's lieutenant governor Sir William Gooch had begun to call for the suppression of illicit "ministers under the pretended influence of new light, extraordinary impulse, and such like fanatical and enthusiastic knowledge." He believed they were a threat to the stability of the colony and might lead the common people into wild delusions.

A similar movement was happening in Augusta County which had significant populations of Ulster Scot Presbyterians. They had divided into what some were calling "Old Side" and "New Side" Presbyterians. The old siders were committed to creeds, dogmas and resisted change in the worship service. The new siders favored emotional conversions and spiritual enthusiasm and their ministers stated from the pulpit the Philadelphia Synod was cold, dead and formalistic. The Tennent family from Pennsylvania provided the original leadership of the New Side movement. But it was Alexander Craighead who brought the New Side form of Presbyterianism to Virginia. He travelled from one Presbyterian Church to another sharing his radical views with anyone who would listen. And they listened by the hundreds with sometimes whole congregations changing their perspective from Old to New. One New Side minister, Samuel Davies of Hanover County had even begun to preach and baptize the African slaves located within his circuit of Presbyterian congregations even though he himself was a slave owner. He sought to introduce them to the Christian gospel which the slaves had largely resisted due to Christianity's association with their white masters. Many slave owners were reluctant to teach the African Americans about Christianity for they feared it might give them radical ideas about equality and freedom. Not all agreed with the new movement. And this would sometimes cause bitter divisions within the Ulster Scot Presbyterian communities that had begun to spring up in the Virginia and now the North Carolina backcountry. The Carolinas had recently been opened up to settlement and once again the Ulster Scots streamed in to obtain free land and freedom from the religious constraints of the established Anglican Church of colonial Virginia.

In the year 1754, war broke out between the Empires of France and Great Britain. This was a true global conflict involving land and sea battles from Europe to the Far East including the colonial possessions in North America of both England and France. Johnny, whom everyone now simply called Junior to distinguish him from his father John, had just turned fourteen. And by this year, the Cleveland plantation at Blue Run was prospering, to John and Martha had been born nine children and all except one had survived their infancy. The eldest surviving child, Mary had married a man by the name of Bernard Franklin and had moved away to Augusta County where they had settled down to begin raising a family of their own. The next in line was Benjamin, who by age 16 was a tall fellow built rather stout with powerful arms and broad shoulders, then followed fourteen-year-old John Junior, twelve-year-old Elizabeth, eleven-year-old Robert, seven-year-old Jeremiah, six-year-old Larkin and finally two-year-old Patty. The Cleveland children were well fed, healthy for the most part and were being educated in their home by Martha on the fundamentals of reading, writing and simple arithmetic. At least that was the case for the boys. It was expected that one of them would eventually take over the small but growing plantation. The girls also were taught how to read the Bible and to write in order to maintain correspondence with their mother when they eventually married and moved off to their own farms. At least that was the plan Martha and John had for their children and for the eldest child, Mary, now twenty-three and expecting their second child, the plan was working. But Martha was worried about her boys. They seemed much more interested in hunting, fishing and playing in the forest then doing their studies, all except John Junior. Contrary to the rest of his brothers, Johnny loved to read, in particular, the Bible, and would often engage his mother or the local parson in questions of a theological nature. In fact, Johnny was always asking questions about things that mattered little to others in the family including his father. Unless, of course, the topic was politics and then usually a spirited discussion would develop with the father taking the side of King and Empire which John Junior would passionately question. But, for the most part, the lives of their children were relatively stable and peaceful. That is until what would eventually be called the French and Indian War occurred in Colonial America. The plantation at Blue Run was no longer on the Virginia frontier. That landmark had moved considerable farther west and that was one of many issues that had ignited the war. Ulster Scots, Colonial English, and Germans were moving up to the mountains and in some cases over the mountains and settling small farms in the various meadows and valleys they could find that might grow a bit of corn or provide enough silage to feed their hogs which often ran free. This caused significant tension with the Indians up and down the Allegheny Mountains and of course the French who had long since claimed the Ohio and Mississippi river valleys as their own were not happy with this encroachment. They would encourage the Indians to make trouble for these new settlers. Last year, Virginia Governor Robert Dinwiddie had sent a 21-year adjutant in the colonial militia by the name of George Washington to carry a stern message to the French who were now settling in the Ohio valley. The royally appointed Dinwiddie warned the French to vacate the land which was being claimed by the British crown. The French refused to move. This year, Dinwiddie appointed Washington a lieutenant colonel and sent him with a force of 160 Virginians to reinforce a British colonial post called Ft. Pitt. However, before Washington's men could arrive there, the French along with their Indian allies had conquered the fort and renamed it Fort Duquesne. Washington moved within around forty miles of the French position and established a make shift fort at Great Meadows which he called Fort Necessity. It was here the first blow was struck for King and country. From this base, Washington was able to ambush a scouting group of about forty French and Indian warriors. And it was this first violent interaction which initiated the events across the Atlantic that ultimately brought global war to England and France. The Clevelands, of course, knew Colonel Washington since John's cousin, Alexander Cleveland worked on the Washington plantation as slave master and keeper of the many horses that Washington dearly loved. George had married well and was certainly using his wife's fortune in land to leverage a higher position in the military than some thought he deserved. But he had proven himself courageous under fire and was indeed a skilled leader of fighting men. Benjamin wanted in the worst way to join up with Washington's forces which now included men from both Virginia as well as North Carolina. But his father would not hear of it.

"I need you here son to help me manage this plantation. Plus, I have plans on making another purchase of a large piece of land in North Carolina. I'll eventually need you to move there and make it a profitable enterprise." John smiled as he looked at his oldest so hoping he would abandon his dream of valor on the battlefield. He knew how much Benjamin wanted to participate in this war but from John's perspective it was not their fight. He had his land. It was making money for him and his family. He saw new opportunities for further accumulation of land. And to a Virginian of English descent, land meant wealth, status and prestige. "We're all deep in debt," he mused to himself, "but who cares as long as there is land to be taken and tobacco to be grown … eventually I'll pay off all my creditors. It will happen but my sons need to play an active part in my grand scheme. And, by God, they will." He thought to himself with such sternness in his countenance that Martha recognized the change in his face and looked at him quizzically.

Benjamin ran away and joined Washington's forces. But due to his age, he was immediately sent back home. After that, things did not go well between him and his father. The one thing John Cleveland would not tolerate from any of his children was an outright act of disobedience. From that point on, the relationship between the two was cool and reserved, more like business partners than father and son and it drove poor Martha into a deep pit of depression and constant worry. She had not wanted this rift to occur between any of her children and her husband but she knew years ago given

Benjamin's strong will and John's demanding character, tension between the two would simmer and then eventually explode.

One morning, Martha rose early to tend to her chickens and when she checked on her children she noticed Benjamin's bed had not been slept in. She immediately ran outside to the barn containing the horses and looked in the stalls. One of John's prized animals was gone and a note had been pinned to the wooden side of the stall. It read, "Dear Momma and Daddy, I'm heading west to join up with some fellas that are looking for a passage into the land of the canes across the mountains. Some fella by the name of Boone is leading the outfit. He's calling it a hunting trip but everyone knows the real reason. Don't worry Momma, I'll be o.k. Tell daddy I'm sorry about the horse. I'll return it in one piece. Love, Benjamin."

Martha could feel the tears rolling down her cheeks as she read her oldest son's letter. She thought to herself, *so it's come to this ... the boy's run off and taken his father's biggest and fastest horse ... Oh Lord,* Martha looked toward the heavens, *please send your angels to watch over my boy and bring him home safely to me.* She neatly folded away the note and stuck it in her dress pocket. She would have to explain all of this to John and the rest of the children and she wasn't quite sure how she should do that other than just come right out with the truth.

Benjamin stayed away for years. Word would occasionally make its way back to the Cleveland plantation at the Blue Run of wild tales of Benjamin's antics. Apparently, he had developed quite a reputation as a hunter and trapper. He loved to gamble and was fond of hard drink. Perhaps too fond if some of the rumors were true. He also had found himself in conflict with the Cherokee tribe of natives located in the mountains of the North Carolina colony. It was the warfare Benjamin had sought as a younger man. The Indians would strike first at some isolated cabin killing all of its white European inhabitants and then Benjamin and his small band of followers would exact revenge upon whatever tribe they could encounter. They weren't always just. Sometimes they caught and killed innocent bands of Cherokees who had never laid a hand upon any of the settlers but to Benjamin and his ruffians "the only good Indian was a dead Indian." This was justice frontier style. Benjamin was developing a reputation as a fierce man with which no person in their right mind would want to tangle.

Back at the Blue Run, things had begun to settle back into the slow and measured pace of the Virginia tobacco plantation. It had become obvious to the settlers of the English colonies the French wcrc losing the war at least on this continent. The great global conflict was coming to an end. French soldiers had vacated much of the Ohio country and parts of the southeast leaving it all in English control and that meant settlers who had been pushed up against the eastern side of the Alleghenies could now safely and legally travel through the mountain passes into western Pennsylvania, and what eventually would become the states of Kentucky and Tennessee although officially they were still considered parts of the colonies of Virginia and North Carolina respectively.

John Junior had stayed close to the farm as he transitioned from boy to man. He was a hard worker and his father appreciated that aspect of his personality. But Junior was different from his older brother. First thing a person would notice was the physical size of the young man. He was not tall like Benjamin nor stoutly built. It wasn't that he was small but when compared to his older more powerfully built brother he lacked the prowess of Benjamin. But he made up for it in his intellect. He was constantly reading. If it wasn't the Bible, then it would be some other theological and/or political treatise which had been published in Philadelphia, New York or Boston and he had been lucky enough to get his hands on a copy. He also often rode into town to learn of the news that had been posted outside the country store or tavern. It was in this way, he kept the family informed of things which were happening outside their little sphere of Blue Run Virginia. Johnny yearned to go to one of the colleges up north but he knew that was not going to happen. With Benjamin's absence, his father depended upon him even more around the plantation and quite frankly the family was "land rich but cash poor" as the saying goes so there were simply no funds available for him to further his education. He felt stuck.

The war had been profitable for many of the Virginia planters but not John Cleveland. Unfortunately, he had gambled with a large shipment of tobacco to England hoping the trading vessel would make it safely to England. Other planters had warned him to simply send his cash crop north to Philadelphia. The market price for tobacco had fallen drastically in Philadelphia, New York and Boston but was holding its own in London and Amsterdam. John knew that if he could just get one major shipment safely to the European tobacco traders he would make enough cash money to pay off all his debts and finally own his plantation outright and maybe even have enough cash left over to buy some of the things his wife

Martha desperately craved. But shortly after leaving the protective coastal waters of the Virginia colony it encountered a French warship which commandeered all the goods aboard and then set the vessel on fire. She sank to the bottom of the ocean in minutes. John Cleveland had lost everything. He became a broken man.

Martha did what she could to hold her little family together but she knew that the future for her sons and daughters no longer lay in the worn-out tobacco fields of Orange County. She would stay with her husband as each year he continued to attempt to eke out a living on soil that was rapidly becoming deleted of all its nutrients. But she encouraged her children to think of the west as the place that held their future.

Life had become difficult at the Blue Run. One Sunday morning, John Junior had hitched up the one remaining horse to take the family to services. Everyone went except Junior's father. After his devastating financial loss, his spirit seemed to die along with his hopes of financial independence. Although he would never say it in public to his wife or children, he blamed God for his misfortunes. After all, hadn't his Calvinistic wife said that God is in control of all things? Therefore, he reasoned, it must be God's plan that I suffer in this manner. So, John Cleveland figured if God had given up on him he was going to give up on God. And that became a bitter and tense issue between him and his God fearing and faithful wife. She continued to every Sunday have John Junior hitch the wagon and take the bunch of them to church where they spent most of the day and Martha weekly made excuses for her husband's absence. Of course, everyone knew what had happened and Martha and the Clevelands became the sad talk behind closed doors of some of the wealthier members of the parish at St. Ann's, which now everyone was calling St. John's. The old parish had split over the evangelistic teaching of George Whitfield. Now the newer more spirit moved and emotional members worshipped at St. John's while the more orthodox members stayed at the old parish of St. Ann's which if the truth be told was slowly dying due to the aging and subsequent deaths of many of its members.

On this particular Sunday morning, John Junior was driving the family to the services when they happened to drive by a small gathering of people gathered close together down by the Rapidan River. To Johnny's surprise he saw a line of men and women all dressed in white robes standing in line waiting to enter the cool spring waters of the Rapidan. And then he heard a booming male voice, "As much as you have professed with your own mouth your belief in the Lord Jesus Christ as your Savior, I now baptize you in the name of the Father, the Son and the Holy Ghost." And then Johnny's eyes about fell out of their sockets as the man with the booming voice immersed each of the people in the line one by one completely under the water.

Johnny stopped the wagon, "Momma that man's trying to drown those people. Where's Daddy's rifle?" he said looking around the wagon bed for the old musket. Martha burst into laughter. "No lad, he is not trying to drown them … he's trying to save them. He must be one of these Baptist preachers I keep hearing about. They believe only adults can truly accept the Lord as their Savior therefore they put no trust in the baptizing of infants."

Johnny looked at the man. He continued to preach even as he was laying the people under the water's surface. "They asked Peter what must I do to be saved and Peter said unto them … repent and be baptized for the remission of all your sins. Come now, Come now to Jesus and be saved." Johnny was mesmerized by the man. He wasn't much older than him and yet had such eloquence in his speech combined with a commanding physical presence. He was a tall man but slender as if it had been a while since he sat down to a good meal.

Martha seemed to read her son's mind, "no, he doesn't look well fed now does he son? Probably been on the run since the Governor outlawed exactly what he is doing right now … preaching without a license and re-baptizing adults who have obviously already been baptized in the Church of England as eight day old infants."

"I want to speak with him Momma. Robert, you take the reins and take Momma and the children on to the service. You can pick me up on the way back home." And just as quickly as he said it, Johnny was off the wagon and heading straight towards the small gathering of Baptists. Martha watched him walk away and in her heart, she knew something at that moment had changed in her son's life and there wasn't anything she could say or do to change his destiny. So … she smiled, nodded her head and looked toward the heavens, "watch over him Father … that's all I ask". Then she told Robert to get the horse moving or they would be late for the service.

Johnny moved to the edge of the folks gathered by the river. He leaned over to one of the people next to him and said in a muffled tone, "who is the man doing the preaching and baptizing?" The younger man answered, "That's the Reverend Johnston and over there standing by the water's edge is his wife, Mollie." John followed the man's glance and was stunned into silence at the beauty of the preacher's wife. She was older than he by about five or maybe even ten years but in his mind, she was the prettiest thing he had ever laid his eyes upon. Just at that moment she looked directly at him. Their eyes met and locked for the briefest moment and then she quickly looked embarrassingly at the ground. Johnny also felt somewhat embarrassed. After all, this was another man's wife and a man of God for heaven's sake. But he could not help but keep glancing at her as her husband preached on and on about the power of the blood of Jesus to heal the sins of man's soul.

Suddenly everything became very quiet. Johnny turned quickly and looked in the direction of the Baptist preacher. He was clutching his chest and suddenly collapsed in the shallow edge of the river's swirling water. A woman screamed and a few people surged forward to help the poor young man. Johnny was as surprised as everyone in attendance but he stayed back away from the crowd. He didn't know if the man was truly hurt or perhaps this was part of the delivery of his sermon. He had heard stories of men and women being "caught in the Spirit" and falling to the ground unable to move or speak and thought that perhaps this is what he was observing.

Apparently, it was not an act, nor part of some mystical religious experience. The Reverend Joseph Johnston had just died. The small crowd that had gathered to witness his preaching and the baptisms was stunned to silence. Only the young woman who a stranger had introduced to Johnny as the wife of the preacher was moving. A couple of the stronger younger men in the crowd had carried Johnston's lifeless body and laid it upon the sand at the edge of the river. Johnston's wife, now a widow, was holding her husband in her arms and the tears were freely flowing down her cheeks. After a short while, someone in the group, one of the older men, began to pray while a black African, apparently someone's slave, began to sing a slow and melodious song about "going home". Others began to join in and soon the small group of approximately fifty souls was singing praises to God for the life and contribution of this young preacher. His wife was now being consoled by other women in the group and eventually they were able to get her to release her hold on the dead man. One of the elderly women helped the young widow into her carriage and asked that the men place her husband's body in the back of a wagon that had been used to store provisions for the day's service.

Johnny finally regained his senses and asked someone close by, "What happened to him? Are they taking him back to his farm for burial?" A young woman in the group stopped and turned to Johnny. "Of course, you are a visitor with us this morning. You would not know the history of Joseph and his wife Mary who everyone calls Mollie. Joseph is or was around thirty years old and his wife Mollie is twenty-six. They had two little boys but both died in infancy. Now, she is all alone." And the woman began to cry. John asked her, "Are they going home to their farm now?" The young woman answered, "No, they have no place of their own. Joseph was a missionary to this part of the colonies and along the western frontier. They stayed wherever people would put them up for a few weeks while Joseph preached the gospel to whomever would listen, white, black or red. He didn't care. He thought they were all in need of the saving blood of Jesus. And now the Lord has taken him home." And she began to cry once again. Johnny realized that his motivation was probably not pure in spirit but he felt a tremendous need to help out the widow Johnston but didn't really know what he could do. So he began walking after the crowd forgetting that he had informed his brother to pick him up here when the family was heading back to the Blue Run after services at St. John's.

The crowd got smaller as the buggy and wagon carrying the widow and her dead husband's body approached a small farmhouse about a mile from where the young preacher had given up the ghost of life. A group of the men had carried Johnston's body from the back of the wagon and gently set it upon the ground outside the small wooden structure that had been the temporary shelter of Joseph and Mollie Johnston. Johnny heard from the others this was the home of old man Carver who had lost his wife to fever the past year. It had somehow been decided on the spot that Johnston would be buried in a grave next to Carver's wife. Johnny thought to himself, "How odd … these two had no home and no church … and no place to place their bodies while they waited on the return of the Lord Jesus upon the Day of Judgment. At least, I have the Blue Run and St. John's." And then the thought struck him, "Why not invite Mollie to come and stay with his family for a while?" He was sure his mother would approve and it might do his father some good to have a young woman with strong religious conviction in the house. Maybe she would be able to "talk some sense" into his backsliding daddy. But he wasn't sure how to go about it. He hadn't even been introduced to her. And for goodness sake, she had just lost her husband. "I must be going mad," he thought to himself.

And then he looked up and saw her looking at him once again and somehow that gave him the courage to do what he wanted to do. He walked up to her and took off his hat. He nodded his head and said, "I'm so sorry for your loss Mrs. Johnston. You don't know me. My name is John Cleveland. I was riding with my family to services at St. John's over by the town of Orange. My father owns the tobacco plantation at the Blue Run about five or six miles due south from here. I heard your husband preaching and saw him baptizing the people in the Rapidan and had to stop and listen to what he said. And then, of course …well … I'm so sorry." John stopped speaking because Mollie had begun to cry once again. She finally composed herself and spoke to John, "Yes, my husband and I had heard of your father's plantation. In fact, Joseph was planning on speaking with your father about holding a revival on his land in a couple of weeks. It would have been for all the folks located in this part of Orange and Augusta counties. We didn't know what the reception would be like. You see, we are often not wanted in this part of Virginia. The governor has tried to have my husband arrested a number of times but so far, we have been able to stay just outside of his grasp. We intentionally stay away from the larger towns and the coastal ports. Joseph felt the calling to preach to the poor folks living on the edge of civilization as well as the Indians and black slaves. But now …" she turned and looked at the body of her dead husband," now, I don't know what to do," and began to weep once again. John looked at the small gathering of local farmers. He knew some of them but most was unknown. They were the poor of this county. They lived in small wooden cabins with dirt floors trying to survive on what little they could grow or hunt. This County was primarily a land of middling to large tobacco plantations and if you happened to not be born into one of the planter's families, life was rather difficult. In fact, most of the poor of Orange and the neighboring counties were heading west and south to join the mass migration of English and Ulster Scots settling in the backcountry of the Carolinas. John suddenly realized that God had decided he was to stop the wagon and listen to the final words of the preacher Johnston. John also thought to himself, "Perhaps it is God's will that I am to take up where this man has dropped off?" He looked at Mollie and before he could think he heard his voice say, "Miss Mollie, my family would be honored to have you as our guest. My mother, Martha is her name, would be pleased as punch to have another woman in the house. I have younger sisters also and they would be tickled to death to have you around … at least for a few weeks until things settle down and you decide what the next chapter in your life will contain. I'm sorry for being so forward but given the circumstances, it seems like it might be the will of our Lord." John looked around at the dirt covered ragged faces and saw some of them nodding their heads while others were indeed frowning and shaking their heads no.

"Mr. Cleveland," Mollie replied. John interrupted, "please call me John or Johnny if you must … my daddy's name is John so they call me Junior or Johnny to keep things straight."

"Oh, alright … John then … I …I need to bury my husband. Would you be kind enough to read a few passages of scripture over his grave and perhaps … say a prayer for his soul? "Mollie responded.

"Yes, of course." John answered. So, for the next couple of hours as the stronger of the men gathered there dug a fresh new grave while the available women wrapped Joseph Johnston's body for burial, Mollie and John spoke about Joseph and his missionary work. John learned that Mollie and Joseph had both been born in Northumberland County close to the Maryland border and alongside the Chesapeake Bay. Mollie had been orphaned as a baby when her parents both died of the fever and she was raised by the Johnston family. Mollie's parents had been McCann's and had travelled from Antrim County in Ulster along with the Johnstons, Maxwells, and other Scots whose ancient roots lay in the border region of Scotland and England. Although they had all been raised as Presbyterian, one day an itinerant Baptist preacher by the name of Daniel Marshal originally from Connecticut had held a three-day revival and Joseph was converted. He announced to the family he had been called to preach the word of God to the heathens of the colonial frontier and on that same day asked Mollie if she would be his wife. That was just four years ago, in 1755. It had all happened so quickly, Mollie admitted, but the Lord had indeed blessed them with two infant boys who they unfortunately had lost soon after their births. Mollie had survived but, she admittedly sheepishly, it looked like maybe they would not be able to have any more children. At this, John lowered his gaze out of humility.

At last, it came time for the burial. John did read a few of his favorite passages from the New Testament. Verses that he thought might bring Mollie some comfort in this time of loss. And then he said a short and simple prayer asking God to take the soul of this dearly loved man who had died while spreading the good news of

Jesus. And then the last shovel of dirt was spread over the grave of Joseph Johnston.

As the small group walked back to the little cabin of the elderly Carver, Mollie suddenly said, "Yes, John … just give me a few minutes to gather up our meager belongings and I shall accompany you to the Blue Run." She turned and gave old Mr. Carver a quick hug and thanked him for his hospitality. Everyone in the group understood it would not be proper for her now to stay with this one old man but some in the small group wondered about this new planter. Who was he? And what were his intentions?

As soon as Mollie's two small bags were packed, they headed back to the place on the Rapidan where John's family had dropped him off that morning. As they made the final turn in the dusty road, John could see his family's wagon. All of them had scattered about the area calling out his name afraid that he had somehow run into trouble. John yelled out to his mother and brother that he was alright and walked straight to the wagon with Mollie following behind. Everyone seemed to notice Johnny and the woman following him at the same time and suddenly stopped in their tracks. Robert was the first to ask, "Junior, who is this lady? And where have you been?" Johnny then spent the next fifteen minutes recapping the days' events. After he finished, he turned and looked straight at his mother, "Momma, I told Mollie she would be welcomed to stay with us for a few weeks while she gets her life organized. I assume you agree?" John asked hesitantly.

Martha looked Mollie up and down and took her time answering. Finally, a smile came to her lips and she said, "Why, of course, lad … what made you ever doubt it. Miss Mollie may stay as long as she needs to … it will certainly be nice to have another female around the farm." And with that, she walked over to Mollie and gave her a huge hug. "I'm so sorry for your loss child. This life can certainly be hard on us Christians but we have the knowledge of a loving God and the hope of eternity … now don't we lass?"

Mollie replied, "Yes, Mrs. Cleveland, yes, we do." The younger brothers grabbed Mollie's handbags and placed them in the back of the wagon. Everyone insisted she sit up front with John at the reins while Martha and the children held on in the back. "Giddy-up," John told the old mare and the wagon lurched forward heading back to the plantation and the Blue Run.

The days turned into weeks and turned into months. Mollie was made to feel as if she were part of the family. Even old John found a bit of happiness with her around. And, of course, Johnny was thrilled to have her on the plantation. Finally, he had someone to talk with about the deeper theological questions he had developed in his own mind upon reading the scriptures. And they talked and talked … from morning to evening … although both had plenty of chores to do around the farm to keep things in working order, somehow, they found time each day to sit be it for a brief moment to contemplate what both considered the more significant questions of life, God and eternity.

Johnny knew that he was in love with Mollie and he felt extreme guilt regarding his attraction and affection for her. She was a widow still wearing black. And yet, when they were together, his soul was at peace. She had a way of bringing him spiritual comfort that he didn't really understand but for which he was grateful. And, of course, he had no idea if the feelings were reciprocal because he dare not approach such a sensitive topic. It was not uncommon for young widows or widowers to remarry soon after their loss but usually there existed an unwritten social rule of waiting at least a year before a new courtship would commence.

One day, Johnny decided he had waited long enough. Mollie was walking towards the hen house. He saw her from his position in the horse barn and slowly walked towards her. "Mollie, I know you are busy but could I have just a moment of your time?" John asked gathering up his courage for what he was about to say.

Mollie seemed a little frustrated with the interruption but managed to smile and say, "Of course, John, what's on your mind. Thinking some more about Revelations chapter 22," which had been their last topic of discussion last evening at supper.

"Well … uh … no … although I did enjoy your interpretation that's not what I mean to speak with you about …" John removed his hat from his head and looked straight into Mollie's eyes. They were about the same height but John seemed to stand just a little taller at the moment.

Mollie smiled and looked expectantly at this young man. If the truth be told, she had grown quite fond of him and considered him her closest friend, which is why she was shocked when suddenly Johnny dropped to one knee and took her hands in his.

"Mollie, I don't know if you know this but I love you. I think, God forgive me, I have loved you from the first moment I saw you. I don't rightly know how you feel about me but …. Oh well … here goes …Mary Mollie

McCann would you do me the honor of becoming my wife?"

Mollie was speechless at first. Then she blurted out, "stand up John or folks will think you are proposing to me or something silly like that ..." She regretted saying it as soon as the words had left her mouth for she could she the impact it had upon him.

"But Mollie ... that is exactly what I am doing ... I'm asking you to marry me." John replied in a male voice that suddenly sounded much older than Mollie had heard before.

"John ... I carry for you very much. You came into my life at the worst possible time and helped me when I had nowhere to go and no one to comfort me. Your family has treated me like one of their own. For that I will always be grateful. But .... John ... I'm a twenty-six-year-old widow and unable to bear you any children. Even if I did love you, I couldn't do that to you." Mollie began to tear up and spoke in a broken voice.

John stepped closer to her and gently put his arms around her waist and pulled him closer to him. "But do you Mollie ...do you love me?"

Mollie looked into the deep brown eyes of this young man and suddenly she knew ... yes, she loved him. "Yes, John, I love you. I've known for some time now but didn't think it would ever amount to much given the difference in our age and the circumstances of our meeting and all that ...." Her voice trailed off.

"Mollie, you are only seven years older than me. And as far as the circumstances of our meeting ... don't you think God had a hand in all of this. Isn't it God who decides when we are to be born and when we are to die? Isn't God in ultimate control of the destiny of our lives?

Mollie, it was God who made me stop that day and listen to Joseph preach. It was God who brought us together when you needed my help. And Mollie … if or if we don't have children … isn't that also up to God. Why not place your trust in Him and be my wife come what may we'll be together until we breathe our last." John stopped talking and took Mollie's tear stained face in his hands and gently kissed her lips. "I love you Mollie … be my wife".

Mollie looked at the ground and then into John's face, "Yes, John Cleveland, yes, I will be your wife and we together will place our trust in He who knows our destiny." They kissed one another passionately. Mollie was the first to break away to catch her breath. John grabbed her by the hand and started to walk back towards the plantation house. "Come on girl … we've got to tell momma and daddy and the rest of the family," John said with a huge smile upon his face. Mollie smiled and placed her arm in his and together they walked up to the big house.

The family was not shocked by the news in fact, most had been expecting it, nor where they shocked when Johnny announced that as soon as he and Mollie were husband and wife, they planned on continuing the missionary work of Mollie's deceased husband. And within a matter of weeks, that is exactly what happened. The Sandy Creek Baptist Association of Guilford, North Carolina had requested that Baptist missionaries be sent west of the Virginia fall and into the Carolina backcountry to bring the gospel to a generation of British immigrants who had not heard the news of Jesus preached since their grandparents had left the mother country. They were also sent to the native Indians and to the black African slaves.

The morning of their departure came upon them sooner than any of them expected or desired. But Johnny knew that God had called him to the edges of British civilization and he had Mollie's full support. The first place to which he was heading was Benjamin's new plantation in Wilkes County. Apparently, his brother had done well, at least financially, or so it seemed. His new plantation, called, Roundabout, named because of the land upon which it stood, land that had been surrounded on three sides by the slowly flowing Yadkin River, was nestled up against the base of the Blue Ridge Mountains. It wasn't particularly fertile land but it was cheap and there was plenty of it for the taking. And the Ulster Scots, English and German settlers were not shy in taking all the available land they could get their hands upon. The Cherokee were pushed further west and south into the Smoky Mountains and as the French were facing defeat after defeat on the continent they were unable to stem the tide of British immigrants into the Carolina wilderness. And it was a wild place. That is why John felt the need to travel there to bring some semblance of order and civility to the backcountry. In addition, The Virginia colony was becoming hostile to dissenting faiths. Baptist, Quakers and Moravians were being hounded, persecuted and jailed. The Carolinas and now Georgia had taken a different view towards the non-Anglican denominations of the Christian faith.

"Good bye Momma. Good bye Daddy. Goodbye everyone, "Johnny said with a wave and never looked back. They all knew they might not ever see one another again. That is the way things were in the colonies. Your children grew up, got married and moved off to find a better piece of land that would provide for them and their children hopefully just a little bit better than the parents. Martha was holding one of the little ones in her arms while tears streamed down her cheeks. John had already headed for the barn where he kept his supply of corn whiskey. The rest of the children ran after Johnny and Mollie's wagon waving and saying "goodbye" and "God be with you" and occasionally "I love you." But Johnny Cleveland who would soon become known as the Reverend John Cleveland kept his hands steady on the reins and face staring straight ahead. Mollie was holding onto his arm tightly and trying to hold back her tears unsuccessfully. They travelled almost thirty miles that day and met up with another Ulster Scot family heading south from Philadelphia. John could tell from their accents they were "fresh off the boat".

"Where ye headin'?" The oldest one in the bunch asked John. "Going to my brother's home in Wilkes County, North Carolina and then … not quite sure … probably up into the mountains. Where you folks heading?" John asked politely.

"Going to a place called the Pendleton District in South Carolina. We heard the land's plentiful, cheap and the game is good. I bought a new rifle in Philadelphia. It shoots straighter and farther than any old musket could ever manage." The man hoisted it up in the air to show John. "Where's your weapon?" the stranger asked.

John picked up his old worn out Bible," Reckon this be it brother … the word of God," and with that statement John smiled at the man and his family.

"Lad, ye may need a bit more than that when ye meet the Redskins for the first time … or a bear" The man laughed and then turned his wagon down the fork of the road that led further into the south country.

John turned to Mollie and said, "We go to the east for a bit now. Until we come to Benjamin's place. But I think we had better be looking for a safe place to spend the night. We'll not get there before night falls."

The night was uneventful but the forest noises kept them both awake for some time. Finally, out of exhaustion, they fell asleep in one another's arms. John prayed for the Lord to watch over them as they slept and to prepare Benjamin's heart for their arrival. He and his brother had been close but times have a way of changing a man and John was not quite sure of the reception that lay ahead for he and his new young bride.

Benjamin saw their wagon first. He had the keen eyes and ears of a hunter and nothing ever got close to him by surprise. His mouth dropped wide open when he saw who it was. "Little brother ... my God ... is it you? ...And who is that pretty young thing sitting next to you?" Benjamin let out a huge laugh. He had been big as a boy but now he was a mountain of a man. He had to have been well over six feet tall and must have weighed at least 250 pounds or more. John pulled the horse to a stop and went around the other side to help Mollie climb down to the ground. Benjamin grabbed John in his huge arms and then looked at Mollie somewhat unsure of what was proper. After John had regained his breath he managed to say, "Brother Benjamin, this is Mollie ... my wife". At which point Mollie extended her hand to politely shake her newly met brother in law but Benjamin would have nothing to do with the extended hand. He grabbed her up in his huge arms and swung her completely around in a circle. "Well, I'll be a skunk's tail ... my little brother has gone off and married himself a pretty young thing. Well let's not stand here in the sun. It's getting up there and today's going to be a hot one. Let's go inside and sit in the cool of the parlor. I'll have one of my house slaves fetch you two something cool to drink." Benjamin turned quickly for a man of his size and marched into the big house barking out orders to everyone inside to prepare for their new guests.

John and Benjamin spent the next few days filling each in on what had transpired since he had left the Blue Run. Benjamin was not surprised to hear of John's decision to enter the ministry but he was a little taken aback about how everything transpired. Yes, he agreed, it must be the hand of God at work. Benjamin was not what you might call a religious person but he did believe in an almighty God who was in control of the affairs of man.

Eventually, the subject of politics came up between them. Their father was loyal to King George and they both knew he would die loyal to the English crown. "But things are different in the backcountry, Johnny … I mean, John. Once a man gets out here in the wilderness and gets a taste of complete and total freedom … well … let me tell you son … there ain't nothing like it on the face of this old earth … freedom … John … can you understand what I'm saying to you … I'm free here at Roundabout. Free to do as I see fit and to live my life without a thought of what good old King George has to say about it. And John, "Benjamin's usual chipper voice became quickly rather somber," it's a freedom I'm willing to die for … and so are the men who I know scattered from here to the Watauga settlement." Watauga was the westernmost point of English settlement in North

Carolina. John knew of it but not much about it. They called themselves the over the mountain men.

"So little brother, where are you heading to next?" Benjamin asked with an unusual tender concern in his husky and manly voice.

John and Mollie had talked and already decided. "We heard some Ulster Scots talk about available land and new settlements in the Pendleton District of South Carolina. I think we'll head there and I'll preach the gospel to whomever I encounter. Who knows? Maybe they'll need to build churches and I can stay on as one of the pastors?"

"You mean a Baptist minister ….my God John … how did Momma and Daddy take the news of your conversion?"

John just smiled and said quietly, "Daddy doesn't much care these days for organized religion and momma was all right with it as long as I kept true to the teachings of John Calvin … she figured if God had called you it didn't really matter how a person was baptized or at what age for that matter."

Benjamin roared with laughter, "That's our momma … a Calvinist to the bone." John joined in his brother's laughter and before long the two were hugging each other. Benjamin was the first to speak, "I reckon you'll be leavin' us soon, then?"

"Tomorrow at daybreak," John replied. Benjamin looked into the eyes of his little brother and gently put an arm across his shoulder as the two of them headed into the big house for their last evening together.

John and Mollie spent the next fifteen years of their lives preaching the word of God to the white settlers, black slaves and red natives of the western Carolinas and as far south as northeastern Georgia. They had established a small farm at the confluence of the Tugaloo River and Chauga River. The farm was actually in South Carolina but John owned former Cherokee land on both sides of the border. And to their surprise, Mollie was able to give birth to many children over the next fifteen years. The first being a son they named John born in the first year of their marriage. A dozen followed. It seemed every year Mollie was expecting a new one and most of them survived into adulthood. Eventually, John's brothers, Jeremiah and Larkin brought their families to the area. There were little Clevelands everywhere on the Tugaloo. In fact, to get from one side of the river, the South Carolina side, to the Georgia side required a crossing on Cleveland's ferry. John's ministry was growing. Little Baptist churches were being planted throughout the region. John's message wasn't always well received and sometimes he was beaten rather severely after or even sometimes during his preaching. But he never wavered from what he believed was God's calling on his life to preach the good news of Jesus to all who would listen.

Things in the backcountry were going well for the settlers who had moved there over the past twenty-five years but the tension between mother England and her colonies had steadily grown and finally exploded way up in Massachusetts. A war for Independence had finally come to the American colonies. While the initial fighting remained in the north eventually the war spread to the southern colonies. And it arrived with a vengeance. What had started in the north as a war against the English crown turned into a civil war in the southern colonies of Virginia, the Carolinas and Georgia. There were people on both sides of the issue and both decided to take up arms against the other. Neighbor fought neighbor. Brother turned against brother. It was as if Satan had released the hounds of Hell upon the land. The Georgia and South Country backcountry were strong supporters of the revolution and would often be called upon to conduct hit and run attacks upon the established British outposts surrounding Charleston and neighboring coastal areas. Finally, Cornwallis had enough and sent a man by the name Banastre Tarleton to "make waste' of the entire backcountry region and he nearly succeeded. He made a fatal mistake however. One of his subordinates, a Scotsman by the name of Ferguson sent a challenge to the Watauga settlement and others scattered through the mountainous region to completely surrender or suffer the consequences.

Benjamin sent word to his brothers living on the South Carolina –Georgia border that they were needed and to bring their long rifles. And they answered the call, including the Reverend John, who was now 40 years old along with his younger brothers Larkin and Jeremiah and plenty of their able-bodied sons. John was made a chaplain in Colonel Benjamin's North Carolina militia while Robert was voted a Captain. They met up with the over the mountain men from the Watauga settlement at a place called King's Mountain. The battle did not last long. Ferguson made the tactical error of trying to defend the flat top of the mountain and left himself and his thousand-strong militia of loyal Tories no escape route. Scores died and hundreds were captured later to be hung as traitors to the cause of revolution. No one actually knows who shot and killed Ferguson but somehow Benjamin Cleveland ended up riding Ferguson's horse back to a hero's welcome in Wilkes County. Or so he claimed later when he got into the local politics of the County and was elected a justice of the peace.

King's Mountain was a pivotal battle of Washington's southern campaign. It forced Cornwallis to seek refuge on the Yorktown peninsula of Virginia where he was finally hemmed in by the French navy and combined militia and regular forces of the America colonists. The impossible had happened. Cornwallis surrendered his sword and the long bloody war for American independence had finally come to an end.

The war may have ended but tensions remained high in the Carolinas for years after wards. People remembered who were Patriot and Tory during the revolution and their memories were long lasting. John returned to the Tugaloo area and continued his preaching. By this time, the Cherokees had abandoned northeastern Georgia and white settlers flooded into the area one of whom would become very important to the Cleveland family and to John in particular. His name was Thomas Gilbert and his family was fairly well off back in the Virginia tidewater region. Gilbert was also a faithful member of the Baptist church. His brother had been an ordained Presbyterian minister in Virginia and Thomas himself would occasionally preach the good news to the local inhabitants. Eventually he and John joined forces and helped to establish many Baptist churches throughout the Pendleton District of South Carolina and what was now being called Franklin County Georgia. Cleveland provided the sermons and Gilbert's contribution was his enormous wealth. Rumor has it that at one time Gilbert owned over 1,000 acres of land and had over 100 slaves which kept it productive. The crop was not however tobacco but corn, hemp and cotton. The cotton market seemed insatiable. In particular, the British weavers demanded ever more growing bales of cotton shipped across the Atlantic and the southern planters were only too happy to supply that constantly growing demand.

John and Thomas became close friends. In fact, Thomas's daughter Comfort would eventually marry John and Mollie's oldest son, John, who was now nicknamed "Cornfield John" because of his uncanny farming knowledge. Comfort was only fourteen when she married and had a son Reuben just a few months after the marriage, so folks around the area would often mutter under their breaths about Cornfield John's ability to sow more than just corn seed. Of course, they never let the good Reverend Cleveland or Master Gilbert hear their gossip. Thomas and John were not happy about the situation but with the passing of time the wounds healed and the marriage between Reuben and Comfort seemed to solidify with time even with its rocky start. The controversy unfortunately followed the Reverend John for the rest of his days. But instead of making him angry and bitter at the sinfulness of mankind, which was often being preached from the many new pulpits of the Tugaloo Association, John was becoming much more compassionate towards those whom the community at large had labeled as outcasts. This never truly happened to Comfort given her father's wealth and influence. He had actually been sent as a representative from Franklin County to the Georgia statehouse and sat on a committee regarding approval of the U.S. Constitution. No, Comfort and Cornfield's disgrace was not what initiated new thoughts in the mind of the good Reverend Cleveland. It was the black faces he saw every day as he traveled from farm to farm and Baptist meeting house to meeting house.

He saw their pain. He saw the scars from their beatings. He saw their families torn apart after a master had decided to sell off a child or a spouse to another planter. And yet, in the midst of all their suffering, they were able to come together and sing of God's glory and grace and the love of Christ. John did not understand it. How could these poor souls who had lost so much still have so much faith and hope in the future? How could they love this white Christian's God? And as John's insight into their condition began to develop and sharpen his sermons began to change. Not significantly at first but as he continued to preach his focus became the love of Jesus for the downtrodden. John was no abolitionist. Like those raised in this area at this point in time he believed slavery was indeed ordained by God and that the Lord was using this peculiar institution to bring the gospel of Christ to the pagan African. No, John was not advocating the end of slavery. But he had begun to preach about treatment of the slaves as brothers and sisters in Christ. He had been quite anxious at first when he began down this theological path but his courage strengthened as he spoke more and more about the love of Jesus for all people; be they black, red or white. Not all received this new message well. John was censured by some churches and one even had him excluded from membership based upon the false charges of excessive drinking. Everyone knew that John rarely took a drink of whiskey and the charges were obviously meant to silence him from speaking further on the humane treatment of slaves by their masters. But others did hear him and it had an impact upon how they began to treat their own and other African slaves.

It was New Year's Eve, 1799 and John and Mollie was in their home on their beloved Tugaloo. Their children and grandchildren had all gathered at the house and everyone seemed excited about the end of the year and the century. A huge feast had been prepared and eaten and now the family had broken off into smaller groups. The children were playing upstairs in their bedrooms. The younger adults were in the parlor listening to two of the family members playing a fiddle and banjo. John and Mollie were seated in their rockers close to the fireplace where someone had just added another log to the flame. Midnight was approaching and it had become a family tradition for everyone to gather out on the front lawn and sing a hymn followed by a prayer by John. The time was approaching. John suddenly stopped rocking in his chair and looked at his wife of forty years. He gently took her hand in his.

"Mollie, I want you to know how much I love you. And I want you to know how happy you have made me. I know it hasn't been easy, living with a traveling preacher like me. I want you to know how deeply appreciative I am of you. Through good times and bad you have always been there besides me encouraging me and giving me strength. I know our first meeting was at a time of great sorrow for you. But I will forever be grateful to the Almighty that he put me on that road by the Rapidan these many years ago, so that I might hear the true good news of our lord Jesus and see the young woman who became the love of my life." There were tears in the long beard of this aged old preacher as he looked adoringly at his bride.

Mollie looked at John and just smiled and nodded her head. "I know John. I know. And I love you too. My life is complete because of you. Thank you and thanks be to God."

And with that the old couple got up from their chairs and walked hand in hand with the rest of the family out on the front lawn to celebrate the passage of time. No one in that little group knew what the future may bring but thanks to the work of this dear old preacher, they all knew who held the future in His hands.

Chapter Fourteen – Talico Plains, Monroe County, Tennessee, ca. 1819

"Shema Yisraeil Adonai Elohim Adonai Echad", the old man muttered under his breath as he sat on a log overlooking the green valley known as Talico to the Cherokee who had lived there for only God knows how many years. The old man's ten-year-old grandson, Philip, looked at his weathered seventy-two-year-old grandfather.

"Granddaddy Moses ... was you saying something to me?" asked the young one respectfully. The two were close. Philip loved him and Samuel Moses adored his grandson.

Samuel looked at the young man sitting next to him. He thought to himself, "he has his mother's eyes but his father's smile ... and thankfully, does not look at all much like me." Samuel smiled and answered his grandson. "I was saying the Shema ... it is the only Hebrew I remember from my childhood."

"What does it mean?" responded Philip.

The old man sat up a little straighter and recited in English, "Hear, Oh Israel ... the Lord is our God, the Lord is One. I used to also know how to say it in German and Spanish. But with the passage of time, I've forgotten what little I knew of both those languages." He dropped his head slightly and shook it ever so gently as if to convey a sense of loss.

"Momma tells me you know how to speak Cherokee?" the wide-eyed grandson asked of his grandfather.

Samuel chuckled, "I used to know a few words ... mainly just enough to conduct a trade with them." He was silent for a moment and then spoke again, "this was their land you know … before we took it from them." Philip sat in silence. He knew this was a touchy subject within his family but at the tender age of ten he didn't truly understand why.

"Those were the days Philip … I can't remember where I put my pipe but I remember those days decades ago when I first came over the mountains and saw this beautiful valley nestled here in these hills."

Philip sat closer to his grandfather. He could tell his granddaddy was about to launch into one of his tales. He didn't often speak of his early years. To many in the family they were clouded in mystery, covered by the mists of time. But, every once in a while, usually when he was alone with him, his grandfather would just start talking about something from his past and Philip would sit quietly next to his side and just take it all in. Even at the young age of ten, Philip knew that his grandfather had seen and heard things that he would probably never get the chance to see or hear his entire life.

Granddaddy Moses began his story, "I can't remember the year … think it must have been around 1765 or 66 maybe. I was in London, England, of all places. I must have been eighteen or nineteen years old. That is when I met her, a pretty little lassie from Ireland by the name of Mary Brown. She was a servant of the house where I was living. It belonged to my great Uncle Jacob. He had made a fortune in trading on the continent. I don't really remember what he was involved in …nor do I much care… he was not a kind man … no sir, not kind at all. In fact, that's how I met Mary. She had done something to displease my Uncle and he was giving her a verbal lashing. The poor thing was trembling with fear. I stepped between them and caught my Uncle's fury. Later told me I should mind my own business and leave the managing of his servants to himself. I don't think the old man ever did like me really. I am thankful to him. He took me and my two brothers in after our mother and father died. We were all just little fellows. I think I was only four or maybe five. I had been born in Aachen Germany... in the northern Rhineland area of Westfalen. And ..." Philip's grandfather lowered his voice, "we were Jews. That's how I know the Shema. I was raised in my Great Uncle's huge London mansion in the Jewish sector of town. It wasn't something we would advertise outside the home. We did sometimes go to the synagogue and I did learn some of the Torah but religion was not a significant factor in my youth. My Great Uncle's business, however ... well, that's what mattered to that old man. Anyway, my youth was spent learning the trading business and I guess I learned it fairly well. I could make a deal as good as any of them ... even with men who were three or four times my age. But my Great uncle taught me well. Even if sometimes he had to beat it into me ... No ... he was not a kind man. Well, anyway, after that day I stepped between him and Mary, he began to distance himself from me and Mary did just the opposite. In fact, we became lovers. It was scandalous or would have been had it gotten out of the immediate family. But Mary and I were pretty good at keeping our relationship private. Just my brothers knew what was going on between us and they had the decency to keep their mouths quiet. But then one day, and I don't really remember what we were fighting about but somehow my Great Uncle had put two and two together. He told me to end it and I told him ... well ... I really don't want to repeat to you lad, what I told the old geezer. But I reckon that was the last straw. He told me to pack my bags. He was sending me to Charlestown in the American colonies. I was shocked. We had our disputes but he had always calmed down after the passage of time but not this time. "

Philip was listening intently to his grandfather. He had never heard this part of the story. He was fascinated with the things his granddaddy was sharing with him. "So … what happened?"

Samuel looked at his grandson. He thought to himself, "this one is a smart one … he listens … and then he speaks. He is going to make a good business man someday."

Samuel continued his story," Mary was an Irish Catholic girl. Well, that's what she told my Great Uncle but if the truth be known, Mary's father was a Presbyterian soldier from Scotland who fell in love with an Irish Catholic farm girl from Ulster. Mary was the product of that union. Unfortunately, both of Mary's parents died when she was young and she was raised by nuns in an orphanage in Dublin. As soon as she was old enough to leave, she left and headed for the big city of London. It was there she found employment with my Great Uncle. You see, there was a lot of prejudice against the Irish in London, in particular, against young unwed Catholic lassies. So the place for her to find employment was in the Jewish part of town. My Greta Uncle used to say, "we Jews … we know what it's like to be persecuted for what you are and not necessarily who you are." Probably the wisest thing the old man ever taught me. Anyway, after my Great Uncle told me I was heading to the colonies, I asked Mary to be my wife and leave with me. She said she loved me and would do so on one condition … my conversion to the Catholic faith. Well …

I wasn't expecting that as a condition of her agreement but at the time I was quite angry with my Great Uncle and as I already said, although we were Jewish, religion wasn't a big factor in my life. So … I said yes to Mary's condition."

Philip let out a soft and slow whistle. He had never heard this story about his grandfather before and was initially surprised and shocked. For as long as he could remember, his family had considered themselves Baptists. His mother drug him sometimes kicking and screaming to the church building every time the doors were open, though his father was an on again off again visitor. And granddaddy Moses had also hopped in the wagon when it was time to go to the service. Now, here he was sitting here right next to him and telling him he was born into a Jewish family in Germany and that he converted to the Catholic faith in order to convince his sweetheart to marry him and accompany him to the colonies.

Samuel continued, "So, Mary found a priest somewhere and he asked me a few questions about how I felt about Jesus. I said as far as I could tell he was a good man who kept the law faithfully and for that he was killed. Well, you should have seen the priest roll his eyes and cough and sputter. When it looked like he might back out and not marry us, Mary stepped in and explained that "I was new to the faith and had a lot to learn" and that she "would promise to teach me all the Christian fundamentals". Finally, the old priest seemed to calm down and proceeded to baptize me and then married Mary and I right there on the spot. And that," Samuel chuckled, "is how I became a Christian … the first time anyway."

Philip looked at his grandfather with a puzzled look upon his face, "the first time?" he asked.

"Well, I've told you this much, I might as well tell you the rest of it," Samuel responded. "Mary and I traveled on one of my Great Uncle's business partners sailing ship from London to Charles Town, what folks are now starting to call Charleston, South Carolina. You see, even though my Great Uncle was quite furious with me over the whole converting and marrying a Catholic affair, he shrewdly saw an opportunity to expand his business dealings in the colonies by me. So, he had the Captain of the ship drop Mary and me off at the port and had one of his contacts arrange a place for us to stay in the small Jewish quarter of the town. At that time, the Carolinas had a pretty tolerant view upon folks of different religions including the Jews. Mary wasn't thrilled. And I told her I hadn't changed my mind. I would still go to mass with her and she could teach me all about the Catholic Church but she needed to understand that for the time being we needed my Great Uncle's financial support which meant I had to keep up the pretense of being a faithful Jew and attend the local Synagogue. Purely for purposes of establishing and maintaining the business relationships. It was a strange couple of years. Finally, both of us had enough of the arrangement. I decided to tell my Great Uncle I could no longer continue this charade and wrote him a letter informing him of our decision. It didn't take long for him to reply. The man had the local authorities literally throw us out of our home with a few meager possessions. So there we were … homeless with little prospects for generating income. I was no farmer. I had lived in the city all my days and had little knowledge of the way of the farmer. And, of course, all Mary knew how to do was to keep the house of the wealthy clean and tidy. Imagine our surprise, when right out of the blue, a man dressed in buckskin asked if we wanted to join him in an expedition over the western mountains into the Tennessee territory. The fellow was an Indian trader and said he could use a couple of young strong people to help him in the wilderness. Having little choice, we agreed and before long we were sitting on the back of a wagon heading west. We went as far as the roads would take us and then our Indian trader said we were to walk the rest of the way. We left the wagon in the care of some rugged looking fellows at the last trading post and tavern. I was a little unsure but the trader seemed to know the men and apparently trusted them with his mule and wagon. Told them he would be back in a couple of weeks with deerskins and maybe a little gold to share with them and that brought big toothless grins from everyone gathered around us. I didn't like these men. They kept staring at Mary and finally I asked them had they never seen a woman before and one of them volunteered not one as pretty as this one. "

Samuel became quiet. Phillip knew to not interrupt his grandfather or that would be the end of the day's storytelling and back to work the two of them would go. Finally, a tear formed in the corner of Samuel's eye and dropped slowly onto his whiskered face. He began, "at first, Mary and I had a wonderful time being together. For the first time in our lives, we were free. I mean completely free. No man or woman shouting at us to do this or that and … we were so in love." Samuel paused …"and then Mary became quite ill. I tried what I could. Lord knows I tried to save her … but …. "Samuel paused once again and wiped the tears from his eyes. "I guess we'll meet on the other side someday." Samuel returned to his quiet introspective state and Philip sat patiently by him.

Samuel began again, "of course, I reckon if Mary had not died, you, little man, would not be here. "

Philip looked confused at his grandfather. Samuel chuckled again and said, "If I hadn't been a single man I would have never met your granny, fallen in love, married and your granny would have never had your daddy." Samuel smiled at his grandson who quickly realized the logic and joined in with a big ear to ear grin of his own.

"I reckon it was in the spring of 1783 when I first laid eyes upon your granny ... Sarah Tewksberry of the Pee Dee River Valley North Carolina. The war with England was winding down and I knew trade with the western parts of the Carolinas and Virginia would rapidly expand as peace returned. By this time, the Cherokee trusted me. I knew their language and their ways. I was even given a Cherokee name ... man with crooked nose ..." Philip laughed at this remark and so did the old man. "Yep ... when God was giving out noses, I guess he had a little material left over." At this comment, Philip laughed uncontrollably and his granddaddy tickled him to make matters worse.

"Anyway, because they trusted me, I would usually get a fair deal. I would take their deerskins and a little gold they had picked up here and there and then travel east to civilization where I would sell their items for things I needed to survive upon and sometimes even some extra Carolina coins. You know back then Philip we didn't have any such thing as a U.S. dollar. That was all in the future. Anyway, one morning I stopped at a little trading post nestled along the Pee Dee and there she was.

Sarah was about my age and had been married once before but her man died in the revolution. They never had any children. She was an Ulster Scot … just like most folks in these parts of Tennessee and a dyed in the wool Baptist although she will tell you she was raised as a Presbyterian and then "saw the light" at one of the many revivals the Baptists were holding just before the war broke out. Well, Philip, I must tell you, though Granny Moses may not look it now, when she was a young thing, man oh man, how the eyes of men would turn and follow her wherever she went. Used to make me so mad but after time I got used to it. What a pair we made. Me short and stocky with a nose you can hang a lantern on and her tall and slim with thick red hair, freckles all over her face, and the greenest eyes I had ever come across." Samuel paused, "now look at her, solid white hair, skin as dark as a Cherokee, and perhaps a little more plump then she used to be." Philip giggled. From his perspective, his beloved Granny Moses was just that … Granny Moses and he had a hard time imagining her as a pretty young woman.

"Any way," Samuel continued," it took some convincing but eventually I managed to win over her heart and she agreed to become my wife and move with me to the Tennessee territory. We all knew Tennessee would eventually become a state in her own right but that didn't happen until six years after your daddy was born in 1796. Back then, it was considered part of North Carolina. But after the war ended, folks flooded over those mountains to our east," Samuel pointed in the general direction of the mountains. "And, of course, that's when the troubles with the Cherokees began in earnest. "

Samuel became quiet again and eventually Philip thought the story telling was over for the day. Suddenly,

Samuel spoke with a changed tone in his voice, "we done 'em dirty ye know … just because they were different from us … we took their land … took their freedom … took everything from them … just because we could." Samuel looked down at the ground for the longest time. "And I'm just as guilty as the next man. I could speak their language. I knew their ways. They trusted me. And the Carolina officials knew they trusted me. So I became the go-between. I was one of the few who would strike the deals between the Carolina government and the Cherokee nation and was told by the powers to be that I needed to ensure the Cherokee felt like they were getting a fair deal but everyone knew they weren't. And me … you know what makes me most ashamed Philip? … Being a Jew, I should have known better. I treated those poor Cherokee like my ancestors … your ancestor's son … were treated for centuries by the Kings and Queens of Europe. The authorities would come into our Jewish villages and take whatever they desired and then force us to move to another land where eventually the same thing would happen over and over again … I guess this had been happening to my people ever since we were kicked out of Jerusalem by the Romans. So … I should have known better … I should have acted better and done the right thing … but I didn't." And with that Samuel became very quiet and sat looking off into the western sky.

"Over yonder somewhere is where many of them settled … places I had never seen but had heard of …places with names like Arkansas and Missouri. Some of them managed to stay here in Tennessee … down around Chattanooga or they moved up into the Great Smokies …getting as far away from white civilization as they could I reckon. But Washington had a plan. He was the first President you know and he wanted the Cherokee as well as the Creek and other tribes down here in the south to become civilized. He offered them a small plot of land if they abandoned their ancient nomadic communal ways and took up land ownership. Of course, others got into the act and before long every peaceful Cherokee village were being overrun with teachers, preachers and unfortunately, a lot of scoundrels. The men in Philadelphia just didn't understand them the way I did. You have to live with a people and learn their ways before you can truly understand what makes them tick. Anyway, with the slow passage of time, a number of them did start to fit into white society. A few of them even became slave owners running large cotton plantations. But Philip, here in Tennessee, the color of your skin had become pretty important by the time you were born. Try as hard as they could, they were never truly accepted by the ruling white planters and they weren't trusted by the poor whites. So … from the day you were born until now, there has been a small but steady stream of them leaving these parts completely or just giving it all up and heading up into the Smokies where they live the old way."

Philip looked at his granddaddy and realized this man had seen so much more of the world and lived so much more of life than he ever would. Perhaps for the first time in his young life, he became appreciative that this old man was his grandfather and represented his connection to another world.

Suddenly, Philip asked his grandfather a question, "So what made you become a Baptist? Was it a condition of Granny Moses?"

"Naw," Samuel replied, "Sarah didn't really care about my religious views, although she did want me to keep the fact that I was born a Jew a secret from our neighbors and such … she said people around these parts would simply not accept me if they knew of it. And since I hadn't attended a Catholic mass since Mary died, that wasn't an issue either." Samuel paused in his dialogue as if thinking about how he would explain his faith to his grandson.

"I guess Philip, I just decided myself one day that Jesus of Nazareth was truly the Messiah that my people had yearned for and that not only was he the Jewish messiah but that he was indeed the Savior of the world. Jesus came to save us all Philip … white, red and black … Jew and Gentile … He came to save us all. Once that though became firmly planted in my head then it just seemed like the natural thing to do was to join in with Sarah and the rest of the folks in these parts. Before long, I had been dunked in the river and proclaimed a member of Sarah's church which I reckon was the first Baptist church in this county. From that day, I have been at peace with my decision." Samuel looked at Philip. He hoped the boy understood how much he meant to him. The boy would live on long after his old body had given up the spirit of life. He hoped and prayed that Philip would remain faithful to the Creator God and attempt to follow the teachings of the Messiah all the days of his life and that his descendants, should God bless him with some, would carry on that faith for generations to come.

"Philip, I think I hear your momma callin'? We best be getting back to the cabin if we want some of her fine fried chicken. Race you back." And with surprising agility for a man of his age, Samuel jumped off the log and started to trot back towards the small Tennessee cabin they all called home. Philip laughed and ran by him as if he were standing still …. "C'mon granddaddy … catch me if ye can".

Chapter Fifteen – Big Bear Creek, Marion County, Alabama, circa 1830

Years ago, this land had been part of the Chickasaw hunting grounds. Although the Chickasaw had initially tried to remain neutral in the war between the colonies and the British, eventually they had to pick a side and as a tribe they joined in with the Creeks and Cherokees in support of Great Britain. After all, the King of Britain himself, George III had promised the five civilized tribes of the southern colonies that their lands would forever remain free of colonial encroachment if the rebellion could be put down. The borders would then be secure. The white man would live on the eastern side of the mountains and the five tribes would stay to the west. That is what was said to the Indian tribes to entice them into fighting on behalf of the Union Jack. But that is not what transpired.

Those were Robert's thoughts as he sat on the porch of his humble but adequate cabin overlooking his fields of cotton. Cotton was King. Everywhere he looked the land was covered with cotton plants. It was the middle of summer and the white buds were showing against the green plant and the red Alabama soil. "Quite a sight", he thought to himself.

His little family was growing. He and Sarah had met and married back in Mecklenburg, North Carolina in 1799. Soon they had been blessed with children, many children. It seemed to the surrounding neighbors that Sarah was always "with child". This year he would turn 44 and Sarah had just delivered her ninth baby. They had only lost two so far. That was much better than others had fared. Robert knew of one family in the community that had lost half their little ones to illness of one sort or another.

It had not been easy. His son, Andrew K. had been born in 1813, the same year that Andrew Jackson went to war with the Creek nation and nearly wiped them off the face of the earth. That had been the last uprising of the natives. Now they simply wanted to survive. A number of them fled to the west across the great Mississippi. But many chose to remain and try to adapt to the white man's culture.

But most were struggling. Many of them had been taken advantage of by huckster's in the Alabama territorial government who paid a pittance for vast tracts of their lands and then offered those same lands to white settlers heading west over the Great Smoky mountains. There were actually two major paths the settlers followed. One was through the Cumberland Gap discovered by Daniel Boone. This led into the fertile Kentucky bluegrass region and the other was a southern route from the Carolinas into north Georgia and then on into northern and southern Alabama territories.

This had been the path followed by Robert Thomas Cochran shortly after his son Andrew K. had been born. Robert had been surprised when he received a commission from the Mecklenburg assembly to scout out and survey this part of northern Alabama. He had been 32 years old, married with a small but growing family. He had a reputation as a good and honest surveyor but a man with a quick temper who was just as likely to settle an argument with his fists versus his words.

Sarah did not want to leave her home but Robert was convinced the future for his family lay in the western frontier in what was eventually to become the state of

Alabama in 1819. And soon others in the community decided that Mecklenburg County was becoming a bit too crowded. Eventually the plans were finalized and several families had decided to travel together under the direction and guidance of Robert. Of course, after the War of Independence had been won thousands of white Americans had or were in the process of moving into what would eventually become the states of Ohio, Kentucky, Tennessee and Alabama. Robert knew that although the journey would have its inherent dangers the group would be safe as they traveled westward. He remembered the families who had come with him. The Kennedy, Self, and Frederick families had decided to join the entourage and as they moved from east to west others, the Boyd, Rowe and Osborn families joined in or soon followed. Soon after Alabama had become a state of the Union, state sponsored banks were created in order to generate capital for the new state government and hopefully enhance economic development. The banks began to sell off so called public lands to incoming settlers from the Carolinas and Georgia. These public lands had been the lands of the Creeks, Chickasaw and Choctaw tribes. This caused an explosion in movement of yeoman farmers, wealthy cotton planters and others seeking a better life for themselves and their families. Robert Cochran and his small entourage were a small part of this vast expansion of white settlers into what was then being called the Mississippi Territory. The rich cotton planters headed for the flat and fertile areas of the territory scattered along the Mississippi river and central Alabama. The Cochrans and their fellow travelers were not poor but not wealthy either so, they and their fellow yeoman farmers headed into the northern highlands of the territory where land was less expensive but unfortunately somewhat less fertile. Yet it would grow cotton.

The commission was to explore and survey the Big Bear Creek area of what would be called Marion County. And that is where Robert headed straight away. The Big Bear Creek had been named by the Chickasaws. Robert used to remember the Chickasaw name they called this winding stream but had forgotten as time erased this bit of information. He knew it was aptly named for they had stumbled upon many black bear in the area as well as deer, bobcat and other creatures of the forest. The stream was a good source of fresh water and full of fish. Unfortunately, the water was also home to water moccasin and surrounding area to deadly rattle snakes. And, for the first time in his life, Robert and his group encountered the dreaded tornado. The first spring a huge one had hit the area and tore a wide swath of destruction through the virgin forests. Robert laughed as he remembered that one of their members had mentioned something about "God clearing out a space for their crops this year".

That was the one thing his wife Sarah missed perhaps even more than her family. There were no churches to speak of in the settlement. Sarah had been a faithful service attending member of the Presbyterian Church back in North Carolina. But this was the wilderness. And the Presbyterian elders demanded an educated ministry. And few if any respectable seminarian wanted to serve the Lord in the wilderness. Not only were there no churches there weren't any clergy either. But into that gap came the Methodist circuit rider and Baptist lay minister. These were not seminary trained men but individuals who had felt called by God to preach the simple and good word of Jesus to whomever would listen and go wherever their horse would take them. The issue was, of course, you couldn't really depend upon them for immediate religious service. They would often cover vast miles of territory on horseback or on foot if necessary. When they came to your area, a huge tent would be set up on someone's farm and people would come from miles around to hear the word of God. The Methodist or Baptist preacher would stay for a few days, marrying and baptizing folks or saying a few good words over the graves of the recently dead and then move on to the next frontier community.

Sarah and the kids would truly enjoy those spiritual moments but then would become deeply saddened when it was time for the preacher to move on to his next spot on the circuit. She would sink into the doldrums and Robert would have to work hard to elevate her spirits. One thing that usually worked was music. Sarah was quite musical. She could sing well and played the mandolin. Robert also had some musical ability and could play the Irish fiddle or even pick out a tune on something the African slaves called the banjo. This was often what this little community of frontiers people would do for entertainment. A date and location would be selected ... often a Friday or Saturday evening and the locals would gather in someone's barn. There would be plenty of good food, music and dancing and, of course, many cups of whisky would be poured and enjoyed. The party would last into the wee hours of the night and then disband with those sober enough to drive their wagons home while others waited until the effects of the alcohol had worn off before hitching up the wagon.

There had not been a lot of slaves owned by this group of people when they lived in North Carolina. Although Robert was not philosophically opposed to what was now being referred to as the South's peculiar institution, they were expensive … expensive to purchase and to maintain. And, of course, there was always the fear lurking in the back of every one's mind of a slave revolt. But as the demand for cotton continued to rise and slowly but steadily prosperity entered the northern highlands of Alabama, Robert noticed more and more slaves being brought to work the larger farms. Robert's farm was over 1000 acres, not really considered large enough to be called a plantation and Robert never considered himself a planter. However, as he planted more and more of his land in cotton he soon came to the realization that no matter how many children he and Sarah produced they would not be able to work all this land without help. In the end and against Sarah's vigorous objections, Robert began to purchase a few slaves to help out in the fields. He tried his best to treat them fairly. He provided a cabin, clothing and food for them. He had Sarah, along with Robert Andrew and Azor, his two oldest children attend to them when they were ill. He did his best but he had heard of mistreatment by others in the area and that had on more than one occasion caused him to wonder where this was leading. He had heard of rumors of slave revolts and he knew that the northern states had given up on the institution in favor of cheap immigrant labor. There was even talk that the Federals in Washington, D.C. were considering limiting where slaves could be bought and sold in the continually expanding western frontier beyond the Mississippi. This was creating quite a stir on the local political scene. Some of the members of the newly formed

Alabama legislature questioned whether Congress had the right to form any legislation concerning the institution of slavery.

It seemed to Robert that the older he got, the more complex life became. He had questions and the potential answers he generated left him with only more questions that generated more mental conflict. For example, he had questions regarding treatment of the native Chickasaws and Creeks and yet had made his living on what was once their sacred land. He had questions about the morality of slavery and yet he himself owned slaves. And, of course, he had questions about politics. Although he fully supported the idea of an American federal government, he wondered if people in far-away Washington D.C. really knew about or cared about for that matter what happened to him and his family here in Alabama. And then there was the ultimate question .... What about God? Although Robert had been baptized in the Presbyterian Church and certainly would accompany Sarah and the children to the occasional tent based revivals led by the circuit riders, he truly wondered about the depth of his faith. He never doubted the existence of God. He reasoned that things couldn't just come about by themselves. Creation was all around him and creation required a creator. And he did not doubt the Bible stories of his childhood ... Adam and Eve, the Flood, Abraham and Isaac and all the rest of it. And he certainly considered himself to be a follower of Jesus Christ, the son of God. What he had questions about was why things were as they were in his world. Why did people have to suffer? Why did two of his little innocent children become ill and die? Why was the world filled with such violence? And perhaps, most of all, why did Robert's son, Andrew K. have these spells where he appeared to lose contact with the world. He wouldn't fall down and jerk around like some did that Robert had known. No, Andrew K. would just suddenly stop whatever he was doing and then he would begin to grind his teeth or rub his leg with one hand. He would do this for a minute or so and then come out of it. After the spell had passed, Andrew K. didn't appear to remember what had happened to him and was often confused for a while. Eventually he would regain his bearings and get on with whatever task he had undertaken. His wife Sarah didn't have any answers for what was wrong with the boy and neither did he. So, Robert had questions for his God. Why? He would gaze into the heavens with tears in his eyes and ask why of his God … and the heavens didn't respond. Robert reasoned that God knew of his situation. "Perhaps," he thought," we've somehow brought this upon ourselves, some sin that has been committed by me or one of my ancestors"? Sarah refused to believe that a loving, kind and merciful God would take out his vengeance on an innocent child. She would say to Robert, "this is Satan's doing … trying to test your faith my husband. Consider the story of Job." Robert would often think about the sorry state of mankind. In the end, he had no satisfying answers. After the tears stopped flowing, he would simply bow his head and say out loud, "thy will be done" and try to move on with his life which meant working hard just to stay alive. Life was a struggle in frontier Alabama.

He saw two of his sons, John and Silas Maxwell, walking up the dirt lane that ran from his cabin to the Orrick's place and then on to the small village of Hackleburg. The town of Hackleburg, what there was of it, was actually just the intersection of two military roads built by General Andrew Jackson, now President of the United States during his fight with the Creek Indians and then a year later, the British. A few families had tried to establish a place to spend the night for travelers heading west or south. It was just a tiny tavern with a small general store attached to the side. Not much really. But they called it a town, gave it a name and hoped for a prosperous future. The land had been originally part of Robert's holdings but he had sold a few acres to the original inhabitants. Sarah desperately wanted them to build a permanent church building but there was little interest by the locals in undertaking this task. It wasn't that they weren't religious … they were. But these original inhabitants of northern Alabama were a very practical people. They weren't going to bother spending precious time and money on a building when there was no guarantee they could entice a full-time pastor to serve and after all, what would they call the church. This particular group of settlers was quite a mix of ethnic and consequently religious backgrounds. The Cochrans, of course, were originally from Ulster and of the Presbyterian faith but there were folks there whose origins were German and they considered themselves to be Anabaptists and those whose ancestors had originated in England had originally belonged to the Anglican church but soon turned to the Baptist or Methodist church for religious instruction and worship. And their total numbers were relatively small … maybe only a couple hundred settlers here in a ten-square mile area. Sarah would just have to wait for her church building to be built and be content with the traveling missionaries.

"What are you two up to now?" asked Robert of the two young men. John had been born in 1805 and his brother Silas Maxwell four years later in 1809. Both had married and had settled down on small farms a couple of miles away from the original homestead.

John answered, "Been to town to read the news".

"And what of it?" asked his father.

"Seems that President Jackson has signed the Indian Removal Act" replied Silas.

"And what does that mean?" Robert responded.

"Nothing good for the Indians … that's for sure," both men chuckled but quickly stopped after receiving a piercing glare of retribution from the father. The boys knew of their father's tremendous respect for the natives and their culture.

"Seriously, daddy, "Andrew K piped in after joining his brothers. The three men turned and looked at the sound of the voice. Andrew K. was now 20 years old and had recently begun spending an unusual amount of time at the Orrick farm. The Orrick's had moved to the area from Tennessee. There was speculation that the old man Orrick had run into some kind of trouble with the authorities but to Robert he seemed like a decent enough fellow and … he had a bunch of daughters who would soon become eligible for marriage. Everyone in the Cochran family knew this is what drew Andrew K. to their farm as often as his chores would allow. Andrew K. continued, "This is good news for us. It will mean all the rest of the land the Creeks and Chickasaws have been holding on to will now go on auction for white settlers coming to northern Alabama."

"And what happens to them … the Indians?" asked Robert.

"Well, according to what I read in town, "John answered, "they will be moved out west … to some place called the Oklahoma territory."

"And they agreed to this …?" Robert asked with a hint of sarcasm in his voice.

Silas responded, "Reckon daddy, they didn't have much of a choice."

"I reckon you're right about that boy", replied Robert with a touch of disdain in his voice. Although Robert didn't know all the details, he was confident that, once again, the natives had gotten the short end of the stick in this deal. He thought to himself, "Where is Oklahoma anyway … how these poor folks going to get there … walk?"

As if he was reading his father's mind, John responded, "I heard at the stage coach stop some men talking daddy … guess the federal troops are going to round them all up and force them to march over land to the Mississippi and then river boats will take them across. They'll continue the march on the other side."

"Sounds like quite a distance. Anyone say how many miles it is from these parts to there?" Robert asked.

John was quiet and then responded with a somber voice, "Man said it was over a thousand miles from the Cherokee lands in eastern Tennessee to the Oklahoma border."

Robert shot a look of disbelief towards his three sons. "A thousand miles," Robert exclaimed. How can any man walk that far without taking ill, and what about the women and children and the old ones? Surely, many will not make it?"

"That may be the plan," John replied.

"Good God", was all that Robert could utter.

The small group of father and sons grew quiet. Finally, Robert broke the silence. "'Tis getting dark. You two best head for your homes and Andrew, you and I had better get on home if we want some of your mama's good cookin'". And with that final statement, the men headed off to their respective homes.

As soon as Robert and Andrew entered the farm house, Robert knew Sarah had heard some news she considered good. She was skipping around the kitchen humming and singing and setting the table with a huge smile on her face.

Robert looked at his wife and smiled. She wasn't always this happy and it did his heart good to see her in such a frame of mind.

He spoke," well woman you look mighty happy, reckon ye got some good news?"

"Yes, indeed, dear husband. Heard from Mrs. Fincher that a Methodist circuit rider is making his way across north Alabama and will be here in Marion county in just a couple of weeks."

The Finchers lived on a small farm just a few miles north of them. Robert thought to himself, "Even with miles between these farmer's wives, news still travels fast." He spoke to Sarah, "so how come you and Mrs. Fincher to meet?"

Sarah replied, "Her man built her a new buggy and she was just out testing it out when she happened to stumble upon me working in the garden. It's a pretty thing, I might add."

"Who," replied Robert, "the buggy or Mrs. Fincher?" and then he chuckled. At first Sarah frowned and then a smile came to her face. She never could really stay angry with her husband. She had fallen for him the day they first met and loved him more today than she ever thought possible … despite his flaws … and there were a few of them. She chuckled at the thought.

"So, where's the tent gonna be set up," Andrew questioned his mother.

"Well … I was hoping this time … it could be set up here on our land." Sarah looked questioningly at her husband.

Robert smiled and stroked his long shaggy beard. He really didn't care for the idea of having a huge tent placed on his land interfering with the farm work. But what he really did not like was the thought of having people from all over the county descend on his place for a week or so. Sure, it was for a good cause and it certainly would make Sarah happy but you never knew who might be showing up at one of these revival meetings and so many times things got a little carried away for Robert's tastes with all the shouting and singing. People would get carried away at these things and Robert found it all just a bit too much. I guess if he were entirely honest with himself, he liked his religion a little more somber and dignified. But … it would make Sarah happy and that is what made him agree to the idea.

"Sounds o.k. to me Sara Cochran. I guess you can have Mrs. Fincher spread the word in her fancy new buggy that the next revival will be held here on Cochran land."

Sarah jumped for joy and gave Robert a huge hug. She then turned back to her tasks at hand setting the table and preparing for the evening meal all the while humming a tune about Jesus and his wonderful saving love.

A few weeks had passed and Robert and his family had spent the time busily preparing his farm for the upcoming revival. They had received a visitor a couple of days ago and now they all sat in the parlor of Robert's cabin talking about the upcoming meeting. The visitor's name was Barnabas Pipkin.

"Well brother Pipkin, will you be doing the preaching this time?" asked Sarah to her guest.

"Oh no sister … I'm way too old and worn out to carry on a camp meeting. The Columbus conference will be sending a new circuit rider by the name Lewis Turner. I hear he is a mighty fine man, knows the scriptures like the back of his hand and can talk for hours if need be on the subject of God's grace and mercy for us sinners." Robert smiled at the thought but inwardly groaned. There were several reasons he could check off in his mind for not having a camp meeting on his land. First, they were highly emotional experiences and sometimes the people attending got a little carried away as far as he was concerned. And then, of course, there were always the troublemakers who attended these things, men who most likely had consumed too much corn liquor and who came not to hear the word of God but to torment the poor preacher. They would stand in the back of the congregation and carry on with all kinds of noise and commotion … sometimes even firing off their guns into the air to frighten the gathering. There was no official authority here … no sheriff or police … so it became the responsibility of the host to try to calm down the hooligans so that the people could hear the preacher. Occasionally these confrontations got out of control and people got hurt. Robert wasn't afraid. He could handle himself in a fight if need be and, of course, he wouldn't be alone. His boys would jump in as well as the local neighbor men who might be in attendance. Sometimes, even the preacher himself, would have to get down off the wooden platform and join in the ruckus in order to bring order back to the meeting. Robert thought to himself, "my goodness, these Methodist circuit riders have a rough life. I've known a couple of them who have passed by down through the years. They are often single men in their mid to late twenties. Their circuits included hundreds of miles of wilderness where danger lurked around every bend in the path. They didn't have to worry as much anymore about attacks by Indians but there were plenty of ruffians in the Alabama woods who were up to no good. And, of course, there were bears and other critters that could be quite a danger to an unsuspecting traveler. But, then again, these men often traveled with a Bible in one hand and Kentucky rifle in the other. These men of God were not like the ones Robert had known back in North Carolina. Many did not have a formal education and some of them were crude in their civil manners. But," Robert thought, "They have given all they can to serve their God and to carry the message of Jesus into the wilderness. And more than a few of them have lost their lives in the process. I have to respect their commitment." Just then his train of thought was interrupted by the Reverend Pipkin.

"So, Robert," asked the preacher, "do you know the Lord Jesus as your savior?"

The room quickly became quiet. None of the gathered Cochran family knew how the patriarch would respond because no one had ever so bluntly asked him this question in public. But Barnabas Pipkin was a rather straightforward religious leader whose faith and been tested and tried on numerous occasions during his tenure as a Methodist missionary to Alabama. Robert's face was stonily silent. He looked down at the floor of his cabin and slowly stroked his long beard. Finally, he spoke," well, preacher, are you asking if I personally know the man Jesus of Nazareth, I would have to say no, I've never met him." Some of the family giggled at this response but were quickly silenced by Sarah's disapproving glare. "Now, if you are asking, do I believe that the man Jesus of Nazareth was and is the Christ, the Son of God … then I would guess I would have to answer … yes … I do believe that to be true."

Barnabas Pipkin looked at Robert with no emotional expression on his face. Then suddenly he broke into a huge grin and began to chuckle. "You had me going there for a second brother. I thought I was going to have lay one of my better sermons on you right here in your own parlor." At this comment, both men laughed and the rest of the family joined in much to Sarah's relief.

Robert suddenly looked at Barnabas and asked him, "why do you Methodists always change your preachers every year or so? My goodness, over the past ten years, there have been … what … at least six different men that I can remember."

"More than six brother. I started here in 1821 and then was followed by Thomas Clinton and B.F. Lidden. They were followed by Wiley Ledbetter and Johnny Lee. Those four all died early on in their work. Then the cross was carried by Thomas Owens and Thomas Abernethy followed by Peyton Graves."

Sarah interrupted, "Oh, I remember the Reverend Graves. Such a good man. Tis a shame what happened to him."

Barnabas lowered his gaze to the cabin floor, "yes, a shame. After that unfortunate incident, Peyton Abernethy returned for a short while and then he was replaced with Isaac Enoch … what a name for a preacher, heh?"

Everyone agreed and smiled.

Pipkin continued, "In 1827, the conference sent two men to this part of the State, Larry Massengale and Jesse Mize and they were followed by Moses Perry. After Perry was transferred the circuit was filled by Felix Wood, then Blanton Box and now Lewis Turner." Pipkin had finished his recital of the brave men who had filled the circuit rider position since his departure a decade ago. He looked satisfied and Robert and Sarah were truly impressed at his ability to recall names and dates.

"That is impressive Reverend Pipkin," replied Robert, "but, again, if I may be so bold, why all the changes?"

Pipkin nodded and smiled. "In the early years, Wesley determined that is was not a good thing for a minister to be connected to any one gathering of believers for too long. It reminded him of the Anglican priests who would be assigned a parish for life and became too embroiled in the activities of the parish families. He also thought it led to temptation … too much familiarity and all that …" Barnabas looked away from Sarah. He was embarrassed to have to mention the sins of the flesh that sometimes overtook the shepherds of the flock. "But, of course, out here in the wilderness, at least in the early years, the reason we had so much turnover was because many of these young men breathed their last in the mission fields of what was then known as the Mississippi territory. Things are tough today but pale in comparison to the conditions the early Methodist missionaries faced in this country."

Robert and Sarah both nodded their heads in agreement. Life was hard here in northern Alabama but things had slowly begun to improve as the cotton market flourished and with it the encroachment of civilization into the highland region.

Pipkin changed the subject of their conversation. "So, when is there going to be a permanent church built in this section of God's kingdom?"

Sarah smiled enthusiastically. She couldn't help it. That was the one thing she longed for in her life. She so desperately missed attending services in a structure built with the sole intention of worshipping God. She remembered the church back home in North Carolina. It wasn't much. Just a simple log cabin but large enough to gather together all the membership and protect them from the elements while the service proceeded. She looked expectantly at her husband. She knew Robert loved to build. He used to say, "We Cochrans have been building churches for a long time." In fact, Sarah knew of an old family myth that the Cochrans had something to do with the construction of the great Abbey of Paisley in Scotland, their original homeland. She didn't know if this was really the case or just some made up story by one of Robert's ancestors a long time ago and then passed down from generation to generation as if it were the gospel truth. Sarah guessed she would never really know but she saw an opportunity to exploit the idea when Pipkin mentioned building a permanent structure for worship.

Without looking directly at Robert's face she answered the Reverend Pipkin's question. "Did you know Reverend Pipkin that my husband comes from a long line of builders of churches?" Robert grunted as Barnabas raised his eyebrows. "No mam … I was not aware of that fact. Is this so brother Robert?"

Robert glanced at Sarah. He smiled slightly. He knew what she was thinking about … the old myth about the Abbey back in Scotland. But he wondered … what if it was true? What if my family has been in the business of building houses of worship? And what if this was the means for my people to show their faith for their God by using their talents and skills in this manner? Was it really in his blood?

He replied to Barnabas, "There is a story in my family that has been handed from old to young. My granddaddy told me it when I was a wee lad. Basically, it goes like this … the Cochrans owned the land upon which the Abbey of Paisley was built and, in fact, helped the first monks that came there from England to build it. Of course, what is not told is that the land was taken by the then King of Scotland and given to the monks. So, I guess we either just stayed put and the monks put us to work or we realized you can't fight the King so we went along with the plan and learned how to work with stone. Only God knows the truth?" Robert smiled and continued, "You weren't thinking of building the thing out of stone now were you?"

Barnabas chuckled. "My goodness no. Just a simple log building would do just fine."

The preacher looked directly into the eyes of Robert. "Are you game brother? Can I count on you to help in the construction?"

Once again silence and tension filled the room. Robert looked at the Methodist missionary then at Sarah. Her eyes told him all he needed to know. She wanted a church. So he would help build her a church.

"Yep … Reverend Pipkin … you can count on me and my boys. We'll help build you a meeting place for your people." Robert replied with a final nod to his children who were gathered around the table where the men sat.

"God be praised, thank you brother Cochran … but please remember those who attend services at this building are not my people … they will be the children of our Lord Jesus. You know, the Anglicans first called Wesley and his followers Methodists because they were so methodical in their approach to the practice of Christianity. The Wesley brothers at first did not refer to themselves that way preferring to simply call themselves Christians or followers of the Lord Jesus but over time the name stuck and now I reckon we Methodists have just gotten used to it." Barnabas was grinning from ear to ear. For ten years, he had wanted to construct a permanent structure in this part of the circuit but had never been able to convince any of the scattered inhabitants of the worthiness of such an undertaking. He looked at Robert Cochran and wondered just exactly why would a lapsed Presbyterian with Ulster Scottish roots want to get involved in such a thing? "Oh well, "he thought to himself, "God does work in mysterious ways."

Sarah spoke, "Well, I think that is enough conversation for one evening. I reckon it is time for all of us to get to bed. Tomorrow is the first day of the camp meeting and people will be coming from miles around. We'll all have plenty to do. We need to rest up for the big event." And with that, the family turned in for the night and Robert blew out the last remaining candle as he lay on the straw mattress next to his wife.

Sarah did not sleep well. She was simply too excited about the prospects of finally having a real church building in which to worship. She was up earlier than usual the next day and was the first to see the lone man walking besides a horse laden with baggage. She thought to herself, "this must be the new preacher … what did Pipkin say his name was …. Oh yes, Lewis Turner …my … he is a young man … can't be much older than 20 or 21 years of age." She hung her apron on the peg by the table and quickly smoothed back her hair from her face. She lifted the heavy latch on the front door and stepped out into the brilliant morning sunlight to welcome the visitor.

"Welcome to our home Reverend Lewis," Sarah smiled and waved at her guest. "My name is Sarah Cochran and my husband, Robert and the children are just now waking up. Can I pour you a cup of coffee … freshly made?"

"Thank you, Mrs. Cochran. May God's spirit bring you and your household His peace. And, yes, I would love a cup of freshly brewed coffee. I've been on the trail quite some time now, walked here with this old mare of mine all the way from Huntsville. That was my last assignment. Now, I'm going to spend my time bringing the good news of Jesus to this part of Alabama and neighboring Mississippi." The Reverend Lewis was not a tall man but not short either. He looked like he needed a wash in the river and Sarah could tell that he probably had not had a good meal to eat in some time.

Just then Barnabas Pipkin walked out the front door and literally ran toward the young man. "Lewis Turner … May God be praised for bringing you safely through the wilderness. I have such good news I want to share with you." The two men shook hands and then hugged each other. They were brothers in the Lord and belonged to a band of brothers fighting the war against Satan and evil in this world. They naturally had a close bond and treated one another as if they were long lost brothers reunited again after a lengthy separation.

Suddenly Barnabas stepped back holding his nose. "My goodness Lewis … you are rather ripe … I would suggest a long bath with some lye soap in Bear Creek." He grinned and chuckled as the Reverend Turner began to sniff the air around him and shook his head in agreement. "Perhaps so, Barnabas, but Mrs. Cochran has offered me a fresh cup of coffee and that's what is on my mind right now."

Sarah had remained on the porch but she had heard the dialogue between the two preachers. "And if you can wait for a little while, I'll soon have some scrambled eggs, fried bacon and biscuits and gravy to fill yer belly."

"My goodness Mrs. Cochran, my mouth can already taste it," responded the young missionary with glee. He turned toward the older Barnabas and said, "Pinch me Barnabas for I think I've died and gone on to glory. Do ye know how long it's been since I tasted homemade biscuits and gravy?" And with that statement, both men laughed so hard they almost cried.

After the young preacher had bathed down at the creek and filled his empty stomach with Sarah's fine cooking, the three men walked down the path to where the large barn was located. A tent had been erected next to the structure and a small platform was underneath the tent. This is where the Reverend Turner would conduct the service.

As they were walking past the open area between the cabin and barn the Reverend Turner noticed the two black men as they headed towards the cotton field. He stopped dead in his tracks and one word escaped from his mouth … "slaves".

The other two men stopped as well and Robert noticed out of the corner of his eye that Pipkin was looking rather nervous. He wondered why but soon found out.

The Reverend Turner said, "If those two men are your slaves Robert Cochran … then we can't hold the revival at this farm." Turner spoke respectfully but with a certainty in his voice.

Robert turned and looked at Turner and then at Pipkin and then back at Turner. He said in a plain matter of fact voice, "Preacher, you are in Alabama … this here's a slave state if you hadn't noticed in your travels?" Robert looked a little annoyed. He was only doing this for his Sarah and now this preacher was going to cause trouble because of his two slaves. It didn't make any sense to him. He started to speak but the Reverend Turner cut him off with a brusque, "I know where I am. And I fully realize that many Alabamians own slaves, but I have never once conducted a worship service on property worked by slaves and I'm not about to start today."

Pipkin finally found his voice and joined in, "but brother Turner, surely you must realize that slavery is a legal institution in Alabama and you can't be seriously thinking you would deprive these unfortunate souls, both white and black, from hearing the gospel because of your philosophical differences?" But Turner was adamant and stood by the two men vigorously shaking his head no to both.

Robert was able to keep his temper in check and asked a simple question. "Reverend Turner … why do you feel so strongly about my slaves … I have many times in my life preachers from different denominations say that the Apostle Paul himself told slaves to obey their masters … isn't that so? Well then, good old Saint Paul saw nothing wrong with it then why would you?"

Turner looked directly into the eyes of Robert and deliberated quite a while before responding. "Robert … I know you to be a good man with a good heart. Let me put this to you with the deepest respect … what if one of those black boys over yonder were one of your sons … would you want them in bondage? You know, as well as any man in this county what happens to their families, how their women folk are sometimes treated by their masters and how discipline is maintained on many an Alabama plantation."

Robert interrupted … "but that's not me Reverend Turner. I've never laid a hand on either of those two nor would I allow anyone else to do so."

Turner replied, "And that is a good thing for you but consider what their lives must be like … having to do whatever they are told whenever they are told it … no freedom to just go for a walk … or take a swim in Bear Creek … or meet and fall in love with a local girl, get married and raise a family without fear their very children might be sold away … never to see them again on this side of heaven … Surely man … put yourself in their shoes … put your sons in their shoes … is that any way to live? Look, I could go into a long and dry dispute with you based upon the teachings of the Wesley's and their opposition to slavery and I could cite chapter and verse that would-be interpretation show you that our Master

Jesus would have never been a slave owning planter but I'm not going to. I want to speak to your heart Robert … slavery may be legal in Alabama and part of the social fabric of the south but in your heart … in your heart Robert, "he paused," you know I'm right."

Robert looked at this Methodist missionary and perhaps saw him for the first time. He was thin and his face was worn and tired. He had sacrificed much to bring the good news of Jesus Christ to this part of the country. He respected him. And his words made him think … truly think about his slaves, Tom and Jeb. "What if they were my boys," Robert thought to himself. And then it suddenly dawned upon him that he didn't know if Tom or Jeb had ever seen their own earthly father or mother. In fact, he didn't know anything about their history. When he had purchased them at auction in Tupelo, he had just assumed they were brothers who needed to get on with the business of living and he put them to work. Granted, the purchase had filled him with a sinful pride. He felt that he was truly becoming a force in the community. After all, he was one of but a very few farmers in the area who could afford the purchase of slave labor. Suddenly, he was stricken with guilt. It overwhelmed him. It paralyzed him with fear. He had been taught since childhood that the African's lot in life had been improved through the institution of slavery. The popular notion was that enslavement in the American south had brought them out of the darkness of their pagan ways and thrust them into the light of Christianity. Yes, he knew it was true what Turner had said. But surely that wasn't the case for all the slaves and slave masters. Didn't even Washington, Jefferson and the great Andy Jackson himself own slaves? How could it be wrong then in the eyes of God? Robert was torn. His mind was a storm racked by first one thought and then another. Finally, he broke his silence … "Reverend Turner … I …I … I need time to think about what you've said … Please don't depart from us until I've had a chance to speak to my Sarah about this … Will you do that? Will you not leave until Sarah and I have talked?"

Pipkin looked hopefully at his colleague. Turner looked at the ground, then the sky and finally at Robert Cochran. "Alright, brother Cochran … I'll give you 24 hours to reflect about it … but then if you remain a slaveholder, I must respectfully ask the tent be taken down and the revival cancelled." And with that final statement, the three men parted company. Pipkin and Turner headed down the dusty dirt road toward the stagecoach and tavern in Hackleburg while Robert walked out into his cotton field looking for Tom and Jeb.

The two black men saw their master heading their way so they stopped their work and waited to be addressed. Both men had removed their hats and were now bowing their heads respectfully in the presence of their master.

Robert spoke, "Boys, put your hats back on … this sun is brutal today. I have some questions for the two of you."

The slaves glanced nervously at each other. Had something bad happened? Massa Robert had never once punished them for anything. He had always been a king and gentle man who had provided them with a clean place to live, clothes to wear and plenty of good food from Massa Sarah's kitchen. Jeb wondered, "What could this be about?

"Let's get out of this hot field and walk over yonder by that big old Cedar tree. There we can sit a spell and talk about something that's on my mind, "Robert spoke slowly and firmly.

The two young black men nodded their heads and followed their master over to the tree. Robert sat on the ground and motioned for the two to join him.

"Alright, "Robert said after some awkward silence, "I reckon there's no better way to start on this but just to get on to it … do you boys know your daddy or your momma?"

And with that Tom broke into a huge smile and Jeb lowered his face to hide the tears that had formed in his eyes.

Tom spoke, "yessa massa Robert, we both knows our daddy and momma. We's brothers... only 15 months between us. Our old massa … he died and his son sold us off at auction in Tennessee to a trader who brought us down from Memphis to sell us once again at auction in Tupelo … where you bought us…. We's so grateful you bought us massa Robert … Jeb and I was convinced we were gonna get split apart and would never see each other again … like what happened to our sisters."

Robert replied, "Sisters?"

Jeb had wiped the tears from his eyes and spoke softly and gently to his master, "Yessa massa Robert … we's had two sisters … Mamie and Nell … when the old massa died his son sold them off too … but we don't rightly know where they ended up … the last time we laid eyes upon them was at the auction block in Memphis … up in Tennessee." Tears started, once again, to form in the eyes of the younger Jeb so he quickly turned his face to the ground.

But Robert saw the tears. And perhaps for the first time saw these two young black men as human beings. "My God," he thought to himself, "what have we done to these poor children of God." Then he suddenly remembered his Sunday school lesson of Noah and his three sons, Shen, Ham and Japheth. He remembered old Mrs. Maxwell telling all the children that the Africans were descendants of Ham and that they were carrying the curse of God and that is why it was o.k. to keep them as slaves. He had always wondered why God had been so severe with Ham … it seemed like a pretty minor transgression to him but when he raised the issue with Mrs. Maxwell, she changed the subject and told him to never ever say anything like that out loud again or she would tell his daddy and a severe whipping would be the consequence.

Robert spoke to the young slaves, "what would you two do, if you were to be set free?"

The eyes of both men widened. Never in their imagination had they ever considered they would someday have a conversation of this nature with Massa Robert and never ever would they think he would bring up the topic of freedom from slavery. The brothers looked at each other and then both spoke simultaneously as if they could read one another's mind. "I reckon we would stay here and work this farm … it's all we knows what to do … where would we go …" Tom spoke, "We's no idea where momma and daddy is or if they's even alive and we wouldn't know where to begin to find our sisters. So … we would stay here with you and your family."

Robert thought about this response. Of course, the boys were right. Where would two free Negro slaves go in Alabama? No one would believe they had been set free and soon they would just end up back on some plantation and probably not lucky enough to be kept together.

Robert's mind was in a state of turmoil. Perhaps for the first time in his life, he did not know what decision was the correct one. He had never experienced indecisiveness of this intensity. He considered his options as he walked back towards the cabin. He knew he had to make some type of decision before he encountered Sarah. He thought to himself, "I can't just free them. They won't survive. I can't just sell them. I need their labor but more importantly, I've grown fond of those two. It would break my heart to see them split up at the auction. If I keep things as they are, the revival tent comes down and Sarah will never forgive me. And … what if Turner is right? What if what we're doing here in Alabama and elsewhere throughout the South is wrong in the eyes of God? I don't want to believe that …. but …. what if what the man says is true? What am I going to do?"

By this time, he had made his way to the cabin and Sarah met him on the front porch. He was surprised to see she was not alone. Standing beside her were the two Methodist ministers, Turner and Pipkin. He started to speak but was interrupted by his wife, "So, Robert Cochran, these two good men have already explained the situation to me and I understand their concerns." She smiled at her husband. Pipkin joined in, "so we have come to an agreement … assuming you will support the action?" Then Turner finished, "I will agree to hold the revival here … if you agree to free your two slaves upon your death." Pipkin jumped back in to the conversation "… Just like President Washington did with his slaves." Sarah then looked at her husband expectantly, "well, my love, what do you think?"

Robert was silent. He stroked his long gray beard. He looked at the ground. He looked at Sarah and then at the ministers, "Guess, that will work." And with that simple statement, Sarah hugged her husband and the two preachers looked at each in relief.

Robert said, "I suppose I need to write that down somehow?" Pipkin responded, "not for us you don't … you are a man of your word … however, I'm sure the two boys will need some type of legal looking document in order to travel safely to wherever it is they end up." Turner stated, "There's an attorney I know over in Winston County. He is … how shall I say this … favorable to our position on slavery. He has helped us out in the past in a variety of ways. I'm almost positive he would agree to writing up something that looked official enough to get the boys out of any difficult situation … should the need arise." Pipkin looked nervously at his colleague. He knew exactly who Turner was referring to and he was glad Turner didn't mention the man by name. They both knew this particular attorney had in the past helped runaway slaves find their way to what was now being called the underground railroad, a series of farms and taverns between here and Cincinnati that would offer food and shelter to slaves trying to escape across the Ohio river to freedom. It was a long and arduous journey and not many who started it here in Alabama made it all the way. But some did. And for that Pipkin and Turner and the others involved in the action were thankful to God for his protection and guidance.

Sarah was excited, "so it's settled then? We can start the preparations and spread the news?" All three men nodded and Sarah offered a quick silent prayer of thanksgiving while saying under her breath' "thank you Jesus".

Within a few days, people from the surrounding area started to arrive at the Cochran farm. Many came from within Marion County but a few travelled from the neighboring counties of Franklin and Winston. Some came from the neighboring Mississippi county of Itawanka. A large contingent of folks arrived from nearby Winston County. What Robert would not discover until much later was the fact that Winston county Alabama contained a significant number of secret Methodist abolitionists. No one really knew why but the county was strong in their anti-slavery position. In fact, years later, when war finally erupted between North and South over the issue of slavery, Winston county originally voted to secede from the State of Alabama and form its own free and independent country. That all changed, of course, when President Lincoln issued his call for troops to prepare for an invasion of the southern states. Although this did not change the mindset of the men and women of Winston county regarding slavery, it did cause them to join in with their fellow Alabamians in the defense of their homeland. But that was all to happen at least thirty years later.

The revival went well. There were the usual rabble rousers but, all in all, the preaching was good with sound Methodist doctrine and many responded to the invitation to accept the Lord Jesus as savior. After three days of almost nonstop worship, it was decided by Pipkin to bring the meeting to a close. Dozens of people had converted and according to Pipkins's letter which he sent to the

Bishop based in Tennessee, "the good news of Jesus has been spread to the wilderness inhabitants of Hamilton county Alabama and much fruit had been gathered for the cause".

It was the morning of the scheduled departure that the Reverend Pipkin and Turner approached Robert accompanied by three other men that Robert only knew in name. They were John Coleman, B.P. Cantrell, and William W. Frederick. Robert knew these three to be local farmers with good size land holdings south of town. He had seen them at the revival and they were often in deep conversation with Pipkin.

Reverend Pipkin spoke first. "Robert, I would like to introduce you to three of your distant neighbors whom you may or may not know well but I do." The four men all took off their hats and shook hands.

Robert replied, "Yes, Barnabas, I know of these men but as you say do not know them well. I was glad to see them at the revival."

Coleman responded, "And we were happy to be there and are grateful to you and your family for your generous and kind hospitality." The other two men nodded their heads vigorously in affirmation.

"So," Robert looked at the four of them standing together on his front porch, "what kind I do for you gentlemen?" At which point Pipkin spoke up," these men have a proposition for you brother Cochran." Robert's eyebrows raised in a quizzical manner. Pipkin continued, "These three men own adjoining farms about one-mile south of the stage coach stop. And they have jointly decided to donate some of their land to God upon which a church will be built. They are not builders, however. Therefore …. They and I would like to ask you if you would be the leader of this project ... to construct a permanent house of worship for the folks of this community. Would you be willing Robert?"

All four men looked expectantly at Robert. He did not hesitate in his response, "Yes, of course, I would be honored to participate in this noble undertaking for the cause of Christ."

This response was met with smiles and a few words of congratulations and praise to the Almighty.

B.P. Cantrell spoke next, "Well ... Robert ... when do you think we could begin?"

Robert was silent for a moment as he thought about what it would take to build a small log cabin structure big enough to serve as a house of worship. "I think we can start as soon as our crops are in .... Sometime this fall ... but before the weather gets too cold. What do you men think about that?"

Barnabas was disappointed. He wanted the group to begin immediately on the construction but the four farmers knew the importance of tending to their fields. Their survival and the survival of their families depended upon a successful harvest. All three men agreed. They would work together to build the church starting as soon as the harvest of this year's crops had been completed.

Robert asked the group, "How many men total will we have?". The three responded that they would help plus between the three of them they had seven able bodied sons who could wield an ax and otherwise help in the construction. Robert added, "and I have three boys who will put in their fair share ... plus I have two black slaves that we could put to work on the project."

And with the statement the mood suddenly changed. The three neighbors nervously looked at the

Reverend Pipkin. It quickly became obvious to Robert that there was an issue with him using slaves to build this church.

Finally, Pipkin broke the uncomfortable silence that had developed, "Robert … the men and I have discussed your slaves and the consensus is we would rather not have them take part in the building of our church … for obvious reasons."

Robert looked puzzled. "What do you mean … our church … I thought the church belonged to Jesus … the bride of Christ …seems like that is how it was described to me once long ago. … And what harm would it be for my two black boys to help on this project. They are good boys … never caused me any trouble … and they work hard and do what they are told exactly as I tell them. … And … what do you mean … obvious reasons?"

Pipkin looked at Cantrell who was obviously the one in the group that had taken issue with slaves working on the construction of the church building. He responded to Robert, "Because they are slaves Robert … surely you must understand we can't have a Methodist meeting house built by slaves!"

"And why not?" replied Robert with a slight indignation in his voice, "not good enough for you?"

"No sir it's not that at all … it's just … well … you see Robert …. ", stammered Cantrell.

Pipkin finally revived his courage and stated, "John Wesley would forbid it. Slavery stands against all that he held near and dear to his heart. I know that it is done. Probably half the churches built in the South were put together with the help of enslaved hands. But, Robert, here in this part of Alabama, we have the opportunity to do things differently?"

Robert turned and looked at the Reverend Pipkin, "May I remind you brother … this here's Alabama and not merry old England. And the last time I checked, the institution of slavery was legal."

Coleman, the tallest and possibly the wisest among the men spoke next, "Legal in the eyes of southern men … yes … but Brother Cochran … legal in the eyes of the Almighty?"

The question hung in the silence. No one responded. All eyes were fixed on Robert.

Finally, Robert stroked his long beard and replied, "alright gentlemen … I won't use the boys. But can they at least fetch water for those who labor in this hot sun?"

The men looked at one another and then all nodded in agreement. The discussion was finished.

It took the organized group of farmers and preachers about two months from start to finish in the construction of the wooden structure that would now serve as the Hackleburg Congregational Methodist church. They had decided to call themselves Methodist for obvious reasons, but the term Congregational had been added to send a message to the Methodist hierarchy as well as the surrounding religious communities that the people who worshiped God in this place would retain some semblance of authority and control not only over each other but also over any Methodist minister sent their way by the Superintendent. These folks of northwestern Alabama were a fiercely independent lot and after having fought in two major conflicts to ensure their freedom, they were not about to relinquish it to any man in authority, be it temporal or spiritual. It was to be the people's church and the doors would always be open to any man, woman or child, be they white, black or red.

The Methodist authorities railed against what they considered to be out right insubordination and antichrist like pride but after a few months, things settled down and life took on its normal slow agrarian pace.

The next spring one early morning Robert was walking towards his newly planted fields when he spotted something moving quickly out of the corner of his eye. Being a seasoned veteran of the Alabama woods he instantly froze in his tracks and slowly moved his head to see if he could make out what it was that was moving through the trees off to his right. He was shocked by what he saw, running as fast as they could were his two slaves toward a man astride a black stallion holding the reins of another large and powerful horse. The man was white. He was wearing a large hat, which prevented Robert from determining who this person was. However, it was obvious what the three of them were up to. Jeb and Tom were running away and this man, whoever he was, was helping them.

Robert let out a shout but this only appeared to encourage the three to move all the quicker. The two young black men were sharing a ride and the two horses were moving quickly away from Robert and into the thick north Alabama woods.

Robert started to run after them but after a few steps realized how foolish he must look. There was no way he could catch three men on horseback and ... even if he could ... what would he do or say for that matter to the boys or to this stranger who was assisting them in their escape? So ... he stopped. His heart was still beating hard from the exertion and surprise when suddenly the horse with his two slaves turned around and headed back towards him. Robert thought to himself, "Are you boys crazy? Here you decide to run away and now what?"

The huge horse came to a stop around fifty feet from Robert. Both young men took off their hats as a sign of respect to their master. Jeb spoke first. "Massa Robert … youse been good to me and Tom. We knows dat. But this white man who lives over yonder in Winston County has told us that if we go with him he can help us make it all the way to Ohio and freedom … dat's what we wants Massa Robert … to be free." By this time, tears were streaming down the faces of both the young men. Robert Cochran was the closest thing either of them had to a father and although the tug of freedom pulled strong, their hearts were broken by the leaving of the only family they had ever known.

Robert was silent for the longest time. He could make out in the distance the white rider. He thought he probably knew who it was now. This fellow would be the attorney Pipkin had spoken about last year, the one who could draw up the papers for the freedom of Tom and Jeb at Robert's death. Was that a ruse? "Probably not", Robert thought to himself. "Pipkin wouldn't lie to him that way. No, probably some unique opportunity has developed along the so-called underground railway and the men in Winston County have decided to take advantage of it."

Robert stood in the red clay of his hard-fought Alabama soil. At first, he was perplexed as to what his next move should be. And then, in a flash, he decided.

"Tom … Jeb … you boys have been good to me. You have worked hard. You have done whatever it was I told you to do and I have never heard a complaint come from the mouths of either of you. You two do not know this but I was going to give you your freedom at my death …. But …. Why wait? I might live for a good number of years yet … and you boys should taste freedom before you become too old to enjoy it." And with that final statement, Robert closed the space between himself and the two young men who had slowly moved their horse closer to him. Robert extended his hand in friendship. He shook Tom's hand. He shook Jeb's hand. The two young black men looked at Robert Cochran and then looked at one another and smiled. Tom was holding the reins of the horse. He quickly put the horse into motion and the two of them galloped off into the woods heading straight for the white man on the black horse.

Robert Cochran watched them ride away. He said a quick prayer asking God for protection and guidance for his two boys and those who were going to risk all to help them gain their freedom. When they were completely out of sight, He turned and headed towards his newly planted cotton field. No one could see him. There were tears in his eyes and a smile on his lips. "Gonna be a good year", he said to no one in particular, "Yep, a good year."

Chapter Sixteen – Boonshill, Lincoln County, Tennessee, summer of 1850

"But momma … I don't know if I actually love the man?" Louisa spoke to her mother with exasperation tinged with anxiety.

"Hogwash," replied Eliza McAfee, Louisa's mother. "What does love have to do with anything? I know … I know … he is not much to look at … but, Louisa, consider the facts. Yes, he is older than you but he is an established member of the community. He owns land, Louisa, in three counties of Middle Tennessee. His family came over the mountains with ours. His ancestors came to the colonies from Ireland … just like ours. He has never been married and to the best of our knowledge has no illegitimate children running around. And, let's face it child, the pickens are rather slim around these parts. And you're not getting any younger. It's time you got yourself attached to a man and began raising a family of your own. And the man did the decent thing … he went to your daddy first and asked for your hand in marriage." Eliza became silent and looked directly at her daughter. "Baby, I know you are scared. I was scared too when it came time for your Daddy and I to get hitched. But that turned-out o.k. and if we hadn't neither you nor your brothers and sisters would be here right now." Eliza let out a quick chuckle with this last comment.

Louisa didn't know where to begin. She had so much to say but didn't know exactly how to express her feelings in words. That had been an issue for her most of her young life. The words came to her in her mind but for some reason they just failed to materialize when she opened her mouth. Throughout her life, she had often just done as she was told even when her mind and her heart told her maybe it was something else she desired. But this was serious. This man, James Carroll Reed, whom she barely knew had rode his horse to her father's humble farm house and asked for her hand in marriage. And she was supposed to do what … just accept it … without at least some semblance of conversation regarding the situation with her parents or at least with James for that matter. He was thirty years old and she only seventeen. Although it was true, he had not been married before surely, he had pursued other women before her? And if no one else would take him, then why should she? Yes, they had spoken on occasion at the Methodist meeting house in Delina or when their paths crossed as they travelled from the county seat of Fayetteville back to their respective farms. And, it was true, what momma said, he did own quite a bit of land here in Lincoln and over in Williamson counties and maybe elsewhere. He even held a few slaves to help work his fields. But he wasn't what one might call a wealthy planter. Those kinds of people lived west of here in the fertile Mississippi flood plains of west Tennessee. The people here in middle Tennessee were a simple folk, with small to middling size farms whose survival depended primarily on trade with the citizens of Nashville to the north and Huntsville, Alabama to the south. This didn't feel right and she had to make her thoughts and feelings known. But she did have to proceed with caution. This section of Tennessee was slowly transitioning from wild frontier to civilized farming communities. Young women, such as Louisa, had to be quite wise when it came to these matters of marriage and family. If you turned down a suitor, there was no guarantee another would follow in his footsteps.

But if you jumped at the first opportunity, you could land yourself in a bad marriage with a man fond for Tennessee whiskey who when intoxicated was not opposed to giving his wife a good thrashing. Louisa had heard the horror stories of some of their neighbors and she had no intention of ever finding herself in a similar situation. But … as momma said … it wasn't as if single men were growing on trees around here. And … he had been very kind to her during their limited interactions and for that matter, she never saw James drunk … actually when she thought about it, she realized she had never seen him even take a drink of hard liquor. "Hmmm," she thought to herself, "I guess it wouldn't hurt to have him call on her a couple of times before she turned him away." She knew her daddy, Jessie, well. He would huff and puff and indignantly strut around the farm house like he was head rooster if she refused James's proposal but, in the end he would acquiesce to his precious daughter's decision. He wouldn't force the marriage on her if she adamantly refused. Other girls in the county were not as lucky and Louisa knew that and she was thankful for her father's love and tolerant understanding. "No," she thought, "I'll just calmly tell daddy I am entertaining the thought but would like to get to know Mr. Reed a wee bit better before I commit." She smiled slyly. She may not be the prettiest girl in the county and she certainly wasn't the most intelligent. She could read and write some but she had not been able to attain any type of formal education beyond what she had learned in Sunday school and at her mother's knees as a young girl. But she was wise for her years and knew that young eligible women weren't growing on trees either. One thing Louisa was exceptionally good at was bargaining. She had learned that skill from closely observing her momma and momma's momma, granny McRae. Those two women could charm a rattlesnake to give up his skin if they put their minds to it.

That evening as the family gathered around the dinner table, Louisa waited for her father to bring up the topic of conversation both knew needed to be discussed, the proposal of marriage to James Reed. Both father and daughter spoke with one another politely constantly smiling and nodding their heads. Louisa was nervous and she knew from her observations that her daddy was as well. Finally, Jesse approached the subject gingerly, "Well, young lady, I reckon you know that Mr. Reed paid me a visit the other day?"

Louisa stopped smiling. Her face took on a serious countenance. "Yes, daddy, momma told me," as she glanced sideways towards her mother who immediately began stacking the dinner dishes for washing. Her mother kept her head down and face turned away from both husband and daughter. This was to be Louisa's battle if it turned into that and she was going to try as hard as she could to remain neutral.

Jesse glanced at his wife. He looked straight into the eyes of his daughter. He thought to himself, "Where has the time gone? Wasn't it just yesterday that this little girl and I would run down to the fields together singing and giggling in pure joy. And now she is to be married?" But he didn't say anything to Louisa. And finally, after the silence between the two of them became almost unbearable, he spoke quietly, "Well lass … what do ye think?"

Louisa looked at her father. He was a kind and gentle man who loved his family and worked hard to provide for them. While Jesse would not call himself a deeply religious man, he was, in fact, highly religious when compared to many of his neighbors. Jesse always sought the Lord's counsel before making any major decision in his life. Throughout her life, Louisa would often find Jesse sitting quietly under some shady tree with head bowed in prayer. She loved that about her daddy. He was a God-fearing man and loved the Lord Jesus with all his heart and soul … as did she. And that is where she started the conversation.

"Daddy, I don't know this man well enough to say yes or no to his proposal. Yes, he seems kind enough and I've not heard any malicious rumors about him. But he and I haven't spent enough time in conversation to see if we are even compatible with one another. Can you understand that daddy? I just need some time to think … and to pray." Louisa knew that last part would touch her father's heart. She wasn't trying to manipulate her father. She was quite sincere when she mentioned the need for prayer. But she honestly knew that presenting her case in that manner would be well received by him.

Jesse McAfee was quiet for the longest time. Then he spoke. "Yes, child, you are quite right. I reckon I was overtaken by the thought of having you starting your own family and Lord willing, making me some grandchildren." Jesse chuckled and Louisa blushed. Eliza attempted to gently chastise her husband with a shocked "Jesse! Let's keep a Christian tongue in that old head of yours … shall we?" But her face had already broken into a smile. She loved this man and constantly fretted over him like a hen to her chicks.

"Then, it's settled. Louisa needs time to get to know this Mr. James Reed. So, I reckon he'll have to wait until you, my precious daughter, are good and ready. So … shall we say, James will come a courtin' on Sundays after church and … perhaps every other Friday night for a while. How does that strike you Louisa?"

It didn't take James long to begin his courtship of the young Miss McAfee. Within weeks, his presence at the McAfee farm was a regular occurrence. Initially, the conversation had seemed forced to Louisa. James was very shy and highly reluctant to engage in conversation. During their first meeting, Louisa thought he might have a stroke from his nerves. He was sweating profusely and although Tennessee summers can get rather warm, on that particular day, the sky was overcast with a cool refreshing breeze blowing in from the eastern mountains. Eventually James was able to remain calm in her presence but rarely would he initiate the conversation. Usually it was Louisa who would select a topic and then ask James his opinion. After a brief moment of silence, he would answer in short concise sentences and then just as quickly as he had begun silence would engulf him with a faint smile upon his lips. Louisa quickly learned that this man was a man of few words more given to action then talk. Louisa on the other hand, loved the art of conversation and was quite talented in this area. And she, through her interaction with neighbors, circuit riding ministers and the occasional traveler heading from Nashville to Chattanooga or Atlanta would learn much of the affairs of the outside world. Louisa yearned to learn of the world outside her little town of Boonshill. Sometimes she was confused by what she heard and would often turn to her father or mother for guidance and further information. Louisa soon came to realize that tension between the northern and southern states was rising due to the issue of slavery; she also came to an understanding that James Reed considered himself a Jacksonian Democrat and had voted for a fellow Tennessean James K. Polk in the last Presidential election. She wondered what it would be like to vote and asked James his opinion of women having the right to vote. That led to a short but rather tense discussion between the two. But Louisa's favorite topic to discuss with James was what some people were now calling the Second Great Awakening a religious movement inspired by the teachings of Barton W. Stone along with the father-son preaching team of Alexander and Thomas Campbell. Although Louisa's parents considered themselves God fearing Christians and regularly attended the Methodist meetings when a Circuit riding preacher would make it to this part of the country, religion was not a major topic of discussion in their household. When pressed by their daughter, Jesse would respond "I guess our people were once members of the Presbyterian Church. But when we came over the mountains to this valley, we had to focus on other things." And then he would go silent as if this statement should be a sufficient explanation for Louisa. Louisa could tell it was not a fertile topic for further discussion so she just accepted things as they appeared to be. However, when Louisa was with her suitor, religion was a common topic of discussion. Her faith was important to her and she wanted to know exactly what James felt about the subject. He did attend the service at the meeting house when a preacher was in town but Louisa realized that many people attended due to habit or the gossip that often spread through the gathering after the service was concluded and folks were gathered on the yard to eat their mid-day meal. Was James just there for the socializing or did it really mean something to him?

One afternoon, as she and James sat on the front porch of the McAfee home, she asked rather directly of James, "so, Mr. Reed … I mean, James (it took a couple of meetings between the two before she felt comfortable calling him by his first name … after all, he was over a decade older) what do you think about the Stone-Campbell movement?"

James, as usual, did not respond immediately. He took out his pipe, filled it with tobacco from his pouch, lit it, and took a few puffs before responding, "Well, Louisa, I reckon they may be on to somethin'."

Louisa was shocked. First, that he even knew anything about their teachings. Second, that maybe he found something of value in what they had to offer. She knew her mouth had opened slightly in subtle shock and quickly closed it while she used her colorful fan to gently blow cooling air on her neck and thick hair. "My goodness, it was certainly warm today," she thought to herself.

Louisa finally responded, "Well, James, what do you mean?"

James took another puff on his pipe. Slowly blew the smoke out into the air and watched as it curled upward until it disappeared in the hot muggy air surrounding them.

"I reckon it was something I read that I think one of the Campbells wrote," the quiet Tennessee farmer said.

Once again, Louisa had to hide her surprise. She did not realize that this man knew how to read. She guessed it had never come up in their conversations before. While it wasn't entirely unheard of Louisa was aware that many of the settlers in this area were not literate or could at best roughly sign their names to deeds, wills and other legal documents. She just assumed James, being a simple farmer, had not spent much time in learning to read. She, on the other hand, had been taught by her own mother how to read with the use of Holy Scripture. But she was wrong about James. Not only could he read but his appetite for learning was insatiable. The man read everything he could get his hands on and knew how to write albeit in a primitive style. In fact, Louisa would have been amazed if she knew that James was in regular correspondence with distant relatives living back in North Carolina as well as a Methodist preacher he had encountered a few years ago who now lived in Davidson county where the man served as full time minister to a growing congregation located in downtown Nashville, the state's capital and fastest growing town.

James spoke once again, "it went something like this … the Reformed Kirk has run so hard to get away from Rome … they have run completely past Jerusalem … or something like that." James scratched his head. His hair was already turning gray and it was obvious that he had already begun to go bald. James was not fond of this ever-present fact of his aging and often wore a hat to cover his head. But, of course, being a gentleman, he always removed his hat in the presence of Louisa. He scratched his beard and took another puff on his pipe. "You know one of the Campbells, I'm pretty sure it was Alexander, was educated at the University of Glasgow in Scotland. He came to America with his mother and siblings to join his father, Thomas, who had come over, I think, around 1807 or so. I believe both men were ordained teaching elders of the Presbyterian Church. I think, if my memory serves me right, they ended up somewhere around Philadelphia where Alexander was ordained by the Brush Run Church. Somehow his father Thomas ended up heading west across the Alleghenies and landed in Washington county, Pennsylvania where he served as religious leader for a number of the churches in that area."

Louisa was spellbound. She had never heard James put more than two sentences together in the short time they had been courting. And she was thrilled. In fact, she suddenly found herself mysteriously drawn closer to this man. She didn't know if this was love but she liked what he was saying and liked how it made her feel. Here was a man who liked religion and apparently knew quite a bit about this latest movement in the Christian frontier of the country.

She finally found her voice and managed to ask, "James, how do you know these things?"

He smiled at her and took another puff on his pipe. "Oh … I reckon … when I have some time to kill … I read things that come my way. No big deal."

But it was a big deal to Louisa. She pressed on, "so, tell me the story, what is this movement all about?"

James looked up at the sky. The sun was about half way between its peak and setting. He knew it was mid-afternoon. "I don't know Louisa. Your parents will be wantin' you to help set the table soon. And I'll have to hitch up the buggy and head back to my place. Maybe this should wait for another day?"

Louisa touched James' arm gently. This was the first time their bodies had ever touched. He arched his eyebrows but remained silent. She said in a gentle quiet feminine voice, "Please James, I enjoy talking with you like this. It's early yet. And momma hasn't called. Please, go on and tell me what you know about the Stone-Campbell movement. I know some folks refer to it as the Second Great Awakening but that's about all I really know … and I truly desire to know more." She smiled at James and, of course, that melted the man's heart.

"Well, I reckon, I can tell you what I know, which really ain't much. In 1809, Thomas Campbell issued what he called his Declaration and Address of the Christian Association of Washington. I think it was a joint effort between father and son. It reads like something a college educated man would compose. To make a long story short, it lays out some simple principles that Thomas and Alexander taught should guide the Christian church. First and foremost, the Bible and the Bible alone was to be substituted for all human creeds. Along with that, the Campbells stated that the commands of God were to be substituted for human legislation and tradition. Piety was to be substituted for religious ceremony and the true practice of religion substituted for the mere profession of it. They taught that the descendants of those who had been converted to Jesus during the first Great Awakening had lost the true meaning of their conversion and were simply going through the motions in order to enter heaven's gate at the end of their lives. They started to call themselves the Disciples of Christ."

Louisa was fascinated and had many questions for James. "James, I've heard this called the Stone-Campbell movement. Who was Stone and what part did he play?"

James stroked his beard and continued to puff away at his pipe for the longest time. Louisa had learned by now this was James's way of gathering his thoughts before he spoke. She was beginning to appreciate the depth of this fellow. He wasn't just a simple quiet farmer but a man with a powerful intellect who chose his words carefully and fully weighed and measured each thought before deciding on what to believe and what to say.

James finally began speaking once again, "I heard Barton W. Stone was his full name and that he was originally born in Maryland a few years before the war with England began. As a young man, he became a candidate for the ministry in the Presbyterian church of Orange County, North Carolina. I don't really know if he had a formal education or not but I reckon so since he taught for a while as a professor of Language at the Methodist Academy in Georgia. Somehow, he ended up in Bourbon County Kentucky serving as the pastor to a couple of Presbyterian churches located at Cane Ridge and Concord. Cane Ridge, of course, was the source of a great revival back at the turn of the century. I've read that somewhere between twenty and thirty thousand folks gathered there at one time to hear the gospel preached by both Methodist and Baptist preachers. Who knows, maybe Stone was one of the speakers? I don't really know but something caused the man to re-evaluate all he believed in concerning the church and what it should stand for and how it should operate in this world. He concluded that religious creeds and traditions were divisive and that the Word of God and it alone should serve as guide for all Christian thought and action. He also had been influenced by the anti-Calvinistic teachings of some of the Methodist ministers and began to question some elements of that particular doctrine. Apparently, this got him into a heap of trouble with the ruling Synod of Lexington and they suspended his membership and license to preach in any Presbyterian church." James fell silent once again and Louisa thought that might be the end of the conversation for this day. But James was just getting his thoughts together. Eventually he cleared his throat and began to speak again, "just imagine Louisa how that must have felt to Stone. Here was a man who had given all he had to help the church grow. And now they turn him out because he has doubts about something a fellow in Switzerland wrote about over two hundred years ago." James chuckled, "I guess the old boy was right, one man's interpretation of Scripture can certainly become divisive. Think about all the trouble old Luther stirred up." James chuckled once again. Louisa couldn't tell if he was honestly amused or if the whole matter somehow made him sad and the laughter was a way to release the emotion he was feeling. Or perhaps it was sarcasm? "No," thought Louisa," this was not sarcasm she was seeing in him. This was important to James. He had studied it much more than she had expected and was fascinated and thrilled by his understanding of the matter. What she was witnessing," she reasoned," was sadness. James was saddened by the divisions that had slowly but surely crept into the church since the early days of the Reformation. And that made her value him even more." And then the thought struck her like a bolt of lightning from the sky, "Am I falling in love with this man?" She smiled and James saw the smile. He thought to himself, "There is something about this young woman that melts my heart."

The two looked at each other in silence for the longest time. No words were spoken but somehow they knew. They both sensed it. Something or some being was drawing them closer to one another and it seemed natural. Perhaps it was their destiny to come together in this way, discussing, of all things, current religious trends, while sitting on the front porch of a middle Tennessee farmhouse during a long and warm summer afternoon.

Suddenly James resumed his story, "Well … what I heard was old Stone came back to his church at Cane Ridge and told them he could no longer lead them as a teaching elder because of what had transpired in his own thoughts and ideas about the church. And, lo and behold, the congregation supported him. Every ruling elder decided to follow Stone wherever he led them. I read that they even composed a so-called Last Will and Testament of the Springfield Presbyterian Presbytery of which Cane Ridge was a part. I've never actually read the document myself but the end result was the dissolution of the Presbytery of Springfield, Kentucky and the creation of what Stone and others began calling simply the Christian church. They decided to drop the title Reverend for the teaching Elder and replace it with simply minister. They said that the Bible and the Bible alone would serve as the only sure guide to heaven. They decided that each individual church should select its own minister and pay for his services out of a free will gathering. And after further deliberation and much discussion among the ruling Elders of this new Christian church, they decided to adopt the principle of a believer's baptism by immersion and that the Lord's supper was to be taken at every gathering of the congregation and not just on selected holy days of the year. Apparently, this document was signed in June of 1804 by the men who had previously led the Presbytery of Springfield. "James suddenly stopped talking and starting fishing around in his vest pocket for something. Finding it, he retrieved a small New Testament, and opened it to the back cover. "Here it is,"

James smiled as he looked at what was written on the cover, "for some strange reason, years ago, when I heard this story I wrote down the names of the Elders who signed ... they were Robert Marshall, John Dunlevey, Richard McNemar, John Thompson, David Purviance and, of course, Barton W. Stone. Funny heh, I reckon I must have been impressed with what these men were trying to accomplish so I wrote down their names but for the life of me I can't rightly remember now the source of this information. So, I don't really know if I got them correct or not. Oh well, I guess God knows and in the end ... that's all that matters ... ain't that so Louisa?" James smiled as he looked at her. And she blushed as she returned his smile. They both knew somehow their relationship had taken on a new nature. Neither of them at that time knew where they would end up but somehow they both knew they would travel the journey of life together.

"Supper's on Louisa," Eliza called out to her daughter from the kitchen. She then scurried to the porch and asked in a quieter voice, "My goodness, Mr. Reed, you must think I'm some type of heathen shoutin' out from the house like so ..." while smiling at him and nodding at Louisa, as if to say, your time today is up young lady.

James jumped up from his seat and quickly bowed ever so slightly in her direction. "I must really be on my way. I've overstayed my welcome as it is."

"Oh, nonsense, Mr. Reed," responded Eliza while continuing to nod her head and smile. Louisa thought to herself, "my momma has done lost her mind ... the way she keeps smilin' and noddin'." Then James turned quickly towards Louisa. "Miss McAfee, would you mind terribly if I return again later on in the week? Perhaps we could resume this conversation … or discuss another subject of your choosin'?"

Louisa moved closer to James and replied, "Why yes, Mr. …er … James…. That would be right nice of you to return later this week. I'm sure that would be acceptable to momma … right momma?" Louisa glanced at her mother who simply nodded her head and headed back into the kitchen saying something about her biscuits were about to burn.

After she left, James gently took Louisa's hand in his, bent down his head and softly kissed the back of her extended hand. He quickly dropped it, placed his hat firmly on his head and without another word spun on his heels and almost trotted down to where his horse had been tied to a tree in the shade. The old mare had been munching on the tall grass and appeared quite content and rather reluctant to have a passenger once more. But soon James was heading down the dirt lane towards his farm. After a few trots he stopped the horse, turned around in his seat, took off his hat and in a manner which he thought rather gallantly swooped his hat to the ground in a salute to the young Miss McAfee. He quickly replaced the hat on his head, spurred his horse and the beast trotted off with James riding rather high in the saddle.

Louisa smiled at this final goodbye and headed inside the house where she knew she would be grilled with questions regarding their conversation.

It was Jesse, her father, who broke the silence at the supper table. "Well, young lady, what do you think so far of your suitor?" Eliza frowned and quickly scolded her husband, "Jesse, give the child a chance to catch her breath and collect her thoughts. After all, the two of them have been chatting up a storm all afternoon." Eliza's face broke into a wide grin. She was just as curious as her man to know Louisa's impressions of Mr. Reed.

Louisa was silent for a moment and then smiled, "I think I like him daddy. He is very quiet but, once we stumbled upon a topic he found of interest he became quite the chatterbox."

"And what was the topic that caused you two to spend so much time discussing?" replied her father.

"Religion," was Louisa's one word response. "Religion?" Jesse remarked with some degree of surprise. I didn't think Mr. Reed was much of a theologian myself. I know he comes to the meeting house on occasion," Jesse stressed the words on occasion, "but he never struck me as the overly religious type."

"Oh, but daddy … that's where you are wrong. Yes, he is a very quiet man… keeps much of his thoughts to himself. But, he is obviously very intelligent, knows how to read and write and even keeps up to date on the recent developments in religious thoughts and ideas." Louisa replied.

"Recent developments?" responded her father. "Such as what recent developments … to the best of my knowledge, there hasn't been much in the way of recent developments in this part of middle Tennessee since we came over the mountains."

"Daddy, I'm talking about the teachings of the Reverends Campbell and Stone." Louisa spoke matter of fact without the least bit of concern in her voice. She was quite taken aback and surprised by her father's reaction.

"Good Lord … don't tell me the man is a Campbellite!" Jesse retorted.

"A Campbell what?" replied Louisa.

Jesse glanced at his wife who was looking at her daughter with anxiety. "They call themselves Disciples of Christ, but most folks I know, at least those who attend the Methodist meetings, refer to them as Campbellites. The two men who gave birth to this Christian sect were both ordained Presbyterian pastors and, I might add, University of Glasgow graduates. Their names were Thomas and Alexander Campbell. They were father and son. They ended up in Western Pennsylvania but their movement didn't really find fertile soil there but it did take off in Western Virginia and Eastern Kentucky and has even found its way to Nashville, here in middle Tennessee. Back in '32, this group merged with the so called Christian church, a denomination started by Barton W. Stone and others."

Louisa was amazed that her father knew so much about what she and James had been discussing earlier that afternoon. "Daddy, how do you know all this? You hardly ever talk about anything related to the church, much less, a brand-new movement." Louisa asked wide–eyed.

"A movement … is that what he called it?" responded Jesse with a bit of sarcasm in his voice. "More like a schism … a way to divide good Christian friends and families from one another. Did Reed tell you about what happened to Stone? That he was essentially kicked out of the Presbyterian church for preaching poor doctrine."

Louisa was surprised by this response since quite frankly what did her daddy care about the Presbyterians … the McAfee's had been regular attenders of the Methodist meetings since they came over the mountains from North Carolina. More importantly, Louisa was perplexed by her father's apparent agitation with the fact that her suitor might not be a Methodist at heart. Or was he? She suddenly realized that although James had told her many new things about Stone and the Campbells, he had actually never stated that he himself was a supporter. She thought to herself, "I think daddy is over reacting but given his Ulster Scots temper, I think I'll just keep quiet for now on this subject" … at least until she got the chance to speak once again to James about what he believed to be true about the Christian faith.

And so, the impending storm like a Tennessee tornado suddenly vanished quickly in the McAfee homestead as Eliza and her younger sisters cleaned up the table and washed the dishes while Jesse and his sons headed out to the barn for some last-minute chores before sundown.

Days came and went with no sight nor sound of James Reed. Louisa knew she shouldn't worry but she did. It was in her nature. "Was he alright? Had he second thoughts about her after their lengthy conversation?" Her mind was plagued with doubts. And then suddenly, early one morning, there he was standing on their front porch with his hat in his hands and a smile on his face.

"Good morning Louisa. I've come to see if you would like to take a buggy ride with me? I'm thinking about buying some more property up towards Delina and I am meaning to head up there today to check it out. Thought you might want to ride along? I've had Bessie, my servant, make extra for the mid-day meal. Perhaps we could find a nice spot along the creek to have a picnic?"

Louisa was excited but also knew that her parents would probably say no. But as she turned to ask them, she bumped into her mother, who was standing right behind her and had, she guessed, heard every word. Eliza looked at her daughter then at this man who had come to take her away. It might not be proper but for whatever reason she trusted James and decided to allow her to take this short unchaperoned trip with him. "But we better not tell your daddy, at least until you are back home safe and sound." The two lowered their conspiratorial voices and nodded at each other. "Alright momma, thank you," replied Louisa.

Louisa spun around and in a cheerful voice, "let's go James." And off they went.

James assisted Louisa into the small but comfortable buggy and then grabbed the reins and they were quickly off on a trot. This horse was quite different from the one James usually rode out to Louisa's farm, for this was a Tennessee trotter, a beautiful tan colored animal with a majestic appearance. Soon they were speeding away down the lane to the Delina Fayetteville road.

The morning went by fast. After James had looked over the potential new property and began the negotiations with its present owner regarding a fair market value, he returned to Louisa who had been sitting patiently in the buggy watching the horse graze on some nearby grass.

"Well, that's done," said James.

"Did you purchase it?" asked Louisa.

"Conditionally," replied James. Louisa looked puzzled. She was about to ask upon what conditions but then decided to change the subject. James seemed to be in quite a good mood and the last thing she wanted to do was bring up the particulars of some business deal he had arranged. She wanted to just sit back and enjoy the ride through the green middle Tennessee countryside. "My, how pretty this land truly is," she thought to herself.

After a short while, Louisa began to hum a tune they often sang during the Methodist meetings. It was one of the many songs written by Charles Wesley, brother to the famous Anglican cleric John Wesley who, along with George Whitefield, co-founded the Methodist denomination. James knew the song and he began to sing the words. She thought to herself, "He has a good, strong and pleasant sounding baritone voice." She joined in and the two of them sang for some time as the buggy strolled along to the rhythmic clip clop of the trotter's gate.

Soon, James pulled in the reins and brought the buggy to a halt. "Over yonder is a meadow with a creek by its side. I thought that would be a nice place to stop for a meal?" James stated.

"Yes," Louisa replied, "looks very pleasant and those tall trees will keep us out of the hot mid- day sun."

The two busily worked together as they prepared a comfortable place to sit and eat the meal that had earlier in the morning been prepared by one of James' slaves.

After taking a few bites of the meal, Louisa exclaimed, "James, this is delicious. You will have to tell your Bessie she did well. By the way, you called Bessie your servant. You meant slave, correct? How many slaves do you own?" Louisa was very curious about this situation. Her family was not slave owners. She wasn't sure about her ancestors but neither her daddy nor momma had ever mentioned holding slaves in either of their families. Wesley and Whitefield both had preached against the slave trade but she knew some folks who regularly attended the meeting house and also had slaves. They would even bring them to the meetinghouse but, of course, they never went inside or if they did, they had to sit in the back of the building. She knew James was a slave owner and she wasn't quite sure what she thought about this aspect of his life.

"Yes, Louisa, I keep a family on my farm. There's Bessie, who tends to my house and does many of the tasks a wife would do and then there's her man, Jacob, who helps me in the fields and then they have three little ones, all under the age of five, I reckon. And yes, they are slaves. I was given Jacob by my father and bought his woman Bessie and their children so the family could stay together. My daddy had sold Bessie and her youngins' off to a trader headed for Memphis. I reckon he was going to sell 'em down the river. I just couldn't let that happen. So I jumped on one of my daddy's fastest horses and caught up with the man about half way to Memphis. I tried to bargain with him but he was reluctant at first. Then, I guess my temper got the best of me and I picked up my Kentucky long rifle and kind of pointed it in the general direction of where he was standing. Reckon he got the message and decided my offer was good enough after all … It was a fair price. The man made a profit. I got a good servant in Bessie and Jacob seemed quite happy when they were all reunited at my farm. That was a couple of years ago. Everything seems to have worked out." James chuckled," Although we haven't seen hide nor hair of that slaver." Louisa started to giggle and then could no longer contain herself. She and James laughed for quite some time. "James Reed … that was a noble thing you did for them … keeping them together like that. God would surely be pleased." Louisa stated after she regained her composure.

"So … Louisa … you're not opposed to what the Yankees call our peculiar institution?" asked James. Louisa started to reply and then stopped herself. If she were completely honest, she really didn't know how she felt about the subject of slavery. It had been a part of her life for all her life. And she knew that in certain circles one had to be very careful in a conversation about this topic. She knew that the folks in east Tennessee, in general, were opposed to the concept. She also knew that west Tennessee planters totally depended upon their slaves working the huge cotton and corn fields of that region. But here in middle Tennessee, things were all mixed up. You might find one farmer holding two or three black field hands living right next door to another farmer who was secretly a dyed in the wool abolitionist. Maybe had even helped slaves to run-away from their Alabama or Georgia masters?

Finally, Louisa responded, "I agree with John Wesley. This type of slavery is not the same type found within the New Testament. And, I personally could never see our Lord Jesus owning slaves. In particular, I could never see him splitting up families like some do … just for profit." Louisa hoped she hadn't stepped over that invisible line that existed in the conversations of Southern gentlemen and their genteel ladies. This was a touchy subject and many a familial relationship had been torn asunder by a conversation of this very nature.

James was quiet for what seemed an eternity to Louisa. She just knew she had gone and said too much. Finally, James spoke, "You know, Louisa, we did not ask to be born in this place or at this time. But … here we are. I reckon we have to make the best of the situation. I know the Yankees want us to free them. And yes, it breaks my heart when I hear the same stories you hear about black families being split apart. But …. Louisa … I don't think we could survive without them. How would we get the crops planted and harvested? Who would do all this back breaking work that none of us white folk really want to do if the truth be known. And … it is such a part of our culture now … No dear … I'm afraid we are stuck. At least that's my opinion. So, I try to do the best I can with what the good Lord has given me. I try to be fair with my servants …er … slaves, treat 'em kindly, feed and clothe 'em well and tend to 'em when they are ill. They don't sleep under my roof, of course, but Jacob and I have built a fairly strong and dry cabin for his little family. And Sundays … that's their day of rest. I figure, if it was good enough for God to take a day off from His labors then so should they."

"And what happens when the little ones grow up?" Louisa asked.

"I reckon I'll figure that I out when the day comes. Who knows, the way some of them Yankees keep rattlin' their sabers, that might be the least of our worries." James said rather somberly.

"Oh James, "Louisa gasped, "you don't think it could ever come to that … do you?"

James took off his hat and wiped his brow and then gently sat the hat on the blanket that was serving as dinner table for the two of them. "Let's talk about something more pleasant, shall we?"

Louisa looked at him and wanted to change the subject but in her heart, she knew that she needed to determine where this man stood on this issue. Louisa's family were not slave owners. And as far as she knew, none of her ancestors had ever owned slaves. But she also realized that many of the families that had come over the mountains into this fertile green valley had over time purchased slaves from the slave markets of Memphis or

Atlanta in order to assist them in their fields. She also knew that some of them simply had slaves because it was a sign of wealth and power. The institution had become a status symbol throughout the south. It was the slaveholders who now held most of the social and political power throughout the southern slave states. And Louisa was old enough to realize that these power-hungry men and their socialite wives were not going to easily relinquish their newly acquired high society positions.

"But James, what about Texas?" Louisa politely but firmly asked him.

James raised an eyebrow, "What of it?"

"You most certainly know to what I am referring," Louisa responded slightly perturbed.

James looked at her and then stroked his beard slowly waiting for the right words to come into his mind. "Texas was an independent country that asked to join the Union. And since it had been settled primarily by southern slave owners it was natural for them to desire to retain their status as a slave holding territory."

Louisa responded, "But the Yankees did not want slavery to spread into the west. Correct?"

"Yep … they sure didn't. Put up quite a fuss in Washington. But in the end … a compromise was reached. Slavery would be legal below a certain latitude and not above it," James stated in such a manner as to let Louisa know that he thought that should be the end of the discussion.

But Louisa was not satisfied. "But the abolitionists are not happy. They want to see an end to slavery everywhere."

James nodded his head in affirmation. "Yep … that's true … they just won't leave us be … which means it may come to armed conflict. I pray not. If it comes to war," James lowered his voice and looked down at the blanket, "it will be bad. Many people will suffer and quite a few will die. And the saddest thing will be … Christian brother fighting Christian brother. Families in the border states will be torn in two. And … we'll lose."

Louisa was shocked with this response. "Lose … how can we lose James."

James looked at Louisa with tears forming in his eyes, "My dear sweet Louisa, we'll lose because our so-called leaders are arrogant men led by their stupid passions. Of course, our boys will fight hard … it's in their blood. But the Yankees will have more factories, trains, food, and …. more of everything. They will beat us due to the sheer numbers of their overwhelming strength in all areas of warfare. Louisa … we don't even have a Navy. How will we be able to safely ship our cotton to Britain? No, my dear, if it comes to war … life as we know it will be finished."

Louisa and James sat quietly hearing only the breathing of one another and the gentle flow of the nearby creek as it made its way over the rocks in its path. It seemed as if even the birds and other creatures of the woods had stopped all activity. Everything was still.

Finally, Louisa spoke, "James do you believe slavery is worth fighting and possibly dying for?"

James looked at Louisa. As usual, he didn't respond immediately. "No, Louisa, I don't … but we may not have a choice in the matter. If the abolitionists have their way in Washington, they may force the government to take some type of military action against the slave holding states. If that happens, what choice will any of us have but to pick up a weapon and defend our homeland?

No, I don't think keeping our slaves is worth the fight but if Tennessee is invaded by a northern army … well then … that changes things now doesn't it?"

Louisa replied, "I pray to God it never comes to that. Think of all the young men who will suffer and die and their widowed wives and fatherless children left behind. No, dear God, let it not come to that."

"Amen" agreed James. "Let's change the subject Louisa. What do you want out of life?"

Louisa at first looked puzzled. But she quickly realized where James was heading with his turn in their conversation. She didn't yet know if she wanted this discussion but decided to see where it led. "What do you mean James?" she answered.

"Well … well … you know … what do you want to happen in your life? Do you want to be married some day? Have children? Be a farmer's wife? Those type of things." James said with more anxiety in his voice then she had ever heard in their previous conversations.

Louisa smiled at James. She liked the fact that he was nervous about the subject of marriage and family. It drew her closer to him, closer then she had expected. Her mind was racing. Was this the moment? Would he ask her? If he did how would she respond?

"James, I do want to marry someday and yes, if the good Lord agrees, have a family. I love children and hope to someday have many of them. The farm life is all I have ever known. What else is there for me to even consider? Moving to Nashville or Atlanta? Or maybe heading up North to Philadelphia or even New York?" she chuckled at this last statement. Imagine me in the city of New York. No, she couldn't imagine how life might be for her off the farm. It was the only life she had ever known and quite truthfully, it suited her just fine.

James spoke, "Louisa, you must know that I have spoken to your father about us?" He waited for a response but she didn't offer one and so he continued, "I know I may not be the man you have dreamt of … I ain't much to look at … but I do have some good fertile lands … and I would treat you well Louisa. I would be faithful to you. I would take care of you as best I could. Provide for you and …God willing … give you many little ones." At this last comment, James looked away in embarrassment and Louisa felt herself blushing. "Louisa, I guess what I'm saying is … Louisa McAfee, will you be my wife … will you become Mrs. James Reed?"

There it was. The question had finally been asked. Now, it was entirely up to her. She didn't know why she thought of it but said it to him anyway, "my daddy thinks you are a Campbellite. And my momma thinks slavery is wrong. But they are practical people and have left the decision up to me."

James looked into her eyes expectantly. Louisa placed her soft and small hand on top of his firm and callused farmer's hand. "James, I will not leave the Methodist church. And you have to promise me that you will never split up your slave family regardless what happens. And … if war does come, you promise me you will stay safe if you are called upon to fight?"

James continued to look into her eyes. Slowly he nodded his head and gently spoke, "Yes, Louisa, I promise to be a faithful and loving husband. I consider myself to be a follower of Jesus of Nazareth, the promised Messiah, the Christ. You can call me a Methodist, Baptist or Campbellite. I don't care … as long as you are by my side?"

"Then yes, James Reed, I will marry you." Louisa spoke and smiled from ear to ear. She was surprised by how happy she felt. She thought to herself, "I guess I do love this man."

James was smiling. He slowly leaned over and gently kissed the side of Louisa's face. Louisa blushed but then quickly leaned toward James and kissed him on his mouth. After a few seconds the two parted and stared at one another in complete silence. An indescribable peace had settled over them. In that moment they both knew that whatever the future had in store for them they would face it together as husband and wife.

"I reckon we better be headin' back to your place?" James finally broke the silence.

"Yes, I think so. Daddy will be starting to wonder about us and momma will be worrying as usual," Louisa smiled as she thought about how she was going to tell her folks she had accepted James' proposal.

James hitched up the buggy while Louisa gathered up their picnic items. He helped her into the contraption, jumped in beside her and grabbed the reins.

After they had travelled a few miles, Louisa asked, "Oh James, what about the property you went to see. You said you bought it conditionally. What were the conditions?"

James turned to look at his new fiancé and burst out laughing … "On the condition, you said yes. It's a pretty piece of land and if you said yes to being my wife I knew we could build a nice house up on top of the small hill that overlooks the nearby fields and woods. Maybe even build it out of stone. Would you like that Louisa?"

Louisa was smiling as she said, "My goodness, you were planning ahead weren't you … why yes, of course, I would love a stone house in a pretty spot where we could raise our family." She was flirtatious with James now. She couldn't help herself. And she didn't care. She was going to be married to one of the most decent, kind and intelligent man she had ever met. The thought warmed her heart.

The discussion with her parents did not go as planned. Louisa was surprised by their response. Her momma was concerned with the fact that James was a slave holder. Her daddy insisted James become a member of the Methodist church prior to the wedding. "after all," he said, "if you two are gonna' raise a family and have your children baptized in the church, then, of course, James will need to become a member in good standing so that you two can be married in the meeting house by the circuit riding preacher. Ain't that so, "Jesse turned and looked at his wife for confirmation?

James stood slightly behind Louisa and was unsure of what he had just heard and how he was supposed to react to this change in attitude demonstrated by the McAfee's. Louisa was also perplexed by her parents. She thought to herself, "You two did not voice these concerns when the subject of marriage to Mr. Reed was first discussed. What has changed?" But she just stood there in the doorway with James standing quietly behind her unable to articulate her thoughts.

Finally, James spoke, "Mr. McAfee, sir, I do respectfully ask you to explain this change in attitude towards me and my proposal for the hand of your daughter in marriage. Surely, Mrs. McAfee, you knew about the servant family I hold that helps me out with the farm? And Mr. McAfee, sir, I do attend the Methodist meetings on occasion but you are quite correct, I have never officially placed my membership with them. I did not realize that would become an issue?"

Jesse quickly replied, "No, I did not realize that you were not a member of the church. Were you even baptized somewhere?"

"Daddy!" Louisa exclaimed as she found her voice. "Neither of you mentioned any concerns at all to me when Mr. Reed ...er ... James initially sought your agreement to his courtship and proposal. Now that he has formally proposed to me and I have accepted ... now ... now ... you raise these concerns." Louisa was obviously exasperated with her parents and though she tried to remain calm her emotions were beginning to overflow into this intense conversation.

The four of them became quiet simultaneously. James broke the silence by stating, "Mrs. McAfee, I can put your conscience at ease. I will sell my slaves, as you call them, to a man in Williamson County who has asked about them before."

"But James," Louisa responded, "you promised me you would never split them up." Shocked by what her future husband had just stated.

James looked solemnly at Louisa, "Yes, I made that promise and that is the promise their new owners will have to keep if the purchase is to be made."

Louisa looked at James and saw hardness in him she had not witnessed before. She wasn't quite sure if she liked this aspect of his personality but quickly realized that James was trying to do the best he could renegotiating with her parents in order to obtain their blessing on the young couple's matrimonial union.

Then James turned to Louisa's daddy, "But Mr. McAfee, I cannot betray my conscience. My parents were not the religious type. I suppose back in North Carolina, they belonged to the Presbyterian Church as all our Irish ancestors did. But it was not the subject of conversation around the supper table when I was a child in their home. I reckon I was baptized shortly after I was born but in all honesty I do not know for sure. As I said, my family was more concerned about survival then going to the meeting house. "Jesse's face was like stone and Eliza had let escape a small yet audible gasp at this latest revelation. Her daughter was going to marry a heathen. Even Louisa was surprised by this newest bit of information on James. She had never thought that he had not been baptized. She just assumed that everyone in these parts had somehow someway been baptized into the church.

The three McAfee's just looked at one another in silence. Finally, James once again spoke, "Mr. and Mrs. McAfee, I do dearly care for your daughter. I promise you both I will do my very best to be a good husband for her. .... I love her ... I always have since the first I laid my eyes upon her at the meeting house." Louisa blushed and smiled. He had not yet said he loved her to her face but here he was declaring his love for her in public to her parents.

James continued, "And I want you both to know that I consider myself a follower of the Lord Jesus Christ but I'm not sure, "James hesitated, "I can be baptized and made a member of the Methodist Church." Louisa's heart sank. Hadn't he just said that it didn't matter to him as long as she was by his side? Was that a lie? Was he just saying that to her to get her to accept his proposal of marriage?

Obviously, James caught the look of disappointment in Louisa's eyes. "Please sir, let me explain. I have been reading the teachings of Barton Stone and the Glasgow educated Campbells. I think they have a point about denominations and how divisive they can become. After all, just look at the four of us, arguing about my lack of membership in the Methodist church."

"You mean your lack of being a baptized Christian'" said Eliza with a great deal of frustration in her voice.

"With all due respect, Mrs. McAfee, I don't know if I have been baptized as an infant or not. Maybe I have and maybe I haven't. But as I have already said, I consider myself a follower of Jesus of Nazareth, the crucified and risen Savior of mankind. Ain't that what really matters?" James asked as politely as he could but there was a tinge of growing anger in his voice. He was a good and decent man. He would make Louisa a good and faithful husband. These two were raising issues that from his perspective should not matter all that much. He reckoned it would be o.k. to sell the slave family as long as their new owners promised to not split them up down the road. But this demand of theirs to join a particular denomination when he wasn't exactly convinced that there was a need for denominational titles in the kingdom of Jesus was quite frankly a step too far and he wasn't sure now if he could back down from his position or for that matter if he even wanted to. He did love Louisa. He wanted her to be his wife. But James Reed did not like to be told what he must or must not do particularly when it came to religion. He had been that way since a child and he knew he wasn't about to change at this stage in his life.

Finally, cooler heads prevailed and Eliza said, "Why don't we all just sleep on it for a night or two. Today's Friday. Why don't we all just meet up this coming Sunday at the meeting house and finish this discussion there after Mr. McAfee and I have had a chance to speak in private with our daughter." Eliz said this with a smile on her face but to Louisa it lacked sincerity. She wasn't quite sure what her momma was up to but she knew that look. It meant Eliza had come up with a plan that might keep everyone somewhat happy and allow her to marry James with the blessing of the family.

From Friday to Sunday morning seemed like an eternity to Louisa. Although she still had a few minor reservations, she was convinced James Reed was the man for her. She was filled with anticipation and excitement as the family wagon took them all the few miles to the Methodist meeting house. The structure wasn't much to look at but it was functional. It kept the congregation dry when it rained and warm during the cooler winter weather. The long-term plans were for a brick or stone structure that would stand the test of time but until that day arrived this simple wooden building would have to do.

Louisa saw James standing by his buggy waiting for them. They greeted one another and headed into the meeting house for the worship service. The Reverend Joseph Smith would be bringing the sermon this morning. Smith was not college educated but like many of his Methodist or Baptist clergy he had "heard the call" from God and responded accordingly. James thought he was acceptable as a public speaker but he didn't always agree with the man's unique interpretation of certain scriptural passages. The service was lengthy as usual but finally it ended and everyone headed outside to the wooden tables that served the purpose of holding everyone's dish they had come to pass. The group ate family style with everyone sharing what each family had managed to bring to the service. As was the custom, certain families were known for bringing meats while others brought baked items such as biscuits and cakes. If James were truthful with himself, this was his favorite part of the Sunday gatherings. It wasn't so much the food, although it was delicious but the friendly conversation and the opportunity to catch up with the news of the surrounding community. Often the circuit rider himself would be able to present to the gathered crowd of people news he had picked up from his travels along his preaching circuit. Who had died? Who had given birth? Things of that nature.

James caught Jesse McAfee speaking to the Reverend Smith out of the corner of his eye. He didn't have long to guess the nature of their discourse as they both turned and headed straight towards him with Mrs. McAfee training behind.

Smith spoke first, "Well, James, it has come to my attention that you want to be baptized and place your membership with our fellowship here?"

James was surprised and his face showed it. Louisa had joined the group just in time to catch what the minister had said to James. "So, that's what her mamma was up to," she thought to herself, "just ambush the poor man here in public so that he had no choice but to do as he was told."

Smith continued, "Jesse here tells me you and his daughter are to be married as soon as you have been baptized and confirmed as a member of our little church here in Delina."

James looked at Jesse who was smiling and nodding his head. He was about to say something when Louisa jumped into the conversation.

"I'm afraid Reverend Smith you may be mistaken." Louisa glared at her parents. "James has made a proposal of marriage to me and I have accepted with no condition that he do anything else then be the kind and gentle man I've come to know …. and love."

Smith looked startled and more than a little embarrassed. Jesse had regained his composure and spoke directly to his daughter, "Louisa, I forbid you to marry this man unless he be baptized and join our church."

Louisa looked at her father and perhaps for the first time in her life spoke exactly what was on her mind. "No, daddy. I know you mean well. But this is my life not yours. He has asked me to marry him and I have accepted his proposal. I love you both very much. But I love this man also and I want to be his wife and God willing have his children." At which point, Eliza smiled. She knew her daughter. Once she had made up her mind, there was nothing anyone could do to stop her from doing tat which she had decided to do. She had been that way since childhood. Eliza looked at her husband and her eyes did all the speaking. Jesse suddenly became silent. He lowered his gaze to the ground and after a few minutes looked up at James and Louisa who by this time were standing side by side holding each other's hand in a tight grip.

James spoke, "Mr. McAfee please understand me that Louisa and I will continue to come to service here and I would never interfere with her decision to remain a member of the Methodist church. And who knows … perhaps God will move in my heart and I will someday join as well. But not today. Not this way." James' voice trailed off as he squeezed Louisa's hand.

Suddenly the Reverend Smith spoke, "Listen y'all. I can't marry you if you are not members of the church."

"But I can," a deep male voice sounded with clarity. Everyone turned in the direction of the voice and saw standing there, John C. Reeves, the Justice of the Peace for the whole of Lincoln County. "You two can be married at the courthouse in Fayetteville. I do weddings on Thursdays."

James looked at Louisa with a questioning look on his face. She didn't hesitate and quickly nodded her agreement.

James looked at Jesse and Eliza McAfee. They looked at their daughter and both realized that this was the happiest they had seen her in some time. Eventually, a slight smile crossed their lips and together nodded their heads in agreement.

"That's settled then," boomed the judge. "I'll see you two in my chambers on this Thursday."

Thursday, June 27th of the year 1850, James Reed and Louisa McAfee became husband and wife.

After the brief ceremony, which was only attended by Louisa's family and James' younger brother, the couple headed north to the Reed farm where the young couple would start out their lives together. The sun was shining. The sky was blue with thin wispy clouds slowly floating by. Louisa looked at her husband and snuggled close to him as he drove their buggy. Neither knew what the future would bring … the joy and the sorrow … but both knew in their hearts they would, with God's help, face it together.

Chapter Seventeen – Chickamauga Creek, Georgia, September 1863

Thomas looked around the campfire which was beginning to dwindle as the night wore on. He could see most of them. These were the men he had fought with for the past eighteen months. They had seen much and suffered much together. And tomorrow, he realized they would, once again, obey orders and follow their flag into battle. As he looked around the group he knew that for some of them, including possibly him, this might be their last night alive. When he joined the men from Hart county Georgia in March of 1862, he had no delusions about what this conflict would involve. No, the men who had joined with him that month … many of whom were friends and family, they knew what lay ahead. They weren't the first bunch to leave. That had happened the year before in 1861 shortly after the first shots were fired. Those young men, and almost all were young men, were quite convinced the war would be a savage yet short affair. His brother Obadiah's son George who was only 18 when the hostilities began immediately left his daddy's farm to fight to "protect Southern rights" as the politicians had so passionately stated. He was quickly joined by his brother Jasper who was only 17. It was like that all over the county. He reckoned it was that way all over Georgia and the rest of the South. Young innocent men filled with themselves marching off to the tunes of Dixie and Bonnie Blue Flag while crowds of young women and sobbing mothers called out their names as their column passed by on parade. He and his wife, Rebecca, were so thankful that their oldest boy, Monroe, was only 13 and too young to go off to war.

But things had not gone well for the South. And soon it became apparent to everyone with eyes to see that this war was going to drag on and on. The next year, in the spring of 1862, the notice went out that more southern men needed to come to the aid of their country. Lee's forces had been somewhat successful but they were up against a fierce opponent with seemingly unlimited resources in men and munitions. The knock-out blow on the northern capital in Washington, D.C. had not materialized. In fact, the Yankees were pushing back and pushing back hard. Kentucky had not seceded. Nashville had fallen quickly as did New Orleans. Lincoln's naval blockade was starting to have its impact felt and although most southerners would not publicly state their concerns, the bedroom conversations of many husbands and wives, father and mothers, were not nearly as optimistic. And so, he reluctantly joined the war effort. In fact, most of the able-bodied men of his county had volunteered their services that year to the Confederate States of America.

On that fateful day in early March, Thomas had joined with brothers, cousins, nephews, brothers-in-law and numerous neighbors and friends. He left behind a wife and six children, Monroe, Elias, Rachel, John Gilbert, Hannah and little Milly, only two years old. They didn't all end up in the same company but many did. Thomas and much of his family and friends were now members of Company A of the 9th Battalion, known as McMullin's Guards. John G. McMullin was their Captain and since they were mainly older men, they had been given the task of guarding southern supply lines and similar objectives. Thomas was one month shy of his 35th birthday. His older brother, Obadiah, was 38. His younger brother, Cornelius, was 28. All had left families and many, like Obadiah, had sons who had been fighting for over a year. Thomas's oldest brother, John Ashley was 43 and although he wanted to enlist was turned away due to poor health. But John Ashley had spoken to Thomas before the train had left the station. Thomas would never forget his haunting words, "Thomas, you watch after my boys. You watch after Dyar and Noel. They are young men. You watch after them and make sure they return home to their momma and me." There were tears in his eyes as he held tightly onto the hands of his younger brother. And, of course, Thomas thought to himself, "I agreed to do something I could not truly do … keep my nephews safe from harm." But he remembered the pleading look in his brother's eyes and yes, promised him he would watch over them as if they were attending some kind of church picnic where the greatest danger might be slipping into the creek or eating too much watermelon. Little did they know what the future would hold for all of them. Of course, John Ashley had told all three of his younger brothers, Obadiah, Thomas Gilbert and Cornelius, that he would check in on each of their families and do his level best to keep all safe and sound.

"That," thought Thomas, "was the last time I saw my brother." He looked up into the night sky as the sun had now completely set in the west and the stars were beginning to shine brightly. "I reckon I am as close to home as I have been since last year. I do hope Rebecca received my last letter. I haven't heard from her since we left the Cumberland Gap last summer. God, how I miss her and my children." He looked up into the air and spoke softly to whomever and whatever was out there "…Are you out there God? If you are and can find it in yourself to do so, I would appreciate you send your angels to guard over my family. Keep them from this evil that has befallen us. Thank you."

Thomas came out of a highly religious Baptist family ... he was named after his great grandfather, Thomas Gilbert, an early Baptist missionary to South Carolina and Georgia. His other great grandfather, John Cleveland, was also a Baptist preacher, whose son, John married Comfort Gilbert who gave birth to Reuben, Thomas's daddy. But Thomas did not really consider himself particularly strong in his faith. Yes, of course, he believed in God. He reasoned that since the world existed it had to have a creator. "Things just don't materialize out of thin air, "he had often thought to himself. But after what he had witnessed since the beginning of this conflict, he had begun to have doubts as to whether God really did care what happened to people.

"We were so ignorant. I was ignorant. I thought I knew what war was like from the stories I had been told. But those old stories did not capture the reality of the horror of watching with your own eyes a man losing an arm or leg to a Minie ball or worse viewing the remains of what used to be a human being after being hit by artillery fire. ... And constantly being in the elements ... the relentless heat of summer or the freezing cold of winter. .... And the food ..." Lately his company had been eating things he would not have fed to the hogs back home.

Thomas gazed slowly around at the men who were either asleep or trying to sleep. The word had come down through the ranks that tomorrow would bring movement of their entire regiment and that could only mean one thing ... battle. So sleep was not coming to many and for those few who had managed to fall asleep it was not restful as their dreams were tormented by what they had already endured … the Battle of Perryville, way up north outside of Lexington, Kentucky, and then the scurrying back from that defeat to Murfreesboro and the Battle of Stones River. "We lost there too," thought Thomas. "In fact, "Thomas thought to himself, "this command of Bragg's hasn't secured a victory since the Cumberland Gap … and Bragg wasn't even in command at that time. He was over at Shiloh losing to Billy Yank. But somehow the man gets promoted to head up the entire Army of Tennessee." Thomas shakes his head in disbelief. It was back in May of this year, his company and other remnants from the Third Battalion were merged into Company D of the 37th Georgia Regiment, led by Lt. Colonel Joseph T. Smith. Smith took his marching orders from Colonel Anthony Rudler, who reported to Brigadier General Bates. Bates reported to Breckinridge, the former Vice President of the United States from 1856 to 1860. Breckinridge had run for the office of President in 1860 but came in third place behind Lincoln and Douglas. Now, after fleeing his home state of Kentucky, he was a field General who reported to Braxton Bragg, head of the entire CSA army of the western campaign. It was rumored that Bragg and Breckinridge could hardly stand to be in the same room together. "Nothing new there," Thomas sighed, "What do you expect, when you put all of these ex-politicians and southern slave owning planters in command. Their arrogance is enormous and they don't listen to each other. Lee, of course, was different. Now, there is a true leader of men." But by now, word had arrived of the disaster that befell the southern troops at a place called Gettysburg in Pennsylvania. The morale had quickly dropped to what appeared to Thomas as the lowest point since he joined. And then the men heard of what happened at Vicksburg … another southern loss. Which meant that Grant would be sending reinforcements to Rosecrans's northern army, the men in blue who were attempting to invade his home state of Georgia. Bragg had decided to leave Chattanooga and take a stand on the east side of this small Georgia creek called Chickamauga.

It was Friday night. All of Thomas's thoughts were of home. It was so close … only 130 miles as the crow flies. But he shook his head as if trying to clear it of those persistent thoughts of Rebecca and the children. "Why in the name of everything that is holy are we doing this?" He never shared this doubt with anyone including his brothers but he could not help what his mind produced. He was not a slave owner. In fact, neither were most of the folks in Hart County. Of course, a few families did have some field hands and one or two of the largest landholders had a substantial number of field and house servants. But was that what this war was all about? Slavery? Not if you listened to the firebrands that made up the political power of the southern states. To them, it was all about states' rights … the freedom of each state to manage its own affairs without federal interference from Washington. Yes, Thomas had heard the argument. He didn't buy into it. "After all, our great grandparents fought for freedom from England in order to govern ourselves … to make a brand-new country in this wilderness and not a multitude of separate pieces. We are one nation. We are Americans." Thomas realized this was the minority position and one that he was very careful to not voice in public. He, of course, shared his thoughts with Rebecca but only with her and not often. He had hoped and prayed that cooler heads would prevail and that a compromise of some sorts could be worked out between north and south. He was deeply disappointed when the war broke out and once again he had hoped for a quick and merciful ending. "And tonight, "he thought to himself, "Here I lie cold and hungry waiting for tomorrow's sunrise in order to take some poor soul's life or lose mine in exchange."

Thomas heard a sound behind him. It was Thornton Sanders, a distant cousin to his wife, Rebecca. Thornton had gotten out of his bedroll and walked over to the dying fire in an attempt to warm up. Thomas rose and walked over to him. Keeping his voice low as to not wake the others he said, "Can't sleep Thornton?".

"Naw … too much on my mind, I reckon," replied Thornton. "Same for you?"

"Yep. Reckon so," replied Thomas. The two men were quiet for some time. Finally, Thornton spoke, "we is close to home … ain't we?"

"Yep" Thomas answered. He knew what Thornton was thinking. They were all thinking of home.

"Wonder what the wife is doing tonight?" Thornton asked to the empty sky above him.

"Reckon she's getting your kids to bed and reading her Bible if I know your wife," replied Thomas with a slight smile on his face.

"Yep," answered Thornton, "that's exactly right. Woman knows her Bible … reads it every night afore bed."

The two men became quiet once again.

"Heard the Yanks are heading this way," stated Thornton.

"I reckon so. Guess that's why we're preparing for battle tomorrow," Thomas answered in a hushed manner.

"Wonder who will go up against this time?" asked Thornton not really caring to know.

"Doesn't matter now does it … they'll be in blue and trying to blow us to kingdom come. … and, of course, we will respond in kind." This caused both men to chuckle lightly.

"Thomas, I want to ask you somethin' and I don't want you to get angry with me." Thornton looked at the face of his fellow warrior. There was still enough light from the embers to make out Thomas's countenance.

"Go ahead, Thornton. We all might be dead tomorrow. No sense keepin' secrets now." Thomas smiled as he quietly said these words.

"Thomas, you ever think of just going home. I mean …." Thornton's voice trailed off.

"I know what you mean brother … and yes, the thought does cross my mind on occasion … but you see those two young men lying over yonder?" Thomas pointed in the general direction. He knew in this light Thornton had no idea who he was pointing to but he also knew Thornton already knew what he was about to say," I made a promise to their father that I would look after them boys … and so far, I've been able to. Things got pretty hot back up there in Murfreesboro but we got out of that alright. So … when this is over … I'm going to enjoy taking those two boys back to their daddy and keeping my promise."

"Do you reckon it's about done?" Thornton responded.

"The war that is … the men are saying with our losses at Gettysburg and Vicksburg … well, I hate to say it … but we're running out of places to run to and …." He didn't finish his thought.

"I don't know about that … I would like for it to be over … but Thornton … if we do lose … it if does come to that … what will we be going home to?" Thomas asked wistfully. Home, the very thought brought a feeling of peace to his soul. Home.

About this time, the two men were joined by John Brown, another neighbor and friend from Hart County.

"Can't sleep," said Brown in his low husky voice.

"Yep," both men replied in unison. The three sat in silence by what was now a smoking remnant of last evening's fire. Finally, Brown spoke up, "Gents, if this battle doesn't go well for us … well …. I've come to the conclusion that it's time to head home." The other two men just silently looked at their companion. John was possibly the oldest man in Company D and looked tired from the impact of months of war.

Thomas was the first to respond, "John, you know you just can't walk on out of here without permission … and anyway … what would the rest of us do here without your funny stories to lift our spirits." John was the eldest and often played harmless pranks on the rest of the men trying to elevate their depressed moods. It often worked and he was well liked by the men. John chuckled … "well … I reckon you're right about that … I couldn't just up and leave you fellas now could I." Then the smile quickly left John's face and the two men to whom he was speaking suddenly realized that John was serious.

Thornton leaned in close to his friend and said, "Johnny … keep those thoughts to yourself. No sense getting the boys all riled up for nothin'". Finally, Thomas broke the tension and said … "Listen brother … none of us is sure what tomorrow will bring … reckon we better try and get some sleep … mornin' will be here afore you know it." And with that the little group of three broke up and headed to their bedrolls.

Saturday morning came with the loud blaring of bugles calling the men to marching formation. They were on the move. Thomas quickly gathered up his meager supplies, grabbed his Springfield rifled musket, and checked his pouch for ammunition and seeing that everything was in order quickly scampered down the hill to the dusty road the men would be marching on that day.

The weather had turned bitterly cold during the night. The ground was covered with frost. The breath of each man was visible in the early morning light. Thomas stood in his appointed spot in the column as they prepared to march north and west to the battleground. He could already hear the cannons in the distance. His nephew Dyar stood next to him with Noel, the other nephew, behind them in the next row back. The column had started its forward motion. Dyar spoke first, "Well, Uncle Thomas, do you reckon we'll see some action today? Those guns sound pretty far away … don't know if we're marching toward them or is this flanking move?"

"Reckon we'll find out soon enough son," Thomas said as he looked at his nephew through squinted eyes. The sun was just then rising over the mountains to the east and Thomas was looking directly into it. They marched on in silence for a while. Each man lost in his own thoughts. Thomas thought about his two nephews. He had stayed fairly close to them throughout this campaign. They had fought together in numerous battles from eastern Tennessee north into Kentucky and then retreating to Nashville, Chattanooga and finally back here in northwestern Georgia. And they were still alive and well. Noel had recently developed a persistent cough but so had half the men in the regiment. There wasn't much Thomas could do about an infection but he had on more than one occasion shot at and hopefully hit Yankee soldiers who had ventured too near his family. By now, the boys had caught on that when a skirmish broke out they could count on their Uncle Thomas to be close by firing away his Springfield as fast as he could reload. And Thomas, like most of the men in his outfit, was a pretty good shot. They had all grown up with a shotgun or Kentucky long rifle in their hands used to put wild game on the dinner table. Sometimes, however, the smoke of the battle became so thick no one could really see what was ahead of them. At those times, the men relied on the commands of their officers and, of course their own battle hardened intuition. So far, it had kept Thomas and the other Clevelands safe. But Thomas had a funny feeling about today.

As they marched north and up Lafayette road, Thomas could hear the distant booming sound of cannons and soon could see the smoke billowing up from the battleground. It was a strange experience. He heard the cannon and saw the smoke and then suddenly he could hear rifle fire and the yells and screams of men falling in battle. There was no mistaking the so called "rebel yell" of the southern troops as they rushed headlong into the fray. To so many on the Confederate side, it was inspiring, urging the men on to victory. To the northerners however, it could be terrifying for they had learned that the yell preceded a massive onslaught of troops against their ranks. But to Thomas the yell was neither inspiring nor terrifying … it was a sad reminder of the death and devastation that was about to happen to hundreds if not thousands of those caught in the middle of this conflict. Yes, of course, he was proud of the courage displayed by his comrades and deeply moved. But that yell and the accompanying bugle and shouted commands of the officers in charge always caused Thomas to reflect on his predicament. The doubt in his mind had started slowly years ago when anger and resentment had begun to build between northern and southern states. But then Georgia, his native state, had decided early on to join the Confederacy and secede from the Union and Thomas managed to dampen down his doubt about the cause. And then it had become his turn to join in the conflict and the doubt came roaring back into his mind and this time would not lessen. In fact, with each battle, and the horrific sights and sounds that he experienced with each of them, the doubt began to grow. By this time, after news of Gettysburg and Vicksburg … after hearing of the deaths of his wife's brothers and the wounding and capture of many of his neighbors and distant relatives … now … the doubt was inescapable. "Why are we doing this to ourselves?" the doubt would question. "When will this madness cease?" it continued. "There is no glory in any of this … just the stench of death and the heartbreak of loss," the doubt answered its own question. But still Thomas marched on. He had made a promise to his older brother and with the help of God he intended to keep it or die in the trying. So he marched on. And soon the dreaded orders came … lines assembled face to face against the enemy … march forward … double time and then finally … charge into the very gates of hell. It was at this very moment during the battle that Thomas no longer thought as a human thought. He had become an animal … a ferocious trapped animal fighting for his very survival. There was no past. There was no future. There was only now. It seemed to Thomas that time had stopped or perhaps just disappeared. Everything seemed to move in slow motion. He heard the yells of the men around him. He heard the whiz of bullets as they smashed into the ground around him or flew close to his hatted head or worse yet smacked into the bodies of his fellow warriors. The lines of blue and gray and tangled together and yet Thomas could somehow stay close to his nephews. The three fought on. Then the bugle sounded retreat and the men on both sides quickly broke and ran for cover behind the assembled lines which were already preparing for the next engagement.

Thomas fought to catch his breath and regain what little energy he had left after the exhausting initial encounter with the enemy. "Noel … you all right son?" Thomas asked the young man who was kneeling in the red north Georgian clay. Noel nodded his head yes. He had no energy left to speak. "Dyar … how 'bout you?" Thomas checked on the other nephew as a mother hen might review her chicks after the fox had raided the henhouse. "Yep, Uncle Thomas," came the reply, "I'm just fine and dandy. I think I might have got a couple of em." Dyar replied with a half-smile on his soot covered face.

Noel answered, "you sure did brother … I seen em fall … sure as I'm standin' here … you got at least two of em … What about you Uncle Thomas … kill any of those Billy Yanks?"

Thomas looked at his two charges. "Reckon so … don't remember if I did or not … don't really matter now does it …. We got some of theirs and they got some of ours and tomorrow … why we'll just march to another God forsaken field and do it all over again … now won't we." Thomas tried not to let the bitterness overwhelm him. These young men didn't need to see that side of him. It did them no good.

Noel looked at his Uncle. He had realized months ago, that most of the men shared the idea that the South had already lost this war and it was just a matter of time before it ended and they all got to go home. "Assuming they lived long enough, "Noel thought to himself. But Noel had not realized the depth of frustration and despondence his Uncle was feeling. Noel had come to depend on Thomas strength and wisdom. He was a lot like his daddy back home and he guessed if the truth be told Noel perceived Thomas as a stand-in father for him and his brother while on the battlefield and in the camps they had established throughout the western campaign of the war.

During this break in the fighting both sides rested as much as they could. Each gathered their wounded and attempted as best they could to soothe the pain and agony of their fallen comrades. Thomas had decided soon after his first battle experience he would rather take a Minie ball between the eyes and be dead before he hit the ground then be wounded and have to endure the agonizing pain of the field surgeon's amputation of limb or the slow death associated with blood loss from an untreatable stomach wound. He had seen many go to God in this way and it was not a way he wanted to leave this world.

The sun was beginning its descent into the western sky and the shadows were getting long. Everyone who had survived the day's conflict were convinced they would be able to pitch their tents and rest the night but that was not to be the case. Soon orders came and the entire regiment fell into a marching column heading north. Thomas soon figured it out. "We're going to try to outflank the Yankees left side. We'll march as far as we have to this evening and then tomorrow at dawn we'll attack them from the north with everything old Bragg can throw at em," Thomas reasoned in his mind. "No rest tonight, "he thought sadly, as he checked over his two nephews once again.

Their regiment along with the rest of Breckinridge's command marched north until they represented the farthest right wing of Bragg's entire army. Thomas had guessed correctly. They were going to attempt to swing around the left flank of the Yankees and catch them in a squeeze between Breckinridge to the north and Longstreet to the south. Longstreet's division had just arrived from Lee's Army of Northern Virginia. Longstreet's men were battle tested and ready to avenge their loss at Gettysburg.

Orders came down the ranks for the columns to rest but be prepared for battle with the rising of the morning sun. Thomas, Dyar and Noel found a giant oak tree a few yards off the dusty road and quickly rolled out their blankets and soon the two young men were sound asleep. Yet for Thomas sleep was, once again, elusive.

It had been around one hour when he finally gave up the battle and stood up. He walked away from the other sleeping men and found an old tree stump to sit upon. He took out his pipe and lit what remained of his tobacco. He had been keeping this last bit for what seemed to him an eternity but in reality it had only been about a month since his last smoke. Tobacco had become difficult to obtain as the war drug on and most of the men had either given up entirely or made do with whatever they could get to light up in their pipes. But Thomas had saved his last few ounces of crushed black leaves. He thought to himself, "tomorrow's battle might be my last … I might as well smoke what's left." And with that lit the last match and held it to the bowl. The dried leaves quickly caught fire and Thomas puffed deeply and fully. It was quiet. After the excessive noise of the day's battle, the quiet was extreme. He thought for a moment that he heard singing coming from somewhere across the open field. "Yep, that's a Yankee singin' an old Baptist hymn, It Is Well with My Soul." Thomas knew the song well. He quietly joined in adding the bass echo to the Yank's tenor during the chorus … It is well (tenor) … It is well (bass) … With my soul (tenor) … With my soul (bass) … It is well (together) … It is well (together) … With ….my soul (together). Silence… Then a voice yelled across the field, "well done, Johnny Reb". Thomas didn't yell back … he didn't want to wake the boys. He felt a smile appear on his face. He thought to himself, "I wish it were true … I wish it was well with my soul. But it ain't. It ain't well and tomorrow this peace will be destroyed once again by the sounds of cannons, guns and the screams of dying men." Thomas was mired in a deep melancholy state of being. He felt abandoned … lost … alone … and scared. Then he thought he heard his name "Thomas …. Thomas," the voice called out to him. But it wasn't originating within the campground and it certainly wasn't coming from the Yankee side of the field. It seemed to be coming from slightly above and to his right. He gazed up and over his right shoulder. What he saw caused his mouth to fall open dropping the still lit pipe to the ground. There shimmering in a grayish white light was some type of being hovering over the ground suspended about three feet above the dirt of the field. Thomas could not tell if it was human. It looked somewhat like a man but also had the soft gentle features of a woman. And the voice was unearthly, not the natural sound a man or woman would make. Thomas immediately sensed he was in the presence of something spectacular … something not from this world … and something holy. Thomas fell to his knees and placed his face on the ground. He could not look upon this creature. He finally geared up his courage and spoke, "Who are you? … What are you? …". The apparition spoke once again softly and gently, "Thomas … Thomas … Do not be afraid and do not bow down before me. Stand in my presence child of the dust. I am a messenger sent by the Holy One."

Thomas stood. "What is your name?" Thomas asked.

The messenger replied, "I am unable to speak my name in your presence. It is holy and given to me by the Holy One. You are a child of the dust, born of woman, and filled with decay and corruption. Should I speak my name, it would take your life. And … I have not come for you yet. It is not your time."

Thomas was awe stricken and could not speak. He once again dropped to his knees and fell face down upon the red Georgian clay.

The being spoke again, "Thomas, arise and stand before me. Hear my words. You are to worship only the Holy One and not me. I am his messenger. You will not die tomorrow Thomas. The battle will be difficult. Many will suffer. You will suffer. But your life will be spared."

Thomas had stood once again. He could not look directly into the face of the being. The light was simply too bright. With head down and eyes cast aside he managed to ask in a hoarse voice, "What of my nephews? Will they be alright?"

The being responded, "I do not know the future. Only the Holy One and the Lamb who sits on the throne of judgement waiting for the call to return knows all. I am just a messenger and can only say to you the message I was given. But I can tell you this … all will suffer tomorrow. Many will die but not you."

Thomas replied, "Why tell me this? What am I supposed to do with this information?" Thomas had recovered somewhat from his initial shock. He was now puzzled. "Why me," he wondered.

It was as if the being could read his thoughts because as soon as the question entered his mind, the messenger responded, "because the Lord Jesus has a message for you … this message is for you and for those who will listen to you."

Thomas regained his composure and now simply waited in silence. He still could not look directly at this mysterious creature and yet, was drawn to him. He could not look away.

The being spoke once again, "Thomas … Thomas … I have been sent by the Lord Jesus, the Lamb of God, to say this to you. Are you ready, child of the dirt who is born of woman? Are you ready to hear this message?"

Thomas nodded and said softly, "I am."

The messenger began, "I am the alpha and the omega, the beginning and the end. Before there was time I was and after time ceases to exist, I will be. I am who I am. I wait now for the final day of judgement. I do not know the time of that day, only my Father knows but, hear me … man born of woman … I am sickened by the violence that has inhabited the earth. Everywhere I look I see destruction, decay and death brought upon man by his fellow man. This breaks my heart. I was there when my father spoke to Noah, a blameless man born of woman. My father's heart was broken by the violence of the men and women he had made. I was sent to the Earth to teach you once again of my Father and His love for all of you. And yet, you did not listen. And now … look upon what you men born of women have done to one another."

At this moment, a small circle appeared next to the heavenly messenger, the angelic being motioned for Thomas to come closer and to look into the floating ball. Thomas did as he was told and immediately wished he had not. For it was as if Thomas was in heaven looking down upon all the earth at the same time seeing all of mankind simultaneously. He watched as thousands, perhaps millions of men and women committed horrific acts of violence to one another and to their children. It was heart wrenching and made him sick to his stomach. Thomas thought to himself, "I am seeing what Jesus sees when he looks upon us."

Immediately the being responded, "Yes, Thomas, that is what the Lord Jesus views when he gazes upon the workings of the children of the dirt born of women. And yes, it breaks his heart. And yes, he cries."

Thomas felt the tears form and drop upon his cheeks. This was too much for him to bear. To witness before him all the sins of all the people who had ever lived or who would ever live. Thomas sobbed.

Finally, the tears subsided. The angel spoke, "Thomas, Jesus loves you. This I know, for he has told me so. That is your message. Go and tell all who will listen that Jesus loves. That is your message. Thomas, you will survive this war. Go and tell all others who also survive that Jesus loves and, that you are to love one another even as he loves all of you. Look now Thomas into the ball …"

Thomas was reluctant. What he had just seen was still vividly imprinted in his mind and would perhaps stay with him for the rest of his days. And yet, the messenger beckoned him once again and Thomas could not resist. He looked. This time he saw a different world. He saw people smiling and holding hands with one another. They were singing a song of praise to God and to His son, the Lamb of God who had taken away the sins of the world. The people were from all over the earth. They wore different clothes. They were different in skin color and spoke in thousands of different languages. Yet, Thomas understood it all. It was the same song of praise sung over and over again. Thanking God for the sacrifice of the Lamb that had cleansed the earth once and for all from all decay, destruction and death. Thomas looked all over the earth and could not find one tear on the face of one person, man, woman or child. For God had come amongst His people. He had removed all their sorrows and there was no more death or sorrow or crying or pain. For the old world and its evils were gone forever.

Thomas looked into the face of the messenger who was smiling. The brightness of the smile shone like a noonday sun. Thomas nodded his head and whispered, "thank you."

And as quickly as it had appeared, the vision disappeared and the darkness of night returned to the farmer's field upon which the next day's battle would soon commence with the rising of the morning son.

"Uncle Thomas … Uncle Thomas … Wake up. Can't you hear the bugles blowin'?" Dyar was shouting at him and shaking his shoulder attempting to wake Thomas from his deep sleep. He was confused and disoriented. He arose from his bedroll. His body was stiff and sore. He thought to himself, "I'm too old for sleeping on the ground like this." And then suddenly, Thomas remembered the visitation from the messenger. He blurted out, "boys, you would not believe …" and then he stopped himself. "That's just it ain't it … no one is gonna believe me … absolutely no one … not even Rebecca." Noel turned and looked at his Uncle, "Did you say something to me Uncle Thomas?" he asked.

Thomas started to respond and then just said, "Naw … just stretching out my old bones. Come on let's get in line. The column is starting to head out. Y'all ready for today's fightin'?"

"Yes sir," they spoke in unison. "Ready as we'll ever be, I reckon, "added Dyar. Thomas thought to himself, "Today is Sunday … the Lord's Day." And then looked up into the sky hoping he would once again see the mysterious being he had seen the evening before. Yet, all he saw was the blue sky, bright yellow sun and clouds that had started to form in the west. "Looks like it might rain," Thomas said to no one in particular.

Noel glanced upwards, "Yep, looks like we're fixin' to get wet." At which point there was a bright bolt of lightning followed by a huge clap of thunder. No one in the column even flinched. They had grown so accustomed to hearing the roar of cannon that the noise produced by Mother Nature paled in contrast.

Suddenly, the column was moving at double time and turning to the west. Thomas thought to himself, "here we go … Lord be with us all." At the moment he had finished his small prayer he heard the first cannon shot. It was from their side and was heading west to inflict its devastation upon the northern troops gathered in front of his column.

Historians would later write the fighting on that stormy Sunday was the bloodiest in the western arena of the American Civil War. And the 37th Georgia regiment was right in the middle of the mayhem. In fact, on that one day, the 37th lost over 50% of its men. Bragg had used the combined regiments of Breckinridge to outflank the northern Army of the Cumberland with deadly effect. The Union forces eventually collapsed under the coordinated southern attack and fled in retreat to the safety of Chattanooga.

It was now evening and Thomas sat before a campfire cooking what was left of his daily ration of beans. He looked at his men. They had fought bravely that day. Many had been wounded and many of them had died on the field of battle. Thomas would not forget the sights and sounds of Chickamauga for the rest of his days. One image, in particular, he could simply not shake from his memory.

It had been towards the late afternoon. The Yanks were retreating running for their lives with Thomas and the rest of the 37th in hot pursuit. He and Noel had chased down one of the Yankee soldiers and had cornered him against a tree. Noel had told him to throw down his weapon and surrender. It looked initially like that is what the young warrior was going to do and then suddenly he removed a pistol hidden from his belt and pointed it directly at Noel. Thomas reacted in an instant but the Yankee soldier had managed to discharge his weapon before Thomas fired and killed the man. Noel had been hit. It was just a flesh wound but it was the first-time

Thomas had been unable to protect his nephew. Thomas had walked over to the dead Yankee soldier and upon close inspection realized he was just a boy of 16 or 17. The Minie ball from Thomas had hit the boy in the heart instantly causing death. Thomas bent down and searched his pockets looking for tobacco or any other item that he and his men might find of value. He pulled out of his breast pocket a small book. He looked at it closely. Tears formed in Thomas' eyes and then slowly ran down into his cheeks and into his greying beard. It was a Bible. "The boy was carrying a Bible," Thomas said out loud although Noel did not hear him as he was tending to his wound. And in a moment, Thomas realized the stupidity of it all. He didn't know this boy. He didn't know anything about him except that he had tried to kill his nephew and Thomas had taken his life in exchange. Thomas knew this boy had a momma at home and maybe a daddy as well if he wasn't somewhere out there fighting for his own life. Thomas had killed men before in battle. He had known the sickening experience of knowing in his heart that some poor momma would never again get to see her boy alive and he was the reason. But this death was different. Perhaps it was the experience of the night before or maybe just the cumulative effect of so much pain and sorrow but something had changed in Thomas. He didn't think he could keep on doing this. He was so tired of the fighting. He missed his wife and children so much the thought nearly drove him mad. And now he had taken the life of a young man who was about the age of one of his boys back home. Thomas dropped to his knees and buried his face in the ground. "Oh Lord … what am I to do? Lord … I plead with you … deliver me from this insanity.

Forgive me of the sins I have committed against man and you, oh holy one…. Please … please … forgive me."

By this time, Noel had managed to stop the bleeding from his shoulder. He walked over to where his Uncle lay on the ground face down in the rain soaked dirt. He could hear him talking but could not make out the words. He gently placed his hand on his Uncle's shoulder and said, "Uncle Thomas, are you alright? I have been hit but I think the bleeding has stopped. Reckon we better head back. The bugler is blowing for us to assemble. This one is over. We won Uncle Thomas … we won."

At this exact moment in time, a rifle cracked in the distance and Noel immediately fell to the ground. One of the retreating Yankee soldiers had turned and spotted Thomas and Noel. He knew it was a long shot but out of sheer frustration raised his weapon to his shoulder and squeezed the trigger. He did not live long enough to see the Mini ball impact the back of Noel for an officer of the 37th on horseback cut him down with a drawn sword.

Noel's body fell on top of his prostrate Uncle. Thomas yelled but Noel was unconscious. Thomas quickly moved into action and swooped Noel into his arms. He started to walk and then run back to the forming infantry column all the while screaming for medical attention for his fallen nephew. He carried Noel for almost a quarter of a mile and finally in a state of utter exhaustion dropped him at the feet of the regimental physician.

The doctor quickly ordered two other men to pick Noel up and carry him to the back of the wagon that was then serving as a temporary field hospital. Thomas kept pleading with the doctor to tend to his nephew but the man was overwhelmed with the crying and screaming of the dying all around him. Suddenly he turned to Thomas and said, "Listen to me old man … this boy ain't gonna make it. The hole in him is just too big to mend … and even if I did stich it up … he would probably die of gangrene once the wound became infected … let go of my arm …you old fool … can't you see …I've got others here to tend to that just might survive … but," looking at Noel's pale face while shaking his head sadly, "I'm afraid there's nothing to be done for the boy." The doctor then moved on. Thomas stared after him in disbelief. He would not accept it. No, he could not. He had made a promise to his brother. He would look after these two as if they were his own.

Thomas picked up Noel's body. He could feel life was still within him but slowly draining away. He carried him another half mile or so back to the rear of the encampment. He saw Captain McMullin lying on the ground, alive but wounded. He carried Noel's body and gently set it down besides the Captain who was conscious and still giving out orders.

McMullin spoke first, "Cleveland, what are you doing here? And who is this you've dropped at my feet?" And then just as soon as he spoke he saw Noel's face and quickly realized what had transpired. He continued, "Alright Thomas, I'll get one of the other doctors to tend to him. Rest easy, we'll get your nephew fixed up good as new." Doubting every word of what he had just said he motioned for his second in command to go and fetch another doctor to tend to Noel's wounds.

Soon Noel was on a wagon heading for the military hospital in Rome, Georgia. Thomas had requested to ride along with him but the request was politely but firmly denied by the Captain. Thomas was upset but he saluted and went to find Dyar. He quickly found his other nephew and explained what had happened. Dyar wanted to immediately steal a horse and ride to Rome but Thomas would not let him. Finally, Dyar regained his composure and the two men now sat quietly close to the cooking fire which also served as a source of heat for the autumn night had turned cold after the passage of the storm.

The two did not speak much to each other the entire evening. Eventually, it became time to sleep. Thomas unrolled his blanket and laid it out upon the ground. He was exhausted and soon fell soundly asleep. That night, Thomas dreamt of home. He could see the gentle rolling hills of his farm back in Hart County. He saw his wife and children. It was obvious from their appearance they were struggling to survive. They were hungry. They were sad. In his dream, he saw his family sitting around the kitchen table. There was not much food on it. He saw them bow their heads in prayer. He heard them ask God to watch over him and to bring him back soon from the war. Thomas could take no more of this dream and suddenly found himself awake with tears in his eyes and heaviness in his heart. The sun had not yet come up and the moon was shining in the autumn sky. Thomas thought, "This is madness. Yes, we won this battle but the North will send more and more troupes. They will continue to pound away at us until there is nothing left. And I must check on my nephew. I promised my brother I would look after him. I can't do that from here. I'm going to speak with the Captain once again. Perhaps he'll let me just go to Rome for a short while if I promise to return to the camp?" And with that thought in his mind, Thomas lay back down upon the hard ground and soon fell asleep.

The next day, Thomas approached Captain McMullin. McMullin was in conversation with the other Captains serving under Lt. Colonel J.T. Smith. Thomas knew not to interrupt these men until they had finished their discussion. He was far enough away that he could not exactly make out what they were saying to each other but it was obvious from their appearance that they were all rather upset with something. Thomas caught bits and pieces of the conversation as the air shift and brought their words closer to his ears … "should have pressed on" …. "Bragg should be relieved of command" … "we had the Yankees on the run and didn't press our advantage" … and so on. "So," Thomas thought, "that is what's going on." He turned and began to walk away when he heard Captain McMullin call out his name.

"Cleveland," McMullin barked, "why are you up here and not down with your men?"

Thomas wheeled around and promptly saluted. "Just wanted a minute of your time sir but I can see you are busy right now."

"Well man, you've got my attention," continued McMullin, obviously in a foul mood. "What do you want?"

Thomas saluted once again and looked his commanding officer in the eyes, man to man. "I need sir, to go to Rome to check on my nephew. I won't be long …"

"Nonsense, "the Captain cut him off curtly. "Permission denied. Orders have just come down from on high. Grant is moving his entire command to Chattanooga. He is bringing in huge numbers of reinforcements from western Tennessee and Nashville. Bragg thinks he is planning on a full-scale invasion of

Georgia and the general says we must stop him here. So … "the Captain's voice softened somewhat," I'm afraid you will have to stay with your unit until we beat Grant and the Yankees once and for all … Listen Thomas, "the use of Thomas's first name shocked him," I know you care deeply about your family. We all do. There is not a man in the 37th whom doesn't have a brother, son or cousin fighting right alongside of himself. I just can't spare a man. I need you Thomas. You are going to have to trust that Noel will get good care back in Rome. Goodness man, your nephew will survive and go home a war hero. Now get back to your group."

Thomas looked dejected but he managed a salute and mumbled, "Yes sir" and then turned to walk away.

McMullin spoke up once again, "Cleveland, if things go well at Chattanooga … well … then you'll have my permission to check on your nephew at Rome. How does that sound?" McMullin was now smiling.

"Yes sir, that sound's fantastic. Thank you, sir. Thank you." Thomas beamed. Thomas thought, "beat the Grant and his blue bellies and then check on Noel. Who knows … if we stop them here, maybe Grant will think twice about invading Georgia and we'll all get to finally go home." The thought was almost more than Thomas could bear. He missed his wife and children so much. The mail had a difficult time finding them due to their constant movement but Thomas had received one letter from Rebecca and he cherished it. He read and reread it every evening. It wasn't anything special. Rachel was a plain-speaking woman. But it was from her. Her hand had touched the paper the words were written on and every time Thomas touched that paper he imagined he was once again holding his beloved's hand.

The next two months the 37th and all the rest of Bragg's Army of Tennessee were constantly involved in movement and battles as they attempted to retake Chattanooga and move on to Nashville. But Grant was a formidable force and would not under any circumstances release any ground his men had won. After Bragg's victory at Chickamauga, confidence returned to the CSA forces and they set out to liberate Tennessee from the invading Yankee army but to no avail. They were defeated on October 28th and 29th at Wauhatchie. They lost on November 24th at Lookout Mountain and suffered a disastrous defeat at Missionary Ridge on November 25th. The 37th had tremendous losses at Missionary Ridge and though Thomas and his nephew Dyar survived the heated battle, Thomas's brother Cornelius had been captured and sent north to a Yankee prison. This was a tragic event for both Thomas and his nephew Dyar and greatly disturbed both men. In addition, Thomas suffered a great loss with the death of Captain McMullin who was replaced by Captain W.M. Clark, a no-nonsense military man who for some unknown reason had a particular dislike for the Cleveland family.

Bragg's army was in full retreat and the southern artillery made that possible through brilliant tactics which allowed most of Bragg's army to escape through the Ringgold mountain pass that led into northwestern Georgia. Bragg was going to move his army back to Atlanta and put up a major defense there against the encroaching northern army.

It was early December. Winter had finally arrived. Snow was gently falling. Thomas and the few survivors of the past few months' battles were like walking ghosts. Their frail bodies were skeletal. They were spent from the exhaustion of war. Their spirits had been crushed by the series of defeats at the hands of Grant's relentless pursuit. And now, it looked to all that Grant's Army was now firmly established in Georgia and would be unstoppable. Men were dying of sickness. Desertions were a daily affair. Men would wake up in the morning and see that the man they had shared a warm fire with the night before had just vanished into the wilderness. No one said it out loud but everyone knew what was on everyone's mind … "Go home … protect your family and farm from this invading Yankee swarm … go home". Yes, even Thomas had these thoughts. But he had made a promise to his brother and he was going to keep that promise. When he had approached Captain Clark about seeking permission to go to Rome and check on Noel's health the request was denied. Clark did not care what McMullin had promised Thomas. As Clark stated in clear to understand language, "Listen Cleveland, Captain McMullin is dead and whatever promises he made to any of you died with him. I'm the Captain now and no one is allowed to go anywhere until we stop these Yankees. Do you understand private?" asked Captain Clark menacingly. It seemed to Thomas that Clark would use any excuse to bring him up on charges and perhaps even have him shot if need be, although that really wasn't happening now as much as it had during the beginning of the war. Even the officers knew the war was in its final days. If the Yankees took Atlanta, there would be nothing stopping them from marching all the way to the sea destroying everything in their paths including the farms and plantations of the men and boys now left here to defend them. Munitions were running low. Food supplies were almost non-existent. And it was cold.

It was Christmas Eve. There had been a break in the fighting. No one really knew why. But the remaining men of the 37th were grateful. Dyar and Thomas were sitting on a fallen log of a large pine in front of a small fire. Yankee snipers were across the valley and the men had to be wary of illuminating the area where they had gathered. Dyar looked at his Uncle and spoke, "Uncle Thomas, you don't look so good. Are you sick?"

Thomas replied, "Yes, Dyar, I'm sick. I'm sick of this war. I'm sick of the cold. I'm sick of being hungry all the time. I'm sick of wondering if the next minute some sniper is going to finish me off. I'm sick of it all. … Dyar, I'm ready to go home, son … to go home."

Dyar looked at his Uncle and then leaned into him and whispered, "Then let's go home."

Thomas looked at his nephew. The war had changed the boy. He was now a hardened veteran of some of the fiercest fighting anyone had endured in the history of warfare. And he was done … finished.

"We can't leave Noel in Rome. I can't leave him. I made a promise to your Daddy …" Thomas replied but Dyar cut him off, "yes sir, I know all about the promise … we all know about the promise … and Uncle, I know you are a man of your word … but don't you reckon Noel's dead … Surely, by now, if he wasn't dead, they would have patched him up and sent him back here to fight on?"

Thomas rubbed his long filthy beard. It had been quite a few weeks since any of them had bathed. He was silent for a long time. Finally, he shook his head and said, "No Dyar … I'm sorry … but I can't go home and face my brother without knowing what has happened to his boy … I just can't."

"Then … let's run off to Rome. Surely, we'll either find him there fit as a fiddle or … they'll point us to his grave. One way or the other, we'll know his fate and then we can go on home. Our kinfolk are gonna needs us for protection against them Yankee invaders. God only knows what these blue bellies will do once they get inside Georgia. Think of Aunt Rachel. Think of my momma and our sisters. Defenseless against Grant's men and …. freed slaves." The last statement brought a chill to Thomas' spine. This was the unspoken but universal fear amongst all southern white men, planter or not … revenge by the slaves for hundreds of years of suffering and sorrow. Thomas and the others of the 37th had been shocked the first time they saw black men in the blue uniforms. It had been at Stones River in the battle for Nashville.

"Alright Dyar … we wait for a couple of hours until most of the boys are asleep and then we'll head out … but … if we find that your brother is doing alright … we return to duty."

"What," exclaimed Dyar, "you must be out of your mind, old man; if we run off without permission … they'll shoot us on sight if we return."

"That's the only way I will agree to this plan, son. If Noel is good to fight again, we'll bring him back to the Regiment. They won't shoot us for returning another healthy soldier. Yes, we might get a good sermon preached at us and maybe even a lash or two but if we come back with your healthy brother … I reckon our misdeed will soon be forgotten … as soon as the shootin' starts up again …. Do we have an agreement?" Thomas waited on his nephew's reply.

Dyar stroked his scraggly beard and then quickly nodded his head. That night they left the camp without permission. Thomas wanted to write a note of explanation but Dyar talked him out if it. Breckinridge's men had been camped outside Calhoun, Georgia. They were in retreat from Dalton on the road back to Atlanta. Rome was only 20 or so miles from the campsite. Dyar and Thomas walked nonstop and arrived late in the evening of the next day. The town was not what they were expecting. There was no actual hospital. The Confederates had simply decided to send their wounded to the town and then utilized whatever available structure to serve as a makeshift hospital. Dyar and Thomas decided to spit up in order to search more the various locations more efficiently. They agreed to meet at the eastern edge of the town in two hours. It was Christmas Day.

It was Thomas who first found Noel. He was in what used to be the town's only school but had been turned into a building overflowing with severely wounded and dying Confederate soldiers. Noel was lying flat on his back with his eyes closed. He looked dead. Thomas slowly walked up to his bedside and whispered his name. Noel opened his eyes. He tried to talk but his throat was so parched from lack of water that at first the words would not materialize. Thomas gave his nephew some water from his canteen.

"Uncle Thomas, "Noel spoke in a slow and halting manner as if each breath was a challenge. By this time in the war, Thomas had seen plenty of men in their dying moments and Noel looked as if he would soon leave be one of those.

"Hush son … save your energy," Thomas urged his nephew while gently patting his shoulder. "I've come to take you home; boy … You're going home." Tears had filed Thomas's eyes but he managed to keep his voice under control as he fought back his emotional response.

"Uncle Thomas … is it over … is the war over?" Noel replied.

Thomas looked solemnly at the young man. He said, "It is for us Noel. The Yankees have beaten us badly at Chattanooga and Bragg is moving his troops back to Atlanta for the winter. He is going to try and hold them there."

"Uncle … why is you here?" asked Noel.

"Like I said … to take you home," replied Thomas.

"Uncle Thomas … I ain't goin' anywhere … 'cept maybe to God … and soon …" replied Noel, "My wound never healed. It's infected. Doc says I got maybe three or four more days … tops. Besides the Minie ball tore up my back … Can't feel anything from the waist down … Ain't no use to goin' home now … worthless on the farm." Noel's breath was shallow and intermittent. The color was leaving his face. Thomas knew he was watching his nephew die.

Suddenly Noel's eyes lit up. "Uncle … I had a dream … or maybe I died … don't know which … listen to me … I left my body somehow … travelled down this long lonely tunnel … then … all of a sudden … I was standing again …I was on the shore of some sea … I was lookin' out towards the water and saw a boat … strangest looking thing I ever did see … had a funny shaped front and back … curved … with the face of what looked like a dragon carved into the front of the wood … had one sail in the middle … and men were at the oars rowin' and pullin' as hard as they could … there was this one fella … he stood at the front of the boat .. He saw me standin' on the shore ... he waved to me ... yelled out something but I couldn't understand his language ... and then mysteriously I understood ... said his name was Thorkil .... Thorkil ... told me to "have faith" ... yes, sir, I know it sounds unbelievable but that's exactly what happened ... and then suddenly I was taken away from that place ... up into the air and the next thing I knew I was standin' outside this beautiful huge church or I reckon what you might call a cathedral ... I was in the front yard of this massive old stone structure ... standin' in front of me holdin' hands ... was a man and his woman ... I assume they was husband and wife ... said their names were Robert and Ann ... spoke to me in what I reckon was some form of English ... at first ... I didn't understand them ... and then once again ...just like the first vision or dream or whatever it was ... I could clearly make out what they were sayin' to me ... told me to "have hope" ... and then ...poof ... they were gone and I was standin' at a busy wharf ... lookin' at this large sailing ship filled to the rim with people and goods ... there was two men standin' there lookin' at me ... They spoke to me and this time I figured out right quick what they were sayin' ... Said they were father and son ... said their names were John ... he was the older man and Alexander ... his son ... they both said the same thing at the same exact time ... told me "to love" and then ..." Noel was fading fast. Thomas could barely make out what he was saying. But somehow he found the energy to continue to speak, "Then Uncle Thomas I was back home ... but it wasn't the farm ... it was wilderness ... like how it must have been in the early days when our people came there ... Uncle Thomas ... I saw the Reverend John ... I know it's hard to believe ... but I did ... I swear I did ... and he says to me ...

"Noel … love is the greatest of these three" … and then he said … "Soon … soon … you will join us … tell your Uncle Thomas when he comes to let love be his guide in all things" … and that was the end of it … and now …," Noel opened his eyes and looked into the crying eyes of his beloved Uncle Thomas ,"you're here … and I reckon I'm supposed to tell you what was told to me … let love be your guide in all things .." and with those final words Noel Cleveland breathed his last.

Thomas stood there holding the lifeless hands of his young nephew. He sobbed. He tried but could not stop the tears. Finally, he regained his composure. At that exact moment, he heard his other nephew Dyar speak to him, "Uncle Thomas … Uncle … I see you found him." Dyar walked up to the still body of his brother. He bent down and kissed his forehead. "Goodbye Noel."

He turned and looked through tear filled eyes at his Uncle. "Too late" was all that he managed to say.

Thomas shook his head, "No son … I heard everything we needed to hear. Your brother is at peace. He is safe now. He is with God and those who have walked before us and I reckon someday he'll meet you and me on the other side."

The two were quiet for the longest time.

Finally, Dyar looked at his Uncle and asked, "Now what?"

Thomas responded, "We take his body home. We are not going to let them bury him here. I'm going to make sure the two of you get back home to your momma and daddy." And with that said, Thomas and Dyar took Noel's body off the table and carried it outside. They saw a wagon hitched to an old mule tied to a rail. They both looked around for the owner but could not see anyone close by. Without speaking to one another, they gently placed Noel in the back of the wagon. Thomas took the reins while his nephew sat next to him on the bench, and before leaving Thomas took out his knife and carved his name on the post where the animal had been tied. It read, "Borrowed your wagon. Will return it in the spring." It was signed "Private Thomas Cleveland, 37th Regiment, Georgia Volunteers, CSA."

The two rode in silence down the road towards Atlanta. They came to a fork in the road. The road to the right took them south to the town of Atlanta. The one to the left headed to the north east where just a few days' journey away lay the farmland of Hart County, their home. Thomas pulled up on the reins and stopped the wagon. He looked at Dyar who returned the stare and finally said, "What do we do Uncle?"

Thomas replied, "We let love be our guide," and took the road home.

THE END